HEATHER GRAHAM

KAREN HARPER

STILL WATERS

MIRA

ISBN-13: 978-0-7783-3045-5

Recycling programs for this product may not exist in your area.

CONTENTS

THE ISLAND

Heather Graham

To Rhonda Saperstein,
with lots of love and thanks.
And to Coral Reef Yacht Club and
its members, with deepest thanks,
especially Fred and Marian Davant,
Teresa and Stu Davant,
Dr. Michael and Kelly Johnson,
Jock and Linda Fink, and the Commodore
and his wife: Eric and Elisa Thyree.

Prologue

"**Y**ou're going to feed them *again?*"

Molly Monoco looked up at the sound of her husband's voice. She had been busy in the galley, putting together a goodie bag filled with substantial meals. Ted, speaking with a growl in his voice, had been at his workstation. Apparently he had just noticed how industriously she had been preparing food.

Her husband appeared both aggravated and disgusted.

He knew what she was up to.

She couldn't really blame him for his feelings. Ted had worked hard all his life, and had earned every bit of the income they were now enjoying after his retirement. They both came from Cuban families who had made the move to Florida long before the refugees had begun fleeing the little island. While Molly's maiden name had been Rodriguez, her first name had always been Molly, just as Ted had been Theodore from the start. Their parents had brought them to the States, believing in the American dream, and teaching them a work ethic that would allow them to achieve that dream.

Ted had started out playing the drums at nightclubs

in Miami, not unlike a man who had become a lot more famous, Desi Arnaz.

He had worked as a busboy, as well, then a waiter, a host and a dancer. From his playing, he had fallen in love with salsa. So he had kept playing the drums, kept dancing, kept bussing tables and being a waiter and bartender until he had made enough money to buy his first studio, totally dedicated to the art of salsa. Eventually he had owned several studios, then sold them for a nice fat profit.

Work. Ted had known how to do it well. He had little patience with those who would not or could not help themselves.

And she did understand.

But she had her goals, too, trying to look after others who perhaps didn't deserve help, but then again, who might turn their lives around with a little assistance.

Now, as a retired man of means, he also had his hobbies, like all the sonar gadgets and other equipment on the boat. After all, he would have noticed what she was up to earlier, if he hadn't been playing around so intently with one of his computers!

She smiled. Even miffed, as he was right now, he was still as attractive to her as the young man with whom she had fallen in love forty-odd years ago. Tall, but not too tall, still fit. The hair on his chest was now gray—like the thinning strands on top of his head, but she didn't care. After all those years of marriage, the ups and the downs, she loved him now just as much as she always had—even if he had decided to name the yacht *Retired!*, despite the fact that she could have thought of a dozen more charming names.

His current displeasure with her wouldn't last. It

never did. Just as she loved the fact that he was always tinkering with some new kind of technology, he was secretly pleased that his wife was concerned for the welfare of others.

"Ted, what else can I do?" she asked softly.

"Quench the maternal instincts," he said, rolling his eyes. "We may well be talking criminals here. Hell, we're *definitely* talking criminals."

"Or misdirected young people who just need a helping hand," she said firmly. All her life, Molly had been involved. Blessed with Ted, her high-school sweetheart, she'd worked alongside him at many a club. Then—when she hadn't been able to produce the family she would have loved—she'd tried to help out where she could, at the church, with the homeless, and for various good causes, raising funds, even working soup kitchens. She could afford to, once Ted began making good money.

And she remained blessed. At sixty-five, she was no spring chick. But she was in good health, good shape, and pleased, mainly for Ted's sake, that people would say what an attractive woman she was.

"It's food, Ted. Nothing but a little food," she assured him. "And the last handout we're giving, since we're setting off on our own excursion."

He sighed, and a small smile crept over his face. Coming to her, he wrapped his arms around her. "How did I get so lucky?" he asked.

"Chance?" she teased, smiling.

He gave her a swat on the bottom. She giggled. Flirting was fun. They were older now, so a pat on the behind didn't lead to an afternoon in the handsome master cabin. Forget Viagra. He had a heart condition; she wouldn't let him take it. When there was this kind of amazing affection and closeness after so many years, nothing needed to be pushed.

In his arms, she thought with wonder what a great life they'd had together, and how wonderful it was that they still had each other—and the *Retired!* They could go anywhere, live out their dreams, explore—wherever the whim took them—and do it all in luxury.

"Okay, woman, we're moving on, so go and be lady bountiful, and then we'll get cracking," he said firmly.

"Right."

Molly headed for the ladder that would take her to the deck, her bag of goodies in her arms. She hummed softly as she emerged topside.

For a moment she just stared, confused. She even started to smile.

Then the tune she had been humming abruptly halted, broken on the air.

Her mouth began to work.

No sound came.

Ted heard, or thought he heard, a slight sound from topside.

"Molly?"

No answer.

"Molly?" he called, a little louder this time.

He felt a little thud against his heart. Maybe she had fallen, taking the dinghy, getting on or off the main boat. Hurt herself. Worse. They were neither of them young. What if she'd suffered some kind of attack? Fallen—maybe unconscious—into the water?

He leaped up, some instinct suddenly warning him of danger.

He ran up the steps to the deck.

And froze.

Two thoughts occurred to him.

What an ass he had been!

And then…

Molly, oh, Molly, Molly…

"Time to talk, Ted," snapped an angry voice.

"I can't tell you what you want to know," he protested, tears in his eyes.

"I think you can."

"I can't! I swear, before God, I would if I could."

"Start thinking, Ted. Because trust me, you *will* tell me what you've found."

1

It was a skull.

That much Beth Anderson knew after two seconds of dusting off bits of dirt and grass and fallen palm debris.

"Well?" Amber demanded.

"What is it?" Kimberly asked, standing right behind Amber, anxiously trying to look over her shoulder.

Beth glanced up briefly at her fourteen-year-old niece and her niece's best friend. Until just seconds ago, the two had been talking a mile a minute, as they always did, agreeing that their friend Tammy was a bitch, being far too cruel to *her* best friend, Aubrey, who in turn came to Amber and Kimberly for friendship every time she was being dissed by Tammy. They weren't dissing anyone themselves, they had assured Beth, because they weren't saying anything they wouldn't say straight to Tammy's face.

Beth loved the girls, loved being with them, and was touched to be the next best thing to a mother for Amber, who had lost her own as an infant. She was accustomed to listening to endless discussions on the hottest music, the hottest new shows and the hottest new movies—

and who did and didn't deserve to be in them, since the girls were both students at a magnet school for drama.

The main topic on their hot list had recently become boys. On that subject, they could truly talk endlessly.

But now their continual chatter had come to a dead stop.

Kimberly had been the one to stub her toe on the unknown object.

Amber had been the one to stoop down to look, then demand that her aunt come over.

"Well?" Kim prodded. "Dig it up, Beth."

"Um… I don't think I should," Beth said, biting her lower lip.

It wasn't just a skull. She couldn't see it clearly, there was so much dirt and debris, but despite the fact that it was half hidden by tangled grasses and the sandy ground, she could see more than bone.

There was still hair, Beth thought, her stomach churning.

And even *tissue.*

She didn't want the girls seeing what they had discovered any more closely.

Beth felt as if the blood in her veins had suddenly turned to ice. She didn't touch the skull; she carefully laid a palm frond over it, so she would recognize the spot when she returned to it. She wasn't about to dig anything up with the girls here.

She dusted her hands and stood quickly, determined that they had to get back to her brother, who was busy setting up their campsite. They were going to have to radio the police, since cell phones didn't seem to work out here.

A feeling of deep unease was beginning to ooze along

her spine as vague recollections of a haunting news story flashed into her mind: *Molly and Ted Monoco, expert sailors, had seemed to vanish into thin air.*

The last place they'd actually been seen was Calliope Key, right where they were now.

"Let's go get Ben," she suggested, trying not to sound as upset as she felt.

"It's a skull, isn't it?" Amber demanded.

She was a beautiful girl, tall and slender, with huge hazel eyes and long dark hair. The way she looked in a bathing suit—a two-piece, but hardly a risqué bikini— was enough to draw the attention of boys who were much too old for her, at least in Beth's opinion. Kimberly was the opposite of Amber, a petite blonde with bright blue eyes, pretty as a picture.

Sometimes the fact that she was in charge of two such attractive and impressionable girls seemed daunting. She knew she tended to be a worrywart, but the idea of any harm coming to the girls was…

Okay! She was the adult here. In charge. And it was time to do something about that.

But they were practically alone on an island with no phones, no cars…not a single luxury. A popular destination for the local boat crowd, but distant and desolate.

It was two to three hours back to Miami with the engine running, though Fort Lauderdale was closer, and it was hardly an hour to a few of the Bahamian islands.

She inhaled and exhaled. Slowly.

The human mind was amazing. Moments ago she had been delighted by the very remoteness of the island, pleased that there weren't any refreshment stands, automobiles or modern appliances of any kind.

But now…

"Might be a skull," Beth admitted, and she forced a grin, lifting her hands. "And might not be," she lied. "Your dad isn't going to be happy about this, Amber, when he's been planning this vacation for so long, but—"

She broke off. She hadn't heard the sound of footsteps or even the rustle of foliage, but as she spoke, a man appeared.

He had emerged from an overgrown trail through one of the thick hummocks of pines and palms that grew so profusely on the island.

It was that elemental landscape that brought real boat people here, the lack of all the things that came with the real world.

So why did his arrival feel so threatening?

Trying to be rational with herself, she decided that he looked just right for the type of person who should be here. He had sandy hair and was deeply tanned. No, not just tanned but *bronzed,* with the kind of dyed-in-deep coloring that true boat people frequently seemed to acquire. He was in good shape, but not heavily muscled. He was in well-worn denim cutoffs, and his feet were clad in deck shoes, no socks. His feet were as bronze as his body, so he must have spent plenty of time barefoot.

Like a guy who belonged on a boat, cruising the out islands. One who knew what he was doing. One who would camp where there were no amenities.

He also wore shades.

Anyone would, she told herself. She had on sunglasses, as did the girls. So why did his seem suspicious, dark and secretive.

She needed to be reasonable, she told herself. She was only feeling this sudden wariness because she had just found a skull, and instinctive panic was setting in.

It was odd how the psyche worked. Any other time, if she had run into someone else on the island, she would have been friendly.

But she had just found a skull, and he reminded her of the unknown fate of Ted and Molly Monoco, who had been here, and then...

Sailed into the sunset?

An old friend had reported them missing when they hadn't radioed in, as they usually did.

And she had just found a skull at their last known location.

So she froze, just staring at the man.

Amber, at fourteen, hadn't yet begun to think of personal danger in the current situation. Her father was a boat person, so she was accustomed to other boat people, and she was friendly when she met them. She wasn't stupid or naive, and she had been taught street smarts—she went to school in downtown Miami, for one thing. She could be careful when she knew she should.

Apparently that didn't seem to be now.

Amber smiled at the stranger and said, "Hi."

"Hi," he returned.

"Hi," Kim said.

Amber nudged Beth. "Um—hi."

"Keith Henson," the man said, and though she couldn't see his eyes, his shades were directed toward her. His face had good solid lines. Strong chin, high-set cheekbones. The voice was rich and deep.

He should have been doing voice-overs for commercials or modeling.

Hey, she mocked herself. Maybe that was what he *did* do.

"I'm Amber Anderson," her niece volunteered. "This

is Kim Smith, and that's my aunt Beth." She was obviously intrigued and went on to say, "We're camping here."

"Maybe," Beth said quickly.

Amber frowned. "Oh, come on! Just because—"

"How do you do, Mr. Henson," Beth said, cutting off her niece's words. She stepped forward quickly, away from their find. "Nice to meet you. Down here on vacation? Where are you from?"

Oh, good, that was casual. A complete third degree in ten seconds or less.

"Recent transplant, actually a bit of a roamer," he told her, smiling, offering her his hand. It was a fine hand. Long fingered, as bronzed as the rest of him, nails clipped and clean. Palm callused. He used his hands for work. He was a real sailor, definitely, or did some other kind of manual labor.

She had the most bizarre thought that when she accepted his handshake, he would wrench her forward, and then his fingers would wind around her neck. The fear became so palpable that she almost screamed aloud to the girls to run.

He took her hand briefly in a firm but not too powerful grip, then released it. "Amber, Kim," he said, and shook their hands as he spoke.

"So are you folks are from the area?" he asked, and looked at the girls, smiling. Apparently he'd already written Beth off as a total flake.

She slipped between the two girls, feeling her bulldog attitude coming on and setting an arm around each girl's shoulders.

"Yep!" Amber said.

"Well, kind of," Kim said.

"I mean, we're not from the island we're standing on, but nearby," Amber said.

Henson's smile deepened.

Beth tried to breathe normally and told herself that she was watching far too many forensics shows on television. There was no reason to believe she had to protect the girls from this man.

But no reason to trust him on sight, either.

"Are you planning on camping on the island?" Beth asked.

He waved a hand toward the sea. "I'm not sure yet. I'm with some friends…we're doing some diving, some fishing. We haven't decided whether we're in a camping mood or not."

"Where are your friends?" Beth asked. A little sharply? she wondered. So much for being casual, able to easily escape a bad situation, if it should prove to be one.

"At the moment I'm on my own."

"I didn't see your dinghy," Beth said. "In fact, I didn't even notice another boat in the area."

"It's there," he said, "the *Sea Serpent*." He cocked his head wryly. "My friend, Lee, who owns her, likes to think of himself as the brave, adventurous type. Did you sail out here on your own?"

It might have been an innocent question, but not to Beth. Not at this moment.

She had been swearing for years that she was going to take kung fu classes or karate, but as yet, she hadn't quite done so.

She always carried pepper spray in her purse. But, of course, she had been wandering inland with the girls, just walking, and she wasn't carrying her purse. She wasn't carrying anything. She had on sandals and a bathing suit. Like the girls.

"Are you alone?" Keith Henson repeated politely.

Politely? Or menacingly?

"Oh, no. We're with my brother. And a whole crowd."

"A whole crowd—" Amber began.

Beth pinched her shoulder.

"Ow!" Amber gasped.

"Lots of my brother's friends are coming in. Sailors…boat people…you know, big guys, the kind who can twist off beer caps with their teeth," Beth said, trying to sound light.

Amber and Kim were both staring at her as if she'd lost her mind.

"Oh, yeah, all my dad's friends are, like, big, tough-guy nature freaks," Amber said, staring at Beth. "Yeah right, the kind that open beer bottles with their teeth."

"They are?" Kim asked, sounding very confused.

"At any rate, there will be a bunch of us. A couple of cops, even," Beth said, realizing immediately how ridiculous that sounded!

Time to move on!

Tugging at the girls' shoulders, she added, "Well, it's a pleasure to meet you. We'd better get back to my brother before he misses us. We're supposed to be helping with the setup."

"We'll see you, if you're hanging around," Kim told him cheerfully.

"Yes, nice to meet you," Amber said.

"Bye, then," Keith Henson said.

A plastic smile in place, Beth continued to force the girls away from the man and toward the beach where they'd come ashore in the dinghy. And where they would find her brother, she prayed. Surely he hadn't gone wandering off.

"Aunt Beth," Amber whispered, "what on earth is the matter with you? You were so weird to that man."

Kimberly cleared her throat, "Um, actually, you were pretty rude," she said hesitantly.

"He was alone, he appeared out of nowhere—and we had just found a skull," Beth said, after glancing back to assure herself that they were out of earshot.

"You said you weren't sure if it was a skull or not," Kim said.

"I wasn't sure—I'm *not* sure."

"But it looked like he just got here, too," Amber said. "And the skull—it *is* a skull, isn't it?—had been there a while."

"Criminals often return to the scene of the crime," Beth said, quoting some program or other, and anxiously moving forward.

Amber burst out laughing. "Aunt Beth! Okay, so you got the heebie-jeebies. But puh-lease. Did you see a gun on him?"

"Or anywhere he could have stuffed one?" Kim asked, giggling.

They weren't such bad questions, really.

"No," Beth admitted.

"So why were you so rude?" Amber persisted.

Beth groaned. "I don't know. I guess when you think you might have found a skull, you become very careful about your own health and well-being, okay?"

"Okay," Amber said after a moment. "He looked like a decent guy."

"He probably is."

Kim giggled suddenly. "He was *hot*."

"He's way too old for you guys," Beth replied a little too sharply.

"So is Brad Pitt, but that doesn't mean he's not hot," Amber said, shaking her head as if it was a sadly difficult thing to deal with adults.

"Right," Beth murmured.

A thud sounded from behind. Beth jumped, ready to cover the girls with her own body against any threatened danger.

"Aunt Beth," Amber said, "it was a palm frond."

Beth exhaled. "Right," she murmured.

The girls were looking at one another again. As if they had to be very careful with her.

As if she were losing her mind.

"Come on, let's find your dad," Beth said to Amber.

The woman had to be one of the strangest he'd ever come across, Keith decided, watching as the threesome walked away.

She'd acted as if she'd been hiding something.

As if she was guilty of...something.

He shook his head. No, not with those two teens at her side. They were far too innocent and friendly for anything to have been going on. Not that teens couldn't be guilty of a lot. But he had learned to be a pretty good judge of character, and those two were simply young and friendly, like a pair of puppies, fresh and eager to explore the world, expecting only good things from it.

But as for the woman...

Beth Anderson. She and the tall girl were obviously related. Both had the same very sleek dark hair. Not dead straight, but lush and wavy. And Beth had the kind of eyes that picked up the elements, that could be dark or light, that held a bit of the exotic, the mysterious. Very nicely built, which was more than evident, since all three were in two-piece suits. She appeared to be in her mid to late twenties, naturally sensual and sexy, though not in an overt way. Athletic. With shapely legs that went forever…

She was compellingly attractive.

And a little crazy.

No. *Frightened.*

Of him?

This was his first trip to Calliope Key. But he surely looked the part. So why had he appeared so menacing to her?

She wouldn't ever have come to the island with the girls if she had been afraid of something from the get-go. So…?

They must have found something.

He looked quickly around the clearing. There was nothing immediately evident that would have disturbed anyone, whatever they'd found had to be right around where they had been standing.

For a moment everything in him seemed to tighten and burn; his jaw locked. The heat of anger filled him, the raging sense of fury that the world was never just, and no effort on his part could change that.

And that was part of the reason he was here, he re-minded himself, though he kept that fact private. Keep your eye on the prize—that was the standing order. There was one objective. Find what they were seeking, and do it discreetly. Then the rest would fall into place. He hoped. He wasn't certain anyone else really believed that, and he would be damned if he even knew what he believed himself.

He heard his name called. It was Lee.

He forced a deep breath, aware that he had to tamp down his emotions over his current situation.

He shouted back, "I'm over here."

A minute later, Lee Gomez and Matt Albright appeared in the clearing. "What's going on?" Lee asked him. Half-Ecuadorian and half-American mutt, Lee had brilliant blue eyes and pitch-dark hair, and skin that never seemed to mind the sun.

"Not much. Met a woman and two girls—they're with the woman's brother, maybe some other people, camping on the island tonight," Keith said.

Matt shook his head, swearing. He was the redhead in their group, quick to anger, quicker to apologize, but at all times easily irritated. "There's more. Two more good-size boats, both anchored not far from us. I saw a dinghy coming in with several people."

"Well, what are you going to do," Keith asked with a shrug. "Boaters have been coming out here since...well, hell, probably since forever."

"Yeah, but dammit, they shouldn't be here now," Matt muttered.

"Hey, we knew we'd be in public view, working around whatever happened and whoever appeared. People are here, so let's make the best of it," Keith said. "And think about it. It's not much of a shock. It's a weekend, the perfect time for boaters to take a little break."

"You don't think we could dress up as pygmies and scare them all off the island, do you?" Lee murmured dryly.

"Pygmies?" Matt said.

"Some kind of tribal islanders, maybe cannibals?" Lee teased.

Keith laughed. "Oh, yeah, that would make us really inconspicuous. Besides, while they're on the island, they're not out on their boats, checking out the reefs. It's a weekend. Let's do like the others. Play tourist. Get to know the folks. Check out what they know—and what they're thinking." And what they're afraid of, he thought, but he kept the possibility that anyone on the island might suspect them of something to himself.

Lee shrugged. "All right."

"So we roll out the cooler and the tent and make like party people," Matt said. He laughed suddenly. "Not so bad. One of the people on the boat was a woman, and man, she sure as hell looked like a hottie. From a distance, anyway."

One of the people on the boat? Keith thought. You should have seen the woman in this very clearing, just minutes ago. And I wasn't any distance from her. None at all.

"Doesn't matter if she's hot as blue blazes, no getting too close to the locals, not tonight," Lee warned sternly.

"Hey, I'm just going to be a party boy. A friendly guy, just looking for fun, a good ole boating fool," Matt assured him.

"Well, you can be a good ole boy later. I'm not hauling stuff off that boat by myself," Lee said. "If we're turning into Boy Scouts and doing the camping thing, you guys can do some of the lugging, too."

"Actually, camping isn't such a bad idea," Keith said.

"No, and getting to know folks from the area isn't a bad idea, either," Lee said. He grinned. "I think I'll own the boat."

"Hey!" Matt protested.

"Someone has to own the boat, right?" Lee asked.

"You can own the boat," Keith said.

"I get to own it next time," Matt said.

"With any luck, there won't be a next time," Keith said. He stared at the other two, and he couldn't help feeling an edge of suspicion.

Lee stared back at him. His eyes were enigmatic. "Ever the optimist, huh?"

"I just know what I'm doing," Keith said.

Lee assessed him for what seemed like an eternity. "I hope," Lee said. "I hope to hell you're focused on what we're doing."

"I'm focused. You can count on it," Keith said, and he knew his tone was grim.

"C'mon, then, let's go play tourist," Lee said.

"Sure. Be right there," Keith said.

"Hey, we're all in this together, you know," Matt reminded him, his eyes narrowed.

"Yup."

They *were* in it together, true. But the other two didn't know that he'd been warned specifically to keep an eye on them.

"Damn, Keith, you're acting bizarre," Lee said, staring at him. "Think of what's happened. Focus is the most important thing here."

More important than human life? Keith wondered. "I'll be right with you."

"He's working on that instinct thing he's got going for him," Matt said, shrugging. "Come on, Lee, let's get started. Wonderboy will be along."

Keith waited until they walked back toward the northern shore.

And then he began to search the clearing.

Oh, yeah. He was focused.

There were certain images a man could never quite get out of his mind. Dead men. Dead friends. Friends who'd had everything in the world to live for. Young. The best of the best.

He stiffened, listening. People were coming. The island was becoming more crowded by the minute. He swore softly.

"Hey there," came a throaty, masculine voice.

A man of about sixty, followed by a petite young woman and two men about his own age, was entering the clearing.

"Hey," Keith replied, stepping forward, a smile on his face.

Ah, yes, the masses had arrived. He didn't know why he was suddenly so certain that he and his associates weren't the only ones traveling incognito.

Beth and the girls emerged from the lush greenery in the center of the island to reach the beach. It was beautiful. Once upon a time there had been a very small naval base on Calliope Key, a research center. It had been abandoned, but back toward the interior the ruins of the old buildings remained, allowing a safe haven of sorts if the weather turned really foul. Today, though, the sun was streaming down, a soft breeze was blowing, and the sea appeared incredibly serene.

Ben was on the beach, barefoot, in cutoffs and shades, dressed remarkably like the man who had just scared Beth. He glanced up when he saw them coming. "Back so soon? I thought you were exploring, seeing if there was anyone else around."

At thirty-four, Beth thought, her brother was in his prime. He had, however, taken the task of raising his daughter to heart. Despite the fact that he had lost his wife years ago, he was still far more prone to spend his nights at home rather than out at the boat clubs—though he did belong to Rock Reef, where she worked as a social director—seeking companionship. Beth actually wished he would be more of a sinner at times. She knew how much Amber meant to him, but she was afraid that he wasn't allowing much room in his life for the future. He had been madly in love with Amber's mom, his high-school sweetheart, and nothing had ever changed his desire to see that Amber had everything he could provide, including his company—whether she wanted it or not, since Amber had reached that age where she wanted to spend her nights prowling the malls with her friends, rather than bonding with her dad. She adored him. She was simply being a teenager.

"We *were* exploring," Beth said.

"We met a guy," Amber said.

"Wicked cute," Kimberly added.

Beth groaned.

"Wicked cute young, or wicked cute old?" Ben asked, a sparkle in his eyes.

"Wicked cute your age, or Aunt Beth's age…well, I don't know," Amber said. "He's not a kid, anyway."

"Ah." Ben winked at Beth. "They trying to play matchmaker?"

"I hope not," she said too sharply.

"So, he wasn't wicked cute?"

"Oh, no, he was good-looking."

"But…?" Ben teased.

"Not my type," she said quickly.

Amber sighed dramatically. "The two of you are hopeless."

"He's a total stranger, and you don't go around trusting total strangers," Beth snapped.

Ben arched a brow. She tended to be the one who nagged *him* to lighten up on Amber.

"Girls, go grab the barbecue equipment, will you?" Beth asked.

"She's going to tell you about the skull," Amber said.

"Skull?" Ben had been fiddling with one of the tent poles. He went still, staring at Beth with a wary question in his eyes.

"Kim stubbed her toe on something, and… I think it's actually a skull," Beth said.

"Did you…pick it up?" Ben asked.

"No, I thought you and I should go take a look. And then, if it's what I think, radio the authorities. I didn't want to dig it up with the girls there," Beth said. She bit her lip. "Except… I'm not so sure we should leave them alone on the beach."

Ben shook his head. "Beth, this island has been a boaters' paradise forever."

"I know that."

"The naval base has been closed for decades—people who come here have boats and are…well, boat people."

"I know that, too."

"So…?" he said softly.

She cleared her throat, glancing at the girls, who clearly weren't about to leave.

"Ben, damn it! Remember that couple… Ted and Molly Monoco?"

"What about them?" Ben asked, frowning.

"They were last seen here, on this island."

He sighed, shaking his head. "So what? They had a

state-of-the-art yacht and intended to sail around the world, Beth."

"They disappeared. I heard it on the news several months ago," she responded stubbornly.

Ben let out a deep sigh. "Beth, a friend called in, worried about them, that's all. They might be anywhere. The news loves to turn anything into a tragedy." He caught Amber's eyes and grimaced. "Maybe your aunt does need to meet a tall dark hunk, huh?"

"Ben!"

"He was blondish!" Amber said, laughing.

"Okay, girls, you stay here and set stuff up, and Aunt Beth and I will go check out that skull."

"I don't think we should leave them alone," Beth said.

"She's afraid of the guy we met," Amber explained.

"I'm not afraid of him," Beth protested.

"It's all right," Ben said. "I just saw Hank and Amanda Mason, and her dad and a cousin, I think. They're just down the beach. Girls, scream like hell if anyone comes near you, all right?"

Amanda Mason. Great. Normally, the concept of Amanda—who could be totally obnoxious—being around on the weekend would have bugged Beth to no end. At the moment, though, she was glad that the Masons were there on the beach.

Within screaming distance.

"You bet," Kimberly said.

"Unless it's a really hot guy with a beer," Amber said.

That brought her father spinning around.

"Just kidding!" Amber said. "Dad, I'm joking. Aunt Beth? Tell him."

"She's just teasing you, Ben. Give it a break," Beth told him.

He rolled his eyes, starting off ahead of her. "Why does she do that to me?" he demanded.

"Because you tend to be completely paranoid, and you're on her tail like a bloodhound most of the time," Beth told him, following him through the brush, pushing palm fronds out of her way.

"Right, and you're not being just a little bit paranoid?"

"Ben, I honestly think we found a skull. I'm worried with reason. If you make Amber crazy enough, then you'll have reason to worry, too."

"You wait 'til you have kids," he warned her, stopping and turning back to her. "She's everything I've got," he said softly.

Beth nodded. "So let go a little bit."

"She's only fourteen."

"Just a little bit. Then she'll come back to you and tell you all the wild stuff going on with her friends. You've got to let her live a little."

He nodded, serious then.

They reached the clearing. It was empty.

"Okay, I don't see any guy."

"I hardly thought he would just stand around waiting," Beth said.

"All right, then. Where's the skull?"

"Right here… I pushed a palm frond over it."

She walked over to where they had been. Tentatively, she moved away the fallen debris.

There was nothing there. Nothing at all. It didn't even look as if the earth had been disturbed. "I…" She looked at her brother. He was staring at her with skepticism. "Damn it, Ben, the girls saw it, too!"

"So where is it?"

"I don't know!" She stared around the clearing. There

was plenty of debris about; area storms could be fierce, blowing hard against fragile palms and pines.

But though she kicked up every inch of the clearing, dragging away every palm frond and branch she could see, there was no sign of anything that so much as resembled a skull.

Then...

"Aha!" she cried, and dug, only to dig up a conch shell.

"There's your skull," Ben said.

"No, this isn't it. Ben, I'm telling you, I saw a skull. And I didn't dig it up while the kids were here because it looked like there was still hair attached, even rotting flesh."

"Come on, Beth. You're too into *CSI* and *Autopsy one-two-three-four-and-up-to-fifty-or-a-hundred-or-whatever-it-is-now*. I'm heading back to the campsite."

"Ben!"

"What?" he demanded, turning back to stare at her.

"I'm telling you, there was a skull. And then there was that guy—"

"You know what, Beth? I'm a guy, a lawyer, and yes, I tend to be a little nervous because I know the kinds of people who are out there in the world. Hell, I have a gun, and I know how to use it. But think about it, Beth. You just saw the guy a few minutes ago. And what you thought was a skull had to be down to the bone."

"Not completely," she murmured, feeling a little ill.

"Beth," Ben argued, "how could a guy who just got here be responsible for a skull that may or may not exist, and, if so, is almost down to the bone? I am not going to ruin this weekend with my daughter and her friend, so please..."

She stood up, dusting off her hands again, lips pursed. She nodded. "I know it's the weekend. I know that it's bond-with-your-daughter time. Yes, we'll have a good time. I promise."

He started back along the trail to the beach.

Beth hesitated. She felt night coming, felt the breeze whispering through her hair.

Could she have been mistaken?

No!

Damn it! She had seen it, and it had been a skull. A human skull. So where the hell was it now?

A chill settled over her.

Had *he* taken it?

Was the skull the reason he had come to the island?

The palm fronds around her began to whisper. She turned quickly toward the trail. "Ben?"

Her brother didn't reply.

She glanced around quickly, then called out again, "Ben! Wait for me!"

With those words on her lips, she raced after him, clinging to the words he had said to her.

I have a gun, and I know how to use it.

But did he have it with him?

And what if the other guy had a gun and knew how to use it, too?

2

"There's your guy," Ben said as they walked back onto the beach. He pointed down a stretch of sand.

And indeed, there he was. Along with two other men, one dark and Hispanic looking, the other a blazing redhead, he was securing a large tent pole in the sand. They had respected the silent privacy rule all boaters who used the island obeyed, staking out their territory a distance away from anyone else. From where they stood, Beth couldn't make out the expressions of any of the men.

The redhead stopped working, however, elbowed Keith, pointed toward them, then waved.

Ben waved in return.

"You're not waving to your new hottie," Ben teased.

"He's not *my* anything," Beth retorted.

"The girls were impressed."

"The girls are young and impressionable," she snapped.

Her brother looked at her quizzically. "What is the matter with you?"

"Nothing. It's just that, no matter what, I know I saw a skull."

"Which we couldn't find."

"No," she admitted. "But I'm telling you, there was *something* there. That guy was there, too. And now the thing isn't there, and the same guy is on the beach!"

"I can walk over and ask him if he just dug up a skull," Ben said.

She glared at him. "And if he did, he's just going to say yes?"

"Beth, what do you want me to do?" Ben demanded, shaking his head.

"Be careful."

"All right, I'll be afraid. Very afraid."

"Ben…"

"Beth, honestly, I'm not ignoring what you said. But don't ignore what *I* said, either. I'm capable of watching out for my own family. I never forget that I have two teenagers in my care when I take the girls out. Okay, you got spooked and you remembered that missing couple. But I read the stories, too. They wanted to explore the world, take off by themselves. They planned on an endless trip, on going wherever they chose."

"But still, they just…disappeared," Beth said stubbornly.

"Beth, it's legal for adults to disappear, if they want to."

"Their friends were concerned."

"Maybe they wanted an escape from their friends," Ben suggested.

"Who would do that?" Beth demanded.

"Beth, please. This is a weekend. We're here to have fun. Just let it go, okay?"

She exhaled loudly in exasperation, spinning away from him and heading toward the girls. The were studying a Hollywood-gossip magazine and seemed to have forgotten that they might have stumbled across human remains.

But Amber looked up when Beth hunched down and joined them in the little outer "room" of their tent.

"Was it a skull?" she asked.

"I don't know. It wasn't there anymore."

A strange look filtered through Amber's eyes.

"Do you think *he* took it?" Kim demanded.

"Shh," Amber commanded. "He's *here*."

Beth's head jerked around. The man who had introduced himself as Keith Henson *was* there—standing just outside the tents, where Ben had been building a small fire to cook their evening meal.

The other two were also there: the tall, lean, redhead and the darker man with the stockier, well-muscled build.

Beth overheard introductions and realized her brother was telling Keith that she had mentioned meeting him earlier.

Beth sprang into action, hurrying out. The girls followed her quickly. More introductions were made. The other two were Lee Gomez and Matt Albright.

Keith was still wearing the sunglasses, allowing no insight to his thoughts. He was smiling, however, and Beth had to admit that he was gorgeous, with classic bone structure that also offered a solidly sculpted strength. Lee Gomez was also striking, with his dark good looks, and Matt, though freckled, gave the initial impression of the charming boy next door.

"Keith was just saying that they brought a portable grill and have enough fresh fish to feed an army," Ben said.

She stared at her brother. He wanted them to join these strangers?

"I've also made a mean potato salad," Lee offered, grinning.

"We must have something to offer, don't we?" Ben asked Beth.

"The salad," Amber answered for her. "We have chips, too, tons of soda and some beer."

"Sounds great. We're right down the beach. Hopefully the alluring aromas will bring you right over," Matt said.

"Well?" Ben asked her.

"Of course," Beth said, seeing no graceful way out of it.

"We met some other people, down the beach on the other side," Keith said. "They said they know you. They'll be joining us, too."

"Oh, the Masons," Ben said.

"That's right. The Masons are here," Beth murmured. She could see Hank's yacht, *Southern Light,* out on the water. She was a fine vessel, forty-five feet, forty years old, but her motor had been completely rebuilt and the interior redone. She was often referred to as the Grand Dame at the club.

"Actually, I'm not straight on exactly who's who yet. Except for Amanda," Keith said.

Of course he'd gotten Amanda right. She was five-five, shaped like an hourglass, with blue eyes and light blond hair. Few men ever missed Amanda.

"There's an older man," Lee said.

"Roger Mason, her dad," Beth said.

"Hank has to be here," Ben said. "Amanda's cousin. The boat's his."

"Yes, right. Hank. And the other guy is…"

"Probably Gerald, another cousin," Beth said. "He

lives just up the coast from the rest of the family, in Boca Raton."

"So...they're all cousins?" Matt asked, a hopeful note in his voice.

"Hank, Amanda and Gerald are cousins—second cousins, I think," Ben said.

He hadn't seemed to notice the hope in the question. He wouldn't, Beth thought. He was always too busy being a father.

"There's a young couple camping just beyond them," Keith said. Even though Beth couldn't see his eyes, she knew he was staring straight at her. "Maybe you know *them,* too. Brad Shaw and a woman named Sandy Allison?"

She shook her head. "The names aren't familiar." Again she looked out to the water.

She had missed the fourth boat because it was anchored just beyond Hank's *Southern Light.*

The last vessel was a small pleasure craft. She looked as if she needed paint, and she probably offered no more than a small head, galley, and perhaps room enough for two to sleep in the forward section. There were lots of small boats docked at the club, and some of those—especially the motorboats—were incredibly expensive.

On the other hand, some of them weren't. One of the things Beth had always liked about working at the club was the fact that the people there were honestly dedicated to the water. They came from all life's corners, just like their boats did. The initial membership fee was steep, but after that, the annual dues were reasonable, so people from all different social strata could afford to join, once they saved up the initial investment. She was also proud that the club specialized in lessons in sailing, swimming, diving and water safety.

At the club, though, no matter how inexpensive any of their boats might be, the members, even the broke ones, took pleasure in caring for them—unlike the sad little vessel out beyond *Southern Light*.

"Four boats," Beth murmured.

"Anyway," Keith said, "we've asked everyone over to our little patch of beach."

"Great," Ben said.

"Come on over whenever you feel like it," Keith said. "We're not far," he said, indicating the short stretch of sand that separated the two camps.

"Want help?" Amber asked enthusiastically.

Beth was tempted to grasp her niece's arm.

"I think we've got it under control," Keith said gravely. "But if you need help hauling chips and salad, you let us know."

He had dimples and a pleasant way with the girls. He wasn't inappropriate or flirtatious—as some older men would have been, just nice. He should have seemed charming, Beth knew, but she was too suspicious of him for that.

"We'll see you down there in a bit," Lee said.

The three men waved and started off down the sand. Ben turned to Beth. "Feel better?" he asked her.

She stared at her brother, shaking her head.

"What? Still scared? Nothing's going to happen. Some of the other members from the yacht club will be with us," he reminded her.

Ben was a member. She was the social manager, and she loved her job and most of the members, who were always pleasant and appreciative.

Then there was Amanda.

Luckily she wasn't there on a daily—or even weekly—basis. Hank was the real boat fanatic. It had been his father who had first joined the club, which had been formed back in 1910. Originally it had been just two lifelong friends, Commodore Isaak and Vice Commodore Gleason, who had gotten together to drink and chat in their retirement. By the 1920s, there had been ten members, rising to nearly a hundred before World War II. With far too many able-bodied sailors in the navy, the facility had been used for a while as rehab for returnees. The 1950s had seen a resurgence in membership, and it had become a casual place in the seventies. When the hippies became yuppies in the nineties, the price of membership had soared. At the moment, there were about two hundred members, a hundred of those with boat slips, and at least fifty who could be considered fairly active. Ben and Beth's father had been a commodore, and with his passing, Ben had taken up the family participation in the place.

Beth, with a degree in public relations, had taken a job.

Had she realized that she would be dealing with the Amandas of the world, she might have thought twice. Amanda was the type to drop a letter on her desk and, without looking at her, tell her that she needed copies. She complained at the slightest mistake made by any of the help. Two waitresses in the dining room had quit in tears after serving her.

Ben didn't jump when Amanda was around; he seemed to be immune to her wickedly sensual charm and oblivious to her frequent vicious abrasiveness.

There was no use trying to explain Amanda to her brother. He would just think it was feminine envy.

"Having them here makes everything just perfect," she assured him dully.

"Amanda," Amber said, making a face.

Ben rolled his eyes. "Is something the matter with her?" he demanded.

"Dad, she's a bitch."

"Amber!"

"It's not really a bad word," Amber said.

"Not like a four-letter word or anything," Kim added hastily.

"Beth," Ben said, "aren't you going to say something?"

She shrugged. "They're calling it as they see it," she told him.

He frowned. "I don't like that language."

"Amber, your father doesn't like that language. Please don't use it."

"All right," Amber said, "Miss Mason is a rude, manipulative snake, how's that?"

"With really big boobs," Kim added.

"Kim…" Ben protested.

"Sorry," Kim said, without meaning it in the least.

Ben pointed a finger sternly. "You will be polite."

"Of course," Beth said. "I mean, she's always so polite to me."

Ben groaned out loud and turned away, walking to the spot where he had pitched his own tent, his back to them. "Maybe you'll like the new people better," he said irritably over his shoulder.

She could hardly like them any less, Beth thought.

It wasn't exactly as if they were going out, but Beth

chose to throw a cover-up on over her bathing suit, and the girls did likewise. They hauled their coolers with sodas and beer, and their contribution of salad and chips, down to the meeting point before any of the Mason family appeared but just after the arrival of the new couple, Sandy Allison and Brad Shaw.

She had sandy hair that matched her name and pleasant amber eyes, a medium build and was of medium height. She wore a terry cover-up and sandals, while Brad, about six feet even, with the same sandy hair but green eyes, was still in swim boxers with a cotton surf shirt over his shoulders. They were both cheerful and hailed from the West Coast, according to Brad.

"Love it here, though," he assured them. "When we're diving, I feel like I could stay down forever."

"Absolutely gorgeous," Sandy agreed, slipping an arm around his waist. "There are areas here when you can practically walk right from the beach to the reef."

"Dangerous for ships. Well, at one time," Keith put in, handing Brad a beer. "The area is very well charted now."

"Well, it *has* been a few years since the first Europeans made landfall," Beth murmured.

Keith looked sharply at her. She should have guessed. His eyes were a deep, dark, true brown, rimmed with black lashes that were striking against the light color of his hair and the bronze of his face.

"A few ships did miss those reefs," he murmured, and turned back to the men. "Lee has some equipment on his boat that would do the navy proud."

"So you're not a boater yourself, Mr. Henson?" Beth asked. She hadn't meant for it to sound as if she was heading an inquisition, but it did.

"I am. We're just here with Lee's boat," he said.

Here from where? she wondered.

She could just ask the question, of course, and immediately spoke before she could think better of it.

"So where are you three down here from?" she asked, hoping she didn't sound as suspicious as she felt.

Lee looked at Matt and Ben, then shrugged. "We're from all over, really. I was born here."

"On the island?" she teased.

"Vero Beach," he said.

"I'm your original Yankee from Boston," Matt said.

"Great city," Beth said, looking at Keith.

"Virginia," he said.

"But you must know something about these waters," Beth said. "This island isn't exactly on the tourist routes."

"I told you, I'm originally from Vero Beach," Lee reminded her. "The locals use the island a lot."

"It's our first time camping out here, though," Keith said.

"So how do you know each other?" she asked, unable to stop herself from probing. "Are you business associates?"

"Dive buddies," Keith said. "Hey, here come your friends."

Whatever her opinion of Amanda, Beth had to admit that the Masons were one attractive family. Roger was fiftysomething but had the build of an athlete, and, so she had heard, competed with the young studs at the nightclubs on the beach. Hank was blond and blue-eyed, like his cousin, but he was all man, with a broad bronzed chest and shoulders. Gerald was a shade darker, but obviously a family member.

"Ben!" Amanda cried, sounding as delighted as if she'd met a long-lost relative. She hadn't bothered with a cover-up and was clad in only a small bikini.

A string bikini at that.

Her hair was loose and falling around her shoulders in a perfect golden cloak.

"She's indecent," Amber whispered from behind Beth.

"Totally," Kim agreed.

"She does it awfully well," Beth murmured, watching the woman.

While Amanda was greeting Ben, Hank looked over her head and saw Beth and the girls. He offered a real smile. "Hey there."

"Hi, Hank," Beth called.

"Hey, you remember our cousin Gerald, right?" Amanda said.

"Absolutely." By then the two men had walked over to her. Hank gave her a kiss on the cheek and greeted the two girls. Gerald took her hand. "Small world, huh?"

"Not really, considering how close we are to home," she told him.

"True," he said with a laugh, then turned to the girls. "Amber, if you get any taller, you'll be giving me a run for the money. And…don't tell me, it's… Kimmy, right?"

"Kim," the girl corrected.

"Kim," he agreed. She blushed slightly. He was nice, not condescending, and it was apparently appreciated.

"Fish all right for everyone?" Keith called out. "We've got hot dogs and hamburger patties, as well, for any landlubbers."

"I'd love a hot dog," Kim called out, hurrying toward the barbecue. A pleasant aroma was already beginning to emanate from the portable cooker. Amber followed her friend, leaving Beth behind with the other adults.

"Beth, how nice to see you here," Amanda said. She walked over, perfect smile in place. "You have the weekend off?" she asked politely, as if surprised.

"Hello, Amanda. Yes, I have the weekend off."

Amanda looked disapproving. "I would have thought they really needed you, what with the tourists and all. I suppose the club really does run itself. Still, I'm surprised the commodore didn't want your lovely face around."

"I'm sure he can manage on his own for a few days," Beth said sweetly. "Have you met Sandy and Brad?"

"Briefly," Amanda said, turning.

It was enough for Beth.

She escaped.

To get anywhere, though, she had to pass the barbecue, since the three men had their tents set up in the other direction, and if she made a point of going around the barbecue, she would be heading inland, into the dense foliage, rather than along the sand.

She had nearly made it past when Amber caught her arm. "Aunt Beth, come see. Everything looks perfect!"

She smiled weakly as Keith expertly flipped a fillet, then shook a mixture of seasonings onto it.

"That looks great," Amber told him, though her enthusiasm sounded forced.

"Are you sure you wouldn't rather have a hot dog, like Kim?" He laughed at her grateful expression and put another hot dog on the grill.

"You guys are ready for all occasions," Beth murmured. She was wedged between her niece and Keith Henson. They were almost touching. Almost. Not quite.

"Well, it's not that I can't—we can't—rough it, but a few conveniences are nice," he said. He looked at her. The sun was slipping lower toward the horizon, and in the deepening shadows, his eyes seemed darker than ever. She felt as if he was staring at her with the same suspicion she felt for him.

"We have two-bedroom tents!" Amber said.

"I'm not really sure you could call them bedrooms," Beth murmured.

"Well, I only have a one-bedroom tent," Keith said. "But it's still a convenience when it rains. What I really like is just to sleep on the sand and stare up at the stars."

"Yeah, that's cool," Amber agreed.

"I think your dad wants you in the tent tonight," Beth said, once again afraid her words sounded sharper than she'd intended.

She saw Keith's lips tighten as he tried to hide a smile. Yes, she was definitely on edge, and it was showing.

"Amber?" Ben called, and she scampered off, Kim following in her wake.

"So, have you got padlocks on those tents?" Keith asked.

She flushed, but stared defiantly back at him. "You're strangers," she said, feeling that no other explanation was needed.

The smile he had been hiding turned into a deep grin that brought out his dimples once again. "So are Brad and Sandy."

"They're not three guys."

"Are you sure we're not going to poison the fish?" he asked.

"I hadn't thought of it," she admitted, but stared at him with a grim smile. "Maybe I should have."

"Ouch. That's a challenge. I can take a bite of yours first, if you want."

"I'll live dangerously."

He looked out across the sand, then at her. "Do you come here often?"

"Yes. Well, usually. Not this year. This is the first time this year." She didn't know why she was stumbling around to explain. She didn't owe him any explanations. She kept talking anyway. "We spent our vacation in the Bahamas this year. This used to be the last weekend of summer vacation. Now, the girls have already been back at school for a few weeks. And for Christmas, we all went to Denver. Even though it's so close, this is the first time we've been out here this year. And you?"

"I've dived the area dozens of times," he said, turning his attention to the fish once again. "But there was never really any reason to stop at the island."

"I thought Lee was the one who knew the area," she reminded him sharply.

He smiled. "Lee knows it best. But I *have* been here before. Just not to this island."

"So why now?" she demanded.

He arched a brow. He was answering slowly, she thought. Too slowly. "Well…" He laughed. "Because it's here, I guess."

"So you're really here for the diving? Not the fishing?"

"Obviously we've been fishing." He smiled and nodded toward the grill.

"But you're mainly here to dive."

"Has it suddenly become illegal?" he queried, laughter in his eyes again.

"Of course not."

"I love diving here," he told her, and she felt that he was being totally honest at that moment. Actually, she couldn't think of anything he'd said that hadn't sounded honest. Was she being ridiculously suspicious? Even if she had seen a skull, Ben was right. There was no reason to suspect that a man appearing *then* would have anything to do with a skull that had been on the beach for days, maybe longer. So why was she so suspicious?

Because he frightened her in too many ways?

"Excuse me. I think I'll get a beer," she murmured, slipping past him, but she intended a smooth exit. She stepped a little too quickly and a little too close. She felt the tension in his muscles, then nearly careened sideways into him.

"Excuse me," she murmured again, afraid she was blushing. She hurried away and walked right past the cooler, then remembered she had said she was going for a beer. She quickly secured one, then went to stand by her brother's side.

Sandy and Brad were telling stories about diving the Great Barrier Reef. She had to admit that she'd never been.

Amanda, however, could agree with them on the beauty of the dive.

"Such a long flight, though," Sandy said.

"Oh, it was really a lovely jaunt for me," Amanda gushed. "We went with some of Father's associates, sailed for months and saw zillions of islands, and then went on to Australia. The week in Fiji was my favorite, I think. Though Tahiti was fabulous, too. We had such a darling little place there. While the yacht was being cleaned, we had charming and very private rooms right on the beach. The sunrises were exquisite, the sunsets even more so."

"Hey, all we have to do is step out of our tents tomorrow morning for the same effect," Keith said, arriving with a large plate of grilled fish. "There are some fantastic sunrises right here." He offered Amanda a broad smile. Flirtatious? Or intended to take some of the sting out of his reminder that their own home offered a world-class beauty.

"Oh, yes, this area is fabulous, as well." Amanda smiled meaningfully at Beth. "Especially when you really can't go anywhere else."

Beth smiled back, all the while envisioning dumping the ice in the cooler over the woman's head.

"Soup's on!" Matt announced cheerfully.

There were a few camp chairs, and Matt had spread blankets out on the sand. A looped palm offered a few seats perfectly created by nature, and with her plate filled with fish and potato salad, Beth found herself claiming the tree as a chair. Hank took the seat next to her, but when Amanda called to him, begging him to get her something to drink, he left, and she found herself being joined by Keith. She wondered if he was seeking her out on purpose. And then she wondered why. She didn't have a lack of confidence, it was just that...well, Amanda Mason was there, and she was the far better flirt, on top of being an undeniably alluring woman.

"So you work for a yacht club?" Keith asked.

"Yes." She waved a hand in the air. "*I* work for it. *They* belong to it."

He laughed. "Are you supposed to be the poor little rich girl or something?"

She shook her head, looking at him. "I like working

there. It's fun." She hesitated, wondering why she kept feeling compelled to explain things to him. "My brother is a member, so if I weren't working there, I'd have all his privileges. Working there pays well, and I get free dockage, which Ben uses, since employees get that perk and members don't, and he owns a boat and I don't. I see some of the most luxurious and beautiful yachts in the world. And meet some of the nicest people. Mostly."

"Mostly?" He offered her a slow, wry smile.

"Mostly," she repeated, refusing to say more. Had the tension in her relationship with Amanda been so evident to a stranger?

"It's always interesting when you get around boats," he said. "Some people are as rich as Croesus and you'd never know it, they're just so down to earth. Some are as poor as church mice, putting everything they have into staying on the water. And they're just as nice. But don't ever kid yourself. The sea can breed demons."

She looked up at him, startled, but he was rising, looking toward the group that had drawn around the fire.

Had he been warning her about something?

Maybe himself?

The light had faded in earnest. No more deep blues, purples, streaks of gold or any other color. Night had come.

In the far distance, a faint glow could be seen, coming from the lights along the heavily populated coast of south Florida. But on the island, there was nothing except for the glow from the fire. Around them, the foliage of the inner island had become blanketed in shadows.

The wind stirred, creating a rustle.

"The girls want to hear some ghost stories," Lee called out to Keith.

"I said pirate stories," Amber said, laughing.

"Pirates would be ghosts, by now," Ben told his daughter, amused.

"Most of the time," Keith said, moving toward the fire. "Except that there *are* modern-day pirates. All over the world."

"Too real," Amanda protested with a shiver. Of course, she was still clad in nothing but the skinny bathing suit. Sure, they were on a semitropical island. But the sea breezes at night could be cool.

Keith noticed her discomfort. He slipped off his shirt and draped it around her shoulders. She flashed him a beautiful smile. He smiled back.

It was a simple gesture of courtesy, but it made Beth lower her head, wondering how she could allow someone like Amanda to irritate her so much.

"Okay, so we want an old-fashioned pirate ghost story, right?" Keith asked. He didn't remain behind Amanda but strode toward the center of the group, closer to the fire. He hunkered down by the flames, forcing Beth to wonder if he was aware that the flames added a haunting quality to his classic features.

"I'll tell you the tale of the *Sea Star* and *La Doña*. Both were proud ships with billowing white sails! But one was English, and the other sailed under the flag of Spain. The *Sea Star* sailed from London in the year of our Lord 1725. Her captain was a fierce man, loyal to the core to the king. England and Spain were hardly on the best of terms, and Jonathan Pierce, the captain, was eager to seize a Spanish ship full of gold from the New World.

"Captain Pierce, however, wasn't sailing alone. Along with his crew, he was carrying a party of nobility. One of them was the Lady Marianne Howe, daughter of the governor of one of the small islands, and he was unaware that a year earlier, her ship had run aground on coral shoals and she'd been saved by a handsome young Spaniard, Alonzo Jimenez. Of course, under the circumstances, despite the fact that the young Spaniard and his crew had simply returned the Englishmen and women he had rescued to the governor in Virginia—asking no ransom, no reward, and ignoring the hostilities between the countries—there could be no happy ending for Marianne and Alonzo. Not only was he a Spaniard, but an untitled one, at that.

"Still, Marianne had managed to keep in contact with him, smuggling out love letters. She was ready to cast aside her title, her fortune and her family, all for Alonzo. He had arranged to hide his ship here, around the curve of Calliope Key—"

"Calliope Key?" Kim interrupted. "Where we are now?"

"Of course. What good would a ghost story be if it weren't about this island?" Keith asked, smiling slightly.

His voice was perfect for the tale, Beth thought. It was a rich, deep voice. She had to admit that she was as seduced as the others.

"Oh, right," Amber murmured.

Beth looked at her niece with a certain amusement. Amber was—and always had been—capable of sitting through the scariest horror movie. Now, however, her eyes were very wide.

Keith Henson—whatever he was really up to—had a talent for storytelling. With the strange fire glow on his face and the deep, intense rasp of his voice, he held them all enthralled.

"Go on," Ben said, his profound interest surprising Beth.

"Well, the young lovers never intended harm toward anyone. Marianne was a strong swimmer. She simply meant to get close enough to her lover's ship to escape into the sea, then find refuge on the island until he could come to her. With any luck, the *Sea Star* would have been long gone before anyone noticed she wasn't aboard.

"But while Marianne was conducting her daring escape into the sea, Captain Pierce was sending spies out in his small boats to get the lay of the land—well, the sea. Just as Marianne was reaching shore, news reached Pierce about the Spaniard hiding past the reefs. He manned his guns. Meanwhile, Alonzo had taken a boat to shore…this shore, right here, where our fire now burns. Just as he and Marianne met, the first cannons exploded. It was a fierce battle, and Alonzo was broken-hearted, watching his friends lead the fight…and die. His ship, *La Doña,* was sunk. Many of his men tried to swim to shore but were cut down by the English before they could reach landfall. Marianne was desperate that her lover not be caught, but Alonzo was brave to a fault. When Captain Pierce came ashore, following the Spanish crew, he prepared to fight. Their swords clashed so hotly that sparks flew. Then Captain Pierce was unarmed. He had lost the fight. Alonzo, however, refused to deliver the *coup de grâce.* He stepped back, and said that all he wanted was a small boat for himself and Marianne. Captain Pierce showed no gratitude for the fact that his life had been spared. His men came upon them, and he ordered that Alonzo should hang. Marianne was hysterical, heartbroken, and ashamed that her countryman could behave with so little honor. As Alonzo was dragged away, Pierce assured her that she would forget their enemy, and that he would be her new lover and her husband. Marianne wiped away her tears and approached him, and no doubt Captain Pierce assumed she was ready to accept his offer. But she reached into his belt and drew his pistol. She shot him dead, but too late to save her lover, for even as the shot rang out, Alonzo swung from the hangman's rope, crying out her name and his love—right before his neck snapped. Marianne, desperate in her grief, turned the gun on herself.

"And as that shot went off, the *Sea Star* suddenly moved…drifting out to sea. The Englishmen on the island, stunned and frozen by what had occurred before their eyes, moved too slowly. They raced for their longboats and made to sea. But neither they nor the *Sea Star* were ever seen again. Sometimes, they say, at night, the ship can be seen, riding the wind and the waves, only to disappear into the clouds or over the horizon."

"Oh…" Sandy breathed.

"And what about Marianne, Alonzo and Captain Pierce?" Amber asked.

"They haunt the island, of course," Keith said. "At night, when you hear whispering in the breeze, when the palm fronds move, when the wind moans…what you hear is their voices as they roam the island for eternity."

"Oh, jeez," Kim groaned.

"Oh…" Amber breathed.

Keith looked at Ben apologetically, afraid that his story had been too effective.

"You're not scared, are you?" Kim demanded.

"Of course not," Amber protested. She laughed, but it was a brittle sound. "Don't be silly. Sandy, you're not scared, are you?"

"About staying on a haunted island?" Sandy asked. "No. I mean, the tents are all pretty close together on the beach when you think about it, right? Of course, I do wish Brad and I were one of the groups in the middle."

"I'm sure we're just fine," Amanda said.

"I think it will be fun," Brad teased. "Sandy's going to be all cuddly tonight, I assure you."

"Oh, my God!" Amber exclaimed.

"What?" Ben demanded.

"Dad…we might have found one of them today. One of the ghosts!"

"It's just a story," Keith said. "You asked for a ghost story and—"

"No, no, there was a skull. At least…we thought it was a skull," Amber said.

Ben groaned loudly. "Girls, one of you stubbed a toe on a conch shell. There was no skull. Enough with the scary talk, okay?" he said firmly.

Beth kept her mouth shut, wincing. And not because Ben was annoyed, but because she was suddenly more frightened than ever herself. The girls had just let everyone know they had seen a skull.

And someone here, someone sharing the island with them, had taken that skull for reasons of their own. Reasons that couldn't be ignored.

"It's easy to imagine things out here," Matt said easily. "I promise you, there are no ghosts here."

"But lots of ghost stories supposedly have some truth to them. There were shipwrecks all around here. I'll bet the story is true, and that the ghosts whispered it in your ear," Amber said.

"Okay, that's a scary thought!" Sandy said, shivering.

"It's getting better and better for me, girls. Please, go

on," Brad said, laughing, but also trying to ease the fear the girls seemed to feel.

"We're in the Bermuda Triangle, too, aren't we?" Amanda asked, rising. "Luckily, I don't have a superstitious bone in my body." She stretched, and Keith's shirt fell from her shoulders. She reached down languidly to pick it up and slowly walked—or sashayed—over to Keith to return it. "Besides," she said softly, "there are a lot of handsome, well-muscled men around here to protect us if we need it. Well, good night, all."

Her cousins and father rose to join her, saying their thank-yous as they rose.

The group began to break up, everyone laughing, promising to see each other in the morning.

As they returned to their tents, Beth was silent.

"Aunt Beth, are you afraid of ghosts?" Amber asked.

"No," she assured her niece.

"Then what are you afraid of?" Amber persisted.

Beth glanced self-consciously over at Ben. "The living," she said softly.

Her brother sighed, shaking his head. "Just like good old Captain Pierce, I carry a gun. And I won't let anyone close enough to use it against me," he assured her.

A few minutes later they had all retired, Ben and Beth to their "one-bedroom" tents and the girls to the large "two-bedroom" Ben had recently purchased for his daughter. None of them were more than ten feet apart, with the girls situated between the adults.

Amber and Kim kept a light on, and Beth found herself hoping their supply of batteries would be sufficient. She could hear the girls giggling, probably inventing ghost stories. She told herself that people were simply susceptible to the dark, to shadows, whispers on the breeze, and the dark intent of a tale told by firelight.

But she was uneasy herself. She reminded herself that she had been uneasy long before Keith's ghost story.

It's just a story, he'd said. A good story, told on the spur of the moment.

And it hadn't scared her. Not a silly—even sad— ghost story.

Yet…she *was* scared.

Despite her unease, she eventually drifted off to sleep. Her dreams were disjointed, snatches of conversation, visions that seemed to dance before her, never really taking shape until she saw, in her mind's eye, a beautiful young girl in eighteenth-century dress, a handsome Spaniard and a sea captain, sword in hand….

The sea captain—arresting, exciting, masculine— took on the appearance of someone familiar… Keith Henson.

Sadly, even in her dream, the beautiful young girl looked like Amanda.

She tossed and turned as the dream unfolded, more like a play with the director continually calling, "Cut!" than a real dream.

And then she heard the wind rise, a rustling in the brush…

She awakened, a sense of panic taking hold of her. Her palms were clammy, her limbs icy.

It was just a nightmare, she told herself.

Except it wasn't just a nightmare.

Nearby, the foliage was rustling. Someone was creeping about in the stygian darkness.

Pirates had definitely frequented this area, once upon a time.

Spanish galleons *had* carried gold.

Had Keith truly only been telling a tall tale?

Because human nature never changed. Piracy still existed. She wasn't frightened by anything sad that might have occurred in the past, because the present could be frightening enough.

Someone was out there. Not a ghost.

Someone very much alive.

3

Night moves.

He had expected them.

Someone on the island was playing games.

Innocent games? Searching for legends?

Or games with far more deadly intent?

Keith rose silently and waited just inside his tent, listening, trying to determine from which direction the noises were coming. There was a breeze, so the trees continued to rustle. But he had heard far more than the subtle movement of the palm fronds in the soft, natural wind of the night.

Whoever it was, they had slipped across the sand and into the dense foliage of the interior.

Looking for a skull?

Or was there something more, something entirely different, going on? Perhaps he shouldn't have told his ghost story. But he had told it on purpose, watching the others closely for their reactions. In the end, though, he'd learned nothing except that everyone seemed awfully easy to spook.

But had he caused this movement in the night?

He eased slowly, silently, from the tent and started

across the white sand. Just ahead, barely discernible, the rustling sound came again.

Suddenly there was a light ahead, as if whoever was there felt they had gone far enough not to be noticed.

With the appearance of the light, he knew for certain he wasn't chasing some nocturnal animal through the trees.

He followed, quickening his pace as he left the beach behind.

Fear kept Beth dead still for several seconds until her instinct to protect the girls rose to the fore.

She almost burst from the tent, to find...

Nothing. Nothing but the sea by night, the soft sound of the gentle waves washing the shore, a nearby palm bent ever so slightly in homage to the breeze.

She went still, looking around, listening.

Still nothing. She told herself she needed to get a grip. She had never been the cowardly type, and stories were just that: stories. There were real dangers in life, but she had always dealt with them. She didn't walk through dangerous neighborhoods alone at night. She carried pepper spray, and she'd learned how to use it. She even knew how to shoot, since their friends included several cops, who'd taken her to the shooting range and taught her how to handle a gun, though she didn't choose to keep one, since her house had an alarm system.

So why was she panicking?

Because in her heart of hearts, no matter what anyone said, she was certain she had seen a skull. And it hadn't belonged to any long-dead pirate.

No one nearby, no sounds now. She still had to check on the girls.

First she looked down the beach. All the fires were out, and she could see the tents, silent in the night. Keith and his buddies had tied a hammock to a couple of palms, where it swung ever so slightly in the breeze. Down from them, another group of tents, and farther still, a larger tent, all of them quiet and dark.

She hurried over to the girls' tent and looked in, her heart in her throat. But both of them were in the second of the two little rooms, and they were soundly sleeping. Their light was still on, turning their small bedroom into an oasis and everything around it into a black hole.

She exhaled in relief and started backing out— straight into something solid, large.

In her, terror rose and she screamed.

Keith heard the scream and froze, his blood congealing at the terror in that shrill sound.

In a split second, he was back in action.

The scream had come from the beach.

Beth!

The light ahead went out, but he ignored it and turned, tearing through the brush, desperate to reach her.

She let out a second, terrified scream; then she swung around, ready to fight to the death on behalf of the girls.

There was no need.

"Dammit, Beth," a voice swore fiercely in the night. "What the hell are you doing?"

She blinked, drawing back with just seconds to spare before giving her brother a black eye.

"Ben?"

"Who the hell did you expect?"

"You scared me to death," she accused him.

"What's going on?" Amber asked nervously, rubbing sleep from her eyes as she crawled from the bedroom.

Kim followed, and the four of them wound up in the small outer room of the tent, tripping over one another.

"Nothing," Ben said irritably.

Just then, as Amber tried to stand, she bumped one of the poles and the tent collapsed on them.

Ben tried never to swear around his daughter, but tangled in the nylon, tasting sand, Beth could hear him breaking his rule beneath his breath.

"It's all right. The tent just fell," she heard herself protesting.

But when she twisted to free herself, she only became more entangled.

Then the fabric was lifted from her, and, looking up, she saw the face of Keith Henson, tense and taut as he stared down at her.

"What the hell is going on?" he demanded curtly.

"Nothing," she snapped.

"You screamed."

By then Ben had managed to escape the mess of poles and nylon and make it to his feet. He was shaking his head disgustedly.

"Sorry, everyone."

When she looked around, still on her back, she saw that everyone was there, flashlights shining. Had she really screamed that loudly?

Well, of course she had.

And she was still flat on her back in an oversize T-shirt riding up her thighs, staring up at everyone. Just as the thought occurred to her, Keith reached a hand down to her. At that particular moment, she didn't think twice about accepting it.

His grip was powerful. She was on her feet before she knew it.

"What is going on?" Amanda demanded, swiping back an errant piece of blond hair. Even at night, Beth noticed dejectedly, Amanda looked great. Like a soap-opera character who awoke in the morning with perfect makeup and shiny teeth.

"Are you all right?" Hank asked, polite as always.

Roger, definitely the oldest in the crowd, set an arm on his daughter's shoulder and looked over at Beth, smiling, as well. "Maybe we should avoid ghost stories at night," he said easily.

She tried to smile. And then apologize. "I'm really sorry. I woke up, and went to check on the girls. And then, backing out, I ran into my brother, who was apparently checking on why I was checking on the girls. There were too many of us in too small a space. I guess I woke everyone. I'm sorry." Except, of course, she was certain that she hadn't awakened *everyone*.

Someone had already been up and creeping around the island.

Who?

It was impossible now to tell, because all of them were there. Staring at her.

Amber started to giggle. Beth stared at her, brows raised.

"Oh, Aunt Beth, I'm sorry, but it *is* funny."

"Yeah, a real hoot," Ben muttered.

"Hey, let's just get the tent back up, huh?" Keith suggested.

Kim stared at him, obviously fascinated. "Oh, sure, thanks."

"I can manage—" Beth began.

"Take the help when it's offered, honey. Then maybe we can all get some sleep." For once Amanda spoke without malice. There was even a teasing tone to her words.

Ben smiled. "Keith, if you'll give me a hand, we'll have this back up in two minutes." He cleared his throat. "Beth, you're in the way."

"Excuse me."

"Me, too," Amanda said, and yawned. "I'm going back to bed. Dad, want to walk me back? Hank? Gerald?"

"If you guys are all set, we'll go catch a little more sleep, too," Sandy said.

"We're fine. Good night all," Ben told them.

Once again they parted for the night. Or what was left of it. Glancing at her watch, Beth saw that it was around four in the morning.

The girls' tent was quickly repositioned, and their group, too, was ready to try for a few more hours of sleep.

Ben thanked Keith, as did the girls. "Hey, Aunt Beth. You could bring your sleeping bag in here, and then you wouldn't have to worry about us," Amber said.

"I'll give you guys your privacy," Beth told her, smiling.

Keith was staring at her, his gaze intent, as if he was trying to read something in her expression.

Then he smiled easily, without suspicion. "You all right?"

"Yes, fine."

"I'm sorry if I scared you with my story."

"Don't be ridiculous. I'm not afraid of ghosts." She couldn't help the feeling that her eyes were narrowing.

And she wondered if he realized she was telling him that she *was* scared, but not of any story—of him.

"Well, then, good night."

With a wave, he started off for his own tent.

"Girls, go to bed," Ben said firmly.

"Good night," Amber said.

"Good night," Kim echoed.

They went into their tent again. Beth winced as she heard them giggling.

"Beth, what the hell was going on?" Ben demanded.

She sighed. "I heard a noise. I was worried about the girls."

He let out a sigh. "What's the matter with you? You never used to be paranoid."

"I'm not paranoid."

"Listen, Beth, we're surrounded by people here, half of the people we know. Nothing is going to happen."

"You scared me," she protested. "Creeping up behind me like that. You might have made yourself known."

"I didn't know who you were," he told her.

"Aha!" Beth declared. "You *were* worried. Admit it."

He sighed. "Beth, nothing's going to happen," he responded. "Trust me, huh?"

"I do trust you," she told him.

"Then act like it."

"Okay."

"Can we go to sleep now?" he asked hopefully.

"Yes."

"Okay. Good night."

"Good night."

Beth realized that he was waiting for her to be safely tucked back into bed. She smiled and nodded ruefully, then crawled back into her own tent and into her sleeping bag, where she lay staring at the fabric above her in the deep darkness of the night.

She rolled over. It was better in that direction—the girls were still sleeping with the little lantern flashlight on.

She tried to close her eyes and sleep.

She had heard something.

Or had she? Maybe it *had* been only the natural rustling of the wind in the leaves. Had she simply made up something in her mind, and become truly paranoid?

Or, on the other hand, was she just being sensible?

Trust me....

She did trust her brother. He would gladly die for his daughter, she knew, and would probably do the same for her, and for Kim.

She just hoped to hell he was never called upon to do so.

She tossed again, yearning to go to sleep.

It was a long time coming.

Amanda Mason was definitely a flirt. She made a point of crashing into one of the guys every time she hit the ball.

Usually himself, Keith decided wryly. He wasn't letting it get to his ego, since she also liked to tease Lee—she'd seen the boat, and they'd all said it was his. She didn't much mind brushing against Brad, either, even though he was here with his girlfriend. But so far, no one had taken their makeshift volleyball game too seriously. So far, everyone was laughing.

He, Amanda, Brad, Lee and Kim were one team. Sandy, Amber, Gerald, Matt and Ben made up the other. Roger Mason sat on the sidelines, being the ref.

So far today, they hadn't even seen Ms. Beth Anderson.

"Outside!" Matt yelled in protest of Keith's serve.

"It was not outside—you just missed it," he returned.

"Where's our referee?" Matt demanded.

"Sleeping, despite the noise," Amanda said, chuckling affectionately as she pointed to her father.

It was true. Roger had leaned back in the hammock and gone straight to sleep.

"It was definitely outside," came a voice.

Keith spun around. She was up at last, yawning despite her late appearance. She held a cup of coffee. Sunglasses covered her unique marble-toned eyes, and she was in a bathing-suit top and chopped-off Levi's pedal pushers.

His serve hadn't been outside, and if she had been watching, she had seen that. He wondered why she had decided that they were enemies from the first moment she had seen him.

Other than the fact that she'd been trying desperately to hide her discovery from him.

He forced a smile. "Hey, Matt, the lady says you're right."

"Beth Anderson, you're blind!" Amanda protested irritably.

"It's just a game, isn't it?" Beth asked politely.

"I'm going to have to speak to the commodore and make sure you don't ref any games at the club," Amanda said, a teasing note in her voice that was meant to hide her still-obvious dislike.

Beth managed an icy smile and an easy laugh. "You do that, Amanda," she said.

"Aunt Beth, come play," Amber urged.

"I think I like Roger's idea best," she said.

"Sure—wake the rest of us up in the middle of the night and then sleep all day," Matt teased. "I don't think so."

"No, of course not, come play," Hank urged. "And you can ref my game any old day," he teased.

"Come on, Beth, play," Ben urged.

"I'd make the teams uneven," she protested.

Roger, who had appeared to be so peacefully sleeping, rose. "I'll join in and make it even," he offered.

He walked past Beth, smiling. "Fifty-eight, and I guarantee I can take on you kids."

It was interesting, watching the group dynamics, Keith thought. Everyone seemed to get along fine except for Amanda and Beth.

Was Beth jealous?

Or was it vice versa? Amanda was petite, ultrafeminine. Beth seemed...

Elegant, he found himself thinking. A strange adjective, since she was in beachwear, as casual as any of them.

The teams readjusted. Beth took the serve.

It was wicked.

From the rear corner, he barely returned it. Ben caught the ball, and Roger, bless him, attempted a slam. Amazingly, Beth caught it low, setting it up for her brother, who went in for the kill.

"Point," Beth said calmly, reclaiming the ball.

The game was neck and neck from then on. Sandy was the weakest link, but she made up for it with her good humor and refusal to give up.

Beth was a superb player, in excellent physical condition. She wasn't just shapely, she was sleek. Perfectly toned. She played not so much to win as simply to play hard. There was a vibrance about her, a love of life, of activity, a passion that seemed to come through in everything she did and said, in the way her eyes seemed to burn like a crystal fire when they met his across the net. She clearly loved a challenge.

He had the feeling she would always meet one head-on.

At last Beth's team took the final point, and they all collapsed, laughing.

"What's up next?" Hank asked, lying flat on the sand in exhaustion.

Lee was up and staring at Keith. "Fishing?" he suggested.

"Yeah, fishing," Keith replied.

They were fishing, all right.

"Not me, boys. I'm for lazing in the sun now," Amanda said, rolling sinuously to her feet.

Ben nodded toward Lee's yacht. "You asking us out on that?"

"Would you like to see her?" Lee offered.

Keith looked at Lee and knew just what he was thinking. Keep the current denizens of the island with them, occupied. Keep an eye on them. Know what they're up to at all times.

Keep them fishing, not diving.

He stayed silent. In the end, there wasn't anything they could do about people diving these waters. Still, if discoveries here had been easy…well, they wouldn't be here now.

"You bet," Ben said enthusiastically. "Looks as if she's got every new electronic device known to man."

"I like my toys," Lee said with a shrug.

"I'm with you," Ben said.

"Hell, I'd like to see her, too," Hank said, grinning.

"Me, too," Gerald agreed.

"Little boys, little toys, big boys, big toys," Amanda teased.

"Me, I'd like to see the hammock again," Roger said.

"I think Sandy and I are going to take a walk, explore..." Brad said. "But thanks for the offer."

"Beth?" Lee inquired. "Girls?"

"I'd love to see the boat," Amber said.

"Yacht," Beth murmured beneath her breath.

"But actually," Amber admitted a little sheepishly, "I hate fishing."

"That's cool," Lee told her.

"Beth?"

"I'll stay with the girls," she said. "But I do appreciate the offer."

"You don't care if I go?" Ben asked his sister.

"Not at all!"

But she did. She cared like hell.

"Maybe I will join you men," Amanda said with something like a purr. "The sun is actually much better on the water. And I can always escape below if all the testosterone proves to be a bit too much. I'll just get my things." She started to walk away, then turned back. "I am not, however, cleaning any fish."

Keith watched her sashay toward her tent.

When he turned to study Beth again, she was studying him. The way she was looking at him caused a little pang to creep into his heart.

She was so suspicious of him.

Well, she had every right to be.

But this was a game he played often. And he knew how to play it.

And he knew damn well that he couldn't let her get in his way.

Her eyes swept over him. Cool. Still assessing him.

Then she turned.

He had been dismissed.

Beth was definitely angry with Ben, although she wasn't sure he knew it. And she wasn't about to lash out at him in public—certainly not with the public that was surrounding them.

He was so big about protecting his family, but show the guy a new yacht with all kinds of cool toys, and he was gone in a flash.

To be fair, he thought she was being paranoid and there was nothing to protect his family from. Maybe she couldn't blame him. There had been nothing in the inland clearing, and last night she had awakened the entire island by screaming because she had run into him.

At this point she wasn't even sure herself just what she had seen. Maybe it had been a conch shell, and what she had imagined, in a stomach-churning moment, to be human tissue only sea grass and debris.

It was so easy to question oneself, especially in the bright light of day. Except that the afternoon was waning.

Sitting on the beach with the girls, she looked out to sea. The dinghies were long gone, bearing the fishermen—and woman—out to sea. Roger was sleeping in the hammock. Brad and Sandy were laughing, and running in and out of the waves, being romantic, being a couple.

Good for them. It seemed odd that they were the only couple among the groups. That Amanda had come on a family outing seemed amazing to Beth, but then, she disliked the woman. Roger and Hank were always decent enough, and though she really didn't know Gerald well, he seemed okay, as well. Was she jealous of Amanda? She probed her own psyche in a moment of introspection.

No. She really, truly simply disliked her. And she really, truly liked most people.

So that, she decided with a wry grin, really, truly made Amanda a bitch.

"Aunt Beth, what are you smirking at?"

"I am not smirking," she protested, turning to her niece. "I'm just…smiling at the day."

"It really is a cool weekend, huh?" Kim said, looking up from her star-studded magazine. "I was afraid of being bored, but…well, those guys are cool."

"Those guys are way too old for you two," Beth said sharply.

"Aunt Beth," Amber groaned. "We know that. Can't they just be nice guys?"

"We really don't know them," Beth reminded them.

"You sound like a schoolteacher."

"Right, well, schoolteachers teach you things you need to know."

Beth stood up, stretching, eyeing the water again. Lee's yacht was almost out of sight. Brad and Sandy were still happily cavorting. Roger was sleeping.

She hesitated, looking at Amber and Kim, and then she headed for her tent. Returning, she dropped the little black pepper-spray container on the towel next to Amber. "If anyone comes near you, you know what to do."

Amber looked at the pepper spray, then up at her. "Really, Aunt Beth. Are you expecting a giant grouper to leap out of the sea and accost us?"

"Don't be a wiseass. Wiseacre," she quickly amended. But not quickly enough. Both the girls were laughing at her.

"Amber, Kim, I'm serious."

Amber forced herself to look somber. "We're taking you very seriously."

Beth really didn't think there could be any trouble, not with the yacht out at sea. She offered a dry smile and started to walk away.

"Hey," Amber called. "Where are you going?"

"For a walk."

"You're going back to look for the skull, right?" Amber pressed.

"No." She stepped back toward them. "And don't go talking about the fact that we might have seen a skull, do you understand?"

Amber let out a great sigh. "No, Aunt Beth. I mean, yes. We won't mention it again, okay?"

"Good. And scream like hell if anything happens."

"Like you did last night?" Amber teased.

"Behave or I'll tell your dad that every young guy in the theater department *isn't* gay!"

"Hey, have a great walk, Beth. We'll be little angels, sitting here. Ready with the pepper spray," Kim vowed seriously.

Shaking her head, Beth started off.

The island was such a strange paradise, she thought, heading toward the path through the pines and scrub brush just behind the area they had chosen to stake out their tents. The beach was pristine, the water clear and beautiful. Of course, just beyond there were dangerous, even deadly, reefs. But those who knew the area and could navigate those reefs knew how to reach a real Eden. But behind the beach, the island became a very different place, the dense foliage creating little nooks and crannies, shadows and an eerie green darkness.

She had always loved it.

Until now.

Today it seemed the island itself was working against her. She lost the trail and almost emerged at the other end of the beach. Retracing her steps, she swore softly.

A large mosquito decided to take a good chunk out of her arm, and she slapped it furiously, taking inordinate pleasure out of the fact that she managed to kill it.

At last she wound her way back to the clearing where she had stood the day before with the girls.

She looked around, trying to assess the area. Fallen palm fronds seemed to be everywhere.

Had there been that many yesterday? She tried to remember exactly where they had been standing.

And then where Keith Henson had emerged from the trees.

In the end, because there were so many palm fronds down on the ground, she decided to examine them one by one.

She tried to make sure she didn't miss an area. She had gotten to her fourth frond when she heard footsteps.

Someone else was heading for the clearing.

She forced herself to pause and listen. After determining the direction from which the sounds were coming, she headed across the clearing. As soon as she reached the shelter of the trees, she spun around, afraid that whoever it was had already burst into the clearing and seen her.

Through the trees, she could see something glinting.

She narrowed her eyes and swallowed hard. Whoever was coming was carrying a knife. A big knife.

A machete.

Staring intently at that deadly glint, she backed farther into the trees.

Suddenly she felt an arm reach around her middle, pulling her deeper into the foliage.

A scream rose to her throat.

But a second hand clamped tightly over her mouth, and no sound escaped.

4

Stretched out on the sand, Amber watched her aunt disappear into the foliage, then rolled again to face Kimberly with a sigh.

"We've got to do something!"

"About what?"

"Beth, of course."

"You're calling her 'Beth' now?" Kimberly queried with a brow arched high in a semblance of mature disapproval.

"No…it's just, we've got to do something."

"She's so cute," Kim agreed.

"And so is he," Amber said.

"Which one?" Kim asked, frowning.

"The cute one."

"Even your dad is cute," Kim said.

Amber laughed, shuddering. "Ugh. Dads are not cute."

Kim shrugged. "I'm sure he is to lots of people."

"I know, but…ugh. No, I'm talking about *him.* And I know you know which one I'm talking about."

"Keith Henson," Kim agreed sagely.

"We need to get the two of them fixed up."

"Amber, they're both here. If they want to get fixed up, they'll do it." Kim giggled. "I mean, they're older than we are. They've got to have some smarts."

"Do you think he has a wife somewhere? Or a girlfriend?" Amber asked worriedly.

"I don't think so."

"He better have, like, a real job. I don't want my aunt working her whole life to support some beach bum."

"Amber, we're not getting them married off or anything."

"But we should get them together," Amber protested. "Seriously, she's so pretty, but she never goes out. She needs a date."

Kim blushed. "You mean she's not getting any?" she asked with a giggle.

"Kim!" Amber nudged her hard.

"Well?"

"We need to set her up. But first we have to check him out."

"How are we supposed to do that?"

"I'm not sure yet. We'll have to see when we get home. Dad has lots of cop friends. We can talk to one of them."

"Amber, we may never see these guys again once we go home."

Amber sat up, grinning, and did an amazing Alfred Hitchcock impersonation. "Have you ever had a premonition?"

Kim laughed. "All right. We'll do a real investigation when we get home. Meanwhile, I'll find out a few things about him."

"And how will you do that?" Amber demanded.

Kim smiled smugly. "Silly. I'll just ask him."

* * *

The yacht was state of the art. Ben loved it the minute he stepped aboard.

"Wow," he said simply to Lee.

He worked hard and earned decent money as an attorney, and he'd been proud of his own boat, but in comparison, *Time Off* was small.

And simple.

What the hell does this guy do for a living? he wondered, though he was too polite to ask. None of the guys seemed like dope dealers, and he'd learned that in Miami, lots of people were simply independently wealthy.

Hank Mason wasn't quite so hesitant.

"How the hell do you afford a puppy like this?" he demanded.

"Family money, I'm afraid." Lee's pride was justified when he grinned and said, "She's something, huh? She's a Hatteras, top of the line, and she's been customized, since most of these ladies aren't set up for real fishing."

Customized to a T, Ben thought. Topside, there was the kind of rigging that made deep-water sport fishing fun. The flybridge offered every convenience from a global explorer to sonar and radar equipment, along with a stereo system and the more mundane racks for drinks and snacks. The upper deck offered complete comfort, and the decking was exquisite, with teak trimming. There was even a small refrigerator. The stern afforded racks for at least twelve diving tanks, and a lift-top seat bore a small sign that read Diving Equipment.

"Come into the cabin. You'll like her even more," Lee told Ben.

"I like her already," Amanda said. She smiled up at

Ben and linked an arm through his. "Now this, I must say, is a boat."

Ben had known Amanda for several years, though never well. She was definitely beautiful, capable of stirring his senses, but also making him uncomfortable. He'd learned a long time ago that when someone you loved died, you lost a part of yourself, but you were still among the living. And being alive, he definitely had sexual urges. Amanda gave a man the impression that she could fulfill those urges beyond his wildest dreams. It would be a lie to say she didn't have an effect on him. The problem was, she gave the same impression to every man. He would never trust a woman like her if he so much as blinked. For some guys, it would be okay. They were players. It was curious, though, that she seemed to be hanging on to him. He knew he was decent looking, fit and made a good living.

But the island, as Amanda had said herself, was chock-full of testosterone. Lee, Matt and Keith were the kind of men women always seemed to go for—well-muscled, tall, with the slightly rough good looks and hard-adventure attitude that seemed to draw women like moths.

So why the hell was Amanda clinging to him?

He wasn't a player. His life focused—maybe too much, as Beth was always warning him—on his daughter. And he had a great career. So unless he found himself falling head over heels in love again, he kept his social life discreet. It actually did exist, which might surprise his sister.

But then, a lot about him might surprise his sister.

"Cool, huh?" Amanda murmured, snuggling a little

closer. She was wearing sexy perfume, and she knew how to press her anatomy against a guy.

He smiled and shrugged, looking down at her. "It's one hell of a boat," he agreed.

"Come below," Lee urged, and the rest followed.

Only Lee and Matt were hosting their excursion. Keith had chosen not to come, and despite his impatience with Beth, Ben had to admit that the guy staying back had caused him a bit of concern. But Brad and Sandy were on the island, as well, as was Roger. Though he vaguely felt he should be concerned about Keith, he just couldn't believe the man had any real evil intentions. He didn't like to believe in instinct—he'd worked in the D.A.'s office long enough to learn that it was unreliable at best—but no matter what logic told him, he didn't fear for his daughter, her friend or his sister when they were with the guy.

"Oh, wow!" Amanda exclaimed, hugging his arm. "This is beautiful!"

The cabin utilized its limited space with sleek elegance. A turn to the left of the steps led straight to an aft cabin, while the steps themselves led into a galley that seemed to offer more appliances than his home kitchen. The galley spilled into a main salon with a desk that held a computer, a radio and a number of electronics he couldn't even name. A table looked as if it could hold up to eight diners, and a hallway led to a forward cabin and the head. Everything was leather, teak or chrome.

"Can I get anyone anything?" Lee asked.

"Beer," Ben said.

Lee moved into the galley, grinning. "Amanda?"

"You have any white wine back there?"

"Sure. Hank… Gerald?"

The other two men settled on beers. After the drinks were served—even Amanda's wine was in a small bottle—Lee led the way through to the aft cabin. The master stateroom held a large, comfortable bed. "It's a trundle," Lee explained proudly. "When you need more space, you just pull it out. Of course, you lose your floor space that way. But it allows for a lot of sleeping space. There are a couple of 'closet bunks' in the hallway, as well. There's a private head here in the master stateroom, too, with a shower. But it's the fishing we're out for. Let's head back up."

Ben thought Matt might have gone topside already, to fire up the motor. But he hadn't.

He had remained in the cabin by the computer desk, radio, and Ben had the oddest feeling that the guy was guarding them.

Amanda was still glued to his arm, but Ben had a feeling she, too, was aware that although the saying here seemed to be *Make yourself at home,* there were certain areas of home that were off-limits.

Why?

His instincts were kicking in again. There was something askew with this picture. But what? For a sick moment he wondered if these guys were involved in a modern piracy ring, if they hadn't acquired the yacht illegally. Then again, if a vessel like this had gone missing, he would have heard about it. The members of the club had associates all over the world as well, and the theft of a craft like the *Sea Serpent* wouldn't have gone unnoted.

So much for his instincts. On the one hand, he was convinced that Keith, back onshore, would never cause the least danger to the people Ben loved. And on the other hand…

"C'mon," Lee urged. "Come see the fish finder on this beauty. We'll be hauling in our dinner at turbo speed."

Amanda disentangled herself from Ben, yawning. "You know, I was thinking maybe I'd take a little snooze." She laughed softly, looking at Ben. "We were all awakened in the middle of the night," she reminded them.

"No way," Lee protested. "We're striking out to sea, all for one and one for all. Everyone topside!"

Amanda pouted prettily. She would have spoken again, Ben was certain, except that Lee was striding toward them, ready to herd them all up, as if he were a friendly sheepdog keeping the masses together.

He wondered if he was just creating a sense of something that wasn't there, more spooked by Beth's unease than he'd realized.

She was worse than he was, worrying about Amber, worrying about him, spending the majority of her time at work. For most young women, the club would be a smorgasbord of rugged, tanned, athletic professional men. But not for Beth, who didn't date where she worked. It was as if she was oblivious.

Tall, tanned, perfectly fit in a feminine way—stacked—with her dark hair and exotic eyes, she was probably the greatest catch on the island. But even here, she was proving adept at keeping her distance.

"You're mean," Amanda teased Lee, and clasping his arm, a pretty moue on her face. "I'm just so sleepy."

"I'll set you up on deck. You'll love it," Lee assured her.

At that moment Ben knew for a fact that his suspicions were correct.

No one, for any reason, was going to be left in the cabin alone.

So just what were they up to?

"Shh!"

Beth found the sound absurdly reassuring. Though she couldn't see the man whose hand was on her mouth, she knew it was Keith Henson. Was it the feel of him? A certain chemistry? It didn't matter. She just knew.

She felt his other hand spanning the bare flesh of her midriff. He was tense but no longer forceful, and the hand on her mouth eased, then moved away. She could feel the thud of both his heart and her own.

As they stood there, silent, strangely bonded, Brad and Sandy appeared in the clearing.

And Brad was the one wielding the machete.

It was a wicked-looking weapon, and yet...boaters planning to put ashore on an island might readily have one. In fact, he was using it for the exact purpose one might expect in such a circumstance—chopping away at the heavy growth.

"I think it was here," Sandy said wearily.

"Here is an awfully damn big space," Brad said irritably.

"Don't be ridiculous. It's a small island."

"Way too small, at the moment. We should have realized. It's a weekend."

"Should we just quit moaning and start looking?"

Beth adjusted her footing ever so slightly. Behind her, Keith did likewise. He seemed to have no intention of letting her go, accosting the pair or letting his own presence be known. She could feel the coiled tension in him. He was listening intently.

Were they looking for a skull?

And if Keith Henson didn't know about the skull, why would he be so worried about a young couple searching a clearing on the island?

She turned slightly, looking up at him as Brad hacked away at overhanging fronds and branches. He shook his head, warning her that she shouldn't move, shouldn't give herself away.

A fly buzzed near her nose. She began to wonder just how long she could stand so perfectly still. Yet, her own heart continued to race, and her suspicions were hiked to the limit, every fiber of her being attuned to danger.

"I hear something," Sandy announced suddenly.

"Don't be ridiculous," Brad told her.

"No, no, I hear something. From the beach."

"They're fishing."

"They're not *all* fishing."

"So what? We're just walking around the island."

"I don't like this, Brad. Let's go back."

"Are you scared?"

"You bet." She looked at him pleadingly. "Come on, they all have jobs. They'll have to get back to work in a couple of days. The island will be all ours again. Please, let's just get out of here for now."

Brad let out a long sigh. Then he slipped his arms around her, letting the machete dangle.

"Ooh, nice sword," Sandy teased.

"You bet, baby."

He started to kiss her. Then, with his free hand, to fondle her.

Beth held her breath, feeling acutely uncomfortable. She could still feel the hand on her own midriff, and watching these two get more and more intimate…

I thought you were scared, Sandy! she longed to shout.
Then things got worse.

"Want to really fool around?" Brad whispered.

"Maybe."

"Then you won't be scared? Worried about getting caught?"

"There's something kind of exciting about it," Sandy whispered in return. Her hand slid from his chest.

Lower. Lower.

Beth could feel her cheeks flaming to a bright pink.

"Then again... I should be punishing you," Sandy said huskily. "You were all over the blonde today."

"The blonde was all over *me* today," Brad protested.

"You didn't seem to mind."

"Hey...she was determined to let me know she was full-bodied."

"You and every other guy there."

"Um, true, but you shouldn't let her worry you."

"No," Sandy agreed. "It's the other one I'm worried about. You were looking at her."

"I was looking at her?"

"Yeah, you know. *Looking.*"

"Well, she *is* really sexy. Legs that go on forever. Imagine what she could do with those legs."

Beth could feel the flames deepen in her cheeks, and she imagined that Keith had to be aware of it, too. She couldn't stand much more of this. Self-preservation had kept her silent so far. Embarrassment might well send her flying from cover.

"Hey," Sandy protested.

"Am I turning you on yet?" Brad demanded.

"Seriously... I keep hearing something."

"What happened to the idea of being caught in the act of being so hot and sexy?"

"Those girls are underage."

"Yeah?"

"Well, the last thing we need now is to be arrested for contributing to the delinquency of a minor," Sandy said.

"Good point," Brad agreed seriously. But then he quickly returned to his lighter tone. "Hey…the tent is exotic and hot, you know."

"So let's get back to the beach—please! In a couple of days, they'll all leave. It will be our island again, Brad. Then we can take care of things."

At last the two of them left, disappearing across the clearing, taking the same trail Beth had used.

Behind her, Keith remained still for what seemed like an aeon. It was all she could do to keep from wrenching away. And yet he was right—they needed to let Sandy and Brad put some distance between them.

Finally, however, she could stand it no longer. He was still touching her, his hand still on her midriff, her body backed flush against his.

She stepped away and turned, staring at him, tense and wary.

"What was that all about?" she demanded.

His eyes were as dark as ebony. He wasn't wearing his sunglasses, but his eyes still gave no clue of what thoughts lurked in his mind.

"Shh," he warned her.

"They're gone," she reminded him.

"The trees may well have ears," he said quietly, studying her.

She lowered her voice. "What were they looking for?" she demanded.

"I don't know."

"Why didn't you accost them?"

"Do you really think it's a great idea to accost a man carrying a machete?" he cross-queried.

"But…" She shook her head. "Now we'll never know what they were doing."

"Maybe, maybe not."

She backed away another step, frowning. "What are *you* doing here?"

"Looking."

"Looking for what?" she demanded sharply.

He leaned back against a tree, crossing his arms over his chest. "Whatever you were trying to hide when we met."

Startled, she hesitated, then came back at him far too late. "Don't be ridiculous. I wasn't hiding anything."

"Then I wasn't really looking for anything, was I?"

She let out a sigh of irritation and started to turn away. Then she swung back and collided with him once again. Embarrassed, she braced her hands against his chest and regained her footing quickly.

"Why aren't you out fishing?" she demanded. "I thought you went out on the boat."

"Obviously I didn't."

"Why not?"

"There was a full crew."

"But you snuck around to come back here," she accused him.

"I didn't sneak anywhere."

"Then why didn't I see you before?"

"Probably because you weren't paying any attention. There was no secret about me staying behind. I didn't jump off the boat when no one was looking and swim back."

She stared at him, shaking her head. "There's something wrong with you."

That brought a wry smile to his lips. "I'm not exactly sure how you mean that, but… You should certainly hope not. You're alone with me on an island, and all help is far away."

She took a step back again.

He sighed, reaching for her. She jumped; he let his arm fall, shaking his head.

"I'm going to give you some advice, whether you want it or not. Stay away from this area of the island. Obviously it's of interest to someone, and we don't know why. Keep your mouth shut about seeing Sandy and Brad looking around here. In fact, if you have any suspicions about anyone, pretend that you don't."

She narrowed her eyes, staring at him hard. "Someone might have been killed here."

"And you wouldn't want to join them."

"Is that a threat?"

"Good God, no. It's a warning."

"Right. And *you* should be trusted?"

"Actually, yes."

She studied him long and hard. He was a man in the prime of his life, muscled and hard. She was suddenly certain that, if he had chosen, he could have wrenched the machete away from Brad without breaking a sweat.

To her discomfort, she also remembered the strength with which he had held her.

She spun around, striding for the trail.

He caught her arm, swinging her back. She didn't open her mouth to protest, only narrowed her eyes at him in serious warning, arching her brows slowly as she gazed from his eyes to the place where his hand rested on her arm.

"I was serious. Keep your mouth shut."

"You know something, so you'd better be planning on talking to the police," she warned him.

"If I knew something, I wouldn't need to eavesdrop on other people's conversations."

"I think we should call the police."

"And tell them what?" he demanded.

She faltered. "That...that..."

"That there *might* have been a skull on the island? That a young couple was scrounging around, looking for something? So far, they haven't done a thing that's illegal. And so far, you haven't got anything at all to tell the police. Guess what? You need to get your nose out of it. You need to keep your mouth shut and pretend that you haven't seen a single thing on this island."

"You *are* threatening me."

"I'm not the threat!" he protested angrily. "But just maybe there *is* a threat out there."

"Then we need to stop them. Now."

"There's this little thing called the law. You think you can just tie up Sandy and Brad and call the Coast Guard, and they'll arrest them for acting in what you've decided is a suspicious manner?"

She felt herself flush. He was still holding her. She swallowed, strangely far more afraid now than she had been at any time before. Odd, it felt far too good, especially under the circumstances. She wanted to close her eyes. Lean against him. Let the moment go on. She loathed the concept of basic instinct, but she realized that she was feeling one right then. There was something so right about feeling his touch. She told herself it was just because she hadn't so much as dated in a very long time, but inside she knew it was because she had simply never felt anything so right.

He released her suddenly. "All right, you don't trust me. Stick with your brother. Tight. And keep your mouth shut."

He wasn't touching her anymore. That should mean that sanity would return. Instead she felt startled, like a doe caught in the headlights.

She stiffened, determined to follow a course based on sense and reason.

He started to walk past her, but she wasn't done with him.

She found herself running to catch up with him, then caught his arm, swinging him back to face her.

"What does all this have to do with you?" she demanded.

"Nothing. I came to this island to camp, just the same as you," he told her.

"Then why were you searching the clearing?"

"I told you. It seemed obvious you had hidden something." He had been impatient, almost ready to pull away. But suddenly he became the one determined to carry on the conversation. He moved toward her. There was a tree behind her, and she backed up against it. He set a palm on the trunk to trap her, leaning close.

"What were you hiding?" he demanded.

"Nothing."

"A skull?" he queried.

"Of course not!"

He pushed away from the tree and once again started

back toward the beach. She followed him, irritated and uneasy.

And oddly determined to keep up with him.

To remain close.

They reached the trail. For a moment Beth was afraid they would run straight into Sandy and Brad, but the couple was nowhere to be seen.

Amber and Kimberly were lying on the beach, exactly where they had been when she had left them. Roger, too, seemed not to have stirred from the hammock.

"Hey, girls!" Keith called out.

Amber rolled over and looked back, seeing Keith. "Hi," she called, smiling.

"Hey, guys," Kimberly said.

The girls looked at him, then Beth, then one another. They smiled.

No, she thought. They *smirked.*

"Did you find any good coconuts?" Amber asked him.

It was Beth's turn to look from him to the girls and back again. Obviously the girls had known that he hadn't gone on the boat. Where the hell had she been?

Not paying attention. A mistake she didn't intend to repeat.

"Hey…that looks like a decent coconut right over there." He pointed in the direction of the hammock where Roger lay sleeping.

"I'll get it," Amber volunteered.

Beth bit her lip, not allowing herself to protest. The girls liked Keith. Trying to draw them away and tell them to be wary would only send them flying to his defense.

Kim jumped up to run after Amber.

Beth's pepper spray lay forgotten on Amber's beach towel.

Staring at Keith, she went and picked it up. He smiled, shaking his head.

"What's that smile for?" she demanded, moving closer to him so the girls wouldn't hear her.

"Pepper spray...machete. Hmm."

"Don't kid yourself, this stuff can blind a man."

"I wouldn't dream of mocking your strength, Ms. Anderson," he told her.

Then he turned and went to accept the coconut Amber had picked up. Beth watched as he slammed it against a tree.

The coconut broke at his bidding. He didn't look back at her, just offered the pieces to the girls. Only then did he turn.

"Sorry—is it all right if they have fresh coconut?"

Amber giggled. "Silly. Aunt Beth doesn't have anything against coconuts."

Beth forced a smile.

She was relieved to see the first of the dinghies sliding smoothly onto the shore, just a hundred feet down on the beach.

The others were back.

"Mahimahi tonight!" Ben shouted. He jumped from the dinghy and dragged it farther up the shore, then reached back to give a hand to Amanda. She accepted it with her usual innate sensuality, managing to bring her whole body against Ben in her smooth effort to step to the sand.

"My recipe tonight," Ben called to Beth.

He sounded so pleased. Their fishing expedition had clearly been a great success.

Once again, she forced a smile, then waved and slipped into her tent.

She hoped her brother was having a good time.

For herself, it felt as if she had taken the night train to hell.

And, she realized, it could only get worse. She was suddenly longing for something she shouldn't have.

Perhaps couldn't have…

But the really scary thought was that he was feeling just the same.

5

Beth sat on the bent trunk of the palm tree, eating Doritos and watching.

It might have been a family reunion.

The light was gone, but three separate fires blazed, and the portable barbecue was working away, as well. The fires, she decided, were mainly for show, for warmth and light, though the moon was full, and the sky was clear, studded with stars. The fires were still nice, she thought.

Ben was talking to Keith and Matt by the barbecue, explaining the secret to his perfect mahimahi, she suspected. A coffeepot was set over one of the fires. Brad was the coffee brewer. Hank, Gerald and Matt were hanging out with him, probably talking about their day on the water.

As she watched, Amanda joined the group, giggling, laughing and, judging by her gestures, telling a story about the way someone had caught a fish. The men were laughing, obviously entertained, and equally obviously enthralled.

Beth was startled when Sandy sat down at her side.

She had a beer in her hand, and she was watching the group at the fire, as well.

"She's got a way with her, huh?" Sandy said a little glumly.

"She's very pretty," Beth said judiciously.

Sandy turned to her, a half smile in place, a wry expression in her eyes. "You're much better looking. Actually, so am I. She just really knows how to turn it on and use everything she has."

"Two of those guys are her cousins," Beth reminded her. Sandy seemed so normal at the moment, but Beth couldn't forget what she had seen and heard in the clearing.

"And two aren't," Sandy said flatly. She shrugged. "I guess some women are just like that. They can't keep their hands off anything in pants."

"She comes from a…a world of privilege," Beth murmured, wondering why she was even attempting to excuse Amanda Mason, who tended to make her skin crawl. Still, she'd made it a point to make sure she never talked badly about any member of the club. She offered Sandy the bag of Doritos.

The other woman sniffed. "Think those boobs are real?"

"Um… I've never asked."

"Enhanced," Sandy assured her.

"Well, lots of people…enhance."

Sandy sighed. "True. It's just that… I mean, she uses the damn things like business cards. And men are so easy."

Beth laughed. "I guess sometimes they are."

"She can't have many friends."

"I don't really know," Beth murmured. She felt like

she was ragging on the most popular girl in high school, and it felt more and more uncomfortable. She decided to change the topic. "So how long have you and Brad been together?"

"Three years," Sandy said. "A long time, huh?" She paused. "I'm still madly in love with him. More or less."

Beth wasn't certain how "madly in love" and "more or less" could actually coincide, and again she felt she'd gone back to high school.

"Well, it's great that you're together, then," she said.

Sandy chomped a Dorito. Amanda had her hand on Brad's arm. Sandy shook her head unhappily and looked at Beth. "You don't think it's too long?"

"Too long for what?"

"Shouldn't we be getting married?"

"Oh. Um. Well, I don't know. I guess it's good to really know a person first. I'd much rather be with a person and know that he's the one I want to spend the rest of my life with than marry in a hurry and have it all fall apart. The divorce rate is so high today."

"Is your brother divorced?"

"No. His wife passed away."

"That's terrible."

"Yes."

"So…you don't think it's a bad thing that I stay with Brad even though it's been this long and we're not married yet?"

Beth hesitated. She hadn't begun to imagine that Sandy would come to her for advice on her relationship, certainly not after what she had seen and heard in the clearing earlier.

"I'm not qualified to give advice," she said. "I don't

think there's anything wrong with staying with someone, no matter how long, if that's what *you* feel is right."

Sandy stared at the group by the fire, eyes level on Amanda. "Do you think he'd cheat on me?"

Beth was beginning to feel acutely uncomfortable. "Sandy, I just met both of you. I have no idea."

Sandy didn't seem to hear her. "She's moving on. Who is she after, do you think? Your brother? Or Keith?"

Amanda *had* moved on. Now she stood between Ben and Keith at the barbecue. She was still laughing, charming, flirtatious.

And once again, she seemed to have enthralled her conquests.

"My brother is in his midthirties," Beth said. "He has to take care of himself, make his own decisions."

Sandy sighed. "Yeah, I guess Keith is all grown up, too. Hey, if Amanda is going to be all over Brad, maybe I should be making a few moves of my own." She stared steadily at Beth again, then shook her head. "You're so moral."

Beth laughed. "How do you know that? We've only just met."

Sandy shook her head. "There are things you just know. Things you see. No matter how long you've known someone." She laughed softly. "Like chemistry. Don't worry. If I make a play for someone, it won't be Keith."

"What?"

"There's chemistry going between you two, and if you say it isn't, well, then you're a liar."

"I'm too moral to be a liar, aren't I?" Beth queried lightly.

Sandy still seemed caustically amused. "Well, he feels

attracted to you. I see his eyes when you just walk by. And to be truthful, that's why I'd never make a play for him. Why bother? He's preoccupied. Actually, I don't play games. And I don't think Brad would, either. She just really pisses me off."

"It seems as if you and Brad do have something... special," Beth said, feeling a little lame but also really uncomfortable. When she looked at the woman, she wanted to shout, What the hell were you looking for today? A skull?

Both women turned to stare at Brad then. Apparently his coffee was perked, and he had gone to the trouble of making Irish coffee; he had a bottle of Jameson's out, as well.

"Hey, I'd actually like one of those," Beth said, ready to get up and end what was becoming too intimate a conversation with someone she didn't know—and didn't trust. She rose. "Come on, we'll both head over there, and it won't look like you're worried in the least."

Sandy flashed her a quick glance, and she realized that the woman *had* been worried. But Brad hadn't done any instigating, and Amanda was being just as flirtatious with every available guy there.

Beth headed over to the fire and told Brad, "That's definitely a different drink for a night on an island. I'd love one."

"Sure. Sandy?"

"Sounds good to me, too. I'd love one."

Brad mixed up two mugs. "Club Med has nothing on us, huh?" he teased, sliding an arm around Sandy's shoulders.

"No, we're just a regular party," Beth agreed.

"Food's ready!" Ben called out. "Someone grab some plates, please."

Roger was the first one to oblige, and he became the official hand-'em-outer. Everyone found seats, in the hammock, on blankets or towels on the sand, or in the few folding chairs they'd brought out. For the next several minutes, compliments to the chef rang out.

"Hey, how about me?" Lee teased. "I led the fishing expedition."

"I know, and it was a hell of a good time," Ben told him.

"Maybe we should have gone along," Sandy told Brad.

"Yeah, maybe," Brad said, grimacing.

"There's always tomorrow," Matt offered.

"Tomorrow. Sunday," Sandy said, and shivered. "Just Monday and then back to the real world. Work on Monday."

"What do you do?" Beth asked her.

"Do?"

"For a living," Beth said.

"Oh, I'm a consultant."

Maybe it was the fact that Sandy had brought up going back to work on Monday when Beth knew she didn't plan on doing any such thing, but Beth didn't believe her for a minute.

"Back to work for you, too, Beth, right?" Amanda asked sweetly.

"Thankfully, I love my job," Beth replied pleasantly.

"I'm not always so fond of mine," Ben admitted.

"Ben's a lawyer," Roger explained.

"What kind?" Keith asked.

Ben laughed, a slightly dry sound. "Criminal. I used to work for the D.A.'s office, but now I get the scumbags off. It's a good living, but…well, I don't know how long I want to do it." He hesitated, glancing over at his daughter. "I'd like to get away from some of the ugliness. I'm thinking about making a real switch into entertainment law or something like that."

Beth turned to Keith and asked pointedly, "What do you do for a living?"

She thought he hesitated for just a second before he said, "I'm a diver."

"And you make a decent enough living?" Hank asked.

"Decent enough for what?" Amber piped in.

Hank laughed easily. "Well, enough to have friends like Lee with a boat like that."

"Hey, the boat is his," Keith said.

"Well, what do *you* do?" Amanda asked Lee.

"Nothing remarkable," Lee said. "Family money."

"I like that," Amanda said, and everyone laughed. The sound, however, had an edge to it, Beth thought.

Apparently Amanda had decided that Lee offered the best opportunity to go on living in the style to which she'd become accustomed. During cleanup, she hung around him, flirting, giggling.

Later Ben sternly vetoed the idea of ghost stories, and the others agreed, staring at Beth. Someone suggested music, and a boom box appeared from somewhere.

As the music played and the conversation went on around her, Beth found herself thinking about the Monocos again. Was there some connection between them and the maybe-a-skull she'd found? Or was she getting carried away worrying? As Ben had said, they were adults, and they could travel the world without reporting to anyone, if they chose.

Whether she'd seen a skull or a conch shell, she was absolutely certain that people were behaving strangely.

The feeling of being in the middle of something she didn't understand sat heavily over her. The rest of them were acting like the world was a great place and everyone just loved everyone. Well, except Ben. Her brother seemed to be brooding, for some reason.

And Keith.

He had managed to hang back and avoid conversation.

He was watching, she thought. Watching everyone.

The thought gave her chills. And yet…despite *his* strange behavior, she was still drawn to him. She should have been wary, but, ridiculously, she sensed in him a kind of strength, an…ethic. Was she crazy? Was it only because she couldn't remember when she had met someone who so attracted her? But if he'd wanted to hurt her, he'd certainly had the opportunity, and he hadn't. Instead, he'd protected her.

She decided that she wasn't going to say anything more to Ben or anyone else about the skull or her sense of uneasiness. But when she got home, she was definitely going to start finding out more about the Monocos.

On the other hand, maybe the need to know that seemed to fill her every waking minute now would ebb once they returned to real life. She would see Amanda and Hank again, and Roger and Gerald. But there was no reason to believe she would ever cross paths again with Sandy and Brad, or the independently wealthy Lee, Matt—or Keith Henson.

The group split up late. Beth tried to act nonchalant as she made her way back to their site, but when she was curled up in her own tent, she realized that she still felt uneasy.

If he hadn't had any idea what Brad and Sandy were up to, why had Keith been so determined not to reveal their own presence?

She felt a hot flush rise within her when she remembered the way they had stood, listening, for what had seemed like aeons.

She lay awake, just listening, for a long, long time.

Then, just when she was finally relaxing into sleep, she heard something. A rustling. The wind in the trees? She strained to hear.

Great weekend. She should have been suntanned and relaxed. Instead she was a nervous wreck, more tired than when they'd started out.

In the night, she imagined that she was hearing all kinds of things.

At last, with a sigh, she untangled herself from her sleeping bag and carefully stuck her head out through the opening of her tent.

There was nothing around. No one to see. The night was silent.

She crawled out of the tent to stretch, then froze.

She wasn't alone.

Looking down the beach, she realized that what had appeared to be a shadow against a tree was a man.

The realization sent a flurry of fear snaking along her spine. She stood still, staring.

The shadow lifted a hand. Said, "Hey."

"Hey," she responded automatically.

It was Keith.

Barefoot, in her oversize T-shirt, she walked down the length of the beach to him. The night wasn't especially dark. In fact, it was beautiful. The moon was out, along with dozens of stars. The breeze was gentle, and it wasn't too humid.

"Enjoying the weather?" she asked.

"It is nice, isn't it?" he asked. He sat down and patted the sand by his side. "Join me?"

She hesitated, then sat. "What are you doing?" she asked him.

"Enjoying the weather, just like you said."

"It's the middle of the night."

"I have strange sleeping habits."

"I'll bet you do," she murmured.

He smiled, handsome face rueful. "Is there a hidden meaning behind that?" he asked.

She shook her head and looked away.

"You just don't trust me."

"No, I don't." She let out a sigh.

He laughed. "By the way, what happened to your brother's friends?"

"Pardon?"

"The guys who were supposed to be joining you. You know, the great big lugs who can open beer bottles with their teeth."

She stared at him with a deep frown, having no idea what he was talking about at first. Then she remembered what she'd said when they met.

"I guess they got…sidetracked. They're not coming."

"And they never were."

"Okay, so I don't trust you much now and I certainly didn't trust you at all when we first met."

He looked forward again and spoke softly. "Well, we're not pirates, if that's what you're thinking."

"I didn't suggest you were pirates. Pirates belong in ghost stories."

He shook his head, looking her way again. "No. Modern-day pirates are very real. Ask your brother. Sail in the wrong direction and you're asking for trouble. Think about it—the sea is vast. You can be close to civilization, but on the water, far, far from help. Don't ever think of pirates as being something from the past!"

She frowned, surprised that he had spoken with such passion.

"Pirates, because of the drug trade?" she asked him.

He shrugged. "Pirates because some men will always covet what other men have." He watched her intently, then turned away again. "And pirates because sometimes what another man has is knowledge that's worth its weight in gold."

The way he spoke sent shivers down her spine. She was sitting close to him, not touching, and she wasn't sure if she wanted to stumble quickly to her feet and say good-night, or move closer into the aura of his warmth. He was definitely a compelling man, built like rock and steel, with his strange easy smile and chiseled features. And chemistry.

She knew she should be drawing back just because she wanted to move so close. She realized in shock that she was envisioning sex with the man.

Not a good thing when she didn't trust him at all, much less what was happening here on the island.

He seemed to be warning her again.

"Go back to your life tomorrow. Forget anything you might have thought while you were here. And for God's sake, don't talk about it," he said softly.

She shook her head. "You're very scary, you know."

"Am I?" He looked away again. "I don't mean to be. It's just a good thing not to get involved."

"A good thing how? And involved with what, exactly?"

He let out a sound of impatience, flicking at a few grains of sand from his knee. "You're trying to make a mountain out of a molehill," he said, shrugging. "Just leave it alone. When you dig for one thing, you may find something else that you don't expect—or want."

The breeze seemed to grow chilly. She was silent for a moment. "Just what is it that you know, or at least suspect? Why were you so determined that Brad and Sandy shouldn't see us today?"

He groaned. "There you go. I don't know or suspect anything. Hey, I'm a diver, remember? I like the sea, the sand, the wind…going down deep where it's peaceful and calm and the world doesn't intrude. I like fishing, islands, Jimmy Buffett and the easy life. So I keep out of things that don't concern me. And that's what I'm strongly advising you do, too."

She stared back at him, shaking her head. "You're talking in circles, and the strangest thing is, no matter what you say, I don't believe you."

"Oh?" He arched a brow, features slightly tense, then easing as he offered her a rueful grin. "Is that a challenge? Or an accusation?"

"Neither. I'm just saying that I don't trust you."

"How amazing. I never would have realized—especially since we've just discussed that fact."

"You're sarcastic, to boot."

"Sorry. If I bug you that much, you might remember that I claimed this tree first."

She stiffened and started to rise.

He caught her arm. "I'm sorry."

"I'll leave you to your tree," she told him, teeth grating.

"I said I was sorry. It's just that you came over here and started attacking—"

"I didn't attack."

"You accused me of…something. I just don't know what you want from me."

She hesitated, feeling his hand lingering on her arm. His eyes were so steady on her. So sincere.

Why couldn't she have met him at one of her brother's small get-togethers? At the yacht club, or on a local dive trip? Why couldn't he have been an old school friend of someone, anyone, who could be trusted? His touch was the kind that made little jolts of electricity tease the bloodstream, and when she was close to him like this, all she wanted was to touch and be touched.

She gave herself a serious mental shake. He wasn't one of her brother's old school friends, and she had met him under very strange circumstances. And she seemed to be having trouble answering him, though he wasn't pressing anything. He was just looking at her, and they were very close. Close enough so that she knew she liked the arch of his brows, the strength of his features, the way his jaw could seem as hard as a rock until his smile changed everything about him.

"Beth, seriously, I don't know what you want—"

"The truth," she murmured.

He released her and leaned back against the tree, looking up at the night sky.

"The truth?" he asked, sounding edgy again. "I don't know anything about anything. My motto is simply to be very careful. That's the truth. I just think you should be careful, too, that's all."

"Because Brad and Sandy were behaving suspiciously?"

"Because you think you found a skull—and you're pretty much letting everyone know."

It was her turn to be aggravated. "There you go—talking in circles again. I *think* I found a skull. If I didn't find a skull, then what is there to be worried about?"

"Maybe nothing. Probably nothing."

"Do you know you're incredibly exasperating?" she demanded.

That rueful smile slipped easily into place again. "Do you know the line that should come after that one? Let's see. 'You're incredibly beautiful. I don't think I've ever met anyone quite like you.' But that wouldn't sound much like the truth to you, either, would it? And it's probably something you've heard a million times before." The fact that he didn't touch her then, or move closer to her in any way, made his words seem all the more compelling. She felt the urge to move closer, but she forced herself to maintain her distance. She felt as if there was at least a grain of honesty in his compliment, and she doubted he was a man who got turned down often.

"Thanks," she murmured uneasily, and looked at the swaying palms against the night sky. She worked with the public herself, knew how to smile and play a part, how to manipulate—and when she was being manipulated.

She turned to him squarely, "Actually, it sounds like the kind of line you use when you're trying to change the subject."

"I've just offered all that I can on the subject that I'd be changing," he told her.

Her eyes fell on Lee's yacht. "Quite a boat," she murmured.

"A seventy-five-foot motor yacht," he agreed. "You should have come aboard. She's one glorious lady."

She turned to him. "You could show her to me in the morning."

He seemed surprised by the suggestion. "I could, yes." He watched her curiously for a moment, a slow smile creeping over his lips. "Ah. You're going to check her out. Look for bodies or evidence of evildoing."

Beth averted her eyes. "No such thing. She's a beautiful boat. I work at a yacht club."

"So you see lots of beautiful boats."

"I love to be able to discuss them with the members."

He laughed easily. "You can check her out. No problem."

"Which means, of course, that if you were concealing something, it would be well hidden," she informed him.

"Did you study criminology?" he demanded. "Or do you suffer from an overdose of cop shows on television? If you've been paying attention, one more time, Ms. Anderson, it's smart to keep out of things that don't concern you."

"So I shouldn't go on the boat?"

He groaned. "You're more than welcome to see the boat. I told you—we're not pirates."

"Does that mean you're not pirates but you *are* some other kind of criminal, or that some people are pirates, even though you and your friends aren't?"

"If I say good-morning when I see you and the sun is up, will you be dissecting those words, as well?" he asked her.

She shrugged. "I don't know."

He stood, reaching a hand down to her. "Well, I suggest we get some sleep and find out," he said.

She hesitated before accepting his hand. As he helped her to her feet, she came up against him. The length of her body brushed against his. When she was up, she remained close, thinking—hoping?—he was going to touch her.

She thought she might lose all sense of reason and reach out and touch him, place her fingers on his face.

"No line," he said softly. "You are...like a flame. I'd give my eyeteeth to be the moth that was consumed."

She blinked. His voice was deep, sincere, and yet he was distant. He didn't even try acting on his words. If anything, they were wistful.

"Don't worry," he assured her, and a dry smile twisted his lips. "I know how to pine from afar." He hesitated. "You really don't need to be afraid of me," he assured her.

"I'm not afraid of you," she lied.

"You're not?"

"Only a little."

"Actually, you should be. I'm dying to touch you," he said.

The breeze whispered. The ghosts of the island, she thought. The cool air caressed her flesh. She was tempted to step forward and tell him that she *was* afraid, but willing to take her chances anyway.

Just to be touched.

To her absolute amazement, she heard herself say, "Maybe *you* should be afraid. Maybe I'm dying to touch you, too."

His hand rose. His knuckles and the back of his hand just brushed over her cheek. His eyes met hers. For once there seemed to be honesty in them. "You're like a dream, perfect in so many ways."

She swallowed hard. "Not perfect," she murmured.

He laughed, dropping his hand, easing back a bit. "Smart, gorgeous, sexy…and good on a boat. That's a dream to me. And I'm insane for saying this. I don't think that I'm what you want. I don't know if I can be." He drew a deep, shuddering breath. "And now we should get some sleep."

They stood there for what felt like forever but was probably no more than a dozen seconds.

"Still want to see the boat in the morning?" he asked.

"Yes. And I'm not a complete coward, you know." What did she mean by that? She wasn't certain herself.

He smiled and stepped back, and she could almost believe she had imagined a moment more intimate than any she had ever shared.

"In the morning, then," he said, and she wondered if his voice was as husky as it sounded, or if she only wanted to think so.

"Yeah…in the morning."

"Should I see you back to your tent?" he teased.

"I'll be fine. It's only a few feet away."

He smiled the rueful half smile that seemed to tear away sanity. "I'll just keep an eye on you from here," he assured her. "Apparently you didn't bring your pepper spray."

She shook her head, studying him, and lifted her hands. "No pepper spray. *Should* I have carried it?"

He groaned, then laughed. "Good night, Ms. Anderson. It's been a lovely evening."

"It *is* a lovely evening," she murmured.

Suddenly he pulled her close, and she thought he was going to kiss her, take her in his arms and really kiss her, and if he did, she didn't know what she was going to do.

But he didn't. He just held her. She felt the electric heat and force of the length of his body, not at all dissipated by the cotton between them. He brushed the top of her head with his lips, then pulled back again. "Go, go on back," he told her.

She stepped away, staring at him.

"Trust no one," he told her.

"Not even you?" she whispered.

"Not even me. Go on."

Husky had been replaced by something that resembled harsh. She backed away for several steps before turning to head to her tent.

When she reached it, she turned back.

He was exactly where she had left him.

Watching.

Somehow, she knew that when she went into the tent, he would remain there, watching—though for what, exactly, she had no idea.

But he would be there through the night. Of that she was entirely certain.

Just as she was certain she was the one who was the moth coveting the flame. In her life, she had never actually planned anything the way she was planning it now.

But there was an ache inside her.

Whether she burned to ashes or not, she had to touch the fire.

Hands off.

That was what he had warned the others. They had business to attend to here.

But there was the other business, as well. And that kept him thinking, curious—and determined to find out everything he could about their fellow campers.

Clenching his teeth, he reminded himself that it was no surprise that tourists had come to Calliope Key for the weekend. But he couldn't allow anger to waylay him, nor could he allow himself any emotional involvement. All he could do was seek justice now. And put an end to it all.

Beth Anderson was a distraction he couldn't afford.

Keith swore softly in the night.

Then he spun, instantly alert at the smallest sound.

Matt, stretching, looking as if his joints ached and he wasn't ready to pull a shift on guard duty, eyed him cautiously.

"Quite a conversation," Matt said.

"I couldn't exactly force her to go back to bed," Keith reminded him.

"She's something, huh?" Matt said, and grinned. Then the grin faded and he shook his head. "It's dangerous. I wouldn't want her to wind up…hurt."

"She won't," Keith snapped out.

"If she—"

"She won't," he repeated.

"Hell of a story you told the other night," Matt said, sounding somewhat sharp, as if the words were an accusation.

"It's a well-known legend."

"Did you tell it on purpose?"

Keith shrugged. "Why not? Throw it out there."

"Yeah, maybe." Matt shrugged, looking out to sea— and the yacht. "Nothing?" he inquired.

"All's quiet."

Matt nodded. "Actually, what else could we expect?"

"Nothing," Keith murmured. He looked at Matt. Neither one of them felt at ease.

"Well, I'm up. You can catch a few winks."

"Yup."

"You're not going to sleep, are you?" Matt asked.

"I'm damn well going to try."

"Don't worry. I know it isn't your lack of faith in me. It's just your nature."

"Trust me. I'm going to try to sleep."

"That's right. You've got a date in the morning, don't you?"

"What?"

"You have to show Beth Anderson the yacht."

"Oh. Right."

Great, just great. His entire conversation had been overheard.

"It will be fine. It's Sunday at last. The working world will return to work," Matt said. "And we'll have the place to ourselves again."

Keith murmured a disjointed, "Not exactly."

"I don't blame you, by the way," Matt went on.

"Blame me for what?" Keith said.

"If Beth Anderson had looked at me with so much as a slightly interested smile, well… I'd forget everything, too."

"I haven't forgotten anything," Keith said.

He left Matt by the palm and returned to his tent.

But Matt had been right.

He lay awake. And listened.

He couldn't help remembering a picture that was as vivid in his mind's eye as if he were back at the morgue again, staring down at Brandon Emery's face. He'd been so young. Twenty-four and so damn good at everything he did. One of the brightest newcomers, filled with all the right stuff, as they said.

Too damn good. He shouldn't have been out alone. Especially when he had seen something, known something. And he *had* known something. Keith could still recall the last email he'd gotten from Brandon, word for word.

I think I've got it. Honest to God, you're not going to believe it. I'm going to check it out, and I'll let you know next time I write.

But there had been no next time.

No next time for Brandon.

Keith had never heard from him again. Not until he had been called to see the body. What had seemed like a fairly easy—even run-of-the-mill—venture had turned deadly, and the image of Brandon Emery in the morgue was one that would never leave his mind.

His body had floated up near Islamorada. His boat had been found drifting a few miles farther north. But he hadn't been anywhere near Islamorada when he had e-mailed.

He'd been here, working off Calliope Key.

And no matter what anyone said, he hadn't simply drowned.

He sat up in a sweat. Swore.

Ted and Molly Monoco. He hadn't known the couple, but he'd read about them. He'd never put them in the same arena as Brandon before. Brandon had been part of his work. Ted and Molly had been retirees, off to see the world.

But they'd been here, too. It might well have been damn stupid of him not to connect everything that had happened in the area. But what was the connection?

Brandon's boat had been no great shakes, and it hadn't been stolen. Had the Monocos' boat been seized? He'd heard rumors that it had been seen. Rumors. And there had been similar incidents in the papers over the last year.

The Monocos had owned the kind of vessel any modern-day pirate might well envy.

Had they died for that reason?

How could that be connected to Brandon's death, or their own quest here? Had the island itself become deadly, or remained deadly through the centuries, a place near enough to civilization to attract visitors, and yet remote enough for anything to happen? A place to kill and…

A place to hide the dead?

He would never sleep. Because now Beth was on the island. Beth, who wouldn't let things rest.

It was chilling.

She would be going home soon. She would be in no great danger, once she returned to Miami. Once she forgot the island.

Forgot the fact that she thought she'd seen a skull…

Gotten over the idea of discovering just what had happened to Ted and Molly Monoco?

6

"Hey, Dad, where's Aunt Beth?"

Ben, who'd been stowing gear, looked up from the tent poles he was arranging as his daughter rubbed sleepy eyes and stared at him.

"Gone," he said gravely.

She frowned, shook her head and rolled her eyes. "Dad, where is she?"

"I'm serious. She went out to see the yacht with Keith Henson."

"What?"

His daughter's incredulous excitement gave him pause. "I said," he enunciated, "that your aunt went out to see the yacht with Keith Henson."

"Oh, Dad. I heard you perfectly."

"Then—"

"Oh, Dad, it's too cool." By then, Kimberly had come up behind her. "Did you hear that? She went with Keith to see the boat."

"Wow!" Kim agreed.

"I didn't think she had it in her."

"She's just so suspicious."

"This is awesome."

"Random."

"Wicked."

By then Ben was frowning. "What are you two going on about?"

"Oh, Dad. He's a hunk."

"Really fine," Kim agreed somberly.

"I mean, there was…like, thunder."

"And lightning."

"Between them," Amber finished.

"We were trying to figure out a way to get them together," Kim admitted.

Ben scowled seriously then. "You two butt out, okay? She's a grown-up, and she's not going off any deep end over a guy just because he's got a six-pack, okay? Don't you two go pushing anything. She went to see the yacht because I raved about it, and that's it, do you understand?"

"Okay," Amber murmured.

"Seriously," Kim agreed.

Then they looked at each other and ruined the effect, bursting into laughter.

"Amber Anderson," he said firmly. "I mean it. Leave your aunt alone."

"He's acting like a male," Kim murmured to Amber.

"All touchy," Amber agreed.

"*He* is standing right here," Ben told them.

"Sorry, Dad," Amber said.

"I mean it."

"We know you mean it," Amber told him. She nudged Kim. "Hey, let's go explore."

He felt a frown furrowing his brow. "No exploring."

"What?" Amber protested.

"Stay on the beach."

"Why, Dad?"

Why? He didn't know.

"Because I said so."

"But, Dad—"

"Because I said so," he repeated.

He turned away, because he really didn't have a better explanation to give his daughter. As he paused to look down the beach, his frown deepened, and he tried to tell himself there was nothing to worry about.

But everyone, it seemed, was looking out to sea.

Not too far away, Matt was standing by one of the palms. His arms were crossed over his chest, and he was looking toward the yacht.

Down farther, Amanda Mason was posed in almost the exact stance, staring out over the water, hugging her arms around herself.

And even farther down…

It was Brad. Staring out at the water, at the little boat nearing the majestic yacht.

A sense of unease filled him, like a little inward shiver.

He literally shook himself, irritated.

He dealt with the scum of the earth, so why was he so bothered now?

With a slight groan, he turned away. Good God, Keith's buddies—including the owner of the yacht— were right there. The Masons were down the beach. Brad and Sandy were unknowns, but what the hell, they were there, too.

Beth was as uptight as an old schoolmarm, worse than he was himself.

Everything was fine.

"Hey there!"

He turned. Lee Gomez was waving to him, heading toward the interior of the island.

"Looking for a few good coconuts," Lee called to him. "Want any?"

"I'm fine, thanks," he returned.

Down the beach, Sandy had moved to stand behind Brad. She slipped her arms around his waist and rested her cheek on his back.

Brad didn't seem to notice. He was intent on the yacht. Then he turned, as if aware that he was being watched, and saw Ben staring at him.

Ben waved.

Brad waved back, then turned his attention to Sandy.

It's all just fine, Ben assured himself.

And it was. They would be getting off the island.

He was amazed to realize he was glad the weekend was nearly over. He usually dreaded going back to work after a break. What the hell. There ought to be some saying about the scumbag you knew and the scumbag you couldn't quite recognize.

He looked good rowing, Beth decided.

She purposely turned her gaze to the yacht they were approaching, dismayed that she seemed to be doing little other than appreciating the physical assets of the man.

Around boats, guys wore trunks, cutoffs, T-shirts, even no shirts. They tended to be bronze, and the club attracted a slew of well-toned, healthy, fit specimens of masculinity.

Keith Henson just seemed to have it all and carry it off just a little bit better.

This morning he was in blue-and-black swim trunks, the kind a million surfers wore, the kind that shouldn't have been the least bit erotic. He had eschewed a shirt, since the day was hot—nothing unusual in that. But his skin seemed to be an unreal masculine shade of bronze, and his muscles flexed with each tug on the oars. Shades hid his eyes from her view, and she certainly hoped her own hid her thoughts equally well. Suddenly she blushed. She had been thinking about how he was dressed, but now realized that she, too, was skimpily clad in a bathing suit and sarong—an outfit that she would have thought nothing of if she weren't with him.

But there was something between them.

She couldn't stop herself from thinking of it as chemistry, though she was sure she never would have felt such a draw if it hadn't been for his smile. Or the darkness of his eyes. Or the keen mind that seemed to lie behind his every word.

His every lie.

"Well, do you like her?"

They had reached the yacht. He stood, rocking the little dinghy, and tied on. The aft ladder had been left down, and he swung on, reaching out a hand to her. With the dinghy bobbing on the waves, she accepted. She found herself noting the ease with which he helped her. The man was strong. Did that make him some kind of a criminal? And if he was, what kind of an idiot was she to be here with him?

She landed on deck with ease and looked around. She estimated the original price of the boat at more than six figures.

"Really, *really* nice," she assured him.

"Come on. I'll show you around."

He took her around the upper deck, then to the flybridge, and finally down to the cabin. She whistled softly.

"It's like a luxury-hotel suite," she told him.

"The great thing is that she can do anything. Despite her size, she's got top speed, and she's rigged for fishing as well as pleasure cruising."

"That's why there's the global positioning system, sonar, radar, communications—and whatever else is up there and down here?"

"We all like to fish," he said with a shrug. "What can I get you? Juice, soda…water? Want coffee? It will only take a minute."

"I'd love coffee," she told him.

He seemed to be involved in the task, but she had the feeling that he was watching her all the while. For her reactions?

Or to make sure that she didn't notice something she shouldn't?

"Make yourself at home," he said.

"Thanks." She took a seat on the sofa in the main salon area. She might have been sitting in the salon of a resort. Beyond the windows, she could see the sea, the sky and a glimpse of the island.

"How long do you think you'll be in this area?" she asked him.

"Oh, a while."

She laughed suddenly. "Do you ever have a direct answer for anything?"

"What do you mean?"

"Okay, how long are you going to be here? A while. A 'while' can mean anything. If someone had asked me about this weekend, my reply would be clear and direct. I go home tonight."

He shrugged, pouring coffee into mugs. "I don't know

how long I'm going to be in the area. When we're fished out, dived out and done, I'll head back."

She let out an exasperated sigh. "Back to Virginia?"

Even then, she thought he hesitated. "Yes."

"Do you have a house there?"

"Yes. There—is that direct enough?"

"What part?"

"Northern Virginia."

"Does your city or town have a name?" she demanded.

He came around and handed her a mug. "Whoops, sorry, did you want cream or sugar?"

"Black is fine, thanks. Well?"

"A fairly well known name, yes. Alexandria."

"There, see, it wasn't so hard. You have a house, it's in Virginia, in the city of Alexandria."

"Do you have a house?" he inquired in turn, perching on the arm of the sofa. Close again. The kind of close that made her wonder why she felt the need to analyze everything. Why not just take a chance? Why care so much about exactly who or what hc was?

Just enjoy the simple things in life, she told herself. Everything doesn't need to last forever. She never just met a man and went with him…anywhere. It seemed that she had never been so emotionally confused before. Last night she had lain awake during all that had been left of the darkness, thinking, tormenting herself. She could…no, no, she couldn't, sure she could, she shouldn't, mustn't…and then, why not? This sense of something hanging in the balance was new to her. This kind of need, this kind of longing… She couldn't actually even remember ever being spontaneous, simply acting on instinct. And yet she was free and single, over twenty-one, always responsible, dependable...

Surely everyone had a right to a moment's insanity, to fulfill a fantasy. It was Sunday and she would head home, back to the real world, and most likely thought she would never see him again.

"Hey, are you still with me?" he asked, bemused.

"I, um...yes, of course."

"Well?"

"Well what?"

He arched a brow. "House. Do you have a house?"

"Oh! I have a town house, yes."

"And that would be where?" he asked.

"Coconut Grove, near the yacht club."

"Nice."

"I like it."

"However—"

"Yes?"

"I've heard that Coconut Grove can be a dangerous area."

"Any populated place can be dangerous. As you said yourself, even sailing the islands can be dangerous. But Miami has a bad rep. People are nice there. It's like any other city. You're most likely not going to be hit by a drug lord unless you're dealing or something like that." She shook her head suddenly, looking into her coffee cup. "You ask a simple question, and I give you a paragraph. I ask a question and get a one-liner. Maybe I'm the one with the problem."

She was startled to realize that he didn't laugh, or even smile, as she had expected he might. He was looking at her very seriously. He reached out and touched her. Light, totally casual. He just touched her chin with the tip of his forefinger. "I don't think you have a problem at all," he said very softly.

There it was. The moment when she was supposed to stand and say, "I have to go."

But she didn't. He eased down from the arm of the sofa, next to her, his scent a mixture of the wind, sea and salt, his flesh still reflecting the heat of the sun, emitting power from every pore, and she didn't move. She waited.

His sunglasses were gone, and his eyes seemed as dark as ebony, as mysterious as an abyss, and he was studying her, long and intently. Once again she thought it was time to back away, because then he would rise, as well, and the moment would be broken.

But she didn't move, and his fingers slipped into her hair, cradling the base of her skull. Then, at last, his lips touched hers. At first it seemed like nothing more than a hot and teasing whisper of air; then the fullness of his mouth pressed over hers. She wasn't avoiding, wasn't protesting; she was set adrift in a sea of fascination and discovery, her arms rising, hands resting on his shoulders, fingertips awakened by the simple feel of skin. He kissed her hard and deep, and she felt an infusion of warmth and arousal.

It was he who broke the kiss, easing away, and his voice was definitely husky when he spoke. "I think you're supposed to tell me that you need to get back."

She nodded. "You should be telling me that this isn't your boat."

He nodded in response. "We should go."

"Certainly. Now."

"Remember, I told you that you should be afraid of me."

She shook her head, studying his eyes. "I should be. But I'm not. I mean, I am. But I'm not."

"Tell me to take you back," he said.

She shook her head slowly. "I guess I'm just not afraid enough."

"Still...we need to...not..."

"You're right."

But neither moved, and when he kissed her again, she let her fingers play down the length of his back, and she felt his hands on her. Then, he broke away again, his voice extremely deep as he said, "I really should take you back."

"If that's what you want."

"What you *don't* want is to be involved with me," he murmured.

"I don't recall saying that I was involved."

He moved away. "Ah, Ms. Anderson, you are far too decent, believe me. So if you'll just say..." His voice trailed off.

She smiled, her senses perfectly attuned, her mind suddenly set upon her course. She moistened her lips slightly, her smile deepening. "You want me to say I should go? I should. Do I want to? No. Am I going to? I don't think so, but then again, that's up to you now."

His groan was deep and shuddering, and then he stood with a suddenness that surprised her and swept her up into his arms.

"We shouldn't be doing this," he said.

"Absolutely not," she agreed softly as she linked her arms around his neck.

Her eyes locked on his, she was barely aware that he was heading for the elegant master stateroom. The bed was huge. He managed to rip off the black-and-white cover without losing hold of her, and when he laid her down, the sheets seemed cool against the sun-touched heat of her flesh. He quickly lay down beside her. Her sarong was a tangle around them both, quickly eliminated, and she would forever remember the contrast between the coolness of the bedding and the warmth and vibrance of his flesh. They met in a passionate, exploratory kiss, lips melding, tongues sliding, mouths locked. His hands were every bit as powerful as she had imagined, his fingers as gentle, his touch as magnetic. His lips fell to her throat, to spots just below each ear, to the center of her throat once again, and lower, the tip of his tongue teasing up and down her collarbone, then lower still. Her fingers slid into his hair, testing its rich texture, blond and then ash, where it had been bleached by the sun. She felt the pressure of his body against her. With his hips and legs pressed to hers, she felt the swell of his arousal, taut beneath the surf trunks. Then his hands, adept at manipulation, released the hook of the bikini bra, followed by his lips, firm against her breasts, and his hands, caressing, cradling. His lips teased after every touch, moving over her areolas, nipples, up the length of her throat again. The frenzy of caresses wet, hot, seemed to send streaks of pure fire sailing through her bloodstream, and rushing with ardent precision into the very heart of her sexuality. She didn't remember ever feeling as she did now, and knew that was because she had never actually felt anything this vital, this passionate, alive, tempestuous…ever before.

He paused, his eyes on hers, smile totally seductive. "This is insanity."

"We've agreed on that."

"You need to go back. You shouldn't be here."

"We've agreed on that, as well," she whispered.

"You shouldn't be involved with me."

"I wouldn't dream of being involved with you."

"One might call this involved."

"One might."

He shook his head. His lips touched down again. For a moment they teased a mere breath above her own. Then the kiss deepened, and their limbs entwined as their bodies met and melded. The naked length of his chest seemed glorious, the sound of his breathing filled her senses, along with the thrum of their hearts. His flesh felt like the sun and the sea, smooth, slick, hot. He moved erotically against her, her breasts crushed to him.

She clung to him, splaying her fingers down his back, along his spine, down to the waistband of his trunks, around in front to the ties. Her fingers weren't as adept as his, not quite as experienced. His hands covered hers, though he never broke the kiss. She was dimly aware when the trunks were gone, acutely aware when the naked length of his body pressed against hers. She felt his fingers slipping beneath the bikini bottom as he effortlessly did away with the last barrier between them, which in itself seemed an exotic ecstasy. She was pressed close to him again, and his fingers seduced a path down her spine, curved over her buttocks, brought her flush against his arousal. His lips continued to caress and assail. Then he moved, sleek, agile, shifting atop her, lips pressing against the hollows of her collarbone, teasing her breasts. His hand glided down the curve of her form, pressed apart her thighs. She felt the stroke of his touch first, and then the taunt of his tongue; felt as if she burned within, caught in a sudden, swift maelstrom of fire. Pure sensual ecstasy exalted her even as the rage of intimacy dismayed her, though for only a split second in the rush of sensation.

He was an incredible lover.

Subtle and bold. Teeth, tongue, lips, touch, all meshed in a passionate dance of sensuality that left her breathless, thundering, quivering somewhere between total vibrant ecstasy and simple delicious death. She arched, writhed, thrashed, cried out God-knew-what....

Trembled, throbbed...begged.

Involved.

Good Lord, yes, she was involved, any more involved and she would be living in his skin. She had sworn to herself that she had sense and reason and knew what she was doing, but this was...

Involved.

She was more involved than she had ever been. More touched, elated, electrified, swept away, taken...

She tore at his hair, dragged him to her, and before she could even meet his lips again with her own, she shuddered with a new sense of sheer carnal elation as the force of his body thrust into hers.

The ship rocked.

God, the man knew how to coerce with the slowest, gentlest movements, and then to thunder and pulse with the force of a wicked gale in the North Sea. She knew there were moments when she literally forgot everything except the burning need to be with him, one with him, feeling the shudder and quiver, strength and power, the slick wet heat, the movement, the hunger....

She must have shrieked, screamed...loud enough to wake the dead and half the ocean. She knew he must have felt the burst of the climax that violently seized her, so euphoric she thought she knew at last what they meant by a thousand little deaths.

Surely he felt, he knew...

And waited, his own climax erupting seconds later— or hours, she wasn't at all sure, she lay in such a damp bath of steam that she wasn't sure she was breathing, or that her heart continued to beat at all anymore.

She had thought she could just walk away. Congratulate herself on a mature affair. On allowing herself adult pleasure, denying the complications of real emotion.

But nothing came without a price, and she knew that. She'd told herself not to get involved...

Too late. This *was* involved.

Easing to her side, he held her, smoothed back her hair. She wondered desperately what their pillow talk would be after such a sudden and volatile interlude. When he rolled her to face him, his eyes were dark and intense, and the slightest smile curved his lips. Again he touched her hair, and she had to wonder what he was seeing in her eyes, how much he could read from her face.

God help her, she didn't know what to say or how to act. She was afraid she would start stuttering, try to explain that she never did things like this, that he'd been unique somehow, and that he'd been more than she had ever begun to imagine.

But there was no chance for awkward words, no reason to promise that of course they would see each other again.

Beth's eyes flew open as she heard the sound of a dinghy approaching, the sound of chatter and laughter.

The girls!

His eyes widened and his brows arched as he heard them at the same time.

"Dear God," she swore, flying up even as she spoke, stunned, horrified.

Feeling like an idiot. Anyone could have come aboard

at any time. What in God's name had she been think-ing? She *hadn't* been thinking. She'd been reacting, and feeling....

She hadn't wanted to get out of pillow talk *this* badly!

"Hey!" He was up, too, and reaching for his trunks in the blink of an eye. She looked in panic at the condi-tion of the bed, and wondered about the state of her hair at the same time.

"Got it," he assured her, tossing over a brush from the nightstand and reaching for the sheets. She tripped back into her bathing suit, fingers shaking so hard she couldn't get the bra top fastened.

"Don't panic, you're a grown-up, you know," he said calmly, fixing it for her.

"That's my niece!" she exclaimed, running the brush viciously through her hair. "*And* her friend, and they're at a horribly impressionable age. I'm supposed to be a role model. You don't understand. Her mother is dead—"

"Don't panic," he repeated softly. "I *do* understand, and we're fine. Get topside. I'll finish making the bed."

She sped out of the cabin. There was a boating maga-zine lying in a wire rack by the table. She nearly ripped it apart in her haste to grab it. Then she sat on the sofa, her heart racing painfully again.

The girls—and whoever had come with them—were just coming aboard.

She stretched out and crossed her ankles, trying to look casual and comfortable. Then she decided she looked too casual and comfortable, and uncrossed them.

She crossed them again, smiling, as Amber made her way down to the cabin. "This is too cool. Way, way too cool," she said.

"Ohmygod," Kim breathed, coming down behind her.

"Like a floating hotel suite, huh?" she said, trying to sound cheerful and welcoming. She decided she was loud and fake, but apparently she sounded all right to everyone else.

Amber turned to her with wide eyes. "Like a floating palace."

"Not that lush," Ben protested, coming down behind the girls. He looked at his sister and grinned—apparently oblivious, she noticed gratefully. But then, he probably thought he knew her. Just as she had thought she knew herself.

Keith came striding breezily out from the stateroom. "Hey, kids. Want a tour? Or would you rather roam around on your own?" he asked.

Amber didn't get to answer. "Would you look at the kitchen!" Kim exclaimed.

"Galley," Amber corrected.

Kimberly laughed, running her hand over the counter and staring at the appliances. "No way. This is a full kitchen," she protested.

"Seriously, it's not a salon, either, it's a living room," Amber agreed, looking at Keith.

"You can go around the world in her, can't you?" Kim asked.

"You could."

"Have you ever?" she asked.

"No. But she does offer all the comforts of home," he said. "Speaking of which, would you like something to eat? Drink? You want a smoothie?"

"You can make a smoothie?" Amber asked.

"Yup. I'll see what we have."

He delved into the refrigerator, and the girls went to

join him. Ben looked at Beth. "You don't mind that I brought them?" he asked.

"Don't be silly."

"We didn't interrupt anything, did we?" he asked, a frown starting to crease his brow.

"Don't be ridiculous," she protested. Then afraid that she was about to blush the shade of a beet, she leaped to her feet, closing the magazine.

"Hey, did you get a good look at the upper deck and the flybridge?" he asked excitedly.

She smiled. Big boys, big toys.

"It's an amazing yacht," she said.

"And to think I thought I had the prize of the seas when I bought mine."

In the galley, a blender roared to life just as she started to answer, so she had to smile and wait.

"You have a wonderful boat, and I love it," she said loyally at last.

"Oh, I love it, too. It's just…well, who wouldn't want to own something like this, huh?" he asked.

"Dad, you want a strawberry smoothie?" Amber called.

"Sure."

"Aunt Beth?"

"Absolutely," she murmured. She followed her brother into the galley and accepted a large paper cup from her niece.

She couldn't help it; she felt wary of Keith. She had to keep her distance. She was afraid even to make eye contact, terrified that at any minute she was somehow going to give herself away. She was certainly over twenty-one, but she felt so responsible toward her niece. She'd always tried to teach her that sex should be special; that it was the most intimate act between two people and shouldn't even be contemplated without sincere emotion, the deepest respect, and a sense of responsibility and consequences.

Well, emotionally, she *was* involved, like it or not. Had she been in the least responsible? No. And as to thoughts of future consequences...

It terrified her to realize just how much she wished there could be one. That he would reappear somewhere in her world, that he would be a responsible member of the human community and not just a diver. Or...a common criminal. Or worse.

A murderer.

No. She knew instinctively that wasn't true. Or else she just wanted to believe it.

Keith didn't have any problem being entirely natural and casual. He chatted easily. Beth wasn't even sure what was being said half the time.

Then they heard the motor of the yacht's dinghy, returning with Matt and Lee and the supplies. Ben said it was time to go, and thanked Keith, then Matt and Lee. They all talked about what a pleasure it had been to meet, said they would undoubtedly run into one another somewhere along the line sometime.

"Beth, you can come back with the girls and me," Ben said. "Save Keith the bother."

"Of course."

"I can take you back—" Keith began.

"The girls and I have already packed up. We don't need to head back to the island, just straight to the boat," Ben said.

"Perfect," Beth murmured.

It wasn't perfect. Perfect would be if they all disappeared, if there didn't have to be any words, if she could just go back where she had been and pretend. Pretend Keith Henson was someone she would see again, someone she had known forever and ever...

Someone she trusted.

She had to trust him. She'd just gone to bed with him.

She felt more awkward than ever. She was at ease saying goodbye to Matt and Lee, but she couldn't meet Keith's eyes, and she only shook his hand, while she'd kissed the others goodbye on the cheek. So much for appearing completely casual.

She couldn't escape quite that easily. He stopped her and took her hands. His eyes met hers. Amused but affectionate, she thought. *Affectionate?* She wanted so much more.

She still felt so ridiculously awkward.

"We'll talk soon," he said.

She nodded, hoping she looked casual, carefree.

"I will find you," he said softly.

"Finding me won't be very difficult," she murmured.

"Strange timing, huh?"

She didn't know exactly what he meant. And she couldn't ask him. She couldn't stand being so close to him any longer, with so very much unsaid.

She had to escape, and she did, reaching her brother's dinghy before the others.

As Ben revved his little motor to life, he laughed with the girls as they raved about the *Sea Serpent*. She was grateful she didn't have to speak. She kept a smile plastered to her face as she lifted a hand in farewell to the men standing on deck.

Soon Ben had set their course for home. She reflected that she hadn't even said goodbye to the others—any of the Masons, or Brad and Sandy. The Masons she would see again, and as for Brad and Sandy...

Thinking of the pair still gave her an uneasy feeling.

She looked away from the yacht at last and turned her gaze westward, toward the Florida coast. It would all come into perspective, she told herself.

She would get home. She would believe she had been silly, that she couldn't have seen a skull. That nothing had been going on during their stay on the island. No one had lurked around with evil intent.

And as for Keith...

She would stop thinking about him eventually. In her mind, he would lose the charismatic appeal that had all but obsessed her. She would remember him as a man. As someone special she had once met. Handsome, virile, exciting...but too laid-back, too ready to enjoy good times with his friends, too lacking in ambition.

It would all come into perspective....

But things always came back around to one fact.

She was certain she had seen a skull.

Just as she was certain there was something about Keith. No matter how appealing the man might be, he simply wasn't what he seemed.

There had been an honesty in the way he'd touched her, but only lies had fallen from his lips.

7

"I admit to still being confused," redheaded Ashley Dilessio said, easing back in her chair at Nick's, her uncle's restaurant on the bay.

Nick's was everything good about the area, Beth thought. Boats came in to dock, houseboats were moored nearby, and anyone was welcome. The tables were rough wood, an overhang sheltered the outside seating from the sun, and it felt like a continuation of island living in the midst of a hectic, overpopulated, multicultural community.

Not to take anything away from the yacht club, she decided a little defensively. The two establishments were just different. And of course part of Nick's appeal was that she'd known Ashley most of her life.

Now Ashley was with the police force, in the forensics department, and her husband, Jake, was a homicide detective.

"Okay, you got to the island. You walked with the kids. You thought you saw a skull. A man showed up— you hid it. You went back with Ben, and there was no skull," Ashley said, her green eyes studying Beth with a slight frown wrinkling her forehead.

"That's the gist of it, yes. Ben thinks I saw a conch shell," Beth said, her tone a little sheepish. "It might be nothing, it might be something. But I couldn't stop thinking about Ted and Molly Monoco."

"I remember the story, but… I thought they were sailing around the world," Ashley said. "No wonder no one's seen them."

"But what if it *was* a skull?"

"You said that whatever you saw was gone when you went back."

"Maybe I just couldn't find it," Beth persisted.

Ashley stirred her straw around in the large glass of iced tea in front of her. "This isn't my jurisdiction, or even Jake's, you know."

"But you have contacts," Beth reminded her.

Ashley nodded thoughtfully.

Beth let out a deep sigh. "Shouldn't someone check it out?"

"Yes," Ashley agreed. "We can get the Coast Guard out there to take a look, if nothing else. But…why would the skull—if it was a skull—have disappeared? Did any of the other boaters seem suspicious?"

Beth groaned. "All of them."

Ashley smiled. "Okay, tell me."

Beth began describing the other campers on the is-land: the Masons, who Ashley knew casually, Brad and Sandy, and the three men in the exquisite yacht.

"Three hunks, huh?" Ashley teased.

"Um. They looked the part."

"What part?"

"Oh, you know, the type who would be out fishing, diving…boating."

"You mean they had beer bellies and could open the bottles with their teeth?"

"Ashley!" She flushed slightly, remembering the way she'd described Ben's mythical "friends" who were due to arrive on the island.

"Sorry, just kidding. But they don't sound like modern-day pirates. Not if they already had such a fantastic boat themselves."

"So there really are pirates out there?" Beth asked, keeping to herself the thought that maybe Lee hadn't been the legitimate owner of that boat after all.

"You bet. There's lots of money—and very little law—once you're out on the ocean," Ashley said seriously. She was doodling idly on a napkin. "Describe your guy."

"Which one?"

Ashley grinned. "The one you're talking about the most, seem the most suspicious of—and the most attracted to."

"Ashley…"

"Beth, just describe the guy. Tall? Dark? Face shape— round…long…?"

"Um, really good bone structure. Cheekbones broad, chin kind of squared, really strong. Eyes…" She watched as Ashley sketched on the napkin. Her friend was good. "Farther apart. And the brows have a high arch. The nose is a little longer, dead straight. The lips are fuller. And the hair…well, depends on whether it was wet or dry."

"Just go for the face."

"A little leaner there, below the cheekbones," Beth said. Then she exhaled, leaning back, staring at Ashley. "You'd think you knew the guy. That's incredible."

Ashley shrugged, sliding the cocktail napkin with

the perfect likeness to the side of her plate. "Let's hope so. I'm being paid to do it."

Beth shook her head, staring at Ashley, thinking of the man whose likeness her friend had just drawn.

"Hey! Look what the summer wind brought along," a masculine voice said, breaking the moment.

They both looked up. Jake had arrived. Winking at Beth, he kissed the top of his wife's head and pulled out a chair. He was a rugged-looking man; he either looked his part as a cop or could be taken for one of her boat people. In fact, he was both. He'd spent years dealing with the hardest, darkest, ugliest secrets of a big city, and still knew how to come home and smile, play with his toddling son and baby daughter, love his wife and enjoy his friends.

"Beth thinks she might have found one of the missing Monocos," Ashley said.

Beth was startled when he looked at her sharply, then at his wife again. "I'm not sure they *are* missing. I just heard a rumor that their boat was seen recently."

"She might have found a skull on Calliope Key," Ashley explained further.

"It disappeared," she murmured, then shook her head. She couldn't be hesitant. "Actually, I'm sure I saw a skull. But I got scared and tried to hide it. Then I couldn't find it. And—"

She broke off, then plunged back in. "Well, if someone else had hidden the skull, it didn't seem like a good idea to make a production of digging it up."

Jake grimaced, looked at Ashley again, and then smiled at Beth. "Don't worry, kid, we'll get on it," he assured her. "I'll call Bobby—Robert Gray, a friend with the Coast Guard. I'm sure he'll help. Will that make you feel better?"

"Yes, and thank you," she told him.

"Hey, are we invited to your next big event at the club?"

"Absolutely," she assured him. "You can come in any-time, you know that. Just use my name. No, better yet, use Ben's. He's the paying member." She grinned.

"Want to hear more about Beth's excursion on Cal-liope Key?" Ashley asked her husband. "Some of her new acquaintances sound fascinating."

"Oh?" Jake said, and looked at Beth curiously.

"She met three hunks. Rich ones, maybe."

"Ohhhh," Jake said.

Beth groaned and stood. "You two are cops—you're supposed to be taking me seriously. I'm out of lunch-time. Call me."

Ashley grinned, shaking her head. "We're taking you seriously, really. The thing is, your hunks do sound in-triguing." Ashley paused, her expression turning serious. "I promise we'll find someone—the right someone—to look into what you saw."

"And we *will* call you," Jake promised.

Shaking her head, Beth turned and left them. But she smiled as she did so. She could trust them. If they said they would see to it that the Coast Guard checked out the island, it would be done.

As soon as Beth had gone, Ashley pulled the cock-tail napkin from the side of her plate, setting in directly in front of her husband.

He frowned and stared at his wife.

"He was out at Calliope Key. Where Beth thinks she saw a skull."

Jake picked up the napkin, but hardly bothered to study it.

"She sounds as if she's paranoid already," Ashley murmured.

Jake shook his head.

"Perhaps," Ashley began, "I should—"

"No," Jake said firmly. "No. She's back here, and she's safe. There's no reason to say anything."

"We both know—"

"Yes, we both know. But we don't know what the hell else is going on. Leave it. I'll call Bobby, they'll check out the island. Other than that, there just isn't a hell of a lot we can do."

"Jake—"

"Ashley, it's out of our hands. And besides, since we don't really know anything for certain, what the hell are we going to say?"

She sighed, still unsure that silence was the right course.

Keith surfaced, lifting his mask, spitting out his mouthpiece. He saw Lee on deck—his binoculars in his hands, looking toward the island.

Hand on the ladder, Keith kicked off his flippers and crawled aboard.

"What?" he asked Lee, shedding the rest of his equipment.

Lee shook his head slowly. "I'm not sure what they're doing."

The day before, they had caught sight of Sandy and

Brad on their old scow of a boat—and the couple had been watching them through their binoculars.

"What does it look like they're doing?" Keith asked.

"Stashing, stowing…getting rid of something. In a hurry."

Keith took the binoculars from Lee and turned slowly, scanning the horizon. *Damn!* He thought as he sighted a Coast Guard cutter. *Beth*. She just wasn't going to let it rest. She'd gotten the authorities involved. The problem was, they weren't going to find anything.

"Take a look," he said softly to Lee.

Lee took the binoculars back and followed Keith's line of vision. "Coast Guard," he muttered. He looked at Keith. "Anything we need to worry about ourselves?" he asked. "This isn't the time to be making explanations."

Keith shook his head.

"Nothing down there?" Lee asked tensely.

"Not yet."

"What was on the radar?"

"An old tire iron."

Lee swore. "Well, hell, let's get ready for guests, then, huh?"

Keith nodded.

He turned, moving down the deck to find the fresh-water hose and rinse down his equipment before stowing it. Lee hurried down to the cabin.

As he worked, Keith was startled to see that Brad had gotten in his dinghy and was motoring quickly away from his anchored boat.

He chose the direction away from Keith and his group, disappearing around the island.

He was gone for only a matter of minutes, back long before the Coast Guard cutter approached.

Brad hadn't even turned on the dinghy's motor, he thought. He had used the oars, but had moved with incredible haste.

Why?

The answer was obvious. To try to go unnoticed. And to get rid of something.

Or some*one?*

On Monday Beth had been hopeful, by Tuesday she had been mad, and on Wednesday she was morose, then angry again, this time with herself.

Keith Henson knew her name, where she came from and where she worked. She realized that she'd had it in her head that he was going to find her, that he was going to say he had to see her again, that he was as mesmerized, fascinated, and in love or lust with her as she was with him.

But obviously he hadn't made any effort to locate her—she was simply too easy to find.

Every time the phone rang, she answered it eagerly, then was disappointed. Since she had come home, she realized, nothing had changed.

She still thought about two things: Keith Henson and the skull on the island.

She realized that she was becoming obsessive, but she couldn't seem to help herself. Despite the fact that Ashley and Jake had been true to their word—they had taken her seriously and gotten a friend to order the Coast Guard to search the island—nothing had been discovered. She should have been happy—there had been no corpse on the island, no body parts.

But she couldn't help wondering where the skull she

had seen had been hidden, or whether at this point it had been removed entirely.

At home—and even at work—she had spent hours online, looking up everything she could find on the Monocos. There were pictures of them alongside their magnificent yacht. There was even an old photo of them—from perhaps fifteen years ago—when they'd been at her club. That meant some of the older members might have known them.

She'd also searched the name Keith Henson on the internet. She found a dozen men of that name who had websites or were mentioned in articles.

He was not one of them.

She was thinking about both the island and Keith now, as usual, tapping a pencil idly on her desk, when there was a knock on her office door and George Berry, the current commodore of the club, poked his head in.

"Beth?"

"Hi, Commodore."

"May I come in?"

"Of course, please do."

He sat in the chair across from her. "I've been worrying about the Summer Sizzler."

"Oh?" She smiled questioningly.

The Summer Sizzler was an annual event, and all new members were seriously encouraged to attend. It was an important date on the club's social calendar. The food had to be the best. The entertainment was expected to be the same. And it was coming up in less than two weeks. She, along with the entertainment committee, had it well in hand.

"Chef Margolin has been working hard," Beth assured the commodore, when he didn't say anything further. "He hasn't given me his final menu yet, but I'm willing to bet that once again, he'll completely outdo himself."

The commodore waved a hand in the air. He was a man in his early sixties, with a head of the most remarkable silver hair she'd ever seen. His wife had the exact shade. They both had twinkling blue eyes, and in Beth's mind, they were adorable. They'd had no children, and for as long as she could remember, they had put their time and efforts into their various boats, charities and the club.

Like the Monocos, she found herself thinking.

"You *are* planning something very special, aren't you?"

She arched her brows, looking at him. *How special?* The Summer Sizzler was like an end-of-the-season party—not as major as New Year's, Christmas or the Grand Ball, when the new commodore was installed each year.

Special?

Of course, there was going to be a great menu. And she'd ordered torches, and wonderful light and flower arrangements for the outside bar area, hired a band....

"Really special," Commodore Berry said insistently.

His concern gave her an idea. "I think you're going to be very happy with my plan," she told him.

"You do have a plan for something special?" he asked.

She saw no reason to tell him that her plan had just come to mind. "Give me a day or two, and I'll lay it out for you, all right?"

"It's going to be incredible, right?" He smiled anxiously. "It has to be, you know. I want to go down in history as the best commodore this club has ever had."

"We'll see to it," she vowed.

As soon as he had left her office, she jumped up and headed for the stairs that led down to the first level, with the dining room and, beyond glass doors, the patio. Just a little while earlier, she had noticed a member she had been anxious to talk to—Manny Ortega.

Manny was in his sixties, just like the commodore. He was a fascinating man, who'd come over from Cuba in his teens—lying about his age in order to enter the States with a conga band. He had worked clubs all over Miami in his day.

She was certain he must have worked with Ted Monoco at some time in his life, and she was more than certain he knew the couple, because, according to an item in the paper, he had called the police about the Monocos, suggesting that they were missing.

"Hey, gorgeous," he said to her as she approached his table. He was sitting, Cuban coffee in front of him, smoking and staring out at the different vessels in their berths.

Manny loved his Cuban cigars. He always had the real thing. She wasn't at all sure how he got them, but she never asked.

"Hey, yourself," she said. "And thank you. Can I join you?"

"Absolutely. What's up? Need an aging drummer?"

She laughed. "You never know when I'll take you up on that, Manny. Actually, I was curious. I happened to be reading some old newspapers the other day. Are you a good friend of the Monocos? Ted and Molly?"

"Yes, I am."

"Have you heard anything from them?"

He shook his head slowly, his mouth downcast. "Not a word."

"Do you think something happened to them?"

"Well, I did. But the police told me the other day that their yacht had been spotted, so I guess I have to respect their right to privacy. Seems odd, though. They've always kept in touch with me before."

"It does seem odd. Do you know who actually saw their boat?" she asked.

He tapped his cigar, studying the smoke. Then he looked at her. "Is there a reason you're asking all this?"

"Oh, we just came back from Calliope Key, and it made me start thinking."

Manny lifted his hands in a fatalistic gesture. "Who knows about people? They tell me that Ted and Molly can do what they want, that they are adults. So…did I offend them somehow? I don't know. Could they show up tomorrow? I suppose."

"But…don't they have bills to pay and stuff? Taxes?"

"Everything is done automatically from Ted's accounts. He set it up when they started planning to sail around the world. I just hadn't realized he was planning on closing the door on old friends."

"So no one has talked to them?"

He looked upset, and she wondered if she was treading on dangerous ground. Manny's feelings had evidently been hurt. He might have started off worried, but whatever the police had said to him must have made him believe that his old friends just didn't care anymore.

She leaned forward. "It doesn't sound like the Monocos to me," she said.

He arched a brow. "You knew them?"

"No, but…they were—or are—nice people, right?"

"The best," Manny agreed.

"Then it doesn't seem right."

"No, it does not seem right. But it is…what is." He stood and stretched. He was a man of about five-nine, compact and wiry, his features weathered. He set a hand on her head. "You're a sweet person. Kind to worry, but don't. It will do nothing but frustrate you, I promise."

But they were your friends, she longed to remind him. She managed not to say anything, in the interest of remaining employed.

She nodded, then, on a whim, asked, "Manny, have you ever met a man named Keith Henson?"

He frowned. "I do seem to recognize the name. In what context, I'm not sure. I don't think I've ever met him, but the name rings a bell." She waited, he frowned. After a minute, he shook his head again.

"How about Lee Gomez?"

"Hey…this is Miami. I know dozens of Gomezes."

"But a Lee?"

Again he shook his head.

"Matt Albright?"

"No…can't say I know that name."

"How about Sandy Allison or Brad Shaw?"

He stared at her, frowning and took a puff of his cigar. "What is this today, Beth? Twenty Questions? All these names? There are three million people living here."

She flushed. "They're just people we met on the island."

"Honey, people have been going to that island for centuries. Lots of them. From all over."

"I know. But the name Keith Henson rings some kind of bell?"

"Yeah. But I don't know what."

"Thanks, Manny," she murmured. "Sorry for bugging you."

"I have to go, big date this afternoon," he said. She had always thought of him as a dapper man, rather an old-fashioned word, but one that fit him. He inclined his head toward her. "Thank you for the lovely company, Beth. See you later."

"Oh, Manny, I'm sorry. One more question. A man named Eduardo Shea bought the studios from the Monocos. Do you know him?"

"Sure."

"Is he…a nice guy?"

"Thinking of salsa lessons?"

"Maybe. Mostly I'm planning something for the club."

"The studios are doing well under his ownership, I have heard. He's a decent fellow, a good teacher. Is that what you need to know?"

"Yes, and thanks for the help."

"My pleasure." He stood, ready to go, then paused. "You are a very nice person, Beth. It's your job, I know, to be nice to people, but there's a real kindness behind everything you do. Don't make life miserable for yourself. Trust me. I don't know if Ted and Molly are alive or dead. I know that my fears make sense, and that the explanations I hear from the police make sense, as well. I've learned that there's nothing I can do. You should learn from my experiences."

"Thanks, Manny," Beth said. "You're pretty nice yourself."

He winked. "You're cuter. Have a good day, Beth."

He left. Beth waved, then rose. Walking back inside and through the dining room, she noted that Amanda was seated at a table with a group of women. She was wearing a white skirt suit and a broad-brimmed white hat.

Only she could carry it off, Beth thought, hoping to pass through unnoticed. But Amanda looked up, and Beth groaned inwardly. She was going to be asked about something. Amanda would do her best to make it appear that she wasn't doing her job.

But Amanda only stared at her for a long moment, then she turned away, as if she had assessed Beth and dismissed her entirely.

Beth returned to her office. As she reached it, she hesitated. Her door stood ajar. She could have sworn that she had closed it. A sense of unease raked along her spine. She gave herself a mental shake. Ridiculous. A member had simply come up to talk to her, then not closed the door all the way. The commodore had come back, perhaps.

She smiled, thinking she was really becoming absurd.

But as she walked into her office, she was convinced that things were…wrong. It seemed that the papers on her desk had been moved slightly. Frowning, she began looking through her things. Nothing seemed to be missing.

She glanced at her computer.

It was off.

Her frown deepened. She hadn't turned it off.

A chill shivered through her. And yet…there was nothing really frightening here. Maybe there had been a power surge. Maybe she had hit the off button without realizing it.

But she never turned it off during the day.

Still…

It was broad daylight. There were dozens of members

and employees in and around the club. There was absolutely no reason to feel a sense of danger.

Yet she sat down slowly, the icy hot trickle of fear refusing to abate.

It remained with her throughout the day, and even followed her into the darkening parking lot when she finally left that night.

Thursday.

Morning dawned.

Keith and Matt stood on the aft deck, looking across the water.

The disreputable vessel belonging to Brad and Sandy remained where she had been at anchor.

Matt let out a long sigh. "Guess they have no jobs to get back to," he said.

"They don't know what we're doing," Keith said with certainty, though their presence had disturbed him, as well. He had explored the area where he thought Brad had dumped something, but he hadn't found anything. Still, the ocean was huge, and water and sand shifted. He hadn't known exactly where to look—or what to look for. He was still convinced, however, that Brad had thrown something into the sea.

Something he hadn't wanted the Coast Guard to find.

"I still don't like it," Matt said.

"I don't like it, either. Frankly, I don't like anything about the two of them. But as far as what we're doing goes… Matt, one of us stays on board as lookout, all the time. We can't stop our work completely just because other people are anchored nearby."

"They've been anchored nearby for too long," Matt pointed out.

"Maybe they're saying the same thing about us."

Matt snapped around, looking at him sharply. "I don't want to leave," he murmured.

"Maybe we should, though. Spend a night among the masses. See if we can pick up any idle gossip, any rumors."

Matt stared at him, eyes narrowed, and shook his head. "Keith, I think you're going off track. I'm upset that Brandon is dead, too. But now you're convinced that some old couple's disappearance is somehow connected, but I don't see how."

"They might be dead, too."

"Lots of bad things happen. Lots of people die. They're not all related."

"Nope, not all of them. But I don't think it would hurt to do a little investigating."

Matt looked like he was about to argue, but then he shrugged. "You might be right." Then he smiled. "I imagine you want to try to get an invite into the domains of a certain yacht club?"

"There are plenty of places to put ashore," Keith said. "I repeat—"

"Yeah, I think we *should* head to that area. Other than Brad and Sandy, those were the people hanging here."

"We'll talk it over with Lee," Matt agreed. "And you're right," he murmured, sounding a bit disgruntled. "It's just damn convenient for you, huh?"

Keith shrugged. Hell, yes, he was anxious to get over there.

He was worried about Beth Anderson. She was home, but he knew in his gut that the Coast Guard had been out here because of her. Still, Brad and Sandy were the suspicious ones, and they were out here, while Beth was safely on the mainland. He shouldn't feel uneasy. But he did.

What the hell were Brad and Sandy up to? Hanging around forever, tossing things into the water.

He wanted to just go over and ask them what they were doing, but he didn't want to arouse suspicion against himself. He reminded himself firmly that a boat-load of Coast Guard sailors had arrived on the island, stayed a good long time and searched the interior—and found nothing.

Beth had not given up. She had gone to someone with the power to make things happen, and what was to say she wouldn't push the issue again?

His smile faded, and he shook his head. She was like a dog with a bone, refusing to let go.

And that could be really dangerous for her. Because something *was* going on out here. He was sure of it.

Brad had been afraid they would search his boat, so he had gotten rid of something in the ocean.

So why were he and Sandy still there, watching them all the time?

It all kept coming back to one thing.

The skull.

8

Ashley surprised Beth at the club on Friday.

"Hey! What are you doing here?" Beth asked when Ashley appeared at her door.

"Letting you take me to lunch."

"Cool."

Ashley slid into one of the chairs in front of Beth's desk. "I don't know why, but now you've got me going."

Beth pushed back the menu she had been going over and looked up, waiting for her friend to go on.

Ashley shrugged a little sheepishly. "Well, I told you the Coast Guard found nothing."

"Yeah. So...?"

"I tried to find out if the Monocos' boat really had been seen."

"And?"

"Your friend Manny actually made inquiries up in Palm Beach County. I checked with the officials there, and no one ever made an official report about their boat having been sighted. And no one ever officially filed a missing persons report."

"I thought Manny did."

Ashley shrugged. "Nothing official. According to

the police up there, there were inquiries made, that was all. An officer might have talked him out of making an official report, because when you're over twenty-one, it isn't illegal to disappear, as long as you choose to do so."

"So where does that leave us?"

"Nowhere. Just that you've made it into a mystery that intrigues me. Now let's go eat, or I'll run out of lunch break."

Beth nodded and rose, and they went downstairs to the restaurant. They both ordered the mahimahi, which, the waiter assured them, had been caught that morning by some of the staff. As he started to move away, Beth suddenly caught his arm. "Henry, who is that, third table down, her back to us?"

"Ah. Maria Lopez. You've met her, right?"

"Yes, but only once."

"She's beautiful, isn't she?" Henry said admiringly. "She was an international dance champion. They called her the queen of salsa."

"I know. Didn't she work out of the Monoco studios?"

"I believe so. She danced all over the world. She's sixty now, if she's a day. She has the figure of a young girl, yes?"

"A well-endowed young girl," Ashley murmured, grinning. "She's striking."

"Excuse me," Beth said. She glanced at Henry and explained. "I have an idea about the club and salsa lessons. Maria Lopez being here today is too perfect. Be right back."

She was obsessed, Beth realized, but it was all right, because she *knew* she was obsessed. Hell, even Ashley admitted that her curiosity had been piqued. "Ms. Lopez?" Beth said, feeling comfortable, because it was perfectly within her duties to greet the woman. "How very nice to see you."

The woman, as beautiful as Henry had said, turned to her.

She frowned slightly, trying to determine just who Beth might be; then a smile, soft and lovely, warmed her face. "Hello, Miss Anderson, isn't it?"

"Beth, please."

"Will you have a seat?"

"It's so wonderful to see you here," Beth said, sitting down.

"I like to come down by the water," Maria said. "The sea and sun can be so rejuvenating, don't you believe?"

"Definitely," Beth agreed. Where, and how, did she plunge in? "In fact, I was just out at Calliope Key, and that made me think of an old friend of yours. Didn't you work with Ted Monoco?"

Maria's dark eyes flashed, and for a moment, Beth was afraid she had made the woman angry. But then Maria said, "Oh, yes. Ted and Molly. Such wonderful people. Those were the days. The studios he ran were the best. He gave people the gift of movement, the gift of dance."

"How wonderful," Beth murmured. "I guess now... he's giving himself the gift of the sea and the sun."

Maria Lopez sat stiffly for a moment, then shook her head. "No, I fear not."

Beth swallowed carefully. "What do you mean?" she asked, careful not to give away her own thoughts.

"I believe something has happened to them. I would have heard from them otherwise, and there has been no word. I miss them," she said softly. "And the worst is...

there seems to be nothing I can do." She forced a smile. "So here I am. Lunching near the sea."

"I'm so sorry," Beth said. She paused for a moment, then asked, "Tell me, do you still dance?"

"Sometimes, yes," Maria said.

"I was wondering if…perhaps…you would consider dancing for our Summer Sizzler here at the club."

Maria arched a delicate brow.

"I'd love to do something extraordinary," Beth explained.

Maria was clearly flattered but not yet convinced. "To dance, one needs a partner. Perhaps you could speak to someone at Ted's old studio, the main studio, on South Beach. All the studios were bought by a man named Eduardo Shea. He does well."

This was too perfect, Beth thought, everything falling into place so casually and naturally.

"So I've heard—Manny told me," she explained. "You know Manny Ortega, I'm sure."

"Oh, yes, of course." She offered Beth a full smile. "Manny is very talented, a lovely man. He knows Eduardo, as well. Eduardo is also quite an interesting man, half Cuban, half Irish. I can dance for you—with a partner, of course. But you should bring dance to your members, as well."

"That's what I've been thinking. That we should offer lessons here."

"Your members will have so much fun. And the single men will do much better with the ladies."

"Maria, what a wonderful idea."

The older woman flushed slightly. "Thank you. Call Eduardo. Tell him that I suggested you speak to him. And if you go through with this, I will dance with his instructor, Mauricio. We will need to rehearse, of course. And if you wish your party to be a real success, you'll need at least two male and two female instructors. I will work with them, of course."

"I don't know how to thank you."

Maria laughed. "You will receive a bill."

"Of course."

"Truly, it will be my pleasure," Maria said, inclining her head, something regal about the movement.

As Beth rose, Maria reached for her bag. "Give me a moment.... I have Eduardo's card, and also my own, so that you may call me with details."

Beth accepted the cards and reminded Maria that if she needed anything, to please let her know. As she left the table, she stopped Henry and told him that she would sign the tab for Maria's lunch. Then she hurried back to Ashley.

"The fish was wonderful," Ashley said.

Beth apologized swiftly. "I'm sorry. It's just that—"

"There was Maria, who knew the Monocos, and you're still obsessed with their disappearance, so..."

"Ashley, I saw a skull."

"Beth, you're not a cop."

"So I should feel in my gut that a murder—no, murders—have taken place and just forget it?"

"The police are on it," Ashley said.

"I hope so," Beth said. "Anyway, I needed something special for the Summer Sizzler. Now I've got it."

Ashley groaned, took a last sip of her iced tea and rose. "Jake and I will be at your Sizzler thing, by the way."

"Thank you."

"God sometimes needs help looking after fools," Ashley told her.

Beth grinned and waved as her friend left the dining room.

When Keith woke up the following morning, Brad and Sandy's boat was gone.

Even though he'd been bothered by their presence, he found their absence alarming.

Once again, he headed out to dive the area where he was certain that Brad had cast something overboard, though he was aware that both Lee and Matt, back on the boat, were convinced he wouldn't find anything.

He was close to shore, and there was a lot of seaweed in the area. Though the seas were relatively calm, the sand seemed to be rising; the area was murky.

A large grouper came quizzically toward him, stared at him, apparently found nothing of interest and moved on. A small horseshoe crab, sensing danger, dug more deeply into the sand. A tang, far from the reefs, shot by.

Hands clasped behind his back, fins barely moving, he went over and over the area, trying to follow a grid. He wasn't deep, maybe twenty-five feet, so he could have stayed forever. But he began to wonder himself if he wasn't crazy. Maybe Brad hadn't really dumped anything. Or maybe the guy was a pot smoker and had tossed out his stash. Fish miles away could be chewing it up by now.

The sound of his own breathing was getting monotonous. He usually liked the sound. It was peaceful, just like diving, but now, he was aggravated, looking for what he couldn't find—just as it seemed he had been doing day after day.

A clown fish darted past his mask. A small eel slithered up from the sand and made a hasty retreat.

Though it seemed pointless, he retraced the area for the tenth time, even as the water began to turn chilly.

Just when he was about to give up in total disgust, he saw it.

At first he wasn't quite sure what he had found. He saw it in the sand. He reached out, dusted sand away, picked it up.

Stared.

Stopped breathing, the cardinal sin in diving.

Gulped in air again.

And knew what he had found.

In the morning, Beth drove out to the beach to keep an appointment with Eduardo Shea.

He was a striking man, not particularly tall, perhaps five-ten, no more. His eyes were a brilliant blue, and his hair seemed to be pitch-black. He was tanned, with fine bone structure and quirky, flyaway brows. He had a smile in place long before he reached her.

"Miss Anderson, welcome."

"Mr. Shea," she murmured.

"Come in, come in. We'll talk in the office."

She nodded, walked into his office and took the chair in front of his desk. The walls were lined with plaques, and the shelves held all kinds of trophies. Her heart quickened as she saw a large picture on the wall of Eduardo Shea shaking hands with Ted Monoco, Molly at her husband's side, beaming.

"I see you like that picture," Eduardo said.

"He must have been a very fine man," she murmured.

Eduardo frowned. "He *is* a fine man, talented, and

also a good businessman. You don't always get the two together."

"Very true," she agreed, then changed the subject so he wouldn't think she was unduly interested in the Monocos. "How long have you owned the studios?" she asked.

"Not quite a year. But we are doing very well. Ted Monoco established a legacy of excellence, and we do our best to preserve it," Eduardo said proudly.

"I had a conversation with Maria Lopez yesterday, and she—"

"Yes, I've spoken to Maria. And I'm prepared to offer you an excellent deal."

"Oh?"

"Maria will dance with Mauricio, though she says she won't teach. But I know Maria—she won't be able to stop herself. We'll send four more teachers. As to the music, I must approve the band, because if the beat isn't right…"

"Perhaps you'll suggest a band," Beth said diplomatically.

"I'll be happy to. Now, as to the cost…"

He laid out a rate scale that was more than fair. She thanked him, a little curious that he was willing to let his teachers work so cheaply.

"I have faith in their abilities. Your people will be coming to the studio to go on with their lessons, I promise you."

"I hope so," she murmured, finding herself looking at the wall again.

"You know the Monocos?" he asked.

"I've seen them," she said vaguely.

"They were so excited to be off on their boat. Ted

loved two things—dancing and his boat. After Molly, of course. They're a great couple, still in love, after so many years. So few people mean 'till death do us part' anymore."

"Some people do," she said.

"Ah, a dreamer. Well, I like dreamers. Though dreams won't come true if people don't create them. Think of Ted. With nothing but his talent, he built up this business—and a fine retirement income."

"Were you friends before you bought the business?" she asked politely.

"Of course. I bought the business because I learned from Ted," Eduardo said. He glanced at his watch. "I have a lesson coming up. I'm delighted we'll be doing business together. In fact, I'll teach you myself on the night of your party. Next thing you know, you'll be taking lessons yourself."

She smiled. He and Maria seemed to have the same cheerful confidence. Nice.

"We'll see. I'll talk with you about final arrangements," she told him.

As she rose, he walked around the desk and in an old-fashioned manner, kissed her hand. She tried to decide if he was sincere or just slick.

On the way out, she paused, looking again at the pictures on the office walls. They had all evidently been taken at various competitions. The men were in tuxes. The women wore ball gowns, elegant, formfitting, beautiful.

And in one of the pictures, smiling at the camera, looking her most devastating, was Amanda Mason.

Beth scanned the rest of the pictures. Yes...there, in one, Amanda's father, Roger. And in another, Hank and a lovely young blond woman. Even Gerald, though he was merely in a group shot where a trophy was being handed to a woman.

"Are you interested in competitive dance?" he asked her. Before she could answer, he said, "Of course. You know the Masons. They're boaters."

"Yes, I know them. They belong to the club."

"Well, they won't be needing any basic instruction."

"I hope they'll enjoy the evening especially, since they already dance," Beth said. "Thank you again, and we'll speak soon."

She hurried out, her mind spinning.

What did it mean?

She groaned aloud. It meant that the Masons enjoyed dancing. Big deal.

She shook her head, wondering what she was doing, what she had accomplished. Eduardo Shea didn't seem worried about the Monocos. Eduardo had known them. The Masons had undoubtedly known them.

So?

She could meet a dozen people associated with the Monocos.

Those who had known them, worked with them, sailed with them, liked them.

And it all came back to…so?

None of it was bringing her any closer to the truth.

The monorail took Amber to school and home again. It was a ten-block walk from the Coconut Grove Station. Usually she got off and walked straight home, then called her father—Mr. Paranoid—who generally got home not long after.

This was an early-release day, though, and she had

forgotten to tell him. Since Kim was with her, and she wasn't expected anywhere, Amber decided that they should walk down to the club.

It was a long walk. They stopped at a fast-food joint near the highway for a soda, but by the time they reached the entrance to the club, they were both sweating.

"Straight to the café," Kim said.

"We should tell Aunt Beth we're here first," Amber said.

"Why?"

"So she knows. Then she can call my dad."

"Water, water. We need water," Kim said.

"Okay, water, then Aunt Beth's office."

"Your dad is a member, right? So we're allowed in with or without Beth."

True, Amber thought, but she felt uncomfortable not letting her aunt know she was there first thing. It was going to be bad enough when Beth called her father to tell him that she'd forgotten an early dismissal.

When they approached the gate, Amber waved to the guard, who waved back.

"Beat you inside!" Kim said, and started running. Amber didn't have the energy to run, and by the time she entered the club and walked through to the restaurant, Kim had disappeared.

Amber went up the stairs, but Aunt Beth wasn't at her desk.

Kim *was* there, a look of pure mischief in her eyes. "Look—her computer is on. She's getting an e-mail."

"Kim, you can't use my aunt's work computer," Amber protested.

"No, no, you have to look! This is totally awesome. It's him. I'm sure it's him."

"Who?"

"What do you mean, who? The hunk from the island."

"Keith?"

"Yes. Would you get over here and look!"

Amber exhaled a little nervously but couldn't resist temptation. She walked around the desk and stared at the computer. The e-mail read:

Beth, I got your address from the switchboard. This is Keith, from the island. I'm asking you again to forget anything you think you saw. Let it go, please. There's a new twist. I'll see you soon and explain.

"Should we answer him?" Kim asked.

"No!"

Kim hit Reply and started typing anyway.

Will I really see you soon? I'll be waiting anxiously.

She turned to Amber and asked, "What do you think?"

The two of them started to giggle.

"We shouldn't be doing this," Amber moaned.

"Oh, come on. She needs a life. Don't you want a really hot uncle?" Kim demanded.

They looked at each other and started to giggle again. Amber smiled slowly, then started to type herself. If I'm not at the club... Once again, she hesitated.

Then she typed in her aunt's address, added Or Private message me and gave her aunt's screen name. With one last determined look, she hit Send.

"Oh, yes." Kim applauded.

They heard a noise that seemed to be coming from

one of the nearby offices. Kim jumped up. "We need to get out of here now."

"Let's go."

They crashed into each other in the doorway in their eagerness to escape the office and their guilty endeavors, then ran down the stairs.

The man reveled in his own strength and a sense of superiority.

Kids, he thought with a sniff. Thank God they were so into themselves, so silly, so unobservant.

He wondered briefly what he would do if a child got in his way. He smiled grimly. He had decided once that nothing would stop him. Still, one simply had to hope that certain snags never entered into a picture, since it was impossible to truly know exactly what one would do until the occasion arose.

He entered Beth Anderson's office in practiced silence and looked around slowly at first. He wasn't afraid; he could easily explain his presence there.

Then he walked over to the computer and pulled up the e-mails, curious what the girls had been up to.

For a moment he felt as if ice was running through his bloodstream. But then he relaxed as he realized there was nothing there that could be held against him. Nothing. He was certain of it.

There were tissues on her desk, the box held in an elegant gold wire basket, the metal filigree artistically designed into the shape of sailboats.

He grabbed two tissues and carefully, slowly, meticulously wound them around his forefingers. Then he wiped the keys he'd just touched and began to type himself.

* * *

Beth was thoughtful as she returned to the yacht club, worried that all her plotting and planning would come to nothing. Maybe everyone was right. Not that she'd been imagining things. She was too sure of what she'd seen for that. But that nothing she did would change anything. Even nature was against her. The ocean was vast. The truth of that was never more apparent than when you were out on the open sea in a small boat. It was easy to imagine that the sea could swallow a boat and leave no trace.

Then again, the sea had a habit of flipping a finger at humanity. Flotsam and jetsam usually washed up somewhere!

But not always.

She waved to the guard at the entrance, not really paying attention, and pulled into her space, close to the main building. Inside, she hurried upstairs. In her office, she tossed her handbag onto a chair, slid behind her desk and sat down. She closed her eyes, leaning back for a minute.

Forget it. Just get back to work, she charged herself.

With a shake of her head, she rolled her chair forward and touched the space bar on her computer to turn off the screensaver.

She nearly flew back in the chair.

A giant skull appeared on the screen, then flashed off as if it had never been there.

It was followed by the words *I'll be seeing you soon. In the dark. All alone.*

She jumped up and ran out of her office, ready to run down the stairs and find the manager or the commodore or anyone.

But as she reached the foyer and looked into the dining room, she came to a sudden halt.

Kim and Amber were there, just inside the doors, heads together as they sipped sodas. They looked up and saw her.

Both girls were talented actresses onstage, but in the real world, neither one of them was much at deception. The eyes that met hers were wide and filled with guilt.

She stared at them. "What are you doing here?" she demanded.

"Early-dismissal day," Amber said, swallowing hard.

The girls exchanged glances.

Beth crossed her arms over her chest, furious. She was sure they hadn't really intended to do anything awful, but she had been scared. Really scared.

"Early dismissal," she choked out.

"I…forgot to tell Dad," Amber said. "So, I, um, came here," she finished weakly.

"To my office," Beth said icily.

Both girls gulped.

"You were on my computer, weren't you?" Beth asked accusingly, forcing herself to keep her voice low, since she was at work.

"Aunt Beth…" Amber began, then trailed off guiltily.

Beth tried hard to control her temper, but she still felt frightened, and that didn't help matters.

She always tried so hard with Amber. It was such a delicate balance. She wasn't Amber's mother and could never hope to fill that void. She wanted her niece to know, though, that someone was always there for her, as a mother figure.

Her real mother would have had the luxury of real

fury and the ability to punish her without losing her, but Beth had to tread a milder path.

"I suppose you thought you were very amusing," she began.

"I—just thought—" Amber began.

"I don't want to know what you thought!" Beth exploded, good intentions forgotten.

"Please don't tell Dad," Amber begged. "I'm sorry, really sorry. I'll make it up to you. Somehow. If you tell Dad, then he'll tell Kim's parents, and then…" Her voice faded. She looked at Beth and whispered, "Please. We really didn't mean to be terrible."

Beth didn't answer her. She had to calm down. She turned around and walked back up the stairs, not knowing if the girls would follow or not.

In her office, she sat down again, shaking.

She looked at the computer, then started to laugh. She had apparently tripped over the cord on her way out. The only thing that greeted her now was a blank screen. After a moment she rose, found the displaced plug and returned it to its rightful lodging.

A week ago she wouldn't have been scared, she would have been puzzled.

Her anger had already begun to fade, probably because she had been so frightened, then so relieved.

She weighed the situation while she logged on and opened up her art program, working on plans to promote the Summer Sizzler and make sure she got everyone in the place excited about the dance lessons.

Do I tell Ben about this or not? she asked herself, returning to the question of the girls and their prank.

Amber would hate her.

Amber would have to get over it.

Maybe she should give the girls a second chance.

She forced her mind back to business. She was going to need a picture of Maria Lopez, which should be easy enough to find online. She pulled out Maria's card to call her for permission.

She found a picture that was sensational and was also able to reach Maria immediately. In an hour her flyer had come along perfectly and was ready for printing. With that accomplished, she sat back in her chair—just as her brother made an appearance at her door, his daughter right behind him.

He was frowning. "You knew you had the girls?" he asked.

She could see Amber's eyes. Pleading.

She shrugged, not willing to outright lie when the girls had done something so wrong.

"They never cause any trouble here, Ben." She stared at Amber. "Almost never," she added with a grim smile.

She saw him relax. She hadn't lied, though she hadn't exactly told the truth, either.

"All right, but I'm supposed to know as well when it's early dismissal," he told his daughter.

"Dad," Amber said, and there was a slight note of reproach in her voice. "You have the school calendar. You just don't always pay attention."

Ben opened and closed his mouth. "Yeah, I have the school calendar," he said finally. He sounded gruff. He turned and walked away.

Amber stared after him, thinking he was still angry. Beth knew better. He was just feeling as if he'd somehow failed as a parent.

Amber stared at Beth again, and Beth was startled

to see tears rising in her eyes. "I'm sorry, Aunt Beth. Really sorry."

"Don't do it again," Beth said softly. "And your dad lives for you. Give him a break."

Kim slipped an arm around Amber as they walked off together.

"Hey," Beth called. "Kim—what's the story? Am I driving you home later, or are your folks coming?"

The girls turned back to her. "I'm getting picked up at five-thirty by the guardhouse," Kim said. "Thank you," she added quickly.

"Right," Beth murmured. "Amber, after Kim's folks have come, we'll find your dad and have dinner before we leave, okay?"

Amber nodded and took off with Kim.

Beth watched them go, forgetting her own anger. This aunt thing wasn't easy, she thought. Of course, life never was.

She smiled slightly, turning back to her work, writing herself a mental note that she should be checking up on Amber's school schedule more than she had been.

Ben wasn't angry; he felt depleted. He was actually a pretty good father. He just sucked at trying to be two parents at once.

He sat at the outside bar, sipping a beer. "Hey," came a call.

Looking around, he saw Mark Grimshaw. As kids, they'd taken sailing lessons together. Then they'd wound up at law school together upstate, and, like their fathers before them, they'd both become members of the club.

"Hey yourself."

"Your latest case is sure making headlines," Mark told him.

Ben must have winced, because Mark quickly apologized. "There's a group of us—and not all attorneys, honest—at the pool. Why don't you join us?"

Ben lifted his beer. "My daughter's here. I think we'll just grab a bite and go home."

"It's early. They're not even serving dinner for another hour. Maybe your daughter wants to hop in the pool, too."

No, his daughter wouldn't want to hang with her old man. But maybe a few laps would tire him out, if nothing else.

"Sure. Let me go to my locker. I'll join you in a few minutes."

Mark nodded, smiling. He was a pleasant guy. Worked on civil cases, had a great reputation. Ben had tried to set Beth up with him. Beth liked him well enough but insisted there was just no chemistry.

In the locker room, Ben shed his coat, eased out of his tie and began to turn the wheel of the combination lock on his door. As he did, he thought he heard a noise and hesitated, looking around.

He wouldn't have been surprised to see someone. Lots of guys came straight from work, changed and headed out to the pool or their boats.

What surprised him was that he didn't see anyone.

He was certain that he hadn't been alone a moment ago.

Working too hard, too much. Worrying too hard, too much. Hell, if life was just a jaunt out on the boat, days on an island…

Hell. He suddenly wanted to give Beth a good shake. He was jumpy because of the stinking island!

With a shake of his head, he turned back to his locker and started the combination over.

Click…click…click.

The lock opened.

He changed and went out to the pool.

It wasn't even dark yet. He'd been ridiculous, thinking he'd heard something. Someone.

Disgusted with himself, he strode out to the pool and dived in. Strong-armed, he did lap after lap. When he came out, dripping, his friends were waiting with a beer.

Amber had come out. She smiled, waving to him. Apparently Kim's folks had picked her up. She walked over. "Dad, think Aunt Beth would mind if we ate burgers out here? I was thinking about hitting the pool, too."

"Sure. Aunt Beth won't care. It's a nice night, and you're right—we should just be casual out here." He left it at that, but inside he was inordinately pleased that she'd wanted to spend some time with him after all.

She smiled again, then scampered off to change. His heart took a sudden plunge.

It was hard to love someone so much and not smother them with that love.

As he watched his daughter walk away, he felt again the pinpricks that had haunted him in the locker room.

Fear.

Irrational but all too real.

He was scared. And he wasn't at all certain why.

It just seemed that suddenly a shadow, something dark, had entered his life, stealing away comfort and ease.…

He looked up.

The sun was still out, brilliantly shining.

The shadows, he tried to tell himself, were all in his mind.

9

Beth was glad she had kept her mouth shut about the girls messing with her computer. When she joined her brother and niece out at the pool, she found a number of families engaged in a game of chicken.

Ben, with Amber on his shoulders, was trouncing the opposition. There was a lot of laughter and camaraderie going on. Nice.

She sat on the sidelines, watching, until Amber saw her and waved, then tapped her dad on the top of the head and alerted Ben to her presence, as well.

The competition tried to take advantage of Ben's distracted state, but Amber turned back, ready to take on the world. Her opponent went down, and Amber laughed delightedly.

Like a child.

Then the two of them, after high-fiving each other in victory, laughed and left the pool, joining Beth on the sidelines.

"Congratulations," Beth said.

"Thanks," Amber said. "You're cool with this, right? Hamburgers okay with you? I'll go put our orders in. Would you rather have fish, Aunt Beth, or the salad bar?"

Beth shaded her eyes to stare at her niece. "Are you suggesting I *should* choose the salad bar?"

"No!"

"I'm going to have a hamburger and fries and iced tea," she told Amber. "Ben?"

"The same."

Amber nodded, grinned and went off to the counter to order.

Ben stared at his sister. "Dancing?"

"You could learn to dance," she said defensively. "Salsa, I've decided. For a party—'Summer Sizzler.'"

"I think it's great," he assured her. "Summer Sizzler—salsa. What's not to like?"

"Good."

"But are you sure that's all you have in mind?" He leaned closer. "Tell me you're not still trying to find out more about the Monocos."

"I happened to see Maria Lopez at lunch. She's a salsa queen. I spoke with her. It will be fun, good exercise, and Eduardo Shea gave me a great deal, because he thinks some of the members will sign up for dance lessons."

Ben let out a sigh, shook his head and leaned back in his chair again.

To Beth's dismay, one of the members, a woman named Tania Whirlque, came over and immediately brought up the same subject.

"Hey, Beth, I hear we're having a dance workshop at the Sizzler."

She hadn't even put the flyers out yet.

"Do you like the idea, Tania?"

"Love it, especially if they're going to arrange for a few teachers. I'm not so sure I'll get my husband out on the floor, though."

"We'll have to work on the guys," Beth said.

"You know, when I heard Eduardo Shea's name, I got thinking about the Monocos," Tania said. She took a seat next to Beth.

Beth couldn't keep from casting a slightly guilty glance at Ben. "It seems that no one has heard from them."

"Quite frankly, I fear the worst." Tania hesitated. "We have friends from Virginia who lost a boat to pirates."

"Really? What happened?" Beth asked, all her suspicions on the alert again.

"They were off Chesapeake Bay, in a forty-five-footer by themselves. They were anchored, sunning… I think Betty was cooking dinner. They were attacked by thieves who climbed aboard in dive gear. They thought the divers were in trouble at first, lost…whatever. Anyway, turned out they were armed. While Betty and Sal were being welcoming, the divers pulled knives, forced them overboard and stole the boat."

"How horrible! But they survived?" Beth said.

"They're both strong swimmers, and they were able to reach another boat in the area. They called in the Coast Guard, but the thieves got away."

"When did it happen?" Beth asked.

"About a year ago now. The boat has never been found. But then, you can disguise a boat just like you can disguise a car."

A year ago. Before the Monocos disappeared.

"Could they describe the…pirates?" Beth asked, finding she still couldn't quite wrap her mind around such a crazy concept.

"One was male, one was female," Tania said. "And that's about it. They both had on wet suits and head covers. I talked to Betty about it. She says when she looks back now, it all happened so fast that she can't really remember much about the incident. Frankly, she's just glad to be alive. Where they were…well, even though they're strong swimmers, they could easily have drowned."

"The thieves probably meant for them to drown," Beth murmured.

Ben moved uncomfortably, obviously disturbed. She wondered if it was because of the story Tania had told or because he thought it would fuel her desire to find out the truth about the Monocos.

"Ben is always armed," Beth said.

"Ben has good reason to be armed—he put away a few unsavory characters when he was with the D.A.," Tania reminded them. "You're a crack shot, right?" she asked him.

He nodded grimly. Then he said, "Let's drop this, please? Amber is coming back with our burgers. I don't want to scare her."

Despite the fact that he laughed and teased his daughter as the evening wore on, Beth could see that he remained uneasy.

Finally she realized it was getting late. "I've got to go back to my office before I go home. I left my stuff up there. See you tomorrow sometime?"

"Probably. Are you working?"

"For a bit. I usually come in just to see how things are going on the weekends. You know that."

"Want me to walk you out to the parking lot?"

"You guys have to change, and I'm tired. I just want to go home, and we have a security guard in the parking lot, remember? But thanks. And, Ben, I'm okay—I haven't gone off the deep end."

Beth said good-night to Amber, then left, hurried up to her office for her handbag and jacket. After scooping up her things, she turned out the light, and headed downstairs and out the front door.

The club hadn't completely shut down for the night. The dining room would still be serving until around ten or ten-thirty, and then it would take another hour to an hour and a half to close down completely. And that night, out by the pool, the snack bar was serving late, as well.

There were still plenty of people around, talking and laughing. Even so, Beth heard her heels click on the concrete.

As she walked, she could hear the breeze as it rustled through the trees and bushes that grew around the borders of the club and the reflecting pool by the front steps.

Suddenly she thought she heard footsteps coming up behind her.

She told herself there was no reason for the sound of footsteps to frighten her. The club was still full of people, one of whom might have chosen to leave at the same time.

Was it in her own mind though, or were these footsteps echoing her own almost perfectly?

She paused, turning back.

The breeze lifted her hair and felt cool against her neck.

No, it felt chilling.

"Hello?" she called. "Anyone there?"

There was no reply.

The bushes, which seemed so benign by day, suddenly seemed thick and dark, able to hide a million dangers.

She straightened her shoulders and gave herself a

mental shake. "Hello?" she called again. Once more there was no reply.

She started walking again, looking toward the front of the lot, where the security guard should have been in his little glass-windowed booth.

She couldn't see him. He might have been sitting, with his head in a book, perhaps.

Or someone might have taken him out.

"Oh, right," she murmured aloud, disgusted that she was letting her mind go off in such a paranoid direction. He was there somewhere. Or maybe he had gone off to help someone who was having car trouble.

Her car was only another fifty feet or so away.

She stared at it, hugging her purse against her side, reaching inside until she found the comforting shape of the pepper-spray canister.

The parking lot was well lit, but bright lights always allowed for shadows.

And those bushes, so big and lush, admired by everyone who came.

She didn't like them anymore. Not one bit.

Aim for the car, she told herself. She had to get over this feeling.

The sounds from the club had faded completely. Click, click. She could hear her heels against the asphalt again, and then...

Footsteps, following.

She turned back once more.

This time she was almost certain she saw a shadow go flying behind a tree.

"Hello?" she called.

No one answered.

The car was nearly in front of her, and she made a hasty decision.

Screw rationality.

Run.

She did, and she was ready, keys in her hand, to click open the lock and jerk open the door as she reached the car.

Quickly she slid into the driver's seat and slammed the door shut. She started to exhale, then remembered to hit the automatic lock.

She let out a sigh and leaned back, allowing herself to feel a little ridiculous. When she looked to the side, she could see the guard in his little booth.

She closed her eyes again, took a deep breath and opened them. She frowned. The guard was gone again. She leaned to look out the passenger window to see where he had gone.

That was when someone loomed up in the driver's window.

Ben knew they should leave, but he was really enjoying the evening. Amber was smiling and playful, almost like she had been when she was younger.

She was a good kid, he reminded himself. Talented, driven. He was lucky.

"Did you notice that yacht anchored on the other side of the *Sea Witch?*" Mark asked Ben.

"Huh? Sorry… I was drifting, I guess," Ben apologized.

"It's a night for that, isn't it?" Mark said.

"I don't think I've noticed any new boats around," Ben said.

"She's a real beauty. I'd love an invitation on to her!"

"What is she?"

"Motor yacht. Looks like she's fitted for anything in the world you could think of doing out on the water," Mark said.

"Oh, yeah? Some guys out on Calliope over the weekend had a boat like that," Ben said.

"Were you on it?"

"You bet. It really was fitted out for anything in the world."

"Well, if it's the same guys and you know them, get me an invitation," Mark said.

Ben nodded. "There were three of them. A guy named Lee Gomez owns her. His friends were Keith Henson and Matt Albright."

"Yeah? What do they do for a living?"

"Family money bought the boat."

"There you go. Can't beat family money."

"Nope. Better to earn it yourself," Ben protested.

Mark laughed. "You see it your way, I'll see it mine. Doesn't matter—I don't have any family money coming my way, so I guess I'll have to go with that damn earning it thing. Well. I'm going to change and get out of here. If you see those guys, though, hang on to them and call me."

"Sure thing," Ben said. He looked over at Amber. She had been lying on one of the nearby lounges, but now she was staring at him. She looked a little ashen, or maybe it was just the light.

"You think it's them?" she asked.

He shrugged. "Could be. I think somewhere along the line I said they were welcome here anytime. I thought you liked them."

"Uh, yeah. I'm going to shower and change, Dad. You about ready?"

"Yup." He rose and set an arm around her shoulders. "Let's go home."

She didn't shake him off. She suddenly seemed glad of his arm.

Somehow Beth refrained from screaming, then was glad she had.

It was just Manny, tapping at her window.

She turned the key in the ignition, then rolled down the power window. "Hey, Manny."

"Hi, gorgeous. I hear we're having a salsa night at the Summer Sizzler." He sounded pleased.

"Yes, do you like the idea?"

"Love it. Maria will be dancing?"

"Yes."

"Wonderful. Well, sorry, I didn't mean to startle you." He started to walk away, but before she rolled the window up, he turned back to her.

"Did you go out to the beach and see Eduardo Shea?" he asked.

"I did."

"What did you think?"

She was startled by the question. "Um, he seemed to have a lot of love and respect for the Monocos, and he also seemed to like my idea. I think he likes the fact that most of our members can afford dance lessons if they like the taste they get at the Summer Sizzler."

Manny was studying her strangely, she thought.

But everything that night had seemed strange. It was definitely her, she decided.

Manny shrugged. "Sounds good."

"I hope so. Actually, some of our members have already taken lessons at the studio."

She was curious to see if he would ask her who—or if he would already know.

"Oh, of course. The Masons dance."

"Right."

"I'm sure it will be a fantastic evening. Good night."

Nothing suspicious there, she told herself dryly. "Good night," she returned.

He walked away. She rolled up her window and, shaking her head, started out. The guard was in his booth as she drove past.

A creepy feeling crawled up her neck, and she threw her car into Park at the entrance to the main road.

She turned, almost dreading what she might find, and looked carefully into her backseat.

There was nothing there.

Her car was an SUV, with plenty of room in the back. She actually got out, circled to the rear and stared into the back, then breathed a sigh of relief when she saw that it was empty of everything other than her mask, fins and a towel.

Feeling like a fool, she hopped into the driver's seat and headed home.

Ben opened his locker and frowned. He wasn't obsessive-compulsive in any way, but neither was he a slob, and something seemed...out of order, somehow.

He looked over everything. His jacket was hanging on the hook. His shoes and suit pants were on the first shelf, his toiletries on the middle shelf. The things he kept on the upper shelf were there, just as they had been. Stuff he kept at the club that was only used at the club.

His silly St. Patrick's Day T-shirt, his Halloween glow sticks and vampire teeth were there, along with the plastic eggs that members put pennies in for the little kids to find at Easter. His schlocky vampire cape was folded over everything else.

He couldn't think of a thing that was missing.

He checked for his wallet and found it right where it should have been, in the pocket of his trousers. His keys were there, as well. There was nothing missing.

He still had the feeling someone had been in his locker.

With a little oath of self-disgust, he got his clothing, slammed the door and headed for the showers.

Beth loved her house. It was a row house, right on Mary Street. Although it wasn't really that old—no more than thirty or so years—it had been built in the old Spanish style. She had a little front yard to go with it, and a matching backyard. The entire diminutive community was enclosed by a high iron fence, with each house possessed of an individual gate for its front walk.

Her yard boasted a palm and a lime tree, and in the little garden area, she had different kinds of flowers in a brick plant bed. Her porch area had a swing seat.

It was no problem to leave her car overnight on the street, since pay parking ended at midnight and didn't begin again until nine the next morning. The Grove was one of those places that wasn't in a hurry to get up in the morning. Few places—other than banks—opened before ten o'clock, and lots of the shops didn't open until eleven.

She parked in front of her house, then opened her unlocked gate and headed for the door, only to discover that whatever paranoia had gripped her at the club had apparently followed her home. As she headed up the little walk, she was suddenly certain she saw a shadow on the street.

A shadow that was there, then gone.

The streets here—absolutely beloved by day—suddenly seemed eerie by night. Coconut Grove was famous for the lush foliage so many home owners encouraged, but by night, especially when there was a moon, there were shadows. And rustling leaves. Always. It was something she didn't usually think about.

But tonight...

She hurried up the steps to her door. On her way, she dropped her keys. She bent to retrieve them and looked back toward the street, certain she'd heard footsteps.

There was a huge oak just down the street.

It seemed that—just as they had in the parking lot at the club—a smaller shadow suddenly merged with the larger one of the tree.

As if someone had slipped behind the oak.

She quickly retrieved the keys and cursed when her fingers shook.

She got the key into the lock and twisted it. The door opened. She stepped inside, slammed it shut and leaned against it, quickly turning off, then resetting, the alarm, and locking the door.

The prickling of unease at her nape remained. She didn't turn the lights on but eased around to the window, kneeling on the couch and just touching the drapes, determined to look out. Her eyes widened.

She hadn't imagined it.

There had been two shadows.

A man emerged from behind the tree.

She could make out nothing about him, other than the fact that he was tall.

And that he was watching her house.

She sat back quickly in the dark, amazed and, oddly, not as terrified as she might have been.

At least she wasn't crazy.

She looked out again quickly, realizing that she needed to watch him, needed to see where he went, what he did.

But when she looked out again, he was already gone.

It was then that fear set in.

Had he already moved closer to the house? Was he trying to find a way in…?

Was he out there, closer still, nearly breathing down her neck?

What to do…call the police?

And say what? There had been a man standing on a public street?

She shook her head, got up and suddenly went into speedy motion, running around the downstairs first, checking every window, running through to the back, checking to see that both bolts were secure, then heading upstairs and assuring herself again that all her windows—and the glass doors to the upstairs balcony—were securely fastened.

She was certain she was never going to be able to sleep that night.

She dragged a pillow and blanket downstairs. In the living room, she set up a bed on the couch, then stood still in the middle of the room.

She had lights on everywhere. That was probably stupid—in fact there was no "probably" about it.

But she didn't want to sit in the dark.

At least she had heavy drapes. Coconut Grove was the kind of place where people walked all the time, where they took out their bicycles and ran with their dogs. She loved living where she did, but she also liked privacy, so her drapes kept her safe from the public eye.

She turned on the television. If she was going to sleep tonight, it would be with the television on and every light blazing. Fine.

As a last precaution, she dragged one of the heavy end chairs from the dining-room table and set it in front of the front door. Foolish? Maybe, but she couldn't help remembering the skull jumping out at her from the computer, and the words that had been written there.

I'll be seeing you soon. In the dark. All alone.

She knew she was being foolish. Amber had written the words. She had admitted it.

Still…

Someone had been out there, and there was nothing wrong with being careful.

Finally satisfied, she lay down on the couch, and hit the channel changer until she got to Nickelodeon. There was little likelihood of anything coming on that might scare her into a further fit of unease.

A vintage sitcom was playing, just as she had expected.

She eased her head against the pillow, smiling a little wryly at herself. This was all absolutely ridiculous. No reason to be afraid.

Then something thudded against the front door.

Sharp, hard, startling.

She bolted upright.

* * *

"Do we really have to go by Beth's place now?" Ben asked, puzzled. "I'll see her tomorrow."

"I have something of hers, Dad," Amber explained. "Something—personal."

He assumed his daughter had taken some of his sister's female necessities and was in a panic to give them back.

Whatever.

It had been a great night, but he was tired.

"Dad, she's only two minutes away," Amber said.

He forced himself to grin at his daughter. "Liar," he accused with fake ferocity. "It's at least five minutes."

"Dad," Amber groaned.

"All right, all right, we're going."

They turned onto Beth's street, and he pulled his car up behind hers.

He frowned. Something seemed to be lying on the porch. A dark...lump.

"Um, Amber, stay in the car for a minute, huh?" he said.

He opened the gate and hurried along the walkway. His heart sank. It was an animal. Bending down, he saw that it was a cat. A black cat, and one that had evidently been in an accident. Poor thing; it had probably crawled off the street and on to Beth's porch. Maybe it had somehow known that a softie lived inside, a woman who would have rushed a strange animal right to the vet, no matter what the cost, if the creature had lived.

He hesitated. He didn't want his daughter or his sister seeing the badly mangled creature.

Amber was starting to get out of the car.

"Stay back!" he told her.

He returned to the car himself and opened his trunk. He tended to keep extra supplies for the boat in the trunk. Paper towels, toilet paper, dish detergent and, luckily, trash bags.

He went back for the cat.

"Dad?" Amber called.

He picked up the dead animal, deciding he would get rid of it without either woman knowing what had happened. "It's all right, honey. Just a mess of foliage," he called to his daughter.

He bagged the cat and walked around to the trunk. As he dropped it in, Amber emerged from the car.

With his daughter in his wake, he headed up the steps again and rang the bell. There was no answer. He rang again, then pounded on the door, which flew open.

Somehow, instinct warned him, and he ducked right before a burst of pepper spray could hit him in the eyes.

"I'm calling the police, you pervert!" his sister swore, just before the door slammed shut.

10

They pulled the dinghy up to one of the club docks. Matt leaped out first, ready to secure the small boat.

"Nice place," Keith murmured, following behind him.

Before Lee had even joined them, Keith heard a cry. "It *is* you!"

Lithe and sleek as ever, Amanda Mason was sashaying down the dock. "How delightful."

"Amanda," he murmured.

She hugged and kissed all three of them, as if they were long-lost relatives.

"I wondered when you all would make it in," she said. She was in a sundress, the kind that showed off the perfection of her figure but also seemed fine for a casual night out.

Her sandals were studded with rhinestones. Her toes were painted perfectly.

"We decided we needed a little civilization," Lee said.

"Oh, honey, no one ever promised to be civil," Amanda said. "Come on in. We were about to leave. Thank goodness we waited. Daddy is here, and both my cousins are here tonight, too. It will be just like old-home week on Calliope. Well, minus Sandy and Brad.

And I th... ...how long its...
come o...

"We...
ing his...
lite and f...
Amanda. A...
be all over a limit. I...
might not have minded, but...
to see the...bad up address, and...
for...ear. It should be arriving the next...

...he...

we...

to...

t...

Handwritten note:

Cold Case
Colorado —
Cassie miles

Hot Summer in
Texas
Delores
Fossen

Texas Target

Barb Han

www.deloresfossen.com

...k
...ll
...d.
...in
...im,
...les.

...had
...ble.

...s spot
...the sil-
ver remain...

Apparently Roger had just arrived as well, Keith thought, though that didn't have to mean a thing.

As the plates were swept away, coffee was being served.

"In from the sea at last," Roger said. Tonight, the patriarch of the clan was in a white suit. He wore it well.

Hank was more casual in a calypso shirt, and Gerald was wearing perfectly starched trousers and a tailored shirt, looking as if he had just shed his jacket and tie.

"So how's life been going out on Calliope Key?" Hank asked politely.

"Fine," Matt said. "What's not to enjoy about beautiful days out on the water?"

"Are you staying on the boat now, or still camping?" Roger asked.

"Mainly on the boat," Lee told him.

"Diving, diving, diving, huh?" Roger said.

"Nice life when you can get it," Keith admitted.

"Discovered anything out there?" Roger asked.

"Clown fish, angels…rays—saw a huge ray yesterday," Lee said.

"No sign of any wrecks?" Roger asked.

"No. Should we have seen something?" Lee asked.

Roger shrugged. "It's shipwreck city in these waters," he said.

"Did you see my girl out there?" Hank asked the newcomers. "The *Southern Light* has her berth here."

"We saw her," Keith said, thanking the waiter who was bringing over more chairs. "She's a beauty. Your club is great, too."

"I've actually been here before," Lee said. "And it is great."

"So, are you vacationing in Miami for a while now?"

"Taking a room anywhere?" Roger asked. "I can recommend some great places."

"Daddy, they could stay with us," Amanda said.

All three men in her group stared at her hard. Lee quickly said, "Thanks, but we're going to stay out on the boat. It's easy to get in and out."

"What are you drinking?" Roger asked them.

"We'll join you for coffee," Hank said.

"Excuse me, I'm off to the facilities," Keith said, rising. "Coffee would be great," he added, determined to escape before he could be followed.

"There's one by the front entry," Roger assured him.

Keith nodded, made his way through the tables out to the foyer, trying to get the layout of the club straight in his head. He looked back. Lee had risen with Roger Mason. The two seemed to be thick in conversation. Amanda had been left to flirt with Matt. Their conversation seemed to be intimate. Hank and Gerald were left to speak with one another. Keith watched the dynamics for a long moment, then hurried up the stairs. Curious that Gerald was here tonight. He'd been under the impression that the man lived farther north along the coast and wasn't around that often.

It didn't take more than a few minutes to find her office. He let himself in and closed the door.

The door flew open a second time.

Beth stood there, looking horrified. She swallowed hard and said worriedly, "Ben?"

"It's all right," Ben grated out. "You missed me. Barely."

"Dad? Aunt Beth, what did you do?" Amber cried out indignantly.

"It's all right," Ben said, straightening. He stared at his sister, stunned. Beth was pale, in shock. Mortified.

"What?" he demanded.

"You scared me," she said. "Oh, Ben," she apologized again. "I'm so sorry." Then she straightened her shoulders. "What the hell were you doing out there? What did you throw against my door?"

He let his shoulders fall as he shook his head. He noticed the large dining-room chair, now moved over to the side of the entry. "Beth, kitchen," he said.

"Hey," Amber protested.

"Get in and lock the door, Amber," Beth said as Ben took her by the shoulder, prodding her toward the kitchen.

He sighed as she stared at him. "Beth, I didn't want to have to tell you—there was a dead cat in front of your door."

"A dead cat?"

"The poor thing had obviously been hit, and it crawled up on your porch to die," Ben told her.

"Ben, someone threw something against my door," she informed him.

"It probably fell against it," he said. "Dammit, Beth. You might have blinded me," he told her.

She exhaled. "Yeah, sorry. The sound just scared me."

He set his hands on her shoulders. "Let go, Beth. Let go of this whole thing with the Monocos, okay? You'll turn both of us into idiots jumping at our own shadows."

She nodded, touched his face. "I didn't get you?"

He shook his head. "Man, I'm tired. Good night, okay?"

She laughed suddenly. "What are you doing here?"

"Amber said that she had to give you something back. Do me a favor—don't tell her about the dead cat."

"Where is it?"

"In my trunk."

She shook her head. "I won't say anything."

They walked back to the living room. Amber was standing there, arms hugged around her chest. "Leave whatever you brought for your aunt and let's go, huh?" Ben said.

Beth stared at Amber, frowning. Amber stared back at Beth.

She wanted to say something to her aunt, Ben realized. Something she wouldn't say in front of him.

It was just going to have to wait until tomorrow.

He swore softly. "Amber, just call Beth in the morning, huh? Let's go."

He walked out the front door. He heard Beth say softly, "Amber, it's all right. We'll talk in the morning."

His daughter followed him. He heard his sister lock her door behind them as Amber headed for the car.

A moment later, exhausted, he drove away.

When Keith returned to the table, Amanda was just rising. "I was about to show Lee and Matt around the pool area. Join us?"

"Absolutely," he said. He took a sip of the coffee that had arrived in his absence and arched a brow to Roger. "Coming?"

"I'll let her show you the way," he said.

"We've seen it," Hank added dryly.

Keith nodded and followed the others out. Amanda caught hold of his arm. "I really want you to meet Maria Lopez. She's outside."

The woman was in conversation with a wiry-looking, older Hispanic man. She was animated and spoke quickly in Spanish, her tone hushed.

Realizing that someone was approaching, they both fell silent. The man rose.

"Manny, how delightful," Amanda purred. As she stepped forward, he took her arms and kissed her cheek.

The woman, very elegant in a dignified, old-world way, waited.

Amanda stepped back. "I'd like you to meet Maria Lopez, a very famous member of our little society, and Manny Ortega, a musician and a talented man! Maria, Manny, let me introduce Keith Henson, Matt Albright and Lee Gomez."

Keith thought he saw a flicker of recognition in the man's eyes. But the older man said nothing, merely exchanging handshakes with them all.

"I'm trying to convince them to come to the Summer Sizzler," Amanda said.

"Yes, you must come," Maria murmured politely.

"Will you be in the area that long?" Manny asked.

"We can arrange to be," Lee said in reply.

"If you're dancing, we'll certainly arrange it," Keith assured her.

She assessed him carefully, her beautifully defined features giving away nothing of either appreciation or dismissal. "It will most certainly be my pleasure," she said.

"Well, I'm showing my friends around," Amanda said. "Will you excuse us?"

"Certainly," Manny said.

As they left, Keith noticed that Manny and Maria didn't resume their conversation.

He was certain it was because they both suspected that Lee's Spanish was excellent.

He followed the group around for another few minutes, then glanced at his watch and excused himself.

As he had expected, his car was waiting.

"I've shown you mine," Amanda said huskily. "Aren't you going to show me yours?"

Matt stared at her blankly. She'd been gone for a while. Said she'd had to feed a dog or something like that. Her cousins had disappeared, too, Gerald taking Lee for a trip around a few of the South Beach bars, Hank claiming to have a date. He'd been left talking to the salsa queen, Maria, and the older fellow, Manny, who had insisted he have a real Cuban cigar.

But then Amanda had returned, anxious to show him Hank's yacht.

The words she had just murmured were a come-on if he'd ever heard one. He was somewhat shocked. It wasn't that he didn't have self-confidence. It was just that in the company of Lee and Keith, he usually came out on the short end. Some men—or women, for that matter—just had an air that attracted the opposite sex. It was sad to admit, but in the company of the other two, he came in last. Like tonight. God knew what Keith was up to. Keith had the leeway to do whatever the hell he wanted; he was the leadman on the job. Lee had taken on the role of getting to Gerald Mason.

Frankly, he'd been feeling like the odd man out.

But now...

Here she was, cute as a button. No, not just cute. Sexy, provocative, petite and yet voluptuous. Her fingers rested on his chest. Stupidly he said, "Show you mine?"

"We've taken a look at Hank's yacht. I'd love another look at yours."

"She's actually Lee's," he reminded her.

"But I'm sure you have all the rights of ownership," she teased. "You don't mean to tell me that you can't ask me aboard? Your friends are gone for the night, right?"

How did she know that? It seemed important to know what this woman was all about. And with both of the others gone, it was his job to watch the yacht. "You want to go to my place?" he queried.

She pressed against him. "I do."

He wasn't a fool, he reminded himself. He could hold his own when he needed to. But…sometimes work and pleasure could collide.

She must have known that he was hesitating, because she grew even bolder. She ran her hand straight down his chest to his genitals. "I like risk and excitement," she whispered, standing on tiptoe to breathe the words straight into his ear.

"They, uh, they could return," he stuttered, testing her. "I can get a room."

"But I like boats," she insisted, pouting.

She didn't want him. She just wanted to get on the yacht. She thought she'd found a patsy. Well, two could play the game.

"Sure, the tender is right over there," he told her.

Beth leaned against the door, shaking. She had nearly hurt her brother. Badly.

She let out a deep sigh, knowing she had to get a grip.

There was a firm knock on the door. She jumped, then caught herself.

Ben. What had he forgotten?

She threw the door open.

There was a man at the door. He seemed huge, looming in the darkness beyond the pool of light where she stood.

It wasn't Ben.

And she no longer had her pepper spray.

A scream rose in her throat as he stepped forward.

She screamed and tried to push the door shut. It met an immovable obstacle and stalled. Then she heard her name.

"Beth. Dammit, Beth. You told me to come!"

She went dead still, only then recognizing the towering form in the doorway.

She just hadn't been expecting him.

She stepped back in shock. She'd spent the first part of the week praying he would call.

The second half of the week, she'd simply been mad.

"May I?" he asked, still standing on the porch.

He was everything she had remembered and more. Dark eyes, a startling contrast to the sun-bleached lightness of his hair. Bronzed. In form-hugging jeans and a tailored shirt, open at the throat.

For a minute she couldn't find speech.

Then she was angry with herself, because she was being worse than Amber and her friends, gawking, letting herself be thrown off-kilter by any man.

"What do you mean, I told you to come?" she inquired curtly.

He cocked his head slightly, a smile curving his lips.

"May I come in? The neighbors will be out soon, if they haven't called the police already," he teased.

She stepped outside, looking around.

She couldn't help but look over to the tree, then back at Keith.

Had he been stalking her? Hiding behind the tree while her brother was there?

Why on earth would he do such a thing?

Maybe he wanted her alone. All alone.

She lowered her head for a moment. To be frank, she wanted to be alone with *him,* too.

"Beth, are you all right?"

She stepped back and repeated, "I told you to come?"

He let out a sigh. "Today."

"I asked you to come today?"

"In your e-mail. Remember?"

Her brows arched; her mouth formed an O.

"I'm going to throttle her!" she said.

"Who?" he demanded, confused.

"Come in," she murmured.

He stepped into the house, frowning and looking around curiously. Then he turned to her, a half smile on his lips. "Great place. Amber, I take it?"

"What?"

"The one you're going to kill. Somehow she got on your computer and flirted with me, pretending to be you."

"I think so. The little rat tried to scare me, too."

"I see." He was silent a moment, surveying her place once more. Then he turned to her again. "Maybe you *should* be a little scared."

"Why?"

He hesitated again. Then he shrugged. "It's a scary world."

"Do you ever just answer a question?"

"When I can."

"You're a liar. You can answer right now. I should be scared…why?" She crossed her arms over her chest. "Because I *did* see a skull on the island?"

"I don't know what you saw on the island, Beth. But everyone there knew you saw *some*thing. And it's obvious that you're scared. Though if you *are* scared of something, it's not really all that bright to go ahead and just answer the door. Actually, you should never just open a door. That's why most of them have peepholes, you know."

"Yes, thank you for the lecture. I answered the door like that because I thought you were my brother."

"You scream when your brother arrives?"

She was glad when the phone began to ring then. She excused herself and went to pick up the kitchen extension.

It was Ashley.

"Hey," Beth murmured, watching Keith Henson in her living room as she spoke.

"I wanted you to know, there's an APB out for those people you met on the island."

She nearly choked. "Which ones?"

"That couple. Brad and Sandy."

She almost gasped in relief. "Um…why?"

"They're wanted for questioning. There's no proof of anything against them, and I probably shouldn't be telling you this, but I happen to know that the nameplate from the *Retired!* was discovered in the water just off Calliope Key. I thought you should know. I mean, I doubt they'll show up around here, and hopefully they have no idea they're under suspicion, but…well, you might have found the remains of one of the Monocos. The powers that be don't want that news getting out yet, because they don't want to scare them off if there's a chance of bringing them in for questioning."

Keith was still standing in the living room. She had the feeling that he could describe the place in detail if he was asked to do so later.

"Um…" She turned away, not wanting Keith to hear her. "Why do they suspect those two?"

"There's a reason," Ashley assured her.

"And that would be?"

Ashley didn't give her a direct reply. Instead, she asked, "Want to meet me at Nick's tomorrow? Breakfast, lunch, brunch—whatever works for you. Maybe you can give me a hand."

Her friend wasn't going to say any more over the phone, she realized. She was just glad for the information she *had* gotten.

If anyone was guilty, it was Brad and Sandy. *Not* Keith Henson or his friends. Not the man with whom she'd already slept, who was standing in her living room, surveying it with what appeared to be a practiced eye.

"Beth?"

"I'm here."

"You'll meet me?"

"Sure. I have to run into the office for a little while in the morning, and then I'll be out."

"See you then. Be careful, okay?"

Beth paused for a moment. "I will."

"See you tomorrow."

"Thanks."

She hung up and found Keith smiling at her. "It really is a nice place."

"I'm glad you like it." She was convinced there was

certainly nothing evil about the man, so why did she feel uncomfortable?

She still didn't know why Sandy and Brad were the ones attracting suspicion when others had been on the island, as well, and the Monocos had been missing for roughly a year.

"Are you in Miami for long?" she asked.

"I don't know. We kind of go with the flow," he told her.

"Must be nice."

He studied her for a long moment. "You're acting very strangely."

"According to you, I'm always acting strangely."

"Sorry. And I'm sorry for just showing up, too. I honestly thought I was invited. Since that evidently wasn't the case—"

"It wasn't, but you—you don't have to go," she murmured quickly.

"You don't seem pleased that I'm here."

She smiled suddenly. "Actually, I am," she told him very softly. Then, because it seemed to her that the tone of her voice was way too intimate, she said quickly, "I'm the one who's sorry. I...well, to use one of Amber's words, I suck as a hostess. Can I get you a drink? I think I have wine and beer. Or coffee? Tea? Water?"

He grinned, walking toward her.

She was startled that she was still standing. She felt as if her bones had turned to liquid, destroying all hope of remaining upright.

Then he was there in front of her. He touched her chin, lifting it just slightly. She met his eyes and felt as if they could make her forget the world, melt into his being.

She shouldn't give so much to someone she had

known so fleetingly, she knew. It was one thing to think she had every right to moments of sex, sensuality and lunacy. But this…

This was frightening.

"I can't stop thinking about you," he murmured huskily, his thumb traveling a path along her cheekbones. "When I should have been thinking about so much else."

She couldn't think of a thing to say to that.

"Should I leave?" he asked.

"Are we going to go through this again?" she asked very softly.

"I only—"

"If I didn't want you here, I wouldn't have asked you to stay. Yes, I know your speech. Don't get involved with me. Well, we're hardly involved."

"You're mistaken."

"We have different definitions of *involved,* then."

"So this means nothing to you?" he queried.

"I didn't say that," she told him. "But involved…that would mean I'd know where you were, not because you owed me explanations, but just because you'd want me to know. Wanting to see me again would be a priority for you, and seeing you would be a priority for me."

"Beth, right now I can't—"

"I didn't ask you to. I'm a grown-up. I've made my choice. I don't want you to go. It's already late. You'll leave too soon as it is, won't you?"

"Yes."

"Well, then…"

His movement always seemed unhurried, easy, as if he were a cat that had long studied its prey and seldom failed to reach its objective. It was in his eyes, as well, in his voice, that thing about him, always so casual, and yet...

What was his real objective?

Tonight, she decided, it was her.

Tonight there was nothing rushed about him. He studied her eyes again for a long time, as if waiting for a protest, knowing there would be none, but still giving her a chance to turn away.

She had no intention of doing any such thing.

At last his lips touched hers, and every remaining bit of resolve she might have felt fled. Her arms moved around him, fingers threading into his hair, and she tasted the kiss, explored the texture of his lips, felt the exhilarating sweep of his tongue.

His hands worked magic, cradling her nape, pulling her closer. The length of his body was a fire, rock-hard strength, something she wanted, needed. And where before it had been anticipation of all that was new, now it was memory of what was real, electric and compelling.

There had been a strange honesty in getting to know him...at least in this. She pulled away and said softly, "I do have a bedroom."

"I'm glad to hear it. And I'd love to see it."

She hesitated. He was giving her another out.

"Are you staying?"

"All night. I have to leave early. If that's all right."

"It wasn't a demand."

He lifted her chin again. "I think I would stay forever if I could."

Strange words. A line? At a different time, that possibility might have bothered her. But not tonight.

She turned, her hand in his, and started up the stairs. He followed close behind. She didn't put on the bedroom light; with him beside her, she liked the shadows, a realm where her own uncertainties could be hidden. With him in her house, she wasn't afraid of whatever lay beyond the door. The darkness offered no threat.

If he wanted light, he said nothing. She stripped the comforter from the bed and watched as he undressed, while she did the same. It seemed so bizarre. She had never had an affair like this before. She wondered vaguely if being together twice constituted an actual affair.

Then she didn't wonder about anything. He came to her in the shadows, touched her, and his naked flesh against her own seemed to be the most erotic splendor she had ever known. She allowed her fingers to play down his chest, feel the beating of his heart, knead the length of his back. The shadows gave her confidence, and from his back she slid the feathery brush of her fingertips lower, teased his buttocks, then stroked the rise of his erection. And then...

She found herself lifted, lying on the cool sheets, startled by the extreme difference between the crisp coolness of the bed and the heat of his body.

The pressure of his body aroused her. Their lips fused, hands stroked wildly. They broke apart, panting in the darkness, came together again. Her fingers moved through his hair. His lips moved to her throat, to her collarbone, below.

The touch of his fingers, the simmering, liquid heat of his lips and tongue, slowly trailed down her body. She writhed as if she longed to become part of him. She was in thrall to a brush, a stroke, a feathered sensation that left her yearning for more, a deeper, firmer exploration of fingers and tongue...acts of sheer intimacy that amazed her, exalted her, ever so slightly frightened her. She was barely aware of her own sinuous movements, flesh erotically sliding against flesh, the twist and curve of her body as she accommodated his, the sleek motion in which scent and movement, heat and pressure, combined, and it seemed that the world revolved upon the rise of her need and the climax he promised.

She let out a soft cry as the first little ripple of pure pleasure seared through her, a shot that catapulted, and continued, a slow tease that radiated. He rose above her, and in a corner of her mind she was ever so slightly afraid. Afraid because she had found the perfect fit, a man who thrilled and excited her, who captured her soul with the sound of his voice, his merest touch, the way he moved, in bed and out. A fear that he wasn't real, that this total consumption of body and soul would never come again.

Then he was in her and around her. She was striving, twisting, turning, hungry to become a part of his very being. Each thrust took her higher on a wave of eroticism, and the feel of his flesh, burning and powerful, beneath her hands, was almost more than she could bear.

Then there was the moment of ultimate climax, darkness shattered, a brilliant burst of light that shot violently into her mind, a feeling of sheer ecstasy so high and complete, that it shattered into a million pieces of crystal. There was one last powerful surge of his body, and then the collapse against her that signaled the volatility of his own climax, followed by the feel of his arms around her, the return of the shadows, the slowing thunder of her heart and a feeling of incredible completion.

His fingers, moving through her hair...

His arms, wrapped around her...

His words, soft and teasing. "Where have you been all my life?"

She moved against him. "Here. Right here." She tried to tell herself that no matter what had transpired between them, she barely knew him. Her feelings were insane. She didn't just want him, she was fascinated by him. Sex was incredible, but sex was not enough. She wanted to get beneath his skin, into his soul, know what made him tick, see his smile, feel wrapped in his laughter....

She'd never been this foolish in her life, falling in love so quickly, so completely, forgetting all too easily that she needed to be wary....

But wariness eluded her. Only one question formed in her mind but went unspoken.

Where will you be *the rest* of my life?

11

Beth woke with a start. Alone. She ran a hand over the side of the bed where he had been, feeling a sense of loss. He had said he couldn't stay late.

And yet...

Alone, with the morning light flooding in and washing away the shadows, she wondered why.

A meeting with the guys?

After a while, she rose, remembering that she needed to run by the club to pick up her design for the flyer so she could drop it off at the print shop to be made into a poster, then head down to Nick's to meet Ashley.

The thought of meeting Ashley jolted her into faster action. Now, more than ever, she was burning to know why Brad and Sandy were wanted for questioning.

If Brad and Sandy had stolen the *Retired!*, and if she had really seen a skull on the island, it seemed likely that the pair must have murdered the Monocos. The thought was chilling.

And had they also been the ones who attacked the couple in Virginia?

When she had showered and dressed, she hurried downstairs.

He had left coffee brewing for her.

Interesting. He was a man who took off at the first light of day, but he left brewed coffee.

She drank a cup, still reflecting on his arrival and Ashley's phone call, then hurried out.

It took only a few minutes to drive to the club. She waved to the guard, parked, then ran up to her office and printed off the design she wanted.

She started down the stairs, ready to head out, when she paused, catching a glimpse of someone she shouldn't have.

Or, at least, someone she wouldn't have expected to see.

Not where he was. And with whom.

She didn't go into the dining room. She didn't need to. She could see just fine from where she was.

It was set for breakfast. In the morning, the restaurant manager used the colors of the flag—red, white and blue—and napkin holders in the shape of a captain's hat. Seated at the table nearest one of the paned doors—open that morning, in honor of the beautiful weather—was Amanda Mason. She wasn't there with her father, or either of her cousins.

Breakfast that morning was a buffet.

So was Amanda.

Keith Henson had apparently come for the buffet, too, though which buffet, Beth couldn't be quite certain. To his credit, he had food in front of him.

He just didn't seem to be eating it. Amanda was talking animatedly. Keith was listening. He was smiling; she was laughing.

There was a dress code in the dining room: shoes and shirts, cover-ups for all bathing attire.

Amanda had followed the code, but just barely.

She seemed to be spilling from the bathing top she wore. Literally. True, she had on a cover-up, but it was sheer gauze.

Belinda, one of the breakfast servers, paused next to Beth.

"You should see the bottom."

"What?"

"Amanda Mason. Her bathing suit. You should see the bottom. Or lack thereof."

"A string?" Beth inquired, surprised. They frowned on such things at the club. This was a family place.

"A two-string. A one-inch square piece of fabric in front and another in back. The strings are on each side. Want coffee? Are you having breakfast?"

"Thanks, but I'm out of here," she said, flashing Belinda a forced smile. "I have plans."

"That's right, it's Saturday. You're off. I guess we're all used to you working so much overtime."

Beth shrugged. "It's not always work. When Ben and Amber are here, I'm just hanging with the family."

Suddenly, she realized that Keith had turned, that he'd seen her. Was watching her.

But he remained with Amanda.

"Well, have a good day off," Belinda said.

"What?"

"Have a good day off."

"Oh, yes. Thanks."

She hurried back out to her car, her head reeling. Once she was behind the wheel, she couldn't quite put the car in to Drive. She just stared out through her windshield.

What the hell was he doing? He hadn't just run into

Amanda. He had said last night that he had plans in the morning. Amanda had been his plan? Then why come to her house?

She gritted her teeth. Maybe she was just mistaken about chemistry and some ridiculous inner sense of honor and decency. She didn't really know him. It wasn't as if he'd gone out of his way to seduce her. She couldn't actually blame him for anything. *She* had wanted *him.*

Angry with herself, she started to drive.

Her radio was tuned in to one of the local stations. The hosts were doing a segment called "Dial a Date." One DJ was telling callers to check out the "hotness" of their female guest on the internet. Then one of the men dialing in asked her about her sexual experience. The guest purred that she knew what she was doing, and yes, if the guy was right—and the dinner good—she definitely slept with a man on the first date.

Beth was pretty sure the phone lines at the radio station were about to start ringing off the hook. She began to wonder if the entire world had come to think of sex as casually as they did breathing. Was that Amanda's take on it?

Was it Keith's?

Worst of all, was the whole thing about something unique, special and honorable—and sheer chemistry—all in her own mind?

Matt woke with a start. Alone.

He sat up, and his head started spinning. He felt ill. "Amanda?"

There was no response. He leaped up, then staggered, holding his head between his hands. Sweet Jesus. Had he really had that much to drink? They'd hit the Jack

Daniel's on arriving…and she'd been with him every second. Aggressive, exciting, quite possibly the most purely carnal experience he'd ever had. Pushing him down, crawling on top of him…

"Amanda?"

He made his way out to the galley. She'd left coffee on, but no note. Matt reached into a cabinet for something to kill the pain. He swallowed six caplets, drank a glass of water. His head was still spinning. He leaned against the counter, fighting the sensation. He needed coffee, a bagel, something.

He didn't bother to toast the bagel but ate it almost savagely. After a few minutes, his brain began to kick in.

He swore and went topside, where his voice rose as he cursed to the morning sun and the sea.

She'd taken the tender in.

He hurried back down to the cabin and searched it arduously. Nothing seemed disturbed. Nothing at all.

Still swearing, he judged the distance to the mainland, dressed in swim trunks and a tank, then went topside, furious with both the woman, and with himself.

He'd been had. Big-time.

He hit the water, glad the sea was smooth that day. As he swam, the salt, sun and sea began to clear his head.

But dull torture remained.

Did he tell the others?

"I'm so glad that you all have decided to visit civilization for a while. Although…" Amanda smiled knowingly. "I can't say I'm all that surprised."

"You expected us?" Keith asked, smiling back. He didn't need to lean in close. Amanda had taken care of that all by herself. She was at a table but somehow nearly on top of him. There was no way out of the fact there was something naked and almost primeval about her raw sex appeal. She practically reeked of female hormones. She'd had money and position all her life, plenty of time and opportunity to hone the "bad girl who could do whatever she wanted" image.

So different from Beth. Everything about her was just as sensual, as gut level, as sexually, sensually appealing. But there was a touch of class inherent in her allure. She moved with supple grace, as sleekly as a feline. Her voice roused the libido. Her eyes seduced with cool intelligence and an underlying honesty that compelled and…

He locked his jaw. This wasn't the time to wax poetic—or simply sexual—about Beth. Or think of the way she had looked at him during their night together.

"What were three handsome, heterosexual men going to do out there forever?" Amanda asked huskily.

Her fingers—nails perfectly manicured—made a fluttering motion down his arm.

"I mean," she continued, "how long can you just dive and fish without some kind of a…break, shall we say?"

He shrugged and eased back slightly. "We were intrigued. So many of you had mentioned this place while we were on the island." He offered her a broad grin, moving in closer again. "So…this is it. And are you here all the time?"

"A lot of the time," Amanda said. "I love boats. The way they rock. Even when they're just tied up at the dock."

The older Cuban man he had met the other night was taking a seat at one of the tables, Keith noticed. Amanda cast him a brief glance, then paid him no mind.

Manny, Keith remembered. He was the friend who

had reported the Monocos missing. He knew now that the Monocos were definitely missing and he was pretty sure he knew how and why. But a piece was still missing. He had a feeling Ted Monoco had known something about his own work out by the island. That nothing was as simple as it looked.

He looked back at Amanda, who was almost on top of him, despite this being a public place.

"You haven't been on board Hank's boat. She's almost as nice as your friend Lee's."

"Where is Hank?" he asked. "And the rest of your family?"

"Oh, he and my dad have some business today. And Gerald doesn't come around as much as the rest of us. None of them will be around for quite a while."

It was as open an invitation as a man was ever going to get.

"You can tell me all about fishing…that rush you get when you land the big one."

She wasn't referring only to fish, he knew.

"And diving. Floating in a different world. A magical world. Making fantastic new discoveries."

Again her words were sexual, but he sensed something more. She wanted to talk. She wanted *him* to talk.

He glanced at his watch, forcing an expression of real regret to his face. "I can't see her right now. I have an appointment with a man about a boat."

Amanda pouted. She touched him again, delicately on the arm. "And you can't postpone it?"

"I wish I could. I'll be back, though."

He rose, made his goodbye.

She waved; he started out.

At the entry, he turned back.

Manny had risen. As Keith watched, he joined her at the table, and the two of them began to talk, heads close, voices apparently low.

He turned to leave again, then noted the dancer, Maria Lopez, at a corner table.

She was watching Manny and Amanda, as well.

Beth parked and walked around the back, to the waterside. Ashley was seated at one of the tables there. She had her sketchbook out.

Though it was a public marina and boats came in and out constantly, it seemed to be quiet at Nick's that morning. A few people were down at the docks, working on boats. Friends chatted. Down one of the long piers, a fisherman was already in with his catch, cleaning it.

It was Saturday morning, a lazy time, except for those eager few who were anxious to get out on the water. The real early birds had already gone out and some had already come back in.

She noticed an old sailor, one of Nick's regulars, at one of the tables, smoking his pipe, sipping his coffee, reading his newspaper. Farther down, a mother fed a pair of toddlers, who seemed convinced all their food really needed to be given to the gulls by the water. Signs begged customers not to feed the birds at the tables—such generosity could lead to a scene straight out of Hitchcock. Once started, the birds did not give up.

There was a couple at another table, wearing sunglasses and looking as if they'd partied a little too hearty the night before. Probably why they looked vaguely familiar, she thought, then headed toward Ashley's table that was in the sun, but protected by an overhead umbrella.

"Hiya," Ashley said, seeing her arrive.

Beth slid into the chair opposite her.

"What's the matter? You look glum," Ashley said.

"I'm fine," Beth said.

"No you're not, but you can tell me the truth whenever you're ready."

"So what's up? Tell me what's going on. Why do they think Sandy and Brad went after the Monocos?"

Ashley thrust her sketchbook toward Beth. Beth studied the picture on top. It was of a couple, faces only, side by side.

"Recognize them?" Ashley asked.

"Are you kidding?" Beth asked.

"Look at the eyes."

She did, and hesitated. "It could be them, I guess."

Ashley looked disappointed.

"Who gave you these descriptions?"

"I started with a sketch done by a forensics artist in Virginia. Then I called the couple and got a little more from them. I didn't really think you'd be able to get anything from this, but I thought I'd give it a try."

"It could be them. But if I had to swear to it, I couldn't. There's just not enough there," Beth said regretfully. "But, please, tell me why the police are so convinced Brad and Sandy had something to do with the Monocos just because the boat's nameplate was found. There were a lot of people out there."

"They were seen dumping something where the plate was found," Ashley said.

"You couldn't tell me that over the phone?" Beth asked.

Ashley seemed a little uncomfortable.

"It was found by some boaters who saw Brad throw something in the water."

"Some boaters? The only other people out there when we left were Lee Gomez, Matt Albright and Keith Henson."

Ashley didn't reply. "Their names probably aren't Sandy and Brad," she said.

"Their boat was practically a derelict," Beth reminded her.

"If you were making money pirating exceptional boats, you wouldn't go running around in them while you were looking for more boats to pirate." She hesitated, turned to a fresh page in her sketchbook. "Describe them to me. One at a time. Start with Brad."

"All right, I can try," Beth said. She took her time, being as detailed as she could. She wasn't surprised when Ashley produced a startling likeness of the man, which became even better once Beth made a few adjustments for her.

"So that's pretty close to what he looks like?"

"Damn close."

"Okay. Now let's do Sandy."

When they were done, they had a good portrait of her, too.

"It's strange," Beth said. "They weren't…unattractive people. In fact, they were both…strangely wholesome looking. But I just realized something about them in these sketches."

"What?"

"They're…not remarkable in any way. Like his wasn't the chiseled face of a powerful man you'd recognize anywhere. She wasn't a raving beauty, she was…cute. I guess that would be the word. They were…"

"Nondescript," Ashley offered.

"Exactly," Beth said. "They were the kind of couple who could…well, blend in, disappear almost anywhere."

"Which is what it seems they've done," Ashley said. "Who knows where they've gone."

"I take it you know for a fact that they aren't on or near the island anymore?" Beth said dryly.

"I'm with Metro-Dade," Ashley reminded her. "But from what I've heard, no. The nameplate was found, but they were already gone. And the Coast Guard looked for them."

"How far could they get in their boat?" Beth mused. Ashley shrugged.

"Maybe they found another vessel to steal and ditched the one they were on."

"Possibly. But I still don't think they're stealing boats and tooling around the seas on them."

"Then what the hell *would* they be doing with them?" Beth asked.

"Bringing them in to a boatyard, disguising them and selling them. It's just like a car theft," Ashley said. "You know, the way cars are stolen here, then sold down in South America."

"Ashley, a million people have a Ford or a Chevy. A luxury yacht is far more noticeable."

"Bigger risk, harder to really camouflage—but the rewards are worth it."

"I see," Beth murmured, then realized that Ashley was staring over her shoulder, looking uncomfortable.

"What?" Beth said.

"Nothing."

Beth let out a sigh of aggravation and turned around. She started.

There was Keith Henson. He certainly had a talent for showing up unexpectedly.

At least he was no longer with Amanda. And with that thought, she couldn't help but wonder if it had been… fast. Had Amanda gotten him out on her father's or cousin's boat?

She gritted her teeth, angry that she couldn't seem to get such thoughts out of her head.

Keith was standing on the dock, talking with the man who was cleaning his catch. When she looked farther down the same dock, she saw that Lee Gomez was there, as well, shirtless, in cutoffs, laughing as he spoke to a couple on a handsome catamaran.

Her eyes were drawn back to Keith, and she realized that she had only seen him because Ashley had been staring at him.

"You know him!" Beth accused Ashley, spinning back to stare at her.

"Who?" Ashley demanded innocently.

"That's Keith Henson you're staring at. You know it, and you know *him*."

"I don't know what you're talking about."

Beth stared at Ashley, convinced that for some reason, undoubtedly connected to police business, she simply wasn't being truthful.

"You've seen his face on an APB?" Beth demanded a little harshly.

"No," Ashley protested.

Beth frowned, watching her friend. "Ashley…"

"I don't know him," Ashley insisted. "But if he's your friend, you're more than welcome to ask him to come over and join us."

"You're lying."

"Beth, if you want to talk to him alone, go ahead."

"Ashley, what the hell is going on?"

"I don't know what you're talking about."

"You're an incredible artist, but you're a lousy liar," Beth said, trying to control her temper. "Is he a cop?"

"Who?"

"Ashley, stop it! Is he a cop?"

"Not that I know of."

"So you *have* seen his face on an APB!"

"Beth, stop worrying. I was looking at the guy because he's so damn good-looking. He'd be great to sketch."

"You are such a liar."

"You're obviously startled to see him. So go talk to him."

"I intend to," Beth said. She rose and headed straight for the docks. Despite the sunglasses, she knew he saw her coming.

"Good morning," she said.

"Hey there." The fisherman who was cleaning his catch looked up, thinking she was talking to him.

She smiled, then turned to look expectantly at Keith.

"Friend of yours?" the man asked Keith.

"Beth Anderson, meet Barney. Barney, Beth. Barney here sails out early and sails back in early," Keith said pleasantly.

"Kind of the way you do?" she asked, still smiling and feeling as if her face would crack.

"So you're an early bird, too, huh?" Barney asked.

"He's a busy man, out at the crack of dawn, places to go—people to see," Beth told Barney.

"Sounds like a good life," Barney said approvingly.

Keith was staring at her, thoughts and emotions hidden by the glasses, his expression just as friendly as her own.

"The best of everything," Beth suggested. "I'm sorry. Am I interrupting something here?"

"We were just talking about boats," Barney said. "Fine ladies, some of them around here. My own *Sheba* is just a rustic old girl, but I catch all the fish I want." He grinned nearly a toothless grin. "Sell 'em to old Nick up there."

"Good for you. Nick likes to make sure his fish is fresh. Would you like to try the catch of the day, Keith?" she suggested.

"Sometime. I've eaten," Keith said.

"Oh, yes. I did see you digging right into that buffet." "I know."

"Well, excuse me, then," Beth said, her voice tightening. "You gentlemen go on and enjoy your conversation. Have a nice day."

With that she turned around and walked away. She was suddenly so angry—with him *and* herself—that she completely forgot Ashley. She walked straight to her car, got in and drove away.

Keith watched Beth leave, frowning. No matter how cool her tone, how casual her words, she was angry, and he knew it.

And he was sorry.

Glancing at the tables, he saw Ashley watching as her friend left.

Then he saw that the couple who had been sitting near the wall of the restaurant in the shade had risen, as well.

They, too, were headed for the parking lot.

He frowned. He'd never seen them before. The guy was bald; the woman had really long dark hair.

He'd never seen them before, he thought again. They were just out for brunch. They'd eaten, and now they were leaving. Odd. He still felt there was something familiar about the pair.

Disturbed, he hesitated. Lee was going to wonder what the hell was going on, but that was just the way it was going to have to be.

Keith headed for the parking lot himself.

Beth didn't know exactly where she was going as she drove out of the lot. Perhaps it was simple habit, but in a few minutes she was heading toward the club.

Once she was there, she wondered what she was doing, but since she'd already waved to the guard and parked in her space, she went in. She regretted the fact that she'd walked out on Ashley. What she'd done was incredibly rude, but then again, Ashley wasn't being honest with her, and she knew it. Ashley knew Keith Henson. Or knew about him. Knew something she wasn't telling.

She was about to go straight up to her office, when she heard her name called. Manny.

"Hey, gorgeous. You're not working today, are you?"

"I'm…just working on the Summer Sizzler," she told him. "Commodore Berry wants it to be so good, so…"

"You've eaten?" he asked her.

"I'm not particularly hungry."

Manny frowned, studying her a little intently. "You look upset."

"No…a few things rushing around in my mind, that's all."

"You should get out on the water," he suggested.

She laughed. "Being out on the water doesn't solve everything," she told him.

He shrugged. "Out on my boat, the world is a better place. I can smoke my cigars and sip my brandy...watch the sea and sky roll by. What's better? Lots of space. It puts everything into perspective!"

"I'm sure."

"You come out with me sometime," he told her gravely. "I promise, you'll feel much better."

"Okay," she told him. "It's a date. But I work all week, remember."

"Start work early, then leave early. We'll cast off around four, four-thirty."

"All right," she said.

"Sometime soon."

"Sure, soon." She smiled, gave him a wave and started up to her office.

As she climbed the stairs, she wondered again what the hell she was doing there. But she had arrived, and if nothing else, her office was a nice haven.

She had left it locked for the weekend. She dug in her purse for the keys, opened the door, walked in and tossed her handbag on a chair.

She closed the door thoughtfully as she reached for the light switch, then turned toward her desk.

Then she saw it.

Her heart seemed to stop in her chest.

Dead center on her desk.

A skull.

12

The guard at the little outpost had seen Keith before. He tried a quick wave, but the fellow frowned and stopped him.

"Yes?"

"Hey," Keith said, offering an engaging smile. "You saw me this morning, remember?"

"Yes?" The man didn't smile. He waited.

"I'm a guest of the Masons."

"Your name?"

"Keith Henson."

"I'll have to call the Masons," the guard told him.

It wasn't as if the man were big and brawny, or as if he had a gun, Keith thought. If he had really needed to get through, he would have just gunned the engine.

But he wanted to keep his presence here on the level.

"Go ahead. Amanda is still here, isn't she?" he asked pleasantly.

The man stared at him again, then relented. "Yes, Miss Mason is still here. Go on."

Apparently Amanda had invited men to the club before. He must have fit the profile of her previous guests.

He wasn't sure that pleased him.

Didn't matter. He parked his car and hurried toward the front entrance. He hadn't been able to move quickly enough to see what car the couple from Nick's had taken from the lot, nor had he managed to follow Beth and discover if the couple had been following her, as well. He wasn't even sure she was here.

As he walked in, he was startled when she came running down the stairs and directly into him.

"You!" she said, backing away as if he had suddenly become poison. He was startled. She wasn't staring at him with the simmering anger she had afforded him just a little while ago. She was staring at him as if he were some kind of heinous beast.

"What?" he demanded sharply.

"Henry!" she called, and he realized that one of the waiters from the restaurant had apparently heard them, and was hovering near the arch that separated the foyer from the restaurant.

"Yes, Beth?"

"Call the police. *Now.*"

Keith's heart sank. What the hell had she found out about him—or what did she think she knew?

"What is it?" he demanded.

"It's amazing, isn't it? I just found a skull on my desk—another skull—and look who's hanging around. Again. Henry, call the police," she repeated.

"Yes, Beth, immediately," Henry said.

"A skull?" Keith said, staring at her hard. Then he walked past her, heading up the stairs.

"Where do you think you're going? Don't you dare touch a thing. The police are on their way!"

He ignored her. She followed him up the stairs, nearly

touching him, she was so close. But he continued to ignore her, reaching her office, stopping in the doorway.

"Where?" he demanded.

"On the desk."

He walked a few feet into the office. There was nothing on the desk that didn't belong there.

"Where?" he repeated.

She stood next to him and stared. "This is impossible!" she exclaimed.

By then they could hear sirens. Henry had obviously dialed 911.

"I'm telling you, it was there."

Footsteps were pounding up the stairway.

"What's wrong?"

Keith turned to see Ben Anderson striding into Beth's office. Several other men were behind him.

Ben gave Keith a seriously suspicious glare and hurried to Beth's side. "What is it? What happened?"

"There was a skull on my desk," Beth said heatedly.

"What?"

"There was a skull on my desk," she repeated.

Keith saw the emotions flickering through Ben Anderson's eyes. Dismay, worry, agitation—and a sense of weariness and annoyance.

"Not again," Ben said softly.

Beth glanced at her brother. "Dammit, Ben. What is the matter with you? When have I ever been a scared-of-her-own-shadow, paranoid storyteller?"

"What are you doing here?" he demanded of Keith, as if it somehow had to be the other man's presence that had brought this on.

"Guest of the Masons," he said softly.

"All right, what's going on?"

This time, the question came from a uniformed police officer, who parted the gathering crowd on the landing and came into the office.

The officer, a man of about fifty with clear green eyes and a very slight paunch, looked around, scowling. "Where's the emergency?"

"There was a skull on my desk," Beth said flatly.

"A skull?" the officer said.

Beth sighed deeply. "A skull, Officer. A human skull."

"Where is it?"

"It was there, now it's gone."

"I see."

"I swear to you, it was there."

"All right, folks. Clear out. Go back to what you were doing. This little lady and I need to have a talk," the officer said.

"I'm her brother. Perhaps I can help," Ben said. Beth looked indignant at the soothing tone of his voice, Keith noticed.

"Her brother. All right, the rest of you, please…" the officer suggested firmly. "Unless anyone else saw a skull?" he queried.

Some of the people who had gathered began to head down the stairs again.

Snatches of conversation rose to the office.

"Someone is playing a joke."

"It's not that close to Halloween."

"Hey, didn't we have a bunch of skulls as Halloween props?"

"Who are you?" the officer demanded when Keith remained.

"Keith Henson."

"Are you a brother, too? Husband? Boyfriend?"

"I'm concerned," Keith said.

"Look," Beth insisted, drawing the man's attention angrily. "There was a skull on my desk. Can't you look for fingerprints or DNA, or something?"

The officer looked wearier than ever.

"Miss...this sounds like a case of mischief to me, and that's all."

Beth appeared outraged. "You mean that you're not going to do anything?"

"I'm not sure what I *can* do," the officer said. "Look, you saw a skull, but it isn't there now. Your friends are probably right. Someone is playing a trick on you. Someone down there is laughing right now. Yes, I'd probably arrest 'em for it, if I could. This is malicious mischief. But I don't know who did it, and I have more important things to be doing than trying to find out."

"There was a skull on my desk," Beth said again.

"I'm afraid it isn't there now," the officer said quietly. "So that's it?"

"What do you want him to do, Beth?" Ben asked in a conciliatory tone.

She stared furiously at her brother, then at the officer. She didn't even seem to remember that he was there, Keith thought—either that or she was still so suspicious of him that she didn't even want to acknowledge him.

"I want to file a report," Beth said. "I want someone to do something. My office had been locked. I cannot believe that I saw what might have been a human skull on my desk and you don't intend to do a thing about it."

Keith had the feeling that the officer—Patrolman Garth, according to his badge—had been involved in crank calls more than once.

Garth walked over to the desk, studying it carefully.

"There's nothing here now. No sign of anything. And, I'm willing to bet, there *is* a master key."

A tall, gray-haired man burst into the office. "What's going on here?" he demanded. "What's this about a skull?"

"Commodore, Beth thinks there was a skull on her desk," Ben explained.

"Officer Garth," the policeman said. "And you're...?"

"Commodore Berry."

"Perry," Garth repeated, as if he was beginning to consider the entire place a joke.

"Berry. Commodore *Berry,*" the man said, highly irritated. "Current elected head of the club," he explained. "Beth, what's going on?"

"There was a skull on my desk," she said.

"But there isn't now?" he asked.

"No," she admitted.

The commodore squared his shoulders. "Miss Anderson is not given to hallucinations."

"Beth," Ben said quietly, "don't you think someone might have been playing a little trick on you? A number of people—including me—have those skulls left over from last Halloween. They were part of the table decorations. And the master key does hang on a hook in the maintenance room. We should be more careful."

"Ah, yes, a *master* key. Hmm. You decorated your tables with skulls?" Garth asked.

"It was Halloween," Ben said.

"Beth, is it possible it was a prop skull?" the commodore asked.

Beth appeared torn. "It's possible," she admitted. "I saw it and...and panicked, then ran downstairs to call the police."

"Why didn't you just call from the office?" Garth asked.

Beth stared at him, lifted her hands, let them fall. "Because there was a skull on my desk! I didn't expect it to pick itself up and disappear."

"How many ways are there up to this level?" Garth asked.

"The stairway from the foyer leads up here," Beth said. "And there are restrooms up here, with stairs from the hallway in front of the office downstairs and from the south side of the dining room."

"I believe, Miss Anderson, that someone was playing a trick on you with an old prop. Whoever it was probably didn't think you'd react so quickly by calling the police. That person came up and took off with the skull after you raced down the stairs," Garth told her. "It was a prank."

"I want something done," Beth insisted quietly.

The officer let out a deep sigh. "We'll file a report," he told her. "May I use your desk?"

"Beth," Ben murmured, "you're actually going to make him do this? Fill out a report—over what was obviously a prank?"

"You bet," Beth said.

The officer sat down. Keith decided that, at that moment, he would definitely be more useful elsewhere.

Wanting to see what Beth had been talking about, he entered the hallway and saw the doors to the restrooms.

He hadn't realized that there was more than one way up here. Foolish on his part. He should have explored every inch of this place immediately.

The men's room was large and clean. At the far end of the hall there was a doorway that led to two ways out. A carpeted stairway led down into the club. Another door led to a balcony area, with an outside stairway.

If someone had been in Beth's office, there were plenty of ways they could have retrieved it after Beth went racing downstairs.

Had it actually been the skull she had seen on the island, though? Or had someone heard about her discovery on Calliope Key and decided to either tease her—or warn her—by putting a Halloween prop on her desk?

He followed the stairway to the balcony. From his vantage point, through the trees, he could see some of the cars in the parking lot. He could also see the acreage next door to the club. It was a public park. Anyone who was careful could come and go without being seen. All they would have to do was slip through the trees.

Had the couple from Nick's followed her, then left their car at the public park? Crawled through the bushes to the club grounds and, somehow, broken into Beth's office?

The scenario just didn't ring true.

He took the stairs down to the dining area. Roger Mason was having lunch with a man in a captain's hat. There was no one else he recognized in the dining room.

He walked out to the porch area. Amanda was at a table by herself, leaning back in her chair, broad white hat shielding her face from the sun, staring out lazily at the boats. He saw her cousin Hank at another table, having a beer with a group of men. Farther down from Amanda, he saw Manny Ortega involved in an avid discussion with Maria Lopez.

Without being totally obvious, there was no way to eavesdrop on their téte-â-téte. He regretted the fact, but knew it was important that he not betray himself.

Looking to the left, he saw that Amber and Kim were by the pool. He wondered if they'd heard about what was going on.

Amanda called out to him.

He strode over to her table. She was grinning wickedly. "So what's going on up there? Has Miss Anderson finally snapped?"

"Pardon?"

"It's all over the club, of course. No one could possibly miss the arrival of the police." She indicated the inside dining room with a wave of her hand. "That's the commodore my dad is speaking with now, poor man. I'm sure he's beside himself with humiliation. We've never had the police here before. Ever."

"I don't think the man is humiliated. I think he's worried about Beth. It's a rather disconcerting thing, don't you think, to see a skull on your desk?" Keith said.

Amanda laughed. "I heard there was no skull."

"Even worse to see one and then have it disappear."

She made an impatient sound at the back of her throat. "Don't be ridiculous. She feels the stigma of her position here, you know."

"Pardon?"

"We're members. She's help. She's crying out for attention."

His temper flared at that, but he controlled it, forcing a casual glance around. "You know, Amanda, I don't think anyone here feels like that. Her father was a member. Her brother *is* a member. I'm sure she could work somewhere else, if she wanted to."

Amanda laughed and picked up the frosted drink before her. "So you *are* sleeping with her. I thought so. Pity. I liked you best, you know." She spoke casually.

"Well, thanks for the compliment, but I'm just pointing out the fact that we're living in the twenty-first century," he said smoothly. "It's not an upstairs, downstairs world anymore."

"So you believe she saw a skull?"

"I believe she saw something, yes. She doesn't strike me as prone to histrionics."

"Please. A skull? A real human skull?" Amanda said disdainfully.

"I believe there was a skull on her desk. Whether it was human or a Halloween prop, I don't know. Are there any known pranksters here at the club?"

Amanda waved a hand in the air. "Who knows? People here like to have fun. Perhaps someone was playing a trick on her. Maybe even her own brother."

"There's an idea," Keith said, though he didn't really believe it. The more he thought about, though, the more he thought that the use of a skull had to be more than coincidence. The prankster had to be someone who had been on the island.

"Ben did keep one of the skulls in his locker, I hear," Amanda said.

"Don't you think he would have admitted that he'd done it?" Keith asked lightly.

"With the police called in already? Doubtful." Amanda narrowed her eyes suddenly. "Why don't you go talk to the little darlings over there?" She pointed. "Amber and Kimberly. The girls are at that age…and they do prowl around Beth's office."

"Maybe I *should* go ask them," he said lightly, and rose.

"Do come back," Amanda invited, her voice husky and amused.

He smiled, and walked over to the pool area. Amber looked up, sensing the arrival of someone. When she recognized him, she started, then smiled. "Hi."

"Hi yourself," he said. The girls were both seated on lounges, but they weren't leaning back, relaxing; they were sitting up, feet on the ground as they faced one another. He sat at the end of Amber's lounge. "I hear I had an e-mail exchange with the two of you."

They both blushed to brilliant shades of red.

He cut right to the point. "Did you put the skull on your aunt's desk, as well?" he asked.

"No!" Amber said with horror.

He stared at her hard. "I'm not going to the police or your father with the information, I swear. I just need to know."

Amber shook her head, stricken. "I swear I didn't do it. I would never do anything like that. Really."

"Honest, Keith, it wasn't us," Kim said.

He believed them. "Do you have any idea who might have done something like that?"

Amber sniffed. "Amanda."

"Miss Rich-Bitch Mason," Kim agreed.

He smiled, lowering his head.

"Do you girls think maybe you have a little bit of prejudice going there?" he asked.

Kim looked away. Amber stared at him sagely. "You think? Or is it true that Miss Amanda Mason just takes what she wants and steps on anyone in her way?"

"Wow," he murmured.

"Good call," Kim said.

"Well, you tried to scare your aunt once."

Amber frowned. "No, I didn't."

"Oh, come on, you said that you were on her computer."

"Yes, I e-mailed you on her computer." Amber was frowning. "I didn't try to scare her."

He frowned in return. "Amber—"

His cell phone started to ring, and he excused himself, walking a few steps away.

It was Lee. Keith listened, his heart thudding, then standing still. "We'll talk later. I have to go," he said to the girls after he hung up.

He didn't wait for a reply but strode quickly toward the parking lot.

Officer Garth was gone. The commodore hadn't stayed while the policeman took the full report but had hurried down to play spin doctor about what had happened. Beth thought that he was a good man; he had some doubts, she was certain, but he also believed she had seen something, and meant to find out who had played such a trick and why.

When Garth was gone, she was left with her brother.

He was quiet, sitting in one of the chairs across from her desk, hands folded idly together, looking down.

"Beth," he said very softly.

"Oh, Ben, get off it. I have not lost my mind."

"I just don't believe it was a real skull."

"You don't want to believe me."

"Well, of course I don't," he said impatiently. "I don't want to think that danger is following me home."

"Ben, this is being done to me, not you."

He offered her a wry grin. "Basically, you *are* my home."

She had to smile at that. But she leaned on her desk,

trying to reach him. "I swear to you, I have not gone mad."

"Okay, Beth. Whatever you say," he said skeptically.

To her surprise, he got up then and started out of her office.

"Ben?" She followed him.

He stopped and turned back to her on the stairway. "I need to check something, and you can't come with me."

"Why?"

"I'm headed to the men's locker room."

She frowned in earnest. "Why?"

"I'm just checking on something."

"What?"

"Beth, stop it. What are you doing in your office today, anyway? Take the day off. Go home. Rest. Watch a movie. Do something."

"Ben, dammit—"

"Okay, Beth, I had a weird feeling in the locker room the other day. I think that someone was in my locker and stole my old Halloween skull. I'm going to go and see if it's still there."

"So you do believe me?"

"What I believe is that your wild story from the island has gone around and someone is playing tricks on you, okay? But just playing tricks, Beth. That's it. You can't keep running around as if you've suddenly become part of *CSI: Miami,* okay?"

"Me, *CSI!* You're a mess. You're acting as if you're frantic!"

"Because I think my skull is missing…. Don't you understand, I have to see if it's really gone. Okay, I am feeling a little déjà vu. It's weird. But I'm just checking my locker."

"Find out if your skull is gone," she said flatly.

"And then you'll leave, please?" he said. "I will, too. I was going to clean the boat, but forget that. I'm getting the girls, and I'm going home, or to a movie. Want to come?"

"I want to find out if your skull is gone."

He sighed. "All right."

She followed him down the stairs to the pool area. As she walked through the dining room, she felt herself reddening. People were staring at her. They weren't talking to her—they were just staring at her.

At least, when she passed Manny and Maria, they waved, though they looked at her strangely at the same time.

Amber and Kim leaped to their feet when they saw her arrive, while Ben headed toward the lockers. "Are you all right?" Amber asked anxiously.

"Of course I'm all right."

"But there was a skull on your desk," Amber said, no doubt in her voice at all.

"Yes."

Amber looked at Kim knowingly.

"*She* did it," Kim said.

"I'd bet she did," Amber agreed.

"Who did what?" Beth demanded.

Amber lowered her voice. "Amanda. Amanda Mason. She wants Keith, but she knows he's into you. She's jealous, and she's trying to make it look like you're crazy."

"Amber," Beth murmured, though she wondered if, catty as it sounded, her niece might not be right.

Except that Keith Henson certainly didn't seem to be denying Amanda Mason the pleasure of his company.

Amber groaned. "Aunt Beth, please stop trying to sound as if such immaturity is impossible among adults."

Beth had to smile. Sometimes her teenage niece seemed old far beyond her years.

"Amber, we can't just assume that Amanda did it, okay?"

Amber shrugged. She and Kim exchanged knowing glances.

"You two just continue to be polite or avoid her entirely, all right?" Beth said.

They nodded in tandem.

Beth looked over to the patio. Manny and Maria had gone to sit under an umbrella, heads close together. She wondered suddenly if they weren't kindling a few sparks. If so…good. She liked them both.

"She's gone," Amber said.

"Who?" Beth asked.

"Amanda," Kim said. She lowered her voice to a whisper. "She left right after Keith came over to talk to us."

"Yeah. Then his phone rang, and he took off," Amber said. Her eyes narrowed sharply with suspicion. "You don't think it was her calling him, do you?"

"Their whereabouts are not your concern, okay?" Beth said. Still, her teeth were grating. What the hell was the man's game?

Ben made his reappearance then, and he looked angry. "I'm going to talk to Commodore Berry and the board of trustees about this. Someone *was* playing a trick on you. The skull is missing from my locker."

"See!" Beth told him victoriously.

"Beth, it was a prank. I still don't think we needed the police."

"You're an attorney. You're the one who told me once that everything should be reported."

Ben sighed. "Girls, let's go to a movie."

"We've got to change," Amber said.

"All right, hurry. Beth, are you going to join us?" Ben asked.

"I think I'll go home," she said. Amber had been staring at her hopefully. "Honey, I'm really tired," she added. Then she realized Amber was afraid she was still angry with her. "Never mind. I'll go to the movies with you. But no horror movies, okay?"

"I can drive and bring you back here for your car later," Ben said.

"Thanks, but I'll take my own car. That way we can both head back home when we're done."

"Okay," Ben agreed. "Girls, go get dressed."

While the girls changed, Beth excused herself to make a phone call. When Ashley answered, Beth said, "Hey. It's me."

"So you have time for me now, huh? What happened to lunch?"

Beth inhaled. "Sorry. I was…angry."

"Great. Take it out on me."

"I really am sorry. It was inexcusable."

"As long as you know it," Ashley said, a teasing note in her voice.

"I need some advice."

"Oh?" She thought Ashley said the word very carefully.

"I found a skull on my desk."

"What?"

Beth explained everything that had happened.

"It does sound like a prank," Ashley said.

"Well, the guy you claim you don't know or recognize—Keith Henson—managed to be here right after it happened."

"I guess he followed you."

"Ashley, will you please tell me—"

"The baby is crying, I've got to go," Ashley said.

"Ashley!"

"Talk to him, Beth. Talk to *him*. I've got to go. Really."

The girls had changed and they were ready to go. Kim decided to ride with Beth, so she wouldn't be alone.

At the mall, they stared at the list of what was playing, argued over it for a few minutes, then chose a romantic comedy.

Beth decided she needed comfort food and ordered a hot dog, popcorn, Twizzlers and M&Ms. Her brother stared at her as if she had gone seriously crazy, but she ignored him.

The movie was good, but Beth was distracted. By the time the movie came to an end, though, she had decided that the whole thing *had* been a prank, and she was angry—determined to find out who had played such a twisted trick on her.

Maybe the girls were right. It could have been Amanda. She was definitely starting to feel more angry than scared.

They had an early dinner at a casual steak place in the mall, and walked to the parking lot together. Ben suggested that she come stay at their house. She thanked him but refused.

Kim looked serious when she said goodbye.

Amber threw herself into Beth's arms. "I would never hurt you, Aunt Beth. Ever!" she vowed.

Beth smoothed back Amber's hair. "I know that," she said, puzzled.

"I would never try to scare you. Really."

Beth frowned, remembering her computer. Amber had admitted to being the culprit who had been playing on it.

"Amber, honey, are we going?" Ben asked. "Beth, you sure you don't want to stay?"

"Yeah, I kind of need to be home."

"I think you're just being stubborn."

"I think I have things to do. Follow me home, if you want."

The girls went to Ben's car; Beth slid behind the steering wheel of her own. She made her way to the street, aware that Ben was behind her.

As she drove, she wished she was back at the movie. She had been diverted there, even though the thoughts of her panic were not too far away. Now everything seemed to be tormenting her at once.

If today's skull had been a Halloween prop, what about last week? Had she seen a skull? Or a conch shell. If she were seated on the witness stand in a court of law, could she really swear to anything? She'd been so sure, but now...

And what the hell was Keith Henson's part in all this? One moment, so sincere, so real, she would bet her life on him.

And then...

She drew up in front of her house. Ben pulled up next to her. She waved him on and blew the girls a kiss, then got out of the car and started for her little gate.

It was then that it struck her like a blow to the head.

The shadow was back.

She wasn't imagining it.

There was the tree...the shadow of a tree...and someone emerging from that shadow.

Someone who was stalking her.

Someone who had waited.

But it wasn't the shadow that got her. The shadow was just a distraction.

She twisted her key in the lock, a wary eye on the shadow, ready to scream...

The attack came from the rear.

A sudden rush of wind from behind her, a gloved hand clamped over her mouth.

Only then was there movement from the shadows.

13

This time Keith didn't know the man who lay on the sterile stainless-steel table.

Though completely antiseptic, the place had a smell. It seemed that no matter what, a morgue had a smell.

"Victor Thompson, twenty-seven, been diving since he was fifteen, been on boats all his life, grew up in Marathon and knew the reefs like the back of his hand," Mike Burlington said. "Made a living taking out charter tours from Islamorada."

"Drowned?" he said, looking from Mike Burlington to the medical examiner, James Fleming.

Fleming had a reassuring appearance. In fact, he would have made a good family physician. He had a rich head of white hair, a pleasant, weathered face, and appeared to be in his early fifties. Old enough to have learned a lot, young enough to maintain his sharpness.

"Yes, his lungs are full of water," Fleming said.

"There was a good fifteen minutes left in his air tank," Mike said.

Mike Burlington was also the type to demand respect. He was tall, lean and wiry, in his early forties. He was the kind of man who had known what he wanted all his life. Coming from a sound but lower-income family, he'd joined ROTC in high school, gone into the military, gone for his degree on army funding, then headed straight into investigative work. He was tough, inside and out, but never lost sight of the fact that his purpose was to protect the living.

"There are no bruises, no sign of force on the body?" Keith asked.

Dr. Fleming shook his head. "Be my guest," he said softly.

Carefully, his hands gloved, Keith made his own inspection of the body.

Just like...

He studied the lividity markings and looked at Fleming again.

"Yes, I think he drowned, was taken out of the water, then thrown back into it. The blood settled forward, so he was transported face downward, then thrown in the water again, all within hours of his death. He washed up on Marathon."

"And his boat?" Keith looked at Mike again.

Mike shook his head. "Nothing like the kind of luxury vessels that have disappeared. He was out on a twenty-nine-footer. A decent enough boat. He took good care of it but it wasn't worth a fortune."

"Has the boat been found?" Keith asked.

"Not yet."

"He went out alone, I take it."

Mike nodded grimly.

"Any suggestion to friends that he was heading toward Calliope Key?" Keith asked.

"The police in Monroe County have done some investigating. Seems he and his friends talked a lot about sunken ships and the wrecks along the Florida coastline. I can give you a list. Anyone know where you are right now?" Mike asked him.

Keith shook his head.

"All right. Keep it that way. At the moment, since we don't know what the hell's going on, I want everything on a need-to-know basis."

Keith considered arguing the point. But Mike wasn't a trusting person. He'd been around too long. He'd seen the best of human nature, courage and loyalty. He'd seen betrayal, as well.

"There's a lot of weird shit going on here, and I'm starting to think it's connected," Keith said.

"Go ahead, explain," Mike said.

"Gentlemen? May we let this young man rest in peace?" the doctor asked.

"For the moment, but his body's not to be released yet," Mike said.

"I'm not sure if the local authorities—"

"I'll deal with it," Mike assured him. He looked at Keith dryly. "Come into my office and tell me everything," he said, leading Keith out to the hallway.

When Keith had given him a full report, Mike said, "Someone is leaking information."

"Not necessarily," Keith argued. "Too few people know about the operation."

"Too many people are dying," Mike said. "Someone knows something they shouldn't."

"That doesn't mean there's a leak. Hell, there are people who know who I am," Keith reminded him.

"Keep an eye on your co-workers, that's all I have to say," Mike said sternly.

"Right," Keith agreed tensely. Yeah, he would keep

an eye on them, just as he'd been doing. But he couldn't believe either Lee or Matt was involved.

He looked down for a moment, then stared at Mike again. "We might have screwed this up. We can still change the procedure. Just do the whole thing up big, warn people, keep anybody else from getting hurt."

"Oh, great. Call the papers. What then?" Mike demanded. "Just forget everyone who's already died?"

"Doesn't look like we're managing to stop the flow of blood the way it is," Keith said.

"We're close, dammit," Mike insisted.

Close?

Close enough to prevent any more loss of life?

"You've got your orders," Mike said flatly.

"Right."

He left, and just as he exited the building, his phone began to ring. He answered, expecting Lee or Matt.

Certainly not the slightly accented voice that spoke to him.

"Mr. Henson?"

"Who is this? How did you get this number?"

"We can all do a little sleuthing, Mr. Henson. I'm talking to you because of a mutual friend."

"All right. Who are you?"

"Manny Ortega. You remember me, yes?"

"Yes. Why are you calling?"

"I need to speak with you. In person. I believe that I can help you. And you can help me. I believe that you will believe me."

He glanced at his watch, uneasy with the time but equally curious. "It's got to be quick, and I suggest you tell me first who gave you my phone number."

He was surprised by the answer, and more curious than ever. "When? And where?"

"There's a boating store on Twenty-seventh. Huge place. Open late. Can you meet me now?"

"Give me an hour."

"I don't need much of your time."

"There's an errand I have to run first," Keith told him. "Then I'll be there."

Beth didn't attempt to turn around.

There was a knife at her throat. She didn't doubt for a moment that it was real.

Nor did she doubt that her attacker would use it.

Her pepper spray was in her purse. Worthless. The only thing she could do was stand there and pray. Even if she could somehow overpower the person with the blade, there was the other one to deal with after. If there was an after.

Because the "shadow" was armed, as well. And she was sure the gun pointed at her could stop her escape cold.

Her blood was racing through her veins; her limbs were rubber. She could make out nothing of the shadow's face, because he—or she—remained at a distance. She didn't even know if the shadow was male or female.

Just as she didn't know if she was being held by a man or a woman.

A man, she decided. The grip was powerful. She didn't think many women—no matter how deadly or well muscled—had that kind of painful strength. She also tried to tell herself that when someone went to the trouble of hiding their identity, it was because they didn't intend to kill. If she could see faces, *then* she would be in danger.

There was no way she could identify either person.

The whisper that slithered into her ear was no more helpful.

"This is a warning. Drop it. Forget Calliope Key. Forget you ever heard the names Ted and Molly Monoco. Next time, you'll die. Don't go to the police. Don't tell the police anything. If you even think about going to the police, remember this—you have a niece. That pretty little girl can die right in front of you, just so you'll know you killed her before you die yourself. Got it?"

Got it? She wasn't sure she had anything. She was frozen. She had been terrified enough—and then they had mentioned Amber.

Suddenly there were lights in the street. Lights from a car, coming to a halt in front of her house.

She was suddenly shoved hard. She went down on her knees, then fell flat. As she fell, she heard the sound of running footsteps.

Her attacker was gone.

So was the shadow.

"Beth!" It was Keith. He was by her side in seconds. "Are you all right?"

"Yes."

Then he was gone, running in the darkness.

Still stunned, she lay still for several seconds. Her heartbeat slowed. She inhaled, and the air was ridiculously sweet. Her first realization was that she was alive.

Her second was that her knees hurt.

She managed to stumble to her feet and get the door open. She nearly screamed again when she heard run-

ning footsteps, and turned, ready to fight off any attacker.

But it was Keith.

"Call the police," he ordered.

"No!" She shoved him away and headed inside. He
followed, and she locked the door, then headed straight
for the kitchen. She poured a shot of brandy, ignoring
him. She stood at the counter, aware of the pain in her
knees, just staring.

He took her by the shoulders and shook her. "Beth,
you have to call the police."

"No!"

"You were just attacked, and the bastards have disappeared. I can't search the neighborhood by myself."

"No," she repeated.

"Then I'll call them."

He reached for the phone. She grabbed his arm.

"No, I'm begging you—don't call the police."

"If they threatened you—"

"They didn't just threaten me. They threatened
Amber."

He hesitated. "Beth, no matter who they threatened,
you need to call the police."

"I will not put her life in danger. If you call the police,
I swear, I'll call you a liar. I'll say you're harassing me."

"You wouldn't."

"The hell I wouldn't. I mean it, Keith."

He swore, turning away from her, running his fingers
through his hair. Beth swallowed a second brandy, and
found that despite her anger and misgivings about him,
with Keith there, she felt safer, with a renewed sense of
determination. She was furious at herself for being so
gullible, so vulnerable, such easy prey.

"I'm going to assume you're not a cop yourself," she said harshly.

He spun on her. "I'm not a cop. But I do know that you can't let people get away with threats."

She turned, reaching for the phone. She wouldn't call the police, but she would call a cop. Ashley. No. Maybe she was being watched. Ridiculous, she was in her own house, curtains drawn, the lock locked—and Keith inside, with her.

It was doubtful that the thugs who had attacked her had the resources to bug her phone, but even so, she didn't dial.

They had threatened Amber. That was terrifying.

Did she dare take a chance with her niece's life? And then there were the events of the day. A skull sitting on her desk and—an entire club full of people convinced she was overreacting to a prank. With her luck, she would get Officer Garth again. She could just imagine the conversation.

"As you know," she reminded Keith icily, "I already called the cops once today. Just imagine what will happen if I call them again. 'You're sure you didn't imagine there was someone behind you? In front of you? Why can't you say what they looked like? It must have been a prank.' Then I could speak in my own defense, 'Look, my knees are cut up.' And the friendly cop could tell me, 'I'm sure you were frightened of a bush, Miss Anderson. You must have fallen and hurt yourself.'"

"Beth, I was there. I saw them."

"Right. You saw them. You went after them, but they'd disappeared."

"This whole area is overgrown. There are a million

places for someone to hide. But that's the point. They're cowards. Someone else showed up, and they ran."

"I'm not an idiot. But we're talking about my niece."

He put his hands on her shoulders. "Beth…"

She wrenched away from his grasp. "Even if the cops come, there won't be a damn thing they can do. I've had it with people doubting me. And my niece is in danger, too."

"Beth, you've been in danger since the day you saw the skull and the girls mentioned it when we were together as a group that night."

"So you're suggesting that someone on the island was responsible for the skull being there?"

"If there was a skull," he said softly.

"Not you, too!"

"Beth, I knew you were hiding something. I searched the area."

"And you knew what you were looking for?" she demanded.

"No, but I would have noticed a skull."

Beth stared at him hard, arching a brow.

He sighed. "All right, Beth, I didn't have a lot of time, I was interrupted almost immediately. But I had known you where you were—I should have found something." Again, that implication. *If it had been there.* Then he shook his head, as if aggravated with himself for that admission, rather than her. "Beth, that night, there were people out and about when they should have been sleeping. I had even expected—been awaiting—that. Something was going on there. But…"

She stared at him. "I'll call my friend Ashley," she said. "She's a cop, and she knows I'm not insane, and that I'm not someone who tends to panic easily."

She hesitated, staring at him, then poured another shot of brandy. No, she didn't panic easily. But at the moment, she needed more fortification.

She drank down the shot, amazed to realize that she relished the burn when it went down her throat.

She still felt uncertain, with no idea what to do. She believed with her whole heart it was wrong to give in to criminals in any way, but...

They had threatened Amber.

She poured another brandy. Keith walked up behind her, taking the glass from her. She spun on him, eyes filled with fury.

"That isn't going to help the situation," he told her.

"Really? And what is?"

"Calling the police."

She backed away from him. "Let me deal with this."

"Beth, listen to me—"

"No. And don't you have something to do, somewhere to go?" she demanded.

She wanted to beg him to stay with her, protect her. But she had a life to live—and obviously so did he. She couldn't ask him to be her personal bodyguard. That wouldn't help Amber. She felt furious, trapped and very afraid.

"I can't stay," he said in soft frustration, as if to himself.

His words reminded her that he seemed to be playing a million different games. "Excuse me, but I don't recall asking you to," she said.

He stared at her hard, then picked up the phone himself. She grabbed it, but his grip was firm. "Stop it. I'm not calling 911."

"Who are you calling, then?"

He took a deep breath. "Jake Dilessio."

She dropped his arm and took a step back from him, folding her arms across her chest. "So you do know Jake and Ashley."

"Yes," he said flatly.

He dialed. "Jake, it's Keith. Sorry for the short notice, but can you meet me at Beth's house?"

Beth narrowed her eyes, watching, listening. Obviously, he knew Jake well. Her sense of betrayal grew.

When he hung up, she stared at him. He stared back. "Want to explain?" she asked.

"You know I'm a diver," he told her with a shrug. "I've been called in to work this area before."

"With the police?"

"Yes," he said impatiently.

She shook her head slowly. "That's all you're going to say?"

"I'm afraid so."

"Were you on Calliope Key…looking for a body?" she asked.

"No."

"Then…?"

"I have to leave when Jake gets here, but I'll be back."

She turned and walked away from him. "Don't bother. I've known Jake a while myself. He's married to one of my best friends. I think I'll rely on him for whatever help I need." And leaving him standing there, she headed upstairs.

If Beth had been afraid of being obvious by having a cop arrive at her door, she needn't have worried, Keith thought.

Ashley dropped off Jake, with both kids in the car, in their car seats.

Keith explained the situation briefly. "And you didn't make her call in a report?" Jake demanded.

"Apparently Miss Anderson is your good friend. You talk her into it. I'd love to see you succeed."

"I'll talk to her," Jake said firmly.

Keith mentally breathed a sigh of relief. He could safely leave—Jake Dilessio was there. Maybe the man could talk some sense into her.

"I'll be back as soon as I can," Keith told him.

When the door closed and locked behind him, he surveyed the area. He cursed, wondering how the hell the two attackers had disappeared so quickly and completely after assaulting Beth. He was fast, but in the seconds it had taken him to make sure she was all right, they'd disappeared. They'd headed down the block, turned the corner and been gone.

He knew he needed to get going to keep his appointment with Manny, but the speed with which the attackers had vanished disturbed him. He strode to the corner and looked down the street. There were more row houses. There was an old single-family residence, set back deeply in a large yard. Across the street, there were more houses. They could have taken off through any of the yards, and done so easily in the time it had taken him to bend over and see about Beth.

He headed for the yard of the house that was set back so deeply and crossed over the grass, his penlight on the ground before him. He traversed the area several times, but it seemed undisturbed. He turned his attention to the houses across the street and made a number of mental notes.

Then he walked back to his car, got in, and shifted into gear to keep his appointment with Manny Ortega.

"You know why we're not finding anything?" Lee murmured, sitting at the computer console in the main cabin, his eyes darting from the screen to a book of charts.

"The damn thing isn't really there?" Matt asked wearily. He was on the sofa, his head on one of the throw pillows. A feeling of guilt and unease still plagued him. Lee had returned from his evening out with a full report—nothing. He'd gotten to see the clubs of Miami Beach. End of story.

That had been the time for him to speak up. Tell the truth. *I was taken for the ride of my life. Sorry, guys. I can't believe she used me as if I were a horny high-school kid.*

Lee turned and stared at him, shaking his head. "It's there. I know it's there. It's just broken up so badly that we're not getting anything. The coral's probably grown over a lot of the ribs and the hull."

"So why aren't we picking up the cannons?" Matt asked.

"That I don't know."

Matt felt a greater guilt. Still, he kept silent.

"Shit," Lee swore suddenly.

"What?"

The television mounted over the doorway to the aft area had been on, the sound muted. Lee reached for the remote and turned up the volume. The news was on. The tragic death of a local charter-boat owner and dive master was being reported.

"Another one," Lee said.

"They didn't say anything about him being anywhere near Calliope Key," Matt pointed out.

"It's time we get our own asses back out there," Lee said. He shook his head. "Keith is crazy, thinking he can find out something at that yacht club. We need to be out there. Watching. Shit. Where the damn hell is he, anyway?"

When Keith returned, Beth's house was dark.

He wasn't accustomed to even feeling uneasy, so it disturbed him to realize he was feeling something akin to growing panic. He dialed her number, but there was no answer. Where the hell was she—and, worse, where the hell was Jake? When the answering machine came on, he felt like an utter fool, but he started speaking. "Jake, dammit, answer. Beth, pick up. You don't have to see me or let me in, but pick up. I see your car. I know you're there, and I'm worried. If you don't answer, I'm going to get the police out here."

She picked up. "Yes?"

"You *are* there."

"Yes." The terms "icy" and "distant" wouldn't begin to describe the tone of her voice.

"Are you all right?"

"Yes. Is there a reason I shouldn't be? Jake is here, remember." If anything, her tone grew harder still.

"You guys didn't answer the phone," he said irritably.

"Jake is in the bathroom, and I'm fine. We don't need to talk right now. It's late."

"Beth, look, I'm sorry. I told you, I had some things I needed to do, and I knew you'd be all right with Jake there. But…we do need to talk."

"I'm not calling the police. And as for you…don't

be sorry. You were around to run them off and now...
now I'm with a friend. So don't be sorry. We all have
an agenda, don't we? I just don't care to see you or talk
about it any more right now."

"Beth..." He hesitated. There was nothing he was at
liberty to say to her.

"Beth," he said, "it was a strange day."

"I just want to be alone, all right? Jake is here. I'm
fine."

She hung up.

He sat there, his phone in his hand, for several seconds, just registering the fact that she had cut him off
so coldly.

Well, what the hell had he expected?

It didn't matter. He was loath to leave. Nothing had
been solved. Jake had a job and a family. He couldn't
just turn his life over to keeping tabs on Beth.

His phone rang. He expected it to be Jake, and he answered quickly.

"Where the hell are you?"

It was Lee, and he was aggravated.

"Busy. What's up?"

"The noose is tightening. We really need to move."
Lee was quiet. "They found another diver. The news just
came out. We need to get back on the boat."

"I know we need to get back out there. I just need a
little more time."

Lee was silent. "I told you before, we need to focus.
There's the project, and that's it."

"I'll be there as soon as I can."

"Listen to me, Keith. We've got to get back out on
the reef."

"I'll be there. I have something to solve first."

"Look," Lee said, sounding seriously pissed, "we need to talk. We have a job to do. You can't go taking care of the rest of the world. We have to be back on that reef by tomorrow morning."

"Where are you now?"

"Right where we've been. Waiting."

"I'll be there soon."

"Really soon," Lee said.

Keith hung up, contemplating the situation. He hesitated, then dialed Beth's number again. She had been attacked. And then there was the skull on her desk. That had to mean something, as well.

Why the hell couldn't he just find the connection?

He closed his eyes for a moment. There was money in this, big money. Maybe Mike was right. Money often meant corruption.

He called the house number, determined to tell her at least some of what was going on, and to hell with the consequences. The machine came on.

"Beth, I know you're angry. You have a right to be. But I'm worried about you. Jake can't stay there forever. Listen. I think that you were followed today, from Nick's to the club. A couple left right in your wake. That was why I followed you. A *couple,* Beth. It might have been Brad and Sandy, in disguise. If they're the pirates, they're dangerous." He paused. "Guilty of murder. Jake has to go home sooner or later. You need to stay with someone."

"What's happening?" she picked up and demanded. "Why did you leave, then, and come back so worried and determined?"

"I had a meeting, that was all. I said I'd be back. Put Jake on the phone, if you just want to fight with me.

Please. Honestly, if I knew what was happening, I'd tell you," he said bitterly.

He heard her sound of frustration. "Listen, Beth, I'll explain everything to you as soon as I can, I promise. For now...please, pack a few things and go with Jake to his place." He was quiet. "I'm not leaving until I see you go with him."

"All right." She hung up on him.

He remained where he was, tense, pondering his next move. Then his cell phone rang. He looked at the caller ID and realized she had hit Redial. "Beth?"

"It's Jake. She's coming back to my place."

"Thanks."

"She still won't agree to filing a police report. I've tried everything but brute force," Jake told him.

"Just keep her safe, huh?"

"You bet," Jake assured him.

Keith remained where he was. He expected a long wait, but it was no more than ten minutes before Jake and Beth appeared. She locked the house but didn't glance his way. Jake gave him a wave as he got into the passenger seat of her car.

Despite Jake's presence, Keith followed. He pulled out his phone and dialed when he realized she was going in the direction of Nick's.

Lee answered. "I'll be there in about another ten minutes," Keith told him. "You can bring the tender and get me at the dock at Nick's."

"Great. Glad you've had your entertainment for the night," Lee said sarcastically.

Keith hung up.

He waited in the car while Beth parked at Nick's,

grabbed her overnight bag and headed toward the rear with Jake. Then he followed.

The place was jumping. It was a Saturday night. Nothing could go wrong with that many people around.

Please, God, he thought. Let that be the truth.

He saw Ashley, her youngest child in her arms, making her way through the tables to meet Beth and Jake.

Once they were all together, Keith circumvented the busy patio and headed out to the pier.

He heard the motor of the tender soon after. Lee had come. The stare he gave Keith spoke volumes.

"No involvements," Lee muttered with disgust. "Yeah, like hell. We came in for information. Not for your entertainment."

"Let's just go," Keith said.

"Hell, yeah. Let's just go. Eye on the prize, pal."

Keith swung on him. "Hey, swallow this, pal. Fuck you. The prize has changed."

If nothing else, it had probably been the longest, most eventful day of Beth's life. By the time she reached the privacy of Ashley and Jake's place, in an ell off the restaurant, she was so keyed up she was ready to scream—and not at all sure of where to start.

"You lied to me," she told Ashley.

"I'm not at liberty—" Ashley began.

"I've already explained that," Jake said, staring at Beth. "Over and over again."

"Oh, come on. You know I would never say anything to anyone else if you told me not to. What the hell is going on here? I can't imagine that you've become buddy-buddy with some kind of criminal, but he keeps denying that he's a cop." Beth stared from Ashley to Jake.

"Shh," Ashley pleaded. "You'll wake the kids."

She let out a sigh. "I'm sorry, I don't want to make your lives any harder, but—"

She broke off, wincing.

But Amber had been threatened. And Keith's words on the phone had hit disturbingly close to home. She had noticed the couple herself. She just hadn't realized they had followed her.

They had probably been following her all day, before staking out her house. She had to pray they hadn't waited around to follow her here.

She stood very still and stared at Jake. "I need someone off duty to keep an eye on my niece," she said softly. "And I mean now. That's the only reason I agreed to come here. You two can help me. I need Amber protected."

"Amber?"

She nodded. "Jake, you've got cop friends coming out of the woodwork. I can pay, but I want Amber protected. Without Ben knowing. I don't want him doing anything stupid." She was angry; her decision was made.

"Does someone want to explain exactly what's going on?" Ashley demanded.

"Beth was attacked," Jake said.

Ashley gasped.

"Threatened is more like it," Beth said.

"Keith showed up, they ran off."

"And you didn't call the police?" Ashley asked incredulously.

Beth groaned.

"I told her she should have called the police immediately," Jake said sternly. "So did Keith."

"They threatened Amber," she said. "And I'm not filing a report of any kind. I mean it. I'm not taking any chances. I want you to help me with this."

"Keith saw a couple here today, while you two were together today. They followed Beth when she left. I'm willing to bet they're the same two who are suspected of pirating the missing boats."

"Here?" Ashley said. "Beth, do you think it might have been them?"

"I don't know for sure, but it's starting to sound likely. And, oh yeah. I found a skull on my desk today, but the cop I called seemed to think I was a paranoid lunatic, so if you don't mind, I'm not speaking officially to any more police today. I think that someone got into my office, *then* followed me. The official cop couldn't see that. Okay? Wait! I don't care if it's not okay. You lied to me, Ashley. You said you didn't know him."

Ashley glanced guiltily at the floor.

"And if he's not a cop, what the hell is he?" Beth demanded, still angry.

"We don't have the right—" Jake began.

"Oh, Jake! What do you think Beth is going to do—post it on the internet?" Ashley demanded impatiently. "He's not a cop. In fact—"

"Don't even try to tell me he's a scuba instructor," Beth snapped.

"Well, actually," Jake said, "he is."

Before Beth could literally scream with aggravation, Ashley spoke, explaining, "He's with a company that specializes in dive rescues and retrievals, salvage and maritime crimes."

Beth stared at her friends, perplexed. "Why couldn't you tell me that?"

"Because we don't know what he's doing," Jake said impatiently. Then he hesitated. "They contract their services to the government. He could be working for the feds or the state. When I see him, I don't ask. Whatever he's doing this time, it's important that people don't know who he is. He often works undercover. So when he doesn't tell me what he's doing, I respect his position and don't ask. I don't want to jeopardize his work—or his life."

Beth stared at him, shaking her head. "Why wouldn't he tell me? Why wouldn't he trust me?"

Jake shook his head. "Beth, when you're undercover, you tell no one. You pray that you don't run into the people who know you. And if you do, you pray they keep their mouths shut."

"Who on earth would I say anything to?" Beth protested.

Jake shook his head. "You wouldn't say anything on purpose, Beth, but what if you accidentally let something slip to Ben? They've already threatened Amber."

"Get someone out there now, Jake," Beth demanded hotly, then added a soft "Please."

"All right."

He went away to arrange it, leaving her with Ashley. Beth still felt angry.

"You could have said something to me," she insisted.

"Beth, the point is, anyone can inadvertently say something. You just learn to keep your mouth shut."

"Fine," Beth said. "Then let's see what I can tell you. It seems that Sandy and Brad—or whatever their real names are—have been stealing yachts and murdering people. They probably changed their appearances and came here to scout for their next victim. They somehow decided that I had them pegged, probably when they saw me here with you, so they attacked me. They're out there somewhere, but Keith Henson—if that's *his* real name—has decided to go back…somewhere. I hope to find them."

"There's already an APB out across the country for them," Ashley said.

"Well, they were here. Right here, on land," Beth said. "And there *was* a skull on the island. Keith was in the clearing right after I discovered it. Did he take it? Did he bring it in somewhere? Did it belong to one of the Monocos?"

Ashley shook her head. "I don't know."

Beth shook her head in disgust. "Great detective I would have made. I figured Eduardo Shea must have had something to do with it…someone who was profiting off the dance studios. Or Amanda. I probably just wanted her to be guilty of *something*."

She fell silent.

Had Keith Henson been questioning Amanda? Had she misread that whole thing?

Jake reappeared. "Amber will be fine," he assured Beth.

"Jake, I don't care what it costs. I'll pay it. You called people you really trust, right?"

"Beth, I called people I'd trust with my own life, Ashley's life—my children's lives," he assured her. "And they're friends, doing me favors. You don't have to worry about it."

"Yes, I do," she said firmly. "But the point is, until…

Brad and Sandy are brought in, Amber has to be kept safe."

She felt deflated suddenly. She'd been so angry, so frightened. And now she felt as if she were a balloon that had been suddenly popped.

"Beth, are you all right?" Ashley asked. "You look pale."

Beth lifted her hands in a shrug. "At least he isn't a criminal."

"Keith? No, he isn't a criminal," Ashley said.

"Beth, the FBI, the local police, the Coast Guard—everyone is looking for Sandy and Brad. They *will* be caught," Jake told her.

She forced a smile and nodded.

Sure.

But when?

That was the question of the hour.

When Jake and Ashley had gone to bed, Beth found that she was still too restless herself to sleep. She went online and looked up the island. To her surprise, there was a great deal written about Calliope Key. Apparently almost everyone since Columbus had put ashore there. Ponce de León had stopped by. The Spanish had claimed it, then the English. Despite its proximity to the Bahamas, it had remained part of Florida after trades between the Spanish and English, the Spanish and the Americans, and the English and the Americans.

When the Spanish had held the island, they had often lain in wait to surprise English ships and lured them onto the reefs. Apparently the welcoming sight of the island, and the sound of the wind on the water and through the trees had beckoned them onward, and thus the name,

Calliope Key. Sadly, the islet had been like a siren, enticing men to their deaths.

There had been too many wrecks to count, but as she read, Beth came across one very specific incident. A battle between an English ship and a Spanish ship, the *Sea Star* and *La Doña*. Captain Pierce had battled Captain Alonzo Jimenez. All had been lost, including the innocent travelers aboard, seeking to reach Spanish ports in Central and South America.

Beth stared blankly at the screen.

The ghost story, the tale that Keith had told that very first night around their campfire, had been true, or at least based on truth.

She was suddenly certain that meant something.

That it just might be at the base of everything else.

But *what* did it mean? Treasure seekers were always combing the coast of Florida. There were so many known wrecks that had yet to be found. The legend of the Bermuda Triangle had sprung up because so many had been lost and no trace ever found.

She hesitated, then began combing the article again. Both ships had been lost with treasure aboard, as had so many ships before their sad encounter. But these treasures had been worth millions, even at the time. Heaven only knew what they would be worth now.

Enough to kill and die for, certainly.

They were still anchored in the bay.

Matt was pacing the cabin. "All right. Sandy and Brad are guilty. They've been stealing yachts. They have a base somewhere, and they've managed to get the boats to this base, where they're being done over. Every law-enforcement agency out there is onto them. So...what is the difficulty now? Why don't we just come out with the big guns—major league underwater equipment?"

"We've got to be back out there in the morning, and we have to find it," Lee insisted. "It's ridiculous that we haven't been able to."

"Maybe our coordinates are wrong," Matt said.

"I don't believe that," Keith said firmly. He was the one who had studied the accounts of the wreck, taking into consideration every storm that had ravaged the area since. He had also been the one to study and calculate what had possibly occurred after they had received the new records, only recently turned over to the United States by the German government. He had figured in time and tides.

Keith stopped pacing. "Why do you think they didn't try to steal *this* boat?" he mused.

"Huge boat, three men. Witnesses," Lee suggested.

"Just two of them," Keith mused. "Tough guys when they're armed, against a retired couple, one friendly diver…"

"But they hung around out there," Matt said.

"Maybe they were looking for the right opportunity," Lee said. "Hoping we'd eventually show some vulnerability."

"They won't dare show up out here again," Matt said. "They must know the law is onto them."

"Maybe, maybe not," Keith put in.

"I just don't get it. Why are we still tiptoeing around?" Matt said.

Keith rose. "Because we work for a company with a government contract and this is what we were hired to do. Not to mention that we've got another dead diver on our hands."

"Who might never have been anywhere near Calliope Key," Matt reminded him. "Plenty of assholes put on dive gear."

"This man was experienced," Keith pointed out.

"And didn't own a yacht," Matt added.

"Accidents happen," Lee murmured.

Keith kept silent on that score. He had seen the body. There had been no accident.

On Sunday morning, the newspaper carried an account of a diver found dead in the Keys.

Beth found herself obsessing over the article, reading it over and over again. When Ashley awoke, she stuck it beneath her nose.

Ashley shook her head. "Beth, everything in the world isn't related to a missing couple and pirated boats. Those two couldn't have been everywhere."

"It was idiotic of them to have been in Miami," Beth said.

"Not really. Think about it. The area is huge, boats everywhere. Hide in plain sight." She looked at Beth. "He didn't have the kind of boat our pirates have been stealing. And, Beth... Jake and I were out one day in the Keys, diving down to the *Duane*. A guy on our boat wasn't in the best shape and shouldn't have been doing such a deep dive. He panicked, popped up to the surface and died. It happens."

"I know."

"So do you have a plan for the day?" Ashley asked, carefully changing the subject.

"Besides just being worried sick?" Beth asked her.

Ashley leaned forward. "They *will* be apprehended. And Amber *will* be protected. Look, Beth, you have a right to be scared. And angry."

"I'm angry about having to be scared. I have a lot to do this week."

"We can get a man into the yacht club, as well."

"Ashley, you and Jake can't go calling in every favor you've earned. You have to let me pay these guys."

Ashley shrugged. "If you were to allow me just to report what happened—"

"No. I will not risk Amber."

"But, Beth—"

"Hey, I reported the skull. Lot of good that did."

"This is different."

"Maybe they'll be caught soon," Beth said. Her cell phone rang, and she excused herself and picked it up.

"Where the hell are you?" Ben's voice demanded angrily.

"At Ashley's," Beth said.

"Why didn't you tell me? What were you doing, babysitting?" Ben asked.

"Something like that," Beth lied. She hesitated. Why not tell her brother the truth? Because he had doubted her over the skull? Because he would panic over his daughter? She didn't like lying to Ben. But for the moment... "So what's up? What do you need?"

Ben was silent for a minute, still angry. His voice was tight when he said, "Amber is anxious about you—I don't know why, and neither one of you seems to want to tell me. I have to clean the hull today, so I'm taking her to lunch at the club, and she's going to swim and sunbathe while I'm working. Will you come?"

She didn't want to do anything but fume and fret and worry, she realized. But that was a stupid course of action to take. She had to trust in her friends, and wait for Sandy and Brad to be apprehended.

They were probably hiding in plain sight, just as Ashley had said. And if so…

They were hiding around boaters. She looked at Ashley. "Want to have lunch at the club?"

"Sure. I just need to arrange a babysitter."

Keith could hear the lulling sound of his own breathing, at forty-five feet down, following the path of the reef. With breaks here and there, it stretched for nearly a mile.

Lee was topside. He and Matt were tracing a grid, with Matt perhaps twenty feet west of his position as they moved south.

Matt looked over at him and made the "okay" sign.

He returned it.

They continued searching the area. In his mind, he ran over and over his conversation—conducted in the fishing rod aisle—with Manny Ortega.

"You had my name and number from Ted Monoco?" had been his own first incredulous and very suspicious demand.

Ortega had given him a shrug and a shake of the head. "You didn't know Ted, but he knew you. Four years ago, you were in the Everglades. A small plane had gone down. People he knew were on that plane. You and your crew rescued their daughter."

Manny continued. "I tried to reach you before. The number Ted gave me was for an office in Virginia, and when I called, they said you were away on assignment for an unknown length of time." He shrugged. "I contacted the police. I believe they tried with what resources they had. But the law in this country is that you may disappear if you choose if you're an adult and doing nothing illegal."

"Go on."

"The last time I heard from Ted was when he mentioned you and gave me your number to try to reach you. He thought he was onto something. He didn't say that he was afraid of anything, he was just very excited. I didn't think much of it until time went on and I didn't hear from him. Then I began to worry. That was when I tried to reach you but couldn't. I finally felt there was nothing I could do. Then you appeared here."

"So how did you get my cell phone number?"

"It wasn't as difficult as you think. You gave it to Laurie Green, the girl you pulled from the plane in the Everglades. I finally thought to call her and ask."

"I see. So what do you think I can do for you?"

"Find Ted and Molly. Dead or alive. Though I'm very afraid it will be dead."

A ray suddenly dislodged sand near the base of the coral, drawing Keith's mind back to the task at hand. The water was murky in the wake of the panicked fish. He nearly kept going.

Then he saw something.

Just the corner of something black that wasn't coral.

He circled, looked. The sand had resettled. Carefully, with just his fingertips, he explored the area. Dusted carefully, trying not to create such a cloud of sand that his vision would be impaired. Patience was needed for this kind of work, and he had learned to practice that kind of restraint through the years.

His efforts paid off at last. He found the object.

It looked like a crusted, big black button.

But it wasn't. His heart skipped a beat. He needed

to get it back up to the boat, but he was almost certain what he had found.

His hand curled around it. He looked over at Matt, who had realized he was onto something.

For a moment he was tempted to drop the object, to shake his head to show he'd been mistaken and come back later. Mike was so convinced that there was someone on the inside....

And Manny Ortega believed Ted and Molly Monoco were dead. So did Keith, but he didn't believe they'd been killed for their boat.

He believed they had found something on or near Calliope Key, then died for their discovery.

Too late.

Matt swam over to him. He produced the object. Matt stared at it, nodded silently, then studiously began searching the area further.

Keith placed the object in a pouch and joined Matt in the search.

They were close....

So close.

He had to wonder, though: Had others been this close before them?

But had those others even known just what it was they were really looking for?

14

It was on the drive to the club that Ashley looked at Beth and said, "You really do need to tell your brother what happened."

"You mean about being attacked?"

"Yes. You're in terror about filing a report because of Amber. He has a right to know."

"He'll tell me that I should file a report. And God knows—he might do something stupid and dangerous."

"You should file a report." Ashley lifted a hand in the air to silence the protest she knew was coming. "Make it official. If Sandy and Brad are what I think they are— tough-talking but only preying on the vulnerable— they're not brave enough to go up against real authority. They were at Nick's, a piece of real stupidity. The place is known for being a cop hangout. I doubt they really know what you're doing—it's unlikely that they have the time to continue to stake you out. They intended to scare you. That's all. Don't let them succeed."

Beth mulled over her friend's words. Then she asked, "They've killed before, so why did they just try to scare me?"

"We don't know that they killed the Monocos, and the couple in Virginia survived," Ashley said.

Beth shook her head. "I'm convinced the Monocos are dead."

"Maybe killing you was a risk they didn't dare take. I don't know, Beth. But I still think that you need to file an official report. Scare them in return. Hell, there's already an APB out on them, which they probably know, so what's the difference if you file a report, too."

They arrived at the club and easily found Ben and Amber at a table waiting for them. Amber still seemed anxious when she looked at Beth, who couldn't help but hug her too tightly. Then she smiled at her niece and tousled her hair, trying to defuse the moment. Ben and Amber both greeted Ashley with pleasure. The Sunday buffet was elaborate, the club filled with members in good spirits, and Beth wished she could go back to a time when all she did there on a Sunday was enjoy herself.

After lunch, Ben went off to work on his boat. Ashley, Beth and Amber went poolside. Beth was glad to see that it was busy, and that she couldn't for the life of her figure out who Amber's secret bodyguard was.

"Where's Kim today?" Beth asked Amber.

"I don't know. She just said she couldn't come," Amber said with a shrug. Then she hesitated. "Aunt Beth, I'm really sorry about the other day."

"You should be."

"I just… I want you to be happy."

"Let me be happy on my own, okay? Now swear you'll never interfere in my personal life again."

"I swear," Amber said.

"And don't *ever* try to scare me again," Beth said.

"I didn't try to scare you," Amber replied.

"Oh? I remember what you wrote word for word. First the skull popped up and then, 'I'll be seeing you soon. In the dark. All alone.'"

"I never wrote such a thing!" Amber protested.

Beth frowned, feeling a new chill seep into her spine.

"Then Kim must have done it."

"No," Amber insisted. "All we did was write back to Keith on e-mail."

"Beth, it's time you reported this. Officially," Ashley said firmly.

"You're going to call the police about Kim and me?" Amber asked, stunned and horrified.

"No, honey…there's been more than that," Beth murmured. She looked around uneasily. There was no one around who might be listening to their conversation, she was certain. There was a group of children playing with a ball nearby, and a few members of the women's charities committee busily discussing their next fund-raiser.

She was startled to see that Maria Lopez was there again. She was elegant in a one-piece black bathing suit, straw hat and sunglasses, down at the other end of the pool. She couldn't possibly hear anything they were saying.

She looked down toward the docks, shading her eyes. A number of the boats were out. She saw Ben, assembling his scuba gear—he meant to go down and clean the hull. As he gave his attention to his tank, a woman hopped to the dock from the deck of a boat farther down.

Amanda.

Dammit, didn't she have any other place to go? From being an occasional visitor to the club, she'd turned into a regular—a very unwelcome one, from Beth's point of view.

As Beth watched, Amanda approached Ben, lightly touching his shoulder.

Ben looked up and smiled.

Beth looked quickly away, but Amber had seen the direction of her gaze. She groaned. "Can we get her arrested?" she asked Ashley.

"Flirting isn't illegal," Ashley told her.

"Simply being that woman should be illegal," Beth said dryly.

"Beth…" Ashley persisted.

"All right, all right," Beth said. "But…let's get through the afternoon. Let Ben clean his boat. And I'm telling you, no one's going to be able to do anything."

That evening Ashley brought Amber to Nick's with her. Jake, Ben and Beth went to the station, where Beth filled out a formal report. Ben was a nervous wreck—and extremely angry with his sister. Beth continued to remind him that he was among those who had kept telling her that she was paranoid. Luckily, with Jake there, they couldn't fight too openly. Both he and Lieutenant Gorsky—the lead officer on the pirating case—tried to remain casual and calming as the two argued.

They left in a state of stiff tension. But it was done. Ben's house would remain under surveillance, and it had been suggested that Beth move in with her brother for the time being.

Great. He was barely speaking to her.

But since their lives might well be at stake, Beth agreed. She knew that the department didn't have the manpower to protect them all as they tried to get through their daily lives. At least, because of Jake and Ashley, extra protection, in the form of off-duty cops, would be afforded to them.

Still, the night was pure misery. Amber was confused, and her father warned her firmly that she wasn't to make a single move alone. Beth tried to be reassuring, but she had to reiterate her brother's words to her niece.

On Monday morning she drove Amber to school, glad to see the officer following them all the way.

He didn't follow her to the club. He was staying downtown, where he would be keeping an eye on the school throughout the day, so Beth was careful as she continued to work. At the club, she noted that the security guard was not alone.

She was nervous, wondering if anyone was inside the club itself or wandering the grounds to keep an eye on things. Midmorning, Commodore Berry came in and sat down gravely. He told her that he'd been contacted by the police and there was going to be at least one officer on duty inside the club or on the property at all times, keeping an eye on things. Since there were known pirates working in the area, he was grateful to have the assistance.

Beth wondered if he blamed her for involving the club. It didn't seem, however, that he ever realized it had anything to do with her. There were so many exceptional yachts berthed there that he seemed to think that was what made them a potential target.

The rest of the day passed uneventfully. She made calls to confirm arrangements for the Summer Sizzler, contacting delivery services and the florist, and talked to the chef and the staff. She called Eduardo Shea's office, and he assured her that he had not forgotten, and told her that he would be in with Mauricio and Maria later during the week.

That afternoon a police tech came to inspect her computer. She went down to the cafeteria to allow him time to work on his own. The club was strangely quiet. There was no sign of any of the Masons.

The tech was a nice guy, encouraging in his expertise. He was convinced no one had hacked her computer from the outside. The sabotage had been performed right in her office.

Chilling information. Whoever had given her the warning had been at her desk, in her chair.

She left early to pick up Amber. The policeman followed them home. She waved goodbye a few minutes later, after he had inspected the house and she had locked the door behind him.

She spent the evening practicing scenes with Amber.

That night Ben kept his distance, and she found herself growing angrier with her brother. None of this was her fault, though he was behaving as if it were.

Tuesday was more or less a repeat of Monday. She felt the growing strain of the situation.

Wednesday was better. When she went down to lunch, she was startled to run into Eduardo Shea in the dining room.

"Mr. Shea," she said happily. "You're here."

"Miss Anderson, your party is this Friday night. I told you I would see you here."

"Yes, of course."

"Ah, there's Mauricio."

A handsome young man with dark hair and arresting green eyes approached, and Eduardo introduced him to

Beth. A few minutes later Maria Lopez arrived in a stunning gown. Short, sequined, it fit her to a T.

"Where will the performance be held?" Eduardo asked.

"There will be a dance floor on the patio. It's being delivered Friday morning," Beth told them.

"That's not good," Eduardo said.

"Oh?"

"They should have more time to practice their number on the actual site," Eduardo said.

"Oh," Beth murmured. "I'm… I don't think we can close off the area until then," she told them unhappily.

"It will be fine, Eduardo," Maria said. She smiled at Beth. "But for now, where may we rehearse?"

"The meeting room," Beth suggested. It was actually part of the dining room, but it could be closed off for committee luncheons and was sometimes rented out to corporations for special functions.

It also had a hardwood floor.

Eduardo wasn't pleased, but he seemed resigned. Disdainful, but resigned.

Beth managed to get Eduardo to allow her to attend the rehearsal. At first she simply watched the two dances in wonder. It seemed unbelievable that anyone could move their hips as fast as Maria did. On the dance floor, she was ageless. Her face glowed; her elegance was visible in every movement.

"Incredible," Beth murmured.

"Come on. I'll teach you," Eduardo said.

"Oh, no, no," Beth protested.

But she found herself standing up with him anyway. "It's all in the timing," he told her. The music was playing again. Mauricio came up to partner her under Eduardo's direction, while Maria stepped behind her to show her how to move her hips. She grew flushed and happy as she began to get the timing, so involved that, to her amazement, she forgot the current circumstances of her life.

Forgot that she had first thought of this because she'd wanted to meet Eduardo Shea, suspecting that he might somehow have been involved in the Monocos' disappearance. To her absolute amazement, she was having fun.

Until Amanda Mason arrived.

Amanda greeted Eduardo with enthusiasm, kissed Mauricio, and did the continental kiss-on-both-cheeks thing with Maria Lopez. At that point Beth excused herself and returned to her office. She was startled when she reached her door to turn around and discover that she had been followed.

By Amanda.

The woman stood there, chin high, hands on her hips—looking much taller than her actual stature—staring at Beth belligerently. "Why do you do that to me all the time?" Amanda demanded.

"Why do I do what?" Beth demanded.

"I walk into a room, and you leave."

Beth stared at her, stunned. Then she replied honestly, "Let's see. Maybe because you treat me as if I were a servant or a lesser being of some kind?"

"I do not," Amanda protested.

"You do, too."

"If I do, it's only because of the way you act toward me."

"What are you talking about?"

"Let's see. You don't do anything overt. That nose of

yours just goes in the air a little, and you look at me as if I were…the trash of the century."

Beth could barely believe the conversation.

"Amanda—" She broke off, shaking her head, not at all sure what to say. "Maybe it's the way you behave."

"And that would be…?"

"I don't know! As if the world was your toy, as if men were there for your amusement, whether they're married, engaged or…taken."

"You're jealous."

"No, Amanda, I'm not jealous."

She expected anger, some kind of scathing retort. But Amanda just stared at her. "Am I that bad, really?"

Beth sighed. "I don't know, Amanda. Maybe it's me, too. I don't know."

She didn't know what she expected then. Certainly not the frown that furrowed Amanda's brow. "I… I'll try to be…" She paused, looking for a word. "Better."

Then she walked down the hallway, and Beth went into her office and sat down, stunned.

Keith waited in the Palm Beach deli. At ten o'clock, Laurie Green walked in, just as she had promised. She saw him at the table, and a smile lit her face. "Keith!"

She rushed over and hugged him fiercely. He hugged her back, then disentangled himself carefully. She had lost her parents when the plane had gone down, and she herself had nearly perished in the muck soup of the Everglades. She had experienced agony and grief, but from the beginning, she had been grateful for her own life. Once on the verge of death, her sandy skin and light hair spoke of her health and well-being.

Slightly embarrassed by her show of emotion, he

managed to get her seated opposite him. "So everything's going okay?" he asked.

She nodded. "I graduate from Nova University next spring."

"That's great. I'm delighted to hear it."

She waved her left hand in front of him, showing him the diamond on her finger. "And I'm getting married in the fall."

"That's absolutely wonderful," he said sincerely.

Then she smiled. "That's not why you called me."

"No."

"What's up? You know that I'll help you any way I can."

"I know that, and thanks…. Do you know if your folks were friends with a couple named Ted and Molly Monoco?"

The smiled left her face. "Have they been found?" she asked.

He shook his head. "So it's true, they were friends of your folks?"

She nodded. "I didn't know them that well. My parents decided to take dance lessons for some event they were going to. Ted owned the studio they went to, and they got friendly. They were nice. *Are* nice. I hope. I don't know what to think."

Keith nodded. "Did you ever meet a man named Manny Ortega?"

"Oh!" she exclaimed, her cheeks reddening. "I gave him your number. I told him I'd gotten it a long time ago, that it might not be good. Did I do something wrong? I'd forgotten all about it."

"No, no, it's fine."

"Are you sure?"

"Absolutely. So you know Manny?"

"Yes, he was a friend of the Monocos. I went to a couple of dance parties with my parents, and he was there, playing with the band. I was sticking out like a sore thumb, and he was nice to me. I can't say that I've seen him in…well, in years. But when he called me, saying that Ted hadn't called in and he'd mentioned something about your name, well… I'm sorry. I didn't hesitate to give him the number."

"It's fine. I just had to make sure," Keith told her. "So tell me about this guy you're about to marry."

He had a firm destination in mind once he left Laurie, and with a two-hour plus—depending on traffic—drive ahead of him, he pulled out his cell phone and put a call through to Mike. "Manny's information checked out," he told his boss.

"Any more finds?"

"Not as of the time I left this morning," Keith told him. "I'm heading down to the Keys. Look, we're searching, doing the best we can with what we have. You need to haul out the big equipment for this one, Mike."

"You need to hang in there. They'll catch that couple soon. They're watching the roads, the airports, train stations…and boats."

"You know how big the damn coastline is, Mike?" Keith asked.

"Yes, I'm aware of the length of the coastline."

"I don't think that catching them is going to solve the entire problem," Keith said.

"It needs to happen."

"Yes, but, Mike, they can't be pulling this off alone."

"You don't think they'll squeal once they're caught?"

"Maybe, maybe not. Mike, you need to get the right

people following the financial trail. Someone in the area is making the arrangements to take the yachts, and refurbish and camouflage them."

"We've been looking into every boat shop in south Florida."

"Start looking at people."

"Want to give me names?"

He did.

"What makes you certain any one of these people is involved?"

"Because I believe there was a skull on the island when we arrived. And I believe that someone who was there that weekend managed to remove it."

Mike was silent for a moment then he said, "You know, we're not really trying to catch pirates," he reminded Keith. "There are other people who do that. Our job is to find *La Doña*."

"I swear it's involved somehow."

"You know you gave me the names of your co-workers, right?" Mike asked casually.

"Hey, you're the one who said you don't trust anyone," Keith said. "I don't have the resources to find out who's invested where. You do."

"I'm not an idiot, Keith. I've already spoken to the FBI. They've been working on the money angle. Thing is, people don't usually write down their ill-gotten gains on their tax returns."

"There's got to be a connection to some kind of boat shop somewhere."

"They're on it, Keith. What's your plan now?"

"First, can you get me a list of students and investors in the old Monoco dance studios?"

"Yes."

"I'm heading to the Keys. Islamorada. I'm going to hang around a few bars, see who knew Victor Thompson, try to find out what he was doing."

"The police have questioned at least fifty people."

"The police can't go down and hang out at a bar as well as I can," Keith said with a little smile.

A moment later he hung up. He hesitated, played with the thought of trying to reach Beth, then discarded the notion. She would just hang up on him, if he was even able to reach her. Of course, if she said hello and answered her phone, he would at least know she was all right. Still, he decided to call Ashley at work instead. She assured him that everything was all right: Amber was in school, Beth was well. There had been no more incidents. "Will we see you soon?" she asked.

"Of course. No news on Sandy and Brad?"

"Not yet."

"You're sure Beth is fine?"

"Yes, there's an officer on duty at the club. He calls in on the hour."

He thanked her and hung up.

Maria Lopez walked into the empty dance studio and looked around. A feeling of deep and poignant nostalgia swept through her.

She remembered the old days so clearly.

She could still outdo many a younger dancer, but the truth was, her glory days were over. No matter how hard they fought it, people got older.

Ted hadn't cared. He had wanted nothing more than retirement. He had always told her to cherish her accomplishments and enjoy life. She did enjoy life. But she had given up so much. Love, a real relationship. She had been too busy when she had been young, too eager to compete. Too determined to hold on to her title—until she had known it was time to bow out, rather than lose. Now she had no children to fill her life. She had traveled, of course. And then she had come back to see Manny at the club. And Manny...

Manny would not shut up about Ted and Molly.

She frowned, thinking she heard a loud voice from the office, and spun around.

Curious, Maria walked in that direction. The staff was gone. Not even the young receptionist was manning her station.

She moved closer to the office door.

And she listened, her eyes widening.

She had wanted to speak with Eduardo about the Summer Sizzler.

No more. She swallowed hard. At first she was afraid. Then she thought again of Ted and Molly and their kindnesses to her through the years, and she grew angry.

In another hour, Keith had reached Islamorada. He found the marina where Victor Thompson had kept his boat and run his charters.

The guy had clearly been well liked. At the spot where his boat should have been berthed, there was a cross, and flowers covered the pier and floated in the water nearby. He was standing there when a man walked up to him. "Friend of Victor's?" he asked.

"Fellow diver, paying my respects," Keith told him. "You were a friend?"

The man was in his late fifties, with a full head of silver-gray hair. Well built and bronzed, he was covered with tattoos and sported a gold skeleton for an earring.

"I taught him to dive. I never taught him to go off alone, though," he said sadly.

"Doesn't make a lot of sense, an experienced diver like Victor," Keith said. "Where was he diving when it happened?"

"I didn't see him the morning he took off, so it's a mystery to me," the man said. He pointed toward a building near the docks, with a Keys-style thatched roof and an outside bar. "As far as I know, he didn't say anything to anyone. But we all hang out up there, at La Isla Bar-A. Some of us are up there now, drinking to Vic. Come join us, buy a round. Man, it's a sorry thing. I just don't understand how we lost Vic. It's a tragedy, and a waste, and I'm angry, I guess." He shook his head.

Keith thanked him for the information and headed for the bar. "I'll be up in a minute," the older man told him. "Name's John, John Elmer. You can buy me a drink, too."

"Sure."

The bar was typical of the area, with lots of tall stools and hardwood tables, chairs and benches. It had the neighborhood feel of Nick's. The woman behind the bar was attractive, but no kid. She was busy, but she handled the load with ease. He decided that the big group at the far end of the bar had to be Victor Thompson's friends. He didn't horn in on them immediately but sat a short distance away. When the woman came to take his order, he asked for a beer, then asked her about the group. "If those are Victor Thompson's friends, I'd like to buy them a drink."

"Sure. You knew Victor, huh?" she said. "So many people cared. He was a great guy. So sad…"

He saw the group at the end of the bar looking up

after the drinks had been ordered. One of them lifted his newly delivered beer and called out to Keith, "Hey, thanks. Join us?"

Keith rose, taking his beer with him. He offered his hand around, and met Joe, Shelley, Jose, Bill, Junior and Melanie. "Good guy, absolute waste," the one named Joe, who had summoned him over, told Keith.

"A real friendly guy. Never met a stranger. That's why we're all here right now," Melanie explained.

"He always said he didn't want a wake, people in black crying over his shell," Jose said.

"Yeah, Vic wanted a party," Joe said. "People remembering the good times, laughing. We're supposed to cremate him, take him out to the reefs he loved."

"Sounds like a fitting way to handle the end," Keith agreed. "Still…" He shook his head. "Funny thing. How could he know the reefs so well, and…"

"We can't figure it out, either," Shelley said, looking morose despite the fact that she was supposed to be partying. Keith's heart took a little plunge. The woman had obviously cried her eyes out.

He got them talking about Victor's destination the day he had died. But they were at a loss, as well. "As far as I know, the day before, he had talked about looking at some new places to take people," Joe said. "But no destination in particular that I know of."

"He wanted to get into a day-and-night thing. Like camping somewhere," Melanie offered. "The Middle Keys are filled with great places."

"Yeah," Keith agreed, thinking Calliope Key might be a great place, too.

"I think he headed south, but I don't really know," Joe said.

"Hey, remember the time he knocked the whole motor off John's dinghy?" Melanie said, and giggled.

"Yeah, and remember the time he fell in love with the Cuban girl in Miami and we all had to take dance lessons?" Bill said, snickering. "Man, did we suck."

"Victor took classes in Miami?" Keith said.

"We all did—he didn't want it to look as if he was chasing the girl," Melanie told him. "And speak for yourself. I was good," she told Bill.

"Where did you guys go?" Keith asked.

"Someplace on the beach," Bill answered. "It was changing hands when we were there…oh, man, I'm losing brain cells or something. Wait. Monoco. The Monoco Studios. They went missing, didn't they?"

"Sad, huh? That old Monoco guy was great. But I heard their boat had been seen," Melanie said.

"Where'd you hear that?" Keith asked.

Melanie looked at him blankly then shrugged. "I don't know. I think some people in here the other day were saying it."

Keith remained a while longer, bought another round of drinks, then left. On the way back, he put in another call to Mike.

It was late by the time he had taken the tender back to the *Sea Serpent*. Lee and Matt were in for the day, and neither seemed glad to see him, though they couldn't argue with his disappearance; since they had been informed by Mike that he was to come in with the coin and make a full report.

"You find out anything?"

Keith shook his head. "You?"

"Seems like we're beating our heads against a brick wall," Lee told him.

"Did you hear anything from your old buddy Hank?" Keith asked Lee.

"No, did you hear from any of your old buddies…like Beth Anderson or Amanda Mason?" Lee asked.

Matt made a choking sound. They both stared at him. "Sorry—swallowed wrong," he said, and turned away.

Keith and Lee stared after him, then Lee shrugged and turned away, as well.

A rift had definitely formed between the three of them. Lee went down to the cabin, while Keith remained on deck, staring out at the sea. His cell phone began to ring, and he was glad that he'd been left alone on deck when he answered it.

Manny. He listened to what the man had to say, weighed it, then replied, "I'll need Beth Anderson in on it."

"How will we manage that?"

"We have mutual friends," Keith said. "I'll check in with them. Beth will come," he added softly, "if you convince her brother and her niece."

He rang off, hesitated, then he put in a call of his own. He would be sticking his neck out in a big way, but he was convinced it was time. When he hung up, he stood very still in the night, listening, wondering if either of his co-workers had made an attempt to hear his conversation.

It seemed that he was alone in the dark vastness of the sea and sky.

Still…

When he went to sleep that night, it was with one eye open.

15

On Thursday, Beth found that she was well ahead on her work. Eduardo Shea, Maria and Mauricio were practicing, and the final rehearsal planned for the next afternoon, after the floor was in place.

She sat at her desk after lunch, going through all the last-minute arrangements. Then she found herself writing down a chronology starting with the day she had seen the skull on the island. She included a paragraph noting that the ghost story Keith had told had been based on a real event. She made a side note with the information about the couple in Virginia who'd had their boat stolen, along with the fact that—no matter what the rumor mill said—the Monocos hadn't been heard from since they'd last called in from Calliope Key.

A diver had turned up dead, which might or might not mean foul play.

Someone had messed with her computer.

Someone had put a skull on her desk.

She had been threatened at gun- and knifepoint, and law enforcement everywhere was looking for Brad and Sandy, who were apparently pirates. They hadn't been at the club—at least, she was almost certain they hadn't been at the club when the skull had appeared on her desk. And she didn't see how they could have gotten there in time to place it there, anyway. She tried hard to remember if the skull had been real or a prop. Ridiculous question. She should have known. But the minute she had seen it, she had panicked, then run to get the police. Smart call, one would think. And since Ben's toy skull had turned out to be missing, it probably had been a fake, anyway.

Both Manny Ortega and Maria Lopez claimed to feel a real affection for the Monocos. Neither had been on the island. Eduardo Shea seemed like an up-and-up businessman with a love of dance.

She pressed her hands against her temples. Did any of it make any sense?

And why, in the middle of all this, could she not stop thinking about Keith Henson? She was so angry with him....

And so suspicious and edgy. Had he just been attempting to get close to find out what she might know? What she might have set in motion.

Yes, she was sick with jealousy, too proud to ask certain questions—or too afraid of the answers? Had he slept with Amanda, as well, eager to know more about her, too?

Why did she wish she hadn't been quite so furious? Why hadn't she allowed a conversation? Why did she feel as if she had...cut away a part of her being? She prayed for a little more dignity. Praying didn't help.

She simply wanted to be with him.

"Hi."

She looked up, so startled that she nearly screamed. Her brother was standing in the doorway. She glanced at her watch. One o'clock. Way too early for Ben to be off work.

"What are you doing here?"

"Early-dismissal day," Ben said.

"Again? They just had one."

"Hey, do I control the Miami-Dade Board of Education?" he asked ruefully.

"You should have said something. I could have picked Amber up from school."

"I know. And I appreciate it. But I decided to get her myself. And now I'm getting you."

She arched a brow. "Getting me to…?"

"We're going diving."

"Diving? I'm working."

"I've got permission for you to leave. Commodore Berry is thrilled to death with your plan for tomorrow night. He said you can take the afternoon off and come with us."

"Who's 'us'?"

"Amber, me, the Masons, Manny and a few others. Actually, Manny was the one who came up with the idea of a nice social afternoon."

"I should go down and watch the rehearsal," Beth said.

"You're too late. They've already finished. In fact, Maria is coming out with us."

"She is?"

"Um. With Manny."

"Ben, I'm not so sure—"

"Ashley and Jake are coming."

"Oh?"

"Beth, I'm not an idiot. My daughter's life has been threatened. I think Brad and Sandy are violent but cowardly, and we've taken precautions, but even so, we're going out with a pair of cops, okay? We're going in a big group. Amber wants to go out on the Masons' boat. That's cool—big group. Got it? I'm *not* an idiot."

She leaned back, smiling. "I'm sorry. No, you're not an idiot. Where are we going?"

"I told you. Diving," he informed her firmly. She glared at him, but when he told her that she was welcome to go aboard Manny's boat or one of the other three vessels making the run, she refused.

Amber was going to be aboard Hank Mason's boat, and that meant she was, too. Along with Jake and Ashley, who weren't just cops but excellent divers.

The trip started off well. The sun was out; there was a perfect breeze. Amanda was actually being a charming hostess, and Beth thought she might actually be sincere when she asked with concern if anyone had discovered who the prankster was who had left the skull on her desk.

"I bet he would have admitted what he did if the police hadn't come in, making the whole thing such a big deal," she suggested, which made Beth wonder if the skull on her desk had actually been a prank, totally unconnected to the very real attack on her. Maybe someone had heard about the incident on the island and thought they were being funny.

"Well, we'll find out soon enough if it was a prank or not," Jake Dilessio said with a shrug.

"Really?" Amanda said. "I thought you were homicide. What are you doing investigating such a silly thing?"

"Hadn't you heard?" he asked her. "There's an APB out on the couple you all know as Brad and Sandy.

They're suspects in the piracy that's been going on along the coast for over a year now, and they were recently spotted in Miami."

Judging by the shocked looks that greeted that statement, neither Amanda nor her family had heard a thing about it.

"Really?" Hank said. "We were sleeping right down the beach from them!"

"Let's hope to God they're apprehended soon," Roger said fervently.

"They will be," Jake said with deadly assurance.

There was silence for a minute. Then Amanda determinedly changed the subject. "You know, I've never dived this site before. Have any of you?"

The conversation turned to diving, and Beth half listened to the stories exchanged. Mostly she found herself watching Amber and being worried.

Hank decided to stay aboard while the others paired up and went into the water. Amanda immediately pounced on Ben, determined to be his buddy.

"Hey, Amber, can I be your buddy?" Jake asked, glancing reassuringly at Beth. "Ashley and Beth can go together."

Beth smiled at him. She could relax if Amber was with Jake.

Hank's boat was fitted out perfectly for diving, with stands and benches for easy access to enough tanks for ten. In fact, she was actually better equipped than many professional dive boats, with medical equipment on board, as well. She was surprised that he had decided to take on the role of dive master above board, since he loved to dive so much himself. Then again, he could head out whenever he chose, so perhaps he had decided that supervising the entire scene would be fun for a change.

It was hardly as if they had the area to themselves. Dive boats from the Keys, Miami and as far north as Palm Beach congregated here, along with private boaters like themselves. The wreck was a well-known and popular site.

It was fun being down with Ashley, and an easy afternoon, with so many divers present that it was almost impossible to be worried. In addition to the wreck, the area teemed with fish, anemones and all kinds of undersea life.

They had barely begun the dive when Ashley glanced at her compass, then beckoned to her. She led Beth away from the wreck, into an area of reefs.

They came to a huge outcrop of coral. Next to the coral, there was a bed of sand and seagrass. There was a diver there, exercising perfect buoyancy, simply sitting on the sand.

Waiting.

It took Beth a minute to register who it was—people in tanks and masks were hard to recognize at first glance. But then she knew.

Keith.

She stared at Ashley, furious at both of them—especially Keith. This had obviously been arranged, even though she had told him in no uncertain terms that she didn't want to talk to him until he was willing to do some explaining.

Ashley was her dive partner, but their group wasn't far away. She could have turned and propelled herself right back to join them, and she was sorely tempted to do so. She didn't understand what his appearance here—

twenty feet down—meant. He could hardly do much explaining where they were.

He gave them the divers' sign to rise, and Ashley nodded, then looked at Beth. Beth lifted her hands. Fine. They would rise.

They surfaced by a boat. Beth was startled to realize that it was Manny's. He and Maria were both there, as if they were awaiting their arrival.

She lifted her mask, held on to the ladder and pulled off her fins.

Keith pulled himself out of the water easily, then reached down to help her and Ashley. Manny stood by, ready to assist, as well. "Welcome, gorgeous," he said, with a smile. "Let me help you with your tank."

"Wait... I need this tank to get back to the boat I'm supposed to be on," she protested, staring at them all one by one, confused and angry. Her last reproving glance was for Ashley. How the hell had this happened?

"No, it's all right. I'll radio over that you and Ashley decided to come up here and visit with Maria," Manny said. "Let me take that. We should go below."

She stared at the sea around them. There were a number of boats around. Dive flags littered the area.

Hank's boat was a good distance from them, no activity evident on board. Everyone must still be down at the wreck, she thought, and allowed Manny to help her with her tank.

"Come on down. I've got coffee and tea ready," Maria said, offering them towels. "Not that it's anything but a lovely day. Still, you're wet, and the air-conditioning is on in the cabin."

Beth followed the others down to the cabin. It was nice, not huge. Manny's boat could sleep two. There was a head, a small galley and a dining/living area, with a table against the port side. Beth stared at Keith, damning both him and herself. She'd hated herself for wishing he would reappear at any moment.

Now that he had, she just wanted to run over to him. But she couldn't let herself. She had to remind herself that the man had an agenda. An agenda that included disappearing whenever he needed to do so and it included spending all kinds of time with Amanda.

He stared back at her with no apology.

"Sit, please?" he said.

"I didn't know the three of you were so well acquainted," Beth said, speaking at last and looking from Manny to Maria and then to Keith once again.

"We've just recently become friends," Keith said.

"Interesting," she murmured.

"I didn't tell Manny anything," Keith said evenly. "He knew who I was."

"Clue *me* in, why don't you?" Beth said, her tone heated and her heart wondering if he'd reveal his secrets to her.

"I'm with a company called Rescue, and most of our contracts are military," Keith explained. "No one was supposed to know who we were or what we were doing," Keith explained.

"I see," she said, looking around at the group. It amazed her that even Maria was in on it, while she had been in the dark.

"Beth, you must understand. I already knew who he was," Manny explained.

"And Maria knew, too. But you couldn't tell me," Beth said icily.

"You didn't want to call the police when you were

accosted at both gun- and knifepoint. If you had, they might have caught Brad and Sandy," Keith said. "There's plenty of blame to go around here."

Beth glared at him angrily. "Not fair. Amber's life was threatened." She stared at Ashley. "And excuse me, but how the hell did *this* all come about?" she asked, gesturing at the group and their surroundings.

Manny cleared his throat. "I arranged for all this to happen today. You needed to see Keith."

She hoped she hadn't given away the fact that she'd begun to feel desperate to see the man. It felt as if her cheeks were burning.

"Why?" she demanded.

She didn't get the answer she had hoped for or expected.

"I need to be at your Summer Sizzler tomorrow night," he told her.

She almost laughed aloud—at herself. She managed not to, and instead stared at Keith, shaking her head. "You've gotten into the club on your own several times. Membership doesn't seem to mean a lot where you're concerned. You're best friends with Manny and Maria. And Amanda would be happy to invite you to the party. You sure as hell don't need me to get in."

"You need to tell her everything you've discovered," Manny said.

"Sit down, Beth. Have some tea. Please," Maria said. She flashed Beth an apologetic smile. "It's partially my fault that you're here."

"Oh?"

"Please, sit, Beth. I'll explain," Keith said.

She sat. He sat opposite her.

His eyes were on her, dead steady. "Beth, Manny

knows me the same way Jake and Ashley do, through a previous situation here in Miami-Dade, that's all."

"And I know about him because Manny told me when I went to him for help," Maria explained.

"Wonderful," Beth murmured, still lost. She looked at Keith. "So you were never on the island looking for the Monocos from the start?"

"No."

She stared straight at him. "Then you were looking for the ship."

"What ship?" Maria murmured.

"La Doña," Beth said flatly, staring at Keith.

He stared back at her. She realized that no one had known what he was really doing—they had just known who he was. And he didn't appreciate the fact that she had spoken.

"It doesn't matter," Beth said, offering Maria a quick glance, then turning back to Keith. "Go on."

"The point is, I want to be at the Sizzler from the start. I need to *watch.* And I don't want anyone to know I'm there. I want access to your office, and I want to get behind the scenes, so I can watch what's going on. Matt and Lee will be there. We've all been invited already."

"The Masons?" Beth asked.

He nodded. "Amanda called and invited us," he told her.

She tried not to stiffen. "I don't understand what you want. You could have arranged this without me."

"Actually, no."

"Why?" she demanded. "What's so important about you being there with my blessing?"

"I told you, I need free access. Everyone who was on the island will be there," Keith said.

She shook her head, a wry smile in place. "Not exactly. Brad and Sandy aren't invited."

"I have a feeling they'll be there anyway."

"They wouldn't dare be so obvious," she protested.

"I think they're confident enough in their ability to disguise themselves to risk it."

"Then the police should be there."

"The police will be there," Keith said, glancing at Ashley.

"Then they can arrest them the moment they see them," Beth said.

"They'll have to know who they are—but it goes beyond just identifying them. Beth, here's the thing. We don't think they're working alone. Or that they just want to get to you. They're looking to get paid."

"Paid!" she exclaimed.

"They disappeared really quickly after attacking you. I looked into the property surrounding your house, specifically at the block around the corner. Do you know who owns most of the houses in the area?"

"Who?" she demanded.

"Eduardo Shea."

Beth stared at him in surprise. "You think Eduardo is in on the piracy? I don't understand."

"Among Mr. Shea's investments are a number of boatyards on the South American coast," Keith told her. "We know that whoever is stealing luxury vessels has to be making them over somewhere. The police have investigated all the local facilities, and everyone comes up clean. It would also make more sense to get the boats far away from this country, where all of them have been registered."

"Now I'm really confused," Beth murmured. "I don't

understand why Sandy and Brad would risk being at the club."

"I think that Eduardo was talking to them on the phone the other day," Maria put in.

Beth stared at Maria.

"Eduardo was distressed. He was threatening someone. Then, he said that he'd see them at the club. I told Manny," she explained. "Manny was very upset. He contacted Keith and said we must tell him."

"But…that's so… I mean, they must know that they'd be in danger of exposure at the club."

Keith shook his head, offering her a rueful smile. "How? They don't know the police will be there. They don't know that Eduardo Shea's finances have been investigated."

"Still, it would be a ridiculous risk!"

"Hide in plain sight," Ashley murmured, joining into the conversation at last.

"I'm sorry. I still don't get this," Beth said, eyes hard as she stared at Keith again. "What is your involvement? Because, according to what you've told me, you were never out at Calliope looking for the pirates."

He sat back. "My involvement is personal. I happen to believe that, if they're apprehended, Sandy and Brad can answer a lot of questions," he said flatly.

"I still don't understand why you need me—why you need to be out of sight," Beth murmured.

He lowered his head for a moment, then looked up. "There are a few other dynamics I need to keep an eye on. I'm asking you—no, begging you—to trust me. And not to demand answers that I can't give you yet. I had Manny set up the dive—and no, your brother doesn't know that Manny arranged all this on purpose—because

I hoped that if you met with Ashley and Manny and me, you would be able to have faith in me."

"I wouldn't go so far as to say that I have faith in you," Beth told him. "But sure, be my guest. I still don't understand. You can have access to all areas of the club and hide out in my office or wherever." She stared at Ashley. "The more cops the merrier." She felt as if her head was reeling, and she didn't understand anything. "Commodore Berry knows the police will be at the club? And the board of directors are aware of what's going on, as well?"

Keith nodded to her.

"Then you really didn't need my permission for anything," Beth said.

He stared at her. "Yes, I did."

The tension seemed heavy. Manny and Maria remained silent. She didn't know on exactly what level he meant his words, or if being with her had been part of his undercover work or also something personal.

She just wanted to get away.

"I think we should join the others now," she said sharply. "The rest of the divers must be up."

Keith stood. "I'm going. I'll see you tomorrow, then."

"Right," she said stiffly.

He went topside with Manny. Ashley took his place at the table. "You've got to understand my position. Please, Beth," she said. "Trust me."

"*I* trust *you*," Beth said, the implication that she didn't care not to be trusted herself quite evident.

Ashley flushed.

"You really need some tea," Maria said.

"I really need a drink," Beth replied.

* * *

Beth was finding it impossible to sleep. Usually, the night after a dive, she crashed immediately.

Not tonight. She was at Ashley and Jake's place, the kids were sleeping. Ashley and Jake were sleeping. And she was tempted to join the crowd hanging out late at the restaurant.

There were sure to be cops among their number.

Then again, Brad and Sandy had apparently patronized Nick's, as well. Still, when she went to the window and opened the drapes, she could see the docks. As late as it was, she could see several people sitting on one of the ice chests on the walk, talking, beers in hand. She craned her neck to look to her right, toward the restaurant. People were still filling the patio seats.

Restless, she dressed and stepped out, locking the door, pocketing the key Ashley had given her. She walked toward the patio and took a seat, then ordered a beer. That might help her sleep. God knew, she needed to sleep.

People at Nick's were friendly. Several said hello. She was asked if she wanted to join in a game of darts but declined.

At last the crowd began to thin out. She rose, heading back to her friends' house.

As she walked, she heard the sound of a chair scraping. She spun back, cursing at herself for being such a goose.

But the feeling remained with her that she was being followed. She quickened her steps, turned back and saw a form.

All she had to do was scream. People would come running. But as she looked at the shadow of the man who had just left the light of the patio area, he was joined by a young woman. She caught his hand, and, laughing, they headed down toward the dock together. She let out a sigh of relief and turned.

She froze. And saw another shadow. It wasn't coming from the patio but from the parking lot. It shouldn't have been there. She stared, trying to figure out whether she was imagining it, maybe seeing the shadow of a large hibiscus. Her breath caught as the shadow grew. She stayed calm. All she had to do was turn around and head back for the patio.

She did so, walking quickly, to her dismay discovering that everyone had left. The serving staff couldn't all be gone, she told herself. Nick himself was in there somewhere.

She started to hurry after one of the waitresses, who was disappearing inside. The door closed as she reached it. She grabbed the handle and found it locked.

Panic was rising inside her. She lifted a hand to pound on the door.

Then she heard her name.

She turned.

Keith.

She gasped softly.

"What on earth are you doing, wandering around out here?" he demanded.

She couldn't breathe for a moment. "I was having a beer," she said finally. "What are you doing, wandering around out here?"

"I was going to have a beer—I guess they've closed," he said. She stared at him. She still felt so distrustful.

And so hungry, even though she loathed herself for it.

"Beth," he said.

She took a step backward. "I really don't know you," she said.

"Actually, you really do. And I know you."

He lowered his head for a minute. The light caught the sun-bleached blond of his hair. He seemed very tall, a striking presence. She suddenly ached to be held, to feel as if she hadn't somehow made a disaster of her world.

To feel as if something was real and solid...

He looked at her again. "Let me just walk you back to the door."

She shrugged. "Tell me, Keith, what do you think you know about me?"

He looked at her, frowning. "I know I care," he said simply. "And I know you are who I want to care about."

He took her arms, turning her toward him. He appeared perplexed. "Please try to understand."

"There are things I can understand, and things I can't," she said.

"And exactly what does that mean?"

She shook her head, turned and walked to the door, then unlocked it. The damn hibiscus still made her uneasy. Or was that really it? "There's beer in the house," she heard herself say.

"Are you inviting me in?"

"Apparently you have as much right to be here as I do," she said, leaving the door open as she entered.

He stepped in behind her. She stopped walking, knowing that his hands would fall on her shoulders, that he would sweep her hair aside, that she would feel his lips and his whisper against her neck.

He didn't disappoint her.

But then he shocked her.

"I know that I'm falling in love with you," he said.

The door closed behind them. She turned in his arms, then wound her own arms around him as his lips found hers. But as the fusion of their mouths grew heated, she forced herself to pull away slightly.

"The...guest...room," she murmured. "They... have..."

"Kids. Guest room," he agreed.

He swept her up. For the moment she forgot that she still didn't know or trust everything about him. In the darkness, in the privacy that lay behind closed doors, she thought only of his naked flesh, the heated explorations of his tongue, the eroticism of his touch.

Miraculously, he had appeared, vital, like a fire, pulsing with life. She knew he would disappear by morning.

At the moment, all she longed for was the night.

He stepped away from the shadows at the side of the house and into the light, staring at the door. He had watched it close. Watched the two of them come together...

And it enraged him.

He'd been so close....

And what?

Dare he make a move tonight? No, no sense in it.

He stretched his fingers, knotted them back into fists. This was insane. Just too tempting. He'd had a beer at Nick's. If anyone had seen him, so what?

Then, just when he had seen her really beginning to fear the shadows, to trust that niggling sensation at her nape, the one that sent chills down her spine and gave him such pleasure...

Keith Henson.

He swore softly.

Then he disappeared back into the shadows.

16

The club looked exquisite. The florists had arrived at the crack of dawn. The dining-room staff began at the same time, and soon after, electricians were out stringing the special lights. The theme was hot and tropical, and by afternoon, the place had been transformed.

Beth came at ten. She'd slept late, knowing she would wake alone. As she left the house, she glanced at the hibiscus bush.

She was tempted to ask Ashley to rip the damn thing out!

Nick's was already buzzing. Cheerful waiters and waitresses called a good-morning to her as she hurried around to her car.

She felt silly for letting herself get so spooked the night before. And elated because she'd been with him. Because he'd said he was falling in love with her. Angry...

Because even though she'd been with him, so little had really been said.

She told herself to forget him for now and try again for a little bit of dignity and distance when she saw him again.

Beth spent the day in an uneasy fog. She ran around as she was supposed to, ensuring that the flowers were right, the tables set and the dais specially arranged for the commodore. Champagne was chilled; the correct wines arrived.

At three she went up to her office, ready to lock her door for a few minutes and collapse into her chair.

She started when she walked in and discovered that Keith was there. She stared at him accusingly.

"You didn't lock it," he told her.

"I don't usually during the day, when I'm up and down. I can see now that I should have."

He heard her tone and ignored it, speaking crisply, "You'll need to lock it tonight, and I'll need a key."

At the moment he was in dock shorts and a T-shirt. There was a garment bag hanging off one of her shelves, next to her own.

"You're here for good, then—I mean, from now till the party's over?" she asked.

He nodded.

"I have one question for you," she told him, trying to keep her distance.

"And what is that?"

"Why isn't my brother in on what's going on?"

"I'm working on a need-to-know basis here," he said, his eyes level upon hers.

"I see. Maria needed to know all about you, but my brother shouldn't?"

He sighed. "Beth, Maria knew from Manny."

"So because they knew who you are, they're in the clear?" she asked.

"No one is in the clear," he said grimly. "Beth—"

She took a step back. "I don't think today is really the time to get into a heavy conversation."

"You're right. Let it go. I'm not accusing your brother of anything. He just doesn't need to have anything more dumped on him right now."

She felt a twinge of irritation coming on. "That's a crock. You think my brother can't be trusted."

"Beth, do we have to do this?" he demanded.

"You asked me if you could be here, remember?"

Something hard touched his eyes. "I'll need a key."

"Top drawer, on the left. It's in a compact," she told him.

"Interesting hiding place."

"I never needed to be all that worried about hiding it before," she told him.

She no longer wanted to collapse into her chair. She left the office. Downstairs, she decided to grab something to eat in the kitchen. The chef asked her to taste the black-bean soup, which was delicious. She was so nervous, though, that she could only manage a few spoonfuls.

When she returned to her office, Keith was gone.

She called Ashley, who assured her that the man watching Amber had called in. Her niece would be getting out of school soon, then heading home and getting ready to come to the club with her father. Beth decided to get dressed for the evening. She headed down to the women's lockers with her clothing.

Extra staff had been hired for the evening, and caterers were working on the patio and dockside bars and chair arrangements. All the permanent staff and extra personnel were wearing tuxedos for the evening, the men and the women. She nodded with approval as Henry waved to her.

There was a large man helping Henry. He seemed a little awkward. He noticed her watching him and came over to her. "Officer Greg Masters, Miss Anderson," he said quietly. "I just wanted you to know we're here. Blending in."

"Thank you," she murmured. Blending in? She wasn't so sure, but he was there, and that was enough.

She crossed the side patio and entered the hallway that led to the women's lockers.

No one was in the area. In the locker room alone, she felt chills along her spine. She went through the place, looking into every bathroom stall, every shower.

She was definitely alone, but she still had the eerie feeling that she was being watched. She showered and dressed quickly, then emerged, still with the uncomfortable feeling of being watched. She wondered why she was so nervous, knowing that the police had already arrived and Keith was there, as well.

What about Lee and Matt? she wondered. They had been invited by the Masons. Were they there already, too? And exactly where was Keith at that moment, and why had he been so determined that he needed to be there so early.

She made a few last-minute checks in the kitchen, the dining room and the bar. The band arrived to set up, and then Eduardo Shea appeared, dashing in an elegant black-and-white salsa costume with ruffled sleeves. She knew she had to behave naturally, and she managed to greet him with enthusiasm. All the while, though, it seemed that her blood ran cold.

"Has Maria arrived yet?" Eduardo asked her.

"No, not yet. But, please, come say hello to Commodore Berry and his wife, and I'll show you where your table is. The band is set up, and everything will be exactly as you requested." She smiled and took him by the arm.

Commodore Berry was standing outside, looking totally the part in his white suit and captain's hat. He was gazing out at the docks with pleasure. He turned to Beth, smiling. "Look, there's a group coming in from the Belle Haven club. Rumor says this is going to be the end-of-summer party to outdo all the others." He lowered his head as if he was about to whisper to her, then noticed Eduardo. "Good evening, sir. Welcome."

Beth fled. If Commodore Berry could carry off his part so well—knowing that police were watching his party for uninvited guests—surely she could carry it off, too.

Ashley and Jake arrived, and then Ben and Amber.

"You all right?" Ashley asked.

Beth stared at her friend. "I guess you saw Keith this morning."

"Yes," Ashley said, flushing. "But I wasn't referring to Keith. I was talking about this evening. But, um, of course, Keith is welcome in my home anytime. But… as to tonight…?"

"As long as you stay right on Amber every minute," Beth told her, "I'll be absolutely fine."

"I'll be with her, I promise," Ashley assured her. She looked at Beth anxiously. "You know…nothing may happen. No one will act if they don't see anything out of the ordinary."

Beth nodded. "I almost wish something *would* happen. Something…so that I can stop feeling as if I were on pins and needles all the time."

"It will be all right," Ashley said, and squeezed her arm. "Everything looks fabulous, by the way."

"Thanks," Beth said wryly. "There's Maria. Lord!"

Maria was in a short sequined dress that hugged the perfection of her body. Her hair was swept back, and she wore a red rose tucked behind her ear. The dress sparkled with her every movement. Beth noted that the short skirt would swirl and glitter as she danced. Maria turned, saw Beth, and nodded gravely.

"People are beginning to arrive," Ashley said.

"Time to play hostess."

"Have you seen Keith?"

"Hours ago. I don't know where he is now. Excuse me."

For the next hour Beth was insanely busy, so much so that she nearly forgot that her sparkling contribution to the yachting club social season had become a charade. Despite the insanity, she found herself anxiously looking for Amber all the time. Her niece wasn't alone. Ashley was with her, as she had promised. Apparently Kimberly's parents had dropped her off to enjoy the event, as well. Both girls were stunning in their fancy outfits and heels.

She caught her brother watching her, as well. He still wore a look of accusation every time his eyes turned her way. They had been so close all their lives. She felt a pain in her heart because now he felt she had betrayed him. She longed to tell him she wasn't at fault, but she couldn't. Not yet.

The other dancers had arrived. Mauricio stood beside Maria.

The Masons were there, ringed around Eduardo, Maria and the dancers.

Then, in the crowd, she saw Matt Albright, and a small distance from him, helping himself to a glass of champagne, Lee Gomez.

Still, no sign of Keith. But then, he'd said he wanted to stay unseen, and apparently he'd meant it.

As she greeted some of the members, Commodore Berry came to her side. "Beth, this is incredible. Already a hit, and we've hardly even started." He lowered his voice. "I know the place is crawling with police, but how can you tell who's who in such a crowd?"

He had a point, she decided. In a moment of panic, she excused herself and threaded her way through the crowd.

She breathed a sigh of relief. Ashley was still with Amber. Sticking like glue.

The band stopped playing just then, and the commodore asked everyone to start taking their places for dinner. People began to file to their tables. An older man, tall and well built, with thick white hair, beard and a mustache, and sea-green eyes, passed her and smiled. She smiled back, though she had no idea who he was. There were too many guests from their sister clubs that night, she decided. She watched the others file into the dining room and take their seats. The dance instructors were together at a table with Manny and Eduardo Shea. The Masons were all in attendance, including Gerald. They were at a table with Matt and Lee.

If Brad and Sandy were present anywhere, she hadn't seen them.

The commodore gave his welcome speech. Beth joined her own family at last. When she sat, she was at Jake Dilessio's side. Ashley was beside her husband,

and Amber was on Ashley's other side, with Ben next to her, and Kimberly next to him.

She tried to relax, tried to eat.

Whoever the man was with the white hair and Colonel Sanders mustache, he must have been a friend of Commodore Berry's, because he had a seat on the dais.

The commodore announced the menu, welcomed the members and guests, and hoped that all the docking arrangements had gone smoothly. He thanked the chef and the staff, and made a special announcement, thanking Beth, as well, and introducing her. She was startled when he demanded that she rise, which she did, and she tried not to feel awkward as she received applause.

Her brother clapped with the others, politely, but he stared at her as if he felt he had nurtured a traitor. She wondered if she would ever be able to fix things between them.

Yet again, she wondered where Keith was.

Dinner was served, and it was as delicious as the chef had promised. Kim and Amber chatted; even Ashley and Jake seemed casual.

As courses came and went, people hopped sociably from table to table. Amanda joined them for several minutes, complimenting Kim and Amber, flirting with Ben. Hank dropped by, then Gerald.

There was a tap on Beth's shoulder. She nearly jumped a mile. It was Matt Albright. "Hi. I just came over to see how you're doing," he said cheerfully.

"Great. Good to see you," she told him.

"Have you seen Keith?" he asked her. "He was supposed to be here with us."

"No, I haven't seen him in here," she answered honestly.

"There's just no telling with that guy," he said, and shrugged. "Well, I hear there's dancing later. Save something for me, huh?"

"Sure. Though I hear it's salsa—and your best partners are over at that table," she said, pointing to Eduardo and his group.

"I have a feeling you'd be a great partner," he told her.

"Well, thanks," she murmured.

Roger Mason stopped by next to greet her brother.

Amber rose. "Where are you going?" Beth asked sharply.

Amber stared at her, surprised by the tone of her voice. "The bathroom, if it's all right."

"I'll go with you," Beth said.

"Aunt Beth, I know where it is."

"I know, but, um, I need to go myself."

"We'll all go," Ashley said cheerfully, rising. "Kim, join us?"

"I don't really have to go," Kim said, bewildered.

"But you don't want to have to go during the dancing, right?" Beth asked. She didn't know why; she just wanted the girls together, no matter what, and with Ashley or Jake at all times.

She didn't understand, either, why she was nervous all the way to the ladies' room and back. The place was swarming with people, guests, members, staff, everyone having a good time. Ashley was as casual as could be, making the girls laugh. Beth thanked God for her friend—and for the fact that her friend was a cop and married to a cop.

Back at the table, she sipped champagne, realizing that throughout the day she had become more tightly wound with each passing moment. She had to calm down or she would wind up jumping out of her chair and screaming.

Dessert was served, and as the flaming soufflés went around, Commodore Berry rose again, announcing their entertainment.

Mauricio escorted Maria to the dance floor out on the patio, open to the dining room and surrounded by additional tables.

The music began.

For several minutes Beth found herself as transfixed as the others. As she had felt earlier, it seemed impossible that anyone could move so fast, that steps could be so sensual and erotic, that anything could appear as miraculously, glitteringly swift and elegant, all in one.

Then the music broke, and Mauricio and Maria stopped dead, dramatically posed. The old cliché was true, Beth thought. She really could have heard a pin drop.

Then the moment was over. The music began again, and the dancers swirled into motion once more until at last the performance came to a halt.

Everyone in the room rose; the applause was thunderous.

Beth blinked. Eduardo was walking forward to thank his dancers. He was carrying a cordless mike, and he announced that there would be lessons for the guests, then introduced the rest of his staff. He had been speaking for several minutes before Beth realized that he hadn't come from the direction of his table, he hadn't been seated during the performance.

Her heart thudded as she wondered if that meant anything.

She looked around. The big cop who was dressed like a waiter was standing by one of the serving stations.

He was still staring at the dance floor. Everyone had been staring at the dance floor. Had anyone seen Eduardo come and go?

"Miss Elizabeth Anderson."

She started when she heard her name. She looked around, certain she must seem like a stunned child to the spectators.

"Come on."

There was a roar of applause. Eduardo was looking at her, an arm outstretched toward her.

"Get up, Aunt Beth. Go!" Amber said.

"Go where? What?" Beth demanded.

"He wants to use you to show everyone how quickly they can learn," Kim told her.

"What?" Beth said. "After that—after Maria, he wants me to get up there?"

"Go on, sis," Ben said, staring at her. "You were the one with the idea to bring in Eduardo Shea, weren't you?"

He had no idea how true that was, she thought. She was the one who had insisted on prying, on putting his child in danger. She knew that somewhere inside, her brother still loved her. But right now he wanted her to get up there and trip over her own feet.

She had no choice. She rose, forced a smile and walked toward Eduardo. She tried to remember everything she had learned in her brief workout during Maria's practice session.

She met the man's eyes. Tried not to betray the fact that she knew he might be conspiring with murderers.

He stepped toward her. Her fingers curled around his in proper rhythm form. The band began to play.

She was no Maria Lopez. But Eduardo Shea was good. No matter what else he might be, he was a great dancer. With him leading, she was shocked at how quickly she fell into the rhythm and how she could turn at his command without missing a beat.

Mauricio's voice rang out as he invited everyone to rise and join them. He walked to the dais and selected the commodore's wife. Maria beckoned to the commodore. The other teachers went to different tables, inviting the guests to rise.

There were evidently, and perhaps naturally, many people in the room with some knowledge of salsa. Soon the floor was so crowded, it was almost impossible to move. Dancers began to spill out onto the lawn, in front of the docks.

Dinner was officially over, it seemed. But the party had just begun.

She was breathless when Eduardo stopped, bowing to her. "Thank you for being such a lovely volunteer! Regretfully, I must dance with others now," he said.

"May I?" someone said behind her as Eduardo turned away.

She turned. Before she could protest, she found herself dancing with Hank Mason.

"Quite a party," he told her.

"Thanks."

"Are you doing all right?" he queried.

"Of course."

"You look a little nervous," he said. "I heard about the prank with the skull, of course. Did you really see a skull when we were on the island?" he asked her.

She shook her head, staring straight into his eyes. "Must have been a conch shell—that's what Ben said."

He smiled. "You still seem awfully jumpy."

"I've got a lot riding on tonight, you know." She looked nervously past his shoulder. Eduardo had led Amber out on the dance floor. "Excuse me, Hank."

She extricated herself from his hold and hurried across the floor. She needn't have worried. Jake had already cut in.

"Beth?" It was Roger Mason. "Do an old man proud, would you?"

Before she knew it, she was in his arms. He knew how to salsa, and once again she found herself moving at the speed of light. She tried to see where Amber was and frowned, unable to see Kim, her brother, Amber or Ashley.

The music suddenly changed, with the singer announcing that they were going to take it down to a rumba.

"Excuse me. If I may?"

Someone else was cutting in, neatly slipping her away from Roger.

Beth was startled to swirl into the arms of the white-haired man she had seen sitting with Commodore Berry.

To her surprise, he knew how to rumba. She knew the basics and was able to move, but she was so concerned about Amber, she was thinking only about escape. "It's all right. Kim's parents are coming for her. The girls are out front. Ashley's with them."

She nearly gasped. She never would have recognized him, as well as she thought she had known him.

She nearly said his name out loud.

"Close your mouth, please. Relax. You can't be that tense for a rumba."

She stared at him, amazed. She wondered where he had learned to do such an incredible camouflage job with makeup. It was impossible to tell that the beard and mustache were false, that the hair was a wig. He was wearing green contacts, she realized. "Your own mother wouldn't know you," she told him.

"That *is* the idea."

"Matt and Lee don't even know you, do they?" she asked.

He was silent for a moment. "No."

"Do you still think something's going to happen?" she asked him.

He shrugged. "Shea got up and started to disappear when Maria and Mauricio were dancing. I followed him. He was getting a beer." He shook his head, looking a little disgusted. "I hope to hell I wasn't wrong. It will be hard to swing law enforcement around to my way of thinking a second time. They can be pretty unforgiving. Like someone else I know."

She arched a brow. "Interesting. Let's see, I have no idea what you're really trying to do—ever. And I realize now that you're as much a chameleon as any criminal out there. I thought I knew you, at least a little bit, but now I don't know if anything I thought I knew is true."

"Could you trust me for a little while? Please?"

She tilted her head, staring up at him. "I just don't know how far you would go to achieve what you're really seeking," she told him. She became aware of a ringing as she spoke, then realized that it was her phone, clipped to her skirt.

"Excuse me, will you? I'm sure there are others you

need to dance with tonight," she said smoothly, and stepped away, quickly slipping through the crowd to reach a spot on the edge of the dance floor, a breath of air and enough semi-isolation to hear.

She glanced at the caller ID and quickly answered.

"Aunt Beth?"

"Amber, what is it? Where are you?"

She heard something that sounded like a sob.

"Aunt Beth, come quick. I need you!"

17

Keith watched her go, feeling an actual pain in his heart. Even after last night, she didn't intend to forgive him.

Had he been an idiot? he wondered. He'd spent the day in various forms of disguise, joining in with the electricians, the wait staff and then the guests. He'd listened in on conversations between the Masons, the dancers, and even Matt and Lee. There had been nothing to hear. The only moment when something might have been amiss had been when Eduardo Shea had risen, and he'd followed the man, only to see him with one of the waiters, getting a beer.

He'd studied every guest. No sign of Brad or Sandy.

"Hey there, handsome!"

He turned to see an attractive older woman in a stunning blue gown that was complemented by the blue tint in her hair. "Spare me a dance?"

He was about to find a way to beg off when he saw that Matt Albright was on the floor with Amanda. He smiled at the woman.

"You must be from one of our sister clubs," she said.

He introduced himself as Jim Smithson, friend of

Commodore Berry. He whirled her on the floor, close to Matt and Amanda. She began to talk as they moved, complimenting the party.

She knew the steps; dancing was not a problem. She was very talkative, which was.

Still, he caught snatches of conversation.

"…and just disappeared," Matt said.

"I had a lovely night. I told you, I really like boats," Amanda replied.

"I saw that," he heard Matt say.

"Don't you, Mr. Smithson?"

He looked down into the eyes of his dance partner. He hadn't the least idea what she had said.

"Yes," he replied, wincing, praying she wouldn't speak again.

"…the boat…but not me, I take it?" Matt said.

"I had an appointment," Amanda said. "Forgive me?"

"What's not to forgive?" Matt said a little harshly. "You took the tender and left."

Amanda giggled. "Sorry about that. I needed to get back to the club. I was meeting—"

"I'm so glad, Mr. Smithson. I think you'll find I have a lovely home," the blue-haired lady said. He realized she was staring into his eyes, enraptured.

"Excuse me?" Keith asked his partner.

"And I'm glad that you feel the way I do about sex for our generation," she said.

"What?"

Matt and Amanda had rumbaed away. "And since we agree that when a couple of our…maturity feel such an urge, there's nothing wrong with acting on it…we can slip away right now," she said.

"I'm afraid I can't, ma'am. I have a commitment this evening. You'll have to excuse me."

Keith apologized, thanked her for the dance and left as quickly as he could. He wandered out to the edge of the patio. The music was loud, the lights brilliant. He saw one of the cops he'd been introduced to and nodded. The cop nodded in return, then accepted an empty glass from a gray-haired woman who was looking helplessly around for a place to put it down.

It appeared as if she was about to approach him. He turned, circling around, searching for Matt. At last he found him, standing out on the dock, staring out at the water.

He strode down to the dock to join him. "Evening," Matt said, though he didn't look as if he was eager for company.

Screw the disguise. "What the hell was that all about?" Keith demanded.

Matt stared at him. His eyes widened. He swore softly. "What was what about? And what the hell are you doing, looking like Colonel Sanders?"

"Watching," Keith said, eyeing him. "Listening."

Matt flushed a brilliant shade of red. Then he winced. "I—should have told you." His shoulders hunched down. "Lee went barhopping with Gerald. I… I wound up with Amanda."

"And you took her out on the boat?"

Matt hung his head and nodded.

Keith stared out at the water. "Well, did you learn anything?"

"I learned she knows how to spike a drink."

"So, you think she was prowling around?"

"God, I hope not," Matt said. Then he shook his head. "Yes, I think so."

Keith was silent for a minute. He felt Matt shuffle miserably at his side. He looked at him. "Did you say anything to Lee yet?"

"I was too embarrassed to say anything to either of you."

Keith nodded. "Keep it quiet for now."

"Now that you know, I feel like I should tell Lee, as well," he said with self-disgust. "Then I can get my feelings of absolute mortification over with once and for all."

"Let's just see how things progress for the time being, all right?" Keith said.

"You're the boss," Matt muttered.

Keith stared at him and wondered.

Beth's sense of panic grew as she searched for Amber out in front, near the driveway, and couldn't find her. She tried Amber's cell phone and got voice mail. Just when she was about to panic, Ashley called.

"Ashley?"

"I'm here. Amber's phone died, and she wants to talk to you."

"What is it? What's the matter? Are you all right? Where are you?" Beth demanded as soon as Amber got on the line.

"With Ashley."

"Are you all right? Is your father all right?"

"Yes."

"Then what's wrong?"

"Oh, Aunt Beth, you're not going to believe this."

"What?"

"Kim broke up with me."

For several seconds Beth stared at the phone blankly, wondering if she had heard correctly. "I'm sorry, what?"

"It was unbelievable. She was here, having a great night. Then, right before she left, she said that she had to talk to me. We came out here—it was all right, Ashley and Jake were nearby—and she told me that it wasn't me, it was her. But we had to break up."

Beth was silent for several long moments. The conversation was definitely startling. She wanted to shout at Amber that she was worried sick about her life and not petty problems, but she couldn't do that. She tried to focus on what her niece was saying, and that was even more confusing. "Um, was there something more to this relationship than I knew about?" she asked after a moment.

"No," Amber protested, and then laughed, the sound a little hysterical. "I mean, that's what makes it so bad. Have you ever heard of a *friend* breaking up with a *friend?* Like…don't even talk to me in the halls at school? I didn't believe her. I started laughing, at first. But she was serious. I told Ashley after Kim left, and she thinks it's bizarre, too."

Beth could still hear the tears in her niece's voice. "Where's your father?"

"I don't know. Oh, Aunt Beth, I know that this is your big party, but…can…can you come out here? Can I go home with you?"

"I've been staying at Ashley's."

"Can I come to Ashley's?"

"If it's all right with her."

"I can't go home with Dad tonight. I just can't try to explain this to him. Oh, Aunt Beth, I don't believe this. I'm so upset."

"Honey, I'm right here…where are *you?*"

"To the left of the canopy."

"I'm over on the right. I'm coming. We'll find your dad…actually, he's not really happy with me right now. I'll have Jake talk to him. Tell Ashley that we need them to convince your father it's all right." She was walking as she talked. She still felt a slight sense of panic, she was so anxious to see Amber. Then, at last, she saw her. She breathed more easily, convinced she was creating demons where there were none.

She hurried over to the bench where Amber and Ashley were sitting. Ashley was looking lost and helpless. She stared at Beth with an I'm-trying-but-I-don't-really-know-how-to-handle-this-one look.

Amber looked absolutely stricken.

Beth reached down, pulling Amber into her arms. "We'll sort it out."

Amber looked up at her, her cheeks tearstained. She threw her arms around Beth.

"Have you ever heard of such a thing?" she whispered.

"It may be no big deal," Beth assured her. "She could change her mind tomorrow." She was trying to give Amber the attention she needed while looking around suspiciously. The three of them seemed to be alone in the driveway. No, they weren't. She could see the big cop down at the other end of the driveway, lighting a cigarette.

"No, it's serious, it's over," Amber said.

"But, honey, you weren't dating…you were friends. Friends don't have to have just one friend. Even if you're a little off right now…well, it can't be that bad."

"It *is* that bad. It's humiliating."

"You have other friends."

"We have all the same friends."

She squeezed Amber's hand. "We're going to have to see what happens, I guess. Remember, I love you. All my friends think you're the prettiest, most talented creature in the whole world. Honestly, honey, it will be all right. Someday you'll get to realize that most things that happen in high school aren't worth a crock of beans."

"That's true," Ashley told Amber, touching her cheek gently. "You're gorgeous, and you're talented, and we're all going to live our lives vicariously through you."

Amber stared at her, trying to smile, clearly not believing a word.

"Listen, honey, you know that I have to finish up here," Beth said. "I shouldn't be out here now, but—"

Amber let out a snuffle and a low wail. "I'm so sorry, Aunt Beth."

"Don't be sorry. It's all right. I'd ditch the job in two seconds for you, you know that."

"But I wouldn't want you to," Amber said softly.

"I know. So we're going to work this out."

"You go back in," Ashley said to Beth. "I can stay here with Amber for now."

"I just need to hang around the entrance, say goodnight to people," Beth said. "They should start heading out fairly soon."

"Can we go to the locker room, Ashley?" Amber asked. "I've got to fix my face." She was trying to put on a brave smile.

"Absolutely. Meet you inside, Beth," Ashley told her.

Keith headed back in just in time to see Eduardo Shea getting a beer from the same waiter—and handing something to the man. The waiter slipped an envelope into his jacket pocket and looked up. He had a black mustache, pitch-dark hair and appeared to be Latino. But there was something about him…

"Hey," Keith said, striding through the club. The waiter looked at him, then started hurrying through the crowd. "Stop him."

To his disgust, people just stared at him curiously but did nothing. Keith started to run after the man, who disappeared behind one of the bars and a huge arrangement of tropical flowers. Keith ran after him and nearly crashed into a man's back.

It was a different man. He turned, looking frightened. He began to speak in Spanish, protesting. Keith shook his head. "Where did the other guy go?"

The man shook his head blankly.

"The other waiter."

The man turned, pointing. There were waiters everywhere. As Keith stood there, his hands on the waiter's shoulders, Jake strode up to him.

"What is it?"

"Shea just gave one of the waiters an envelope."

"Which one?"

"I don't know. The one who's already half a mile away, probably," Keith said, and swore.

"Where's Shea?" Jake asked.

"Headed back inside."

"Maybe it's time to ask a few questions," Jake said. He went striding through the crowd, and Keith followed. Shea was heading for the exit.

"Mr. Shea?" Jake called.

Shea had definitely planned to make a break for it. It appeared as if he intended to keep going, at first. But then he turned, a brow arched as he waited. "Yes?" he asked.

"Let's speak outside for a moment, shall we, Mr. Shea?" Jake said.

"I'm sorry; I'd rather not. I'm quite exhausted by the evening."

By then Jake had produced his badge. "Police, Mr. Shea. Detective Dilessio, homicide."

"Homicide? Surely our dancing wasn't that bad."

"Very funny, Mr. Shea," Jake informed him.

Other people were beginning to note the conversation.

"Shall we go outside?" Jake suggested.

"I told you, I'm going home."

"I can take you in, you know," Jake said very politely.

"On what grounds?"

"Questioning. I've got twenty-four hours to hold you, sir, before I press charges."

"Charges for what?"

"Conspiracy to commit murder," Jake told him politely.

"We'll go outside—if you insist. You've got nothing on me, and trust me, I'll see you sued for false arrest," Shea threatened.

Jake took him by the elbow, leading him out. As he did, he said pleasantly, "Actually, I believe that a quick phone call to the FBI is all I need to assure myself that I can't be sued for anything, Mr. Shea."

They reached the outside of the club. "Mr. Shea, I believe you own a large amount of property on Mary Street. Would that be correct?"

"It's illegal to own property?" Shea said.

"And you have major interests in several South American boatyards," Jake continued pleasantly.

Shea began to frown. "I don't know what you're suggesting, Detective." He nearly spat out the title.

"You know exactly what he's talking about!" They all started. Maria Lopez had come out of the club, a shawl clutched around her shoulders. "You killed Ted and Molly, you *bastardo*," she accused him.

"Maria, please," Keith said softly.

"I heard you. I heard you on the phone. You were yelling, saying they were not to be cowards, that they were to show up tonight, that they must not go near the studio to ask you for money. I heard you."

As he stood by, Keith looked out toward the parking lot. He saw a man in a tuxedo looking around furtively. "Shit," he swore, and he began to run.

The man turned, saw him and began to run himself.

But this time there was nowhere to disappear, no crowd in which to hide, no mass of tropical flowers to veer around. Keith was down the drive, shouting to the security guard. The "waiter" saw the guard and hesitated a split second too long before veering into the bushes bordering the park.

Too late. Keith tackled him. They both went down hard. The man stared at Keith, who was ready to rip at the man's mustache. Then he realized it wasn't a fake—the man wasn't Brad.

He stared up at Keith, wide-eyed. Caught, he lifted his hands.

By then the security guard had come running. "What's in your pocket?" Keith demanded. He was losing his own mustache. He ripped it off, leaving only his beard. The man's eyes widened.

"Your pocket!" Keith said again, rising, grasping the man's arm, dragging him to his feet. He felt in the man's jacket. There was nothing there. It didn't matter. With panicked eyes, the man pointed at Eduardo Shea.

"That man should be arrested for assault and battery," Shea protested, staring at Keith.

"You're going in for questioning," Jake said firmly. "Feel free to call your lawyer."

One of the plainclothes officers was standing nearby. "I have a car, Detective," he told Dilessio. Jake nodded. "I think this silent gentleman needs to come in, too," he said.

"The man has nothing on him," Shea protested. "By all means bring him in. Let him file charges, too."

Keith suddenly felt an urgent need to get back inside.

"I can take them both in for questioning," Jake told Keith. "But I'm going to need solid evidence."

"You have Maria's testimony—"

"An overheard conversation. I'm going to need more. Unless you can get the feds in on this," he said. He followed the officer escorting Shea.

Keith turned to head back in.

The band was playing on until the bitter end, and there were a few straggling members who intended to stay until that bitter end. Beth had a splitting headache by then. She stood beside the commodore in the main dining room, feeling as if the salsa beat was now smashing into her head.

She was startled when Ashley came up to her, alone.

"Where's Amber?"

"With her dad. Beth, a man will follow you to my place. You have your key, right?"

"What's happened? Did—did they catch Eduardo… doing something? Sandy… Brad?"

"Not really, but… Eduardo Shea is going to be questioned at the station. I think Keith is calling his boss so they can come up with something to hold him on. Anyway, I need to get down to the station, as well. You have one of our friends, the big waiter, on guard duty. I'll be home as soon as I can get there."

"Ashley—"

"Beth, that's all I know right now. When I find out anything else, I'll call you, I promise."

Ashley murmured good-night to Commodore Berry and started out. Beth looked at him, ready to explain that she needed to be with her niece, then decided not to bother. He would know about the entire events of the evening soon enough, she was certain.

She walked outside. Her brother was nowhere to be seen. The party out here had broken up. A waiter was wandering around, picking up fallen glasses. "Ben?" she called.

Her brother didn't answer.

Panic seized her. "Ben!" she called again, louder.

Still no answer. She tried to calm herself. Amber was Ben's child. He might have insisted that they head home. She called her brother's cell phone. No answer. She tried Amber's, then remembered that Ashley had said it was dead.

She cursed, and tried her brother's phone number again. Still no answer.

Then she saw Amber. The girl was striding along the dock. Idly, it seemed at first. She looked up, seemed to see something and started to walk faster. And where the hell was Ben?

"Amber!" Beth called.

Amber apparently didn't hear her. She kept moving

along the dock, her long-legged stride taking her quickly down to the farthest pier. Beth followed. Amber didn't stop at the dock that hugged the shore; she had seen something that had drawn her attention. In a minute she was almost running down the length of the dock that jutted out to the sea.

"Amber!" Beth called again, following as quickly as she could. It was hard to run in her ridiculous heels, and she wondered how on earth her niece was moving so fast. But then, Amber had mile-long legs.

Down the length of the pier, past sailboats, motorboats, big boats and small, Amber at last came to a halt. Beth had been running so desperately in her wake that she couldn't stop when Amber did. She nearly plowed into her niece. "Look," Amber said, pointing. "It's their boat."

Beth stared at the boat. It didn't look familiar at all. It had a fresh coat of paint and was of moderate size, about twenty-six feet. She frowned, looking at her niece. "What are you talking about?"

"That couple who were on Calliope Key—they've decided to clean her up. She looks good, huh?"

Chills raced up and down Beth's spine. Amber was right, she thought, though she couldn't be a hundred percent sure. It looked like the same boat...but different. Fresher. It was the size and make of the beaten-up vessel they'd seen off Calliope Key.

"Amber, we've got to get out of here," she said urgently. As she spoke, she started to turn. Then she screamed as something wet and cold slapped against her ankle. She looked down just as a man sprang up.

It was Brad—or the man she had known as Brad. Bald now, clad in a drenched tux. He had managed to shed his shoes, and the dark toupee he had worn to blend in with the other waiters was askew. He must have seen Amber coming and slipped into the water. Maybe he'd intended to hide. Maybe he'd hidden intending to accost her the second he had seen her look down the dock and start toward his boat. She opened her mouth, ready to scream, determined to protect Amber no matter what.

"Don't do it," Brad said, producing a knife. He lunged toward Beth; in a second, he had pulled her tightly against him, the knife to her throat. She met his eyes. He smiled. They both knew it didn't really matter if she screamed or not—the band would drown out any sound from the docks.

Despite the blade against her throat, Beth ordered, "Amber, run."

"Amber, don't even think about it," Brad said harshly. "Move and she's dead."

"Amber, run!"

"Amber, step aboard the boat," Brad said. "Or she's dead."

"Amber, I could be dead one way or the other." Beth started to protest further, but her words ended in a little gasp when the knife bit into her flesh.

"No, don't hurt her!" Amber sobbed.

Brad just smiled into Beth's eyes as Amber hopped immediately onto the deck.

18

Keith hurried into the foyer and then the dining room. He was certain he looked ridiculous without his fake mustache and beard, but he didn't really give a damn. He saw Commodore Berry, still smiling, still wishing his members a good-night and a safe trip home.

"Where's Beth?" Keith asked the man.

"I don't know. And quite frankly, this is all becoming a bit of a fiasco. Miss Anderson should be here, saying good-night with me. Whatever you people were so certain of tonight certainly didn't happen—"

Keith ignored him. "Where are Ben and Amber?"

"Mr. Henson, I'm afraid I don't know, and I'm still quite busy—and you look a mess."

Keith walked past him, continuing to search the area. His blue-haired dance partner glanced at him and gasped.

Shaking his head, he hurried to the patio, since the closest door led out in that direction. There was no one there, but the door to the men's locker room was ajar. Keith ran toward it and burst in.

He was stunned to see a figure on the floor. As he

hurried over, he heard a groaning sound. He was stunned to discover Ben Anderson, struggling to sit up.

"Ben, what happened?"

Ben shook his head. "I was in here… I don't know. My head. I came in because I'd left my watch in my locker…must have tripped. I was walking toward it… look, it's open." His eyes widened. "Amber… Amber was waiting for me, by the door. I told her to wait—not to wander off. Oh, God, she didn't wait. She wandered. She didn't listen. She didn't realize…wouldn't believe it could be dangerous here!" He stared at Keith. "My daughter! You have to find my daughter."

Keith straightened. "Have you seen your sister?"

"No."

"I'll get you help," Keith said.

Then he was out the door, shouting. He ran into a waiter in the patio and grabbed him by the lapels. "There's a man hurt in there—get help. Get the police."

The waiter paled and turned to do as he'd been told. Keith raced down onto the lawn. A few people were straggling out to spend the night on their boats. He searched through the crowds on each pier.

In the distance, he saw Amber Anderson getting on a boat. He frowned. There was someone else on the boat… and on the dock, but he couldn't tell who.

Amber probably knew most of the people who had boats here, he reminded himself. But even so, why wasn't she waiting for her father, the way she'd undoubtedly been told to do?

Amber's father was lying on the floor of the men's locker room, after being struck by someone, for some reason.

Keith started ripping off his dinner jacket as he raced down the pier.

* * *

"No! Don't listen to him. Get out of here," Beth insisted. She was terrified but trying desperately not to sound it. Her mind was racing. She knew that if she didn't somehow force Amber to escape, they would both be prisoners and probably end up murdered.

"She's already listening to me, honey," Brad said.

It was true. Amber was already on the boat.

At that moment Sandy came out of the cabin. She had stripped down to the white shirt worn by the caterers beneath their tux jackets. Tonight, she was wearing a disheveled red wig, and she'd designed a perfect smattering of freckles over her nose. She wore big, thick-rimmed glasses.

"Brad, what—oh!" she began.

"Get on the boat," Brad told Beth.

"Amber, get off the boat!" she cried.

There were tears in her niece's eyes then. "Aunt Beth, he'll kill you."

"Amber, he'll kill us both!"

"No," Sandy protested suddenly. "Get on the boat. Please, just get on the boat. We've got to get out of here." She turned pleading eyes on Brad. "Brad, don't hurt her. Get on the boat, just get on the boat. Please, nothing will happen to either of you if you'll just get on the boat. Brad?" she implored.

"What the hell do you want me to do? They'll both go screaming for help. We've got to get out of here now—with them aboard," Brad replied roughly. "Get the lines, kid," he said, addressing Amber. "I've seen your dad's boat—I'm sure you know what you're doing. I don't want to hurt your aunt—Sandy there likes her a whole lot. But this is a pretty desperate situation you've caused for us. Tell your aunt to get her pretty rump on the boat so I don't have to kill her, and help us get out of here!"

Beth wasn't even sure that Brad cut her on purpose, but the knife moved against her throat, and she choked out a small sound of pain.

Amber jumped like a rabbit and did as she'd been told. Sandy stepped up to the rail as Brad prodded Beth forward, forcing her to either step or fall onto the deck.

Once they were all on board, he grabbed Beth by the hair, dragging her down to the small cabin. "If you hurt Amber in any way, I swear I'll kill you," she said, her voice shaking despite the bravado of the words. She didn't consider herself a particularly brave person, but she had discovered a deep-seated maternal instinct. She would fight to her last breath for her niece.

Keith got close enough to see the knife at Beth's throat before the boat headed out. He swore, weighing his options. If cornered, they might kill one of their hostages, as a warning to back off.

He reached for his cell phone; it was gone. He'd lost it in the scuffle out front. Swearing silently beneath his breath, he started to move again, kicking off his shoes as he ran to the end of the pier, then dived into the water. He surfaced, then paused briefly to reconnoiter.

The boat was just moving within the speed limit of the law and following good boating etiquette. They were obviously trying not to be noticed. That was his first piece of luck. He swam hard.

His second piece of luck came when he realized that they'd been in a hurry and careless of the lines. One was trailing in the water. He caught hold of it just as the boat began to increase its speed. He strained to pull himself up closer, fighting to clear the motor. As the boat began to scud across the water, he held on for dear life.

"Tie her up!" Brad shouted to Sandy.

"You are not going to—" Beth began. She stopped. The knife again. She swallowed hard. "I'll do anything if you'll just let her go," she said quietly.

"Sandy, quit screwing around. Tie the kid up," Brad insisted.

"No!" Amber shrieked.

"Shut up, kid, or I *will* kill your aunt."

Beth couldn't see what was happening, but she was surprised when the knife didn't bite into her flesh but instead eased away from her. "Stop," Brad hissed to her. "I don't want to hurt you *or* the kid."

"What makes us any different?" she asked.

"We haven't killed anyone," he said harshly. "Yet."

He sounded honest. Oddly, disturbingly honest. She held still. His hold eased again.

She heard Amber whimpering, but she didn't dare turn to look. "I swear, let her go and I'll help you do anything."

Sandy came into the cabin. "Is the kid tied up?" Brad demanded.

"Yes."

"Okay, now this one."

"Brad, this is insane. Why did we take them?"

"Are you nuts? They'd have had the cops after us in two minutes. They know, Sandy. That bastard was a liar."

"I don't know anything," Beth said. It was a lie—and yet, paradoxically, also the truth.

"You didn't get the envelope?" Sandy demanded.

"Hell, yes, I got the envelope. And if we're caught, so help me God, that bastard Eduardo is going down, too. He said the money would pass from hand to hand. In the end, some fool stuffed it into the pocket of the kid's father's jacket by accident. Can you believe that? I had to cream him to get it and get out. You know what's in the envelope?" he demanded of Sandy. "Do you want to know? Go ahead, look inside."

Beth wasn't tied up, and Brad was paying attention to Sandy. Beth tried to figure out how she could get the knife.

"Look in the envelope!" Brad raged.

Sandy did, then cried out in dismay, staring at Brad in disbelief.

He wasn't looking at Beth. She twisted, biting his arm as hard as she could. He dropped the knife with a loud scream. She shoved a knee into his groin, and he screamed again, doubling over in pain. Beth turned to run to Amber.

But Sandy was already there, and she had grabbed a frying pan. It cracked against Beth's skull, and she went down.

Lee had just brought the tender back to their vessel when he saw one of the little boats from the yacht club leaving, something trailing in the water behind it. He turned and hurried down to the cabin. "Matt? Matt, you back yet?"

He paused, stunned. Matt was back. But he wasn't alone. "What the hell are you doing here?" he demanded of their visitor.

With tremendous effort, Keith made it over the side. Amber's eyes were wide as she watched him appear.

Emerging from the surf and the darkness, he must have been a frightening sight. She looked as if she was about to scream, but he brought his finger to his lips to silence her and hurried to her side. She was tied up, her Summer Sizzler finery in disarray.

He worked hurriedly at the ropes Sandy had tied around her wrists and ankles. "Where are they?" he mouthed.

"In the cabin."

Keith judged the distance to the shore. It was becoming greater every minute. "Can you swim that?" he asked her.

She nodded. "But Aunt Beth—"

"I'm here, and we'll have a better chance of saving ourselves without worrying about you. There's a life jacket. Wear it. You're not afraid? You've got to get to shore and get help. From Jake, from the real cops, no one else, okay? Find Jake and tell him to get a hold of Mike. He'll know what you mean. They'll get everything on the water out after these guys. You can make it? You're sure? We're a half a mile out in night waters."

"I can make it," Amber swore tearfully.

"Then get out of here. Now."

He grabbed one of the life jackets and handed it to Amber. Looking down into the cabin he saw no movement.

That worried him.

"Go!" he told Amber.

She turned back once, her eyes tearing up.

"Honey, go. Get help."

She nodded. Apparently aware of the need for quiet, she slipped into the water. He afforded himself a split second to curse the fact that he'd sent a kid into the water at night, a half mile from shore. But if anyone could do it, it was Amber Anderson, he was certain. He turned, hunched down.

Beth was in the cabin.

And the cabin was far too quiet.

Beth awoke feeling a thudding pain in her temple.

Memory flashed back. She remembered Sandy wielding the frying pan. She laughed inwardly at the irony.

She had eluded a man with a big knife, then been bested by a woman with a frying pan. She opened her eyes slowly, aware that she was still at sea and moving quickly. She was on a bunk.

She tried to move. Her hands were tied. She began working at the ropes with her teeth, then froze when she heard a racket topside.

"What the hell is that?" she heard Brad cry out.

"The kid?" Sandy suggested.

"You stay here and mind the helm. I'll go see," Brad said.

Then there was nothing. Beth remained dead still, listening in terror.

Suddenly there was a thump.

A moment later Sandy came rushing into the cabin where Beth lay. She reached into a drawer, drawing out a gun. Smith & Wesson .38—yes, the same gun Ben kept. The woman sidled over to the bunk and knelt down beside Beth, putting the muzzle against Beth's temple.

Beth swallowed, feeling the cold bite of the metal, imagining the bullet ripping through her head.

Amber? What had happened on deck? What about Amber?

After a while Sandy grew restless, tired of waiting.

She stepped to the small doorway to the cabin, ducking. "Brad?"

Nothing. Sandy stepped out, but a second later she was backing into the cabin again. Beyond her, Beth could see that someone else was aboard the boat.

Her eyes widened. Keith. Soaked and dragging Brad by the collar.

"Brad!" Sandy cried out.

"I don't want to kill him," Keith said. "So you'll give me the gun, Sandy, and then you'll turn this boat around."

Again the gun was pressed to Beth's temple. She saw Keith's lips tighten, his flesh take on a paler hue. But he held his ground. "Trust me. You shoot her, I'll snap his neck. I can do it, and I'm pretty sure you know it."

"I can shoot you and then her!" Sandy said, turning the gun on Keith.

"Do you really have the nerve?" he asked her. "And you know," he said, sparing a lightning glance at Beth, "Amber is on her way home."

"She'll drown."

"I don't think so. She's a strong swimmer. And she has a life vest."

Beth's heart took flight. Amber *would* make it. She was a survivor. She would get help. Adrenaline burst through her. She gritted her teeth and wrenched at the ties binding her wrists. She felt a surge of sheer joy and power as her arm swung free, catching Sandy right across the jaw. The other woman gasped.

And the gun went off.

"You are going to explain this, aren't you?" Lee demanded. They were already in pursuit of the smaller boat, but they were keeping their distance. Lee didn't want to alert them to the fact that they were being followed.

"Honestly, we were just talking," Amanda said, giving Lee her sweetest smile.

Matt was up, restless. "There's got to be more we can do," he murmured.

"You want to take a chance on spooking them, so they kill Keith and whoever else they've got?" Lee demanded hotly.

Matt shook his head.

Lee looked at Amanda. "I'm really sorry, but you're here for the duration."

"I'm fine," she assured him, blue eyes excited. "Where do you think we're heading?"

Matt spun around, looked at Lee. "I think I know where we're going," he said. "The island."

Lee glanced at their headings. "Seems like a damn good guess to me," he said.

The bullet ricocheted wildly, hitting the brass lamp, a metal mirror backing and a bedside-lamp mounting, rather than thudding into the wood.

Then Keith let out an oath and, one hand to his temple, sank to the floor.

For a moment both Sandy and Beth were dead silent. The gun had fallen to the floor, forgotten.

"Oh, God!" Sandy cried out, rising.

To Beth's amazement, she raced over to Keith. Brad remained groaning on the floor while Sandy grabbed a towel, dabbing at Keith's head. She stared at Beth. "You might have killed him!"

Beth sprang to her feet, her heart in her throat. She

pushed Sandy aside, falling to her knees beside Keith. He wasn't dead; he was breathing. His heart was beating. The blood...

Sandy dabbed at the wound. "Give that to me," Beth said. Taking the towel, she applied pressure to Keith's temple. She sensed movement around her, but she paid no attention, determined to stop the flow of blood.

Keith's eyes opened. One green contact was still in; the other had been lost somewhere. He stared blankly at her, dazed, and groaned. "What the hell happened?" he demanded. Relief filled Beth. At least he was still alive. His eyes closed. "Oh, yes. I remember. Bullet... out of nowhere."

"Sandy, can I have some water?" Beth asked.

A wet towel was stuffed into her hand. She washed the blood away and was relieved to see that he only had a surface wound. She looked around. The bullet had come to rest in the wood of the door frame.

"Can you sit up?" she asked.

Groaning again, he did so. Then he looked up. Beth did the same, then gasped softly, backing up against the wall. Brad was back on his feet, and he had retrieved the gun she had so stupidly forgotten.

"Brad..." Sandy said anxiously.

It was all...out of focus, Beth determined. In her struggle to help, she had nearly killed Keith. Sandy, who'd been acting like a cold-blooded killer, had been terrified that Beth might have killed the man she'd been threatening just seconds before. And Brad...

Brad looked really angry.

"Brad," Sandy said.

"What?" he snapped. "She bit a hole in my arm and nearly broke my Mr. Jolly. This asshole gave me a black eye and a knot on the head. And you want me to be nice?"

"They think we're going to kill them," Sandy said, fighting on their side, it seemed to Beth.

"I'd like to!" Brad muttered.

Keith was staring at them, a deep frown furrowing his features. A trickle of blood ran down his face. "What do you intend to do with us?" he demanded.

"Just hold you—until we get our money," Sandy said.

"Will you kill us then, the way you did the others?" Beth demanded.

Brad looked furious. "We didn't kill anyone! We take a few boats. We get them down to South America. And we get paid. That's all."

"You stole the Monocos' boat. And neither Ted nor Molly has been seen since."

Sandy was impatient. "They weren't anywhere near the boat. Brad and I went aboard, and they weren't even there. We took the boat, yes. We didn't kill them."

Keith studied her. "Where's your money?"

"Don't tell him," Brad snapped.

"What difference does it make? They're going to know anyway." She shook her head. "That bastard Eduardo kept telling us we could get it in Miami. But he's paranoid that he'll be seen. Tonight it was supposed to be in an envelope. And do you know what he sent us? Again? A damn note saying the money is in the clearing on the island. He's such an asshole."

"So that's what you were looking for," Beth whispered.

Keith, at her side, was silent, still studying the pair.

"Please, quit fighting. When we've got the money,

we're leaving, period. And we'll let you go," Sandy pleaded.

"Tie them up, Sandy. And do a better job this time, please," Brad said wearily.

He turned the gun on Beth, smiling, but he addressed his words to Keith. "Let Sandy tie you up good and tight. Or else I won't kill Miss Anderson, I'll just see that she has a few shattered bones. How would that be?"

Beth winced.

"Get up," Brad told Keith. "Hands behind your back."

Keith obliged. Sandy shoved him toward the bunk. "Get in." She giggled. "It's actually kind of sweet. You can have your girlfriend just as soon as she's tied up, too."

A few minutes later, both securely tied—their bonds approved by Brad—they lay on the bunk, side by side, alone in the dark, while the little boat shot through the water.

For a moment they were silent. Then Beth exhaled. "I'm so sorry."

"Hey…you were trying to save both our lives," he said.

"But…in a way, I shot you."

"Yes, you did," he mused. "So much for my attempt to rescue the woman I'm falling in love with."

She was silent. "What constitutes love in your book?" she whispered.

"Wanting to spend my life with you, every waking moment, you know, that kind of thing. The bullet-in-the-head thing…well, I'd just as soon not have that happen too often."

Tears sprang to her eyes suddenly. They might be about to die. She had to know.

"What about your work?"

"I like my work. Usually it involves saving lives," he said a little bitterly.

"But you were willing to do almost anything in this current…search."

She could sense him slowly smiling in the darkness. "Amanda?" he said. He turned to her. She felt the warmth of his whisper against her face. "I never slept with her. I wouldn't have slept with her. I spent time with her, talked to her—she and her family were on the island."

She inhaled. "If we survive…"

"You're going to owe me for this one."

"Do you think…could they be telling the truth? That they didn't kill anyone?"

"Let's hope so," Keith said softly. "Turn around."

She did so and felt him edging down her back. "What are you doing?" she demanded.

"Sorry, nothing erotic. I'm pretty good with my teeth, so I'm working on the knots."

She had no idea how far he had gotten when, what seemed like an eternity later, she felt the boat begin to slow.

"We must be at the island!" she told him.

"Turn around and hold still," he warned her.

The door to the cabin opened. The light was turned on again. They both winced against it. "Get up and behave," Sandy said. "We're taking you ashore. If you're good, we'll leave you alive and well on the island. Maybe we'll even leave you a little water. But move now. We've got to hurry."

Keith gave a pretense of struggling to his feet, giving Beth time to grasp her wrist bonds with her fingers, so no one would suspect she was free. She rose carefully, face forward, and stood in front of Keith. Sandy led them past Brad, who was in the main cabin, his gun on them.

They got into the tender, carefully.

Sandy took the gun. Brad rowed. They were all silent. Then Sandy said, "There's a boat coming…a big one, Brad."

"Nice? You think we can take her?" he asked.

"I think we need to find the money fast and get the hell out of here!" Sandy said.

They beached. Awkwardly, Keith and Beth got out. Brad turned on a flashlight. The moon was high in the sky, but not bright enough to light the interior.

"Let's move," Brad said.

"The boat is still coming. Hurry," Sandy urged.

They started walking. Apparently Keith wasn't moving fast enough, because Brad prodded him forward.

"Eduardo Shea is under arrest, you know," Keith said over his shoulder.

"Good. I hope he rots."

"The police are looking for you, along with the FBI."

"We have plenty of places to go in South America," Brad assured him. "Move."

They reached the center of the island. Sandy ran ahead and started kicking palm fronds around. "Do you think the bastard stiffed us?" she wailed in dismay. "Help me, Brad. We've got to hurry."

Brad swore and headed across the clearing. "Stop running around like a headless chicken. Organize what you're doing. I'll come from the east, you start from the west."

In a minute the two of them were intent on their quest.

Beth stared at Keith. He nodded to her, then inclined his head toward the west. She frowned, then understood.

Someone else was coming. Brad and Sandy were so intent on their quest that they hadn't heard the stealthy movement through the brush.

"Now," Keith mouthed, and he and Beth moved furtively, heading toward the barely discernible trail through the western foliage. Then they began to run.

"Hey!" Sandy shouted.

There was the sound of a gunshot. A bullet whizzed by Beth's head, so close that she felt the rush.

Brad hadn't been the one to fire, though. The bullet had come from the other direction. Beth kept running, tearing into the brush.

"Get down!" Keith warned her.

Brad screamed in agony after a second bullet burst loudly in the night. Sandy let out a horrible howling sound.

"What the hell are you doing?" someone shouted.

In the brush, blind, Beth nearly collided with Keith. Her hands were free, though, and she steadied herself, then started working on the ties at his wrists. She fell to her knees, tugging at the ropes, her heart thundering as she listened to the events in the clearing, far too close behind them.

She glanced up. She could see that Keith was tense, listening, and she suddenly realized that the man who had spoken was Matt Albright.

"Where are they?" another voice demanded.

Sandy sounded hysterical. "They're alive, I swear. You shot him! You shot Brad. My God, you've killed him!"

"Where are they?" Lee repeated. Then Sandy screamed.

Beth didn't want to think about what had happened to her.

"Dammit, Lee," Matt protested again.

"They took Keith, Beth and the girl," Lee said.

"They ran," Sandy cried, barely coherent. "They ran…except the girl… Keith got her off the boat. I don't know how."

"You're lying."

"I'm not."

"Keith?" Lee shouted. "Where the hell are you?"

Beth was certain he would step forward. He didn't. Instead, he looked down at her and shook his head. "No," he mouthed in the moonlight.

They crept closer, close enough to see what was happening in the clearing.

"Lee?" Matt said.

Lee spun on him suddenly. Raised the gun.

"What are you doing?" Matt asked, stunned.

The direction of the muzzle moved. Lowered onto Amanda Mason. "You just had to bring her on the boat, didn't you, Matt? Now I've got to kill her, too, and Hank isn't going to like it. I think it better look as if you killed her."

Beth's eyes widened in disbelief.

It was then that Keith moved. Like a shot in the dark, he catapulted himself out of the trees, slamming against Lee's back before the man could turn.

The two of them went down. Beth saw the gun go flying.

The fight was bitter. She saw Matt running to get in

the midst of it. She saw the other two men rolling, fists flying viciously.

Beth rose, hurrying to the edge of the clearing to hide in the thick foliage. Just as she got there, Keith emerged victorious, straddling Lee Gomez.

But then another shot blazed through the night. Hank Mason came striding through the clearing, followed by Roger. Hank strode closer, aiming the gun at Keith's chest. Keith was breathing hard, his features stony. "Get up," Hank ordered crisply. He looked around. Brad lay dead. Sandy was bloodied and still sobbing silently. "Get up."

"Yeah, I'll get up. But I wouldn't trust him anymore. He was going to kill Amanda," Keith said.

"Like hell," Hank said.

"Daddy!" Amanda cried, seeing Roger. She raced over to him, and Roger stopped, uncertain. "What the hell is she doing here?" he demanded.

Lee stared up at Keith venomously. "She was on the boat," he said. "I had no intention of killing your daughter, Roger. Now get him off me!"

Hank didn't seem to give a damn about his cousin. He coldly eyed Keith, who rose slowly. Lee rose, as well, swinging a hard punch, belting Keith squarely in the midriff.

"Hey!" Amanda protested. "Dad, what are you doing here?"

"What are *you* doing here?" Roger demanded. He turned to Lee. "Well?"

"I saw Sandy and Brad taking off with our very own Jacques Cousteau here," Lee said, wiping blood from his mouth. "It seemed like the opportune time to do away with him and let the sea thieves take the rap. Should have been perfect."

"I still don't get it," Amanda said plaintively.

"Allow me to explain, Amanda," Keith said. "Brad and Sandy were working for Eduardo Shea, who had something more than dancing going on. He led them to the Monocos' boat, but they didn't kill Ted and Molly. And they didn't kill a good friend of mine, a great kid named Brandon. Nor did they kill a young diver who stumbled on something here recently. Brad didn't even know why those people died. But your father, Lee and Hank do. Hey, is Gerald in on this?"

"What do you care? You're a dead man," Lee told him.

"So humor me," Keith said.

"No, Gerald just comes around sometimes, and since he's innocent, he makes us all look good," Hank said.

Amanda gasped, staring at her father. "You...you pushed me into sleeping with Matt and exploring the boat because..."

"Your father is a pimp, Amanda," Keith said softly.

Roger stared at him coldly. "And you're a dead man. Hank, do it."

"Daddy!" Amanda cried in astonishment.

"Wait," Lee commanded sharply. "Beth Anderson is out there somewhere." He gritted his teeth. "That bitch stumbled on good old Ted's skull. I'd gotten rid of the rest of the rotting corpses when they washed ashore, but I hadn't been able to find that damn skull." He looked at Keith, shaking his head. "And that got you going, didn't it?"

"Actually, Mike has been suspicious for quite a while. After all, someone knew where Brandon was and killed him. It was you, you sorry bastard. You killed that great kid, just so you and your buddies could have the treasure all for yourselves."

Flat in the palm fronds now, lying dead still, Beth held her breath.

"Are you sure you know where to find it now?" Roger asked suddenly. He pointed at Keith. "He's the one who—"

"Found a coin. I know," Lee snapped. "I can take it from there."

"He can't dive worth shit," Keith said. Beth gazed across the clearing as Lee took another swing at Keith. Matt had been backing up, unnoticed. Now he saw her. He looked ill. He was unarmed, she knew, and he was stunned by the recent events.

Lee's gun was just inches away. She stretched her fingers, her arms, silently, desperately.

"I'm going to enjoy killing you," Lee told Keith.

"We need to find Beth Anderson," Roger reminded him.

"And you think he's going to go get her for us?" Lee mocked.

Hank took aim. But Keith was lightning fast. He grabbed Lee and thrust the man in front of him just before the bullet exploded.

In the confusion, Beth reached for Lee's gun. Matt raced forward, tackling Roger Mason's legs as the man fired off a round. Roger spun, noticing Beth, and tried to take aim again.

"No, Daddy!" Amanda cried, reaching for her father's arm.

Her action gave Beth time to grab the gun. As Keith thrust Lee's now-dead body forward, hard, at Hank

Mason, Beth fired at last. It was a big gun, heavy; she didn't even know what it was, and she was amazed that she could aim it. The recoil sent her sprawling into the bushes.

But she caught Hank in the arm.

He howled, and his gun flew. In a split second, Keith was on him. Moments later, it was over.

Suddenly there was silence. Dead silence. The smell of gunpowder filled the air. Then they heard Sandy, sobbing softly once again. Lee Gomez and Brad were dead. Hank was unconscious, and even Roger was dazed. Amanda began to cry loudly at her father's side.

Matt was the first one to speak. "Imagine. Amanda just came aboard to apologize, to tell me she thought she was really in love at last. With Ben Anderson."

"Beth!" Unbelievably, as if on cue, Beth heard her brother shouting her name.

Her knees gave out, and she sank to the ground just as the Coast Guard came bursting into the clearing, Ben running frantically in their wake, along with a tall, hard-bitten man in a camouflage suit, shouting orders.

Her brother reached her. She looked at him. "Amber?"

He smiled, but his smile faded as he looked around, then fell to his knees at her side. "She said you saved her life. You and Keith." Ben dragged her into his arms. She hugged him tightly, then drew away. "Brad said that… that…he knocked you out."

"I'm fine."

They both looked over at Brad and Sandy. She was keening softly, her eyes glazed.

Amanda was hovering over her father.

"Oh, God," Ben said.

"She was innocent. She helped save our lives," Beth

said. Ben stared at her blankly. She smiled. "She's going to need a lot of help."

"I already have some help," she whispered. Ben nodded, stood and went over to Amanda. Beth smiled, feeling the hand that fell on her shoulder. She was drawn up, and strong arms came around her.

"We made it," he said simply.

South Florida had seen plenty of bizarre scandals and mysteries, and far too many stories of greed and murder. But this one dominated the media for weeks, mainly because there was more to it than Beth had known the night she nearly died because of it.

Far more than Spanish gold had been at stake. Documents recently given to the American government by the German government told a tale she had never expected.

The crew of a German U-boat had taken refuge on Calliope Key when their vessel had begun to fail far closer to the American coastline than the government had wanted the public to know at the time.

The ship had carried the makings of a small atomic bomb, but they hadn't had all the time they'd needed to assemble it. Knowing that they were in danger of being taken by the Americans, the captain had ordered the components hidden before they attempted their escape.

Two men had been forgotten on the island. They had thought themselves dead, marooned. But their comrades had been blown up while heading north, and they had been rescued by British sailors. One of them had written a report for the German government, which had lain long forgotten in a secret vault. When it had been recently brought to light and given to the U.S., the American government hadn't known if it was a hoax or a strange and terrible truth. And Rescue had been brought in.

It was terrifying to know that a man like Lee Gomez had teamed up with a financier like Roger Mason to heist such a discovery. There was no telling where the bomb might have ended up, since their only concern had been the highest bidder.

A week after the rescue, Keith and Beth were finally back together again. She'd spent days trying to tell everything to the satisfaction of the officers with the various different agencies questioning her. It had been worse for Keith, since he'd had to file reports in any number of places.

At first, when she saw him, Beth had no desire to speak. She greeted him at her door. Whispered hello, dragged him in.

They didn't actually talk for hours. When they did, she asked him at last, "So what will happen now? Now that the world knows *La Doña* is out there, and that there's more on her than gold?"

He was silent for a moment, meeting her eyes. "I found the location."

"When?"

"Before the party. I knew that someone in our group was on someone else's payroll. Remember that I mentioned Brandon? He was like a kid brother to me. It was the worst waste in the world that he was murdered." He shook his head. "I kept making the connection to Eduardo Shea, but he was small time. The Masons were using him, though, getting information. Anyway, I reported exactly what I found to Mike, with all the coordinates. Lee and Matt knew I'd discovered a coin, but they didn't know that I'd figured out why we couldn't find the remains of the ship."

"And why couldn't you?"

He smiled. "Hide in plain sight," he said. "The ship had become the reef. Once you figured that out, you could begin to trace her timbers—and the cargo hold. I won't be going down on that particular dive anymore. They'll put other guys on it. I have some time off."

"I'm not sure if I do or not," she said ruefully.

He rolled over, staring at her. "Quit."

"Just like that?"

"If they can't give you time off for a wedding and a honeymoon, quit."

She fell into his arms again, smiling. "For you? Just like that," she whispered.

She was incredibly grateful to be alive. And so was Amber. But being grateful didn't always make living all that easy.

Despite surviving "Sail Into Terror!" as the newspapers had dubbed the event, Amber still had a serious dilemma.

"I think he's really falling in love with her," she told Beth, horrified.

"Well, she really did come through for us. She made a move against her own father. She helped save our lives."

"I'm trying not to hate her," Amber told her. "I mean, she might be my stepmother."

"You both have a lot of wounds to get over. But I think she's actually in love with your father and ready to change her ways. And you can always spend lots of time with Keith and me."

"I *am* in the wedding, right?"

"You bet."

The wedding fell in the middle of October, on a perfect fall day. The sun was brilliant, but the air didn't have the touch of fire that made the summer months so hot.

Beth couldn't have imagined anything more perfect, couldn't have imagined feeling a greater happiness.

They were married at the club, in a field of exquisite flowers. Everything was gorgeous.

After all, she did know how to plan a good party.

She was insanely in love with her husband, and when he looked at her, she still trembled, knowing he felt the same. They were married as the sun set in the western sky, surrounded by family and friends.

And when the champagne had been sipped, the toasts raised and the last of their excited hugs goodbye given out...

They chose not to sail into the sunset.

They honeymooned in Vermont.

* * * * *

BELOW THE SURFACE

Karen Harper

As ever, to my greatest supporter, Don

1

When Briana Devon surfaced, her boat was gone. Something—besides the fact that the gulf had gone rough since she'd begun her dive—was terribly wrong.

She struggled to keep her underwater camera and strobe from being ripped away by the waves. Her tethered plastic slate with its latex rubber pencil she used to make notes underwater smacked her face; she thrust it behind her.

She kept the regulator in her mouth, clenched between her teeth. Still sucking in the air from her tank, she heard the hiss of her more rapid breathing mingled with the howl of the increasing wind. Since she was fairly low on air, her single tank yanked back and forth on her BC, the vest-style buoyancy compensator that supported her in the water.

This was impossible! Had she come up in the wrong place? No, the pelican float she'd deployed bobbed wildly, riding the waves. She was where she meant to be, but where was Daria and their dive boat? And how fast the distant storm had come up.

Holding on to her gear and using her flippers, she spun in a circle. Maybe the *Mermaids II* was just blurred by the darkening horizon. No, all she saw were clumps of clouds, not even other boats, with that storm coming in much faster than the weatherman had predicted. But Daria would never have left her out here.

Despite being a veteran diver, panic pulsed through Briana for herself and her sister. Bree and Daria Devon were not only twin sisters but had been best friends since they could remember.

Bree put more air in her BC to keep afloat and fought to calm herself. After all, she'd been diving for twenty of her twenty-eight years and swimming these waters even longer. Every week, she and Daria dived the artificial reef made by the wreck of an old trading boat to check on the growth of pollutant-endangered sea grass and marine life. The grass was a bellwether for the health of the gulf waters in general. It had all been routine until now.

Bree had not noticed whether the anchor had been pulled up. She'd only been intent on doing her work well and quickly. Just take the photos, make the notes, get proof. The results were bad news that was going to upset a lot of powerful people. She'd only come up early because visibility was lessening, and that meant the waves were kicking up. But she'd never imagined this churning, gray sea and gathering storm.

The twins had always buddy-dived unless they were just scraping barnacles off hulls at the marina, but there were two reasons Daria hadn't made the dive with her today. She'd suddenly developed a bad toothache, which would have made the underwater pressure excruciating for her. And someone had to stay with their dive boat: Daria had given Manny, their only employee at their search-and-salvage shop, the afternoon off since he'd been having so much trouble with his daughter. Actually, Daria hadn't been diving much this past month anyway, since she'd been so busy concentrating on her accounting class.

Bree's arms ached from trying to hang on to her camera and strobe in the increasing turbulence. She had never feared this vast stretch of water, only respected it, but now terror immobilized her. Alone. Abandoned? She should probably start swimming in, but she was over four miles out and she'd have to ditch her precious gear. She should have taken it as a bad sign when she saw that bull shark cruising past the reef instead of the usual resident grouper. Bulls became disturbed whenever the water was riled, and they were known to attack humans. How many times had she warned someone not to swim alone or far from shore, and to avoid splashing?

Bree had a whistle to summon help, but there was no one in range to hear it. She could set off her strobe to try to attract attention, but holding it above the waves would wear her out. Reluctantly she let her strobe lights and camera drop, hoping they would snag somewhere near the wreck and she—they—could retrieve them later. The camera was worth big bucks; they'd scraped a lot of barnacles off yachts to buy it.

The twins' co-owned marine search-and-salvage shop had been struggling, but things were on the upswing lately. They did everything from underwater surveys to hull maintenance to retrieval of lost items or sunken vessels. It could be dirty, hard, even dangerous work, but they both loved it. They knew what was below the surface of the gulf off southwest Florida almost as well as they knew each other.

It had been a surprise and a thrill when the prestigious Clear the Gulf Commission had hired them—not their larger rival across the bay—to record the difficult comeback of off-the-coast marine life under siege from toxic runoff. The whole local ecosystem was being poisoned by fertilizers from sugarcane fields, golf course fairways, and polluted water releases from just too many people.

To save her strength, Bree decided to dive again and get as far as she could underwater before she'd have to ditch her tanks and weight belt to swim in. Though she saw no watercraft, perhaps one would be heading for safe harbor and she could hail it. She upended and kicked down until the turbulence seemed to lessen.

The Gulf of Mexico, off Naples, Marco Island and Turtle Bay, was a shallow body of water, at least compared to the Atlantic. The bottom was fairly flat for a long way out: after an initial drop-off, it deepened about two feet per mile and was broken only by small ledges and man-made reefs. But because the depth was fairly shallow, the gulf could get violent fast. It was the underwater storm of sand and silt that had tipped her off to the one above. Though she did a lot of close-up, well-lit macrophotography, even that was looking grainy today.

Most people—especially tourist divers from "the frozen North," as their dive friends called it—thought the water off Naples was not great dive territory. But the twins had always loved it more than the glamour spots of the Keys or even the Caribbean. Fifteen feet of visibility in this part of the world was a great disappointment to some, but in the summers, the sea often went flat and turbulence was minimal. This part of the gulf was not crowded with divers, so it seemed pristine, with an abundance of wildlife like grouper, tarpon, rays, sea turtles, beautiful shells and, unfortunately at times, sharks. They also loved the gulf because that's where they'd learned to dive. It seemed so untouched, with the exception of the fact the reefs were man-made. But then, the natural coral reefs on the other coast were as endangered as the sea life would soon be here, if their project didn't help turn things around.

As she swam toward shore, roiling sand and silt and the thickening clouds made it too dark for her to be certain in what direction she was heading. Mostly, she went with the surge of the waves, which should take her in. Unfortunately, the tide was flowing out and the wind was fighting that, churning the water into a soupy maelstrom. She couldn't even read the luminous dial of the compass dive watch Daria had given her for their birthday last month. Daria and the boat… She could not imagine what might have happened, why her sister would desert her during a dive.

Surely nothing could have capsized *Mermaids II,* not a twenty-four-foot skiff with a flat bottom. There was no so-called Bermuda Triangle on this side of Florida. Yacht pirates and drug dealers wouldn't want a slow diver's boat. Smugglers had begun to bring in desperate refugees fleeing Cuba, and boats involved in the horrible human trafficking trade imported poverty-stricken Guatemalan women as domestic drudges or even sex slaves on both sides of the state. But those boats sneaked in at night to avoid being spotted or caught. Even if Daria had become ill, she wouldn't leave her. Nothing made sense.

In the murky water Bree could not read her air-pressure gauge, but she could feel the air through her mouthpiece becoming more difficult to breathe. Realizing her air was quickly running out, she surfaced. The waves were four feet now; she rode them up, down, sliding with their strength. It had started to rain. Which way was the shore?

She accidentally took in a mouthful of water, then spit it out. Swallowing salt water always made her nauseous. She was getting sick to her stomach anyway, furious and fearful. Dad had always said never to let your emotions rule your head, not when diving. In a way, after Mother died, that had become his credo for life. Just keep busy, so busy you don't have time for feelings, suffocating, desperate, drowning feelings...

Bree dropped her weight belt, ditched her tank with the quick-release straps and began breathing through her snorkel. The tank went under with a loud gurgle. She felt lighter—better, she tried to buck herself up. She could make it in. Keewadin Island, long and narrow, must be ahead somewhere, maybe three miles or so. Thank God, she hadn't been at some of the more distant dive sites like Black Hole Sink or Naples Ledges, which were around thirty miles out.

She tried to convince herself that this was only the usual, quick afternoon summer storm, which would pepper the gulf, bathe the Everglades, then depart to leave a warm, humid evening. When would this summer weather break? Was she going to break?

Bree tried not to swallow water. Swimming was suddenly exhausting; despite her desperation to get ashore, she had to pace herself more. She slowed her strokes and kicks toward what she was certain must be land.

Stroke, stroke, stroke, breathe. Despite the outgoing

tide, she was certain the waves must be pushing her along. But it was so far in. Hard to get good breaths. And then she heard it, the thing she feared most.

Thunder rumbling, coming. And that meant lightning.

Oh, no. Oh, no. Just last week, she had sat on their veranda at Turtle Bay and watched a storm like this. Forks of lightning had stabbed the gulf and then the bay just beyond the docks, coming closer, closer. As usual, the power had gone off for a while, but the twins weren't air-conditioner addicts like their older sister. Amelia almost never opened her windows, even in good weather. That would make her house dusty. Her poor kids, whom she kept so clean, could use a little dust and dirt.

Bree's muscles began to burn. She could hear Dad's voice telling her and Daria, "When in doubt, get out." Out, she wanted out. She wanted to be on the *Mermaids II* with Daria. She wanted to be home, safe and dry. She loved the water, loved the gulf, but not out here alone, tiring, so exhausted. *Lord, please keep me safe. Daria, too. What happened? Daria, where are you?*

A wave took one of her fins, and she had to kick the other off to avoid swimming askew. On, on, pull, pull, breathe, flee the thunder and lightning coming closer. She was starting to feel in the zone, like when she jogged several miles, but she was getting light-headed, dizzy, too.

The first distinct crack of lightning struck so close she flinched and shrieked into the mouthpiece of her snorkel. And then she saw another reason to scream. A big bull shark was swimming with her.

Cole DeRoca was shocked by how fast the storm came up. Usually, you could set your watch by the afternoon storms off the gulf, but this one was early, fierce and dangerous. Though his custom-made sloop was all wood, he wasn't about to have his single mast be the tallest thing in the area. After all, *Streamin'* had copper and brass fittings, and sailors knew lightning could be erratic and deadly.

It would be crazy to try to make it back to the mainland. He'd have to beach the sloop on Keewadin Island and hope he could get her off the sand later. The wind was a good twenty-five knots, whistling shrilly in the rigging. Ordinarily, he'd love racing at this speed, but he needed dry land fast.

To his amazement, the boat nearly heeled over on her side and started south. He felt shoved, grasped in a giant's grip. A riptide? Yes, a narrow but deadly one along here, caused by the battle of the waves and wind.

He went with the flow for a little ways, like they tell you to do when swimming, then fought it to head back north, tacking back and forth. Finally, the long, beige beach of the barrier island of Keewadin appeared through the slate-gray of slanted rain. Cole retracted the centerboard as the sloop neared the shore. With good speed from the driving waves, he released the main and jib sheets, but they began flogging wildly. His primary thought was to save himself and the boat at the likely sacrifice of his nearly new sails.

As he approached the shore, he tripped the jamb cleats to release the halyards and began tugging at the thrashing sails until they both dropped to the deck, finally free from the force of the wind. He felt a wave thrust the bow of *Streamin'* up, then down, as she slammed onto the beach with a thud. Waves pounded the aft of the stranded vessel.

At least it wasn't a deadly riptide this time, just the sweep of surf. He jumped into foaming, waist-deep water and struggled to turn her prow in and get her higher on the shore. Thunder rumbled and lightning crackled. *Get out of the water,* he told himself. *Get out now.*

Cole loved this boat he'd made with his father, the only one he'd helped him build before everything went wrong. Though he was thirty-four now and had been out on his own since he was twenty, sailing still made him feel closer to his dad. Their family tree boasted five generations of boatbuilders, beginning in Portugal, then the Bahamas, onward to Key West, then Sarasota and Naples. Bahamian sloops like this one had once been used throughout the tropics, but now they were like an endangered species. He often dreamed of ditching his luxury yacht interior trade and take a chance on his own boatbuilding. He'd love to build boats like this one again. America had a throwaway culture, but these babies were built to last, even in a storm, though he'd never seen one as quickly fierce as this.

He tried to set the soles of his running shoes firmly in shifting sand. Both hands on the stern, he shoved. *Streamin'* slid her sleek length farther up on the beach. Keeping low, holding the metal anchor by its rope so he didn't have to touch it, he secured the sloop. Then, his shoes filled with water and sand, he slogged behind the line of mangroves and hunched over, crouched on the balls of his feet. He knew not to lie flat, where you'd have more of your body in contact with the ground if it was hit. Thank God, he'd made it safely out of the gulf, because this was one hell of a howler.

Bree wanted to just close her eyes and give up. A countercurrent swept through here, maybe a riptide that would carry her away. Despite her silent fear of her toothy companion, she swam on. She could stop moving to see if the shark would go away and to save her strength, but what if she got pushed farther out? What if lightning…or that shark…

A fierce, elemental terror flooded her; she wanted to scream and scream.

But then—dear Lord in heaven, was she seeing double? No, there were two of them, two big gray bodies with white underbellies, the dorsal fins knife-edged. The newest bull shark was at least seven feet long, his small, flat eyes staring at her each time he came near the surface. She stopped swimming. Should she just hang still in the water and let herself be taken out to sea? Bulls were aggressive and commotion bothered them. Maybe the rough water would keep their attention off her.

Was this a sheer, stark nightmare? If lightning or the sharks hit her, they might never even find her body. Had Daria been caught by these devouring depths, too?

Bree let the current take her for what seemed an eternity, then, when its powerful pull seemed to ease, swam on toward shore again—sharks still alongside. Each time she kicked, each time she pulled her arms through the water or even turned her head to breathe, she feared the jaws of her companions, feared being fried by another lightning strike so close.

A blast of something hit her hard, jerked her through the next wave. The riptide again? Shark? Jaws of a lightning bolt? She spit out the mouthpiece of her snorkel and screamed.

Bloodred colors exploded before her eyes, in her head. Something huge lunged at her. Then came only blackness.

2

Cole was soaked to his skin. The wind lashed him, and rain stung his shoulders and back through his sopped shirt. The narrow key seemed to shudder with each roll of thunder. Yet, through it all, he thought he'd heard a shriek.

He lifted his head. It wasn't just the shrill of wind through the boat's rigging. Something almost human...

Squinting into the rain, he peered around the thick patch of mangroves to check on his sloop. Though *Streamin'* had listed from the pounding of the surf, she looked all right. But something was sprawled on the beach beside the hull, as if there had been an accident and the prow had hit someone.

Still keeping low, he went to see what had come in. His breath huffed out as if he'd been hit in the gut; his heart pounded even harder. A woman—it looked like a drowned mermaid!

No, no, of course not, he told himself as he bent over the sprawled figure. The short-sleeved, full-length, silvery-green wet suit clung to her curves so tightly it looked painted on. It was designed with a fin-and-scale pattern to look as if she had a tail. Long legs, that was all. Her shoulder-length, auburn hair clung to her head. Her graceful, limp arms were in a ballerina pose, as if she would dance. Was she dead?

Afraid to roll her face up—instinct in case she had spine or head injuries from hitting his boat—he felt for the pulse at the base of her throat. She felt cold and, despite her tan, her cheek and chin looked pale and waxy, almost as if she were a life-size doll. She had a faint pulse, but she was so still he wasn't certain she was breathing. Carefully, he turned her over, faceup.

She had marks on her face from a diving mask, but he knew this woman! Or else he knew her sister. She was one of the twins who owned the Two Mermaids Marine Search and Salvage Shop in Turtle Bay, not far from his own business. He'd had an impromptu lunch with one of them—Briana—the day she'd been scraping the hull of the Richardson yacht when he was paneling the salon with Santos mahogany. He'd been going through the divorce then and was only dating his sloop, or he would have called her. Thank God, she was alive, but she might not be soon if she didn't take a breath.

Ignoring the slashing rain and continued threat of lightning, he pulled her carefully up out of the slosh of the surf. Hunched over her, just beyond the breaking waves, he started mouth-to-mouth resuscitation. He hadn't done that on anyone since he'd tried to save his father when he'd found him on the floor, and that was too late. What had happened to this woman? Surely she hadn't been swimming in the storm.

She seemed slender and small, but he knew she was a vital, strong woman. *Come on, baby. Come on back.*

Breathe for me. Let my lips warm yours, sweetheart. Come on, come on.

It had amused him, then impressed him, that two women would run such a rough-and-tumble business, especially when their competition across the bay was a gruff, tough guy who pretty much had a monopoly on search and salvage in the area. The women mostly did light salvage, none of the heavy stuff with dredging and demolition like Sam Travers, but search and salvage was always a risky business.

Come on, baby, I know you're spunky. Take my breath. Come on, you beautiful little mermaid!

He started to panic, his sweat mingling with the rain, even in the cool rush of wind. After what seemed an eternity, her mouth moved against his. He stopped and looked down into her face, glazed by rain and gulf water. Her thick eyelashes, plastered to her ashen cheeks, flickered. She frowned and moaned.

"Hey, mermaid!" he said, feeling like a fool, but he couldn't remember her last name and wasn't sure which twin this was. Still, he used the name he knew, one he'd remembered for months now because it had seemed to suit her. It had reminded him of the word *brio,* for her enthusiasm and verve that time they'd talked and eaten together. He'd felt an instant attraction to her, a surge of desire that he'd tried to control by being overly polite and teasing that day. "Briana?" he said, his voice shaking. "Briana!"

She slitted her eyes open. "Daria?" she said, and started to cough up water.

He rolled her over slightly and braced her with one arm around her. One hand held her forehead steady like his mother used to do for him years ago when he threw up. It wasn't until he saw the burn marks on her limp left wrist, like a big bracelet around her dive watch, that he realized she might have been hit by lightning. He laid her back down on the sand, leaning over her, trying to keep the rain and wind off her with his body.

"Where's Daria?" he asked. "What happened?"

No answer. He gasped when he saw her eyes were dilated, the huge, black pupils eating up the gray-green of the irises, the color of the sea. He had to get her medical help—now. He couldn't wait for the storm to end. But there was no way to get an EMS vehicle out here, and a medical chopper couldn't fly in this mess. He could get on his radio and Mayday the Coast Guard, but it would take them time to get out here and he could have her into Naples by then—if all went well.

He had to hurry. His mermaid had evidently fainted or gone comatose at his feet.

He put his hand on her chest to be sure she was still breathing. Yes, shallow but steady. Though he hated to take the chance with the sloop, he had to risk sailing in with her right now. At least in an all-wooden boat—if he could get it off the beach—they might be able to escape the lightning. It would be rough going, but he had to try.

Praying she had no broken bones or internal injuries, he lifted her into the sloop and gently lashed her down. He stripped off his polo shirt and, though it was soaked, too, laid it over her upper torso. One of his customers had been hit by lightning on a golf course, and his doctor had told him that fast medical help had saved him from severe complications. He could not bear it if this beautiful, bold woman were permanently hurt. That old adage about being responsible for someone if you saved their life hit him hard, but he hadn't saved her yet.

Straining every muscle in his body to get some lift for *Streamin',* Cole tried to time pushing the sloop off the sand with the roll of the surf, but the power of the waves and wind beat it back. Waves could easily swamp or capsize a boat leaving a beach. His fourteen-foot sloop, which he knew more intimately than he knew any woman right now, fought him hard.

But he saw the wind had clocked around to the north. He could use the power of the sails to propel the sloop off the beach. In a hand-over-hand effort, he pulled the main halyard until the sail had reached the top of the mast. Then with a grunting, grinding heave, Cole pushed the bow of the boat off the beach toward the pounding surf. As the little sloop swung her bow through the wind, the sails filled, and she moved into deeper water. He pulled himself into the cockpit and grabbed the tiller in one hand while securing the mainsheet with the other. As he lowered the centerboard, the sloop began to feel her sea legs. She quickly picked up speed on a beam reach and cut through the water like a race car.

But it was brutal sailing. He had to step over his mermaid when he played the mainsheet and sit outboard to balance the heavy heeling. He feared a broach roll and had to adjust the tiller constantly. Every time the boat heeled, water sloshed over the side to soak Briana. She came to again, shoved her head and shoulder up by one elbow and screamed, "Sharks! Daria, sharks!"

"Lie down!" Cole shouted. "Down or the boom will get you when we tack. You're with me, you're all right. Lie down! There are no sharks. I won't let them get you or Daria!"

That seemed to calm her, and that trust clenched at his heart. He had to get her to safety, see that she was taken care of. She was out of her head, and his friend had said amnesia and brain damage could be some of the aftereffects of a lightning strike. If he could just let go of the tiller and sit still a second in this raging chaos, he could call for help, have someone meet him at the marina with a squad for her. But he couldn't tell where he was. To the pier yet? He didn't want to hit the pier.

As for the sharks, she could not possibly have seen them just now, but she was dead on: he glanced ahead and saw several bull sharks racing right with them, just like the ones in the picture in his office. The Winslow Homer painting called *The Gulf Stream* was the reason he'd named his company Gulf Stream Yacht Interiors, the reason he'd named this sloop *Streamin'*. But these sharks almost bumping the boat were no work of art— this race was life and death for real.

3

"Mayday! Mayday! Mayday! This is the sloop *Streamin'!*"

Cole never took his cell phone out sailing with him since he kept a two-way radio on board. More than once, he'd lost his cell in the gulf or gotten it soaked. His handheld radio was waterproof, and he managed it one-handed. Finally, someone answered his call for help.

"*Streamin', Streamin',* this is the U.S. Coast Guard Station, Naples Harbor. I read you, sloop *Streamin'.* Say your location. Over."

"U.S. Coast Guard, this is the sloop *Streamin'.* This is Cole DeRoca sailing solo out of Turtle Bay. I put in on Keewadin during the storm, but I'm heading for Naples—Port Royal, I think." Adrenaline poured through him; he hoped to hell he was making sense. "I have a half-drowned passenger who washed in or swam in on Keewadin. She may have been hit by lightning, too—in and out of consciousness."

"*Streamin',* do you have a GPS on board?"

"No GPS, it's still thick as pea soup out here. Wait—

I see the seawall at Gordon Pass, the rock wall to the south—"

"Put in just north of the pass. We'll send an E.R. squad...."

Cole dropped the radio and slammed both hands back on the tiller. He fought the rush of inward tide that was trying to smash them into the stone break wall of the pass he'd navigated so many times. The outward flow of the Gordon River here crashed into the rising tide. With the wind, it almost capsized them.

He leaned out, away from the hull, using his weight against the lunge and roll of the vessel, wishing he'd had time to get in a trapeze harness. "Come on, baby!" he shouted. His mermaid stirred again, cried out something, but the sloop had to come first now. In these crazy crosscurrents, one wrong move and they'd both be fighting for their lives in the surf. It would be doubtful that he would survive, but Briana would never make it. Above all else, he was desperate to save her.

Cole gritted his teeth and strained to counterbalance the weight of wind and sail. For one terrifying moment, he actually had to steer the tiller with his foot as he hung on to the wire rigging and mainsheet with his hands. The rope cut into his flesh and made his hand go numb. He felt the cords stand out on the sides of his neck; every bone and sinew and muscle screamed at him as he strained to keep the sloop from making a death roll.

Yes! The hull cleared the rocks by about ten yards! He swung *Streamin'* toward the shore, scrambling back into the boat, and readied himself for the crunch of her prow on sand and shells. He threw himself next to Briana and held her to him as the sloop came to a precarious, jerking halt. Her body hit against his, but he braced them both.

Miraculously, as he clambered out, it seemed the storm had lessened. Maybe he was just getting used to the deluge of stinging rain. No, it seemed to be letting up, the lightning and thunder rolling away inland over the bay and the Glades. It was like being given a prize for surviving his struggle with the sea.

He reached over the woman's prone form and retrieved his radio. It still worked. He called the coast guard again and told them his position was about six beachfront houses north of Gordon Pass. They assured him they'd called 911 for him and a squad was on the way.

"One more thing," he told the officer on the line. "Tell them this woman is Briana—don't know her last name—who owns the Two Mermaids Search and Salvage in Turtle Bay, and she mentioned her sister, Daria. If anyone can locate Daria, please let her know about Briana's accident. I'm not sure, but she might have been out in the water with her."

"If that's the case, that Daria or her craft are missing, let us know immediately. Over and out."

"Will do," Cole said, suddenly sounding so weary to himself. "Will—try to," he muttered to himself as he snapped the radio off and bent over Briana.

He cradled her in his arms across his lap, trying to keep her warm. She opened her eyes once, those hugely dilated gray-green eyes that didn't seem to see him, and cuddled closer. His insides flip-flopped. It had been a long time since he'd held a woman and longer since she was someone who needed him.

It seemed both an eternity and yet too soon when he heard a siren screaming along Gordon Drive. He did not let go of Briana until the medics appeared between two houses and came down on the sand carrying a stretcher. They bent over her to take her vitals and put a needle for a drip in her arm. Cole moved back, then off the sloop to give them room.

Several people with houses along the stretch of beach came out into the diminishing rain. A short, elderly man swung a too-small Windbreaker around Cole's shoulders. It was only then he realized he was shaking.

"If I go to the hospital with her, could you watch my boat?" Cole asked him. His teeth were chattering from the chill, and nerves.

"Sure, sure. What happened to her? She your wife?"

"A friend."

"Sure. Beautiful old boat. Don't worry about a thing. I mean, I'm sure she'll be fine—the girl and the boat."

Manuel Salazar, whom everyone called Manny, slammed the door to his old Ford truck, darted through the last raindrops and unlocked the front door to the Two Mermaids Marine Search and Salvage Shop. His fourteen-year-old daughter, Lucinda, trailed him in, yakking all the way. Lately she talked to her parents only in English. Everyone else in the family was proud to speak in *Español,* but not Lucinda. He'd laid down the law to her that she was having the traditional *quinceañera* celebration for her fifteenth birthday, a huge party which announced to friends and family that she was entering adulthood. Most *chicas* couldn't wait for that celebration, which was better than any American birthday or sweet-sixteen party, but not his daughter. Lucinda had suddenly gone from being his angelic, younger daughter to someone he didn't even know.

He walked to his desk to see if there were any phone

messages. Nada. With this storm, he wondered where
the shop's dive boat, *Mermaids II,* had ended up. His
stomach knotted.

"But it's so expensive, Papa. Think of all you and
Mama could do with the money." Lucinda tried another
tack to win her argument. "I overheard you say to her
you couldn't afford it, that you'd have to find a way,
but why should you?" Dark eyes flashing in her pert,
round face, she stood with hands on her hips, glaring at
him. She looked so much like his sainted mother sometimes, though his mother would never have been caught
dead in torn jeans and skinny-strap top that showed too
much skin. "My friends—my American friends—" she
plunged on, "think it's really old-fashioned."

"So, they not your friends then, *sí? Caramba,* don't
you look down on your Latina friends. I never know a
chica crazy enough pass up a *quinceañera!* Your Latina
friends all happy 'bout their parties, dance with boys,
make parents, godparents and *padrinas* happy, *sí?* And
you just ask your Americana friends, what 'bout ethnic
diversity and all that?"

"Man, you go from sounding like a shrink to priest
to politician, Papa. I'm an American teenager, and they
have some say in their lives. Sure, most *chicas* want a
quinceañera party, but not me! You want to spend some
money for me you don't have, how 'bout a new car I
could use to get a job in town when I'm sixteen—that's
the age Americans look forward to."

"No car! Tell your American friends don't come if
they don't want a good time with Mexican dancing and
food and—"

"I can't even talk to you and Mama anymore!" she

exploded, smacking her hands on her thighs. "Carianna didn't have to have one!"

"*Have* to have one? Your older sister give anything, if we could have pay for party for her, invite all our friends and family. But now I got this job with Briana and Daria. They even be *padrinas,* help us pay for things—"

"So it's a party for them? No, this whole thing's for you and Mama, even Carianna and Grandmama Rosa, not for me!"

"Me, me, me!" he mocked, throwing up his hands. "Now that what an American teenager all about! When your mama and I was your age—"

"I'm not you and Mama, and I don't still have one foot in the great country of Mexico where we were all starving! Why can't you just listen?"

"You shut your mouth, American girl! You gonna have *quinceañera,* honor your mama and grandmama. You make your family proud or you gonna find a new family. Now sit there till I find that video camera."

She turned her back and flopped into the padded chair at Bree's desk. Muttering under his breath, Manny walked out of the small office space into the large, concrete-floored back room where dive and rescue gear was stored. A sign over the doorway read The Water is Our Office, and on the far wall hung a blown-up poster of the twins in their mermaid wet suits with scuba tanks at their feet and the words Love That Bottled Air! Another large picture at the back of the room showed only the twins' mermaid tails as they dove below the surface and read, Bottoms Up!

Wall Peg-Boards displayed depth charts, diagrams of the various artificial wrecks in this area of the gulf, and handmade drawings of the precious turtle sea grass the twins tended out by the Trade Wreck. On the floor, separated by aisles to walk between, were gears, winches, capstans, marker buoys, metal detectors, lift bags, underwater lights, pelican floats, wreck reels, cutting tools and cameras.

His area was toward the back of the shop, where the heaviest equipment—especially anything to do with motors—was stored. Manny also handled in-water ship repairs and serviced dive equipment. He had a deal with the twins that he didn't dive with tanks, only shallow stuff with a snorkel. Too far under water and he went nuts—"claustro-hydro-phobic," Daria had labeled it. Still, he loved the look of this place, the very smell of it. His greatest goal in life was to own the business someday and run it his way. He'd take on the rival salvage company across the bay and, once and for all, shut up its big brute of an owner, Sam Travers. You'd think that since Travers also did industrial dredging, demolition and pile driving, he'd leave the lighter stuff to Two Mermaids, but Sam resented the twins, especially Bree.

This big back room always looked like organized confusion, much, Manny thought, like his employers' busy lives. How he envied them for building this business, though he'd helped too and thought he was worth more than they paid him. But he'd recently found out that he would inherit half of the shop if anything happened to either of them, and since then, he'd made some big, hard decisions.

Caramba, he might even have to force himself to dive to get what he wanted, instead of just operating on the surface. He grunted as his eyes searched for the camera to film the inside of the big, fancy Garcia Party House he had rented for the *quinceañera.* He wanted to show his *madre* how good things were going before cancer took her. She'd given up so much for him. He had to make her proud of him before she died, whatever it cost.

He found the camera and took it out of its plastic underwater casing and rejoined Lucinda, who was twirling herself dizzy in Bree's chair. Finally, his *chica* had shut her mouth. But in a way, the silence got to him, because he had to be doing something to keep himself from going loco waiting to hear about Bree and Daria.

For once, Amelia Westcott was glad to see her own driveway. She hated driving in the rain, hated these months of weather so hot and humid you had to run from AC to AC. At least her sons would not be home from Cub Scouts yet and she could take a cool shower and calm down before they showed up. Her meeting with Daria had been disastrous; later, the docent's tea at the art gallery had gone on much longer than she'd expected, partly because the lights had gone out from that boomer of a storm. Ah, sometime this month or next, the weather would clear and she could breathe again.

If she hadn't married Ben, who was now the prominent and very busy prosecuting attorney of Collier County, she probably would have moved north to the Carolinas. It might have helped her escape painful memories of her youth in this area. She did love Ben and their lifestyle here, and she was very proud of her husband, although sometimes she wished she had a career—a cause—of her own that would *really* help other people, something that mattered more than her committees, however philanthropic their purposes and however much they helped promote Ben's career. Then she could look beyond these very luxurious four walls and the messes her boys made. A stay-at-home mom who didn't want to stay at home, that was her.

The moment Amelia closed the garage door and went into the house, she heard her message-waiting beeper. Maybe the day had been changed for the Clear the Gulf Commission meeting tomorrow. At least her membership on that had made Bree and Daria admit she was good for something, though it was Florida Congressman Josh Austin who had suggested them for oversight of the sea grass and marine life report.

"You have one messages," the recorded voice told her when she pressed the play button. With all the world's modern technology, why couldn't they teach a digital chip good grammar? Heaven knows, her laptop underlined every darn spelling and grammar error she made in the numerous letters to the editor she wrote.

"This important message is for Amelia Devon Westcott," the recorded woman's voice said. Amelia's stomach went into free fall. She never used her maiden name. "One of our E.R. doctors mentioned you're on our fundraising guild committee here at the hospital, so that's how we traced you. Mrs. Westcott, I'm calling because your sister—we believe it is Briana Devon…"

Briana, Amelia thought. *Not Daria?*

"…has been brought by emergency squad to Naples Hospital from an accident out in the gulf, and we're hoping you could come into the E.R. to identify her and be with her."

Bree! Bree? An accident? Identify her? Were they trying to break the news to her that Bree was dead? It couldn't be—couldn't be Bree!

The voice went on, "We have been informed that she lives with another sister, but no one at Briana and

Daria Devon's place of employment and residence knows where Daria is, so we have been unable to reach her."

As if she were speaking to a real woman, Amelia whispered, "I've never been able to reach either of them, no matter how hard—how *desperately*—I tried."

Cole paced the E.R. waiting room like an expectant father. He knew he looked like hell, still in soaked shorts, sopping shoes that squeaked when he walked and a borrowed Windbreaker that was so small he couldn't even zip it. The distractions of people in trouble here unnerved him, too: a distraught mother with a kid who'd swallowed a quarter; a young man in terrible pain evidently waiting to be admitted to pass a kidney stone; elderly people who looked like death warmed over. The place was packed, but at least they'd taken Briana back through the swinging doors into the depths of curtained alcoves right away. He'd already bugged the triage nurse more than once. Why didn't they come tell him something?

This sent him back to the terrible night of his dad's sudden heart attack. He'd known his father was dead, but he'd called an ambulance. Rather than pronounce him dead at home, they'd done CPR and rushed him to the E.R. in Sarasota, only to tell Cole what he already knew. But Briana had to be all right. She was strong to have lasted out in that brutal gulf, evidently swimming with sharks, too. Cole had practically forced his way into the E.R. vehicle, but they'd shut him out here.

Shut out—the story of his life since his divorce last year from Jillian. He hadn't realized until she cut him off from their friends—or those he thought were their friends, but were really hers—that he'd given up too much of his own world for hers. It hadn't helped his client list to have his social contacts shrink like that. At least it had given him an excuse to quit playing country club games. But what he'd learned most from the biggest mistake of his life was that, after two years of their marriage, Jillian had not really been an integral part of him. He just didn't miss her. He felt sad and bad their marriage had failed, but he didn't feel her loss. Strangely, he'd feel worse if Briana were lost, and he'd only spent one lunch months ago and then this horrible day with her.

He was surprised to see Amelia Westcott, a woman he served with on the Clear the Gulf Commission, rush in the double glass doors and head for the triage nurse at the front desk.

"You called and told me to come right in," Amelia said. She was out of breath, but her voice carried clearly. "I'm Briana Devon's sister. But is her other sister, her twin Daria, here yet?"

Cole went over. "Amelia, I didn't know you were Briana's sister—I mean I don't know why I would—but I'm the one who found her half-drowned on the beach at Keewadin Island and brought her in—"

"Half-drowned? I'll bet she was with Daria. She's always with Daria on some sea search, some underwater mission. I can't believe they were out in that storm."

Though he could tell she was concerned, she spoke with an undercurrent of bitterness. The older he got, the more he saw family problems everywhere, though most simmered just below the surface of people's daily lives. He used to think his messed-up family was unique, but now he knew it was almost normal.

The triage nurse was on the phone, checking on Briana's status. Finally, some answers, Cole thought. He stuck tight to Amelia while she folded her arms and seemed to collapse within herself. She was a good-looking woman, a platinum blonde with every hair in place and icy blue eyes, in contrast to Briana's natural auburn hair and gray-green eyes. Even now, Amelia looked perfectly put together, with makeup worthy of a photo shoot, while the few times he'd seen the twins around they'd seemed windblown and often wet—a sexy combination. Amelia was obviously older than the twins and, he guessed, uptight by nature as well as from the situation. Rather than taking a deep breath, even when he urged her to, Amelia narrowed her eyes and breathed out through flared nostrils as if she were a bull waiting to charge. That reminded him about the bull sharks, but he decided not to spring that on her, at least not yet.

It wasn't long before a thin, balding doctor came out and went straight for Amelia. The man—his badge said Dr. Micah Hawkins—flipped through papers on his clipboard and asked, "Mrs. Westcott, you are next of kin for Briana Devon?"

Cole felt his knees go weak. Had Briana died? She couldn't have died!

"Yes, her sister—one of them," Amelia said as the doctor gestured her to walk with him. Cole kept right up.

"She swallowed a lot of water, but worse, we believe she's been struck by lightning while in the gulf and that can lead to complications. And you are?" Dr. Hawkins asked, squinting at Cole.

"Cole DeRoca, the friend who found her and brought her in. I gave her mouth-to-mouth and got her breathing again. She's going to be all right?"

"You are to be commended, Mr. DeRoca—you prob-

ably saved her life. If Mrs. Westcott doesn't mind, you
can come along. We'll need to run a battery of tests, call
in a neuropsychologist. She keeps slipping in and out of
consciousness and asking for Daria."

"Oh, she would," Amelia said. "But, you mean Daria
hasn't been found?"

"That's her twin sister. Briana was evidently out in a
boat with her," Cole explained to the doctor. "But Briana must have fallen in."

"Dear God, Daria can't be missing—out there, too,"
Amelia cried, gripping Dr. Hawkins's wrist. "Doctor,
call in whatever specialists you need. I'm not sure about
Briana's insurance, but I'll take care of all that."

Cole's dislike for Amelia softened a bit. But when
she said nothing else, as he followed the two of them
deeper into the maze of curtained cubicles, he asked,
"But if Briana was out in the gulf with Daria, where is
Daria now?"

Was she dead? Briana wondered. She slitted her eyes
open, just barely, trying to keep the bright lights out of
her dark brain. She felt loggy, helpless, at the mercy of
the sliding, shifting sea. Up, down, all around... But the
sky looked whiter now, too bright, one big cloud floating over her with more than one sun in it. *Ceiling lights.*
They hurt her eyes, and even when people spoke across
the room, it seemed they shouted at her.

People's faces, unfamiliar, swam in and out above
her. The sharks were gone. Had they been real? Daria,
her mirror image, where was she? She didn't like to dive
alone, she wanted Daria, her other self, there when they
stepped together through the looking glass into the wonderland of the deep.

Someone forced her eyelids apart and shone a bright light into the depths of her brain. She jerked away. She tried to lift her hands to shield her face, but one of her arms was heavy with tubes and the other was bandaged and hurt like heck. A man—a doctor—leaned over her. Oh, Amelia was standing beside him. Why was Amelia here? And who was the tall, handsome man with dark eyes and black hair, his face so worried as he looked her over? His clothes showed he was not another doctor. Had he been swimming with her?

"What happened?" she tried to ask, but she didn't sound like herself and no one answered. What was the matter with these people? And where was Daria?

"She sustained no burns except on her left wrist, where she wore a stainless-steel dive watch," the doctor was telling Amelia and the man. "Actually, it's probably a skin lesion—an inflammatory response—which may disappear in a few days. I've already ordered a CT scan and an MRI, and we'll have her in a room as soon as possible, so we can monitor her better. We'll do some functional scans but call in a specialist for that."

"Functional—function of the brain?" the man asked, his deep voice a soothing whisper compared to the others.

"Precisely. Aftereffects can vary widely. And although her pupils are dilated, I want to assure you that does not necessarily mean brain injury, Mrs. Westcott." He leaned closer, very close. "Briana, I'm Dr. Hawkins. Can you hear me?"

She could hear him, all right. She heard every sound in this place, even the dripping of that bag above into her tube. "Yes," she said with great effort, because she didn't think she had the strength to nod. Her lips felt stiff and cracked. "Where's Daria?"

The tall man spoke again. "Brianna, can you tell us where you last saw Daria?"

She fought to form her words. They had to help find Daria.

"When I dove—off our boat—at Trade Wreck—before the storm."

Amelia gasped, a sound that pierced Bree's eardrums. "You mean she could be lost at sea?" her sister demanded, but the man put his hand on Amelia's arm to keep her quiet.

"Was she still on the boat when you saw her last?" he asked.

"Yes. Yes!"

"Then she'll be all right," Amelia said. "She probably had to ride out the storm, or put in somewhere else." She squeezed Bree's shoulder and moved away with the doctor.

No, Bree wanted to scream. Didn't they know Daria never would have left her? Not of her own accord.

"We'll look for her and find her," the tall man said, and put his big hand lightly on her shoulder where Amelia's had just been. His hand was warm, solid. Where had she seen him before? "Just try to rest now," he said.

If Amelia and the doctor thought they were whispering when they moved away, she heard them anyway. The doctor was saying that a lightning strike near her in the water—a side flash—must have given her a concussion. He told Amelia she might have sporadic amnesia or become moody, distracted, irritable or forgetful.

Exhausted as she was, Bree vowed never to forget what had happened to Daria. But what *had* happened?

At least that man said he would help. He said "we" would find Daria. She should know who he was, but she could not recall. She felt both fearful and furious, so the doctor must be right about her moods, but she could not have amnesia, not about Daria.

Though Bree was afraid if she closed her eyes again she'd see the horror of the sea, the sharks, she pressed her eyelids tightly closed. Amazing how these bright lights hurt her eyes and how she could hear even the shuffle of the nurses' feet on the floors. Other people's voices and moans, cries of pain. Was she really hearing those or were they deep inside her?

The occasional screech of the curtains' rings across the metal rods almost deafened her. She could hear the man ask Amelia for her cell phone and then take it outside the curtain to make a call to the coast guard to tell them about Daria and their dive boat.

Exhausted, sick, she felt so strange, but Bree knew then what she had to do, even if that man had promised to look for Daria, even if he was calling for help. When Amelia and the doctor weren't looking, she had to get out of this bed, get another boat and go find her sister somewhere out on the dark, devouring sea.

4

It seemed to Bree that the nurses tried to keep her awake all night, not that she had time to sleep anyway. She wanted to get out of bed, find her clothes and find Daria. But nurses came in to check her eyes, shining pinpoints of light into them. They took her blood pressure and checked her drips. She heard them come and go, heard one chewing gum. And always, she thought she heard the roar of the wind and waves.

Despite her desire to stay awake and get up, each time they walked away, Bree slept the sleep of the dead. Had they drugged her? Had someone drugged Daria, too? Had she seen drug dealers trying to make a drop and they knew they had to silence her? Had the horrible people who brought in women for the twentieth-century slave trade called human trafficking come upon her and taken her prisoner, too? Daria would never desert her. Bree knew Daria as well as she knew herself, didn't she?

Fighting a riptide of fear, she swam from nightmare to nightmare, but was suddenly aware that someone sat by her side. A woman. Amelia, when Bree wanted it desperately to be Daria.

"So strong, the water," she said, once in the midst of a waking dream in which she was trying to tell her handsome rescuer what had happened. She was safe in his arms, huddled against him for protection. She never thought she'd need or want a man that way. Who was he? Shouldn't she remember?

"Just a minute. I'll get you some water," Amelia said, evidently thinking she'd asked for a drink. She held up a glass with a straw to her lips. Bree saw that it was barely dawn and she was in a private room. Light poured through the window as bright as noon sun.

"Any news? Did they find her?" she asked, then drank greedily. She knew one of the tubes in her arm was to hydrate her, but her throat was so dry.

"They're going to do a wide search at first light, so that's right now. The coast guard's starting with the co-ordinates your boatman gave them and did an initial sweep of the area last night."

Manny. If only Manny had been with them as usual, this never would have happened…and then Daria's sudden toothache… Bree ached all over.

"My boatman's name," she told Amelia, exhausted from the little effort of drinking, "is Manuel Salazar—Manny. Please call and tell him I'm okay."

But what was the name of that other boatman, the sailor? She felt she should know him—wanted to know him.

"They're going to do an air search, too," Amelia went on, hovering over her. "I'm sure they'll find Daria with your boat. I'll bet the motor didn't work, the anchor line broke and the storm drove her into the Ten Thousand Islands. They'll find her."

"Thanks for being here with me."

"Where else would I be when you or Daria need me? I'm sorry if it took this accident for you to realize that."

That edge to her voice, so familiar. When it came to Amelia, Bree remembered too much she'd like to forget. Amelia was six when their mother died of eclampsia in childbirth, delivering her twins. Now, as adults, they understood how their older sister could dislike them, even blame them. Their widowed father had thrown himself into rearing his twins, whom everyone oohed and aahed over. Amelia, a timid soul and a real little lady at heart, though she could be snippy, felt left out when Dad took the younger girls fishing and taught them to swim and dive. He'd always tried to include Amelia, but she'd have no part of it and ended up spending a lot of time with her maternal grandmother while the tomboy twins went to sporting events or dived with Dad.

"Amelia, what's the name of that man who helped me? I know I've met him. I'm just a little foggy on some things—a few recent things."

"You may have a concussion, or maybe that lightning did scramble your internal wires a bit. You've just got to relax or they'll have to give you a sedative, as soon as they rule out a concussion. That will calm your anxiety and make you forget how traumatic it must have been to—"

"I don't want to forget! Of course, I'm anxious, because we've got to find Daria! I've got to go help find her!"

"You're not going anywhere," Amelia told her, gently patting her arm as if she were a child. "They're going to run some brain function tests today with a specialist from Fort Myers before you can be released. But the knight in shining sailboat who rescued you is Cole

DeRoca, who serves on the Clear the Gulf Commission with me."

Amelia went on, explaining that the commission was meeting today and that the twins' accident would be the talk of the group and she wouldn't be there to answer their questions.

Yes, Bree thought with a little flutter in her belly. Cole DeRoca, the guy who worked with rare woods and specialized in installing custom-made yacht interiors. Bree had been scraping barnacles off a hull in the marina when he'd been working on the same huge yacht, and he'd shared a sandwich and some wine from the galley with her.

She'd found him shockingly handsome in a rugged way. His deep voice had seemed to vibrate into the very core of her being. When she was working, Brcc usually gave little thought to clothes, hair or makeup, but she'd wished that day she'd done better than an old, tight wet suit and saltwater-soaked hair yanked back in a ponytail. Cole had worn faded jeans and a black, sawdust-speckled T-shirt but still managed to look like an ad for owning a yacht, not working on one. His angular, hard body was sun-bronzed; he made her perpetual tan look pale. When he smiled or laughed, he got a cheek dimple and narrowed his dark eyes under thick but sleek eyebrows. Even as he'd chatted amiably, he'd managed to look her over thoroughly and she could still feel the impact of that down to her toes. If she could recall all that and Cole's initial impact on her, didn't that prove her head and body were still working well?

Other details of their brief time together came cascading back. He'd said he worked alone, measuring, ordering, cutting and fitting the imported woods. He loved being hands-on, he'd told her with a devilish grin. He'd told her his wife hadn't wanted him to work with his hands and had a fit at a party when he called himself a carpenter instead of a yacht interior designer. And he'd said he was getting divorced, didn't he?

"I already talked to Manny at your shop," Amelia was saying, "but I had some trouble understanding him. He has a really thick accent. No wonder you took all those Spanish classes. You and your Hispanics."

"If you're including Cole, his grandfather was a boat-builder from Portugal," Bree told her as even more images and snatches of their conversation came back to her from that hour they'd spent together months ago. Yes, she was remembering him so distinctly that there was no way her brain could have been short-circuited by a lightning strike. But why hadn't she placed him instantly when she saw him yesterday?

Granted, she was perceiving light and sound more strongly than was normal, but surely she could handle that. She didn't intend to share those concerns or her erratic memory with anyone right now, because she had to get out of here and help look for Daria. She needed to speak to the coast guard and the civil air patrol in person. She had a friend who flew for the volunteer patrol, and she wanted to call him. She had some ideas about where to look for the *Mermaids II*. But what terrified her was that some of those sites were underwater.

After being taken—in a wheelchair, no less—for a battery of neurocognitive tests early the next morning, Bree lay back in her hospital bed, her eyes closed, even more exhausted. The specialist was to be in soon with the results.

"Your knight in shining sailboat brought you this," Amelia told her, "but they didn't let him get farther than the nurses' station on this floor—family only now, especially since there are reporters downstairs who would swarm you." Bree turned her head to see a beautiful, orange-hued orchid plant. Tears filled her eyes at Cole's kindness. In the midst of dreadful memories of storm and sharks and the fear of loss, the blooms looked like small, hovering butterflies. Hope—they reminded her of hope. And the plant was in a stunning, striped, dark and light box, made of a kind of wood she'd never seen.

"He's divorced now, you know, and quite a catch, if you ask me," Amelia said, smoothing the bedsheets as if she'd remake the bed with Bree in it.

"I'm not looking for a man, but for Daria!"

"Of course—I know. It's just you haven't had anyone serious since Ted. Since before Ted died, even. Darn, sorry to have brought that up."

"It's all right," Bree told her, though she would have liked to bandage Amelia's mouth shut before she stuck her foot in it again. "Just don't ever bring him up around Sam Travers, because he still blames me for his Ted's enlisting and his death."

"As if I'd ever be around Sam Travers," Amelia muttered, perching on the chair next to the bed. "And how ridiculous to hold it over you just because you broke up with his son and he enlisted and died. But then, people do hold grudges for years when someone or something dear is lost. I can sympathize with that."

Summoning up what little strength she had, Bree worked the controls to elevate the back of the bed, then got the TV remote from the bedside table. Talking about loss or death right now was the last thing she could bear.

As ever, despite how kind Amelia was trying to be, she was getting on Bree's nerves.

Bree switched on the TV, which sat high on a narrow, suspended shelf across from the foot of her bed. It was almost noon, and the local stations always covered search-and-rescue efforts in the gulf. Search and salvage. If only she could go search for her sister and salvage her from any possible harm right now.

The TV came on with a political commercial, the kind everyone was sick of already, and the election was still almost two months away. This one was for Marla Sherborne, the incumbent, conservative U.S. congresswoman who was adamantly antigambling. The ad, like most of hers, warned against the dangers of letting casino boats into the area, because it would open the doors to "unbridled outside control of huge amounts of dirty money." A wealthy Miami businessman named Dom Verdugo was trying to bring a casino boat into Turtle Bay, but it hadn't been approved yet and everyone was arguing about it. A gambling boat would bring more business to local restaurants and shops, but hordes of outsiders could run up property prices and ruin the already endangered old Florida ambience, not to mention create more abuse of the gulf itself. The visuals on this ad even tried to tie the casino boat to water pollution that had endangered marine and plant life below the glittering gulf.

Ironically, there was a tenuous—and doubly tension-filled—relationship between Marla and her opposing candidate in the U.S. senate race, Josh Austin. The scuttlebutt was that Josh Austin's wealthy sugarcane-baron father-in-law, a longtime widower, was having an affair with Marla. If anything came of the relationship, Josh could be trying to unseat his step-mother-in-law.

See, Bree tried to encourage herself, her brain was working great, filled with names and details from days, weeks, months—years ago. So why couldn't she summon up much of what happened during her own rescue by Cole? Could they be giving her that sedative already? She had to remember everything to help find Daria.

"The commission doesn't completely trust Marla Sherborne's claims of being so gung ho about the environment," Amelia put in, pointing at the TV. "Not since everyone says she's literally in bed with that sugarcane baron, Cory Grann, and the fertilizer run-off from their fields is such a problem."

There was a quick knock on the open door followed by a voice Bree recognized instantly, though he still stood out in the hall. "Do I hear my father-in-law's name being taken in vain?" a jaunty voice asked. "They're not letting even the press in to see you, but I pulled a few strings."

"Josh!" Bree cried as he popped his head around the door and came in. She was so glad to see their old friend. A politician one could trust, Josh Austin had the ways and means to solve any problem. She felt better already.

"I hope you didn't hear what we think of all these ads, because yours will probably be on next," Amelia told him. Both sisters knew Josh from years back, when he had dated Daria. Even when Daria and Josh had split up—definitely Josh's decision—all three sisters had wished him well, though they had seldom seen him in person over the years since. But all the locals were proud of Josh Austin.

"Hey, I have no choice," he said, his voice still upbeat. "A necessary evil, a sign of the times. I hate the damn things, too."

"It's good to see you, but we need your pull to make something happen for Daria," Bree told him. "We've got to find her."

"That's why I'm here. I'm doing everything I can. I've already made some this-is-top-priority calls to the guard and the air patrol."

He shook hands with Amelia, then strode toward the bed and bent to kiss Bree's cheek. Indeed, one of his campaign ads ran in the background, touting his views that, with stringent oversight, a clean gulf could coexist with controlled gambling to pour more jobs and money into the local economy. And *that* meant more money for environmental protection. The ad ended with a shot of him and his beautiful wife, Nicole, also a lawyer, holding hands and walking toward the camera on the beach. They had no children, or they would certainly have been in the ad. Daria had said she'd heard that Nicole, whom Josh called Nikki, had suffered two miscarriages.

"I had to see you when I heard," he said, putting his hand on her shoulder. "Nikki sends her love. She's down giving the reporters lying in wait for you a sound bite or two about me so they'll leave you alone."

"I'd talk to them if I thought it would help find Daria. Be sure to thank her for me."

"She's being a real trouper right now. Just between us," he said, whispering now but shaking his head, "she thinks once I'm in congress, the White House is a small step, and that's her idea of a dream home. But enough about that. I'm sure they'll find Daria. Oh, here, I brought you the morning paper about your rescue," he said, producing a folded copy of the *Naples Daily News* from under his arm and handing it to Amelia. "You and

DeRoca both did what you had to do. I admire both of you for your courage."

Josh Austin was a wonder, and not just because of his vitality and boyish good looks that never seemed to change. He had always amazed Bree and absolutely awed Daria, who had dated him three years in high school, long before his statewide glory days. In high school he'd been in charge of everything and was voted most likely to succeed. He had, too, leaving everyone behind in his stardust as he married a wealthy man's daughter whom he met at Florida State, became a successful business-man and the youngest state representative in Tallahas-see. He was now in a neck-and-neck race to unseat Marla Sherborne for her U.S. senate seat. Everyone in the area liked Josh, including Daria, even though he'd broken up with her before he'd left for college, long before Ted and Bree had split up. But what a fun foursome they had been years ago. Ted was gone now, but not, she prayed, Daria, too.

The three of them watched silently when the cov-erage of the search for Daria and their dive boat came up as the lead story. An interview with a coast guard spokesman led, then a sound bite from a member of the civil air patrol, who had been flying the coastal islands all morning and found nothing but normal storm debris on various beaches. And then an interview with Cole.

She hadn't realized he was so tall, but he made the reporter look like a shrimp. He wore swim trunks and a black T-shirt that showed how muscular he was. It was obvious he hadn't shaved or slept. It made Bree mad that the hospital staff had turned him away from seeing her, for she owed him her life. If he could only locate Daria, she'd owe him for both of them.

Cole's thick, swept-back hair shone dark in the sun, and his narrowed eyes looked almost black under his arched brows. His chiseled features were half-handsome, half-craggy, almost foreboding when he frowned. Bree shifted her legs under the sheet. As weak as she felt, the mere look and thought of him poured adrenaline through her body.

Cole and the reporter were standing on the dock of the Turtle Bay Marina. "I've been out with friends looking for Daria Devon and her scuba-dive boat," he said into the mike thrust at him. "Especially near Keewadin Island, where Briana Devon was swept in, though she evidently swam a long way to get there."

"Do you consider yourself a hero for saving Briana Devon?"

"She saved herself by managing to swim in during that sudden storm. I'm no hero, just someone deeply concerned and trying to help."

Bree's heart went out to him. He was on edge, frustrated and worried, she could tell.

"Quite a guy." Josh's voice interrupted her agonizing. "His ex-wife was on my initial feasibility/exploratory committee. Bree, how are you doing, really?" he asked, turning to her when the coverage ended. He leaned against the edge of the bed and bent down to take her hand in his. "Your inner strength, I mean, your ability to face all this. I know how close you are to Daria."

"I'll be all right," she vowed, blinking back tears and gripping his hand harder than she meant to. "The doctor will be in with a report soon. They think a lightning strike might have scrambled my thinking some, but that's not true. I'm fine! I'll be fine if we find her."

Now he held her hand in both of his. "Just stay out

of it and let the authorities do their thing, both of you," he said, glancing at Amelia. "I promise you, I'll pull all the strings I can and I'll stay in touch." He bent to kiss her cheek again. As he moved away, Bree saw his wife out in the hall, looking in. Before she could tell Josh, he hurried out. The room suddenly seemed silent and small again. Then Josh popped back in, pulling his wife behind him. Obviously, Nikki Austin had more influence getting where she wanted to go in the hospital than Cole did.

Nicole Grann Austin was even more striking in person than on TV, in the newspapers or on the glossy brochures the postal carriers delivered in droves these days. Her long, honey-hued hair framed her heart-shaped face, her teeth looked like an ad for whitening strips, and, even now, she looked dressed to kill.

"Nikki says the press in the lobby are really getting restless," Josh said. "Bree and Amelia, I don't believe you've met Nikki," he added, making introductions all around. Nikki whispered something to him. "Yeah, good," he told her, then turned to Bree again. "Look, we have a friend who does a lot of PR for us and pilots our plane. He's a triple-threat man, because the truth is, he's also a bodyguard. With this tough race and in this day and age, you just never know. Mark Denton is out in the hall waiting for us, and I'd be glad to loan him to you for a while to keep the media at bay, if you'd like. We're staying in town tonight and don't need him to fly us back to Tallahassee until tomorrow."

"That's really kind of you, but that's okay," Bree said. "I certainly don't need a bodyguard." She thought of Cole again. If he would just be willing to help her...

"You call us, if you do," Nikki put in. Bree saw that the woman was studying her avidly. Maybe she was curious about what someone who had been hit by lightning looked like. Yet there was an edginess about her, or was that just energy and excitement in her big, blue eyes? "Here," Nikki went on, "I'm going to write down both of our cell-phone numbers for you in case. And I'm a lot easier to reach than 'the man' here, if you need anything at all."

Bree took the piece of paper from her, despite the fact Amelia also reached for it. With more good wishes and promises of help, they were gone. Bree caught a glimpse of their companion, Mark Denton, who reminded her of those buff, secret-service types who hovered around the president. That joke Josh had made about the White House—she didn't put it past him or Nikki either.

"Now you just take his advice and get some rest, because I'm sure he'll help us," Amelia said as she opened the folded newspaper he'd brought and a glossy You Can Trust Josh Austin brochure spilled out on the bed. "See?" she said, pointing at it. "For once, truth in advertising."

Finally, Bree was alone. After a detailed, positive report from the Fort Myers's neuropsychologist about her tests, which had included simple memory quizzes, an IQ and an organizational-ability puzzle, no medical personnel were in the room. Amelia had gone to meet her boys, six-year-old Jordan and eight-year-old James, when they got home from school and take them to a neighbor's before she came back.

Amelia had washed her salt-water-stiffened hair for her, chattering about how she used to wash her and Daria's hair when they were little. The dressing on Bree's wrist burn had been changed and the nurse had taught her how to tape a plastic sleeve around her arm so that she could take a shower, which she'd done before Amelia left. Actually, Bree had lifted several other plastic sleeves off the nurse's cart, because she was going to need them.

She had to get out of here. Forget this staying in for further observation. She was the one who needed to do observation of the entire gulf if she had to. She was going to get Manny to take her out to the Trade Wreck so she and one of her scuba-diving friends could start to trace Daria.

Bree hated to be sneaking out, but she was certain, except for her strange perceptions of light and sound, that she was all right. Dr. Hawkins had said if she had any ringing in her ears, it would probably lessen, so she expected her other problems would end soon, too. He had insisted she needed at least another day of observation and then several days of rest, so Amelia was determined to have Bree go home with her.

Since she was not only burned but burned-out, Bree knew full well the doctor and Amelia would try to stop her from diving. She'd probably have to lie to Manny and whomever she called to help her dive about being given a clean bill of health, but she would do whatever it took to find her sister. What could they do? Arrest her? Lock her up? Nothing mattered but finding Daria. No way could she wait for the possibility of being released tomorrow. That might be too late; it might already be too late.

Bree had racked her brain for clues to what might have happened to her twin. The first thing she could think of to do was to learn whether the boat's anchor chain was still planted near the Trade Wreck. Had it been pulled up or thrown over? Second, she had to find and salvage her camera. While Bree suited up, Daria had shot some sample pics off the side of the ship. What if there was some hint on that camera, maybe of another watercraft lurking nearby? And she had to call her civil air patrol friend, Dave Mangold. She needed a clue, any clue!

Even though Sam Travers hated her, she was going to ask him to use his large search-and-salvage vessel to look for Daria. She'd hire him if she had to. The coast guard and the civil air patrol obviously could use the help. Sam had that expensive echo sounder, too. If it could spot schools of fish and find anomalies, even wrecks on the bottom of the gulf...

She covered her face with her hands and sucked in a sob. It horrified her even to consider that *Mermaids II* might have actually gone down in the storm. It couldn't be, but she had to try everything, had to get the answers no one else was giving her. Losing Daria would be almost like losing herself.

She got out of bed slowly. A bit light-headed, not really dizzy. Man, she hated these hospital gowns. At least they'd untethered her from those hanging tubes. She'd forced herself to eat lunch, tomato soup and half a grilled cheese sandwich, to get some strength and convince Amelia and the nurses she was recovering physically from her ordeal.

Bree shuffled over and closed the door to the hall, hoping that might signal she was sleeping. She knew where the street clothes were that Amelia had brought. She'd be crazy to try walking out of here in her mermaid wet suit. In the tiny bathroom, she put slacks, shoes, a blouse and matching jacket on—you might know Amelia wouldn't bring any of her more casual work clothes— when the phone on her bedside table rang. She'd have to answer it. Besides, it might be the coast guard or air patrol.

She picked up the phone on its fourth ring. "Briana Devon."

"Briana! Cole DeRoca. I'm down in the lobby with a friend of yours who heard me ask if you could have visitors this afternoon, a guy named Manny. They say you can't and that they can't even release how you're doing because of privacy laws."

Her heartbeat kicked up. Her prayers—some of them, at least—were being answered.

"Cole," she said, trying to keep from crying in relief. This was obviously a sign she should forge ahead with her plans. "You're a godsend, because I'm leaving and I'd appreciate a ride home. Amelia's not here right now. I'll be down in a minute, but ask Manny to hang around, would you? And if there are reporters in the lobby—"

"Three of them, two with cameramen."

"In that case, get Manny to meet us at the shop in Turtle Bay and wait for me by the E.R. entrance, okay?"

"Will do, but are you sure you're strong enough?"

"Strong enough to do whatever it takes to find my sister," she said, and hung up before he could question her more about her sudden release.

Making for the door, Bree felt like a felon escaping from the penitentiary. At the last minute, she turned back and scribbled her nurse a note, telling her she was fine and had gone for a walk. That was true enough; somehow, she was going for a dive, too.

As she peeked into the hall, then strode out nonchalantly, she carried Cole's gift of the orange orchid in her arms.

5

"Is Amelia coming to your place to stay with you?" Cole asked as he drove her away from the hospital. They turned onto the busy Tamiami Trail and headed south toward Turtle Bay. She wanted to recline the seat and go to sleep, but she sat erect, cursing the fact Amelia hadn't brought her sunglasses. The light, the sounds of traffic—too bright, too much.

"She's with her two little boys right now," she told him, pulling down the sun visor on her side. "I'm sure she'll be over soon." She couldn't decide whether to just level with Cole or to get home first before she sprang her desperate plan on him and Manny. Cole had helped her before, but would he help her now? Besides, just his presence, his closeness, was making her even more nervous than she already was.

"Have you ever scuba dived?" she asked.

"Strictly for recreation, but I can hold my own. The last time was in Tahiti for a wedding anniversary. I'm single now."

"Sorry." She wasn't sorry, but she had no time for such thoughts.

"Don't be. Definitely the best for me and her, too, since she left me."

A woman had left this man? The entire world was crazy.

"Briana, you look shaky. You aren't going to be sick?"

"Sick at heart. I'd warn you before I'd upchuck in this beautiful car."

He was driving a big burgundy sedan, probably one he used to impress his clients, because it didn't seem like him and it certainly didn't seem like Turtle Bay. This was a man she didn't really know.

The village of Turtle Bay was a fairly secluded enclave between the Tamiami Trail on the east, the Gulf of Mexico on the west, the city of Naples to its north and Marco Island to its south. Turtle Bay had been built up years ago, with two clam-canning factories that were now defunct, and the usual condos and luxury waterfront homes had not intruded yet. A lot of locals feared the proposed gambling casino boat here could change all that. One of the old canneries was now quaint shops and seafood restaurants; the other had been converted to Sam Travers's Search and Salvage. Tourists and fishermen came and went daily in Turtle Bay, but returned to their luxe hotels in Naples when the day's jaunt was over. It was a tidal bay, so the main marina was built up on high posts, as were some of the modest houses, even those built farther back off the waterfront. Everything from dinghies to yachts and all sizes of sailboats bobbed in the bay.

Manny was waiting for them at the Two Mermaids with the door open. Thank heavens, no reporters were in sight. "Let's go upstairs," she told the men and, though every muscle of her body ached, she tried to lead them upstairs gracefully.

Her and Daria's two-bedroom apartment above the shop was a light, airy and pleasant place with white wicker furniture, bright floral pillows and open vistas of the marina, bay and gulf. Without Daria, it seemed oppressive, so she was glad to have their company.

She took the orchid Cole had carried up for her and put it on the glass-topped coffee table, which was cluttered with the books Daria had been studying for her accounting class. They'd finally admitted they'd been too careless with the financial end of their business. Manny had volunteered to handle that, but they'd decided one of them should specialize in it, and Daria had cheerfully volunteered. She'd seemed obsessed with the course work ever since. In college—Dad had insisted they go to his alma mater in Miami—neither of them had taken courses in anything like accounting or business. Bree had studied languages, and Daria was a philosophy major. The truth was, both of them had majored in giving scuba lessons and getting a tan on trendy South Beach.

"Please sit, both of you," Bree said, and went into the small galley kitchen. When she was certain they couldn't see her, she grasped the edge of the countertop and leaned against it, stiff armed, staring at Daria's latest note—dated last Friday—on the bulletin board over the sink: *Don't worry about me. Going to study w/ friends after class and might be in late.*

She could not cry, Bree told herself, could not dissolve in frustration or fear. She must find strength she did not have, courage she did not feel. However hurting and exhausted, she had to get moving.

She gulped a glass of orange juice, then poured Coke

into three glasses, dumped a bag of taco chips into a bowl and carried all that in on a tray. She wanted desperately for these men to see her in control. Cole sat on the sofa, and Manny had taken her rocking chair, so she sat in Daria's. They were talking about how Manny never dived but oversaw the shop, their two boats—the larger of which was now missing—and the heavy equipment. Man, Bree thought as she drank down half of her soda, but she needed this sugar and caffeine to stoke her strength.

"So, what you planning?" Manny asked her. "I know you. Want me to get the coast guard and the air patrol on the phone?"

"I'm going to call them, but I want to talk to both of you first."

She forced herself to look directly into Cole's narrowed eyes, because she figured she could get Manny to do what she wanted. Yes, despite the dire situation, the instant arc of energy and tension crackled between them as fiercely as it had the day they'd had that impromptu lunch on the yacht months ago. She had to admit that Cole DeRoca was still the great unknown, deeper than the sea. He had been nothing but kind and caring, but she well knew there could be unknown fathoms beneath. She felt so intensely drawn to the man that she feared her spinning senses could too easily swamp her usually sensible nature. She couldn't afford a distraction right now when she needed to be self-disciplined. She needed the man to help her and had to shut everything else out.

"To try to find Daria," she told them, gripping her sweating glass hard in both hands, "I need to figure out if she left the dive site of her own accord or unwillingly."

"Caramba," Manny exclaimed, flinging gestures, "for sure, it was unwilling."

"So you plan to do what?" Cole asked, putting down his glass and leaning forward with his wrists on his knees.

"I need to see if our boat's anchor is missing from the seabed near the turtle grass meadow. I dived down the anchor line as usual. But when I was ready to go up, I didn't even look for it and just made the ascent from where I was."

"Yeah, you done that before," Manny put in.

"But was the anchor there," she went on, "and I just didn't see it in the increasing turbulence and lessening visibility? Is it still there? And if so, was the anchor chain hauled up properly or shoved off in a hurry? We paid good money for that new anchor and chain, because we've had them pull loose, and twice our rope was cut on something. If Daria didn't leave under duress, she would have hauled it in."

"What you thinking?" Manny demanded. "That more than a storm made her leave you there?"

"Of course it was more than a storm that made her leave me there!" Bree exploded. "That was bad, but it wasn't a hurricane! Sorry," she added more quietly, covering her eyes with one hand. "I'm just on edge, and I know you've been, too, Manny, trying to handle your mother's illness, Lucinda's attitude and everything."

As she lowered her hand and looked at him, he shook his head. "Lucinda's craziness *nada* compared to this," he said. "Anyhow I can help, I help."

"Good," she said. "I'd like you to go down to our slip at the marina and make sure *Mermaid I* is ready to go and that scuba tanks are filled—for two divers, if Cole will come along. It still stays light pretty late. At least the storms missed us today, so maybe the underwater visibility will be better."

"You're going diving *now?*" Cole demanded. "Look, Briana, I'm sure you know a lot of local divers who could search for—"

"I need to do it! I know the area. Besides, if I could just retrieve my camera, it could have something on it. I had to let it go in the storm."

"You got photos of something strange?" Manny asked. He clenched both fists. Even with his brown skin, Bree could tell he was flushing. His voice rose as he got up from the couch and took a step toward the door. "You really thinking someone did something dirty?"

"I don't want to think that, but I know she wouldn't just leave, storm or not, toothache or not. I know Daria as well as I know myself!"

Manny bent to swig the rest of his soda and went out. She could hear him thudding down the stairs, muttering to himself.

"Briana—"

"You can call me Bree if you want."

"The thing is," Cole went on, "even if the doctor cleared you to leave the hospital, that hardly meant you could go diving right away."

"He didn't clear me," she blurted. "I cleared myself and cleared out. I have to do this!"

She jumped up, making Daria's chair rock back and forth on its own as if a ghost sat there. With a shiver snaking up her spine, she moved to the French doors, which had a view of the bay. The sight of the sunlit marina and the gulf beyond almost blinded her. Pushing the double doors open, she stepped out onto the veranda where they kept a wrought-iron table and two chairs. She grabbed sunglasses Daria had left there and shoved them on to mute the slant of late-afternoon sun. Not only had her heightened perception of light not worn off, but she was certain that, beyond the normal bustle of the marina, she could hear the seductive sounds of the sea.

Bree decided she'd need to start wearing earplugs, not when she dove, but when she was on terra firma. She'd often had to wear them to sleep. Unlike Daria, she couldn't fall asleep anywhere. On their overnight flight to Greece for their college-graduation gift, Daria had conked out right away and arrived raring to go, while Bree had wasted an entire night's sleep just being annoyed that Daria was lost in sweet dreams. Daria…lost… in dreams that were really nightmares…

"Bree," Cole said, following her out and putting his big hands gently on her shoulders from behind, "under ordinary circumstances, I'd tell you you're nuts. You've got a lot of professional people looking for her. Besides, the police have a dive team—though, I suppose, they won't deploy it until they're convinced of foul play, even if we ask…" His deep voice trailed off.

She turned to face him and found herself staring at the beating pulse in his strong, bronzed throat. He was half a head taller than she, but his broad shoulders made him seem larger than that. His eyes were a rich mahogany hue, framed by long, thick lashes. She could see her reflection there, could almost drown in their depths.

For one crazed instant, she longed to throw herself into his arms and just hold tight, to beg him to take this burden from her, comfort her, let her hide in his strength. But she did none of those things. Tackle a problem head-on, Dad would have said. It was the way she was and

Daria, too. But had Daria, out on that boat in those rough waves, tried to take on something—or someone—she could not handle?

"Cole, I know that area and the currents like the back of my hand. I have to do this or I'll never forgive myself. I'm certain I would feel something if she weren't... weren't alive. But I do sense she's in danger. Call it women's intuition or a sister's sixth sense. I just have to go check the dive site."

"Then I'll go with you—on one condition. If you begin to feel ill down there or I see anything I don't like, that's it, we're out. And we're not going to do any kind of wide sweep for the camera if it's not near the dive site. Promise me," he said, gripping her upper arms, "because I mean it. I'll pull you right out of there—again."

"Yes, all right, I promise. I owe you doubly. I really think God sent you to find me, and to help find Daria."

"Then I just pray I'm up to pleasing all three of you," he said and surprised her with a hard hug before he let her go.

While Manny was preparing the skiff and putting air in their tanks and Cole drove to his workshop where he kept his own diving gear, Bree made four quick calls. She phoned the hospital main desk to officially check herself out. They were very upset and said they'd inform Dr. Hawkins immediately, but she hung up before they could page him. Bree knew Amelia would try to stop her from diving, so she called her at home and got her answering machine. That was what she'd hoped for, since Amelia should be picking up Jordan and James from their private elementary school about now. She left her a message that she was feeling much stronger and had decided to come home.

She then phoned the coast guard emergency contact number and, after no news there, the civil air patrol information line. She was disappointed and dismayed to learn her pilot friend, Dave Mangold, was out of town and had not participated in the air search. There was no sign of Daria or their boat, but both organizations would keep her informed.

Informed. She was terrified to get a call from either of them.

Realizing she'd left her mermaid diving suit at the hospital, she donned an old pink spandex wet suit and hurried downstairs. Though she didn't intend to tell Cole, she felt strange, kind of floaty, but she had to do this and now. Surely, this almost out-of-body feeling was not related to Daria's fate.

Dad had told them once that, even though he was outside in the waiting room when their mother died in the delivery room, he knew the exact moment when she'd gone because he felt kind of like he'd taken off from the ground. It was so bizarre, he'd said, like the feeling when you ride a roller coaster and go over the highest drop. There was no thrill, only an awed sense of doom. But Bree didn't want to remember all that, didn't want to think of that.

As she went to check her desk phone for messages, she heard heavy footsteps and turned to see if Manny or Cole were back. Big, burly Sam Travers, who ran the rival business across the bay, stood in the doorway, not in, not out. He seemed to block out the light and air.

With a bulky build and a face and body hardened by years of physical labor, Sam stood slightly over six feet tall. His hair had been gray for years, and he wore it cut tight to his head, which emphasized his prominent ears and narrowed eyes. Crow's feet perched at the corners, matching his deep frown lines. Sam had never given in to wearing sunglasses or caps.

Bree recalled from years ago when she and Ted used to hang out together all the time, that his father, now a sixty-four-year-old proud Vietnam War vet, looked angry even when he wasn't. Since she'd broken up with Ted, though, anger was his perpetual mood around her.

Sam had never been able to forget or forgive that she had broken up with his only child after going steady with him for almost five years, two and a half in high school and then the first two of college. That had started what Sam called a fatal chain of events. But once she was away from Turtle Bay, even though she and Ted were at college just across the state, her world had expanded and Ted's had not.

He'd been jealous of her new friends and her snorkeling and scuba students, even of the time she spent with Daria. He'd wanted to drive home most weekends, when she had things to do in Miami. He hadn't really liked college, and she'd thrived there. Maybe he'd become so stridently possessive because his mother had deserted him and Sam while Ted was still in elementary school, but it didn't do any good to try to analyze him. It just wasn't working for Bree anymore, but when she'd tried to reason with him, tried to back away, he'd stormed out and joined the marines—the foreign legion, Daria had called it—without even telling Sam.

So while Ted had gone through basic battle training at Paris Island, South Carolina, Sam Travers had begun his war with Bree. He'd blamed her entirely when Ted was killed by a roadside bomb thousands of miles away in Iraq last year. And when he'd been buried with military honors, Sam had exploded at her, telling her to stay away from the funeral, and Daria had gone alone. Things certainly had not gotten better when she and Daria had opened a competitive search-and-salvage shop, though much smaller and more specialized, on Sam's turf.

Now he stood in her doorway, glaring at her. Ordinarily, she'd be only too happy if she never saw Sam Travers again, but she needed his help.

"Yo," he said in his usual strident voice, which seemed even louder now. "I was looking for Manny the man, 'cause the TV says you're still in the hospital. Just wanted to tell him I been out looking for Daria."

Bree stayed behind her desk. "Thanks for anything you can do. I was going to call you, but I've been talking to the coast guard and the air patrol about the rescue efforts."

"They're good at talk. You want to find something— in this case, someone—you call Sam. You and I had some bad spots, but I got nothing 'gainst her. I'm going out again."

Bad spots? she thought. During these past three years after Ted enlisted, Sam had ranted at her, especially when he was drinking, and she'd come to fear him. However much she sympathized with his loss and grieved Ted's death, she'd even considered getting a restraining order. Ben, her prosecutor brother-in-law, had suggested it, but she didn't want to admit weakness to Sam, who sometimes seemed right on the edge of becoming a stalker. There were times when she and Daria thought he turned up everywhere.

"I can't thank you enough for helping," Bree brazened, though her voice shook. "I know if anyone can find Daria and *Mermaids II,* it's you."

"Yeah, well, bodies might not surface for over a week, but wrecks only give up a trail of bubbles for about twenty-four hours. Time's awastin'. You facing up to the fact I been using my echo sounder?"

"I'm sure she's all right...not—the skiff's not sunk. She put in somewhere. She's safe, I can feel it."

"Yeah, I was sure Ted would be all right, too, big guy like that, body armor and all. A well-trained, gung ho marine riding shotgun on an armored tank. Maybe I'm doing this for him, huh, since Daria was his friend, even if you never really were."

He went out and slammed the door.

6

On the way out to the dive site in the boat, *Mermaids I,* with Manny at the wheel, Cole's thoughts were flying as fast as the white wake they left behind. He'd been trying to come up with additional arguments for why this dive was a bad idea, but he knew he'd do the same thing in Bree's place. Unless he tied her up, he figured he couldn't stop her, so he had to go along to be certain nothing happened to her. He knew she was going, with or without him.

Then, too, she'd convinced him that she could sense that Daria was alive. He knew nothing firsthand about that intense kind of simpatico relationship with another person, but he'd read identical twins could be that way, and he'd never seen twins who were more mirror images of each other. He'd studied a framed photo of them in their apartment, a formal, posed picture where they were evidently bridesmaids at someone's wedding. They were beautiful women. If he ever saw Briana smile, he could probably tell one from the other, because one of them had a slightly lopsided grin, with a sort of bet-you-can't-guess-what-I'm-thinking look.

He was coming to know Briana, and he figured he

knew Daria a bit, too, so this felt doubly personal to him. Another reason that he was literally along for the ride, even though he should have been installing Brazilian cherry in the salon on a big yacht in Naples today, was that he'd quickly come to admire Bree so much. She had not gotten hysterical and had seemed in control, when most women he knew would be frantic wrecks by now. Jillian's first response to any trauma had been tears and tantrums, so he was totally impressed with this woman. Impressed and just plain turned-on, even in these terrible circumstances.

Cole tried to listen carefully as Bree told him things he should know about the dive. Though she was speaking over the roar of the motor, she wasn't talking loudly enough, and sometimes he had to almost read her lips. Like Cole, Manny seemed to be straining forward to hear her. Instead of facing her, Cole moved to sit beside her, edging her over a bit.

"Motor's too loud to hear you!" he told her, only to see her cringe. "What is it? What's the matter?"

"I agree about the motor. Your voice—I'm hearing sounds sharper than I did before, that's all. It's nothing. Okay, I'll start over. First off, if you're used to diving in the Caribbean or even in the Keys, the water's going to look really different here, not so clear. We'll both take dive lights. Manny brought two dive lights along, didn't you, Manny?" she asked, craning around toward the back of the boat so he could hear her.

She almost bumped noses with Manny since he was leaning so close to her. "Always got two of everything on board," Manny told her, sitting up straighter. "Usually for you and Daria."

Bree just nodded. When she turned back toward him, Cole saw she had tears in her eyes.

"Go on," he prompted. He was grateful she seemed to be thinking clearly, despite the fact her emotions were right on the edge.

"We're only going down to thirty feet," she explained, "so we won't have to decompress, but we'll take a three-minute safety stop at fifteen feet, both entering and ascending. The wreck lies in a small, natural trough."

"What's the visibility at that depth?"

"Vis varies a lot out here, from six inches to sixty feet, but since we evidently aren't getting a storm today, it could have settled down to ten or twelve, especially since the incoming tide will bring in clearer water. I've got to find that camera."

"Let's just say we'll check for the anchor today. Set reasonable goals. We can't search a vast area on this dive."

As if she didn't hear that, when he knew she did, she continued. "The camera's in a plastic housing, which mutes the red color I've painted it, especially since all reds disappear about fifteen feet down. At the depth we're diving, everything will look green, yellow or blue."

"I remember. Bree, we should keep this dive short."

"We need to cover a certain area," she countered.

Cole was not used to being told what to do. Damn, this woman was stubborn, but maybe that came with being strong.

"I never would have done a dive alone that day," she admitted, suddenly changing the topic. She kept fussing with her mask she held in her lap. "But Manny needed time to patch up the generation gap with his daughter and couldn't go. It was the fifty-seventh dive we'd made at the Trade Wreck without incident, photographing and recording the growth of the turtle grass there. Daria had a really bad toothache that came on fast, so I said I'd go down alone. It only takes about twenty-five minutes. The storm was a distant line on the horizon, and the marine weather forecast hadn't mentioned it could come in so fast or hard."

"I know. So you anchored nearby but not where the anchor could disturb the site," Cole said, when she frowned out over the water.

"Right. The submerged aquatic vegetation—SAV—is very delicate and not doing well. We always joked that our motto for this Clear the Gulf Commission project would be Save Our SAV."

Her voice trailed off and her eyes took on a faraway look. Was she seeing a scene with her sister? He bumped her shoulder gently, and she seemed to come back from wherever she'd been. He was going to have to stick close to her down there, though she was obviously the more skilled diver.

She went on. "The report we were preparing to give the commission—and the media—next week would not be good news. The poor and declining quantity and quality of the sea grass indicates that the whole marine ecosystem here is still struggling from the increasing industrial and toxic runoff. Too many people means too much pollution, and that extends to the Trade Wreck sea grass meadow, which we're using as a sort of touchstone and symbol for the health of this entire area of the gulf. And it's sick."

"A dire report could mean cutbacks, penalties and political fallout for lots of important people. When the foundation of the marine food chain is screwed up, it's trouble for every living organism all the way up to humans, and that equates to millions of dollars in fishing, real estate and the tourist trade. Had you told anybody about your findings already?" he asked.

"We weren't keeping it a secret," she admitted. "You're thinking someone might want to warn us or stop us from releasing that? But everyone with interests in those things you just mentioned would want the environment to stay safe. They'd want to know what our report says so the situation can be fixed by concerned citizens, environmentalists, scientists, politicians—everyone."

"Back to our dive. We can't search the entire area for a camera."

"I'm hoping it snagged on either the Trade Wreck or another artificial reef nearby."

He nodded. "I heard there's one about three miles off Keewadin, where you came in."

"Right, the Stone Reef. That one's not a wreck but limestone boulders. I don't know if the camera would just go to the smooth, sandy bottom and stay put, or if the tides and currents would move it south until it snagged in one reef or the other."

"So what's the Trade Wreck like?"

"It's a supply ship sunk in the late 1930s, made of wood and metal. It broke apart but what's there is pretty well preserved."

"Do you use GPS coordinates to locate the site? I don't see that equipment on board."

"Our only GPS is on the bigger boat, but we've been out here so much, it's half instinct and half compass coordinates. You'll be glad to know it's ordinarily a safe dive, with no sharks out here. I think the rough water or sudden change in barometric pressure from the storm yesterday stirred them up."

"I was wondering if you still remembered the sharks. You must have swum with them. Some followed us into shore in the sloop."

"I don't want to think about that," she said, shaking her head. "At least the only big fish usually around the Trade Wreck is a resident grouper Daria and I named Gertie…"

She sniffed hard. Tears welled up in her eyes again, and she bit her lower lip. He wanted to put his arm around her, but he just held on to the rail tight as Manny turned them in a slow circle and killed the motor.

Bree usually felt at one with the sea and completely relaxed during her dives. But not today. She wore a high-volume mask that had more airspace and side ports so she could see sideways without turning her head. She'd worn this old Day-Glo-pink wet suit partly because it had a pocket on both upper thighs for a dive knife. She carried two knives, hoping Cole didn't find that strange and that Manny would keep quiet about how abnormal it was.

But *everything* was abnormal. She had the worst feeling something evil was lurking underwater. At least she had Cole along. Though she didn't like to think of Cole as a bodyguard, she felt much safer near him. It was obvious that Josh and Nikki Austin felt that way with their pilot-PR man-bodyguard, so why shouldn't she admit the same to herself? In ordinary circumstance, the idea of this compelling, virile man guarding her body would be to die for—damn, why had she thought of it that way?

She'd used a plastic sleeve to cover the bandage over

her burn and wore her old dive watch on her right wrist. She'd have to call the hospital to ask where the one Daria gave her went, because it might be the last gift...the last...

She turned back to her preparations. They screwed on their pressure gauges and checked the air fill, then hooked up their regulators and sucked on them. Bree heard the familiar hissing of gas and the click of the valves, but so much louder than usual.

They back-rolled over the boat rail and went under in a rising blur of silver bubbles. When the cloud cleared, Bree looked for Cole and saw he was above her with only his big body visible, as if he had been decapitated. He must have stuck his head out of the water to say something to Manny.

Waiting for him to join her, Bree racked her brain to recall if she had looked up at the surface or even over at the anchor yesterday while she took photos, made measurements and took notes. When had *Mermaids II* left? If a second hull had loomed above, she would not have seen it in the low vis and increasing turbulence, but she should have heard an unfamiliar motor. Or had she been too rushed, too intent and busy to note sounds? Usually, even the bothersome little wave runners zipping here and there made a distinctive sound, and she was good at differentiating motor reverberations, from buzz to hum to roar, depending on the size of the vessel.

Cole upended and kicked down to join her at fifteen feet for their safety stop. They were diving the anchor line, but didn't hang on to it, just near it. From watching him come down and reverse his position to stay stationary beside her, she could tell he was a good diver.

They hung suspended, facing each other, kicking

slowly in unison, barely moving but nearly touching. There was something intriguing and intimate about being here like this with him, hidden, close, almost motionless, suspended as if they lay side by side. Although the vastness of the sea was her favorite place to be, Cole DeRoca made her feel small. She wanted his protection, but the turbulent sensations he stirred in her made her also feel out of control and she could not afford that, especially not now. Find clues, she told herself. Find clues to find Daria.

Through their masks, they looked below toward the two gray, shadowy, separate sections of the fifty-foot wreck. Yet their gazes returned to hold each other. Bree forced herself out of the deceptively peaceful lull. She nodded and they swam down toward the wreck with her leading.

The supply boat, named the *Charlotte G. Loher* but referred to by most local divers as the Trade Wreck, had sailed out of Tampa bound for Key West with cattle in the pre-highway days of southwest Florida. Caught in a hurricane, it had broken into two sections. The stern had settled on its hull, but the midship and the prow lay on its port side. With several entrances into the interior of the ship, it had long been an attraction for divers, though it was labeled a hazard dive now for its rusted, jagged edges and unstable structure. The twins had a theory that the increasing pollution in the gulf had accelerated the disintegration of its wood and metal. One of the wreck's bizarre attractions was that occasionally, even now, the skull of a steer would float loose from the innards of the ship to gape eyeless out a porthole in the hull or emerge from the dark entry to a mazelike corridor. The twins had never taken one for a dive trophy, but they knew more than one bar or family room that boasted a skull from the Trade Wreck. Bree realized, too late, that she had forgotten to mention that to Cole.

As the wreck loomed closer in the shifting soup of the sea, they clicked on their lights. Bree startled. She was used to things looking twenty-five per cent larger underwater, but she hadn't been prepared for the increased brightness even here. Perhaps her heightened perceptivity of sound and light could be a blessing. The backscatter of tiny, drifting marine organisms stood out brilliantly. Their slow, swirling movement made her dizzy, but she shook that off. Anyway, this close to possible answers, she was not turning back.

A three-foot sea turtle swimming above the debris eyed them, then glided away. When they swam over and hovered above the sparse sea grass meadow, tiny, spidery arrow crabs with fuzzy topknots seemed to stare at them, but they saw no Gertie the grouper and no camera snagged anywhere here or on the sand flats.

Bree noted that the storm had pulled a few strands of grass loose. Of the fifty-two species of marine sea grass worldwide, only about four of those were widespread in Florida. Her precious turtle grass—fancy biological name *Thalassia testudinum*—was the most hardy, with its deep root system and sturdy runners from which grew blades of graceful, bright green grass. Most of the sea grass meadow stood about fourteen inches tall and shifted its gentle, ribbonlike blades in harmony with the currents. It should love the relatively shallow waters here but, as she'd told Cole, it was struggling to survive here—just as she was, she thought.

But she had no time for her beloved project right now. They swam back toward the wreck, playing their yellow beams ahead of them. Sometimes Cole's shaft of light seemed to dance with hers. If only her camera had caught here on the exterior of the ship, and if only it had captured some clue to what happened on the surface.

Bree motioned to Cole, and they swam the area around the wreck in broadening circles, searching for the camera and the anchor. Cole was not letting her out of his sight. When she motioned he could go one way and she the other, he shook his head and swam right on her tail.

And then they saw something. Both their beams shone dully off the links of a chain, which they followed to the half-buried anchor itself. Yes, their new anchor and chain! It was at least thirty feet from the position of the anchor and rope from their smaller skiff today. When Cole held his hands up in a questioning gesture as if to ask her if that was her anchor, she nodded, but her heart sank.

Daria never would have thrown the entire chain overboard, not unless something terrible—more than an approaching storm—had made her flee fast. Or had someone else thrown it over? And if that someone had wanted the *Mermaids II,* would they have also thrown Daria overboard?

The find filled her with frustration and fury. She had to locate that camera now at all costs, even if it meant going a ways into that broken, rusting old wreck.

She led Cole back in that direction, and they swam the entire length of where the camera might have drifted down or been snagged against the ship by the incoming tide. It was just over twenty-four hours ago now. How could so much have happened so fast? Twenty-four hours—like Sam had said, a new wreck only released a trail of bubbles for that long. *Daria, even if the boat went down, tell me you didn't go with it! I made it in. You must have, too!*

They saw no sign of the camera, so they started back, this time peering into nooks and crannies where it might have caught. Bree berated herself that she hadn't somehow kept the camera with her in the storm, however heavy and bulky. Using both their lights, they illumined each dark entry spot until—

Bree jerked back. Oh, it was just one of those cow skulls, bobbing on the other side of a thick glass porthole. When they'd first dived this wreck with their father years ago, the portholes had been covered with algae, but that, too, had been done in by the lack of oxygen in what some called dead water.

She tried to fight off the images that being this close to the wreck often triggered in her. Whenever she could, she ignored the ship's ruins and just concentrated on the sea grass meadow. She and Ted had dived this wreck just before they'd broken up, the summer before their junior year of college. The two of them had always called this wreck the *Titanic,* not because of its size, but because they'd seen the movie just before they'd first dived it together.

As bold as Bree was underwater, that movie had shaken her to her core. The scene where Kate Winslet and Leonardo DiCaprio had stood together at the top of the ship as it was sinking into the cold Atlantic had not just scared her but haunted her ever since. The first time Sam berated her for being the reason Ted enlisted and died, he'd said she'd *scuttled* and *wrecked* his son's life. And in her nightmares about Ted's death, he wasn't killed by an improvised incendiary device in Iraq but

was sent down to his death on a sinking ship, while—
like the woman in the movie—Bree survived and lived
her life. Then guilt hung heavy in her heart, until she
could convince herself once again that Ted had made
his own choices and that his loss—like her mother's
death—was not her fault.

Now…now, when that nightmare stalked her, in sleep
or awake, would she see Daria going down with the
ship? While Bree still lived and breathed and walked and
swam, would it be Daria she saw, doomed and clinging
to *Mermaids II* while it slipped into the dreadful depths.

Cole tapped on his tank and gestured about the skull.
She tried to motion back to him that cows had been the
cargo. He nodded, and they went on, swimming about
five feet apart, peering as far as they could see into en-
tries of the wreck. It didn't take long to determine that
the camera was not snagged against the upright stern,
but she knew it could have settled into numerous nooks
in the tipped fore parts of the ship.

And then Bree saw it! A glint of new metal! It was
lodged in a small cranny that had once been clearly
marked but was now faded: Fire Ax and Hose—Break
Glass. No glass now, and someone might have taken
the ax head for a souvenir, but the ragged remains of an
old fire hose hung there below the rotting ax handle. It
looked like the plastic housing had come off the corner
of the camera, but she reached for the piece of metal
she could see.

And yanked her arm back. From behind the remnants
of the hose, a moray eel lunged at her, barely missing
her hand. Bree backed away fast; the eel retreated partly
into its lair. Her heart was thudding so hard it sounded
like a bass drum was in her mask.

Morays loved to hide in rocks, tall grass or small cre-
vasses to wait for their prey. Frightening in appearance,
they had small eyes and a protruding snout, but worse
was their always-open mouth, with their powerful jaws
and long, sharp teeth. Their skin was scaleless and they
had thick, mucous-covered, patterned bodies so they
could hide from their prey. This one looked about four
feet long, dangerous and hidden...like someone who
may have hurt Daria.

Cole took her elbow and pulled her farther away. She
pointed at the edge of the camera and he nodded. He
swam over the moray's lair and carefully retrieved the
half-rotted wooden ax handle. With it, he hooked the
edge of the camera and pulled it out. The eel lunged at
the metal, then retreated once again to protect his piece
of property.

Bree was relieved until she saw that what had lodged
there was the strobe lights she had released and not the
camera.

She held the strobe up and shook her head. Cole
squeezed her shoulder. *Is that yours?* he gestured, and
she nodded. Their eyes met through their masks. Bree
fought back tears. She did not dare cry or the mask
would be a mess. She motioned to him that if the strobe
was snagged on the wreck, the camera could well be,
too. He shook his head and pointed to his watch, though
she saw they'd only been down twenty minutes and they
had much more air. When he pointed toward the surface, she shook her head and gestured with both hands
and her fingers spread: just ten more minutes to peek
inside the open entryways.

Another of the common safety sayings about diving,
one her dad had stressed, popped into her head. *Only*

fools break the rules. She was not a wreck diver and she hadn't brought either a wreck reel or a penetration line to help find her way out once she was inside the decaying wreck, where pieces could be loose or block an exit. These lights were good for a thirty-foot dive but not for diving blind inside a wreck—another rule about taboos. Still, when she hit the button on the strobe, it flashed its nearly blinding light. That would have to do to guide her just a little way, to find the camera, which she'd let go of in the same spot she'd dropped the strobe. The risk of moray eels be damned.

She gestured for Cole to follow and swam quickly toward the Trade Wreck with her strobe in one hand and her flashlight in the other. She did not look back. Just a short glimpse inside this corridor and then she'd quickly back out when she was sure the camera could not have been swept farther in.

She heard not only her dad's words this time, but his voice, too, loud over the hiss-hiss of her own breath in her ears. *Only fools stretch the rules.* She was a fool, then, a frenzied fool. But if Dad were here, he'd understand why she had to find the camera, find any clue to find Daria. He'd agree that the motto for now was *Daria's lost, and must be found at any cost.*

Cole was quick. Bree felt him make a grab for her ankle, but she kept kicking. She shot the strobe off repeatedly to see as she swam inside the sunken ship.

7

Bree was desperate to find the camera, and it was too narrow and too late to back out now. In and down she swam, headfirst into the rabbit hole of a dangerous wonderland. Everything seemed alien, even when she lit the dimness only by her single shaft of flashlight beam. Each time the blinding strobe flashed, the rust-encrusted depths of the long-sunken ship made it seem as if its metal skin was bleeding. The dizzying whirl of floating particles caught in the weird currents toyed with her equilibrium.

In this section of the ship, the port-side wall was the floor of the wreck, so the vessel's ceiling swirled past on her left and its floor on her right, making her feel even more disoriented. She swam over portholes that living souls had once peered out on their fateful voyage. This world—her entire world—had gone topsy-turvy. Had any of the crew's bones been trapped here like their living cargo's? Had something or someone sunk *Mermaids II?*

Bree saw no more cattle skulls, though several strange sea creatures peered at her and a small lobster scuttled away. But there was no camera. When the corridor turned and she peered beyond to some sort of galley, she maneuvered around to go back out and was amazed to see Cole, so close that she jerked back and clunked her tank into a bulkhead.

In the small, enclosed space, Cole seized her wrist and pulled her toward him. *Out of here and up to the surface,* he motioned, shining his light on his gestures. Shadows from his hands leaped across his face mask; with his beam at that sharp angle on his strong, sculpted features, he seemed to wear a fright mask. It made her think she really didn't know this man, yet she needed him badly.

Bree knew he was right to make her get out; she'd decided to leave anyway, now that she'd checked for the camera here. But, as if in protest, she accidentally hit the strobe button again. It flashed close in his face. His grip on her tightened, powerful, determined, and he took the strobe from her. Using only his flashlight beam, he gestured, *Out! You first.* She nodded and started out, using her light again. When they emerged into the relatively brighter water outside the Trade Wreck, she saw he had cut his wrist and was bleeding green blood, because at this depth, crimson always looked green.

She tried to motion that she hadn't known he was cut and hadn't meant to flash the strobe in his face. He just jerked his thumb up again. She took the strobe from him so he could stem the blood—she could not tell how bad the cut was—and they quickly ascended with no rest stop and no more communication. They both knew what a tiny bit of blood diffused in a vast stretch of the water could mean, and they didn't want those bull sharks back.

Bree felt light-headed. Those sharks…could they have

attacked Daria if she had fallen in or been pushed off *Mermaids II?* Bull sharks...the bones of bulls, the skulls of steers caught inside the Trade Wreck... Bree's life, wrecked without Daria... Daria trapped, her life maybe ruined, sunk...gone.

In a whoosh of foam and bubbles, they broke the surface together and swam to the skiff's ladder. Manny hurried over to meet them. Cole surprised her by giving her a one-handed boost on her bottom. She spit out her regulator and shoved her mask up on her head. "No, you're hurt. You first!"

"Get up there!" he ordered, his deep voice rough. "From now on, if we dive together looking for clues, I'm the dive boss. I don't care if you're the better diver! You're distraught right now, so I'm giving you a pass, but you're not going down there again without someone else in charge and you following orders!"

She climbed out with him right behind her. "How did you get cut?"

"Following you into that rusted bucket of bolts!"

"Since the strobe was there, I just had to look a littler farther in."

Trying to get a word in, Manny bent over them as they collapsed to sit side by side on the deck. "You find the camera?" Manny asked. "What 'bout the new anchor and chain? You find anything suspicious, any clues at all?"

Briefly, Bree updated him as she worked on Cole's cut with disinfectant from the first-aid kit. "I think you'll need a few stitches. I hope you've had a tetanus shot," she told him.

"Working with hammers and nails—and a crazed female diver—I'd better."

"I'm sorry this happened while you were trying to

help me again. I can drive you into an urgent-care clinic if you need stitches. I'd rather not face the E.R. at the hospital again right now."

"Yeah, it needs a couple of stitches, but I'll take care of it. Your burned wrist and now this," he muttered. "We're a pair."

We're a pair.

He'd said it quietly, but she heard him clearly. She looked into his dark eyes, so close, with the bright, setting sun on the gently rocking boat. Manny still hovered, asking more questions, but none of that registered as the physical and emotional impact of the man she tended hit her hard. She barely knew Cole DeRoca, her hero and rescuer, yet he cared about her and she for him.

We're a pair. That was a cliché she and Daria had used more than once, but now the words meant something different. This sweeping sensation hardly resembled the bond of empathy and synergy she and Daria shared. This was raw energy and power—a fierce magnetism—something she had never felt before, even with Ted, with whom she'd once been so infatuated. This was deeper, almost dangerous. But the timing was terrible, when she had to use anything and anyone, including Cole, to find her sister.

"I'll ask some local divers to help search," she said, when the silence between them turned awkward. "But if you could continue to help, I'd be so grateful. I have a supply of plastic sleeves to cover a hurt wrist." She finished daubing the antibacterial cream on the jagged inch-long cut. Maybe it wasn't as deep as it had looked at first. Thank God, it was on the side of his wrist and not the soft, inner skin, where he would bleed a lot harder.

Bree jumped when Manny started the motor. She'd

been so intent on Cole she hadn't realized Manny had moved away; she'd forgotten he was even here. Looking away again, out over the gulf that held sacred secrets, Bree pressed her lips tight together. Again she longed to throw herself into Cole's arms, but then she would explode in the hysteria she felt pressing down on her like the weight of water.

"When Daria and I were kids," she told him, raising her voice to be heard over the motor, "we once cut our wrists and swore a blood oath to be friends forever— very childish and very dramatic. Also stupid and dangerous, though we didn't know that. We were only about eight. We got in all kinds of trouble for it, and Amelia told her friends we were total flakes who didn't know you were only supposed to prick fingers."

Her voice broke, and she cleared her throat. She blinked back tears as she smoothed the edges of the big bandage onto his skin, tanned and flecked with crisp black hair. They were kneeling now, face-to-face, their hips and shoulders steadied against the rail by the ladder to keep from bouncing against each other as Manny headed the ship toward shore.

"Cole, I'll never be able to pay you back—I can't thank you enough for everything," she blurted, then scrambled to her feet and turned away to pick up some of her gear. Her emotions were so jumbled she was afraid she was going to burst into tears. She sat on the front seat, facing away from him, hunched over the strobe she held across her lap.

Cole came to sit beside her as they sped back toward Turtle Bay. "When this is all over and we've found Daria," he said, bending toward her so only she could hear, "we'll think of some way you can thank me."

* * *

At dusk that evening, Bree sat at the table in the apartment, poring over a marine map that detailed every reef, contour and cranny offshore in this area of the gulf. As she'd promised Cole, she'd made numerous calls to diving friends for help to search the gulf underwater tomorrow. Everyone—some were even taking personal days off from work to help—was going to assemble at her shop at nine in the morning. She jolted when her doorbell rang. Probably someone else from the media, she thought.

She almost wished she'd taken Josh and Nikki up on their loan of Mark Denton for a while. He was evidently good not only at protection but at handling press releases. Bree had given a brief statement to the man from the *Naples Daily News* and the Fort Myers ABC-TV reporter when they'd caught up with her earlier at the marina, but she wasn't going to answer the doorbell if it was more of the same.

Yet, what if there was word from the search teams— good news? Sometimes the media caught wind of things before those who should have been told first. Or what if Cole had returned? He'd said he would go have his wrist cared for, though, and wouldn't be back until tomorrow morning, unless she wanted him to sleep on her sofa tonight. She had wanted him to, but she'd told him she was all right. Several times today, in her desperation, she had done things she shouldn't have and she was afraid of what she might do if she could cling to Cole.

Bree peered out the side window that looked down onto the street to see if she could spot a TV van. There stood her brother-in-law, Ben, looking up with his arms crossed over his chest. His premature silver hair and white, long-sleeved shirt folded up at the elbows seemed to glow in the dusk. As usual, his edgy, stiff body language said everything about his steely backbone. Bree waved at him and hurried down to let him in.

She was proud he was such an upright, unbending county prosecutor, but she thought he too often brought an adversarial stance home from the office and courtroom with him. Ben was up for election in November, just like Josh, and had been bemoaning the fact there had been no high-profile cases to keep him in the public eye lately. Unlike other elected officials, he seldom paid for campaign ads—name recognition and frequent sound bites for the media seemed to be all he needed.

No doubt Amelia had sent him, though he'd probably be happy to lecture his maverick sister-in-law on his own.

"You didn't need to come all this way," she greeted him as she let him in. "I'm hanging in. You could have called me."

"Your cell was busy for hours. Besides, I had to see someone nearby—actually, our casino mover and shaker, Dom Verdugo. All we need is the whiff of organized crime around him, and he'll be on *my* hit list. I wanted to tell him privately to keep his nose clean. He invited me to go along on the casino boat's first cruise to show me he's on the up-and-up. But I wanted to see *you,* not only for your and Daria's sake but Amelia's, too."

He gave her a quick hug, then released her to close and lock the door behind him. "Bree, I realize you're upset and anxious, but you really distressed your older sister by just leaving the hospital today."

"Come on up, then you can call her to say I'm okay," she suggested, and motioned him toward the stairs. With a barely perceptible grimace toward the shop, he followed her.

Ben had ditched his usual suit coat and his tie was gone for once. His leather briefcase, too. Still, he managed to look like a ritzy real estate ad from *Gulfshore Life* magazine, whether he was garbed for the courthouse or his own house. He was a driven man, talented and ambitious, a crusader against breakers of the letter of the law. The more high-profile and gruesome the case, the better. It terrified Bree to think that might come in handy if they didn't find Daria safe and sound.

"This is exactly the kind of thing I'd warned both of you about," he went on, sitting upright on the edge of the sofa. "Something was bound to go wrong with all the risks you take."

"You warned us that Daria and our newest boat might go missing in a storm sometime?" she countered sarcastically, propping her hands on her hips and still standing so as not to feel at a disadvantage to him. With Ben, she always felt she was being grilled on the witness stand, and she'd found the best defense was to be a bit offensive.

"Not precisely," he admitted, frowning, "but I've warned both of you about behavior unbecoming of your brains and beauty."

"Thanks for the backhanded compliment."

"Hate to put it this way, Bree, but you're in too deep. You needed a couple more days under doctors' care, and you shouldn't be on your own right now. You should never have chosen to get into a business with so much danger involved."

"There was nothing dangerous about checking the sea grass meadow for the fifty-eighth time!" she exploded. "I appreciate Amelia's help in the hospital and your continued concern, but—"

"Just listen for a second. You need a level head here, so I called both the coast guard and the air patrol and told them to report to me if they learned anything."

"Oh, no…oh, no!" she cried, and collapsed onto the sofa with her head in her hands. "And they called you? Did they find her? The boat?"

"No, but the fact they didn't isn't good news either. Calm down," he went on, turning toward her and putting a hand on her slumped shoulder. "Amelia and I just want to help. This pipe dream, this search-and-salvage endeavor of yours, should be left to the likes of Sam Travers. You know he contacted me last year about buying you out, and I counseled you to take the offer."

She was angry now. Not only had Ben scared her, maybe intentionally, but he was still doling out advice she—they—didn't need or want. And now he was trying to become the kingpin in the search for Daria, taking over like he did everything and everyone.

She forced herself to inhale deeply, slowly.

"Ben, I know you don't approve of what Daria and I chose to do, and that's your business. But this search-and-salvage shop and finding Daria is *my* business, though I thank you for sideline support."

He leaned back on the sofa, one bouncing ankle crossed over his other knee as if he hadn't heard or heeded a thing she'd said. His voice was soothing, as if he spoke to a child, and that grated on her already raw nerves.

"Come on now, Bree. Why don't you get some things together and come on home with me for a couple of days? It would do you and Amelia both good, and the boys would love to see you, though I'd appreciate it if you wouldn't tell them all those deep-dive stories or promise them scuba lessons again—not until they're ready."

"Which won't be until you and Amelia are ready and that might be never. I know you have friends in high places, so I repeat, any support you can lend to keep the search going is much appreciated, but I will be the contact and the spokesperson. Now, can I get you some coffee? It's all ready," she said, standing.

"Have you been drinking it to stay up? You need your sleep? You look like hell."

Bree spun back to face him. "That's because I'm in hell on earth until I can find my sister!"

"*You* can find her?" He sat up straight again. "That's exactly what Amelia's worried about."

"It's not just me. I've got volunteers who are coming to help tomorrow."

"You'd better not get in the way of the professional searchers. I've seen a lot of missing persons cases, and the best advice I can give you is to keep calm and keep out of it. Sure, stay informed, but let the authorities—"

"The authorities need my help. I know that gulf out there, and I know Daria as well as I know myself. I realize you've seen a lot of dire situations, and if someone has deliberately harmed her, you'll be the first person I'll ask for advice. I know you're the prosecutor for the entire county. You do realize I'd think of that, at least?"

"Fine, I hear you. If that turns out to be the case, all I can promise is that we'll find whoever's to blame and prosecute him or her to the full extent of the law. And Amelia and I will keep in constant touch."

Bree nodded, but she wanted to scream at him that

she didn't care about the law, or his levelheaded rules, only about finding Daria any way she could.

It was nearly nine at night by the time Cole had six stitches in his wrist and got home to shower and chow down a hamburger. Despite that, he drove back to the Turtle Bay Marina. He parked along the dock and glanced up at Bree's lighted apartment. He was totally tempted to see how she was doing, but he hesitated. He'd called her from the urgent-care clinic, and it might be overkill to stop by like this so late. She needed sleep, though he figured she'd be hard-pressed to get any.

He leaned against the wrought-iron lamppost, then squinted up at the second-floor veranda and double doors. Two figures stood within the apartment—Bree and a silver-haired man.

"And why not?" he muttered to himself, and shoved away from the pole. "She has friends and needs them now." He knew that she'd arranged a search of other possible spots in the gulf by local divers tomorrow, and he and Manny were going to be there at the crack of dawn to help. But it bothered him that another man was with her tonight.

Besides, Cole told himself, he had come to talk to Dom Verdugo, not Bree. Although "the godfather of offshore gambling," as the local paper had dubbed him, had not dared to bring his one-hundred-eighty-foot floating casino into its berth at the end of the main marina dock yet. He kept his private yacht, the *Xanadu,* there. Just as Cole had noted before, the sleek ship seemed to sprout its own bodyguards.

"Hey, how ya doing?" the stocky young man who was obviously standing sentinel near the gangway asked as

Cole approached. He had a shaved head, which seemed planted directly on his shoulders with no neck. His black T-shirt and dark pants made him almost blend with the night.

"Not doing too bad," he told the guy. "I'm Cole De-Roca. Mr. Verdugo asked me to panel the main salon of the casino boat, so I thought I'd have a word with him about it. It's after office hours, but I figured it was worth a try."

A second man, who looked like a clone of this one, materialized from down the dock. With a nod to his friend but his eyes assessing Cole, the first man said, "I'll check."

Cole tried not to judge the situation in a negative way. The anti-casino-boat locals insisted a flock of security people reeked of organized crime, but those who were pro offshore gambling argued that any rich man with an expensive yacht would want some protection these days.

Personally, but privately, Cole was antigambling, because he'd seen how it could ruin a family—his own. He used to hate his mother because she'd gambled so much of their lives and happiness away, but ever since she'd died, several years before his father had, he regretted he'd shown her anger and not understanding and love.

Cole was an only child, and he'd once adored his beautiful, vibrant mother. Still, he'd never been able to forgive her for her lies and deceit over her gambling addiction. Time after time she'd sworn she wouldn't squander family funds again, get them in debt, or hang out with people who only wanted her money. She'd drunk too much, too, and had been drunk when she'd gone swimming late at night and accidentally drowned—at least, Cole and his father had told themselves it had been an accident. Surely, she would not have taken her own life, no matter how guilty she'd felt—and how upset she was they could not understand the sickness that made her risk all her husband had worked for and continually gamble away her only son's esteem and maybe his financial future, too.

But it was not the promise of money that brought Cole here today, considering a job from a man whose glittering gambling empire could ruin people's lives. His offer from the Miami business mogul was to panel the large central gambling salon of the casino yacht with Caribbean rosewood. Though the job was worth big bucks, Cole had planned to turn it down in protest of Verdugo's hell-bent push to bring gambling into the Turtle Bay area, one of the few regions left with old-Florida ambience.

But because of Cole's feelings for Bree, he was considering giving this a try, however much it went against his grain to deal with the devil. If there was anyone Cole could think of who might have the means, the might and maybe the motive to keep the Devon sisters' dire ecological report from being released next week, it was Verdugo. The man had been pouring money into promoting the new jobs and tourist benefits that would come from voting his way. But if the twins and the Clear the Gulf Commission made a big deal about the gulf waters not recovering from pollution, the swing vote might turn against a big gambling cruise boat making numerous trips in and out of Turtle Bay.

As Marla Sherborne, one of the candidates for the U.S. Senate, had put it in a brochure he'd read, "Verdugo's Fun 'n' Sun Cruises are unregulated, and such ships dump waste right off Florida's pristine shores."

Besides helping Bree by keeping an eye on Verdugo, it perversely pleased Cole to think a gambler would be paying him. He could use the money from this lucrative job. He wanted desperately to set up a sailboat-building business and get out of doing luxury yacht interiors. Florida was the center of the universe for handcrafted wooden boats. Since net fishing was illegal now, the sloops he'd make would be strictly for pleasure. For years, far too much of his own money had gone down the sewer hole of paying off his mother's massive gambling debts.

"Okay, he'll see you now," the first guard called from behind the polished mahogany rail of the main deck. "Mr. Verdugo's having a drink and says come join him."

The second, silent man gestured he should board. As Cole walked up the gangway and followed the first guard to the stern stateroom, he heard a woman's whining voice on board somewhere aft. He'd seen bigger, plusher yachts, but not in Turtle Bay. The *Xanadu* stuck out like a manicured thumb in a handful of unpolished nails compared to the other vintage craft moored nearby.

As he entered the golden glow of the stateroom, Cole recognized Verdugo from newspaper photos, though they'd managed to obscure his stature, perhaps intentionally. Short and portly, the fiftysomething entrepreneur greeted him with an outstretched hand. "I hear you're the hero of the hour, DeRoca."

"For rare woodworking or breaking news?"

He followed his host into a room larger than most landlocked living rooms. A huge horseshoe couch of ivory leather arched around a freeform glass-topped table; what appeared to be two authentic Picassos overlooked a grand piano. The paintings, a scattering of throw pillows and a large aquarium built into one wall were the only real color in the room of ecru and white with metallic touches. A round area rug muted footsteps. Soft music—an opera?—played in some sort of surround sound.

"You bet, the rescue of that woman—what did I hear she was? Oh, yeah, the ecology photographer," Verdugo said, his voice naturally gruff but bearing no foreign accent as Cole had expected. "Any word of her sister or the missing boat yet?"

"Unfortunately, no," Cole said, noting that Verdugo had twice said he'd "heard" something, as if he had eyes and ears out getting information for him. Did the man watch TV, or did his lackeys keep him informed? Or did he somehow know things firsthand?

"I woulda volunteered this boat, but I didn't want to get in the way of the official search. That storm must have capsized the other sister. Man, can you imagine surfacing from a routine dive and you're all alone? Is Scotch all right? Neat or on the rocks?"

"Rocks would be fine." Cole was going to ask him where he'd heard the twins were out on a routine dive, since he hadn't heard or seen that in the media, but Verdugo pointed at a huge metal bowl and spoke again.

"Have some caramel popcorn with it. People think I'm nuts, but they go together great. Love this stuff," he added, and grinned to show perfect teeth—probably perfectly false—as he tossed some popcorn in the air and adeptly caught it with his mouth.

"So look," he went on, pouring drinks behind a metal and white leather bar, "I assume you've decided to take my offer to panel the casino ship, or you surely would not be here. Right?"

"I'm here to discuss the possibility."

"Okay, then," Verdugo said, and pointed again to the bowl of popcorn as he carried the drinks toward the couch. Cole leaned over, took a small handful of the popcorn and ate some. He studied Dom Verdugo as he handed him a drink and sat on the curved couch, facing him across the glass table.

The man wore tailored Bermuda shorts and a muted silk print shirt, tails out. He was barefooted and deeply tanned, perhaps not as much from the sun as from his obvious Latin heritage; his hooked nose looked Italian and his narrowed, deep-set eyes were just plain hawk-like. He led some small talk, mostly about Cole's work. The guy was as smooth as the Scotch, and Cole had to remind himself that Verdugo bore watching. He wondered if he had been watching—or "hearing about"— the twins and knew about their coming report, but he couldn't figure out a way to broach that subject without giving his intentions away. He was probably just overly suspicious, since he'd become so attached to Briana so quickly and, damn it, deeply.

After his first sip, he swirled the Scotch in his glass, chewed on his popcorn and tried not to stare at the beautiful wood paneling on the grand piano. From here it looked like Mexican cocobolo wood, and that stuff was difficult to harvest. Verdugo's wealth—and the additional fortune he could no doubt make from getting a toehold in southwest Florida with lucrative gambling cruises—made Cole realize he'd probably never harm anyone directly. He'd just have one of his hey-boys do it.

"Actually, I'd like a chance to see the cruise-ship salon before I accept your offer," he told Verdugo, since the other man had started to talk as if Cole's employment was a done deal.

"Money's not an issue."

Cole swallowed hard at that thought. "But my doing an excellent job for you is. I can see from the stunning surroundings here you have excellent taste."

"Nothing but the best," he said, and lifted his glass as if in toast to Cole. "And that's what the Fun 'n' Sun Casino Cruises will bring to this area—jobs, the best new restaurants and upscale stores, even more luxury yachts that need rare wood paneling, eh? Our critics call my other floating casinos 'pay for play' boats and 'cruises to nowhere,' but I beg to differ. We give the customer what he or she wants—craps, blackjack, slots, booze, live entertainment, lots of laughs, you name it. It's not a cruise to nowhere, no way, but a cruise to fun and profit for everyone."

You name it...a cruise to nowhere. The words caught in Cole's mind. He agreed to drive to Miami by Monday to see the cruise ship's salon and decide whether or not to take the job. If Dom Verdugo could give his customers anything they wanted, he could surely give himself the same. How badly did this man want to stop a negative report on the local environment from coming out? Cole wondered. He'd never tell Bree, but since Daria and *Mermaids II* were still missing from a storm they should have been able to ride out, he expected the worst. At any rate, if he took the job, he planned to keep his eyes and ears open around Verdugo.

As he reached his car, he saw Bree's lights were still on. Surely her visitor had left by now. Cole leaned his arms on the top of his car and gazed out over the sailboats and motor craft nodding from their perches on the inky bay. A single small vessel was heading out past the lighted buoys with its fore and aft lights glowing until the blackness of the gulf devoured it.

Cole shook his head and shuddered. Had Daria Devon somehow taken a cruise to nowhere?

It was almost ten-thirty when Amelia heard Ben drive into the garage. She met him in her nightgown the minute he came in through the laundry room.

"She's not with you," she greeted him. "I knew she wouldn't want to come stay with me—even now."

"I tried, but I guess my powers of persuasion only work in a courtroom. She's obsessed with finding Daria, and I can't blame her for that, at least." He walked into the kitchen. Amelia hurried barefoot behind him. Flopping his briefcase on the counter, he kissed her cheek. "You've been crying again."

"Of course I've been crying. Daria's my sister, too, not just Briana's. I should go to her, sleep on her sofa, keep an eye on her. I've got to know what she's planning. You never know what she'll do."

"She seemed totally distraught one minute, but full steam ahead the next. When I was leaving, she told me the guy who picked her up in his sailboat is going to help her run a search with other divers tomorrow. It sounds to me as if he's keeping close tabs on her. I thought they didn't really know each other before the storm, but they sound…close."

"Actually, they had met once briefly," she said. "He's her rescuing angel," she muttered, "and I hope not her avenging angel."

"What's that about revenge?"

"I didn't say revenge. It's nothing."

Ben reached for the door of the fridge but turned back and put his hands gently on her shoulders. "Bree's really going to need you when they find Daria."

"Find her body, you mean."

Her stomach cramped. Tears blurred Ben to make two of him—like the two of them, little Bree and Daria, always the center of attention, of Dad's world, of everything in the damned universe. Even her boys were ecstatic when her sisters came over—no doubt to see them, not her—as if Santa and the Easter Bunny and every *Star Wars* character they adored had all rolled into one and come to visit.

"Yeah, I'm afraid I do mean find her body," he said with a sigh as he pulled her into his arms. "The odds aren't good they'll find Daria afloat on a piece of board or shipwrecked on one of the Ten Thousand Islands."

"I've been racking my brain for what could have happened to her," she said, leaning against him with her head turned on his shoulder. "Even crazy thoughts like maybe someone found her on the boat alone and kidnapped her, but then wouldn't we have received a call about ransom? Or what if those horrible people who steal those poor women for labor and sex—"

"Human traffickers?" he interrupted. "Hell, I'd love to prosecute one of those modern-day slave traders who import girls from South America and force them into labor or prostitution. That's been growing in Miami, and now they're avoiding law enforcement across the state by coming in here at night, since this coast is darker and less populated. No, I don't think those boats come in during the day."

"But if they were waiting offshore to land and then the storm was so bad…"

"That's too much of a long shot, honey," he said, hugging her tight. "I'll bet if there's a culprit, it's the storm. Still, we've got to hold out hope with Bree. She's tough and she's determined."

"Oh, yes," she said, pulling away to get a tissue to wipe her eyes and blow her nose. "She's that and more. You admire her—everyone does. Daria was even more willful, just for the heck of it, but Bree always had some burning purpose. They were—are—different, as well as being like the two peas in the proverbial pod."

When he stood there, staring at her and frowning as if she were a defendant who would blurt out her guilt to him à la Perry Mason, she pushed past him to open the fridge and take out a carton of orange juice for him.

"Not that," he said.

"You want some fresh squeezed?"

"Just hand me the soda. I need something a little stiffer than a jolt of Vitamin C."

"You've been busy at work," she said, trying to change the subject so she could get hold of her emotions.

"Actually, it's been deadly dull. I could use some face time on TV and some coverage in the papers. Hate to think I'm going to have to pay for all that this time around in the election."

"Your name is well-known. People respect you, and they'll vote what they trust."

"What they trust?" he said almost bitterly as he got a bottle of whiskey from the top cupboard above the fridge. "I don't think most people trust anyone on a ballot anymore, so I hope and pray they don't put me in the politician category. Let Josh Austin and Marla Sherborne fight that stigma as well as each other. Prosecutors are public servants. Hell, I could make ten times as much in private practice."

"I know you could, but we do just fine. You love what you're doing. It's your calling in life."

"You and the kids come first," he corrected her, but she wasn't certain she believed him. If her own father hadn't really loved her, how could Ben?

He mixed himself a stiff drink while she stared at herself in the window above the sink with only dark night beyond. It was like looking at her reflection in a black mirror. She did resemble the twins somewhat. If she'd let her hair go natural, she'd look even more like them. But she looked worn down by worry: guilt weighed heavy on her heart and mind and soul. She felt she was in a stupor, like she was slogging through water—damn, why did she have to think of it that way? She should never have gone to see Daria alone, thinking she could divide and conquer the two of them. And then it had suddenly gone so, so bad.

8

Early the next morning in the office of the Two Mermaids Search and Salvage Shop, Briana stood in the circle of her diving friends and acquaintances, fourteen at last count. Most already wore wet suits. Some had dragged in their gear, though others would have to go back to their cars or boats to get suited up.

Manny sat on Daria's desk, hunched over, elbows on knees, staring at his feet. Behind her guests, Cole leaned next to the closed front door with his arms crossed as if to keep any reporters from getting in. A TV van with a satellite dish on top was already parked down the street, so they must have somehow gotten word of this hastily called meeting.

"I can't thank all of you enough for coming to help on such short notice," Bree told them. "As you have heard, this may indeed be a life-and-death search." Her voice shook, but she went on. "Manny has already handed out the diagrams with coordinates of underwater sites we would like to have searched for any signs of our dive boat, in case it broke apart in the storm. I'll let you decide among yourselves which site you'd like to check for possible..." Her voice caught, and she cleared her throat. "For possible debris since you may have places you're more familiar with than others. Many of you know what the *Mermaids II* looks like, but just in case—" she held up a piece of paper "—this is a photo of it you can pass around. We've already had an extensive official search which, unfortunately, I've been informed will be called off at noon today. But the coast guard and civilian air patrol have obviously not been looking under—"

Biting her lower lip, she blinked back tears behind her dark sunglasses. She felt weird wearing them inside, but her eyes were bloodshot and any sort of light bothered her. When she saw Cole leave his post to come forward as if to take over, she cleared her throat again. "Although Sam Travers has used his boat's echo sounder, no one has actually done an extensive search underwater."

As if just saying his name could summon him up like some evil spell, the bell attached to the front door rang and Sam and two of his divers stepped in to join the group. When Bree nodded her silent thanks, several heads turned Sam's way. He glowered at her, but she was still glad to have his help. Manny saw him come in, too. Like a loyal watchdog, he stood with his arms crossed over his big chest, glaring back at Sam.

"I hate to admit it," Bree told everyone, "but it is possible the ship broke up or sank in the storm and my sister is afloat on a piece of it somewhere. So if you should find any signs of the *Mermaids II,* please let us know here right away, even if you do contact the coast guard, or—or the police."

Again, through her sunglasses, her eyes met Cole's intense gaze. He'd come even closer, next to her desk, as if he and Manny stood sentinel on either side of her. In a way, this search was Cole's doing, because he'd made her promise she wouldn't dive again unless she had some sort of lead. She was praying these people would give her that—anything to go on.

"And last but not least," she said, picking up her old camera in its plastic housing. "When I swam back in from the Trade Wreck in the storm, I had to drop a camera much like this one in the water. It's painted red inside the housing and is quite new. If anyone sees it, please retrieve it for me. Daria took some shots on it before I dived, and I'd like those back." Bree had decided not to share her fears of foul play. Besides, she couldn't bear to believe it herself, so she just concluded with, "On the back, the camera's etched with the initials B & D D.

"I guess that's it," she told them as they circulated the picture of the missing vessel and heads bent briefly over it. She could hear individuals whispering. Someone near the back of the room murmured, "Like a needle in a very big, wet haystack."

"Again," Bree said, "I'm so thankful for your help. For those of you who just arrived, we're using this office as a command post. Cole, Manny and I will be here monitoring the radio frequency and the cell-phone number we've written down on the dive sites handouts. Any questions?"

Guy Russel, a friend of a friend she'd never seen before today, asked, "I know you were twins, but did she look like you?"

The man's use of the past tense jolted her. She wanted to scream at him, but she said calmly, "This is still a search mission, not a recovery one. Yes, Daria does look like me, except for little things such as her hair's a bit longer and parted on the other side—my mirror image."

With a hard sniff, she gestured that they could get started. After they'd left with encouraging words or a hug—except for Sam and his duo of divers, who just walked out—Cole put one arm around her waist. He felt so warm and strong when she was cold and shaky.

"That guy who made it sound as if Daria was permanently gone didn't mean it that way," he whispered. "He wasn't thinking."

"It's all I've been thinking," she told him, shoving her sunglasses up on her head and pressing her palms over her aching eyes. She leaned back into him, her head resting against his rock-hard shoulder. "Let's face it, if we're desperate enough to look for the boat underwater and no one's found Daria by now, washed ashore in the way you found me..."

Cole gave her a sharp hug. "Stop thinking that way until you absolutely have to."

"We should contact the border patrol." Manny had suddenly come so close that Bree thought at first he meant to push Cole away from her. His body language said he was angry. He didn't look either of them in the eyes but stared at Cole's arm around her. "They track down illegal aliens," he said, "so how 'bout they can help track down Daria, no? What if she got in the way of those bastards smuggling in Cubans, or she see something she shouldn't? Big money, so smugglers get more dangerous 'round here. We got a few border patrol agents on this coast now. How 'bout we call them, get more help, yes?"

"I think," Bree told him, "we have pretty good clout with Josh Austin and Marla Sherborne. Senator Sherborne phoned this morning to say she'd be stopping by. If worse comes to worst, my brother-in-law will help. He stopped by last night."

She heard and felt Cole give a sigh of relief, but when he said nothing, she went on. "Josh and Senator Sherborne may be fierce political opponents, but I'm willing to play both sides. And, Manny," she added, putting her hand on his arm, "I don't think smugglers—or yacht pirates, if they've been in the area—would want a dive boat like ours."

"Caramba!" he said, shaking off her touch. "What I mean is the storm could have panicked smugglers, they needed a small boat and they play rough."

"I appreciate all your help," Bree said, trying to calm him as well as herself. She stepped away from Cole but turned back to face him. "People like Manny," she told Cole, "who came into this country legally and are willing to do what it takes to make a good life here for their families, are just as upset about illegals as many Anglo citizens are."

"Yet you know desperate people take risks, Manny," Cole put in. "The refugees, I mean, as well as the smugglers."

Manny surprised Bree by smacking his fist into the palm of his other hand. The strain of Daria's plight was rubbing his nerves raw. The poor man had enough trouble, with his adored mother so sick and his daughter's rebellion, none of which Cole knew about.

"Yeah, Manny Salazar—he knows that, all right," Manny muttered, glaring up at Cole.

To Bree's dismay, Manny shoved past them and stalked out into his cluttered realm of the back room.

Sitting at the two desks, Bree and Cole drank coffee all morning and jumped to answer a call whenever one came in. Too many of them were from reporters or well-wishers. Four had come from the groups of divers so far, and the word was that they'd found nothing. Amelia called and was relieved to hear that Bree herself wasn't diving. It annoyed Bree that Amelia still seemed miffed about the fact she'd left the hospital without telling her, when there were so many more important things to focus on right now.

Manny mostly banged around in the back room, but emerged from time to time to get fresh coffee and see what was going on, especially when Cole went to use the bathroom out in the storage area or to make more coffee upstairs.

"Manny, I'm sorry if you felt I didn't listen to you or Cole insulted you," Bree said during one of those times she was there alone. "I know you're blaming yourself about Daria, too."

"What you mean?" he demanded, crossing his hands over his chest.

"That you weren't on the boat when something terrible must have happened. Ordinarily, you would have been there."

"Yeah, that's true. Sorry I snapping at you. Sometimes, even stuff planned out, it don't go like it should."

They both turned as the bell on the front door rang when it opened. If only it could be good news, or better yet, Daria walking in, a miracle, Bree thought, looking up.

It was a woman about Daria's height and, for one insane moment, Bree's insides cartwheeled before she saw it was Senator Marla Sherborne. No way Daria would ever wear a conservative, gray pantsuit like that or the big gold starfish pin on her shoulder. Gypsy skirts with peasant tops and clunky shell jewelry when she was dressed up, that was Daria.

Bree had met Marla Sherborne at several fund-raisers for various ecological causes, but hadn't seen her since she'd become Josh's opponent for her U.S. senate seat. At forty-seven, Marla was a striking woman, blessed with a beautiful heart-shaped face, gorgeous skin and, evidently, eternal energy. If the rumors about her affair with Cory Grann were true, that certainly added some spice to a rather bland reputation up to now. That would really be sleeping with the enemy, since King Sugar in this state had often been blamed for fertilizer runoff pollution problems, which Marla was always attacking.

"Senator Sherborne," Bree said, rising and coming out from behind her desk to greet her. "I'm very grateful for your concern and anything you can do to keep some sort of official search going. It's being called off right about now."

"Briana, I'm so sorry about everything," she said as they shook hands. "No word yet?"

Bree explained about the dive search they had organized today.

"Then you're facing possible bad news."

"Let's just say, I would never forgive myself if, even underwater, I left any stone unturned."

"Actually, it was Josh Austin who mentioned the tragedy to me. I must admit I get so busy sometimes that I rely on aides to monitor TV news and scan the papers for me. Again, I am so sorry for all you are going through. And you were struck by lightning, Josh said. But there was no real fallout from that, evidently."

Bree didn't mention her acute hearing and sensitivity to light. She'd told no one but Cole. It was amazing how she felt closer to him than to anyone right now, including Amelia. She prayed she wasn't leaning on him because the person she'd always been nearest and dearest to was gone. No, she still felt Daria's presence—didn't she?

To shift the subject, she said, "I'm happy to hear you and Josh are not always in some sort of debate or disagreement."

"Not at all," she said with a decisive nod and a hint of a smile, which lit her blue eyes to make her look even younger. "Both of us are working as best we see fit to help our constituents in this beautiful part of our world, and that certainly includes you and your sister—Turtle Bay's two mermaids and champions of our ecological future. Besides, Josh and I have some very good friends in common, and one can't always legislate one's heart. I understand that Josh once dated your sister."

"He told you that?"

"I believe I overheard his wife mention it. I see her sometimes, since her father's a dear friend of mine. You look surprised I admit that. I supposed you know I mean Cory Grann. He's a longtime widower, you may have heard, and I've always been too busy—and too ambitious, I admit that—to marry, though I don't know what's in the future for either of us. He and I have been at odds in the past over some issues, but in this case, opposites attract. Besides, I don't completely blame big sugar for our pollution problems. It's much more complex than that."

"Yes, I understand. So many things are not all they seem."

"Exactly. The sugar industry has poured money into ecological causes and has greatly cut back on toxic pesticides. But that is a topic for another day and not why

I'm here. I just want you to know that the work you and your sister are doing for the Clear the Gulf Commission is important, our linchpin for change. Although finding and returning Daria safe and sound is the top priority for all of us, that Trade Wreck ecological report of yours may be your legacy—both of you. And, I must admit, your plight and hers will draw much more attention to that report."

"I hadn't thought of that," Bree admitted. "Perhaps something good coming out of all this terrible mess."

"Briana," the senator went on, taking one of her hands, "I'm hoping that, whatever happens, you will be willing to stand behind that report, however disheartening its findings. I intend to make it a battle call to action, both here in southwest Florida and on a national level."

As Bree nodded, she noticed Cole had come downstairs, or rather, she felt his presence. As she introduced him to Marla, she couldn't help but wonder if the woman was here because she cared about finding Daria or just about protecting her precious report. Everything she said sounded like a beautifully prepared and written speech.

Bree jerked when the radio static became a voice. "Travers here, Sam Travers, over. Briana, you read?"

She rushed to her desk and bent over it to pick up the mike, then pushed the button to talk back. "Sam, Briana here, over." Her heartbeat accelerated. Of all the searchers who had gone out today, Sam was the least likely to call unless he really had something.

"One of my guys found your camera. They dived the Boulder Reef, and it was there. It's got your initials on the back."

"Sam, thanks! But nothing else?"

Static crackled for a moment. Bree's heart fell to her

feet. Was he breaking her in easy? Cole came to stand beside her and put his arm around her again. Manny came charging in from the back room. Marla Sherborne hovered.

"Someone got something?" Manny cried.

"Nothing else," Sam's voice came loud and clear.

Bree didn't know whether she felt relief or grief, but at least she could look at Daria's pictures on that camera now.

Briana's hands shook as she took the camera from Sam's diver, the freckled, redheaded one, at the front door of her shop. "Boss says, let him know if you find anything that helps," he said, and was gone.

Bree cradled the camera in her arms. It looked so normal, so undamaged, even dry. Both she and her gear had been through the ravages of the storm and sea, so maybe it was a sign Daria would soon be home soon, safe and sound, as Senator Sherborne had said. She'd been gone for almost an hour now, promising to keep in touch.

"Let's download whatever this camera holds and have a look at it," she told Cole and Manny. She was heading toward the corner of the office where she kept her computer, scanner and printer when her desk phone rang. She ran to get it. Manny's wife, Juanita, was on the line.

"*Hola,* Briana," she cried, evidently recognizing her voice. "I so sorry 'bout Daria. I been lighting candles at Our Lady of Guadalupe for you get better, her be found."

"Thanks for your support, Juanita," Bree said. Looking instantly more worried than he already was, Manny stepped closer.

"At this time, I hate bother you but Manny there?"

Juanita said, her voice breaking. "Our Lucinda—tell him I think she run away!"

"Oh, no. Let us know if we can do anything to help. Here's Manny," she said, and thrust the phone at him.

"My mother worse?" he said into the phone in Spanish, then frowned as he spoke loud and fast.

Bree didn't mean to eavesdrop, but her Spanish was good enough that she could tell what Manny was saying as he raked his hand through his hair. He insisted Lucinda would not dare run away, so had someone taken her? The conversation was all a horrible echo of her own fears for Daria. Juanita was now screaming so loud, Bree could actually hear her through the phone's mouthpiece, telling him something about a note. No, a note from Lucinda, not for ransom, Juanita was shouting as Bree and Cole moved away to give him more privacy.

"Caramba," Manny said. *"Sí,* I told her if she's not proud of us to find a new family, but I didn't really mean run away."

"Manny," Bree told him, "go on home. Tell her you'll be right home."

"I coming home right now, pronto," he told his wife, digging his truck keys out of his jeans pocket.

"And call if you need help," Bree called after him as he raced for the door.

"May *Nuestro Señor* and the Virgin help us all!" he cried, and slammed the door behind him to leave only the jingling of its bell.

In the sudden silence, Bree and Cole stood staring at each other.

"I was going to say," she whispered, "when it rains, it pours, but that seems worse than a cliché right now.

Every time I think the nightmare can't get worse, it does."

She realized she still clutched the camera to her. "Let's take a look at these pictures," she told him, anxious to be doing something. "Especially the few Daria shot before I dived."

He followed her over to the computer table. She opened the camera's plastic housing and downloaded the pictures to her desktop PC. In a moment, the screen displayed the array of pictures in three rows.

"Great!" Cole said. "They're in good shape."

All but the first three were underwater close-ups of the turtle grass meadow. But the first three were Daria's shots off the boat before Bree dove.

"I'm going to enlarge those," she said, clicking the zoom icon as Cole leaned over her shoulder. Despite the intensity of the moment—or maybe because of it—she could smell the tang of his aftershave or cologne. She could hear his deep, even breathing. Everything about him emanated strength, and she needed that—needed him.

Taken over the bow of the boat, Daria's first photo was of the northwest horizon toward the storm.

"The water's still quite calm, and the storm far off," Cole observed. "The wave height is what the weather guys call a light chop, two-to four-foot waves, like what I started sailing in. Man, that baby came up hard and fast. So if someone boarded your boat after you were underwater, he or she—"

"She? Ben said that, too. I guess it could have been a woman."

"So whoever didn't know the storm would be that

bad, either, that it could cover up a crime if one was committed. But I see no other boat on that horizon."

She selected the second picture and enlarged it as big as she could. "One very distant boat," she said, squinting at the screen, "but it seems to be heading southeast— probably toward either Gordon Pass or the Marco River. And what's that in the sky? A pelican?"

Cole leaned even closer, his brow brushing her hair. "That or a plane. Can you move the cursor around and blow up that part more?"

She did but they couldn't tell. A speck, maybe even a flaw on the camera lens, though it didn't appear in the next two photos they examined minutely.

"She was just trying to be sure everything worked before I went down," Bree said, her voice sounding small and shaky again. "If these are the last pics she ever shot, I'll frame them."

Blinking back her tears, she skimmed through the shots she'd made below the surface. Good pictures of a bad result. Even before the storm pulled up some of the turtle grass by its roots and roiled the underwater visibility, the sea grass meadow was sparse, with puny growth and skinny, brown-tinged blades when it should be— used to be—flourishing. Yes, Marla Sherborne would have the explosive, negative report she obviously coveted. But, Bree supposed, a lot of others would be upset. Would their report be enough, as Cole had once implied, to rile some important people?

"I'd just like to rip the whole world apart looking for her," Bree admitted, putting her head in her hands so she didn't have to look at these normal, calm, beautiful pictures anymore.

"Maybe that's it," he said, kneeling by her chair and

wheeling her in a half turn to face him. He pulled her hands from her teary face and held her wrists hard.

"What's it?"

"When you said 'rip apart' right now, I thought of something we've both been ignoring. When I tried to make it in to shore in the *Streamin'*, I had to fight my way through a riptide the storm and currents had somehow concocted."

"A riptide. I think I swam through one, too. Yes, I remember! It tried to take me south, toward Marco Island. I went with it, then finally found my way out."

"So if Daria and or *Mermaids II* tried to get into shore—or if the boat was even adrift at that point—they could have been caught in the current and taken a lot farther from the area that the authorities and your friends have been searching."

"And that means the Ten Thousand Islands, which are like a jigsaw puzzle."

"Or, if she didn't get taken that far, she'd get caught by those crosscurrents where the Marco River comes out into the gulf."

"Big Marco Pass."

"Can we radio your dive teams to move farther south?"

"Not after the day they've already put in. We agreed their search would be over by one o'clock, and it's almost that now, with nothing found but the camera. But you could be right."

He jumped to his feet, and she leaped out of her chair. "I'll call the coast guard and talk to them about the possibility," he said.

She seized his arm. "Let's do that only if that site pans out. Otherwise, with them calling off the search at noon today, that would be like us immediately crying wolf. Come upstairs and look at an underwater marine map I was studying last night. Maybe the combination of storm and tides made a vicious current that isn't usually there—the perfect riptide."

As they thudded up the stairs to her apartment, she tried to shove away the memory of the tragic scene in the film, *The Perfect Storm*. Everything terrible had converged to sink a sturdy ship with a skilled crew, sink it in towering waves and howling wind.

She seized the map and turned it toward them. They didn't even sit but leaned over the table on their elbows. "See," she said, pointing. "See this trough the Marco River makes at Big Marco Pass? It can be deep and choppy even in normal conditions, but with extra wind and tide…"

"A lot of water traffic goes in and out of Marco Island there. Maybe someone saw something."

"I'm praying that our boat's motor simply stalled and the storm ripped the anchor with its chain off the boat. She was injured or had no way to get to me if the storm shoved her in—maybe to here," she cried, pointing to small outer islands just north of Big Marco Pass. "She could be marooned anywhere here, maybe hurt. Or, like you said, a boat could have capsized right here where a riptide or rogue current shoved it into the battering of river, tide, currents and storm. And there are rock and stone jetties in that area. Cole, we've got to go look, just make a quick dive to be sure, then check islands and beaches."

"Call some divers back, because you're not going down with just me. Call Travers to use his echo sounder."

"He hates me—blames me for his son's death in Iraq,"

she blurted as she ran into her bedroom to grab some clothes, then continued to talk from her bathroom as she pulled on a one-piece bathing suit, then a spandex dive suit. "We dated for years, high school sweethearts, then went to the same college. But I broke up with him and Ted enlisted!" she called to him. She tore back out into the living room. He did a double take when he saw she was dressed to dive.

"Bree, I said, call somebody else for help. The riptide—your coordinates—it's just another possibility."

"I'm going. I'm sure our other boat has been returned by now. Just a quick look, then a call to the coast guard and/or the police dive team. They'll really check it out—if I see anything there…"

"If you *and* the others you're going to dive with see anything there," he corrected.

He grabbed her by both arms to halt her path toward the door and gave her a little shake. "For starters, we need somebody to man the boat if we're both going down."

"You'll go with me? I promise, no surprises like the dive into the Trade Wreck. But we'll have to get close up to see things, because the vis will be low there."

"I think it's a good place to check, but—I don't care what you say—I'm calling Travers. We need someone to stay on the boat and someone else to go down with us."

"You're right," she said, nodding. Anything to get him to go down with her—to let her go. "My dad used to say only fools break the rules, and I got you cut doing that yesterday. All right, we'll call Sam. However much I used to think I couldn't trust him, he's been helping me now, because he said he didn't blame Daria for what happened to his son."

"Meaning he still blames you." He looked down intently into her eyes. "I guess it's none of my business, but did you really love Ted Travers? That's a lot to handle. His death, now—"

"Now Daria's?" she challenged, hands on hips.

"I didn't say that. I was going to say her being missing."

She gripped his wrists hard, feeling sinews, muscles and bones, so solid in her trembling world. "I keep clinging to the fact we are so close—Daria and I. I'm hoping I'd feel—I'd know—if she were really gone. But she can't be gone. I won't *let* her be gone!"

"Then let's get some help and get going."

"All right—yes," she said, and gave him a quick hug. She started to pull away, but he anchored her hard to him.

They clung full length, both holding tight, Bree standing on tiptoe with her arms clamped around his neck and his around her waist. She turned her face into the side of his throat and felt his pulse pounding there. Her blood pressure was surely off the charts. The top of her head fit perfectly under his chin. Her breasts pressed flat to his hard chest and her thighs to his. She was toned, but his flesh was harder, his entire body like the wood his big hands fashioned. She felt swept away, outside herself.

She had not answered his question about loving Ted. She guessed she had once, an adolescent love, fierce then faded. Although she'd been with Cole only three days now, they'd been in such a seething cauldron it seemed she'd needed and wanted him forever. But it was the impact of her own desire that stunned her. This man, she told herself, as they finally, shakily stepped apart, made that jolt of lightning that had hit her seem like nothing.

9

As they left Turtle Bay in the smaller of Sam's two slow barges, Cole almost wished he hadn't pushed Bree to call Travers for help. It wasn't so much Travers's bleary-eyed employee who captained the sluggish vessel nor the two divers who worked for Sam that worried him, but the spearguns they were cleaning.

Cole had never hunted with spearguns, and these babies looked fierce. "State-of-the-art," one guy boasted, and explained to him how they worked.

The weapons had small carbon-dioxide bottles slung beneath their shafts, so a squeeze of the trigger released a burst of gas and fired the spear with a velocity that could not be matched by older guns. The spearheads were bulky and contained .357 magnum cartridges that would explode on impact, driving the shafts deeper and springing out the prongs they proudly demonstrated to Cole while Bree was talking to the captain in the engine house. They showed him how the shaft clipped to their weight belts.

"You aren't going to dive with those today," Cole said, more a statement than a question.

Ric, who looked like a young Arnold Schwarzenegger, muscles and all, just nodded. Lance, the thin, red-haired guy, said, "Usually do, in case we see something we don't like—or something we do, for dinner."

"With four of us diving in murky water, it doesn't sound safe," Cole countered.

"Nothing too safe about looking for debris in soupy water in a boat channel anyhow," Ric said. "But I guess we can leave the guns on board for once. If we have to pass up a big grouper though, it'd be real nice if you'd spring for a fish dinner."

Cole could not believe they'd consider fishing on a dive as critical as this one, but it must be just more business to them. "You guys and Sam have been very helpful. Yeah, I'll do just that," he promised.

He was glad Bree hadn't overheard the conversation. She was standing at the stern now, staring into the water, so she didn't hear the divers or his agreeing to their bribe. But then, maybe she did hear, because he was amazed at how acute her listening powers seemed to be. It had worried him when she'd said she'd heard and seen more things than she should after Daria went missing. At first he thought she meant she was seeing ghosts, or some sort of visions of her sister, but that wasn't it—he hoped.

He walked aft and leaned on the taffrail beside her. Partly blocking their view, heavy wire cables and a big hook hung from the winch spool; he wondered how much dead weight this barge could lift out of the water, but he didn't feel like asking Sam's divers. For some reason, Sam had not been able to come along, but said he'd be out in a smaller boat soon to see how they were doing. Cole's protective instincts about Bree made him want to tell Sam he ought to let bygones be just that, where Bree was concerned.

Sam had told his captain to anchor on the north side of the channel and float several dive flags. Hopefully, those would slow boats and Jet Skis coming in and out of the Marco River even more than the No Wake and Slow—Manatee Zone signs already did.

"I'm glad we're in this scow, even if it is a bit slow," Cole told Bree, intentionally trying to lift her spirits. Her fierce determination had ebbed to a quiet moodiness. "In the crosscurrents there, it will give us a stable diving platform."

"Despite its flat bottom," she said with a sigh, "a boat the length of *Mermaids II* would have been anything but stable there in that bad storm."

"Do you sense something?" he asked. "I mean, that we're getting closer to answers—to the boat or Daria?"

"Not exactly that," she said, frowning out at the churning wake of the barge. "It's just that she *has* to be alive. I know she is. I want answers and yet I fear them. This possible scenario seems so possible. I've seen wrecks in the gulf, both ships and airplanes, but it just can't be *my* boat and *my* sister! But then," she said, her voice softer, "I'll bet poor Manny and Juanita are saying it can't be *their* girl who ran away."

"You don't mean that you think Daria could have run away, staged something…"

"No, no!" she said, covering her ears like a child. "She has no reason to. She's not the type to do that. I know my sister like—like the back of my own hand. Except," she added, staring dazedly at the back of her hand in the bright sun, "one of the mirror-image things about us was that I'm right-handed and she's a leftie. Lefties always feel a little different from others. It was the earliest thing that made us feel we weren't one and the same."

He took her hand in his. "Bree, why don't you stay on board with the captain and let me go down alone with Sam's divers?"

"Because having a fourth diver could make a difference in low vis. If you reported nothing was there, I'd have to prove it to myself. And if something is there, I'd have to be on-site, look for clues of how the boat broke up."

She tugged her hand back and hit both fists on the rail, then, obviously fighting tears, whispered, "Cole, I don't know what I would have done without you, even after you got me breathing again and to the hospital. You've been my life preserver in more ways than one, but I know you have a life to go back to."

"I do need to drive to Miami soon to look over a yacht for a big client I might take on. Actually, it's Dom Verdugo's casino cruise boat. I was going to turn him down flat, but I think he bears watching and that would be a good way to keep an eye on him. To tell you the truth, my mother was a gambling addict and ruined her life— and almost Dad's and mine—that way. I'm not sure, but her accidental death may have actually been suicide. Beyond needing this big commission, I'd like to see Verdugo's plans and boat stopped somehow."

"I'm sorry about your mother. I can imagine how terrible that must have been—losing a mother tragically," she whispered, squeezing his hand.

She sniffed hard and abruptly turned away to check her gear, which she had laid out behind her on a metal bench. He raked his fingers through his hair. He was a selfish jerk to bring his own family problems up right now, but that had just spilled out. He'd kept what Dad had called their "dirty linen" secret for years, penned up inside, without even telling his wife much about it, yet here he was sharing it with Bree.

As Cole started to recheck his gear, too, the boat began to rock and roll, as he always called such movement in crosscurrents. On the barge the motion was subtle, not like in a sailboat where the helmsman could feel every shift and shake intimately.

He admitted to himself that he was yearning to be that way with Bree, to be able to read her, to sense her movements and moods like a sleek ship under his command, although he knew he'd never control her any more than he could the sea. Still, like the best sailing on the *Streamin'*, it could be a beautiful union. But the shaky ship that was Briana Devon right now was in rough waters, and he prayed she wouldn't break apart. Cole shook his head to clear it, but Ric's voice cut short his agonizing.

"We're here," he yelled. "Let's dive."

For Bree, it was like being in the storm again.

Even with all the diving she'd done in low-vis water, she was not prepared for the impact of this dive on her body and her brain. She felt the heavy, gray weight of the water and the push and pull of powerful currents as if she swam through an Everglades swamp. All around in the wide channel that was the mouth of the Marco River, where it met the tides and waves of the gulf, eddies of sand and silt shifted and resettled. The dark bottom was like a writhing, living being, devouring things then spitting them back up.

Ordinarily, if a diver stopped kicking and swimming for a minute, low-vis water would clear a bit but not here.

She could see only about four feet ahead, even with the high-powered lights Sam's divers had provided. Thank heavens, they each had a writing slate tied to their weight belts, because even hand signals from the others were hard to read.

So she stuck close to Cole, or he to her, she wasn't sure which. The four of them meticulously followed the typical search-and-salvage spiral-pattern grid they had agreed on before they'd left Sam's dock. After marking their starting point on the bottom in the middle of the channel, at two arms' width apart, they swam side by side in a widening circle. Occasionally, they switched positions because the divers to the east and west took the brunt of the buffeting currents.

They also had to swim low because yachts with deep drafts occasionally went overhead, though even with the biggest, the divers had almost fifteen feet of clearance. They'd swum about forty feet from their dive boat to begin; they would have to be even more careful when they surfaced to come up at the site they'd marked.

However much Bree had always loved diving, even under challenging conditions, and despite the fact it was at her insistence this search had been set up, she was suddenly panicked to get out. She should have listened to Cole about not diving. This was a desperate, stupid scheme. The coastal waters of the gulf were huge—as big as the gap between Amelia and the twins, as big as between poor Manny and his daughter right now. Daria and the boat could be anywhere out here.

Bree's acute hearing was bothering her. She should have worn plastic earplugs. The ping-ping or low, rever-berating buzz of motors overhead, the occasional clank of a dive knife or gauge into a tank down here, the sound of all their bubbles fighting toward the surface—the shriek of fear in her own head and heart...

When someone's dive light accidentally swept her way, it almost blinded her as the glare stabbed deep into her brain. Even the dull reflection of a beam off Lance's face mask was too bright. Yet maybe, since she was seeing better than she would have otherwise, it would help her to find things down here. She forced herself to try to pierce the swirling waters just as they all made a turn to the south.

Her eyes caught the grayish glint of metal. It could be anything thrown over or lost from a boat. But it looked to be a curved aluminum handrail, like the one that led up from the diving platform to the stern deck of *Mermaids II*. She gave a kick away from the men and touched the cold metal, half-buried in sand and silt.

Dented and bent, broken, it seemed to point a bit farther out, luring her on. Cole swam with her, behind her; she wasn't sure where the other two were, only that she had to go on, off their search grid, off the ends of the earth, if she must.

Then she saw a four-foot piece of gleaming white metal, also partly buried, but it looked new or well cared for, like their dive boat had been. She brushed sand away from a part of it and uncovered a jagged piece of what was once the stern of a boat. Her and Daria's boat. She was certain, because part of the name *Mermaids II* was there in the bent and broken metal, painted bold and bright in the beam of her light: *MA D I*

Bree gasped so hard, she choked on her mouthpiece and almost spit it out. Cole grabbed her wrist, but she yanked away and swam on, sweeping her light right and left, down, around, as if something drew her like a powerful magnet. Ahead, looming large, in the deepest part of the channel, at a slight tilt, rested the main deck and wheelhouse of their dive boat. It looked fairly intact.

Good, she told herself. That surely meant Daria could have weathered the worst of the storm and gotten to shore before it went down. But this area was so heavily populated, why hadn't someone found her by now?

But then…then…

Awed, horrified, Bree swam closer, upward to peer in through the side window of the wheelhouse. Trembling, she trained her light through the glass to look inside.

And there, floating near the top of the ceiling, her hands lifted and her hair shifting in the water as to hide her once beautiful face, her sister, her other self, was trapped inside.

Cole could barely keep up with Bree; for a moment he'd lost sight of her in this thick water. All at once, she'd seemed to know where she was going, kicking hard toward he didn't know what. But he was certain they had found the wreck of the boat.

And then he saw the bulk of the sunken ship. The hull had a huge piece missing, or was just caved in, but the small upright, half-glass wheelhouse looked intact. Intact—and within… Daria?

Floating inside, her hair streaming loose and free, was a woman, or what had been a woman before being trapped two days in the graveyard of the sea. Her skin looked loose and greenish, mottled. And he saw Bree meant to go inside to her.

He kicked harder and reached for Bree. She tried to shake him off. She dropped her light and put both hands to the doorknob, braced her fins on the side of the wheelhouse and tried to wrench the door open. Cole seized both her wrists, shoved her feet off the metal, got his mask right next to hers and shook his head, no. No!

He would never forget the look in her wide eyes: shock, terror, fury and tears. *Up!* He pointed. *We go back, get help,* he tried to gesture.

To his surprise, she reached for her slate and scribbled, "Can't leave her here," then shone his light on it.

Without going for his own slate, he wrote on hers, "Crime scene?"

He was grateful when she nodded. Then she broke his heart, going closer to the window of the wheelhouse and putting both her palms against it as if she gave some sort of blessing—or as if she could embrace her sister's body through the barriers of glass and death.

On board, after holding out hope and pushing herself for so long, Bree collapsed in tears. Cole led her into the small supply room aft on the barge and, leaving the door ajar for air and light, sat on a huge coil of ropes next to her. She didn't want to be held, but she kept a tight hold of his hand. She was shaking, in shock, he figured, but he knew she'd never agree to go ashore right now. Besides, until Sam or the authorities showed up, he had no way to get her there.

Sam's men radioed both the coast guard and the Naples Police dive team. The already busy waterway quickly became a hub of activity. Gawkers lined the edge of the river and boats huddled close; the press arrived by boats, trying to get video and interviews. Bree and Cole hid out, but they could hear Ric and Lance answering shouted questions. Finally, Sam arrived.

"Sorry for your loss," he told Bree gruffly as he stood

in the doorway of the small supply room, arms crossed over his chest. "Obviously, I know whereof I speak, losing someone nearest to you."

Cole glared at the man. Although they had him to thank for the means to discover and recover the ship, it was hard to feel grateful to him.

Sam plunged on, "Don't know if foul play has a part in this, but there's always something foul about the death of a healthy, vital, young person, especially one dearly loved. In a ways, someone's always to blame. I've known that for years, even if you're just finally learning it."

"Stow it," Cole demanded. "Have a heart, man."

"I had one once, but got it shattered," he said. When Cole made a motion to rise, Sam left them alone again.

"I don't suppose he's right about foul play," Bree said in a monotone, the first time she'd spoken for an hour. "He was probably only trying to make his point about my screwing up Ted's life again. The evidence will probably point to her not handling the storm somehow and the boat going down in it."

"With that storm, it will be hard to convince people of anything else, but I'm sure they'll do an investigation."

"If they don't, I will. She was good with the boat—with swimming, too, you know."

"Of course she was, but you need to concentrate on a funeral and getting your life back together."

"But…without her, it may just seem like half a life. I need to call Amelia and Ben. Could you get my cell in my stuff?"

"Sure. Be right back."

When he returned, a Naples Police officer was talking to her. Though he stood back, Cole overheard what they were telling her, especially the word he'd been afraid to say—*autopsy.*

"I understand," she was saying in a terrible monotone that didn't sound like her. But he remembered mourning, the out-of-body feeling of it where you moved and talked but weren't really there. With a sick-in-the-gut feeling, he pictured again his mother's body, drowned, though she hadn't been in the water as long as Daria was. He and his dad had put their arms around each other and sobbed.

"How long," she was asking the officer, "before I can have her—have her back and we'll know the cause of death?"

"I can't tell for sure, Ms. Devon. It will be up to the coroner, but of course, as soon as possible."

When the man moved away, Cole returned to sit beside her and handed her her cell. The moment she turned it on, it played "Under The Sea," the bouncy tune from a Disney animated movie. For a second, he couldn't recall the movie's name or why he'd seen it. Oh, yeah, he remembered—*The Little Mermaid.* He'd taken a client's kids to see it when the parents had the flu a couple of years ago.

"Lots of missed calls," she told him, swiping at tears on her cheeks. "Can word have spread that fast already? Amelia will hear it from someone else. I should have called her right away, because she's all I have now…but I want to go back down to Daria. I want to be with her when they bring her up."

"Sweetheart, you can't. They'll take good care of her, bring her up in a body bag so no one can see. It's out of your hands now—"

"I know. I know."

Suddenly, she exploded into sucking, gasping sobs and threw herself across his lap and clung to him. With his foot, Cole closed the storeroom door and, tears running down his face, held her hard to him.

That night, Bree swam from dark dream to dark dream. She and Ted stood together on the deck of the *Titanic* as it went down into icy waters—no, that was Daria beside her, going down, down under the sea... voices somewhere... Ben, Amelia. Had they drugged her? Was she back in the hospital. No, this was her own bed.

She dived again, swimming hard to get to the wreck of her life. The sign with the boat's name was still there, broken, distorted: *MA D I*

Only one mermaid left now, just Bree alone. And she was mad. "I am mad," she changed the sign to say, scribbling on Cole's slate. I am furious and I am crazed with anger and pain. She beat her fists on the glass of the wheelhouse to get Daria's attention. Wake up, wake up! Swimming around inside, she was swimming when she should have been steering the boat. Had the storm killed her? The iceberg? Or something else?

Daria turned to her and waved, mouthing the words, *Come on in. The water's fine....*

Bree tried to pull the wheelhouse door open. Tried and tried, but Cole wouldn't help her, and Daria shook her head and tried to hold it shut.

"No, I have to go to her!" she screamed at Cole. "I have to find her, find out what happened!" Someone shrieked those words so close that it woke Bree up.

It was her own voice. Thank God, just a dream! But waking reality was just as bad.

She sat up amid the sheets she'd churned to huge waves around her. The bedside digital clock read 3:00 a.m. and her bedroom door was ajar. Lights came on in the hall, and Amelia rushed in, wearing silk pajamas. She had huge half circles of black mascara under her eyes.

"I'm here, I'm here," Amelia said, sitting on the bed and reaching out to hug Bree. For one moment, Bree just stared at her.

That's right, Amelia and Ben were here, though Bree had hated to see Cole leave.

"You—are you sleeping in her bed?" Bree stammered.

"No, of course not. On the sofa. Ben said not to touch anything of hers."

Maybe he thought something was strange about Daria's death—or else he was just being himself, a trained criminal lawyer who was now a prosecuting attorney. Amelia kept saying over and over, "Bree, I'm so sorry— so, so sorry! So, so sorry…"

So Bree pulled Amelia into her arms and comforted her.

10

Manny was furious that the police refused to start looking for Lucinda for at least forty-eight hours. They'd said she was just another teenage girl who'd left a note she was running away, and they saw that "all the time." Not with my daughter, Manny had insisted, but he knew this was all Lucinda's fault.

Still, all afternoon, and again when the high school let out, he drove the streets of Immokalee, looking for her. He stared at clumps of kids as they walked home, boarded buses or hung around. Lots of *chicas* resembled his youngest daughter—but none were. Didn't Lucinda know that human trafficking was a growing problem in South Florida? Sure, most of the girls abducted and forced into prostitution were from Guatemala, but it could happen if she was found wandering the streets. She looked as Hispanic as those poor women who were either sold by impoverished families or just plain abducted. Didn't Lucinda know she could ruin her life, much worse than she was ruining his?

When he'd gotten home, he'd learned Juanita had called Lucinda's Latina friends. They weren't sure who

her Anglo friends were. Like poor Bree, he was out looking for a lost girl, when the news he'd been expecting
and fearing came over his car radio.

"Boat debris and the body of missing Turtle Bay resident, Daria Devon, has been discovered underwater in
Big Marco Pass. Although the coast guard and civil air
patrol have been searching for her since she disappeared
during the storm on Tuesday, the discovery was made
by her identical twin sister and business partner, Briana
Devon. Authorities, including the county coroner, are
now on the scene. Daria and Briana Devon owned and
operated the Two Mermaids Search and Salvage Shop,
and are sisters-in-law of Ben Westcott, Collier County
prosecuting attorney. Daria Devon and her sister were
currently overseeing the Save Our Sea Grass project for
the Clear the Gulf Commission and…"

Manny pulled into the parking lot of Our Lady of
Guadalupe Church and, gripping the steering wheel,
pressed his forehead to his hands. They—*Bree*—had
found the body. Now came worse suspicions and, maybe,
accusations. He could only hope it would be ruled an
accident to avoid all that.

Despite his trials, Manny hadn't cried for years—
not *macho*. But now, tears ran down his wrists; some
plopped onto the knees of his jeans. Too much…too
many things out of his control. He owed it to Bree to be
with her, to help comfort her, even though she'd gone
starry-eyed over Cole DeRoca. And she had her other
sister and her big-man husband to call if she needed
them. *Caramba,* if there was any hint of someone hurting Daria…

"An autopsy will be performed," the radio voice went

on, "to discover the cause of death and rule out any possibility of foul play."

Foul play—foul play! Play was a *stupido* word for such a horrible thing.

Manny jumped when his cell phone rang. He swiped away tears with his sleeve and reached for it on the passenger seat. It would be his wife on the line, probably to tell the bad news about Daria—or, God forbid, something about Lucinda.

"Que pasa?"

"It's Lucinda," Juanita said in her quick Spanish. "She came home because she heard Daria is dead. Did you hear?"

"Sí. Muy malo! At least something good can come of that if the news brings Lucinda home. Give her the phone."

"She says she's sorry. She went right into your mama and told her she is very sorry. She's been with friends—her Anglo girlfriends, no boys, she says."

"I'm coming right home, then I have to go see Bree, help if I can, after…"

"After what?"

"I'll be right there. And that *chica* better be waiting," he muttered and punched off.

On the short drive home, he berated himself. He'd caused Daria's death, and Bree knew it. If he'd just been there, she'd said. But in a way, it was his defiant daughter and his beloved mother who had caused it. Too much pressure on him. He needed control of his family and he needed money. *Es necesario!* And half of the salvage business was now his. He'd done what he had to do.

Fists clenched, blood pounding, he banged into the house, furious with himself, his daughter and the world.

Juanita met him at the door, holding up both hands to halt his steps.

"Get her out here," he ordered, walking past Juanita, then turning back to face her in the small, cluttered kitchen. He lowered his voice. "My sick mother does not need to hear this. Lucinda's not hiding behind her or you. I said, get her out here."

"I said she's very sorry. She learned her lesson," Juanita pleaded. "Don't let your temper get the best of you, because it can be the worst of you."

By the next afternoon, Bree had sobbed herself sick, then gone stoic. When their pastor dropped by, she had asked him if they could use the little Turtle Bay Community Church for the funeral. The twins loved the church, with its seaside ambience. When they stood up to sing a hymn, they could see the bay and God's great sea beyond, and the congregation was so Deep South friendly. But Pastor Wallace had been right to suggest that, weather willing, they hold the funeral in the back of the church on the lawn, overlooking the bay. "The family of the bereaved," as he put it, had many friends, and with the publicity, a lot of strangers might also come to pay their condolences.

Would someone who wished her or Daria ill because of their report about the toxic gulf water be among those strangers? Bree had wondered silently. Surely, not among those who knew her.

Bree had put in a few frantic hours. She had met with her and Daria's lawyer about Daria's will. Because of the sometimes dangerous work they did, they both had wills with each other as the beneficiary. If they were both deceased, there were bequests left for Amelia's sons. They'd used the only lawyer in Turtle Bay because they feared Ben would try to control everything. At Daria's suggestion, they had recently added a codicil that, should one of them die or leave the business, Manny would become a full partner.

After her visit to the lawyer, Bree, Amelia and Ben picked out a coffin and arranged for a funeral home and the burial of Daria next to their parents, though Amelia kept protesting that she should have her own grave site, even if it was in the same cemetery. The grave site their father had bought when Mother died had a third plot next to her grave, although they weren't sure why. "Maybe the deal was for three plots, so your dad just bought the extra," Ben had said.

All this, and they still didn't have the body released for burial—nor did they have answers, Bree thought. She promised to drive to Ben and Amelia's to have dinner with them and see the boys later, but as soon as they were gone, Cole came over.

"No word on when we'll hear," she blurted when she saw him at the door. They hugged in greeting, and he kissed her cheek. He looked exhausted.

"I probably taste as salty as the gulf from crying," she told him.

"Blood, sweat and tears."

"Something like that."

"How are you holding up?"

Arm in arm, like old friends or contented lovers, they walked toward the sofa. "Cole, I'm just praying the coroner and police come up with a foolproof ruling of accidental death. I—I can't believe it could be anything else." She sat next to him, turning toward him with one leg bent, and hugged a throw pillow to her chest to keep from crawling into his lap as she had on Sam's barge.

"Surely not," he said, covering one hand with his. "Have you been through her things?"

"Ben said not to, in case it does become a criminal investigation. He—it's just that he's trained to think that way. He's seen too many bad situations. I can't be wrong in thinking that this is just a horrible, freak tragedy. I know I was wrong in thinking she was alive all this time when she obviously wasn't, but it's just that I couldn't bear to accept she could be lost—dead."

"I suppose when you've been so close to someone, it's hard to admit that as adults, your connection might not be quite as strong."

She frowned at him. "We may have liked some different things and had some different friends, but we knew all that about each other. It has to be an accident, for heaven's sake! People don't just stroll up and surprise you miles out in the gulf. I still can't recall hearing a boat motor. I didn't even hear her start our boat's motor, and I'm very familiar with its sound, even underwater."

The street doorbell rang, and Bree jumped up as if it had been a fire alarm. "Maybe one of our friends," she said, starting for the stairs. "They've dropped off enough food to feed an army, but Amelia still insists on cooking tonight. If it's another reporter, I'm not opening the door."

She heard Cole come down the steps behind her. It was strange—she'd only known him for three days, but she trusted him completely, just as she did Manny, Amelia and Ben. She crossed the office, running her hand along Daria's desk, and glanced out through the locked door. A good-looking middle-aged couple stood there with serious, almost pained looks on their faces.

"You know them?" Cole asked behind her.

"No."

"I can tell them you're not seeing anyone."

"Since I'm seeing them and vice versa right now, I'll just ask them what they want." She unlocked and opened the door. "May I help you?"

The woman spoke. "We're Vivian and Frank Holliman, friends of Daria's from her accounting class."

"Oh."

"Of course, the entire class and instructor send their deepest sympathies, and we are so very sorry for your terrible loss. But we're here to speak with you about something that can't wait. Perhaps Daria didn't mention our names to you, but of course, she told you about her plans to be a spokesperson for Shells Eternal."

"No. What is Shells Eternal?"

"Oh, dear," Vivian Holliman said with a roll of her blue eyes. "You see, she made plans for her own burial at sea."

Cole couldn't believe Bree asked the couple upstairs or was listening to them with rapt attention as the Hollimans sat on the sofa and Cole and Bree took the wicker rockers. Bree had hers tipped forward, almost upright. When they'd announced the reason for their visit, Bree had looked completely stunned. She must have thought at first that they meant Daria had planned her funeral ahead, then committed suicide. Now she looked as if she was seething but keeping the lid on her temper. The whole damn thing smelled like a con game to him.

The Hollimans had explained that they represented

a business that sank large, sculpted, concrete seashells onto the sandy floor of the gulf. In carefully constructed niches, the shells sheltered the cremated ashes of people. Accompanying plaques served as headstones.

Cole studied them as they did the fast talking. Viv, as she asked to be called, had pure white hair but a young face and a great body for her age; Frank was bald and was the better dresser of the two, including his expensive wristwatch and diamond-and-onyx ring. Bree had started out by demanding how well they knew Daria before they segued smoothly into a well-honed sales pitch.

"We really are an ecology-conscious business, and that appealed to Daria," Frank went on. "As her business partner and a fellow diver, I'm sure it does you, too. And the fact that Daria loved the sea, made promotion for Shells Eternal a perfect match for her. She agreed to be our spokesperson in exchange for a fee and a gratis eternal shells resting place when she passed on."

"Of course," Viv went on as if they were a tag team, "we—and she—didn't expect that she would actually have the need for that for decades. But the point is, she was extremely taken by a photo we showed her of one of our beautiful shells—"

"Offshore at Tampa," Frank put in, "though the next one will be near Naples."

"Our goal is for the shells to be covered with algae, barnacles, soft coral and small sponges, except for the bronze plaques with names and dates of the deceased. Of course, being a diver yourself, you could easily visit the site. A person who loved the water, the gulf, that much should surely have her cremains rest there, even though she can't be our spokesperson now. Actually, we were hoping *you* might consider our offer now—in honor of Daria's wishes."

"Her cremains?" Cole said when Bree just stared at them.

"Cremated remains," Viv explained. "Our ads urge our ecologically minded customers to think outside the box, and Daria did that. I'm so sorry she didn't mention to you that she was interested in a partnership with us."

Cole could almost read Bree's expression. She'd been struggling to smother her emotions since her hysteria in his arms on Travers's barge, but her eyes widened and she looked as if she'd throttle these two. Somehow she managed to unclench her fists and grip her hands together as if in prayer.

"Daria didn't mention it," she told the Hollimans, "but I assure you, your offer is so…unusual that she surely would have told me about it. We lived together, we shared our business and—"

"But she took the accounting class alone," Viv put in, starting to look miffed. "We were hoping you would honor her wishes."

"I assume, since this so-called partnership was so far advanced, you have a contract or some sort of written agreement from her you could show me."

"We were preparing one for her to sign," Frank said, sitting forward on the sofa. "We can bring you a copy of that, of course, or amend it to suit you."

"What would suit me is for you to leave now," Bree said, rising. "Our family has already made burial arrangements, and I'm not interested in Shells Eternal."

The couple stood, reluctantly, even angrily, Cole could tell. He couldn't believe their gall.

"It's not unusual, you know," Viv said, "for someone

as young as Daria not to want to upset those dear to her by talking about death."

"And I assure you," Frank put in as they moved toward the door of the apartment, with Bree leading and Cole bringing up the rear, "that this is not some sort of scam, though I can tell you think so. You can check our website, talk to the families of those who already rest under the sea."

"Our search for Daria, and now her death—" Bree choked on that last word "—have made Daria quite high-profile. Anyone could read about her background."

"I repeat," Viv said, "we are sorry for your loss and deeply regret you cannot honor her wishes. I would have assumed she shared this with you."

Cole figured the Hollimans were lucky Bree didn't just shove them down the stairs.

The bell gave a last jingle as she closed the door to the street firmly behind them and leaned against it.

"Do you believe that?" she asked, smacking her hands on her thighs. "If I wasn't so desperate for any lead about what could have happened to her, I would have thrown them out the moment they said their motto was Think Outside the Box." As they went back upstairs together, she went on. "You don't think those people are bizarre enough that they would harm someone just to get publicity for their concrete shells, do you?"

"I can check them out online. They would hardly have said all that if it was totally bogus. My guess is the business is legit and they just thought they could use a high-profile former scuba diver to give them sympathy and credibility. And they could get you, Daria's look-alike, to be in their emotion-packed ads."

"They said they were in her accounting class, so

that's easy to check." At the top of the stairs, he put his arms around her and felt her shudder. "What scares me," she said as she laid her head against his chest, "is that suspecting those off-the-wall people of harming Daria makes as much sense as suspecting anyone else. I don't think she had an enemy in the world—but if she did and if someone could possibly have hurt her, have I inherited them now?"

Being with her nephews lifted Bree's spirits, though both James and Jordan telling her they were going to miss Aunt Daria pierced her heart. "Now you and Mom get to be best friends, 'stead of you and Aunt Daria," six-year-old Jordan told Bree. Amelia stopped stirring the spaghetti sauce; her eyes met Bree's over the steam.

"Yes, that's right," Bree managed.

"Okay, you two," Amelia told her boys, "go put those *Star Wars* action figures away, wash your hands and come back down for dinner. See if Daddy's off the phone yet, and tell him to wash up, too."

"But we aren't done yet—Anakin is going to turn into Darth Vader and be really bad soon," Jordan, the younger, protested. "See, Anakin used to be good but he's going over to the dark side."

Amelia turned to face the kids. From her seat on a stool at the breakfast bar, Bree thought Amelia looked absolutely stricken by something they'd just said.

"I don't want to hear that kind of thing," she told them, her voice as stern as her face. "Why can't you play with something that has good people in it?"

As if to defend his younger brother, James said, "Luke Skywalker and Yoda are good, and Chewbacca. Sorry, Mom, I know you been crying a lot."

"Yes," Bree said, reaching out to put a hand on each of their heads. "Your mother's tired and sad, so you two go do what she says, all right? And when she works hard on a meal like this, you can both help by eating really well."

"And wash those hands until you've sung all the Birthday Song," Amelia shouted after them.

"The Birthday Song? What's that about?" Bree asked. It felt good to be talking about little, normal things, though her pain and loss sat so heavy on her chest it was an actual physical pain. Surely, that was why Amelia was so strung-out.

"Their idea of washing hands is zip, zip. If they sing 'Happy Birthday To You' all the way through, they get some of the grime gone. Bree, that was really weird about the Eternal Shells stuff—bizarre. Had Daria ever, ever talked about cremation instead of burial?"

"Only in a general way, that for some people it might make more ecological sense, but I don't think she ever felt visiting Mom and Dad's graves was morbid. We always thought it was pretty and peaceful there. We went once in a while and left flowers, tried to concentrate on the good things and happy memories."

Amelia pressed her lips together before she gave the sauce another swift stir and turned back toward the kitchen sink. Bree could see her face only in the reflection of the window. "It's good you two went," she said quietly. "I—I just can't face that place any more than I could being under all that water when you two used to dive with Dad so much."

The front doorbell rang, the chimes beautiful. But then, Bree thought, everything in this house was beautiful and beautifully kept. "Are you expecting anyone?" she asked.

"No, and if it's those Eternal Shells people trying to get to us now, they'll get a sieve of wet pasta dumped on them. Ben will get it. He said he'd man the phones and watch the door. The neighbors have been really nice about dropping things off to eat, but I just needed to make something myself tonight for us, for you. As if there's any such thing as comfort food at a time like this."

Bree heard voices, a man and woman. Surely, the Hollimans had not come here. Ben appeared in the kitchen door, his face solemn.

"What? Who is it?" Amelia asked.

"Josh and Nikki Austin," he said, looking at Bree. "Josh says he's been pushing the coroner for a fast decision and he has something to tell us."

Bree's legs went weak as she followed Ben into the living room and Amelia followed. She went to the broad staircase and called up it, "You two can play a little longer, and I'll call you when you can come down!"

Bree could not read Josh's expression. All those years she'd known him, and she could not psych out what he was going to say.

Nikki looked as if she hadn't slept, with smudges under her eyes as if she'd been crying. Bree was touched that she was evidently taking a stranger's death so to heart, but then perhaps something else had upset her. Nikki's jaw was set hard, as if to keep herself from dissolving in emotion. Bree empathized with the woman; she felt the same herself.

Josh hugged Bree while Nikki hugged Amelia, then Bree. Nikki smelled of expensive perfume. She hugged quickly and lightly, then stepped back to perch on the edge of the deep leather couch beside her husband.

Some movement outside caught Bree's attention through the window behind the couch. In the gathering dusk, standing beside a dark car by the street curb, waited the Austins' jack-of-all-trades, Mark Denton, whom Bree had briefly glimpsed in the hospital. Was he their chauffeur, as well as PR man, pilot and bodyguard?

"As I told Ben," Josh said, "he's not the only one who's been pulling strings with the coroner for quick answers, for all of your sakes, as well as to just get this settled."

"We're grateful for your concern."

Josh nodded. "At least I have some answers for you. There will probably be a few other results later—blood and toxicology tests, for example."

"She wasn't drinking or on drugs," Bree put in.

To her surprise, Nikki spoke, uncrossing then recrossing her long legs. "Of course, Josh is always concerned for all his constituents, but as Briana and Daria were childhood friends, this is especially important to him."

Daria was much more than a childhood friend to Josh, and Bree recalled that Nikki knew that. Marla Sherborne had said she'd mentioned that Josh had dated Daria.

"I admit," Josh said, "because Briana and Daria have been at the forefront of the efforts to monitor the problems with the gulf water, I've gotten more deeply involved than I might have otherwise. I know you have a key report to unveil soon, Bree, and it would be best to have things settled and Daria at rest before that. And, for your sake, Ben, too. With the election coming up, you need answers and closure."

"We all do," Bree said. "Just tell us the coroner's ruling."

Josh exhaled through flared nostrils. "Accidental

death. The autopsy showed she hit her head very hard in the back. The shape of the skull fracture suggests she fell against the steering wheel and was knocked unconscious, perhaps in the rough sea. The medical language says, 'a compression fracture in the occipital region of the skull with internal hemorrhages.' The exact cause of death, though, was drowning, no doubt when the boat drifted ashore, hit the concrete breakwater wall—they think they've found the place—and went down in the choppy channel of Big Marco Pass. They've decided not to raise the wreck, so it will remain there as a memorial of the tragedy. Officially, the wreck of *Mermaids II* is off-limits because of diving dangers in Marco Pass."

Nikki put in, "Of all the terrible, possible scenarios for the accident, that ruling seems the best, at least."

Nothing was the best, Bree wanted to shout, but at least now, surely, with this accidental ruling, she could put her mind at rest.

11

It was nearly ten o'clock that night when Bree entered Daria's room. She had phoned Cole to tell him the results of the autopsy. He'd told her not to do anything until after the funeral, now scheduled for Monday, and had volunteered to put off driving to Miami to check out Dom Verdugo's casino boat tomorrow so he could be with her.

She had insisted he go ahead with his plans. She knew she had to let him get on with his life, though she didn't want him to go back to a life without her in it. If anything good had come from the tragedy of losing Daria, finding Cole was it. And, perhaps, a better relationship with Amelia down the long, tough road without her twin, her other self.

"I'll see you when you get back. I'll be here and I'll be just fine," Bree had assured Cole, though the truth was that she was anything but fine.

As Bree began to go through her sister's possessions, she felt her presence so strongly it was as if she were in the room. She could almost believe Daria would appear in the mussed bedsheets still shaped to her form. When

Bree glanced through the medicine cabinet, she felt as if her sister might emerge from behind the shower curtain, her hair soaked, as if from the sea.

Bree gasped when she caught sight of herself in the bathroom mirror. Her mirror image, indeed! It was as if a distraught Daria stared at her from beyond the fragile barrier of the glass.

She forced herself to look away and put both hands on the washbasin to steady herself. "Dead woman walking," she whispered. A shiver snaked up her spine. She shuddered, recalling the old superstition that people felt a chill when someone walked over their grave. Ridiculous, absolutely crazy and in her own head, she scolded herself. But, in a way, the image of her dead sister would always be with her, aging, changing. What would Daria have looked like at age forty or fifty or sixty? All Bree had to do was glance at her reflection in a mirror or lean down to look at the surface of the water.

She got hold of herself and started in earnest with the dresser drawers. The top one was the catchall junk drawer and held the usual: extra truck, car and boat keys; some dollar bills; a few old photos, including a faded copy of their parents' wedding picture; a pair of earrings that hadn't made it back into her jewelry box; sunglasses; a few souvenirs of places they'd been; and a coaster advertising an unfamiliar bar, the Gator Watering Hole, a bit north of Turtle Bay on a back road off the Tamiami Trail on the edge of the Glades.

One side of the round cardboard coaster had a dancing alligator wearing sunglasses, with a cigarette in one hand and a beer bottle in the other. The place claimed to have "Great domestic beers, fried grouper and gator sand's, and the Old Florida Laid-back Feel."

Bree pictured Daria's last note. She'd be studying with friends and might be back late. But at a place like this?

Daria had often said she preferred the wine bar scene in Naples to the seedy bars Manny talked about. The Gator Watering Hole sounded like a hangout for Glades fishermen and hunters. Bree looked it up in the phone book; it wasn't even listed. So strange—Daria was gone and it was as if this place no longer existed either. What had the place meant to her that she'd kept this?

Bree flipped the coaster over. A list of beers, all domestic. Scribbled in small print on one side was the message, *"Luv ya,"* and opposite that, written in the other direction, as if each were to be read by a person across a table, *"Ditto, babe!"*

Tears blurred Bree's vision. The *"Luv ya"* was in Daria's writing. It must have been a happy, swiftly forgotten moment of fun in her too-short life. Daria had dated several guys in the last few years, but no one seriously and no one lately. And no one, as far as Bree knew, who she'd write *"Luv ya"* words to, even in fun.

Blinking back tears, she put the coaster back in the drawer and went through the rest of the bureau, including her cluttered jewelry box. Nothing unusual. She looked in Daria's purse and found their dentist's name, number, and an appointment time—the morning after the storm—scribbled on a piece of paper. Since the accident had been so public, evidently the dental receptionist had not phoned to remind her of this appointment nor, afterward, to ask why she had not come.

In Daria's purse she also found a calendar the size of a checkbook, one she hadn't seen before. She flipped through its pages. Blank but for big stars drawn on certain dates—oh, yeah, these were the days she had her accounting classes. Now, why hadn't Daria put her dental appointment in here? Daria had worked really hard at learning the financial ins and outs of keeping small business records, but big stars? And then she noted there were several times scribbled on a couple of the starred pages. Not the time of the classes, though—these were later.

"Oh, probably when she studied with the others after class," she said aloud. Had she met someone from the class she liked—or "luved"—and studied with? But why wouldn't she have mentioned that?

As Bree sat down at Daria's computer, she saw a brochure for Eternal Shells half-hidden by the mouse pad.

She gasped. Had the Hollimans been telling the truth? She began to shake again. What else hadn't Daria told her? It was a beautiful glossy brochure. The Hollimans must have indeed assumed that Daria had shown her this.

More frustrated than ever, Bree tried to read Daria's email and check sent and deleted mail, but the password she was sure Daria used—Mermaid2, instead of Mermaid1, because Bree had been born first—didn't work. She'd evidently changed her log-in info and hadn't mentioned that, either. Well, of course, she tried to tell herself, passwords were personal, but even that had not been a secret between her and Daria—until now.

She got off the computer. Maybe she could find a techie who could get around the password. From reading about one of Ben's high-profile prosecutions, she knew that even deleted documents could be recovered. Bree searched the rest of the room, but she was so exhausted she felt near collapse.

She lay down on Daria's bed and stared up at the whirring ceiling fan as her sister must have so often done. Of course, there were probably things she hadn't told Daria, too, but something was very wrong. That Eternal Shells brochure. That coaster from a place she'd never mentioned…and those haunting, even if brief, words, *Luv ya*. Those times scribbled down for after class. Bree had prided herself that she'd known her twin sister almost as well as she'd known herself. And now she was supposed to accept that Daria had evidently hit her head, and the storm had taken the boat and crashed it into a concrete breakwater and she'd drowned.

What was true and what wasn't? She should just go on with her life after Daria's burial. Get back to building the business and, hopefully, build a relationship with Cole. Resurrect ties to Amelia. Present that important environmental report and not let dreadful, doubtful thoughts torment her.

But had she really known her sister well? Had Daria died in a freak accident? Am I my sister's keeper? a voice in her head taunted Bree. Am I my dead sister's keeper?

"Yes, I am," she whispered to the cluttered but very empty room. "Yes, I am. Was she seeing someone? Was Daria hiding something? And was her death, for sure, an accident?"

The huge, white canvas sign swagged across the port side of Dom Verdugo's one-hundred-eighty-foot casino boat, *Fun 'n' Sun,* tied up at the Miami marina read, "A fabulous time with great food, entertainment and gambling—You Can Bet On It!"

To Cole's surprise, there were no goons on guard, and Verdugo himself greeted him. Cole had thought Verdugo was over at Turtle Bay, but he'd heard the man owned a private plane that took him coast to coast in a flash. He still could not shake the feeling the man bore watching.

"Hey, Cole, my man," Verdugo said with a firm handshake as he stepped aboard. "Sorry to hear they found the body and boat of that Turtle Bay scuba diver. Please give my regrets to the sister."

Again, Cole thought, Verdugo had *heard something*. It worried him that the man was aware of Briana and seemed to know that Cole would be seeing her.

"Where are your guards?" he asked.

"This is my territory," Verdugo said with a shrug. "In Turtle Bay, not yet. But I'm fine here with just my onboard staff."

"It will obviously be worth millions if you can get the Turtle Bay venue."

"Oh, yeah, for sure. I make no bones about the fact it's big biz, and I'm glad you are—literally—on board," he said with a tight grin.

"As I said, I'd like to see the extent of the job first."

"Sure, that's partly why I'm here. I'll give you the personal tour. Anyway, you think that girl's death will delay the report on the quality of the gulf water?"

Verdugo was a smart guy and a smart guy wouldn't bring that report up so blatantly if he'd had something to do with Daria's death—would he? Or did he figure he already had Cole in his hip pocket? Probably. Not many people said no to Dom Verdugo. But the whole idea of this man bringing gambling, an addiction that ruined some people's lives, ruined families for years to come, into Turtle Bay sickened him. Hell, panel the luxury gambling salon on board? He'd really like to sabotage the whole boat.

"I'm only asking," Verdugo said, "'cause I hear you're

on the Clear the Gulf Commission. I don't want you to think I've offered you a lot of money to do this job as a sort of bribe about how that all comes out. I don't operate that way."

Cole was suddenly more furious with himself than with Verdugo. He'd been so obsessed with helping Bree he hadn't even thought of how it would look for him to take Verdugo's lucrative contract. But even if he turned him down in the end, maybe he could first determine whether Verdugo had had anything to do with scuttling the *Mermaids II* to derail the Devon twins' damaging report. If he could prove that, it would also set back the gambling in Turtle Bay. He was flooded by memories of his parents fighting over his mother's debts, his own struggle to continue to pay them off over the years—

"You still game?" Verdugo interrupted his agonizing as they walked along the deck and turned into the gaming salon.

Cole just nodded. He was game, all right, although he was risking his reputation if he accepted. But strangely, nothing mattered more than trying to help Bree. He must, he figured, either be insane or in love.

Bree was horrified to wake up snuggled in Daria's bed. Light was streaming in the window, and she sat up abruptly. She had so much to do today. If Manny had called about Lucinda, she hadn't heard the phone ring. Or was he downstairs in the shop, waiting for Bree to appear? She'd been so exhausted—how late was it?

She rolled over and groaned to see the bedside digital clock said almost ten o'clock. Though she'd been drained since her swim during the storm, she could not believe she had fallen into a dead sleep. She'd slept almost ten hours!

She rushed into her own room, jumped in the shower, then ran a brush through her hair. Pulling on capris and a *Mermaids II* T-shirt, she called Daria's dentist to explain why Daria had missed her emergency appointment.

"Sorry, Ms. Devon," the receptionist said, after offering her condolences, "but the appointment you're referring to was to get her teeth whitened. It wasn't an emergency appointment, but one she'd had for a while."

"Daria Devon? Teeth whitening?"

"Definitely. I remember the call."

"Thank you," she said, feeling foolish. Perhaps Daria had just decided to use her whitening appointment to get her toothache taken care of, but that wasn't what she'd told Bree. It was so unlike Daria to give a darn about whiter teeth. Besides, both of their smiles looked good—at least, Bree thought so, and Daria had never said any different.

She went downstairs in a daze. Manny was not there. The place was silent, but the message lights on her and Daria's desks were blinking. Her phone said twelve messages; Daria's just one. For a moment, Bree imagined the lone message could be Daria, saying, *Come get me. I want to come home.*

"Are you going nuts?" she scolded herself. "Stop it!"

She punched Play on Daria's answering machine.

"Bree, Manny here. I called in on Daria's line, 'cause I figured my message might get buried on yours with all that's going on, just like on your cell. Didn't want to call the 'partment case you trying to get some sleep. Lucinda came back, says 'cause she heard about Daria. I know we closed the shop till after the funeral, but I'll come in after lunch, try to do what I can to help. Juanita stood up for her, but Lucinda's grounded for the rest of her life, far's I'm concerned. Tell you more later. *Vaya con Dios. Adios.*"

At least, Bree thought, Daria's death had brought Lucinda back. She bent to scribble a note to Manny: *Gone out for a while. Don't worry about me. Take care of your own—life is short. B*

She ran upstairs to grab her truck keys and purse, took a breakfast bar and her water bottle and copied the address to the Gator Watering Hole off the coaster before returning it to the top dresser drawer. She rushed back downstairs. First, she was going to Daria's accounting class. The group met at different flex times, some mornings, some afternoons, some evenings, so working people could attend at least some lectures. She wanted to see what else the Hollimans or anyone else knew about Daria, and then she was going to check out the Gator Watering Hole.

She stood in the doorway and stared outside. She'd been so out of it, she hadn't realized it was starting to rain. The wind had kicked up, which made her uneasy. But nothing was stopping her until she got some answers—and she wasn't even certain of the questions.

To Bree's dismay, the Hollimans were not in Daria's class when she poked her head in the door. She had gotten wet darting into the building from her truck, but even if she'd had an umbrella, it likely would have gotten turned inside out, the wind was gusting so hard. The instructor had evidently dismissed the class a bit early.

Too late, she realized her mistake of showing herself so suddenly. Several of the students gaped at her and one pointed. She couldn't blame them. After all, she had even startled herself looking in the mirror last night.

Loudly enough for everyone to hear, she introduced herself to the instructor. "I'm Briana Devon, Daria Devon's twin sister, and I just wondered if I could talk to you for a minute."

"Of course," the tall, young man said. His crew cut and open face reminded her of the photo she'd seen of Ted in uniform, the one in the paper that went with his obit and the story about him. "We are all very sorry for your loss," he told her. "I'm Seth Johnson."

They shook hands. Several other class members expressed regrets on their way out. "Daria mentioned the Hollimans—Viv and Fred," she told him, surprised she'd lied so smoothly. It was easy when you wanted something badly. Is that why Daria had lied? "I see they aren't here," she added. "I wanted to extend an invitation to the funeral to them."

"They missed today, which is unusual. You know," Seth said, "I can't say the same for your sister."

"What do you mean? Daria attended class religiously. It was very important to her!"

"I'm not criticizing," he said, holding up both palms at her outburst. "After all, this class is set up with flex time, with some online assignments, to suit the needs of our busy adult students. But she had conflicts, especially the night classes, which is when most of the students can make the lectures. As she may have told you, we flip-flop key lectures and exams between this hour and two evenings a month to allow people to attend."

"And she—she didn't? I'm not sure what you're saying. Do you keep attendance? I just—" She could not think of a lie to cover this bumbling question. "I just would like to know."

He showed Bree his records. Daria's attendance had been spotty, especially the night classes, always the first and third Tuesdays for the last two months. Damn, Bree thought. Daria was moonlighting to earn more money—for teeth whitening, the new dive watch she gave Bree for their birthday. Or—and this she refused to believe, because they'd always shared girl talk—she was meeting someone. But that must have been it.

Shaken, Bree thanked him and started away, then turned back at the door. "The Hollimans—do you know anything about their Shells Eternal business?"

"Everyone in the class did," Seth told her. "They were like walking, talking advertisements."

She went out into the corridor. Walking, talking advertisements—that's what they had wanted Daria to be for them. Now Daria wasn't walking or talking anymore, and the Hollimans had uncharacteristically missed tonight's class.

Before she went outside, Bree leaned against the thick floor-to-ceiling glass window next to the back door of the school and looked past the puddles in the parking lot. Everything looked wet and gray, almost as if the entire place was underwater. Daria, she agonized silently, why did you lie about these little things? Did you really have a toothache that kept you from diving with me that last day? Manny's not being there would have been reason enough I had to go down alone. Come to think of it, Daria hadn't dived much the last several weeks. Why did she miss classes and not mention something as strange as Shells Eternal? And why hide a new man in her life?

Bree glanced down at her watch. However dark it

looked outside, it was not even noon on this Friday yet. TGIF day for many people, and among the laid-back locals, that could start early. The Gator Watering Hole had the *Old Florida Laid-back Feel,* as Daria's souvenir coaster read.

The rain seemed to be letting up a bit, but it was so hot and humid that she'd probably be just as wet as if the rain continued. She'd go to that place in the Glades and ask around to see if Daria had ever been there. And if so, with whom?

12

Amelia knelt on the thick, wet grass with rain and tears dripping off her nose and chin. She bent close to her mother's headstone in the cemetery she had never set foot in since the day of her father's funeral four years ago. The area looked so different now, no tent, no fake grass blankets laid at the lips of the grave, no metal framework holding the coffin before it was lowered.

The cemetery workers had not yet dug Daria's grave. If they had, she might have thrown herself into it, so deep was her despair. She didn't like it that Daria would be buried here on Monday. The twins should be buried somewhere else, together. Since Ben insisted he wanted to be cremated, Amelia wanted her eventual resting place to be here by her mother's.

"Mommy, I think Daria's death is sort of retribution for yours," she said in a trembling voice. She swallowed a sob. It helped to say things out loud where she was certain no one would hear. "I found that medical report about your death years ago Dad had hidden. The fatal cervical rupture was from the birth of the second child, not that Briana wasn't partly to blame. After you died,

Dad forgave them, even favored them. It's not my fault they were his favorite. What happened—" here she emphasized each word "—wasn't my fault!"

She gripped her hands together, trying to find the right words to stop her pain. "I thought that when I had my two boys, everything would be better, but it isn't. I try to want to do things with both of them, but they are so loud and get so dirty and they want to swim and snorkel, and you know where that leads. But I didn't mean to shout at Daria and hit her that last day…"

She almost choked on those words she hadn't meant to say. Was she sorry? Her guilt was making her physically sick, so didn't that mean she was sorry? At least now, she and Bree would be closer, wouldn't they? That is, if Bree ever got over losing Daria.

It began to pour. Her hair stuck to her head and rain ran down her neck and throat. Bree had said Daria's hair had been streaming loose under all that water, holding her and the boat down, holding it down to drown…

Amelia squeezed her eyes tightly shut, but the images of herself trapped underwater wouldn't go away. It was like in the nightmares she'd had since Mommy died, worse when Dad and the twins went scuba diving. Trembling, she forced her eyes open. Tears, rain, deep water, even blood—it was all the same.

"I'm sorry, Mommy. Really sorry…" she whispered.

When she heard a low, distant rumble of thunder, she knew she'd better get going. Thunder might mean lightning, and she had no intention of ending up in the hospital like Bree, or worse.

That fear was surely rational. That meant she was coping, that she wasn't clinically depressed, didn't it?

"What happened could have been worse," she whispered to herself as she got to her feet. "Bree could be dead, too."

She bent to stroke her mother's wet, gray marble tombstone in farewell, but she couldn't bear to touch her father's.

Bree drove south on the Tamiami Trail through fitful rain and gusts of wind until she reached the turnoff to Cypress Road, heading east into the Everglades. A small runway with a few prop planes huddled by a single hangar at the intersection. She had to wait before making the turn as a string of cars came at her from the other direction. Although most people drove Alligator Alley to cross the state toward Fort Lauderdale or Miami, traffic was still heavy on this older route linking Tampa and Miami. She glanced across the airport tarmac; even in the rain, one man was working on an airplane. If the Gator Watering Hole wasn't too far down this road, it was possible that pilots stopped for a few drinks there. Now that was a scary thought.

After her turn, the tires crunched wet gravel; she drove slowly on a road barely wide enough to be called double lane. She was immediately on the edge of the Everglades, where shallow water surrounded grass on both sides of the road and cypress trees and their knobby knees poked through the so-called river of grass. She passed some slightly elevated islands called hammocks, from which sprouted pine and palms. Vegetation grew so thick in the heat and humidity here that she felt she was almost driving through the seaweed world on the bottom of the gulf.

She wondered how their—now her—precious turtle grass was doing at the Trade Wreck site. It needed to be monitored and photographed again, but who would be her dive buddy now? She'd have to give the Clear the Gulf Commission their "state of the sea grass" report alone next week. And it was going to be dire enough that all hell could break loose over that, too. She sniffed hard and grabbed a tissue from her purse to wipe her nose.

Although Manny was great with motors, machines and technical problems, he'd never make it as her new diving buddy. If he couldn't see all the way below the surface, he wasn't going down. He couldn't speak for their sea grass project. She might have to hire someone for dives—that is, she and Manny might—but she couldn't bear to think of running Mermaids without Daria. Funny, how she'd hardly given a thought to the business since that fatal day.

If—just if—someone was behind Daria's death, did they assume that, deserted at sea in rough waves and an approaching storm, Daria's twin would die that day, too?

About a mile off the highway, Bree saw a hand-painted sign for the Gator Watering Hole. The actual hole was a water-filled ditch surrounding the building and small parking lot on three sides like a moat. That could indeed hide an alligator or two. In these parts alligators made their way into golf course lakes, ornamental ponds, canals and ditches. People had to keep an eye on pets and children, not to mention themselves.

The tavern or bar—whatever it would dare call itself—looked like a dive out of the backwoods boonies, which it was. Its roof was part sturdy old Florida tin over the main section and part ragged palm thatch over the full-length porch, like the Seminole Indian–style *chickee* huts which had been made fashionable on cabanas and pool bars at ritzy hotels. But there was nothing ritzy about this ramshackle place.

Bree was pretty certain this was a wild-goose chase. Even if it was a short drive from Daria's accounting class, she couldn't fathom her sister meeting someone here. And it would be pitch-dark out here at night. Bree decided she'd have to go back to the next accounting class and ask if the students had gone here as a group. Or else Daria had just found the coaster, it had intrigued her and she'd kept it. But those *Luv ya, babe* notes bothered Bree. Who had written that back to her sister? She needed answers now, before they buried Daria, so that she could go on with her own life. Since she was here, a quick question or two in broad daylight—or cloaking rain—could help to settle her soul.

Three vehicles were parked in front and one in back, all pickup trucks, two in various stages of rusting out. One of them displayed a Confederate flag and a gun rack in its back window, not uncommon in these parts. One had balloon tires like locals used for what they called swamp buggy races through mud-filled obstacle courses. Bree parked off to the side so she could stay away from the other vehicles.

It boosted her courage to see a woman step out onto the porch and light up a cigarette. She had too much hair, too much makeup and too-tight shorts and halter top, but at least it wasn't all good old boys inside. After just a couple of puffs, she tossed the cigarette in a puddle and darted back inside. Maybe she was the cook or waitress.

Bree backed in against the palm tree trunk barrier at the top of the east-side ditch so she was parked heading out. As her wheels bumped against the barrier, something she'd forgotten hit her.

Up until the time they were in their teens, Dad sometimes used to teasingly pronounce Daria's name like *Dare*-i-a, because of the risks she sometimes took. He'd dubbed her his daredevil, "The Evel Knievel of the Deep," known for too fast a descent or too deep a dive. Only when his little daredevil almost choked to death from swallowing chewing gum underwater did she slow down. That's right, Bree thought, *Dare*-i-a had once been so sure that nothing could harm her that she reveled in taking risks.

Bree had always been more circumspect. She wasn't going to take any chances in this place, either. Just a quick question or two and she was out of here.

As she headed toward the building, a quickening breeze shoved clotted clouds overhead, and the rain increased. The wind was coming from the same direction as the storm that had killed Daria.

The rain beat incredibly loudly on the tin roof. Other than that, the place was quiet, the lighting lousy. No TV blaring, no canned music. Stepping into the building was like stepping back in the past. An old jukebox half blocked the entryway but it sat silent. Plain, mismatched wooden tables and chairs were clustered around the edges of the small room; a row of rattan stools lined a long bar. There was a worn-looking pool table in the corner.

The clientele was negligible, as she had hoped. Two guys who looked like denizens of the deep Glades played foosball, and one man hunched over a table, apparently asleep. The woman was not in sight. From behind the bar, through a small opening with a serving counter from what must be the kitchen, drifted the smell of frying burgers. The walls had no neon-lighted beer signs, just some Florida State Seminoles and Miami University Canes football pennants and blow-ups of the stadiums.

Actually, the dominant decor could be called early alligator. At least ten gator skulls, with open jaws flaunting razor-sharp teeth, were nailed high on each of the four walls. They seemed to grin at her.

Suddenly everyone looked at her; the men stopped talking and playing foosball. The only sound was the rattle of rain on the metal roof and the swish of palm fronds against it.

Here we go again, she thought. They think they're seeing a ghost. Her heart careened to her feet. That meant Daria must have been here.

"You're here way off schedule, honey," said the bartender, a tall, gaunt man. "You want the usual?"

Hadn't they heard Daria was dead? She guessed it was possible. Glades guys were not like boaters and divers, totally attuned to what went on in or near the water. In that case, she wouldn't be dead woman walking, but live one talking.

"Sure," she said, deciding to be Daria to see if that got her more info than the way she'd intended to proceed. "Change of plans about my schedule," she told him, and dug in her purse for some money. The foosball game picked up again, along with the other conversations. "When were you expecting me?"

"Next Tuesday, like always," he muttered, slapping down a tall, old-fashioned Coca-Cola glass on the bar.

Bree's eyes widened when he poured it half-full with lemonade and half with foaming beer. Daria loved what the Brits called shandies; she'd learned to drink them when she'd dated a snowbird from Toronto.

"Okay, then, this one's for here, and these beers are

for the road," he told her with a smile that was missing two prominent teeth. "Or for the guy you're meetin' out back, like always."

Bree's pulse pounded as he produced two bottles of Mountain Brewed beer. "Tell me what he looks like," she said, trying to sound coy as she put money on the bar. "I just might have the wrong guy in mind."

"Never really seen him, and you know it, but Bess—" he gave a toss of his head to indicate the kitchen "—or a little bird musta told me, well-built, dark hair. Out here it's see no evil, speak none neither. Say, you two goin' parkin' in the Glades in this wet mess, since it's nearly dark as night outside?" he asked with a laugh.

Bree realized her mistake now. She might insult him if she explained who she really was and started to grill him. Having pretended she was her sister, she could hardly ask more about the guy she was meeting. Well-built and dark haired? Someone who called Daria "babe" and liked Mountain Brewed Beer? And someone who didn't come in here for his own drinks?

She drank half of her shandy down, just because she was suddenly so thirsty, then spilled most of the rest of it on her wrist when a clap of thunder sounded. It seemed to echo off the metal roof and inside her skull. Lightning! She had to get in the truck and get out of here.

"Thanks," she said, stuffing the two beers in her big purse and heading for the door.

"Don't he want them opened this time?" the bartender called after her.

"No. I'm—we're fine," she said, realizing it was probably a good thing they thought she was meeting a man outside.

Even with her sensitivity to light, Bree was surprised

to see how much darker it had become outside in mid-afternoon. She prayed it would not turn into another one of those afternoon deluges like the one that had trapped her and Daria. She had to get home and think through all she'd learned. She wanted to come back here with Manny or Cole, maybe even Ben, though she didn't want him to know she was investigating on her own.

Daria obviously did have someone she was meeting secretly. A married man? Had she rekindled a flame with Josh Austin? No way, not with a stunning wife like his and his high profile, not to mention how busy he was.

Holding her big purse over her head for a break in the rain so she could see, Bree ran for her truck.

"You run away like a dog, you spend Saturdays with me on a short leash," Manny told Lucinda as they entered the Two Mermaids. He handed her a broom and pointed toward the back room.

"That's a big place with lots of junk in it!" she dared to protest.

"I don't care. Just do it and not complain—same with that *quinceañera* party. Now that Daria's half of this business come to me, we have more money for a nice one."

"Yeah," she said, taking the broom from him with a frown, "but without Daria to dive with Bree, your profits will be down, won't they?"

"Maybe we hire a part-time diver. When the mourning for Daria is over, we advertise more. But this been a lot of publicity already."

She just shook her head, glared at him and stomped into the back room. The swish, swish of the broom convinced him he'd at least had a small victory with her.

The front doorbell rang, and Manny saw it was one of Sam Travers's workers, the red-haired one named Lance. He carried a pair of green fins. It looked strange to see him alone. He was usually with his diving partner, Ric, a real stud who evidently worked out a lot.

"Your boss left these on Sam's barge," he said without a greeting.

Manny was tempted to tell this man he was partners with Bree now, but it hadn't been announced and he hadn't even reminded Bree of it yet. He didn't want to seem too pushy when she was grieving.

"Thanks," Manny said, taking them and putting them on Bree's desk.

"I can understand why she forgot them," Lance said, folding his arms over his chest. "Hell of a thing—bad enough her sister was dead, but to find her like that? The whole scene was surreal."

Manny wasn't sure what *surreal* meant, but he could guess. "We are grateful for Sam's help," he told Lance.

"Considering that you're our business rivals?" Lance asked, as he headed for the door. He stopped and turned back. "Or that he blames Briana for his son's death?"

"You know that, too?" Manny asked. Lucinda's broom had stopped. He had to check on her.

"Sam hardly makes a secret of it. Man, I'd like to get a glimpse of that attic shrine he's made to his son. Talk about whacked-out… The way he really feels about Briana, I wouldn't be surprised if he isn't up there sticking pins in a voodoo doll of her. Know what I mean?"

Manny wasn't clear on what a voodoo doll was, either, but he got the message. And he was going to make sure Bree got that message when she returned.

* * *

Bree ran toward her car so fast that she slipped in the mud and sprawled to both knees and both hands in the mire. Her keys got coated with muck. Cursing but moving carefully, she got to her feet and wiped the keys off on one of the few clean spots on her jeans, then looked around.

For a moment, through the slant of gray rain, she felt disoriented. Was her truck where she had left it?

Of course it was, straight across the tiny parking lot. She'd gotten turned around and was looking the wrong way. Was she losing it?

With a nervous glance, she walked toward it, telling herself to watch her footing. Any thought she'd had of walking around back to talk to Bess in the kitchen or to try to find out why Daria met a man "out back," as the bartender had said, flew right out of her head. She was getting away from here.

In the driving rain, she tried to get her key in the door lock, but she was shaking so hard it didn't go right in. At least the rain cleaned the last of the mud from her keys.

And then—she wasn't sure where he'd come from— she saw a man striding straight for her, as if he'd emerged from the ditch or the swamp. He wore all black, jeans and old running shoes, Windbreaker and a billed hat. The neck of a second black T-shirt was pulled up around his face for a mask. And he held a huge, raised wrench in one hand.

13

Bree ducked the man's first swing with his wrench and didn't wait around for a second. Where had he come from? Was he one of the guys inside?

She screamed but a clap of thunder drowned her out. With the rattle of rain on that roof, people inside might not hear. *Save your breath to run. Someone will come out or along the road to help.* Hoping she could beat him to the other door of her truck, Bree dashed around the back with her key out. She and Daria had taken a self-protection class; Ben had insisted on it when they'd moved to the apartment above the marina shop. Hold your car keys between your fingers as a weapon. But nothing she had could take on that wrench.

He was too fast for her. He came around the front end and lunged at her again. Who? Why?

Sidestepping him, she tore for the door of the bar, but he caught up and yanked her back. He didn't swing the wrench this time, but turned her away from him—so strong—and clamped a hard, dirty hand over her mouth. His arm was so tight around her waist she couldn't breathe. She tried to bite his fingers, but he smacked her mouth. Her teeth cut the inside of her lower lip and she tasted blood. When he tried to drag her toward the ditch, she elbowed him in the ribs, then just picked up her feet.

They toppled over, side by side. She screamed, but the rain on the tin roof drowned her out, drowned her... Horrid images leaped at her: Daria trapped in that flooded wheelhouse underwater...her hair wet and waving...her hands upraised, as if for help. Another wayward thought hit her. What if someone—this man?—had tried to hurt Daria? What if her skull had been struck by a wrench and not the boat's steering wheel?

Her attacker half rolled, half jumped to a standing position and dragged her to her feet. She clawed at his wrist with the keys. He let her go but blocked her path toward the bar door. Knowing the woman was out in the back room, Bree tore around that way.

She evidently took him by surprise and got a little lead. Behind the place were picnic tables, two big, shell-shaped planters for cigarette butts, and a crude bridge over the back part of the ditch. Thick, wet vegetation loomed ahead.

Bree heard him coming, his feet fast, his breath loud. She cursed her acute hearing, because her pulse pounded in her ears.

He got to her before she reached the back door. The building had windows here, too, but the louvered wooden shutters were down in the rain.

"Hey, babe," he said, his voice a low rasp, but the words screamed inside her skull and her soul.

Babe? Could this be the man Daria had met here, the one who wrote on the coaster? Had their affair gone wrong, and he'd killed her? And now meant to silence someone who looked like her or someone asking too many questions?

The last thing in the world Bree wanted was to run into the Glades, but he would be slowed by the standing water. She was used to it and could handle it, was more sure-footed, she was certain. Then she could go around toward the road, circle back to her truck, or maybe someone would come by. It was only about a half a mile to that little airport, and she'd seen a man there. And on the highway, there were plenty of people to flag down, people who would never turn down little Cypress Road.

She veered away from him and sprinted toward the bridge. She made it that far. It was the first time it registered that she still had her heavy purse over her shoulder, pressed under her arm and that her cell phone was there. If only she could put a little distance between them, she'd call 911. And she had two beer bottles for weapons.

But out on the rickety bridge, he had her by her wrist. Rain tattooed the water in the ditch and enveloped them in a gray, slanted curtain. Bree reached for one of the bottles and threw it at him. Beer sprayed over both of them as the bottle broke on his head, maybe dazing him, but his cap and the T-shirt that covered his face kept him from getting cut. If she could just yank that mask down! But then, if she knew who he was, he would surely kill her. She was hoping he might only mean to scare her. He'd done that, all right.

But she felt power pump through her. She'd aim her keys for his face this time or swing her purse at him. Moving a little slower, he raised the wrench again.

Bree swung her purse. The wrench went flying into the ditch, but he slammed into her. She opened her mouth to scream again, but they broke through the wooden bridge railing and splashed into the ditch.

Water enveloped her with a surge and a smack. She hit her head against something. Was she diving? She'd gone off the boat backward. But no tanks, no regulator, no mask. She held her breath, so dizzy at first. Under the sea, under the sea, Bree and Daria, under the sea.

But it wasn't deep. Her bottom hit bottom, and she bounced right up for a huge gasp of air. A few feet from her, her attacker was trying to stand, sputtering, splashing. Dear God, she prayed, don't let there be gators in here.

She had the choice of either daring to pull down his mask or scrambling out to run.

Clawing her way up the bank, she slid back twice while he reached for her ankles. His fingernails raked her leg. Amazingly, her purse, full of water, was back over her shoulder.

She kicked the man away, lost a shoe, then clambered out and ran, dripping wet, her purse sloshing, her soaked hair flinging water. Gut instinct told her not to run back inside but to get out of here. She had a head start. Beat him to her truck this time!

She glanced back once as she turned the corner of the building. Her attacker's hat but not his mask had come off. He was floundering out of the water, shaking his head and spraying water off dark hair as if he were a dog. She didn't even recognize him bareheaded, but she had water and her own hair in her eyes.

Run!

Gasping, she made it to her truck and steadied her right hand with her other to turn the lock and throw herself in. She slammed the door, locked it, praying he didn't come, hadn't found that wrench to knock out her windows. Could fingerprints be taken from a wet wrench, if it was found later?

Her right hand, which had clutched the keys the entire time, seemed frozen into a claw. She was shaking so hard she almost couldn't shift gears. With a screech, she turned the wheels to roar out onto the small road.

She sped back toward civilization. Throwing water in the rain, the windshield wipers whipped across her vision, *whap-whap, whap-whap.* She should not have tried this alone. She needed Cole or Manny, even Ben.

At the stop sign to the Trail, she didn't see anyone following and had to wait for traffic again. She put her forehead on the steering wheel and sobbed. Maybe Daria, with her good sea legs, had not slipped and hit her head on the boat's steering wheel, no matter how rough the water was. Maybe someone had boarded the boat and hurt her. No matter what Josh Austin reported or the coroner ruled or other people accepted, she had to look into that horrible possibility. Could the storm have cleverly been used to make a murder look like an accident?

After hugging her, then holding her at arm's length, Cole took to furious pacing while she told him everything, starting with the fact Manny had warned her that Sam Travers was as unforgiving as ever and then working up to the worst by blurting out about her attack.

As he walked back and forth, Cole alternated between clamping his hands under his armpits or gripping them on top of his head. Bree could tell he was livid, not only with Sam and the man who'd attacked her, but also with her. She figured he kept his hands constrained so he wouldn't give her a good shaking.

She was just lucky she'd had time to clean up and change out of her wet clothes, so he didn't see what a mess she'd been, but she hadn't had time to shower or wash her hair. She'd toweled it dry but tiny flecks of green algae clung to it, pond scum like the bastard who had attacked her. After she'd dived into the depths of the Trade Wreck with the strobe, she'd seen Cole angry, but he was a lot angrier now. His dark eyes were narrowed; every muscle in his face looked chiseled from stone. A pulse beat at the side of his throat, and his big body seemed coiled tight, ready to strike.

"You said you'd stay here, and that you'd be fine," he interrupted. "Go ahead, tell me the rest."

"I'm sure I didn't know him," she concluded, still clutching a cushion to her breasts as she sat cross-legged on the sofa.

"He was masked."

"I would recognize you in a mask—or Manny, Sam Travers, Ben, Josh Austin. Lots of people," she protested.

When he finally sat down beside her, his weight toppled her into him. He lifted and turned her chin to make her look at him. The cut inside her mouth made her flinch. That and the scratch on her leg were her only physical injuries, however achy and black-and-blue she might be tomorrow and for the funeral, two days away.

"So," Cole said, "it couldn't have been someone from inside that place because you're sure no one left after you entered."

"Unless he was out in the kitchen with Bess."

"Yeah, I want to talk to her."

"The thing is, my attacker fits the vague description of the man Daria was evidently meeting. He could be the one who wrote on the coaster. He called me 'babe,' too. It's the only thing he said—'Hey, babe.'"

"It could connect, or not. Lots of guys are muscular and dark haired—including yours truly."

"He wasn't as tall as you."

"Great, then it wasn't me," he said, his voice suddenly dripping sarcasm. "We've narrowed the suspect down to someone we know, such as one of Verdugo's guards—they all look like that. Or Ric, Sam's worker, though his choice of weapon seems to be a speargun, not a wrench. Then there's Frank Holliman, for all we know, not to mention a gazillion guys we don't know. And saying *Hey, babe* doesn't mean much. I could say that to you, too, as a come-on and not a threat."

"Why are you tearing down everything I say?" she demanded, and threw the pillow at him. He swatted it away as if it were a mosquito.

"I'm not. I'm just a little upset—you could have gotten yourself killed. And I don't want you jumping to conclusions that just because you were attacked, Daria was, too. Don't assume we have more answers than we do."

He'd said *we* again, she thought. As frustrated as he was making her, she loved that.

"Cole, I admit I shouldn't have gone in there, but you surely shouldn't, either."

"Why the hell not? I'll take Manny with me, talk to the bartender and Bess, check for that wrench, though you're right. It can't have prints on it if it's in the ditch."

"I don't want you to get in trouble over this."

"What's the diff?" he muttered as if to himself, shaking his head. "I'm already in over my head with Verdugo—and you."

"Me?"

"Yeah. I'm furious with you—again—for losing your head, and here I've lost mine over you."

"Oh."

"Oh? Is that the best you can say?"

His hands on her shoulders were more than firm. He bent to nuzzle her cheek, then dipped his head to trail his lips down her throat, which she mindlessly arched back for him. He kissed the hollow between her collarbones, then moved up the side of her neck to her left ear. He nipped at the lobe, then darted his tongue inside the shell of her ear, thoroughly, just once.

Every nerve in her body jumped to attention, screaming for more. She sucked in a sudden breath, teetering on the edge of beautiful oblivion. She was acting like a schoolgirl, she scolded herself, as if she'd never had a man near her before. But this was so different. Cole's merest touch set off a torrent of insane sensations clear down to the pit of her belly.

"I know you hear things too well lately, so I'm whispering now," he said, his mouth moving against her cheek. "And I'll make it quick because, as luscious as the rest of you is, your hair smells like…gator water."

She almost laughed. Amidst all this terror, he had the power to take her on a roller-coaster ride of emotions, and that both scared and sobered her.

"Two things," he said, his voice deadly serious. "You stay put until I get back. And, however helpful he's been, stay away from Sam Travers."

"He may come to the funeral. After he helped us look for Daria, I can't tell him to stay away."

"I just mean you don't go near him, okay?" he said, putting her back at arm's length to look hard into her eyes. She wasn't used to taking orders, but from him, she was starting to welcome them.

"All right. I won't go near Sam."

"Meanwhile," he said, releasing her and frowning at his hands while he flexed them, "I'll take Manny to cover my back and you can babysit his daughter. I feel the urge to go order a Mountain Brewed at the old laid-back, good-time Gator Watering Hole."

Bree tried to keep her mind off her own problems by listening to Lucinda's woes, but she was really worried about Cole. With Manny, he was going to do her dirty work, to find out about the man who met Daria on the sly, but also, she feared, to pay someone back for attacking her. She couldn't bear it if he or Manny got hurt.

Lucinda seemed happy to have been rescued from sweeping the back room downstairs and from her father's presence. After Bree showered and washed her hair, they sat at the table in the apartment eating shrimp salad and the brownies one of the church people had dropped off. Bree was too uptight to feel hungry, but Lucinda had a good appetite. She was a pretty girl with lively brown eyes, just on the verge of becoming plump, but that gave her a voluptuous figure. No wonder Manny was trying to keep an eye on her. She chattered on about things, then something she said brought Bree back from her agonizing with a jolt.

"Swear you won't tell my dad something, Bree?"

"If it's something bad or dangerous, you really shouldn't put me in a position like that. Manny's an employee but also a friend."

Lucinda's sleek eyebrows lifted. "Yeah, but won't he be a partner now?"

"Yes, when everything is settled. I didn't realize you knew all that."

"A bunch of stuff I overhear—like what that guy who brought your fins back said about you. But yeah, Dad told our whole family all that about the partnership a long time ago. It's really a good thing, too, 'cause we can *so* use the money. Is it okay if I just ask you a general question then, not tell you a secret?"

Bree knew the entire Salazar family. Lucinda was the only one who really sounded Anglo and that bothered Manny. In his opinion, his daughter was too much an American teen and Bree didn't want to interfere with that, not considering how strict Manny was with his family.

"All right, Lucinda, shoot," Bree said, deciding not to quiz the girl about what else Manny might have said about becoming a partner.

"First of all, you can call me Cindi if you want—with an *i* at the end. I like to dot both *i*'s with little hearts or happy faces, know what I mean?"

"Sure. But in front of your dad, I might stick to Lucinda."

"Oh, yeah," she said, rolling her dark eyes. "I mean, it's *so* good to talk to a straight-up adult who understands me. So, let's just say a friend—a Latina—falls for an Anglo guy—I mean, about as American as he could be. This guy is *da bomb*—blond, great body, tall, on the basketball team. A real hottie. Let's say his parents are not real happy either, 'cause they think Hispanics are all a bunch of illegal immigrants—and Catholic, 'stead of Baptist, which is true. Anyway, I'm asking you for her, 'cause I know you dated Sam's son in high school and Sam didn't want you to."

"No, that's not quite it," Bree said, shoving her plate away and leaning back wearily in her chair to rub her eyes. "Sam Travers was all for me dating his son, even marrying him, but I broke it off when we were in college. Ted got really upset and enlisted in the marines and was killed in Iraq. Sam Travers blames me for the fact Ted was there—and got killed."

"Man, that bites," Lucinda whispered, frowning and shaking her head. "You don't blame yourself, do you?"

"Ted Travers made his own choices, but I feel like I've got a big target on my back when I'm around Sam. Listen to me, Lucinda—Cindi," she said, sitting forward and taking the girl's hand across the table. "My sister dated someone in high school for a long time, too, but when he broke up with her, she just went on with her life. No one blamed anyone, ran away from home or did anything crazy. So trust me on this and just tell your friend not to think her relationship with this boy has to be the end of the world. If it works, it will have to take time, patience and understanding. If it doesn't work out, life goes on and maybe there's someone, Anglo or Latino, even better for her a little ways down the road of life."

"So you mean your sister—she got over the guy she dated in high school?"

"Yes, exactly."

"And found someone else to love. She must have been so hurt by the guy breaking it off—even if she didn't show it."

Bree frowned. Since Josh, Daria had dated several men and had been the one to break it off with every one of them. Was she afraid of commitment, or did she think she'd better break things off before they dumped her? Could that have been the fallout of her loving, then losing, Josh? And why hadn't Bree thought of this when Daria was alive?

"I know," Bree went on, her voice shaky, "it's hard to take advice from older people, especially parents, and especially when they get all upset and yell, but that's only because they care about you so much. Cindi, please try to treasure the time you have with your parents and your sister, because you won't have your family forever. And don't be in too much of a hurry to give your heart—or your body—away. Sometimes, in a way, you might just not get either back."

Bree jumped up and took their dishes to the kitchen before the girl could see she was going to cry. Time with parents didn't last forever, let alone with a sister. Had Daria ever gotten over Josh Austin? Bree thought she had...she was *sure* she had. But now she wasn't sure of anything, including the fact that she had known her identical twin sister, the person closest to her in the whole world, at all.

Cole and Manny looked around the property of the Gator Watering Hole before going in. The sun had come out after all the rain, and they felt as if they were in a steam bath.

They saw where Bree and her attacker had fallen through the railing of the bridge. They also saw a couple of gators sunning themselves near another part of the ditch, so they decided to fish around for the wrench later—a lot later. There was no way it was going to have prints, and no promise that the police would even try to ID them, if there were.

Shaking his head, Cole muttered, "She almost

drowns, swims with sharks around her during the storm, gets hit by lightning, then barely missed the gators."

"How many lives they say a cat got?" Manny asked as they headed around the bar toward the front door.

"Nine, so I'd like to think she's got five to go."

Manny just grunted.

They ambled in and sat sideways at the bar so they could scan the entire front room, which was a lot busier than when Bree had been there earlier. From Bree's description, Cole could tell the bartender was the same guy. He could tell the guy didn't especially like Manny here, as if one Mexican would begin an onslaught of them here in redneck heaven. Just to get his attention, Cole ordered in Spanish. "*Dos cervezas aqui*—Mountain Brewed."

The man raised one shaggy eyebrow. "Don't sell many of those 'round here, but get in a case now and then for a special customer."

"That right? Maybe a friend of mine. Dark-haired, works out all the time?"

"Could be," the guy said, nervous now. "Never comes in, sends a friend." He grabbed a bottle opener and bent the first metal cap.

Cole considered playing dumb about the fact Bree had been here, but that probably wouldn't work. He decided to try a plain, old man-to-man approach and hoped he didn't have to get rough, even if he was ready to. He figured, one wrong move here and they'd be taking on almost every man in the bar.

"We're friends of the woman who was in here earlier today," he said, keeping his voice low. "the one you made a shandy for and sold the two Mountain brewskis."

"What's the deal with the guy you're all looking for?"

he asked. "Swear to God, don't know his name or why a class act like her took to meeting him here—yeah, well, I guess I do," he added with a snicker.

"Did Bess get a good look at him?"

He seemed startled Cole knew the woman's name. "What's the prob, I asked," the guy demanded, still not raising his voice either. "He leave her and she wants him back? Or what?"

"Yeah," Cole said. "Or what. Can I talk to Bess just for a sec?"

"She's pretty busy, fryin' fish."

"You see, we've got other fish to fry, too. If I can just talk to her, I won't feel I need to make a police report that the woman you're referring to was attacked by a guy with a wrench when she walked out of here in the rain today. Her attacker might just fit the description of the man I'm trying to trace, but I can just let the police take over and come out here to snoop around, check your liquor license, question your customers, and—"

"Lay off, I hear you. Come on out in back. And we don't need no health inspector here lookin' at the kitchen neither, if you was going to bring that up next."

Bess's description of the mystery man was the same general, nondescript one the bartender and Bree had given. "But there is one thing I thought was kinda funny," she added, after the bartender had gone back out and Cole and Manny were about to leave.

"What's that? Anything might help."

"More 'n once, I think she met a different guy. Like maybe she was really getting around, meeting clients here or something. You know—johns. If you're involved with her, I'd try asking her about it."

Cole smacked his hand down so hard on the counter

that her pile of knives jumped and clattered. She grabbed one and held it in front of her.

"I didn't mean nothin' by it, just telling the truth," she muttered. "If that don't do no good, just get on outta here 'fore I call Jerry."

Manny went way up in Cole's estimation when he automatically covered his back by facing the door, in case she did call Jerry in. Cole clenched his jaw and gritted his teeth.

"Can you describe anyone else she met?" he asked, trying to keep calm.

"Listen, mister, it's pitch-black out there at night. I'm standing here doing dishes or fixin' food. I just glance out, that's all. It wasn't the same guy all the time. There were at least two different ones, one taller and thinner than the other, that's all."

Cole raked his hand through his hair. "Thanks for your help. I appreciate your honesty," he told her as they went back out through the bar.

But he was considering lying to Bree.

After the rain stopped, Lucinda wanted to go sit on the lanai to watch what was happening at the marina, but Bree felt afraid. Until Cole learned something about her attacker, she was hesitant to even sit outside.

Such a feeling infuriated her. She was not going to become a victim or prisoner. Sure, she'd be more careful now, but whether or not her attacker's purpose was to scare her into silence or shut her up for good, she wasn't going to cooperate. The best defense was surely a good offense.

"Why don't you pour us both a glass of OJ from the fridge, and I'll be right back," Bree suggested. "But the furniture on the veranda will be soaked, so we'd better just open the doors to the patio and sit in here for now. The doors are locked, but I'd appreciate it if you unlock them so we can get the breeze and see out better."

As Lucinda headed for the kitchen, Bree went to the bathroom, popped into her bedroom to brush her still-damp hair, then hesitated in the hall to stare at the closed door to Daria's room. Manny had said he'd heard Sam had a sort of shrine to Ted, no doubt with cherished mementos and photos. Bree didn't want to become obsessed like that, nor would Daria want her to.

Still, after the funeral, she'd go through her sister's things again. She'd give some away to the church for their collection for migrant workers, keep precious things, of course, and offer some to Amelia. When Bree had searched the room so thoroughly yesterday, she'd noticed a few new clothing items of Daria's she hadn't even worn yet. Maybe she would keep a few things for herself. Wearing them would make her feel closer to Daria. How often they'd shared clothes over the years.

Something compelled her to open Daria's door and glance in. She gasped, clamping both hands over her mouth so hard she felt her cut against her teeth.

True, Daria had left the room in disarray, and Bree had moved things around, but it was even more of a mess. No one had been here when she wasn't, so what had happened?

The pillow on the bed was out of its case. Other subtle changes caught her wide stare, a picture they had taken in Greece aslant on the wall, a sock hanging out of a drawer Bree had carefully closed. And two pairs of shoes, which had been under the bed skirt now peeked out.

Trembling, she glanced behind the door, then looked

under the bed and into the closet, which looked rearranged. Bree opened the bureau drawers she'd gone through. She rifled through the top one, as she was certain someone else must have done.

The Gator Watering Hole coaster was gone.

She almost called Cole on his cell, but she remembered that she'd given Amelia a key to the apartment. It had been almost as if Bree had presented her with the Holy Grail, she'd been so pleased. Maybe Amelia had wanted some remembrance of Daria and had just come over, though she didn't believe that was likely. At least she would have left a note. Of course, Manny knew where the extra apartment key was downstairs in Bree's desk. He'd been here all morning, while she was gone and Lucinda was sweeping the back room.

Shaken, she rejoined Lucinda, who had two glasses of juice waiting on the coffee table next to the orange orchid Cole had given her in the hospital. As Bree had asked, Lucinda had the veranda doors open to the warm breeze off the bay.

"Sorry I took so long," Bree said.

"No problem. By the way, the doors weren't locked like you said." She turned to Bree and smiled up at her. But her smile faded, and she went wide-eyed. "You okay?" the girl asked. "You look like you've seen a ghost."

14

"I'm not sure I want you to see the painting in my office," Cole told Bree as he unlocked the front door of his Turtle Bay shop, which had *Streamin'* and a yacht he'd been working on moored right out the back door. "I know the old pickup line is come have a look at my etchings, but this one may give you a jolt."

They had just returned from a Sunday brunch at Amelia and Ben's house where Cole had fallen in love with their two sons—in a much different way from what he was feeling about Bree. So fierce was his desire to protect her that he'd talked Manny into not telling her that Bess had insisted Daria had been meeting more than one man. There had to be a good explanation for that, and he wanted to break it to her gently. Maybe he'd find the right time once they were out sailing this afternoon.

It was a windy but hot, sunny day again, and he was going to take her out to leave a memorial wreath over the Trade Wreck site, where she'd last seen Daria. He knew she needed any kind of shoring up she could get. Not only was she grieving for the mysterious loss of her beloved sister, but Bree was deeply shaken by her discoveries that she hadn't known Daria as well as she'd thought.

"A painting?" she said. "What about it? Naked women or something? We thought about getting one of mermaids for our front office, but all the ones we found were topless, and we figured it would give the wrong mess—oh, I see what you mean."

She stood silent at first, staring at the large reproduction of the painting as he closed and locked the door behind them.

"I've seen that before—in a book somewhere, I mean," she told him, leaning lightly back against him as he put his hands on her shoulders. "Such wonderful movement and power."

"It's a great reproduction of my favorite painting of all time, a Winslow Homer done right around the turn of the nineteenth century. It's called *The Gulf Stream,* so I named the sloop and my business, Gulf Stream Yacht Interiors, for it. It's kind of my inspiration for my philosophy of life, especially in tough times."

His pulse picked up. Maybe he could break the bad news to Bree right here, but before he could say more, she interrupted. "Those are bull sharks swimming along with the sloop, right?"

"Right. But what I really love about it—the only reason I brought you through this way, when the sloop's out back—"

"Is because this is a sloop very similar to yours. And, like the day you rescued me, it protects the sailor from those sharks."

"True, but I always liked the way the sailor looks calm. The mast is broken, but the sloop's not sinking or even taking on water. Despite the looming storm and the danger in the water, he knows he'll get through it all."

Standing in his loose embrace, she turned to face him. He wanted to pull her to him, but he said, "There's one other thing I need to tell you about what Manny and I learned at the bar yesterday. Bess swears that Daria met at least two different men out in back there. It was dark, and she couldn't give a good description, but saw enough to know it was two men."

"What? But then—then there were two beers the bartender knew to give me. One shandy, two Mountain Brewed."

She didn't get the implications of what he was saying, Cole thought, and perhaps that was just as well, but he added, "Not two men at the same time—different times."

"Maybe she met a couple of guys from her class afterward," she went on. "I'd hate to go back to the school and make some general, public plea for information. Besides, why would both guys be so secret or taboo that she met them out in the dark in the boondocks?" He could tell she was on a roll now, probably to keep from admitting Daria could have had an entire secret life built on lies. "Or, you know," Bree plunged on, "Viv Holliman's hair is really short. Maybe the Hollimans are the ones who met Daria there—to discuss business…at different times…but…"

Her voice trailed off. He saw her shudder. She must know she wasn't making sense.

"You think I'm clutching at straws," she said. "If—if," she stammered, "she was meeting more than one man and they found out and were insanely jealous or something like that, wouldn't they have gone after each other?

You're thinking one of them might have wanted her to pay for two-timing him, then things got out of hand?"

He pulled her to him. Despite the fact she held the wreath she'd made, she put her free arm around him.

"I don't know what I'm thinking," he admitted. "So far we're still fact-finding and don't have enough to form a theory to act on. We've got a damn multiple-choice quiz going."

"I don't know if I can get through the funeral tomorrow," she admitted, her lips pressed to his shoulder, "especially with this new, dreadful possibility. I mean, if there was some sort of attack on Daria like there was on me…we'd have to convince the police of that. Cole, maybe she accidentally fell and hit her head during an argument with someone, but then, when he left the boat alone to drift and crash, it became sort of—of indirect homicide."

"Manslaughter."

"That's it. If any of that could be true, that it wasn't an accident, I've got to know, to get justice for her. And what if her attacker's at the funeral? I've heard that killers sometimes are drawn there or to the burial place of their victim. Who hurt her? Who hurt her and why?"

He cupped her face in his hands and wiped tears from her cheeks with his thumbs. "First of all, let's concentrate on getting through the funeral, and then we'll do what we can to find enough evidence to get the cops to open the case. Keep Daria's room sealed, and we'll try to get someone in there to take fingerprints, though if someone is truly clever and desperate, don't get your hopes up. Hey, the good news is that, when I agreed to do the job for Dom Verdugo, I talked him into moving his casino yacht from Miami to the marina here. That way I can stay around to help you. I suggested to him it would be good PR if he had the boat here for people to see. I think he's even planning a party cruise on it soon for influential people—without the gambling, of course."

"I know you want to keep the gambling from coming in here."

"I do, but I think he's also a good candidate if there was foul play in Daria's death, and I've spoken with more than one of his employees who could fit the description of your attacker."

"I'd put Sam's diver, Ric, on the list, too, even if he did make that dangerous dive to find Daria with us. All right, let's go, Captain. Bon voyage, ship ahoy and all that," she said, cradling the flower wreath to her. "Oh, I left the pelican float to keep the wreath in place in your car."

"I'll get it. Go on out in back and choose a piece of wood you like so we can float that better."

He kissed her quickly and headed back to his car. When he glanced through the front office window, he saw her still staring up at the picture of the sloop sailing toward the storm with the sharks chasing it.

"Why hasn't seeing more of Bree cheered you up?" Ben asked Amelia as they sat by the side of their screened veranda pool, watching the boys race little wooden sailboats in the shallow end. "I don't mean that the loss of Daria is something you'll get over quickly, or ever, for that matter, but you've been spiraling down. Even Bree seems on a more even keel than you, and she's lost more than—"

"How dare you say that!" She shoved the book she'd

been reading about the grieving process onto her chaise longue. Ben had been going over a stack of affidavits.

"I just meant Bree was her twin, lived with her... Honey, I'm going to call the doctor and have him prescribe something to get you through the funeral tomorrow."

"No," she said, reaching over to grab his wrist and trying to keep her voice down. "I won't be drugged so I say something I shouldn't."

"Like what?"

"I just mean your friends will be there, and a lot of important people, I'll bet. The Austins, maybe even Marla Sherborne. It's going to be a media event, and I won't have everyone staring at me because I look comatose."

Ben shifted his work aside and swung his legs down between their lounge chairs. He bent over his knees to lean closer as Jordan shouted from the pool, "Dad, my boat won that race. James says it didn't, but I did!"

"You two get along now or you're getting out of there!" Ben told them. "I'm trying to talk to your mother."

"Trying to," Amelia noted. "Meaning, you're not being very successful at it."

"Let's not argue. I know you're under stress and I underst—"

"You don't. Not really. Ben, you're a lawyer and my husband. I have something to tell you, part of the reason I'm feeling so awful about Daria."

Instantly, his expression changed. His concerned gaze seemed more guarded, she thought. His shoulders tensed. But she had to tell someone some of it or she was going to go right out of her mind and be a raving harridan by tomorrow.

"I saw Daria the day she died," she blurted.

"And didn't say so? Why?"

"Please don't read too much into that. You know her birth caused my mother's death...."

"Yes, but there was hardly any intent on her part."

"Would you just listen?" she said through gritted teeth. She wanted to scream at him, but the boys would hear. "I know you're used to firing questions at people, but just listen." He nodded, curious now, but he looked like he was holding his breath.

"I made a date to have a late breakfast with her at the Grog Shop at the far end of Turtle Bay Marina that morning. I asked her not to tell or bring Bree. I guess I just thought I'd try to divide and conquer them, or something like that. Anyway, when we met outside on the dock, I told her I was tired of being shut out. That Dad had always shut me out, maybe because I looked so much like Mother, as if he couldn't bear to see a reminder of her."

"Go on," he prompted when she just gripped her hands tightly together.

"And she said, if anyone was the reminder of Mother's loss it was her and Briana, and they'd gotten along with Dad just fine."

"That's all?" Ben prompted when she said no more.

"I—I don't know what got into me, but I told her she was selfish—that I hated her. Then she got right in my face and said, 'Amelia, you've got to get over your crazy ideas Dad didn't love you and grow up.' Crazy ideas, she said. Then I—I shoved her and she shoved me back so hard I bounced into a mooring post and could have gone right into the water. I could have been crushed by one of those big boats tied there, for all she cared. And don't tell me I started it first, like I'm some kid. She—both of the twins are the ones who started all my problems, first losing my mother and then, in a different way, my dad!"

He stared at her a moment. She could see his wheels turning, assessing her story, probably looking for flaws, discerning motives. "There's no more?" he asked. "That's the last time you saw her, so you're feeling guilty about the way you parted?"

She nodded, kept nodding. Her entire body was shaking.

"I wouldn't tell anyone else about that unless it comes up somehow," he said. "You obviously didn't go in for breakfast together after that, so no one saw you eating with her. Amelia, you have got to find the strength to bury these deep-seated feelings. And don't argue with me when I make an appointment for you with a therapist I know. There's nothing else, is there?"

She realized she was still nodding. "No," she said, and shook her head side to side. There was more to tell, but she was hoping that bleeding out this much of the festering poison would help her get through tomorrow. How ridiculous were those courtroom dramas or funeral scenes, where the guilty party shouted out what they'd done in front of everyone.

"Dad, Mom! He's looking at me really funny, and he's splashing me!" Jordan shouted. "Make him quit it! It's his fault."

"That's it!" Ben told them. "I'm coming in to play policeman and the first one of you who messes up is going to his room!"

He leaped up and cannonballed into the deep end to the squealing delight of their sons. Amelia stared at the

big splash he'd made as her son's words—"It's his fault...
fault...fault..."—echoed in her head.

"I picked this piece of dark wood since black's the
color of mourning," Bree told Cole as he came into his
back workroom with the pelican float from his car. She
loved the rich smell of this well-lit workroom, piled high
with various exotic woods in long trays. His workbench
looked out over the far end of the marina next to the
Grog Shop Restaurant. Cole had told her he ate a lot of
his meals there, when he didn't get takeout or delivery.
A man who was dedicated to his work, she thought, just
as she had been.

"African wenge wood," he said of the stark piece.
"That's a good choice. It's very hard wood with not much
grain." He took a minute to attach the peach and yellow hibiscus and blue plumbago blossoms to it so they
wouldn't break up, then they headed out the back toward the *Streamin'*.

At least it was a cloudy day. Sometimes she thought
her hearing was not as acute as it had been at first after
the lightning strike, but she was still overly sensitive
to light. Perhaps that helped her to see better in low-
vis water—Briana Devon, the X-ray-eyed underwater
superwoman. Maybe that was why she had spotted the
broken piece of *Mermaids II* and then the wheelhouse
with Daria inside, when the other divers didn't see things
as clearly.

The *Streamin'* headed out into the bay at a good clip,
as if she yearned for a race. Bree didn't doubt that Cole
could make this sloop move, even if it was dead calm.
Bree and Cole had life preservers nearby, but she didn't
feel she needed one with him at the helm. Still, she

warned herself, as the sails bellied out and they moved from the bay into the gulf, after all she'd learned about Daria since her death, she should know better than to totally trust anyone now. Love might never change but the trust at its foundation could.

The wind tugged at her hair and shirt; they were almost flying. She loved to escape the land and ride the waves, but she could hardly escape her grief at sea. In a way, her sister was and always would be a part of the deep and its mysteries. This great water had given Daria joy and purpose, but it had taken her life—or so the authorities said. She might have drowned, Bree thought, but she was becoming more and more certain that the sea was not the real killer.

She wondered if she should have let Daria's remains be buried at sea. She could have agreed with the Hollimans' Eternal Shells offer, but she couldn't trust them. Too much the shysters, but then, she wasn't certain who wasn't. Someone, maybe someone close to Daria, and to Bree, too, could have caused her death.

"You said you can find the spot by heart now," Cole called to her.

By heart, she thought. Yes, she'd always be able to find the spot she last saw Daria alive by heart, a broken heart.

"It's right about here," she told him. "Just a sec, and I'll eyeball the land coordinates."

She looked back toward shore and picked out the Naples pier and Gordon Pass to the south, then triangulated those by the reddish roof of the Ritz Carlton Hotel to the north.

"Yes, this spot is good," she told him, "but go a little farther south before you anchor so you don't catch the turtle grass meadow. Which reminds me, I'll have to get someone to come out here to check it with me Tuesday morning before my report to the commission that afternoon."

"You think you can handle the dive and the report alone—without Daria, I mean?"

"Yes, I can," she said, her voice strong. "I have to see that all through. Maybe it will flush someone out."

"Not with you as the bait! And I won't let you dive alone. I'll go down with you, if you promise to stay out of the wreck."

She nodded, but he wasn't looking as he furled and tied the sails and dropped anchor. As she readied the wreath, he came to help her. How sore she felt from the beating she'd taken yesterday. She was turning black-and-blue—even greenish-gold—in places she couldn't show Cole.

She appreciated how he let her guide the placement of the wreath, just lifted it to keep its weight off her hands as she balanced everything on the side of the sloop. When the boat listed a bit toward their weight, he leaned farther aport, leaving her to bend over the side of the sloop alone.

For one moment, Bree wasn't sure she could bear to let it go. How would she ever get through the funeral if she couldn't even let go of a wreath she'd made?

She gently placed it on the water, threw the pelican float's sixty-foot tether line in, then dropped the round metal anchor she had tied to the piece of wood. The float bobbed to the surface, its red Day-Glo rings bright and bold. The wreath looked lovely on the wood. It started away, then bobbed almost in place as it rode the waves.

She was grateful that Cole gave her this moment

alone, yet she longed to cling to him. Staring down into the gray-green depths, she mouthed the silent words, *I love you, my Daria. I'll always love you, but what did you do? What did you get mixed up in?*

She remembered again that she hadn't heard a motor in the water that day. How had someone approached *Mermaids II?* Maybe in a sailboat?

At that thought, she jumped when Cole came close again. They sat on the floor of the sloop with his back against the stern seat. He'd been sailing that day of Daria's death, she thought. Others could have been, as well. That could be why she hadn't heard a motor.

When he pulled her into his arms, she leaned against him, grateful for his concern and strength. "Did you see any other sailboats out last Tuesday?" she asked. "Since the weather guys were really off that day, others—especially people with big sailboats—might have gone out."

"I saw a few, at least early. But they seemed pretty distant."

"From you or from this position?"

"I get where you're going, but I'm not sure how we'd check into that. Area marinas seldom keep track of when vessels permanently moored at their facilities put out, and a lot of sailboats, just like power boats, are in private berths up and down all the canals."

"I suppose," she said with a sigh, "I could inquire of the civil air patrol, but they already put in so many hours. When Dave Mangold, my pilot friend from the patrol, gets back in town, I can have him ask around if any planes were flying the day of the storm and saw any watercraft of any kind. It all just seems like such a long shot. Cole, she must have known whoever approached her. I'll bet whatever boat came up to her, she recognized someone and let them board our boat or get too close to her. It's creepy to think of her out here in this exact spot, while someone crept up or tricked her somehow..."

"Don't think about it now. You're here to honor her memory today. You need to relax before tomorrow."

She nodded fiercely and turned so she had her back against the inside of his knee for support. He had one arm around her waist; her bent legs were draped over his other one. It eased her lower back pain to lean into him, and it eased her heart just to touch him.

"Cole, my voice of reason," she said, putting her head on his shoulder. She knew she was setting herself up to be kissed: she hoped so, the cut on the inside of her mouth and sore muscles notwithstanding.

"I don't ever feel very reasonable about you," was all he said before he bent to cover her mouth with his.

It was their first real kiss of mutual, meshing needs and desires. He'd comforted her before; he'd protected her. Now she wanted more.

The boat moved under them in a rhythmic cadence, and they seemed to roll with it, first one way, then the other, their weight toward her, then him. He slanted his mouth over hers and his hard hands pulled her closer. As she wrapped her arms around his neck, his free hand skimmed over her, shoulder, arms, waist, hips, thighs, back up to cup her breast. She arched under him, breathing with him. His merest touch seemed to heal all her body's aches and pains, if not those of her heart.

The *Streamin'* yanked against its anchor and dipped its masts. The lines creaked and the waves rustled incredibly loudly.

A ship sneaking up on us? Bree thought. As she jerked

bolt upright, her head bumped his chin. She twisted away from him to look all around.

"What?"

"I just—sorry. I thought I heard something, that there was another boat. Sorry."

"Yeah, me, too. I wasn't sure if that was the boat rocking or the entire world. I'd better bring her around."

Bree steadied herself as he scrambled for the tiller. She saw that the wreath took the push of the waves but stayed firmly in place. That's what she would do, too, she vowed. Cole brought up the anchor and unfurled the mainsail. "Watch out, or you'll see where we get the saying, Lower the boom."

She ducked and he brought the ship about and headed them back in. He'd handled both the sailboat and her skittish behavior smoothly. Amazing that she'd only been with this man off and on for five days, and yet felt she knew him. The same mistake she'd evidently made with Daria.

15

It was a blessing that the day of the funeral was cloudy with a sea breeze, or it would have made the temperature in the little church where Daria's family stood in a receiving line unbearable. So many attended that the line came up the center aisle and snaked around the side, leading past the closed casket.

"This funeral brings back memories of someone lost too young," Sam Travers told Bree.

She instantly felt on alert. Ric and Lance were with him. Bree stared hard at Ric, trying to see if he avoided her gaze. He didn't, but his left cheek had a cut on the same side where she'd hit her attacker with the bottle. Of course, it could be from anything, and salvage diving was too often a contact sport.

"Yes," Bree said to Sam, deciding not to give in to his subtle badgering. "Very happy memories of my life with Daria, which I will always cherish. I wouldn't want to let bitterness consume me. And I do thank you for all your help in the search for her."

"Oh, so nice of you to come…" she said to the next people in line as she turned away before Sam could fire another salvo. As if she had sent Cole a mental SOS, he suddenly appeared, shouldering Sam slightly aside and offering her a glass of water.

"Thanks for being so thoughtful," she told Cole as Sam glowered and moved on.

"I heard," Cole said, speaking quietly and quickly, "that Sam's firm has taken a job in Sarasota to help demolish the supports of an old bridge, so he'll be out of town for the next few weeks."

"Good! Sam would go anywhere in the state for a demolitions job. Ted used to talk about how his dad was a Vietnam War hero, setting charges to destroy bridges and underwater barriers to troop movements. His specialty has always been combat or commercial explosives. That's probably made it much harder for him to accept that Ted's death was from a bomb. I wish he could let it go, but I am starting to understand his pain."

Cole took her water glass and moved away again. He seemed to be everywhere in the room, yet kept an eye on her. Anytime she looked his way, he was watching, even when he had her two nephews practically hanging on to him in their mutual admiration society, which they had formed swiftly. That had deeply touched her. Cole was good with kids. Everything about him seemed so good.

"Mayor Dixon," she said, greeting the next person in line, "thank you so much for coming. Daria would have been honored…"

During their wait to speak with the family, visitors viewed photos Bree had selected of high points in Daria's life. It was hard to find ones that she herself wasn't in, too. She made sure most of the early pictures had Amelia in them.

"Josh and Nikki, you've been a great support through all of this," she greeted the Austins as they exchanged hugs.

"It's the least we could do for an old friend of Josh's," Nikki said. "And for you, too, Briana. Oh, I'd like you to meet my father, Cory Grann from Clewiston. And I believe you've met his friend, Marla Sherborne."

Politics might make strange bedfellows, Bree thought, but this was quite a crew. Cory Grann was extremely handsome. He would have made a good Marlboro man, and he would have fit in a Clint Eastwood gritty Western. Yet he was dressed like the captain of a yacht with white slacks, a natty navy blazer and an ascot, no less. More than anyone else here, he seemed to be cool and collected as he gave his condolences. This, she thought, was the so-called sugar baron ecologists loved to blame for pollution runoff.

"Oh," Nikki said, gesturing toward a thirtysomething man who brought up the rear of their group, "and this is Mark Denton, our campaign aide and pilot."

Bree shook his hand. His shake was so firm she fought to keep from wincing. She was still sore and had covered several bruises with makeup today. She noted that Nikki left out that Denton was also a bodyguard, but then others were leaning in, trying to hear what the celebrities of the gathering were saying.

"Sorry for your loss," he told her. His lips barely moved when he spoke, as if he was the master of the stiff upper lip. If he was skilled at PR, it was probably all in written releases and sound bites.

Surprised that Josh hadn't spoken, Bree turned to him. It wasn't like him to be so quiet. He looked ashen. Either he was ill or he was grieving for all he and Daria had once shared. Tears in his eyes, he clasped her hand until Nikki put her arm in his and he abruptly let go.

"We're staying for the funeral," Nikki told Bree. "And we'd love to have you visit us someday, especially if you want a change of scenery for a while. At our retreat near Clewiston, I mean—in Tallahassee we do nothing but run around in circles, both in different directions. But we have a house on my father's grounds near Clewiston and Lake Okeechobee. Nothing but boring sugarcane for miles, but it's amazingly relaxing. We could even send Mark to fly you over."

"It is just lovely there," Marla put in.

"That's very kind," Bree told them, deeply touched.

"Sure, no problem, picking you up," Mark Denton said as if to fill an awkward moment when Josh still didn't speak. "My employers' wish is my command." Marla and Cory Grann were already talking to Ben and Amelia, and the line moved on.

Friends and friends of friends went by in a blur. Bree had a chance to ask Daria's accounting instructor if any of the students went out together after class, but he said he didn't think so. She asked the same of Viv and Frank Holliman.

"We suggested it once—twice, didn't we, Viv?" he said.

"But Daria always had to get home and left very promptly, though we did spend time chatting with her before class, when she was there."

"I saw her copy of your brochure," Bree told them, still embarrassed she hadn't believed them at first. "Eternal Shells looks like a fascinating opportunity, but I really needed to pass on it for my sister."

"After all, our earthly shells are delicate and we need

to think in terms of eternal ones," Frank said, quoting exactly a line from their brochure. "Well, keep it in mind for yourself—someday."

Bree could not shake her instinctively uneasy feeling around them. Despite what they had said about never meeting Daria after class, Frank was built a lot like her attacker—and perhaps like the man Daria had met out in the Glades. He could have worn a wig to help disguise himself, and he could have cheated on Viv. But surely Daria couldn't have been attracted to him—at least, the Daria Bree thought she knew.

After greeting guests, who must have numbered at least two hundred, and making sure that the reporters at the front of the church were kept at a distance, the family led everyone outside in back for the funeral itself.

It was standing room only, after the family and closest friends filled the chairs that church volunteers had set up. The view of the gray-green bay and gulf beyond the coffin, then the pewter-hued horizon, was magnificent. Bree had left the photos inside, for they would just blow away, but she'd placed some of Daria's favorite seashells and her diving mask on the casket next to the family's spray of white roses, with the ribbon which read *Beloved Sister and Aunt.*

James and Jordan were on Ben's far side, swinging their little legs and shifting in their wooden seats. Briana was on the center aisle at Amelia's right side, with Ben on Amelia's left. Bree thought that Pastor Wallace said all the right things, comforting things, uplifting things. But she still felt so lonely and low.

"I'll read now from Psalm 107," the pastor said as his simple black-and-white robe fluttered in the breeze.

"Those who go down to the sea in ships,
Who do business on great waters,
They see the works of the Lord,
And his wonders in the deep..."

He went on reading about those at the mercy of the sea, who cry out in their troubles. He said everyone was grateful that they had not lost Briana that dreadful day, too. *Was* everyone grateful for that? she wondered.

The pastor segued into a message on Daria's too-short life, on the gifts she took from the sea and the gifts she gave the sea, including a mention of the report that would be made public tomorrow. "Daria's sea grass project endeavored to protect God's great and precious sea, just as God now protects her soul forever. Daria—with her twin sister at her side—loved God's creation, both above these waters we see even now and far below their surface."

When Amelia kept fidgeting more than her sons, Bree realized she should have asked the pastor not to overplay their twinship, but then, he knew little about the third sister. So many people had remarked about how much Bree looked like Daria, how it was as if she still moved among them, and Amelia had looked more shaken each time she overheard that.

The funeral director had asked Bree and Amelia if they would like to view the body before closing the casket, but they'd both declined. Bree wanted to shut out the horrid picture of how Daria had looked when they'd found her body, and Amelia just repeated, "I can't. I'm so sorry, so sorry..."

Bree tried to concentrate on the service, but she kept wondering whether her attacker—and maybe Daria's

murderer—was here. Fred Holliman was the perfect
height, but would a wig have stuck to his head after a
fall in a ditch when his baseball cap came off? And that
bruise on Ric's cheek. She had no doubt Sam Travers
would give everything he had to see Bree suffer as he
had since Ted died. No, she was going crazy, carrying
everything too far. Where was the line between self-
protection and paranoia?

Over Amelia's protest, Bree had insisted the Salazars
sit just behind their family. Manny was deeply grieved
today, and his wife, Juanita, kept crossing herself. Lucinda sat next to her older sister, Carianne. Their family was all in black and wearing large crucifixes, even
Lucinda.

The members of the Clear the Gulf Commission
were here and sitting together, except for Cole, who kept
prowling the perimeter of the church and now was standing off to the side as if he'd been hired to keep order.

The congregation sang "Eternal Father Strong To
Save," which Bree knew as the Navy Hymn, with its
resonant, haunting chorus of "O, hear us when we cry
to thee/ For those in peril on the sea."

Oh, yes, she could cry right now. Amelia was sobbing silently, her shoulders shaking despite the fact Ben
had a firm grip of her left wrist. Bree clasped her other
hand. Crying would do no good. It was finding out who
had possibly hurt Daria and making that person pay
that would bring some closure. Bree would find a way
to forgive, but only after truth and justice had its way.

She stared at Daria's favorite diving mask on top of
the casket. The diffused sun glinted strangely off the
plastic as if two bright, unearthly eyes stared out from
behind it. Someone here was wearing a mask. Someone

here might be pretending to be grieving and be staring at her even now. Had Daria's murderer meant to kill her, or was it an accident and he or she had simply fled before the boat was taken by the storm and bashed on the seawall? Had that same killer come after Bree? And the most terrifying thought of all: could the murderer have meant to kill Bree but mistook Daria for her twin?

The benediction was from a Bible verse Bree and Daria had always liked because it seemed to them it asked for the Lord's blessing on daily work. Starting out their business, they'd needed all the help they could get.

"So teach us to number our days
That we might have a heart of wisdom...
And let the beauty of the Lord our God be upon us,
And establish the work of our hands for us;
Yes, establish the work of our hands."

After a final prayer, Pastor Wallace announced that everyone was invited to stay for a luncheon served by the women of the church here on the lawn, after which there would be a private burial for family only. Everyone stood while the pallbearers carried the casket to the hearse for now.

Bree took Amelia's arm and walked her inside, with Ben on her other side and both boys keeping close. Amelia was trembling so hard that Bree's heart went out to her. She had denied coming into their apartment and searching Daria's room for mementos. Bree believed her, but even that inquiry must have shaken Amelia. Her older sister must also be mourning the times she had never had with Daria, and the lack of precious memories to cherish.

"I just can't face everyone right now," Amelia said, pulling away. "I'm going to ask the pastor if there's someplace I can lie down."

"I'd go sit with you," Bree said, "but someone besides Ben has to mingle."

"Yes, of course. Besides, everyone's feeling sorry for you, not me."

"Amelia, I—"

"It's all right, Bree," Ben said. "You boys stay with Aunt Bree until I get your mother settled down."

"Not much wailing and no kneeling, not like when Grandpa died," Lucinda told her family in English as they ate sandwiches and salads on the lawn between the church and the bay. "Feels funny not to have a mass, too."

"It is their way, and it's okay," Manny told her.

"Glad you can accept different ways of thinking and doing things," Lucinda muttered.

"Don't start!" he said, shaking a finger in her face.

"Don't either of you start," Juanita said. "She set you up for that one, *si?* Let's just get along today, all right? This the United States of America, and thanks to Bree, we accepted here right with the money and power people."

Manny just glared at Lucinda as he finished his lemonade. "Maybe when word gets out I'm Bree Devon's partner, people 'round here won't like that," he said, wiping his mouth with the back of his hand. "When I went with Cole to that place I told you 'bout, if looks could kill, I be dead. And that backwoods bar not even up to Turtle Bay."

"Shh!" Juanita scolded. "It bad luck at a funeral talk

about your own death. It mean, if you not die within the next year, the next of kin of this one buried today be dead."

Manny rolled his eyes. "Sometimes, *mi* Juanita, I see why our Lucinda want to run from our ways. Next you be telling me just 'cause this a sad day, our *quinceañera* for her be cursed. Let's say *adios* to my partner Briana and head home, *si?*"

When they made their farewells, he was surprised that Bree and Lucinda hugged each other. And annoyed when he heard Bree say quietly to her, "Remember what I said, Cindi."

The ceremony at the grave site was blessedly brief, because Amelia was still a wreck and that was destroying Bree's hard-won poise, too. They all walked to their cars. Ben put Amelia in theirs—the boys had gone home with a friend—when Bree said, "I'm staying until they close the grave."

Ben turned to face her. "It will depress you even more. You don't have to do that."

"I know. But I came into the world with her, and I want to see her settled and at peace, as they say."

He took her arm and walked her away from his car. In the distance they could see the funeral director talking to the cemetery crew with their waiting backhoe.

"Bree," Ben said, obviously fighting to keep his patience, "she's at peace. Now you have to work on that, too, not keep causing waves."

"That's a good one," she said. "Not causing waves."

"You know what I mean. I can tell you're not really letting the dead be dead. I'm not the county prosecutor for nothing, and I can read between the lines about what you've been thinking all of a sudden. If you pursue a half-cocked murder scenario, you're only going to get yourself upset or worse, hurt."

She pulled away from his hand on her arm and turned to face him squarely. She was tempted to tell him she'd been attacked, but she didn't want him insisting she stay home or with Amelia. And what he'd just said almost sounded like a threat. "Hurt, meaning?" she asked.

"To use another cliché, you're going to stir up a hornet's nest if you go around suspecting people of some sort of wrongdoing, accusing them—"

"I *will* accuse them if I find out someone staged that so-called accident. I thought a county prosecutor might call a possible murder a little more than 'some sort of wrongdoing.'"

"Amelia said you think someone broke in and searched Daria's room. If I get a CSI tech to come out there and take prints, will you lay off?"

"I'd appreciate that. I was going to try to get the police to do that."

"I said, will you lay off then?"

"No. Someone clever enough to pop the lock on my veranda doors and desperate enough to climb up onto the second story to do that needs to be stopped. But if CSI does turn up a set of prints other than mine or Daria's, will you pursue it?"

"Of course I will. Look, I'll see if I can call in a favor and send someone over tonight. We wanted to have you come back to the house, but Amelia needs to take a tranquilizer and go to bed. She's never gotten over what she considered desertion by her mother, then her father."

"That's not the way it was."

"But if she thinks it's true, it's reality to her, and I

can't risk her losing you on top of Daria. There's my bottom line."

So he wasn't actually threatening her. He was just worried about Amelia, and that was completely understandable.

"And another thing," he said, in what seemed a lame attempt to change the subject so she wouldn't argue about Amelia and their father, "is Cole DeRoca."

"What about him? He only saved my life and has been more help to me than anyone. Please don't tell Amelia that, but it's true. Jordan and James like him and—"

"I like him, too, but think about it. He's overly possessive and protective of you, and you've only known him a week. I'm advising, in the emotional state you're in, not to get either psychologically or physically involved with him."

That advice reminded her of what she'd just told Lucinda, but this was different. She was not some adolescent girl in rebellion against her parents.

"Actually," she told Ben, "I had met Cole once before. I even had lunch with him, but he was going through a divorce and nothing came of it right then."

"See, then he might be emotionally vulnerable right now. You know—the rebound effect."

"Thank you, Dr. Phil."

"I admit it's a blessing that he found you on the beach and saved your life. But he's too convenient. He's always in the right place at the right time. His office and workshop are right next to the Grog Shop at the end of town, right?"

"Yes. And?"

"Are you positive he didn't know Daria, if he'd bumped into you before?"

"What are you implying? He knew of Daria, because he's on the Clear the Gulf Commission. But we were given our assignment to observe and photograph the sea grass meadow without actually appearing before the commission. My report tomorrow will be the first time I've been there live, so to speak. Ben, you're wrong about Cole. If I can't trust him, I can't trust anyone."

But those last words tasted bitter in her mouth. If she hadn't known her own twin sister, her lifelong best friend, could she really trust a man she'd known only a week?

16

True to his word, Ben sent a CSI tech to Bree's place that night. Foolishly, she had been expecting someone like she'd seen on the various TV shows featuring forensic scientists, but it was a young, plain, overweight woman. Her ID card hanging on a bright blue cord around her neck read Marilyn Davis but she asked Bree to call her Mari.

"You'll see this makes a bit of a mess," Mari said as Bree led her toward Daria's bedroom, "but I want to lift a lot of prints, then eliminate yours. If you have something you're sure your sister touched—a glass in the bathroom you haven't cleaned yet, something like that, I'll eliminate hers, too. Oh, this place has really been tossed, hasn't it?"

"I'm afraid so. I had searched it earlier but someone else did, too, and those are the prints we hope to identify."

"Did you report the B and E—breaking and entering?" she asked as she tugged on latex gloves and got to work, leaving small pools of dark powder here and there.

"No, because several people had keys. Evidently nothing of value has been taken that I could report."

"Okeydoke," she said, her voice darkening with disapproval. Bree almost told her that Ben hadn't suggested reporting it either, but it was none of her business.

"You know," Mari said, perhaps eager to change the subject, "I've never dusted a place where identical twins were involved. A lot of people figure they have identical prints, but that's not so."

"We've been asked that more than once over the years," Bree told her as she leaned in the entry to the bathroom and watched her work. "The prints are supposed to have similarities, though."

"True. Identicals have the same genetic makeup and their DNA is virtually indistinguishable, but fingerprints are not completely a genetic characteristic. They're partly determined by each separate embryo's environment in the uterus. Their ultimate shape can be influenced by position in the womb and a few other things I can't recall from my forensic classes."

Bree went into the bathroom to get Daria's drinking glass and gingerly took Daria's mascara and powder from her makeup drawer. She could see visible prints on both plastic cases. Many more cosmetics were here than Bree had recalled her using, including seven tubes of lipstick, when she almost never wore that. But she was getting used to being surprised about her sister. There had been a man in her life she had not wanted to tell Bree about. She only hoped that she hadn't done something that kept Daria from confiding in her. Surely, it was something about the man himself that made Daria remain silent, and she needed to find out what that was.

She rifled through the rest of the cosmetics drawer

but found nothing. Perhaps she'd find nothing, prove nothing. She was becoming more and more certain that someone had harmed—killed—Daria, and that now, somehow, she'd become a target, too. Her stomach fluttered in fear, but she beat the feeling down as she put the items in a towel and took them to Mari.

She stared at the thin white gloves encasing Mari's busy hands. Maybe the person who'd searched this room had worn gloves, too.

"I appreciate your taking care of this so quickly," Bree said, leaning in the doorway again. She couldn't stand the silence in the room as Mari moved about like a ghost.

"Orders from the top."

"My brother-in-law, Ben Westcott?"

"Him and some other big brass."

"Josh Austin?"

Bending intently over a brass pull of the dresser, she shrugged her shoulders, but admitted, "The whole CSI unit is amazed at how fast the autopsy report was completed and released. At least, most of it."

"What do you mean, most of it?"

Mari straightened. Her eyes widened, as if she realized she'd overstepped, however much Bree knew about Ben and Josh pulling strings.

"Probable cause of death was the key thing, that's all."

"But what else wasn't released yet?"

"Forensics differs with different situations. I'm sure you'll see everything in black and white soon."

She'd obviously clammed up. Was there something else about Daria's death? Surely she had not been beaten or assaulted, because no one could pass that off as an accident. What else could an autopsy reveal? Could she have been hiding some sort of serious, even terminal, illness? Maybe if word of that got out it might look like she'd committed suicide and neither Ben nor Josh would want that. No, impossible. People with fatal diseases didn't make appointments to get their teeth whitened. It all came back to the fact that Daria would never have left Bree alone out in the gulf. *But,* a little voice taunted her, *the woman who died that day was not the woman you thought you knew.*

As soon as Mari finished and left with her collection of prints, Bree locked the place up tight and drove to Ben and Amelia's. Good. Lights were still on in their spacious home. She hoped Ben hadn't gone to bed, because she planned to question him about the rest of the autopsy report.

She knocked instead of ringing the bell. The porch light clicked on, then off, and Ben opened the door. She gasped when she saw he held not only the evening paper but a pistol at his side.

"Don't mind this," he said, putting it down on the table in the hall. "When I answer the door late at night, it's just a precaution. In my position—"

"In your position," she interrupted, following him into the den, "you tend to play God."

"What? Did the CSI person come? What are you talking ab—"

"Don't blame her, but she let something slip about the rest of the autopsy report—you know, the rest of the story."

Leaning over the back of his tall, leather chair, he frowned. Hands on her hips, Bree faced him.

"What about it?" he asked. "You and Amelia didn't need to see all those chemical readouts of blood, bladder and stomach tests, ad infinitum, or diagrams of dissections. She wasn't on drugs, she wasn't drunk, she wasn't ill, so—"

"I want to see it, all of it."

"A lot of that stuff takes days. I thought it best if the family got her body back and had her laid to rest. The county medical examiner could have held her body for up to ten days when it needed to be embalmed, not just refrigerated, especially in this hot weather. There. You wanted the facts, you've got them. It was hard enough as is and didn't need to be dragged out."

"I'd like to drag the truth out of you!"

"Now look," he said, pointing at her and raising his voice before he lowered it again. "My goal in all this— to protect Amelia first, and then you."

"Amelia, fine, but you have no right to make decisions for me or for Daria. And, of course, none of this has a thing to do with protecting your reputation, especially with the election less than two months away."

"That didn't even enter my mind."

"Let's say I partly believe that, but I want to see the autopsy report. Do you have a copy here?"

"No."

"Then I'm going to the Collier County Medical Examiner's office first thing tomorrow, before I dive the Trade Wreck, and demand to see—"

"All right, damn it," he said, and finally came around his chair to slump in it. Bree was horrified to see how ashen and haggard he suddenly looked. It was as if he'd been drained of fight and energy. "You asked for this," he said, "so just sit down and brace yourself. Swear to me you won't spring this on Amelia, because she's really shaken—grieving for all she's lost over the years, as well as for Daria."

Bree perched on the edge of the smaller leather chair facing his. As she gripped her hands together in her lap, every nerve in her body tensed.

"The autopsy revealed Daria was about seven weeks' pregnant."

A great silence crashed into the room. Bree could hear her heartbeat, feel her blood rushing through her veins. Yet her mind went blank. At first those words seemed to bounce off her, as if they were in a foreign language. She didn't move, she didn't breathe. Strangely, the first thought she had was that she now knew why Daria had avoided diving these last few weeks—why she'd lied that she had a bad toothache the day of the storm. It wasn't wise for pregnant women to scuba, since too much water pressure could harm a fetus. Daria had known she was pregnant and had wanted to protect her baby!

Bree wanted to scream, but she amazed herself by speaking calmly—it seemed to be another person's voice. "Can a DNA test ID the father?"

"A DNA test of the fetus would indicate paternity—if you had the father's to match with it. But I didn't want her body dissected in that way. And having Daria disinterred now that she's buried would be crazy and cruel."

She wanted to argue that he was the one pushing for a quick autopsy and burial, but she said only, "It might lead us to her killer."

"Bree, stop it! It would also make all the papers and stir up scuttlebutt. I—I take it you didn't know."

"Of course I didn't know! Not about a pregnancy and not about who could be the father. Why would I know something like that? I'm only her roommate, twin sister, lifelong friend, the person closest to her in the entire universe—at least, I used to think so."

She was tempted to tell him that she'd been attacked at the Gator Watering Hole, but she was coming not to trust Ben. Even if he'd sent the CSI tech, he hadn't urged her to report the B and E, and now the report of the prints would go to him before Bree saw it. He had claimed that protecting his own reputation played no part in all this, but he'd just blurted out he was trying to avoid scuttlebutt. He must have realized that the unborn baby—her niece or nephew, who had died with Daria—was a motive for murder, depending on what the murderer had to protect. Ben was the county prosecutor, for heaven's sake! But he was trying to gloss this over, stonewall things. Just to spare Amelia and her, as he had said?

She glared at him, unable to hide her anger. "Ben, you know very well that whoever's child it was, whoever she was meeting secretly, could have killed her."

"In the middle of the gulf in a storm?" he challenged. "You said you didn't hear a motor. Maybe he walked on water or swam out three miles."

"I never thought I'd live to see you obstruct justice," she accused. She rose and started out of the den. Ben jumped up and grabbed her arm, swinging her back around.

"And you're going off the deep end!" he accused, his grip tightening.

"Last time you said I was making waves and now I've gone off the deep end. You've got lots of deep, rough water on the brain. Now let me go! I'm devastated and horrified and furious, yes, at her—and you—and at myself for not knowing. I'm going home to bed to sob my eyes out—again."

She shook loose from him. "Is there anything else I should know?" she demanded.

"Just that even the surprising fact of her pregnancy does not warrant your demand that this become a murder case. I'll let you know about the fingerprints, and I'm monitoring things."

"Oh, I see you are," she said, and strode for the front door. As he caught up and opened it for her, she added, "Will you tell Amelia?"

"Since you've taken it out of my hands, yes."

His pistol lay on the hall table. She had the strangest sense she should take it with her, for her own protection. Just like those sharks, something *was* swimming just below the darkening surface of her life, but she couldn't tell what.

When she finally fell into a fitful sleep that night, Bree sank into the sea. Its black depths reached for her, powerful and violent, and pulled her down, down.

At the bottom of the gulf, the stormy currents swept her into a glass coffin, where she held her breath and tried to fight her way out. She had no scuba tanks, no regulator, no air. Where was her mask?

Water filled the glass coffin. Her hair drifted in her face like her dying turtle grass. It stuck to the skin over her eyes, blinding her like the water in a ditch. She struggled to see.

She raised her hands to get out, to fight against being drowned, against being attacked by a man with a raised wrench. But the wrench was shaped like a concrete shell just outside her glass coffin. People waved from outside. Her parents. Ted. Daria, with a baby floating in her arms.

Someone else appeared on the other side of the

glass. Sam, smiling through his mask, happy to see her trapped. He shouted at her, but her good hearing had gone and her hair half blinded her.

Daria, where are you? Daria…who scuttled the ship? Who drowned you?

Scuttlebutt. Ben was outside, too, shouting that he was trying to protect the family from scuttlebutt. He, too, wore a diving mask that hid his face, but she could see he had his gun. He was not pointing it at her, but at something in the depths, the dark depths of the sea….

Where was Cole? Cole could come to save her.

Though she was trying hard to hold her breath— her last breath—she screamed Cole's name. A man in a black mask wanted her to drown, but someone was shaking her and she shoved her hair away and sucked in a huge breath.

"Bree. Bree! Sweetheart, you're having a nightmare," the deep voice said. "Wake up, it's Cole."

It was real. He was here, smoothing her hair away from her face, which was wet with tears.

Yes, she remembered now. She'd called him after she drove back from Ben's. Cole had come over and insisted on sleeping on her sofa. Last time she'd had a nightmare, Amelia had run to her, but this was Cole. Thank God, it was Cole.

He held her until she stopped trembling. "Want to talk about it?" he whispered.

"No, it's too bizarre. I just want it to go away, to forget it, forget everything."

He wore his shorts but no shirt. His bare chest seemed so broad with its expanse of muscled skin and crisp, curly hair. He felt cool compared to her.

"Running away," he said, "is not how you've been handling any of this. You know that would never work."

"I know. I know. I'm so glad you're here."

"After all this is settled, I'd like us to spend time together of a different kind."

She hugged him. "Yes."

"I'm trying really hard not to take advantage of the fact that you need me now. We hardly know each other under normal circumstances."

She knew he was trying to talk himself out of climbing into bed with her, but she didn't want to make that easy for him. She held him tight. Sure, she was insane, dancing on the edge of the same sort of desire that must have hit Daria so hard she had to hide things. She clung tighter to him.

"Bree, sweetheart, I can hardly breathe."

"That's the way it was in my nightmare. Sorry."

She loosened her grip on him slightly and sat up straighter, though they still leaned against each other. Since Bree had heard Ben say Daria was pregnant, nothing had sunk in. Even in explaining it all to Cole, it had not seemed real. The sister she would have sworn she knew seemed to slip further away than even death could take her.

Now Bree fought to clear her head. First thing tomorrow, she had to check the Trade Wreck sea grass meadow, photograph its sorry state one last time before she found the strength to give her report without Daria by her side. But Cole would be with her during the dive and there at the Clear the Gulf Commission. Why couldn't she clear her head and forget the nightmare that clung to her as hard as she had to Cole?

She shifted slightly away from him and swiped at

her slick cheeks. He handed her a tissue from the box of them on her bedside table. Nodding her thanks, she blew her nose and wiped her eyes, then took a drink from the glass of water he handed her.

"A part of me," she admitted, "does want to run away. Take a cruise, drive down to the Keys and sit on the beach, but anywhere I could see the water would haunt me. Maybe I should take Josh and Nikki up on their invitation to have Mark Denton fly me across the state and stare at nothing but boring sugarcane fields, as Nikki put it."

"Do you mean it?"

"No. I've got to see our sea grass project through, even if it will create a lot of fallout. That turtle grass is in worse shape than I am. For Daria and the future of everything around here, I've got to see it all through. The meadow is dying from toxic pollution—and that means the entire biological chain and this whole paradise are endangered. Sorry. It seems I'm delivering my report already." She tried to smile through her tears. "I'm sorry I woke you up."

"You didn't. Despite the hum of the AC, every sound outside jolts me awake."

"You're too tall for the sofa."

"I'm fine. You think you can sleep?"

"I've got to. I can't go into that meeting looking like a witch."

"Not you, not ever, even now. My mermaid is like those beautiful sirens that lured Odysseus's ship right into them."

"To crash into the rocks, you mean."

He kissed the top of her mussed head and slid off the bed, reluctantly, she could tell. Yes, she needed him, and she was pretty sure she loved him, too. But had Daria thought that and made some sort of colossal mistake with a man she desired? A fatal error?

17

It seemed strange to dive without Daria, yet so comforting to have Cole with her, and Manny at the helm of the boat. The sea was calm, the water unusually clear. The flowers had washed off the memorial wreath she'd left, but Cole's piece of dark wood still floated in place. Perhaps they should retrieve that and the pelican float before they left. It would be no good to have a boat run into it, nor to have the site marked so that someone else could easily find and potentially damage the struggling sea grass meadow.

As she and Cole descended near the anchor line, Bree held the camera tight, as if she could lose it again. They made a standard safety stop, gazing into each other's eyes through their masks, but even that reminded her of her nightmare again. Had her subconscious been trying to warn her? Against Sam? Against Ben's meddling? When the man with a mask raised the wrench in the dream, it was in the shape of the Hollimans' eternal shells. She'd been confined in a glass coffin, reminiscent of the way Daria had been trapped in the wheelhouse. Some people believed dreams foretold the future, but she would not let herself be trapped as Daria must have been. Never.

She fought to focus, because she had much to do today. Get these final pictures, prepare the rest of the PowerPoint presentation she and Daria had already done some work on. She was tempted to dig up a plug of the sea grass to show everyone, but she couldn't bear to harm the sparse growth that was already suffering below.

Cole reached out and took her free hand in one of his. She nodded she was fine, so they upended and swam down.

As usual, they'd dropped anchor away from the grass so it wouldn't get torn up. Gertie the Grouper greeted them, a good sign this day would go well, Bree thought. The early-morning sunlight slanting through the water gave it a greenish tint. She wondered if it was this bright for Cole, or if it was her extra perceptive sight again. Was that permanent after the lightning strike, a strange gift—or curse—with her increased hearing ability, for surviving all that had happened since that disastrous day?

They swam past the Trade Wreck and headed for the familiar site of the meadow. When the findings were released, the media would hype everything, and both the pro-environment side and the economists who wanted increased business and tourism on shore at any price would be up in arms. The green earth activists would clamor for more stringent pollution and building construction controls, to return the gulf to its once-pristine condition; their opponents would argue that the demands of increasing population were worth temporary setbacks in nature. And she would be in the middle of all that cross fire.

For her presentation this afternoon, she would begin with a slide dedicating the report to Daria's memory, then juxtapose the earlier photos with these latest ones of the declining—

Bree gasped and almost choked. Up ahead—it couldn't be!

She kicked hard to get closer and stared down as Cole joined her. Hovering, she just gaped at first. The grass couldn't have flourished this fast. In one week, after being damaged by that rough-water storm, the meadow had come back from oblivion? It looked green, healthy, hardy. Surely, she wasn't at the wrong site, because the Trade Wreck was right there where it should be. Manny had put them in the same spot as ever.

She shook her head to clear it. Though this was the site she and Daria had tended for months, it was not the same sea grass. Turtle grass, yes, but it must have been planted here. The site had been resodded!

Cole was gesturing, asking her what had happened. She motioned to him that someone must have dug up the old grass and put this in. He shook his head, then pivoted to look all around them as if someone unseen could be lurking.

Slowly, careful not to disturb the bottom and kick up silt or sand, Bree upended again to get her face close to the edge of the sea grass plot. She swam its entire circumference. Then she crisscrossed it, back and forth, while Cole held her camera and just watched.

Too neat, too new, she thought. In a few places someone had tried to make the edges of the meadow look ragged. On the interior, large tufts of turtle grass had been planted with great care in random fashion to make it look more natural. And the bed of grass was a bit smaller than what had been replaced. This must have come from an entirely different area of the gulf, or perhaps even the other side of the state.

Where had it come from? More importantly, who had the know-how, money and nerve to plant it? Who had this much at stake in her report today? Their entire, precious project could become a waste and tarnish Daria's memory, as well as Bree's business and reputation.

She was tempted to defiantly ignore this, because, surely, the ends of her original report would justify the means. Whoever had done this would not dare step forward to challenge her. But all her claims could be easily disproved if someone dived here. Except for Cole, though—and Manny, of course—she wasn't sure who would know the exact coordinates of the site. No, damn, they'd left that memorial wreath on the surface.

Shaking, she took the camera from Cole and began to photograph the grass from many angles, especially the tidy edges of the bed. As ever, she got macrophotography close-ups. With her diving knife, she cut out a six-inch square, which Cole cradled in his hands on the way up.

"Get what you want?" Manny called when they surfaced.

She yelled to him, "Not what I wanted or expected, but more proof that someone has a motive to want our report to be a good one. Practically overnight, that sad bed of sea grass looks as if it has resurrected itself. Whoever hurt Daria must have taken up deep-sea gardening when he couldn't stop me with a wrench."

Things got even worse back at the shop. "Manny, you haven't been using this computer, have you?" Bree asked as she tried to retrieve her earlier pictures of the turtle grass meadow. She had downloaded the new pictures with no problem, but her photo software seemed to be acting up.

"You know I hate those things. No way. What is it?"

"I can't believe this—or maybe I can. Someone has deleted the pics, even Daria's last shots that I just downloaded five days ago."

She frantically tried other folders, scanned lists of documents, did a search by keywords. Nothing. Had messing up Daria's room been a diversion for this tampering and theft? She hadn't been able to access Daria's new password, but had someone hacked into this machine—possibly without even being here? Still, the Gator Watering Hole coaster had disappeared, so someone had thought searching Daria's room was important, too.

Though she had no more tears left, Bree felt sick to her stomach. Months of important work gone, her and Daria's legacy to the gulf they loved sabotaged. She leaned back in her chair. Manny hovered over her, speechless for once. Cole had gone home to change for the commission meeting. He wouldn't believe this. *She* couldn't believe this.

Bree ran to her desk to check the bottom drawer where she kept her backup CDs. Gone. Someone had been here in person. She raced upstairs into Daria's room to look in the drawer where her sister had kept her copies of backup CDs for the computer downstairs. Why hadn't she thought to check these before? When she couldn't get into Daria's e-mail, she had abandoned the idea of Daria's computer.

Gone. Not only Daria's SAV backups, but all her others. Stunned anew, Bree bent over and hit her fists on her knees. Now she was even more afraid. Whoever was behind all this—and, no doubt, Daria's death—was clever, powerful and maybe wealthy. Dom Verdugo, as Cole suspected? He'd want a good gulf report. He had the motive and the manpower to try to stop a bad one.

"What you gonna do?" Manny asked, standing in the hall. His presence and question jolted her.

"I'm tempted to go dive to find some other sick sea grass to show the committee, so they can see what the Trade Wreck meadow actually looked like. But instead, I'm going to try to blow someone out of the water. I'm going to tell the truth, even if that angers someone dangerous very, very much."

"And now, the report we've all been awaiting," Marv Godwin, the chairman of the Clear the Gulf Commission and member of the local Visitor and Convention Bureau, announced to the crowded room with a nod toward Bree. She was sitting at the front table with him, nearest the podium. She had been trying not to stare at Cole, even though she felt stronger when she glanced his way.

The rest of the commission members sat in the front row. Looking at Amelia—who seemed so haggard and nervous that Bree was shocked she was even here today—did nothing but make her more upset and uneasy. Ben sat in the chair behind his wife, as if to keep an eye on her.

Sam Travers was here, sitting in the back of the room, flanked by his divers, Ric and Lance. Bree had expected them to be on that job in Sarasota already, but Sam would do anything to help protect the gulf he loved and needed for his work. Josh Austin and Marla Sherborne were in attendance, both managing to sit in range of the cameras. Bree was trying to ignore the hoard of state-wide media, with their microphones on poles that they thrust toward the podium. Several cameramen sat cross-legged on the floor in front, as if this were some presidential news conference announcing peace or war. In a way, around here, maybe it was.

"Of course, we are all deeply saddened," Chairman Godwin went on, "by the tragic loss of Daria Devon, and we continue to extend our condolences to the family. We are grateful Briana can be with us today at this difficult time with her findings on what is essentially the health report of our precious Gulf of Mexico. Briana?"

Applause, no less. She wasn't sure the chairman would be so grateful when he heard her report. Cole and Manny were the only ones who knew what she intended, because she thought Mr. Godwin might completely discount her report or try to stop her. After all, he wanted the outcome to be a healthy gulf that could handle more development and a casino yacht. Speaking of that, as she glanced at the crowd, she saw Dom Verdugo was here.

Standing in front of everyone, she teared up at first, picturing Daria here with her, wishing fervently this would still go well, even after some bastard had tried to pull the sick-sea-grass rug out from under her.

Her hands shook as she put her index cards on the podium and reached for the remote control that would run her now all-too-brief presentation. She put the first slide up on the screen. It was all black with the words in white: This Report Is In Loving Memory Of Daria Claire Devon, 1978–2006.

"Thank you, Mr. Godwin, and all the commission for your support and kind words about my twin sister. As you know, for the last six months, Daria and I have closely monitored and photographed the turtle grass meadow near the Trade Wreck, approximately four miles out in the gulf. Mr. Godwin is now passing around a handout with information on our fifty-eight dives and a chart indicating the health of the grass, a consistently downward trend.

"We used to call this our grassroots project, but later called it SAV for Submerged Aquatic Vegetation. I don't need to remind you that sea grass roots are key to the ecohealth of the entire area. Sea grass roots hold the sea bottom in place, and the grass itself produces oxygen and shelters marine life. Yet our gulf sea grass is dying."

The occasional camera flash from the media bothered Bree. Even when she wasn't looking directly into the flashes, they bored into her brain. Her own voice over the microphone seemed much too loud, though no one was reacting that way. People were leaning forward, intense, listening to each word. Despite the icy air-conditioning, she felt herself start to sweat, but went on.

"Before I show you some slides, I want to make two major points. First, I want to reiterate that, in the six months Daria and I studied the site, the grass went from bad to much worse. As a result, other marine life is greatly impacted, even endangered. Life on shore suffers, too, and not just because we can catch fewer healthy fish to eat or swim in less clear waters. Secondly, I must tell you something else almost as upsetting to me."

She cleared her throat and darted a look at Cole. His big body was tensed up; he was frowning. He'd argued at first that she should not throw down the gauntlet, that she would make herself more of a target. She'd convinced him that, in a way, she was buying herself life insurance. How obvious would it look if something strange happened to the second sister who was making a stand against pollution, including that from a casino cruise ship, in this area?

"Someone," she said, "is out to sabotage the proof of our findings. Only this morning on a last-minute dive, I discovered—along with Cole DeRoca of your commission—that the shrinking, browning and fading sea grass meadow had been dug up and an area of much more flourishing grass put in its place."

Murmuring. A few gasps. A lot more strobe flashes. Bree gripped the edges of the podium and stared the audience down.

Josh Austin looked stunned. He whispered something to Mark Denton, who was madly taking notes. Mark nodded. Marla Sherborne's mouth had dropped open.

Sam seemed to register no emotion at all. It hit her then. One of the logical recommendations would be the necessity of deeper dredging to make more tidal cuts, which would induce seawater flushing. And Sam's business would profit from that, in a big way.

As for Dom Verdugo, he looked almost smug as he tugged the cuff-linked wrists of his shirtsleeves down under his blazer. Yes, he would want a healthy-looking sea grass meadow so he could insist the gulf was stable and could take the demands of his big boat and the people it would bring in. And he had the money and a jet to bring in more robust grass from across the state or even from the Caribbean.

"Also," Bree plunged on, though her voice sounded too strident to her, "someone hacked into my computer, which held six months' worth of photos, literally hundreds, so that I would have no visual proof and look discredited. Our triple backups were also stolen. But I can show you one slide of my sister and me that we had printed up *before* the digital ones were taken."

She put a slide on the screen of the two of them, hovering over the sea grass, smiling through their masks. Daria had used the camera's automatic timer to get that shot; it had the name and number of their shop underneath. They had planned to use this photo for publicity, but decided at the last minute that the sea grass looked too sick for their big smiles. How strange that hidden, rejected photo had saved the day. Was the person who was playing with their lives hidden, too? Was he someone she knew—someone here today?

"Please ignore the Two Mermaids promotion," Bree said, "and take a look at the sea grass just under us and behind the lettering. This picture is about three months old, halfway through the project, but you can still see how puny and brown the sea grass looks, compared to the excellent shape of this newly sodded grass, which would do a Naples golf course proud."

She ran a series of slides, calling attention to an especially straight edge of the bed and to a view showing that the grass had been planted below the level of the rest of the surrounding sand. "Note also," she added, "that you do not see tiny sea life, such as arrow crabs, clinging to the new, flourishing grass. When it was dug up and taken out of water, those creatures perished, and no new ones have had time to find a home here. In closing, just let me say that not only I, but also Cole DeRoca, can testify that these are two very different sea grass beds—the one my sister and I were hired to monitor and the transplanted one some enemy of truth has gone to desperate lengths to deceive all of you with. *Desper-*

ate lengths," she emphasized again, almost shouting, and sat down before she could blurt out her suspicions about Daria's death.

The room exploded in questions. Marv Godwin jumped to his feet, holding up both hands to quiet everyone. "All right, we promised you a Q and A session," he said. "As for Briana Devon here, let's remember she's only the messenger...."

And what, Bree thought, was the rest of that saying? Oh, yeah, don't kill the messenger. Had she protected herself today or set things up so someone would try to do exactly that?

18

Bombshell At Clear The Gulf Commission Hearing, the headline in the *Naples Daily News* read the next morning. A photo of Bree at the podium took up a quarter of the front page, with the slide of her and Daria underwater in the background. The article didn't accuse anyone but mentioned that the fallout might include temporary restrictions for onshore building and might "sway even more voters from backing at-sea gambling." If that was the ultimate fallout, Bree thought, and Dom Verdugo became a suspect in the turtle grass switch, he would be even more furious at her than before.

Bree's report about someone replacing the sea grass meadow was also the lead story in the local morning newscasts she checked. Mark Denton phoned to tell her the story was being carried statewide and he and "the candidate" admired her courage. An e-mail from Senator Marla Sherborne, one of nearly a hundred sent to the shop's Web site, said that "the ripples" were being felt even in Washington.

It was not, Bree thought, as she sat at the table with her head in her hands over her barely touched breakfast, the way any sane person who had been attacked in more ways than one should keep a low profile. But she'd decided to flush out whoever was hurting the gulf—and whoever had hurt Daria. Would that be the same person?

When Cole emerged from the shower after another night on her sofa, his hair was slicked to his head. He pecked a kiss on her cheek as if they were an old married couple and poured his own coffee. He'd already eaten.

"Any more phone calls?" he asked.

"I turned my cell off, and the TV. The e-mail count keeps going up. Everything's exploding," she said, turning the paper toward where he sat across from her. As he bent over the article, she pointed to the word *bombshell*.

It annoyed her that he looked so good, compared to the way she felt. She'd spent half the night awake again, afraid of bad dreams and going over and over candidates who might have substituted healthy sea grass for sick, and for possible fathers of Daria's child. Of course, there were many unknowns, but something Manny's daughter had asked about Daria kept sticking in Bree's brain. *Had* Daria gotten over Josh? Or had they run into each other somewhere and *boom!* Old passions had exploded? Even if that were true, it seemed the man was seldom alone. Nikki was on the campaign trail with him, and he always had Mark Denton at his elbow.

Yet Bree kept recalling that Daria had told her once out of the blue—no, they had just seen one of Josh's TV ads, where he and Nikki were walking the beach hand in hand—that Nikki had suffered two miscarriages and they were desperate to have children. How long ago had that been? Certainly, in the last seven weeks or so. At the time, Bree hadn't even wondered where Daria had come up with that intimate information. Just gossip, that's what she'd passed it off as. But was it firsthand knowledge? And would someone like Josh, who seemed to have almost everything he wanted, need to prove he could father a child?

"A million dollars for your thoughts," Cole said, looking up from reading the article.

"I thought they were only worth a penny."

"Not anymore," he said, putting his coffee cup down. "Inflation plus your fifteen minutes of media fame's upped the ante. I can't wait to get working on the paneling for the *Fun 'n' Sun* today to see how Verdugo is reacting. He looked pretty smug for a while at the meeting, but I saw him storm out."

"Cole, remember how I said I'd like to get away?"

"You can't run now. Besides, I've committed to get that casino yacht project going so I can keep an eye on Verdugo and his boys. I couldn't go with you."

"I think I mentioned that Josh and Nikki Austin invited me to spend some time at their place in cane country? Clewiston's not far, and I wouldn't stay long. Maybe just for the day, if they'll fly me there like they said."

"Bree, Josh may not be as high on our watch list for hiring your attackers as Sam Travers and his divers or Verdugo and his goons are, but he—"

"He bears watching, and that's exactly what I'd like to do. Or, barring that, since he's so busy, I'd settle for picking Nikki's brain."

"So you're thinking whoever fathered Daria's child might be a more important lead than someone desperate to stop your report on an endangered environment?"

"I don't know what I think, except that those are the two most obvious motives and I've got to keep pushing at possibilities. Even if Josh were somehow involved, I can't believe he'd ever harm Daria, especially if she was carrying his child."

"Haven't you ever heard the saying that absolute power corrupts absolutely? The man is a politician with big ambitions. Despite the Hollywood morals in this country today, an illegitimate child by his old flame could ruin his marriage, which is no doubt tied to big sugar money in his campaign coffers. It could sully his reputation, when he's built up this 'you can trust Josh Austin' facade."

"But I've known him for years and believe he can be trusted to…"

Bree covered her eyes and burst into tears. She heard Cole scrape his chair back. He came around the table and pulled her up into his arms. Then when she got up to head for her bedroom, he sat in her chair and tugged her into his lap.

She forced herself to stop crying. She got the hiccups but kept talking anyway. "I didn't know that was coming," she said, wiping her eyes with her napkin. "It's all I do lately, swing from heroics to hysterics. It's just that I was going to claim I know Josh well, when I obviously didn't even know my own twin sister."

"Just rest this morning, okay? Then walk over to the *Fun 'n' Sun* to meet me for lunch, and we'll go to the Grog Shop. Let Manny run things downstairs while you check the e-mail, in case there's anything there that would give you another lead. Call me on my cell if something turns up. And I'll try to psych out Verdugo."

"Aye, aye, Captain," she said, trying to sound in control again. She gave him a weak salute as another hiccup jolted her.

"Somehow, sweetheart," he said with a sigh, "I don't

think you're the kind of first mate—or any other kind of mate—who takes orders well."

"Something here for you," Manny told Bree as she went downstairs to check the e-mail on the Two Mermaids Web site after Cole left. "That red-haired diver, Lance, the one brought back your flippers, just dropped it off. A sealed letter from Sam Travis, something to do with business."

As if it were a letter bomb, she took it gingerly from Manny. He sat at Daria's desk. Bree saw he'd put a new nameplate and his family pictures where her sister's things had been. His morning cup of yerba maté was in a mug Daria had always used for coffee. A screwdriver and wrench lay there, as if his realm of the back room had begun to migrate to the front office. Biting her lower lip, Bree went to her own desk and slit the envelope open. In Sam's bold handwriting, the note read,

I know you're still shook but think about this. It's a good time for you to sell out to me, like I offered last year. Remember your brother-in-law was all for it. Have your lawyer contact mine. I'll take Manny on, raise my earlier price, and buy out your property there, if you want to move and move on. S. Travers

She could not believe his gall. Red pulsating lights seemed to explode behind her eyes. With all she and Daria had worked for, did he think she'd turn tail and run? She had a good mind to rip this to shreds, but it might be evidence later of a motive for Daria's death if Sam was involved in any way.

"What is it?" Manny asked, getting up from Daria's—his—desk.

"Lock this place up. We're going to see Sam Travers in person. I take it that they haven't left for their big demolition job in Sarasota yet."

"His guy said tomorrow. What is that?" he repeated.

"Sam's second kind offer to buy us out and to hire you, too."

"No way. *Caramba,* I work hard to get this far here, and I'm not taking orders from him neither."

Bree bit her lip again. She didn't like the way Manny had put that. She was tired of giving him the benefit of the doubt because he was under so much family pressure. Damn it, so was she! But there would be time later to discuss who was the senior partner here. Right now she was going to give Sam Travers a piece of her mind and hope he didn't keep insisting on a pound of her flesh.

Manny locked up hastily and followed Bree out onto the street. "We not taking the truck?" he asked.

"It's not that far. I'm walking. Maybe I'll work off some of this anger."

She was surprised that so many people called her name, thanked her for taking a stand on keeping the gulf clean, or wished her good luck as she strode past. Yes, she'd done the right thing to tell the truth and take the sea grass plot public. Now, if she could only get a credible lead on what had really happened to Daria.

As she approached Sam's large, three-story building, which she used to know inside and out when she and Ted were dating all those years, the first person she saw was Ric, up a ladder. He was repainting the Travers and Son Search and Salvage sign. Sam had never changed the business's name after Ted's death. Even now, it looked as if Ric was just brightening the colors, not changing the wording. Ted had promised his father that when he came back from the service—if he didn't decide to make the marines a career—he'd work with him here, and Sam had immediately put up the sign as if they'd already sealed the deal.

She noticed something interesting about Ric, besides the fact that he was obviously adept at scaling ladders to second stories.

"Manny, how many guys do you know who paint with gloves on?" she asked. She noted they were diving gloves, which made it even stranger, because they were expensive to get splotched with paint.

"Que sera sera," Manny muttered, evidently not following what she meant.

A ladder and a pair of gloves! After the commission report yesterday, Ben had told her that the CSI tech had turned up no "foreign" fingerprints. The intruder might have worn gloves.

"Don't walk under that ladder—bad luck," Manny said, and grabbed her elbow.

"Great. If I walk around it, I'm sure my luck will make a big U-turn for the good," she said, instantly regretting her sarcasm.

"Hey, Briana!" Ric called down. She was still so angry she was tempted to just keep walking, but maybe it would be a good idea to talk to this guy. Her dad used to say you could catch more flies with honey than vinegar.

"I thought you'd be setting off underwater detonator caps in Sarasota by now," she called up to him, shading her eyes in the morning sun.

For a guy who seemed so muscular, he came lithely

down the ladder. Yes, she thought, as he stood on the pavement between her and Manny, he was just the height of her attacker at the Gator Watering Hole. Now to get some info, without giving her suspicions away.

"All of us are going first thing tomorrow," Ric said, his eyes assessing her. "We'll be gone a couple of weeks, blowing old bridge buttresses, then sinking or salvaging the debris."

He smiled at her, more a tight quirk of the sides of his mouth. He wore no sunglasses and she saw he had dark eyes—also the color of her attacker's. As he talked, he pulled off his gloves. He had manicured hands, no less, and a handsome ring on his right pinkie finger. Maybe that explained the gloves. Why hadn't she tried to memorize something about the masked man's hands? If Ric had been her attacker, why would he risk getting up close and personal with her right now? Maybe he planned to earn her trust, then get her off alone and finish the job he'd botched at the Gator Watering Hole.

"Sam's skilled at demo work from his years in 'Nam," Ric went on. "He's taught us a lot, Lance and me. Used to be part of a unit they called frogmen, the ones now called the SEALs. I think they should have named them sharks or barracudas."

"Pretty dangerous work, isn't it?" she asked as Manny frowned at them. "But then, I suppose that's part of the thrill."

"True, the adrenaline really gets pumping," he admitted, his eyes flickering over her again. "Pays better than regular diving, too, time and a half. Sam calls it combat pay. Listen, Briana," he said, turning his back on Manny, who grunted but shuffled a couple of steps away. "I'm really sorry about your sister, and I'm glad I could be there to help when she was found."

He twisted his gloves between his fists as he spoke, almost as if he were wringing someone's neck. He lowered his voice and leaned slightly closer. "After I come back, you want to go diving somewhere different, just for relaxation—for fun? Down to the Keys, maybe? I know it's been terrible for you, but you've got to start living again—for yourself and her, too, now."

Bree suddenly felt at a loss for words. The last thought, that she could enjoy life in memory of Daria, moved her deeply. She wanted to be angry, not to get conned into liking this guy. He ought to go moonlight for those super sales reps, Fred and Viv Holliman.

"That is," he went on, "if you're not tied in real tight with DeRoca. I don't mean to be pushy or poach on someone else's territory."

"Thanks for the offer," she said, trying to sound noncommittal. She wanted to get away or she was going to lose it again. She looked up at the sign he'd repainted. "It's strange to see a diver up a ladder," she said.

"Jack-of-all-trades, master of none," he said, with a shrug and a smile that made him seem self-deprecating and almost charming. Except, she reminded herself, his trades might include B and E and attacking women with a wrench, if not worse.

"Thanks again for your kind words," she said, "but I need to have a few unkind words with Sam right now. Good luck on your demo dives in Sarasota."

As she started away, Manny whispered, "Oh, you thinking he might be the one broke in—and almost broke your bones at the Gator Watering Hole."

She didn't have time to answer as he opened Sam's front door for her and they stepped inside.

"I can't believe you're home right now, the busy man of power lunches," Amelia told Ben. She'd heard the garage door go up, and had been surprised to see his car turning into the driveway. "Are you feeling all right?"

"Actually, I came home to be sure you were."

"I'm holding my own. Can I fix you something for lunch?"

"Sure. How about just plain old *PB* and *J,* like we used to live on while I was finishing law school?"

"It used to be necessity food, now I guess it's comfort food." She started getting things out on the counter.

"Actually, I need to tell you a couple of things," he said, getting two diet sodas from the refrigerator. "First of all, the fingerprint tech said only Bree and Daria's prints are in the bedroom."

She stopped unscrewing the top to the peanut butter jar and stared straight ahead at the cupboard, as if she could read something in the wood grain there. "Strange, isn't it," she whispered, "that Daria can be gone and her prints remain? There are so many places she touched... Sorry, I didn't mean to sound like some sappy greeting card. What else did you come all the way home to tell me?"

"There's more that turned up on the autopsy," he said, popping the tab on a soda, a sound like an exclamation point. "There was some mystery man in Daria's life. She was pregnant."

Amelia sucked in a sob. For one moment she had thought he was going to tell her that the report stated that someone pushed Daria shortly before she died or that they could tell who had pushed her into the steering wheel on her boat, but that was ridiculous. That was her guilt talking again. Pregnant! In a way, that meant there were two deaths, one of a niece or nephew she would never know. She fought to steady herself because she thought she might throw up right here in the sink.

"So Bree has no idea—who?" she asked.

"No, and I believe her. But she's on a crusade because she thinks whoever fathered the child might have harmed Daria."

Amelia gripped the counter. From behind, Ben put his hands on her waist. As if the kids were home and he didn't want them to hear, he whispered, "I got you an appointment late this afternoon with a good doctor, a kind of a family counselor."

"A psychiatrist, a shrink," she countered, not moving, feeling frozen where she stood. "How nice a doctor can see me at the snap of your fingers."

"Honey, I asked him as a special favor to work you in. The appointment's kind of late in the day, but I can take you there the first time. He'll be someone to talk to confidentially, like talking to a lawyer."

She nodded stiffly and tried to process all he had told her. Bree might have been right that someone wanted to silence Daria, someone besides her own, older sister, who'd wanted to shut her up for the cruel things she had said. A man now had a motive for wanting to get rid of Daria. But after all, Daria's death was by drowning.

"You're taking this much better than I expected," Ben said, sounding wary. "Much better than Bree did."

Amelia nodded. It was best if Ben thought she was doing better, and best if the psychiatrist thought so, too. She had no intention of telling anyone she'd gotten Ben's pistol out of his desk drawer in the den this morning and just stared long and hard at it, until she'd realized it was almost noon and heard the garage door. Or that she'd been desperate enough to rent a boat she hardly knew how to steer and go out to continue her argument with Daria, who had said she would not be diving with Bree that day the storm came up.

For Bree, being inside Sam's shop was always like stepping into a time warp. He'd kept the front office the way it was when she and Ted had been dating. They'd both worked here as kids, and, after his mother's desertion and his parents' divorce, Ted had lived here with Sam for a while, over the store. As far as Bree could tell, their private rooms—Sam lived somewhere else now— were still accessed by the same outside stairs she and Ted had sneaked up more than once.

But there were a few different things now. A new guy worked here, manning the phone and computer, one of Sam's concessions to modern technology, like his echo sounder and GPS systems on his boats. And a large poster—actually, just of a saying of some sort—hung behind the front counter. It read,

For want of a nail, a shoe was lost,
For want of a shoe, a horse was lost,
For want of a horse, a battle was lost,
For want of a battle, a war was lost,
For want of a war, a kingdom was lost.

"Can I help you, Ms. Devon?" the guy behind the desk asked. She didn't recognize him, but everyone knew her face—or Daria's—lately. Before Bree could answer, Sam came in from the back room. Without another word, the man cleared the way for him.

"Like that sentiment?" Sam asked, jerking a thumb at the poster. "It means one little thing can ruin eternity for someone."

"I get the point."

Bree remembered Manny telling her that Sam's other diver, Lance, had said Sam had a shrine to Ted's memory in the attic here. Obviously, this poster, like everything in Sam's life, was tied to the loss of his son. Though she hadn't intended to start with him this way, she asked, "How easy was it for you to tell Daria and me apart, Sam?"

"What's that have to do with anything? Her smile was a little more lopsided, and she was jumpier than you, least till lately. As for looks, hard to tell. But I know she wouldn't have dumped my son the way you did."

She ignored the jab. Then it was possible Sam could have come after her on the water that day and hurt Daria by mistake. Or he'd sent Ric, who couldn't tell them apart. Would the slow engine on a barge register underwater?

"Then let's just pretend," Bree plunged on, "I'm here to speak for myself and for Daria. We turned down your offer of a buyout before, and I'm turning it down for both of us again. Manny's my new partner and he agrees."

Sam didn't even glance Manny's way as his gaze burned into Bree's. "Suit yourself," he said with a shrug, though the frown that sliced between his narrowed eyes showed he was hardly shrugging this off. Her eyes widened when she saw Sam had a wrench in his pocket, protruding as if it were a silent threat. Thank God, she'd brought Manny with her, because when Ric came in the front door with his paint can, she felt surrounded.

"That's all I came to say," she told Sam.

"Far's I'm concerned, that's all there is to say," he muttered, crossing his arms over his chest. "I made that offer in good faith to help you out and get you outta the area where I don't have to hear, see, or think about you. Get on outta my shop then, 'cause you're trespassing and always were."

Bree spun and strode out, vowing silently that she'd be back when Sam, Ric and Lance were gone. Maybe there would be something she could use against him in that upstairs shrine, where he worshipped the memory of Saint Ted.

19

Bree stormed back to her office with Manny in her wake, only to find Nikki Austin getting out of a large, dark car in front of the shop. She was alone.

"Bree, I just wanted to see how you're doing," she said, and surprised her with a sincere hug that wasn't just a touch and a jump back this time. "Josh and Mark are at a Rotary Club breakfast in town, so I took the car to pop over. The news coverage on your report is amazing!"

Especially amazing, Bree thought, with Josh giving interviews about it right and left. She said only, "I ought to be running for office. Everyone seems to know my face and name. Can you come in?"

"Actually, I was wondering—Josh, too—if you'd like to leave the media questions to the professionals and take us up on our offer to get away for a while."

As Manny unlocked the front door and went in, Bree hesitated. Nikki's arrival was like a sign she should pursue a visit with them, wasn't it?

"That's so kind, but I know you're both busy."

"Josh has a full docket today and won't join us until this evening, but Mark's going to fly me across the state in about—" she dug her cell phone out of her purse and glanced at the time on it "—an hour and a half. A change of scene might do you so much good."

Bree knew this would upset Cole, but the opportunity was too ideal to pass up. She had to take risks, just as Cole was doing by hanging tight to Verdugo.

"I'd love to, especially if it's just for the day and night."

"We'll be back here early afternoon tomorrow—for a rally at your and Josh's old high school, no less. Rah, rah, Austin for senator! Listen, Briana, you'll love sugarcane country, with its miles and miles of fields to get lost in. Believe me, there's something about the place that makes sorrows easier to bear."

"Looking good," Dom Verdugo's voice came from behind Cole. "That custom rosewood's gonna add a lot of class."

Ever since Bree had called and they'd argued about her going across the state, Cole had been furiously working on installing the paneling. He was so preoccupied that he hadn't even heard footsteps. He'd been almost listening at keyholes earlier, so the fact he hadn't noticed Verdugo's approach upset him even more.

"Glad it suits you, and we're still on for this deal," Cole replied without looking at him. "You seemed pretty teed off after the commission meeting yesterday. I didn't think you'd still be so optimistic that having a casino boat in Turtle Bay is going to go your way."

"I have a talent for working things out."

Cole finished nailing the baseboard, then stood and faced Verdugo. "So did whoever installed that all-new turtle grass meadow."

Verdugo's expression didn't change. "Meaning?"

"You realize some will point the finger at you."

"Let them. Nothing will stick, not when there's a list long as my arm could have done it."

Was that an admission of guilt? Cole wondered.

With a finger jabbing the air, Verdugo went on. "An entire coalition of store owners and builders are dying to develop this area, and this boat will bring in the tourists and dollars they need. No one can stop progress, not in South Florida. Besides, you think I'm the kind of guy who'd do something that blatant? Whose side you on, DeRoca?"

"I'm on Briana Devon's side, and she's distraught about her and her sister's work, not to mention the loss of her sister."

"I can understand that, sympathize. But tragedies happen, ones no one can explain, and don't forget it."

That sounded like a threat. Cole stared back at Verdugo, not letting his gaze waver.

"But, hey," the older man said, producing some of his ever-present caramel popcorn as if from up his sleeve, "I came to tell you I sent out invitations to the local powers-that-be, including the Clear the Gulf Commission members and some political people, to take a cruise on this baby Friday evening. It'll be a shakedown cruise, so to speak—no gambling, of course, but eats, drinks, live music. I want to explain the *Fun 'n' Sun*'s clean-water system, how all refuse is handled on board and unloaded later ashore."

"So you'd like the paneling done by then."

"Only if it doesn't push you. Actually, I'd like to invite you—bring Briana, too, if she's up to it. It'll be great PR for you, as well as me."

* * *

"Which do you prefer doing, Mark?" Bree asked. "PR, piloting, or escorting the candidate and his wife?"

Mark Denton was flying Bree and Nikki across the state in a white, four-seat Cessna pontoon plane. Nikki said she had a speech to write and had put Bree in the copilot's seat to enjoy the view for the one-hour flight. After they left the Naples suburbs with its tentacles of new housing projects reaching outward, the Everglades swept under them, the water reflecting the sky. Shortly after they'd crossed Alligator Alley, they had flown over the Seminole Indian Reservation, then fields of vegetables and citrus, and were now heading northeast toward Lake Okeechobee and cane country.

"I took up flying fairly late," Mark answered her question. "Media and public relations were my first love."

As before, Bree thought that for a man in his position, he didn't seem glib or especially friendly. But his real talent might be in writing speeches and press releases.

"Family?" she asked.

"Married to my work for now."

Though she made a point of staring out the windows ahead and beside her, Bree tried to study the man. His well-shaped head was covered with dark stubble; with his buzz cut, he reminded her of a marine. Slashes of brown eyebrows arched over brown eyes, now hidden by his aviator sunglasses, which reflected Bree whenever he looked her way. His nose was a bit crooked where it must have once been broken. Usually, he spoke without seeming to move his thin-lipped mouth. She had the feeling he didn't like her, but maybe he just thought the

Austins should be sticking to business and not entertaining some bereaved friend.

Despite the drone of the engine, Bree knew that Nikki, sitting directly behind her, could hear what they said, for she occasionally chimed in. Now she leaned forward between their seats to say, "Mark's going to pilot the Austin machine clear to the White House someday."

"Graduate to flying Air Force One?" Bree asked, trying to go along with the joke. But she remembered Josh had told her Nikki was ambitious, her hopes set on going to Washington with him and climbing the power ladder.

"I thought maybe press secretary," Mark said, sounding entirely serious. "One who doesn't just parrot the party line but helps to make policy. What do you think, future First Lady?" he asked Nikki, and she playfully punched his shoulder. "Hey, that's Clewiston, America's Sweetest Town beyond, but this is the start of the Grann sugarcane fields," he said, pointing as he began to take the plane lower. Descending through the blue, blue sky and skimming over the waving green plants reminded Bree of diving the depths of some lovely underwater spot—not, unfortunately, off the coast of Naples.

She had seen sugarcane before but had paid little attention to it. The plants were tall and green with woolly beige plumes, but that was all she recalled. Now, she was in awe. Field after field of cane, swaying in the breeze, stretched for miles through rich, black soil. Train tracks glittered in the sun, ones she knew must lead loaded rail cars to the sugar refineries.

"Are those big machines harvesters?" she asked about the metal monsters parked near a tin-roofed shed.

"That and cane choppers, and you want to stay way clear of those," Mark said. "Most of the harvest starts in about two weeks, but some of it's ready now. Got to satisfy America's sweet tooth. Grand Sugar, which Nikki's father owns, is the third biggest sugar supplier in the nation after U.S. Sugar and Crystal. And beyond, on the horizon, Lake O," he said, sounding conversational now, as if he was loosening up a bit. "It's so close to the Grann property that we just land on the water, taxi to their dock and take a Humvee waiting there."

"I've never seen Okeechobee from the air," Bree said, marveling at the stretch of blue water that ran through the Glades to the gulf. She wondered if people ever scuba dived in Okeechobee. "What does that name mean?" she asked.

"Seminole for big water."

"Makes sense to me."

It was also starting to make sense to her that the wealth of King Sugar, as she'd heard it called, had a very long reach in the state. Not only to satisfy America's sweet tooth, as Mark had mentioned, but, as Cole had said, to fill political coffers. And maybe even reach deep into the gulf to erase evidence that would help prove pollution from these cane fields played a part in poisoning gulf water.

Bree stared in awe when Nikki and Josh's home came into view at the end of a lane, lined with live oaks, about a mile from her father's plantation home, which they'd already passed.

"It's beautiful," she told Nikki, who sat beside her in the backseat of the Humvee Mark drove. "Tara from *Gone With The Wind!*"

"Just don't be looking for Rhett Butler inside," Nikki said with a laugh. "You know, I always hated that movie for its unhappy ending. That stupid woman loved the wrong man."

"That's what I always thought about it," Mark put in, "but then, despite the fact that it takes place right in the middle of the Civil War, it's really a woman's movie."

Rolling her eyes at that, Nikki said, "Actually, I patterned this house, a wedding present from my father, after one Josh and I saw on our honeymoon in New Orleans. But to make it look right, I had to import live oaks and Spanish moss and get rid of a lot of palms and all those air plants that usually cling to trees around here."

A sort of phony Tara, Bree thought. If she'd gone to all that trouble with tiny details, Nikki Austin, like Amelia, was a control freak of the first, and worst, order.

As they pulled up, Bree saw that the big-pillared porch was a sort of false facade, too, for the house wasn't as large as it looked. With a promise to show her around after she rested, Nikki escorted Bree up the sweeping central staircase to the guest suite and left her alone.

Bree put her small overnight bag on the padded bench at the foot of the big four-poster bed and stared out the window. The view, probably the same on all four sides, overlooked miles of densely planted, twelve-foot-tall sugarcane, which began just across the small lawn and narrow garden. In a way, it made her feel claustrophobic. The sugarcane had waves like the sea, but even from this height, she felt enclosed rather than enraptured.

On the oak table by the bay window awaited a silver tray with a pitcher of iced tea, surrounded by small cut-glass bowls with packets of Grand Sugar, lime and lemon slices and extra ice. On a flat crystal plate, with a yellow hibiscus bloom in the center, was an array of exotically hued hard candies. Ah, the lifestyles of the rich and famous, she thought, and wondered if the allure of any of this could have turned Daria's head while Josh flip-flopped her heart. But the money behind everything here was from Nikki's family, not Josh's. Even if he'd tried to leave his wife for Daria…no, she was being ridiculous.

But that secret teeth-whitening appointment. Nikki Austin had teeth that almost glistened. Did Daria feel the need to compete with her rival's beauty? What about those extra cosmetics in her drawer? Did Daria discover the only way she could win out over the stunning, wealthy, married Nikki was by having Josh's baby? And, if so, how was Bree ever going to get the truth of a secret liaison out of Josh?

To Bree's surprise, Nikki's father drove over in a golf cart to join them for a late lunch. He spoke again of her loss, asking if there was anything they could do to help ease her pain and grief.

"Nikki's been very kind and helpful—Josh, too," she assured him.

Despite the fact it was delightfully cool with the air-conditioning inside the house, the three of them sat out on the warm, screened-in back veranda and were served cold raspberry soup and crab salad by a middle-aged, Haitian-born housekeeper-cook named Lindy who spoke with a French accent. The table was set with linen and silver; the centerpiece was a charming combination of blue plumbago blossoms floating in a dish that had hard candies in the bottom, which Bree thought at first were marbles.

As Cory Grann played host in Josh's absence, Bree could certainly understand how Marla Sherborne had become involved with him, even though he must have started out as enemy number one to her beliefs and political platform. The wealthy widower was not only conversational and handsome, he focused his complete attention on anyone he spoke to, whether it was the housekeeper, Bree or his daughter. But it didn't take Bree long to wonder if she'd been brought here for a purpose, just as she'd come for one.

"Big sugar's been blamed for years for everything that goes wrong in the Glades, and now we're also the major whipping boy for gulf pollution," Cory Grann said, somehow working that into their conversation and looking intently at her.

"Which is ridiculous," Nikki put in, "since the cane farmers no longer use heavy fertilizers and toxic pesticides. There's big cattle farming north of Lake O, and they seldom go after them."

Cory nodded. "Lee and Collier county officials should stop blaming us for their poor river and gulf water health and tackle pollution sources in their own backyards. Same with the ecofr—folks," Cory amended. She was sure he was going to call them ecofreaks, as some of their opponents did. "It's just that we're an easy target for anything that goes wrong. And it's very difficult and dangerous to be a target," he added with a decisive nod at her.

Bree felt a slight shiver race up her spine, but she tried not to react visibly. Were those words a subtle threat, disguised by all this luxury, kindness and politeness?

"I know you've converted Senator Sherborne," she said.

"Marla knows how much money we've donated for

cleanup." He leaned slightly closer across the table. "And for this state's other green causes."

Bree had read that big sugar had donated twenty-two million dollars to various Florida election campaigns and to fund lobbyists, as well as to sponsor some down-home television ads that were pro-sugar. Despite their lack of nutritional value, what would Americans do without their sweet fixes? She and Daria had always loved candy.

And then it hit her that, more than once, Daria had brought candy home she'd said she'd bought, and it was just like the citrus-flavored, brightly colored hard balls displayed in nearly every room of Josh Austin's house.

Yes, as pretty and sweet as everything seemed here, she was certain these people meant to play hardball with her.

20

Bree was surprised to find she'd fallen asleep on her bed.

"But," Nikki said when she knocked on her door to tell her Josh would be here in a half hour and they'd have drinks before dinner, "that's why you're here—to relax. Believe me, I know it takes a long time to deal with such losses. For me, it helped to get busy—to fight back, in a way."

Bree thought she would say more, but she darted down the hall.

Bree showered, changed into slacks and a carefully selected blouse and headed for the stairs. The door to the bedroom next to hers stood ajar. She hesitated a moment before walking past it and downstairs. It was—or was meant to be—a nursery, with pale yellow walls and rainbows on the wallpaper, and yellow carpet, too. But it was bare of furniture, an empty box of a room, like a present that was never opened however bright the wrappings.

Daria must have been right. Nikki and Josh had lost two pregnancies, and if they'd had a nursery ready, that might mean Nikki had been pretty far along. Was it as devastating to lose a hoped-for baby you never knew—twice—as it was to lose a sister who was the person closest to you in the world, even if you didn't know her as well as you thought?

Bree's stomach knotted as she went downstairs and heard Josh's voice mingled with Nikki's, but she couldn't tell what they were saying. When she joined them, she saw she'd interrupted a private moment, for he had his arm around her, though she had her outside arm propped on her hip as if she'd been trying to make some point.

"Bree, glad you could join us for some R & R." Josh greeted her and pecked a kiss on her cheek before stepping back. She saw his eyes fill with tears he blinked quickly back as he turned away. Either he was very glad to see her, or he and Nikki had been speaking of something emotional. Or maybe he was taken aback by the fact she looked like Daria. She had intentionally chosen a blouse she knew her sister had worn more than once, supposedly to her accounting class, but evidently to meet a man at the Gator Watering Hole. Bree was dying to challenge Josh about that, but she had no idea if he was the one with the information she needed.

"All right, ladies," he said, rubbing his hands together, "we are going to make our own caipirinha drinks with home-grown *cachaça* before dinner."

"Our own what, with what?" Bree asked. "Something Mexican? My Latino business partner—" there, she'd said it "—drinks a pick-me-up called yerba maté all the time."

"This is the national drink of Brazil," Josh said, taking each of them by the arm and steering them outside and down the front steps, "and it's catching on here, especially in Miami. Who says exhausting statewide campaigning doesn't have its perks?"

Bree could tell he was forcing his light tone. He walked them over to a wooden table set up on the lawn at the edge of the eastern cane field. Several trays held three tall glasses, and bowls of lime wedges, sugar and ice. From the grass below, Josh picked up a thick stick, a sharp knife and a huge, curved machete with a wooden handle.

"It looks like someone's about to declare war," Bree observed, but her voice sounded shaky. She jumped behind Nikki when Josh picked up the machete and swung it in a wide arc. It whistled in the hot, humid air.

"This," he said, "is the way they used to cut cane."

With a tremendous swipe, he sliced through two cane stalks, toppling them toward the women.

"Timber!" Nikki cried, and Bree smelled liquor on her breath already. Each woman caught one of the twelve-foot stalks, despite being half-buried by its leaves.

"Man, using this thing makes me feel good," Josh said, and with a quick laugh, started to decapitate the heads of other stalks, then swung lower to make yet others crash down.

"Be careful, or you'll cut yourself!" Nikki cried. "You don't need to be all bandaged up at your alma mater tomorrow."

That's right, Bree thought. Josh was speaking at Lely High School tomorrow. If she could just risk getting him alone, that might make a good entrée into getting him to reminisce about Daria.

Josh walked back toward them, the huge arched blade still in his hand. He bent down, took the cane Bree held and dropped it onto the ground, then hacked it into three equal pieces at its lowest joints.

"Sugarcane school, lesson number one," he said, holding up one of the joints for her to see. He dropped the machete on the grass and, with the knife on the table, peeled back the husk to reveal what looked like hundreds of wet straws inside the piece of cane. "Bite on this," he told Bree.

Keeping an eye on the machete and knife, Bree touched the severed straws with her tongue. Sweet juice flooded her mouth.

"Spit out the rest," Nikki said. "The chewy stuff is the bagasse. But the liquid's a great source of energy—and of sugar."

"Now, lesson number two," Josh said as he peeled another piece, then put it on a plate and chopped it even smaller before he jammed it in one of the glasses. He took the big wooden stick from the table—it was over a foot long and barely fit in the glass—and mashed the cane.

"Obviously," he said, "the best bartenders across America do not carry on like the madman demo you've just seen. The sugarcane distillate we just made by hand comes in a variety of brands, some of which are aged in cognac barrels or oak casks in France, no less. But I think we should start bottling and aging our own cane into this *cachaça*."

He mixed three drinks with the ingredients and then tapped Nikki's and Bree's glasses before they drank. "To the future of cane and a great senatorial election," he said. "Now watch it, because this stuff can sneak up on you, just like rum. Here, I've got some extra made."

"Before dinner, let's show her our secret getaway

from our big-house getaway," Nikki said as Josh took a swig of his drink.

"And she doesn't mean our little pied-à-terre in Tallahassee. Sure, let's go."

"Lead the way," she said. "Lindy will ring the bell for dinner."

"Onward! Ever onward! Josh Austin for senate!" Josh cried, and raised the machete before him as if it were a flag they could follow. Nikki just shook her head and picked up the tray with more mixings for the drinks. Bree thought the caipirinha was delicious—sweet, yet tart and refreshing—but it had such an alluring kick that she silently vowed to furtively pour hers out along the way. She had no intention of getting drunk and then being questioned by Josh about how much she knew. No, she was hoping he'd have too much so she could set him up for a heartfelt talk and, maybe, a confession. Besides, she had to keep her wits about her, since they seemed to be leading her into the labyrinth of deep cane, and Josh still had that massive weapon.

Amelia was grateful that the doctor hadn't asked her to lie down on a couch, although there was one in the room. "So this doctor-patient information is entirely privileged, like with a lawyer?" she asked Dr. Scott Nelson. Ben had assured her of that, but she was double-checking. The man had a kindly face and soft voice that exuded compassion.

"Absolutely," he said, folding his hands on one crossed knee. They sat in facing chairs as if they were just here for a friendly chat, but she had no intention of falling for that. Oh, no, she fully intended to keep up her guard.

"I could be subpoenaed," he explained, "but I'd refuse to testify and my records would stay sealed. I'd go to prison before I would betray a trust from a patient."

Testify? Go to prison? His mere word choice evoked horrible images of his clients being arrested. And Ben was the prosecutor who would be responsible for bringing a murderer to justice.

Ben had not exactly answered the question of how close he was to Dr. Nelson, to get her an appointment this quickly. She decided not to ask the doctor if information was also kept private from a family member. More than once, she'd seen Ben worm things out of his own clients or other lawyers. She'd already told him too much. She could only pray that he—or Bree, in her crusade, as Ben called it, to find out who had hurt Daria— would not check around the marina and discover that Amelia had rented a boat.

Despite her fears of open water, she's gone out into the gulf until she'd spotted *Mermaids II*. She'd cut the motor and let the boat drift closer, because she figured if Daria heard her, she'd order her to keep away. The rental motorboat was almost on top of the dive boat when Daria had seen her and helped her grapple the two crafts together so Amelia could climb aboard, telling her off the whole time.

And then, it had all happened so fast. More arguing, the push that made Daria slip and crack her head against the steering wheel in the dive boat's little wheelhouse. Daria had said she'd been nauseous and a little dizzy, and now Amelia knew why. Daria shouldn't have slipped from that little push. She must have been dizzy from the first trimester of her pregnancy. Maybe the nausea was why she really hadn't dived with Bree. Everything was really Daria's fault, not hers, Amelia assured herself.

She had scrambled off the boat, back to her own vessel, panicked that Daria might be dead and she'd be
blamed for what was an accident. Because she was afraid
Bree might surface if she heard a motor, she let the boat
drift away again before starting it. She had to get back
in, because the storm was starting to kick up. Surely
Bree would surface and help Daria. They had always
stuck together, so let them take care of each other now.

But to the kindly faced, soft-voiced psychiatrist, she
was saying nothing. Even if he were a trusted Catholic
priest—and there were fewer of them than ever lately—
in a soundproof confessional booth, Amelia would never
tell him or anyone else. Despite the fact that Daria's
death had been ruled a drowning, despite the fact she
blamed Daria for her predicament, Amelia feared she
had killed her own sister. And no one—not even Ben,
trial lawyer extraordinaire—could ever defend that.

Although the sugarcane was planted in rich-looking,
mucky soil, they followed a twisting, narrow gravel path.
The song "Follow The Yellow Brick Road" ran through
Bree's mind as she walked behind Josh and Nikki into
their own land of Oz, hopefully one with no flying mon-
keys or wicked witches.

Bree felt curious but nervous. The leaves of the thick
cane rustled and rattled; the field seemed to sigh as if it
had a life of its own. As startled birds burst into the air,
Bree startled in turn. She scolded herself that she was
getting paranoid. Insects buzzed around her and she
swatted them away. When she was certain no one was
looking, she dribbled some of her drink, as delicious as
it was, on the ground.

She'd argued with Cole that she was certain the Austins would not harm her. If Josh had not been involved with Daria, there would be no problem with her visit, she told him. And if Josh *had* been involved, he'd try to keep a low profile. That certainly would include winning Bree over and not harming her. Daria's death had become her life insurance. But where were they leading her?

"Fear not," Nikki called over her shoulder, as if she'd read Bree's mind while they walked the path between towering, endless stalks of sharp-shaped leaves. "We just want to show you our private waterfront property."

"You're kidding. In here?"

"And since it's not polluted," Nikki said, taking a big swig of caipirinha, "King Cane cannot be blamed for hurting your sea grass hundreds of miles away."

"Was that King Cane or King Kong, my dear?" Josh asked, his cleverness sounding too forced. "This reminds me of the scene where the big ape comes out of the jungle—"

"You're not getting another one of these," Nikki said, taking yet another swallow of her own drink.

Suddenly, the green cane curtain ended in a big circle. Before them lay a large pond edged by reeds, with ibis wading for fish and cormorants spreading their wings to dry.

"This day is full of surprises," Bree admitted.

"You ain't seen nothing yet," Josh said. "This is the hundred-acre detention pond, which filters out the phosphorus and nitrogen from the farm's runoff before it even flows through the Glades to the gulf."

"Mandated by the ruinous Everglades Forever Act in '94," Nikki added. "As wonderful as it sounds, its purpose was to punish cane growers for giving Americans exactly what they wanted. Sugar—so they could all get obese! And, over here, our Shangri-la away from home."

Bree looked left where Nikki pointed and saw they'd erected a screened-in dome, large enough for a table and four chairs. A hammock hung inside, too. The cane field they'd just come through backed up tight against it, but on the other side was a great view of the pond. As they headed for it, a distant bell began to toll.

"Damn, I told Lindy to hold dinner," Nikki said, pouting. "Do you have your cell, Josh?"

"Nope. This wouldn't be paradise if I dragged contact with the outside world in here. Bree?"

"Sorry. I left mine in the house. I had no idea we were going anywhere but to the veranda for a drink."

"I'll jog back and tell her not to expect us for a half hour or so," Nikki said as Josh opened the screen door and she deposited the drink tray on the table. "It won't take me ten minutes, and I'm carrying that machete with me. I'll bring a cell phone back."

"No cells!" Josh called as she hurried away. "No emails, no interviews, no statements, no press releases!" His voice trailed off as his wife disappeared around the twelve-foot-high, green corner of cane.

"Sometimes," he said with a sigh, "I'd rather be raising cane here than on the campaign circuit."

His pun seemed as flat as his earlier stabs at humor. Of course, he was tired, Bree realized, and trying to be a good host. But, like Nikki's false-fronted house, was he covering up something?

"That reminds me," Bree said, as she took the wooden chair Josh indicated and he sank into the one next to her, "did Mark fly you here, too? Nikki and I could have waited for you."

"Yeah. He's back and forth a lot," he told her, rubbing his eyes with his thumb and index finger. "He has an apartment at Nikki's dad's house here, but he's on call to us 24-7 since I've been running." He looked over at her and forced a smile. "Like the Energizer Bunny, running, and running..."

"I'm sure the strain of being onstage all the time is grueling. Everyone watching, never any private time—except here with Nikki. You'd never get away alone with anyone but her or Mark."

He didn't answer but frowned out over the pond. Several red-beaked gallinules were fighting and others skimmed across the water's surface, half running, half flying, as if to cheer on their favorite. Bree wondered if this convenient time alone with Josh was just a gift from God—or orchestrated by the earthly deities who seemed to rule this cane kingdom. Either way, she was not going to let this ten minutes Nikki had mentioned go to waste.

"I'm sure it will be really emotional going back to our high school tomorrow, especially after Daria's loss," she said. "You two shared so many good times there—so many memories and, once upon a time, plans for the future."

"I hadn't thought of the event that way. It all seems a long time ago. I'm in and out of the place in an hour and a half, with a speech to the whole school, then a Q and A with the government classes. Mark got some newspaper coverage."

"I know I'd be thinking of Ted—picturing him there—if I went back. And then, of course, recalling all that came later between us."

Josh shifted in his seat and took another swig of his caipirinha. The cane close behind them rattled its leaves, the sound almost like distant clapping. Bree's hands tightened around her sweaty glass, resting on the arm of her chair.

"But now Ted's dead," she went on, "and Sam blames me. It's hard to have that on my head and heart. Sam acts as if I actually physically harmed Ted."

Josh sat up ramrod straight. "Bree, I know you're grieving for her—I am, too, of course. But obviously, my emotions weren't tied to her like yours, except—ah, you know…from the past."

The silver-tongued Josh was fumbling for words. Had she hit a nerve?

"The truth is, I really, really regret," he said as every nerve in her own body tensed, "that Sam Travers has been such a jerk to you over the years."

That wasn't where she'd wanted the conversation to go at all. How could she get him back on Daria without giving everything away?

"I can handle Sam, but—"

"He's only happy blowing things up lately, but that's what he's always done," Josh insisted, "personally and professionally. He wanted to control Ted's life from the moment Ted's mother walked out. I shouldn't have spoken up for him to get that Sarasota demolition job, but I thought you might like him out of your hair for a while."

"You arranged that job? As a favor to me?" Or, she thought, as a ploy to get Sam's backing for your senate run.

"Yes, and he mentioned he'd like to buy you out. I told him it had better be a fair price. Had you thought about that?"

"He asked. I said no. I'm surprised both you and Ben think you can try to push us into that, though."

"Who's us?" he said, ignoring her testy tone and veering off her chosen path again. "You're talking as if Daria's still with you."

She'd meant Manny, of course, but she saw another way to shake Josh up. "You know how identical twins are," she said, leaning on the arm of her chair to turn her whole body in his direction. She wanted to shriek at him, to demand to know if he'd had an affair with Daria and fathered her child, but then he'd surely clam up. And Nikki might be back soon. She had to do this quickly, quietly, but take a risk.

"How identical twins are?" he repeated her words, narrowing his eyes and staring her down. "Meaning what?"

"We always shared everything, no matter what we told others. We even knew what the other was thinking, feeling."

Lies, lies, she told herself. She'd learned that the hard way in the eight days Daria had been dead. But surely Josh didn't know that.

"You're not suggesting some sort of ESP with her, even now?" he asked, his usually assured voice gone almost breathy.

"I don't believe in ghosts, Josh, and yet I think someone could have harmed her. I believe she's at peace, but I can't let it rest."

She let her voice hang. She was starting to panic. Nikki would come back and she might not get Josh alone again, though she supposed his affair could be known to his wife. No, impossible. Not the way they carried on together.

She tried the only other tack she could think of. "Josh, did you consider that the autopsy might show more than just cause of death? Daria was pregnant—and I can't help but wonder if that could have, in a way, been the cause of her death. Not that the pregnancy went wrong, but that someone wanted to hush it up. I know you and Ben were trying to keep some things under wraps. I was going to mention it to you and Nikki later, but—"

He looked angry, but also puzzled. "Who was she seeing?" he asked.

"I don't know. Do you?"

"Are you crazy? You think it was me?"

"It was someone she felt she couldn't tell me about, for some reason."

"But you just said you shared everyth—"

"I know what I said."

"Are you trying to set me up? You *do* think she was seeing me! Well, she wasn't. And I don't need you mentioning that Daria was pregnant to Nikki. She's had two miscarriages, and I don't want her suspicions running wild when there is no basis in fact. Bree, damn it, I trust you, and I expect you to do the same. I am not the father of Daria's child. Hell, I'm not the father of any living child! And my only part in getting the autopsy results was trying to speed things up so you wouldn't have to suffer longer than you were."

That was the thing about golden boy Josh Austin—he always had the right answers, Bree told herself as she apologized to him and said she'd been grasping at straws. "I only know how much she loved you once," she said, looking out over the lake. "I had to know."

"Now you do. I repeat, I'm trusting you to be fair about this and not spread any sort of ugly rumor that would tarnish my reputation or Daria's memory."

Or your marriage or campaign, she thought. His voice

had wavered, perhaps because she'd surprised and upset him. Before she'd discovered Daria had lied to her, she supposed she would have given Josh the benefit of the doubt, but now she wasn't sure. Did she really think he would have admitted an affair to her when that fact could ruin his marriage, his financial backing and tie him to a possible murder?

Then again, she had to admit, there was no murder investigation but in her own heart and mind. Ben passed it off as untenable; Josh hadn't made that leap when he denied the affair. Only Cole seemed to be in her corner, and he always played devil's advocate.

"I'm baa-ack," Nikki called, and Bree saw she had Mark with her. "Guess who I found, hoping for a hand-out at dinner?"

Josh didn't look any too pleased to have his aide here, but then, Mark Denton was the ultimate symbol of the campaign Josh had come here to escape, even if for a few moments.

As the sun sank and the tall cane cast long shadows across the pond, everyone chatted amiably, though she could tell Josh was seething. She knew she should regret that she'd abused her host and longtime friend with her fishing expedition, but she didn't. If she'd been careless or headstrong, too bad, because she was getting more desperate yet determined by the minute.

21

As soon as Mark Denton dropped her off at her apartment, Bree headed straight for Dom Verdugo's yacht to talk to Cole. It was just after noon, but she was exhausted. All night, she'd dreamed of Josh swinging machetes and cutting off heads, of sharks swimming out of waves of tall green sugarcane to devour her.

Did those crazy dreams mean something? Should she heed them and, despite the fact the Austins were criss-crossing the state campaigning, try to keep an eye on them? Cole was doing the same thing with Dom Verdugo, and she'd have to watch what she said on his casino yacht, too.

The huge banner draped across the side of the boat read You Can Bet On It! Bree shook her head. There didn't seem to be much she'd be willing to bet on lately. She felt she was fighting the riptide again. Every time she thought she could get closer to answers, she was hit with another powerful pull of water trying to yank her under. And, in her worst nightmares, Daria still floated within the windows of the wheelhouse as if she were trying to escape from a glass coffin.

Bree was met at the bottom of the gangway by a young man with such bulky shoulders that he seemed to have no neck. Cole had said there were a couple of men here who, physically, at least, could be candidates for her attacker at the Gator Watering Hole. Her assailant had had a T-shirt mask covering his neck, but this man's build and height fit. Before she could open her mouth to tell him who she was and that she was here to see Cole, he said, "Ms. Devon, right? Mr. DeRoca said you might stop by. Right this way."

She followed him to an entry amidships. It was a beautiful craft with inlaid teak and mahogany, polished rails, gleaming brass fittings, and velvet drapes covering windows. She could hear music floating from somewhere aft and pounding, probably Cole's, just ahead.

"Have you worked for Mr. Verdugo long?" she asked, wanting to hear this man's voice again. She'd like to put him in a lineup, along with Ric, with black T-shirts wrapped around their lower faces and wrenches in their hands and have them all repeat the single word *babe*.

"Not long, ma'am."

"Are you part of the crew?"

"Bouncer in the casino, once things get going."

"Do you think the gambling vote will go your way?"

"Never put anything past Mr. Verdugo."

He led her into a spacious area with several so-called one-armed bandits sitting in the middle of the floor, crowding crap tables and roulette wheels so that Cole could work on the walls. She didn't see him until he rose to his feet across the cluttered room and their eyes met. As ever, clear down to the pit of her belly, she felt the jolt of his stare, the sensual impact of just being near him.

"See, you're a lucky man without even gambling, Mr. DeRoca," her escort called to Cole and left them alone.

She ran right into his arms. Lifting her off her feet, he held her tight and kissed her hard. They seemed to breathe in unison, both suddenly out of breath. Cole's body felt as hard as the wood he crafted with his callused hands, which skimmed her back and cupped her bottom.

"Mmm," he said finally, "I'm getting sawdust all over you."

"I don't mind."

"Yeah, but a little more of that and you'll be a walking giveaway of what happened in here, with sawdust all over your backside."

She felt herself blush hot. This was crazy. She was hardly a teenager like Lucinda, and when she had been, she'd never felt like this.

"Besides," he added, whispering now, "this place may have eyes and ears, for all I know, so save anything privileged for when we go to lunch. Let me wash my hands, and I'll get out of here for a while."

But the moment he returned, another man appeared with a quick knock on the door frame. "Mr. Verdugo told me that when the banging stopped—" Bree bit her lower lip and flushed again "—to tell you two that lobster salad and wine is waiting for you on the stern deck."

Bree was both touched and annoyed. She wanted to get away with Cole, to tell him things about her trip across the state that she'd been afraid to say over the phone, in case Josh could eavesdrop somehow. For one moment, she sensed Cole tense up and thought he was going to refuse the offer, but she was wrong.

"That's really nice of him," Cole told the man, who was also rather muscle-bound and the right height for her attacker. "I need to keep my nose to the grindstone here to meet the deadline for the party cruise anyway. Tell him thanks."

At least, Bree saw when they walked out onto the open deck, the table was set for only two. It was as beautifully arranged as everything in cane country had been, and spoke equally of money and power.

Cole signaled her to keep quiet, then picked up his plate and wine, motioning for her to do the same. They carried them off the boat onto the dock, down to the wooden stairs meant for boarding smaller boats without gangways. They put their food down and took off their shoes as she filled him in on Josh's denial he had anything to do with Daria's pregnancy. Dangling their feet in the water, they had their private, impromptu picnic.

"That *was* a nice table for two," she admitted as they kept an eye on the boat.

"For all I know," Cole told her through a big bite of lobster salad, "the table was bugged."

"We're both getting paranoid."

"Just careful."

"But we're eating Verdugo's food, drinking his wine."

"He's not going to poison anything except the gulf and people he hooks on gambling. He thinks he can buy anything. Tomorrow night he's invited the powers-that-be in the area—us, too, if we want to go—for a cruise party. If he could pay for individual pro-gambling votes, he would."

"How is your paneling deadline going, then?"

"I've had two holes in wood that I thought were just knots, but they weakened the entire plank as if I'd exploded a piece right out of it. I'll have to complain to my supplier."

"That reminds me, another thing Josh told me is that he's the one who got Sam the job blowing up the bridge in Sarasota."

Bree thought again of how the newspaper headline had described her report to the Clear the Gulf Commission: Bombshell. Her eyes lifted at the sound of a commotion down the dock, and Cole turned toward it, too. Two young men in an old rowboat had somehow hit into the end of the dock and staved a hole in their hull. They were cursing, laughing and bailing madly.

"Need some help?" Cole called to them.

"No, we're okay!" one called back, still laughing.

Bree gasped. "That's it."

"That's what?"

"I know the police said they thought they'd found the place where *Mermaids II* scraped the concrete breakwater and sank, but the newspaper also said someone on the shore near Marco Pass thought they heard a bang. Of course, that could have been the dive boat hitting the wall during the thunderstorm. We saw that the stern had been broken."

"Yes. So?"

"I guess, in that storm, the stern could be heading in first. But what if a detonator cap was set to go off and that's why she—the boat and Daria—went down there? We should have looked more carefully, and so should the police. Once we found Daria, no one looked further at that piece of the stern to see if it was broken or blown in."

"And if explosives were involved, that would mean Sam Travers is, too?"

"Yes, or one of his men. I told you Ric could have easily gotten into my apartment with his ladder, then worn his diving and painting gloves so he didn't leave prints."

"So that Gator Watering Hole coaster could lead to him. But that's a stretch to tie him to being the father of her baby."

"I don't know. I just know that I have to dive Marco Pass again to look at that boat. If it hadn't been so tricky there, the police or someone could have salvaged it and then they would have seen what happened. Maybe Sam or Ric were banking on the fact they wouldn't bring the boat up."

"But Sam and Ric helped in the search when she first went missing."

"Searching where the boat wasn't until we asked for help at Marco and they had no choice."

"Bree, I dived with you twice when I didn't think it was wise, but—"

"If we can show an explosion happened on board, we can get the police involved."

"But there have been explosions from time to time on board boats for normal reasons, accidents. Someone poured in too much gas trying to start the motor, someone just—"

"I know! But I still don't think this was an accident!"

"Keep your voice down," he said, looking back toward Verdugo's yacht. "If we do dive there again, we should take some other divers, but hardly the two we took before."

"No other divers, just a lot of light power so we can see down there. We need to do this alone. If I'm wrong, we don't need someone else talking about it. If I'm right…"

"When would we dive?"

"Because of the low vis, we could dive after dark and

see just as far. And there would be less boat traffic. We could even dive from the seawall and not from the boat."

"Not take Manny?"

"I'd feel better if he drove us to the seawall. He could keep an eye on things while we dive."

"Okay. Let me get a few hours of work done, then I'll get my gear and meet you at Mermaids about six. I hate to say it, but the possibility of an explosion makes sense. The wind and thunder could have mostly covered up the sound. Give me your plate and goblet and you get going. I'm going to go find Verdugo to thank him. That way I have an excuse for sneaking up on him. I've managed to case most of the vessel that way, at least above the main deck."

"Be careful. See you at six," she whispered.

When Bree got back to her shop, she let herself in. Manny was out on a job, repairing a speedboat engine. She hadn't even unpacked. She had a lot to do, so she headed toward the stairs.

The front doorbell rang. She peered out and saw Manny's daughter and a tall, blond boy. Bree unlocked and opened the door.

"I know Dad's not here," Lucinda blurted. "This is my friend, Luke, and I wanted you to meet him. It's teacher conference day at school so we got off."

"Come on in," Bree said, though the last thing in the world she wanted right now was small talk with kids, when she had so much to get ready for their night dive. "Luke, it's nice to meet a friend of Cindi's," she added, shaking his hand.

"A good friend," she prompted, rolling her eyes behind Luke's back, as if Bree didn't get that this was the "friend's boyfriend" she'd talked about earlier.

"Sorry about your sister and all," Luke said. "Losing her like that really bites."

"Thank you, Luke. It sure does."

He was a head taller than Cindi and quite a contrast to her dark, cute looks. Thin, almost Nordic looking, a bit gawky and very serious. What would their kids look like? Bree wondered, before she caught herself and came back to facts. Manny would have a raving fit if he found these two here and knew Bree had invited them in. But, if she could control Manny, what would she want him to do in this situation? Definitely build bridges for these two, not blow them up.

Hoping Cindi didn't hate her for this, Bree said, "I'm sure looking forward to Cindi's *quinceañera* party. What a wonderful tradition, like a great foreign import. But it's also cutting-edge American these days. It's kind of neat to be setting new styles, don't you think?" she asked Luke.

"Oh, yeah, sure. I mean, I didn't think of it like that."

"My sister and I were asked to be some of the patrons for Cindi's big party, so I have a stake in everyone having a great time. You will be there, won't you? I know Cindi's looking forward to dancing with you. Cindi, if you want to ask some of your school friends over to learn some of the special dances, I'm sure your dad and I can clear out some of the back room for a practice area. We'll call it a combination of *High School Musical* and *Dancing With the Stars*."

Cindi managed to smile and nod, but she almost turned blue from holding her breath.

"If I have time—and that's only if," Bree added, up-ping the ante when Luke simply stared at her, "I can give four or five of you a scuba lesson or two after practice." She was on a roll now, afraid to give the boy too much time to react or reject things.

"Luke," she plunged on, "the food will be fantastic with neat, new things to try, and Cindi will look like a fairy princess. It's better and bigger than any prom, you'll see."

"Well—yeah," Luke managed, looking as if he'd been hit by a tidal wave. "I'm cool with that."

Bree chatted them up some more, got them soft drinks, showed Luke Manny's desk, talked about him being a partner and his realm of motors and engines, which obviously intrigued the boy. She promised Manny would show him around the back room next time and got them out the front door just before Manny came back. With a sigh of relief for Cindi, if not for herself, Bree took that as a sign the rest of the day would go well.

But she didn't push her luck. Before she sat Manny down to tell him about Cindi and Luke's visit, she got him to promise he'd drive her and Cole to Marco later. She supposed she did make it sound a bit as if Cindi had come to introduce Luke to him. Now it was up to his Lucinda to play her part well at home.

Bree tried to take a nap but couldn't. She ended up pacing and looking at the clock. Three hours yet before she would meet Cole here for their dark-water dive.

She told herself that she had to get back to work on Monday. Clients understood a period of mourning, but her recent publicity had interested new clients. She had to get this place back on its feet. Back on its feet…she was dead on hers, yet she couldn't rest until she had answers. Manny had gone out on an emergency call, but her entire life seemed like an emergency since Daria had died.

The words—the reality—still staggered her. Daria... was...dead.

She leaned her shoulder against the double doors of the veranda and looked out over the harbor. Through the bare-boned forest of the masts and spars of moored sailboats, she could see the roof of Travers and Son Search and Salvage Shop. She'd love to look around in there, now that he and his staff were away. Had they taken that guy at the front desk, or was he still there to oversee things?

No matter, because she knew the back way to the upstairs, even where a key was hidden, if it was still in the same place after all these years. Since Sam seemed unwilling to change things, she'd bet it was. Sam, she was sure, had sent Ric to pilfer Daria's room, or else Ric had done it on his own. Turnabout was fair play. Besides, Sam didn't live there anymore, so she would only be trespassing in his shop—his shrine—not in his home.

Feeling bold, she locked up and walked the waterfront of Turtle Bay, just as she'd done yesterday with Manny in tow. This time she didn't even approach the front of the shop. Instead, she walked between the main building and the big boat-storage shed, as she and Ted had done years ago. A tall, wooden pole with a four-foot flat deck for an osprey nest, a nest rejected by the birds for years because it no longer had a clear view of the water, still stood there. Partway up the pole, in a chink, was a key to the third-floor attic entrance. The key had to be reached by climbing the outside stairs, which she did.

Yes. Sam really should have changed some things,

taken down the *and Son* sign, moved this key. He should have admitted Ted's own decisions had put him in danger's way and have gone on with his life without hatred and revenge eating at him.

But as she leaned over the railing to reach for the key, she felt weak kneed. Could she go on without Daria? Admitting she was dead had been hell. And could she break and enter?

No, she told herself, she wasn't breaking in at all. She had a key, and it fitted quietly and perfectly in the keyhole. She had to do this.

The door creaked. Bree froze, but evidently no one heard her. These rooms were quite a climb from the office downstairs, even if Sam's employee was manning the desk there. She tiptoed in and closed the door behind her. The window slats were slightly open, casting thin bars of light across the floor. She jammed her finger under her nose to keep from sneezing. If Sam wanted to keep this intact, didn't he ever clean it?

This was the room that had once been Ted's, at least for several years after his mother left. Now it was a small museum, a long closed-up tomb. It reminded her of photos she'd seen of King Tut's tomb, the Egyptian boy king who had so many jumbled relics buried with him to take into the afterlife. Everything here was coated, not with centuries of desert sand, but with years of harbor dust.

Her wide eyes took in Ted's bed, desk and a chair with a pair of jeans thrown on it. An unlaced pair of dirty Keds. His catcher's mitt, tickets to Disney World, some favorite T-shirts tacked to boards—yes, she remembered that one from the Collier County Fair. Two big posters, one of them autographed, of football players from the Miami Dolphins. And everywhere, photos, photos, photos, ones Sam must have added.

She looked closer. In the early pictures of Ted, someone had been carefully cut out. His mother, of course. Bree hadn't known her, but she didn't think much of a woman who would leave her son, even if she did desert Sam Travers.

Awed, Bree looked further, past an array of Boy Scout badges, a lineup of bowling and Little League trophies. Then, tacked on a bulletin board, she saw some pictures she recalled. Like Sam's wife, Bree had been cut out of each one. She felt sick to her stomach.

Bree pressed her hands over her mouth, scratching her cheek with the key she still held in her hand. Did she now hold the key to who had killed Daria, either to make her suffer Daria's loss or because he thought he was killing Bree? He'd admitted yesterday they looked so much alike. But then why had Sam offered to buy her out? Why had he offered his barge to help search for Daria? It wasn't that he wanted to be there to see her pain, because he didn't arrive at the barge the day they had found Daria until they had discovered her body. Some things seemed to fit, but other facts didn't.

Ted's old stereo set was here, with its big boom box speakers. But it remained a boy's room. There was nothing of his days as a marine, nothing of his death—until she went into the next room, that had once been Sam's.

Bree gasped and jerked so hard she hit her knee on a chair. A life-size mannequin was arrayed in full marine gear, Ted's dress uniform, beret to boots. Its limbs had been bent into a near salute.

And on the opposite wall, a flag she recalled Ted had brought home with him just before he'd gone to Iraq.

Semper Fi, it read, then in Ted's handwriting under it, *Always Faithful.*

Bree sucked in another big breath as she caught sight of something in the dull, dusty mirror behind her. She swung around. It was a picture of her and Daria. Written across Bree's face, in Sam's writing, was *Never Faithful.*

She started to cry. She couldn't help it. Sam hated her that much. Whether he felt she had deserted Ted, as his wife had deserted him, didn't even matter now. He'd been eaten up by revenge.

Sam had wanted to make Bree suffer, and he'd succeeded. He must have killed her sister, either by design or mistake. There was no reason to search this room for some other kind of proof. The room itself was proof enough. Somehow, she was certain she'd find that one of Sam's detonator caps had blown a hole in the very heart of *Mermaids II*—and her own heart. Did he think the bomb would bring him justice for the bomb that had killed Ted?

But perhaps she could find what sort of detonator caps they used now, then match whatever they found diving to that. Sam used to keep his explosives separate from everything else that was in his big storage room downstairs. There had always been a room on the second floor she and Ted were not to enter, which Ted jokingly called the "boom room."

She tiptoed along the tiny attic hall past the bathroom and opened the door to the stairs. She could hear the muted voice of a man but couldn't tell what he was saying. So Sam's front office man was here. No problem, because she wasn't going onto the first floor and if he kept talking, she could tell exactly how distant he was.

The stairs to the second floor creaked, so she walked

down the edges of the cracked plastic treads. But she was only partway down when a voice came much closer than the other. She froze, pressing herself to the shadows on the wall as someone walked below into the very room she'd been going to enter.

Ric! It was Ric. Why wasn't he in Sarasota? Had Sam come back, too?

He was on his cell phone, talking to someone. Thank God he didn't glance up the flight of stairs when he walked past.

"Yeah, I'm on-site, getting more blasting caps and primacord. That bridge is one mean bastard, but these babies will work great if I just get them calibrated right."

He must be talking to Sam. They hadn't taken enough demolition material, and Ric had to come back for more.

"Yeah, a detonator, too, don't worry."

Should she go back upstairs or might he hear her? He was making some noise in there and, of course, his own voice or Sam's might cover any sound she made. Slowly, carefully, she started to go back up the stairs.

"Okay, see you later with everything you need. And remember that little raise you promised this time."

Sam could be bribing Ric for his silence on Daria's killing! Or for doing his dirty work, like trying to scare her away from solving Daria's death. If she testified to what she'd just overheard, would it be admissible in court? Probably not. But none of that mattered. She and Cole would find evidence underwater now, because they knew what to look for in the broken, blasted body of *Mermaids II*.

22

They dove at dusk. Boat traffic in the Marco Pass was lessening, though vessels went by from time to time with their running lights on, coming in from the gulf. The wind was gentle, the waves a light chop.

They'd walked half a block from where Manny had parked Bree's truck in a visitors' spot at a large, beach-side condo community. He seemed more nervous than Bree and Cole as he rolled their tanks and gear along in a two-wheeled shopping cart.

They would each take two battery-run dive lights down with them, tethered lightly to their wrists to be sure they didn't get dropped or float away in the murky dark. Bree carried the penetration line, which they would lay down as they went in so they could follow it out. A pen line made for slower swimming, but they could surface where Manny was waiting and not make the mistake of ascending in the channel.

They had all been quiet, but Bree spoke as they neared the concrete seawall. "I still consider *Mermaids II* my property, and I intend to try to bring up any evidence of explosives we can find, so I've brought two lift bags."

"You should have called your brother-in-law to check whether that would be tampering with evidence," Cole said, "especially if we can get the police to open this as a murder case."

"And let him know we're doing this? I've had enough of his lectures and taking over things he had no right to control. He should take care of Amelia, not worry about me."

"But I can tell Amelia worries about you. She wants the two of you to be closer."

"I know. I think we can be, but right now, I've got to do this. I used to think that Daria couldn't rest in peace until I could prove who hurt her, but I'm the one who can't rest until this is over."

"I checked the fill in these tanks two times," Manny told them, as he helped them gear up. "You should dive at dawn," he muttered, half to himself. "Not many boats then neither."

"By dawn," Bree told him as she tightened the straps on her weight belt, "I hope to be knocking on the door of the Naples Police Department with proof of a murder."

They eased into the night-dark water side by side, tethered to each other's weight belts by a ten-foot rope. That was the only separation they would allow themselves, they had vowed as they'd kissed for good luck. But now there was no more talking, only the sound of bubbles and the hiss of their breathing. They had not even brought slates to write on. Hand signals and a common purpose—and having been here before—that's what they were relying on.

Yet as they descended, Bree found the low vis suffocating, as if the solid walls of a coffin were closing in on them. Still, her eyesight was acute; the dive lights worked well, giving them about a four-feet radius of sight, and they both had compass watches to take them approximately to the spot where the dive boat lay. The day they'd stumbled on Daria and *Mermaids II,* neither of them had thought to take a compass reading.

This time they located the main body of the ship before the stern, which had been—Bree was sure now—blasted out. How strange it must have been for Ric to see what their explosives had done that day he'd helped to recover Daria's body. If she'd not been so distraught, Bree could have noted how they reacted. Cole had only spoken to them before the dive, while they were cleaning and loading their spearguns.

From the dark depths loomed the majority of the sunken boat, as if it were a ghost ship sailing straight toward them. But that was just a trick of the swift current, lit by their lights. They peered into the wheelhouse where they'd found Daria's body.

It struck Bree that the glass was still intact. Wouldn't a blast have shattered the windows? No, Sam or Ric would know to use whatever strength it took to blow a hole in the hull without creating debris that would float in as evidence. More than one person had told her Sam Travis was skilled at sinking an old boat or a bridge and leaving everything else around it amazingly intact.

Bree heard a boat's slow motor whisper past in the channel overhead. Her hearing was still sensitive from the lightning strike.

As they started away from the wheelhouse, her light caught something, and she turned back. Cole felt the tug on their rope and came back. It was only a grouper hovering near the wheelhouse, one that looked to be the size of their old pet Gertie from the Trade Wreck. She'd like to think that Gertie had come here to keep watch over the place Daria had died.

They swam lower, right along the bottom, still laying the pen line toward where they were certain they had spotted the piece of the boat before.

Yes! There it was! The grayish glint of metal, the curved aluminum handrail that pointed toward the broken stern. Bree was confident that piece of white metal should show up in their lights. But where was it? Could the shifting sand and silt here have buried it already?

Bree motioned to Cole that she was sure it must be here. He nodded and started to brush the bottom away with both hands. Ordinarily, that would lessen visibility, but it hardly mattered where they could only see four feet anyway.

Then, there it was, the piece of *Mermaids II* that had borne its name and now read, *MA D I*. They quickly uncovered more to see if the edges were jagged or pierced.

Yes! Something from outside the hull on the stern had blown the metal inward into a gaping hole the size of a watermelon. The first time she'd seen this, that section had been under sand and silt. She supposed, even if the police took a look at this, they could insist it was caused by a collision with the concrete seawall. No, surely they could tell it had been caused by what she'd overheard Ric call a blasting cap.

Chills raced through her. She blinked back tears to avoid fogging her mask. Somehow this hole had been made below the waterline. Perhaps the perpetrator had placed the device on their boat while it was docked, hoping the small, attached bomb would not be seen. Or perhaps the bomb had been placed when the boat was at sea by someone under the surface. Was another diver in the water besides her that day? Or had the explosive been attached after the boat either drifted or was towed away? If it was towed, why didn't Bree hear the motor or the craft doing the towing?

She looked at Cole, who nodded. He understood! Answers at last. Evidence which would lead straight to Sam Travers and his men. It all fit now, but first they had to retrieve this big piece of metal, get it up to the surface. It was so heavy that she might need both lift bags. Then she had to hope it didn't surface where a boat was going through the pass—

A barbed shaft from a speargun zinged off the metal inches from her hand. Cole's big body jerked; he pushed her away, yanking their tether taut. As he turned to follow, another stainless-steel spear raced past them in a blur of bubbles.

They'd been followed. By the killer? Now she knew who and why.

They could see no one, but someone could see them. Or were there two shooters down here, both Ric and Lance? Maybe the strong currents warped the speargun's trajectory.

They turned off the dive lights that made them targets. Utter blackness closed in like a trap. Keeping the ten-foot rope between them taut, Bree kept shifting her position. She was certain Cole was doing that, too, however much he kept putting slack in their tether.

Bree's breathing, her clicking regulator, her heartbeat and pounding pulse were like drums beating in her head. She couldn't so much as see her own bubbles now, let alone Cole.

Suddenly, someone gripped her upper arm and pushed her up, up. *Cole.* It must be Cole. Yes, they had to surface, then wait to see who else came up. But she hated to leave this evidence down here. It might disappear like her sea grass meadow. She reached down to touch the metal piece from her lost boat again before Cole yanked her away.

For one moment, she feared it wasn't Cole, but if she couldn't see him, she could sense him. To her surprise, he forced her fingers below his mask. His regulator and mouthpiece were gone, and air gushed out of his torn hose in a blast of bubbles.

A spear must have cut through his breathing gear. She took a big breath, then pulled her mouthpiece out and pressed it toward his lips. He pulled her closer as he evidently took a breath. They could buddy breathe, but that was difficult under the best of circumstances. They'd have to ascend fast. At least they weren't so far down that they'd get the bends. Two reasons now to get out fast.

But as Cole thrust her mouthpiece back at her, a big light blinded them. Now that their lights didn't make them targets, their attacker needed his.

Cole shoved her one way and went the other as a spear slashed between them. Their tether pulled loose or broke, or had Cole cut it? Someone came at her—not Cole—as she started away, struggling to get her bubbling mouthpiece back in her mouth.

Up. Up! *When in doubt, get out,* but there was no doubt about this.

The man grabbed at her, got a fin. She kicked at him, hit her ankle on his dive light, so it went off. Was she down here alone with the enemy? Cole was out of air, out of time.

Bree jackknifed and kicked the man with both feet,

hitting him in the chest. She dumped her weight belt and kicked hard, clawing at the water, fighting for the surface. She came up closer to the gulf than she wanted, but not more than twenty yards from where Manny must be.

Cole. Where was Cole?

She spun around. Nothing. Without a light, how could she go back down? She had no idea where he could be now.

In a whoosh of white water, Cole surfaced, sucking in air.

She spit out her mouthpiece. "Cole! Here!"

"Get out! I lost him!"

Yes, Bree thought as they both swam toward the seawall and Manny came running toward them, but the killer had lost them, too.

Manny grabbed under her armpits and helped pull her out. She was gasping like a beached fish, but she tried to explain what had happened to him. "A diver down there—shot at us—speargun. Hit Cole's hose. Tried to buddy breathe, had to surface but—found a hole blasted in the hull—below waterline."

Still sucking in huge breaths, Cole climbed out beside her, then staggered to his feet and stood to look out over the inky stretch of water. Bree scanned it, too. Nothing. No boats, no diver surfacing—nothing.

"I can't even spot bubbles in this dark," Cole muttered.

"It's got to be the same guy who attacked me at the Gator Watering Hole. And the same one who blows holes in boats and bridges for Sam. At last, we know Daria's killer! I wonder if Ric could be the father of her child."

Bree heard Manny grunt then swear under his breath.

In all the chaos, she should have told her new partner about that, but now it would have to wait until later.

"Manny," she said, noticing his bare feet and the pool of water where he stood, which could not have come from her or Cole, "you're soaking wet."

"Fell in," he said, his voice gruff. "*Caramba,* I think we all got in over our heads."

Here came Bree, down the stairs. Manny had been expecting her.

After she had fed both men, Cole had fallen asleep on the sofa, where Manny heard him say he was going to spend another night. At first light, Bree and Cole were going to call the police to see who they could go talk to about retrieving the piece of bomb-blasted metal—if it was still there, Bree had said. They'd waited over an hour, pacing up and down the seawall, but no one had surfaced and they saw no boat nearby from which someone could have dived.

Manny insisted on eating at his desk downstairs while he got ready to close up and go home late. He'd called Juanita to tell her not to worry. She'd said that Lucinda wanted to bring her friend Luke over to meet them on Sunday and he was to keep his temper and be kind to the boy.

"What did you mean earlier by 'we *all* got in over our heads'?" Bree asked him bluntly.

He'd been sitting at his desk, chin on his hands, staring into space. He guessed if Bree could turn Lucinda around, even a little, he owed her some of the truth, at least.

"And I'm sorry," she said, sitting on the corner of

the desk so she seemed to loom over him, "that I didn't tell you earlier that I'd found out Daria was pregnant."

He cleared his throat. "I knew that."

She gasped. "Since when? Who told you?"

"Not sure when. A month at least. Daria told me— more or less."

Bree looked as if someone had slammed her in the gut.

"Overheard her take the call. From her doctor," he went on. "She stepped into the back room 'cause you were at your desk, I guess. She didn't know I was there, working on my knees on some stuff. *You're sure? You're sure I'm pregnant?* I hear her say."

"But she never knew that you had overheard her secret." Bree said that like a statement, not a question.

He sighed and shifted on his chair, suddenly aware it had been Daria's. "Nah, dropped a wrench."

"So you said you'd keep her secret. Did you ask who the father was?"

"She just tell me it very complicated. Yeah, that's the word she used."

Bree's hands slapped her thighs. "Damn it! Why didn't you tell me earlier, when she was missing, at least?"

He shrugged. "Honoring the dead, her last wish to me, in a way. If she was gone, nothing can be done about the baby."

Bree jumped up and started to pace with her arms folded over her chest. Thank the blessed Virgin, he thought. She'd assumed he'd simply volunteered to keep Daria's secret. Truth was, he'd suggested to her that he'd keep quiet if she'd turn more and more of the running of the business over to him during her pregnancy. She'd told him she was having and keeping the baby. He admired her for that, but he'd still blackmailed her, in a way. He hadn't asked for money, but she'd offered it. As ashamed of himself as he was now, he'd taken it, a couple of hundred dollars, which he was pretty sure she got from her lover. But if Bree learned all that, she just might find a way to kick him out of here.

Cole sat on Bree's veranda drinking coffee the next morning as she made the call to the police. He could catch occasional things she said, her voice impassioned.

That's how he'd felt about her from the beginning, impassioned. Had it only been ten days since he'd found his mermaid washed in on the stormy shore? He felt as if he'd known her—wanted her—for years. Since their mutual drive to find what had happened to Daria might be over now, would she need him less?

He did not feel the relief she did. Yeah, everything pointed toward Sam and Ric, and Cole was glad the investigation would soon be in official hands. He still didn't trust Verdugo, but maybe that was because he hated what he stood for, escape from reality and easy money through gambling. It had ruined his mother's life, his dad's and his, leaving a legacy of only loss.

He frowned in the direction of Verdugo's yacht, where he was going to finish the paneling today so the place would look good for the shakedown cruise—the PR party, as he'd heard Verdugo call it. Cole agonized that he had sold out to Verdugo. He'd only wanted to help Bree by keeping an eye on the man, and the paneling deal had fallen into his lap as the perfect way to do that. But he still longed to chuck it all and start up a boat-building business of his own.

He'd agreed to go out on the casino boat tonight, but only so he could search an off-limits storage area he'd noted below decks yesterday while Verdugo was distracted by his guests. Now, he was also looking for diving gear and spearguns. The police could focus on Sam Travers and his divers, but Cole could not shake the gut feeling that Verdugo was dirty, too.

Bree came out and sat across the little table from him. She was almost smiling. That tilted the corners of her gray-green eyes and made her look less exhausted.

"Finally," she said, and sighed so hard her shoulders rose and fell.

"They're going to open the case?"

"A Lieutenant Mike Crawford is going to get a search warrant for Sam's house and shop and put in a request that the police dive team retrieve the stern piece from *Mermaids II* in Marco Pass. I told them I hoped it was still there, because of what happened with my sea grass report to the commission. I said I'd dive with them, but they said absolutely not, that my description of the layout would be enough. And that they would interview both of us at length tomorrow morning."

"Great!" he said, reaching over to clasp her bare knee. "I hope that now you can relax a bit."

"For the first time, I admit I feel totally wiped out. I couldn't let up before, not until we found Daria, buried her, then found her killer."

"But if it *is* Sam or his divers, the question remains whether he meant to kill you."

"If that was his plan, he could have done it several years ago, probably closer to when Ted died."

"Maybe it took time for him to get to the point where he'd risk it, time to lay plans."

"Maybe time to realize he'd get more vengeance not by eliminating me but Daria. I believe he wanted me to suffer for her loss as he had suffered with Ted's. Then, when Daria and I dared to open a business that was competition to him, even though he could almost buy and sell us—and tried to—he just bided his time until he could make it look as if Daria had an accident. Maybe he came upon her in the storm and took his chance, maybe he stalked her. I don't know, but I hope the police can get it out of him."

In a way, he wanted her to go with him on the casino boat tonight, but he wanted to be alone when he searched the storage room he'd seen Verdugo's men go in and out of.

"Verdugo said I can bring you tonight," Cole reminded her, "but I thought you might want to just crash—sorry I put it that way. Are you okay with being alone?"

"I've already decided not to go. Don't worry, Manny's coming over to play bodyguard, since we have a lot to discuss about our new partnership. And," she said, sounding lighthearted for once, "I'll wait up for you, and you can tell me all about it. Besides, Lieutenant Crawford promised to call me here with an update this evening."

"I like the sound of that, not just the police being on the case, but you waiting up for me."

He pulled her closer and kissed her, lingeringly at first, then intensely. Her lips opened; a jolt of desire nearly shot him off his chair. Her fingers moved across his temple and through his hair, stroking it. He felt swept away, as if he was sailing full blast, skimming over the water to parts unknown but deeply desired.

When they finally broke the kiss, with her mouth moving along his cheek, she said, "I realize I've said this before, but I don't know what I would have done without you through all this. Take care of yourself tonight. We might have survived by being in your boat when the sharks were in the water, but I'm afraid on that yacht, you'll actually have some sharks on board with you."

23

Manny was late. He'd called to say he'd had a flat tire on Golden Gate and had spun off onto the berm. Bree realized she was still suffering from the residual effects of paranoia. She should have asked him if he was all right, but instead she blurted, "You're sure it was just a flat? No one's tampered with the truck?"

"I know tires like I know motors. Be there as quick as I can."

"Make sure you're far enough off the road so no one hits you."

"Yes, boss."

"'Yes, partner,' will do," she said as she punched off on her cell. She was hoping to use tonight to patch things up with Manny and set out some mutual rules for working together, because they had to get the business back on its feet. She was pretty sure a lot of Manny's problems with his daughter and with her and Daria had been that he was from a culture—and a gender—that didn't like taking orders from women. They'd have to really talk that one out, or else their partnership would never work.

Bree decided to call Amelia to update her on Lieutenant Crawford taking Daria's suspicious death case, but knowing Ben, he was probably already up on the latest developments. For all she knew, the judge who signed the search warrant had reported right in to him. But the voice who answered the phone was not Amelia's.

"I'm Mrs. Westcott's sister," Bree said. "This is the Westcott residence, isn't it?"

"Oh, yes. This is the babysitter, Johanna. I thought it might be my mom."

"Please tell Mrs. Westcott I called and I'll phone again tomorrow."

"No problem. They went out on a big boat at the Turtle Bay Marina tonight. The boys are being really good," the girl added, as if she had to give Bree the parent report.

"Tell them 'hi' from their aunt Bree, and that I'll see them soon."

She should have known, she thought as she put her cell on the table, that the A-list of movers and shakers around here would include Ben Westcott. She was glad Amelia was well enough to go. Patching up things with Manny was one thing, but Bree knew she had a long way to go with Amelia. She hoped she could help her believe that she was loved and had always been loved. She hoped they could help each other.

As much as she was finally starting to relax, Bree jumped when the downstairs doorbell rang. Maybe Lieutenant Crawford had stopped by in person. Deciding not to turn on the inside office lights until she saw who it was, she hurried downstairs.

It was Nikki Austin, dressed to kill, as usual. Mark stood behind her, looking pretty natty, too, leaning against the car as if the part he would play tonight was chauffeur. Snapping on the main office light, Bree unlocked and opened the door.

"Wow," she said, admiring Nikki's jade-green, strapless, silk cocktail dress. "You look fabulous."

"We're going to meet Josh on board the casino boat for the big show-and-tell party, where Verdugo *shows* the powers-that-be how he's lily-white in the pollution department and *tells* us to get the voters to see things his way. Marla Sherborne's attending, too."

Bree almost told them Ben and Amelia would be there, but she decided to stick with Verdugo. "At least you're on to the casino king," Bree said. "Cole will be there, but, as you can see," she added, gesturing at her shorts and T-shirt, "I'm staying put."

She considered telling them about the police taking the case, but she decided she'd wait on that, too. It still was possible that Josh, not Ric, was the father of Daria's baby. Then again, Daria could have met Ric on a diving job and not told Bree about their developing relationship because he worked for Sam. Even in their brief encounter, Bree had seen how charming Ric could be.

Mark came closer behind Nikki. "We saw your lights and thought we could give you a lift over," he said.

"You know," Nikki added, pointing to her stiletto-heeled sandals, "no one can walk far in these things. We'll wait for you to change. Mark can drop us both off."

"Thanks, but I'm really not going. Enjoy yourselves."

Bree's office phone started ringing. She'd had it on speaker earlier and forgotten to take it off. It might be Cole, and she didn't want everyone to hear what he said.

"Excuse me a second," she said, but she didn't get to the phone in time. A man's voice—not Cole's—spoke. "Bree, Dave Mangold here. I'm so sorry to hear what happened with Daria and that I wasn't here to fly with the civil air patrol for the search."

It didn't matter if Nikki and Mark overheard this, Bree thought.

Dave's voice went on. "I've been to visit my daughter in Memphis and I didn't even learn Daria had been lost until I got back today. I got your messages on my phone here. I did see something strange when I was flying out that afternoon. Racing ahead of the storm, I saw a pontoon plane towing a boat that could have been your dive boat—not sure, but it was really weird. They were heading toward Marco Pass, I think…"

His message continued, saying he'd call back later. The reality of what he'd said hit Bree like a rogue wave out of the dark. A pontoon plane, no doubt the very one she'd been in. She'd heard no motor when she was underwater because an amphibious plane's motor was above the water.

The timing could not have been worse. Nikki and Mark had heard everything, so there was no faking her response with them. Her stomach went into free fall as she turned to stare at them, standing close to each other now, intimately so.

"Too bad we can't convince you to go to the party, then," Nikki said, her voice now solemn rather than solicitous. "The entire Clear the Gulf Commission will be there, I hear."

"My sister and her husband are going, so I'll get a blow-by-blow from them," Bree said, trying to find a way to brazen this out. "They're stopping by to say hi any minute now."

"Nice try," Mark said, aiming a small gun at her. "Nikki just talked to Josh on board and the Westcotts are already there, though he hadn't seen your watch-dog, Cole, yet."

Could Cole be coming back for her? How long would it take Manny to get here?

Bree's mind raced over possibilities. Were these two working with Josh or against him? She was furious with herself for not reading things right, for being sucked in by the Austins and their so-called bodyguard. And what was the real relationship between Nikki and Mark? Bree's voice came sharper than she intended; it didn't sound like her.

"Have you decided to stoop to using a gun now instead of your more bizarre weapons, like a wrench or speargun—or a detonator cap?" she asked Mark. "You've set Sam up to be a suspect in Daria's death, and with my help."

Mark's grimace was more of a grin. "We were still trying to just scare you off at the Gator Watering Hole," he said, his voice calm and controlled as he walked closer, hit the play button for Dave Mangold's message again, then deleted it. "By the way, the piece of blasted stern from your dive boat has gone the way of your sad sea grass meadow. The same way you're going to have to go now—bye-bye."

"Then after killing me, you'll merrily go sailing with everyone?" Bree challenged.

"You're way off base again," Nikki said as she pulled on a pair of white gloves and walked away to lock the front door. "Since you've missed the boat, so to speak, I'm afraid you're going to commit suicide by drowning yourself out by the Trade Wreck where you last saw Daria. And we're not going out on the casino yacht because in—" she glanced at the time on her cell phone

"—less than sixty minutes, an underwater explosive attached to the boat is going to take it and everyone on board to the bottom of the gulf."

"You mean Bree's not on board?" Amelia asked Cole. He'd been busy showing people his woodwork, especially after Dom Verdugo had pointed it out to everyone in his opening remarks. "I thought I'd get to spend some time with her."

"She's really anxious to do that, but she's exhausted," Cole told her, raising his voice to be heard above the buzz of conversations in the main salon.

The man certainly cleaned up well from the time he'd waited with her in the hospital, Amelia thought. He'd looked like a sea captain that night at their house, but he had stepped right out of the pages of *GQ* magazine tonight. If she were Bree, she'd have come along just to beat the women off. It certainly would do Bree good to have a man in her life—but then, maybe she wouldn't need her older sister any more than she ever did. Bree and Daria, Bree and Daria—she could almost hear the way they'd chattered to each other from the moment they could talk.

When other people came up to talk to Cole, Amelia took a shrimp appetizer from the circulating server— the shrimp had a small edible orchid perched atop it, no less—and wound her way through the crowd and out on deck. Ben was so busy talking to Josh Austin he wouldn't miss her.

Josh's wife had just phoned him to say she had a terrible headache, that she was just going to lie down at their local campaign headquarters. Word was that the Austin power couple hoped to emulate Bill and Hillary Clinton someday. Now wouldn't that be something? Maybe Josh would put Ben in his cabinet.

As the boat left the harbor, Amelia ate her appetizer but saved the orchid. With a pink cosmo in her hand, she leaned against the wooden railing, then edged around the back of the yacht. As they left the shore lights of Turtle Bay behind, the stars popped out overhead, but she preferred looking down mesmerized, into the white wake in the dark water.

This gulf had swallowed her sister, drowned her. If Daria had not been unconscious, would she have died or saved herself? And then, would she have blamed Amelia—hated her even more? If she told Bree what had happened that last day, would Bree ever forgive her? How did it feel to slip under the sliding waves to die?

The buzz of voices and laughter floated to her, mingled with the murmur of the sea. Her drink glass slipped from her fingers and disappeared into the silvery wake.

"A toast to Daria," she whispered, and tossed in the tiny orchid. They seemed to be heading in the direction of the Trade Wreck where Bree and Daria used to dive together.

Why had she always been so afraid of the waves and water? Amelia asked herself. But she'd been brave enough to go out in a boat to talk to Daria, who had told her to grow up and get over things. Dr. Nelson had said the same, in a more convoluted, quiet way. He'd said her perceptions might not be reality, at least for other people.

Amelia leaned out even farther, looking down, down into the silken surface of the sea. Again, she assured herself that the coroner's report stated that Daria had actually died from drowning, not from the blow to her head. And that had been an accident—she'd slipped, just slipped in the heat of their argument. But guilt pressed Amelia down, down, drowning her....

Bree's eyes darted to the clock on the office wall. A bomb to go off on the hull of the casino boat—no doubt under the waterline—in less than sixty minutes. Cole gone. Amelia and Ben. Verdugo. Josh and his opponent, Marla. All those others. Yes, these two had to be lovers or else Nikki would not let Josh die.

Somehow, she had to do something, and fast. The minute hand of the clock was moving so quickly. If she could keep them talking, Manny might come, but how long would that take? She had to get to a phone and get the coast guard out there to intercept Verdugo's boat.

Bree said to Nikki, "I'm shocked to think you're planning to get rid of Josh, your ticket to Washington and the halls of power."

"I would have been behind him all the way, before he betrayed me," Nikki said as Mark handed her the gun and went into the back room, clicking on the lights. The man knew his way around here, but then, he'd probably been downstairs, as well as upstairs, searching Daria's room.

"But it was best that Daria be eliminated," Nikki went on, "and now Josh, too, for what he's done. Haven't you heard about the widow's sympathy vote platform? Congressman Sonny Bono dies in a tragic, publicized skiing accident, and his widow gets elected in his place. Years before, Congressman Boggs goes down in a plane crash and his widow takes his office. The third time's the charm."

Bree's jaw dropped. Her gaze met and held Nikki's.

The woman looked rock steady and icy cold. Forget the tactic of trying to work on her emotions or sympathy.

"If you're thinking the explosive on the boat will make Sam a suspect, you're mistaken," Bree insisted. "He's in Sarasota, so he has an airtight alibi."

"Wrong again," Nikki countered. "He's been called back by Josh to speak at a luncheon tomorrow about saving the gulf. Briana, I know you and Sam don't get along, but you should know he's spoken out for your sea grass stance. But I'm glad you suspected him as the mastermind behind Daria's death, just as we had hoped."

Bree just gaped, stunned anew. She'd tried to blame him for all of this and now she might not be around to testify when he took the fall for Nikki and Mark. "Then Ric's working for you?"

"Oh, yes, he's working with us and for us. He's worked closely with Mark."

"Shooting a speargun at Cole and me. Helping Mark break into this place and search Daria's room—and tamper with our computer?"

"It *is* quite a list, isn't it? But we have to end it all now. Ric won't talk, because he's an accessory. Besides, Mark's going to be my chief congressional aide—at least until we can find the appropriate time to get married. So I'll need a new strong arm, and Ric's agreed to become that."

Bree could have sunk through the floor. She'd assumed Ric was talking to Sam about a detonator cap and explosives on the phone yesterday. But if Nikki and Mark had killed Daria, were they purchasing those items from Ric on the sly? Josh had said he'd arranged for Sam to get the job blowing up a bridge in Sarasota. He'd probably told Mark or Nikki how Sam had a vendetta against Bree, or maybe Ric, their supplier, had filled them in on that.

A damn spiderweb, but one that looked like it would hold. Bree felt not only helpless but furious. Think! Think, she told herself.

"How did it happen—with Daria? Did you and Mark know she'd be alone on the boat?"

"She brought it on herself—with Josh's help, of course. I don't totally blame her. Blame fate, if you must. I just happened to overhear Josh take a call at our home in Tallahassee when she called him on his business phone. She probably thought I'd never intercept a call coming into his office. But I picked up on the line and heard her tell him she was pregnant—pregnant with his child, when two of mine had died!"

The gun shook in Nikki's hand; she gripped it so tightly her fingers went white. Bree could hear Mark in the back room. What was he doing? She almost wished he'd come back to calm Nikki down. Surely they didn't want to shoot her, at least not here. But Nikki seemed to get hold of herself as she spoke again.

"You were such a smart girl to grill Josh at our little getaway in the cane field by the pond. You were on the right track."

"You didn't go back to the house," Bree accused. "You eavesdropped from that thick cane. It was all a setup."

"*You* were trying to set Josh up. Mark and I both heard every word you two said. Well, you can guess why I got off the handsome, the clever, the *lying* Josh Austin's bandwagon, when he lied to you. Believe me, he's lied to me for months. And, in the middle of a key election, managed to spend time with your sister. Looking at you right now makes me sick—Daria revisited, Daria déjà vu."

"I may look like her, but I am not my sister. I didn't even know her as well as I thought." Bree meant every word she said. Daria had not deserved to be killed, but she'd made a mess of things.

"Mark had told me of Josh's affair earlier—or let's say, I managed to entice it out of him," Nikki went on, as if she had to rid her soul of her guilt in this defiant confession. "But neither of us knew about Daria's pregnancy until I overheard that phone call. Daria told Josh she was going to make up a story to get you to dive alone while she just stayed with the boat. Here's a good one for you—the rocky sea didn't make her ill, but Josh's baby did. Anyway, she was surprised that it was me in the plane, with Mark, instead of Josh. She thought her lover boy had come to surprise her. Mind you, she'd fallen and hit her head and was barely conscious when we arrived. Mark set the detonator and we towed her into Marco Pass before it went off in that fierce storm. I knew she wouldn't resist our plans when she called me by your name and said she was glad you were there."

Tears blinded Bree. If Daria thought her twin sister was with her at the end, maybe it was some comfort to her. It comforted Bree, though it came from the demented woman who had caused Daria's death. Bree hugged herself around her waist as if to hold herself up. "But when you and Mark became lovers, that was the same deceit you detested Josh for."

"His was worse! He deserted me because I can't have children. Mark and I joined forces to clean up the mess Josh had made."

"I can understand how you felt betrayed—especially

because of your two losses." Stunned by all this and desperate to warn those on Verdugo's boat, Bree knew she was struggling for words.

Mark came back out into the office, carrying a big salvage net with a long handle and a length of cord he must have cut off a lift or buoy. "That's not going to work," Nikki said, pointing at the rope. "We can't have ligature marks on her if she went out in her boat and drowned herself. Take off your shirt and tie her wrists with the sleeves of it."

Bree's mind seemed to clear. She kept a dive knife under the backseat of *Mermaids I,* but it would do her little good with her hands tied behind her. After Mark shed his sports jacket and stripped off his shirt, she thrust her wrists out in front of her.

"Turn around," he said, and shoved her toward her desk. She had no choice but to obey, though she knew it might be better to take a bullet here that could be traced. A shot from the distance Nikki was standing couldn't be construed as a suicide, whereas her drowning would. She could see the headline now: Despondent Over Sister's Loss And Failure Of Sea Grass Project, Briana Devon Drowns Self Same Night Casino Boat Is Blown To Pieces. And there would be no one—Cole, Amelia, Ben, even Dom Verdugo—to say different about her.

Then Bree heard the distinctive sound of Manny's old truck. He was here! Could she warn him, or would they shoot her to shut her up? Her heart pounding, she strained to hear his footsteps and his key in the lock. What was taking him so long?

When Bree heard him approach, she opened her mouth to scream. Mark must have heard something, too, for he jammed a handkerchief in her mouth and shoved her to the floor.

"Get over here—cover her," he ordered Nikki, and darted out from behind the desk. Nikki knelt behind Bree, pressing the gun to her neck. The woman's hand was shaking. Bree dry heaved, choking into her gag.

Manny unlocked the door and the familiar bell rang.

"You upstairs or in the back room, partner?" he called out. "Light's on back in th—"

With a sickening thud, Bree heard Mark strike Manny and his body crumple to the floor.

It was hard to slip away, but Cole finally managed it. Verdugo probably expected him to keep pretending to be part of the *Fun 'n' Sun* team, but he was done with that. He wondered if the guests were swallowing Verdugo's promises of no pollution from this boat half as easily as they were swallowing free drinks and the lobster and lamb entrées.

Keeping an eye out to be sure none of Verdugo's lackeys were on the lower level, Cole went below decks. As far as he could see, the coast was clear.

A glimpse out a porthole he passed revealed a calm night. Stars, no moon yet. He wished he was with Bree to enjoy it and wondered what she was doing. Waiting for Manny or Lieutenant Crawford's call? He was tempted to phone her, but he needed to check out this storage room first, then decide if he was going to search further. He'd have to calculate the timing, the risks.

The storage room was locked, but there was a closed flat cabinet on the wall with keys. Yes, this one was for that storage space. Twice he'd seen Verdugo's goons take keys from here and go into the room. Glancing up and down the corridor, he unlocked the room and darted in. Even when he found the light switch and clicked it on, the small, windowless room was dim. It took a moment for his eyes to adjust.

Not a storage room, but a bedroom. And a naked, Latina-looking young girl was gagged and tied to a single bed, her eyes wide with fear.

24

"Her man coming in here is an unfortunate complication," Mark told Nikki.

Bree strained to listen. As far as she could tell, Manny hadn't moved. Was he unconscious or dead?

"Since we're eliminating anyone who might get in our way, what's one more?" Nikki said, standing and taking the gun barrel from Bree's neck. "It's still best if she commits suicide. Maybe he tried to stop her, and she hit him over the head?"

"Let's go with that. Or maybe Sam came back, stumbled onto this guy and knocked him out."

This was all her fault! Bree had to get them talking to her again, but they ignored her muffled protests as they dragged Manny behind her desk and relocked the front door. Bree tried to catch a glimpse of him as they pulled her to her feet. He lay facedown, a dark pool of blood spreading under his head. When he'd come in, he'd called her *partner*. They would have worked things out, and he would have worked things out with Lucinda.

Mark pulled Bree to her feet. When she balked, he dragged her through the back room, out the door and down the dock toward her boat slip. Nikki followed, carrying the large net and the key to the boat. Bree had finally put *Mermaids I* in the dock space where the larger, newer boat used to be, the one that had become Daria's coffin. She was the last mermaid left, and *Mermaids I* would be the hearse that took her to her grave.

"Say goodbye to Nikki, because she's not coming," Mark told her, shoving her into the boat on her belly. She saw he was going to pull the dinghy behind them so he could get back in after staging her suicide. "She's going to campaign headquarters to lie down with a raging headache, while I get rid of its cause for her. A few volunteers are working late tonight, so they'll be a good alibi. I'll walk over there later, and everyone will assume I was with the car the whole time."

Bree was barely listening. She was near enough to see the knife, but she'd never reach it with her hands tied behind her back. Why didn't someone come along the dock? Nikki kissed Mark passionately—"for good luck," she whispered—and hurried away.

Everything they did went off like clockwork. Clockwork, like the timed bomb they must have put on the hull of the *Fun 'n' Sun,* where no one would see it.

Cole covered the trembling, naked girl with his suit jacket and carefully pulled the masking tape off her mouth. Despite all that, she spread her legs for him and he had to shove them together. He whispered to her in Spanish that he was here to help her.

Tears filled her eyes. *"Cuidado! Cuidado!"* Careful, she kept whispering.

She was afraid to say anything at first, evidently thinking he was another of Verdugo's guys who had access to her. Finally, he coaxed out of her that she was from Guatemala, where he knew most of the women involved in the human trafficking trade had been taken from their homes or sold by their destitute families. She'd been promised a job as a waitress in a Miami casino, but *Señor Verdugo, he bring her here for his boys.*

It was enough to make Cole throw up, but at least it proved he'd been right about Verdugo. Sam might be behind everything else, but Verdugo was dirty, too. He'd get years, not on a luxury yacht but in the state pen, for this.

Cole explained in Spanish that there were some important people on board who could help, but he would have to leave her here for now.

"No, señor! No, por favor!"

Thank God, no one was in the hall, because he could kill Verdugo and his men with his bare hands for this. Wait until he told Bree he'd found a way to stop Verdugo and it had nothing to do with gambling.

Wearing gloves, just as Nikki had, Mark took *Mermaids I* out of Turtle Bay toward open water. As she lay facedown in the boat, Bree felt the vibration of the motor, the rush of water against the hull as they cut through the bay.

Back to the place where this horror began, she thought. The Trade Wreck, where Daria's and her life was wrecked. If he'd just untie her and throw her in, she could swim in again. Piece of cake—no storm, maybe no sharks. But she knew, with the way he and Nikki had set everything else up, he would not just toss her into the water.

And then, as she saw the handle of a large, long-handled retrieval net he'd brought, she realized his possible plan. Maybe he meant to keep her underwater with that net until she drowned. Could she hold her breath long enough to convince him she was dead? If he untied her hands before he threw her in, could she yank him in or swim down and away from him? Did he have the gun or had Nikki taken it? If only she could get control of the boat, could she make it out to the casino yacht in time to tell everyone to get off? How much time was left? It had to be less than half the sixty minutes Nikki had mentioned.

Too soon, they reached the site of the Trade Wreck. Mark cut the motor and let the boat drift.

"Sorry about this, really," he said as he hauled her to her knees. "If you had just let things go, not played detective after your sister was dead, this never would have happened. You should have taken the warning at the Gator Watering Hole, but we couldn't have you running around knowing what Josh did, because that could point to Nikki in Daria's death. Soon, everyone will point to her as the next senator from Florida, then on to the stars."

Bree looked up at the stars through her tears. So beautiful but cold and distant. He finally pulled the gag out of her mouth. Her throat was so dry she could hardly talk.

"If she turned on him—she'll turn on you," she rasped. "In D.C., a stunning and ambitious woman like that, she'll meet someone who can help her move up more than you. Her father won't want her to marry a mere—"

"No," he interrupted and gave her a shake. "Everything we've done together bonds us for good."

"She got someone to get rid of him, didn't she? She'll get—"

"Just shut up. That's it."

He *was* going to use the net to hold her down, and he did not untie his shirt from her wrists. He planned to take it back later, when he was sure she was dead. Could she twist out of the shirt in the water? Could she get free from the net to swim down instead of trying to come up for precious air?

The boat rocked as Mark half picked her up, half rolled her in. She hit backside down and fought to right herself so she could dive, but he put the big net over her. It was a strong-webbed one, meant to bring up large, heavy items. He yanked it down over her and twisted it to entrap her so she couldn't dive or escape.

Then, he shoved her underwater and held her there.

"Amelia, are you all right?" someone asked. She jolted back to reality and jerked away from the rail. It was Cole DeRoca. He looked upset.

"I'm fine."

"You don't look fine, any more than I do. Would you do me a favor and get Ben out here without drawing attention to it? I have something I have to tell him."

"Sure," she said, and started away, then gripped the railing because she felt unsteady. "Is it—not something about Bree?"

"No. Hurry, would you?"

She was back with Ben in less than a minute.

"I was checking a storage room downstairs," Cole told them, "and stumbled on a young woman tied up there. She's been abused, she's naked and she's terrified. Says she's from Guatemala and Verdugo's keeping her here for his guards—for the whole damn crew to rape, for all I know."

"Got him!" Ben said, smacking his palms together. "I don't care what kind of lawyers he pays for, I'll get him at least ten years for harboring a sex slave. And we get rid of the casino boat at the same time. Bingo!"

"But so we don't have a knock-down drag-out fight when they realize we've found her," Cole said, "we'll have to leave her there until we get back to the dock or get the coast guard out here."

"You can't leave her there for one more second!" Amelia cried. Both men had obviously forgotten she was here. But how dare Verdugo or anyone else treat a poor girl like that!

"...so let's come up with a story," Cole went on, "that someone's ill, and Verdugo needs to head back in early."

"I can do that," Amelia told them. "I'll claim an appendix attack, but I'd like to help that girl afterward. Yes, Ben," she interrupted as he started to speak again, "I know she'll be handed over to the authorities, but someone's got to be her advocate. You'll be busy with media interviews galore when all this hits. Cole," she added, patting him on the shoulder, "you've saved another woman from destruction. Wait until Bree hears this. That young woman must be traumatized, maybe suicidal, and I know I can help her."

Bree fought. Grabbing the metal frame of the net with both hands tied behind her, she tried to yank him in. Is this how a netted fish felt, pulled from the realm of the sea where it could breathe only drowning air? *Daria, is this how you felt in the wheelhouse when our boat went down?*

Cole. She'd wanted to have a life with Cole. She

wanted to build bridges with Amelia, teach the boys to dive.

Should she not struggle, save air? Just accept this? Needed a breath, save air...save herself.

Strange colors pulsated before her eyes, blues and greens, bright gold. Like a lovely underwater dive. Like the sun in the sky with the sea beckoning beyond...

Going to suck in seawater now...going to die...just hold Daria's hand and sink into the soft earth under all the sea grass with her... Cole, smiling, sailing away with Cole... The bright colors in Bree's brain were fading, fading to gray and black. She had been certain she could fight death below the surface. The sea was her friend, but it had taken Daria, and now...now...

With a whoosh, someone pulled her up. Her head broke the surface. She sucked in a huge breath of air.

Had Mark changed his mind? Was she hallucinating? Was she dead?

Bree blinked water from her eyes, took another deep breath into her burning lungs. Not Mark, but Sam Travers. He hauled her over the side of his dive boat, scraping her belly, but she didn't care. If Satan himself had saved her, that was just fine.

Bree lay on her back, gasping in blessed breaths as Sam unwound her from the sopping net.

"Where—you—come—from?" she got out.

"I wanted a quiet boat ride, and I saw the bastard take your boat. Thought he was stealing it, so I followed him. When I figured out he had you in that net, I yelled at him. The SOB took a shot at me, so I shot him with a speargun someone stupidly left loaded here in my boat."

Perfect justice, she thought. Her head cleared in a flash as she sat up and saw Mark Denton's body, sprawled against the prow of *Mermaids I* with a spear in his chest.

"I should have let him drown you, of course," Sam went on as she was finally freed. "Here I come back to help Josh Austin with your cause and find out I've been served with a search warrant. If you had anything to do with th—"

"Sam, I know we've had terrible times, but you have to help me," she said, getting to her knees and then her feet. She was dizzy, but she scanned the horizon beyond the Trade Wreck site. Thank God, Verdugo's big yacht was heading in, not out.

"What time is it?" she asked.

"What?"

"Time! I can't explain now but to say the guy you just shot has planted some kind of bomb—the same kind that blew a hole in Daria's boat—aboard that ship. He got the supplies from Ric."

Sam swore only once, then seemed to go into combat mode. "It's nine twenty-three," he told her, glaring at the luminous dial on his watch.

"Then we have twelve minutes to get the explosive off the hull."

"Twelve minutes? They put a timer on it? Even at full speed, they won't make it in. And I'll never get a diver, let alone the bomb squad, out here by then."

"Sam, I'm the diver and you're the bomb squad," she said, grabbing one of the two tanks she saw on board and seizing a mask someone had left near the speargun. She spit in it and started wiping off the plastic to clear it. "And we have to catch that boat while you tell me how to get rid of a demolition cap with a primer cord, like you use to blow up bridges."

"It's Primacord," he said. "Just pray we catch that yacht." He started his motor, leaving *Mermaids I* with the dinghy Mark had planned for his escape in their wake.

"I'll bet you had assignments harder than this in Vietnam!" she shouted. "And I'll bet Ted did in Iraq, too! No matter what you think, Sam, I was proud of him and what he did there."

Their eyes met. She thought she might have made a mistake mentioning Ted, but Sam nodded fiercely and revved the motor on full speed. "Wish I could have gone after Ted's killers the way you did Daria's!" he shouted.

Fighting tears, Bree nodded and braced herself in the bouncing boat, struggling into the unfamiliar gear and checking the gauge on the tank. Not much air in the tank. "Lights?" she yelled at Sam. "Do you have dive lights?"

"Portside storage under the seat!"

Bree knew she was exhausted and yet energy poured through her, as it had the day she swam through the storm. Sam had taken an angle where they were closing on the boat, but surely two more minutes must have gone by. Why was the yacht coming in earlier than expected? Could they have learned about the bomb?

She tried to concentrate as Sam shouted instructions to her.

"If it is one of my detonator caps—"

"It is!"

"It's actually a form of TNT. It's stable, relatively insensitive to shock, so don't be afraid to pry it off. But do not jimmy the Primacord if it's visible. It will be stuck on the hull by what looks like kid's clay, in a bright color, maybe blue or red. It will have metal end caps and one end will be threaded for insertion of the detonator. For a boat as big as that, they may have used a booster of tetryl."

"At least that's a fairly new boat. It can't have a lot of barnacles yet to obscure the cap. I'm going to look near the hull, since that's where they blew up *Mermaids II.*"

"Who did?"

"Later. Look! Someone's outside on the deck!" She saw two men, one as tall as Cole. Yes, it was Cole!

Sam buzzed the port side, blowing an air horn she hadn't seen. Bree was screaming but it drowned her out.

Cole saw them. He leaned out. Josh was outside, too. Poor Josh—poor everyone, in about seven minutes.

"Stop the vessel!" Sam was commanding through a bullhorn. "Bomb aboard! Bomb!"

Josh disappeared. It seemed to take forever, and the big waves from the yacht kept pushing them away, but the yacht finally stopped dead in the water.

Dead in the water, Bree thought, as Sam took them closer, under the higher deck of the larger vessel.

"Bomb?" Cole shouted down. "Has Sam changed his mind and told you—"

"He's here to help!" Bree shouted up to him.

Sam reversed their direction and motored them back closer toward the stern. Cole ran along the railing to stay over them. Bree had so much to say to him, but it would have to wait.

"Not much time," she told Sam as she fitted her mask and stood up to jump in. "Get as far away as you can, just in case."

"No, I'm backing you up. Just get it off and drop it into the depths, because there's no time to defuse it. You'll do fine."

The entire world had gone mad. Sam Travers was

backing her up and telling her she'd do fine and she believed him. Sam had given her her life back once already. At least that was one good thing to come from this terror.

"Get all the deck lights on!" Sam was yelling through the megaphone to Cole and Josh. "Get everyone up on the decks or front of the ship! And don't let anyone jump off."

The last things she heard as she descended into the water were, "Bree, be careful!" from Cole and Sam bellowing, "Tell everyone to brace themselves and call the coast guard, just in case…"

Bubbles and her lights gave her vertigo at first, but she righted herself. The sea around her lit up. They must have turned on more deck lights. How far under the surface would Mark have put the bomb?

Her dive light skimmed the newly painted dark blue hull, up and down. It was so shiny she could glimpse a muted reflection of herself, as if Daria dove with her.

How much time left? No one usually knew how much time was left in their lives. Daria had not known, Mark either.

Nothing here at this level. Try the starboard side, the one that would have been toward the dock. Yes, the dock would have sheltered Mark when he planted it.

Time ticking away. At Daria's funeral, the words, *So teach us to number our days that we might have a heart of wisdom…*

Everyone's days were numbered. How many would die here if she didn't find the bomb?

Then, there it was. Two small, circular metal things, close together and stuck firmly to the hull. No cord was visible but it had to be here. With her dive knife, she pried the red adhesive off, not touching the detonator or the booster or whatever she was looking at. She'd seen movies where people had to cut the correct colored wires to stop a timer, but this seemed so primitive, so simple.

Yes, one was loose. Despite how cool the water felt, sweat was stinging her eyes within her mask and it was fogging up. Time must be gone. It was going to go off with her right on top of it, but she had to try. Try to save Amelia and Ben so their boys would not be orphans. Save Cole, even Verdugo. Josh, though, when everything came to light, might wish he was dead.

When she got the second metal piece off the hull, Bree let go of her dive knife rather than resheafing it. Then she dropped her dive light so it wouldn't hold her back or bump the pieces. She was trembling so hard she might set them off herself.

She jackknifed and upended, taking the pieces, one in each hand, kicking down, down.

Then she let them go—somehow letting all her fear go, too—and kicked and clawed madly for the surface.

She saw the lights above her and was almost to the surface when a muted boom and a fist of water thrust her upward. The sea roiled, and she thought she was back again at the day this all began, fighting to make it to shore.

Her ears hurt. Then hard hands grabbed her and Sam hauled her up and over the side of his boat as Cole jumped, feetfirst, into the water and clambered on board, too.

Dizzy but delirious with relief and joy, Bree stripped off her mask, while Sam unstrapped her tank. Holding tightly to each other, Cole and Bree sprawled, soaking wet on the floor of Sam's boat, while Sam patted her on the back, saying, "You all right? You all right?"

Despite the fact that she kept shaking, Cole's embrace was rock steady. She was definitely more than just all right.

25

Two months later

Bree dived cleanly into the swimming pool on the patio of their new house. Cole knifed in behind her. Though she knew the chlorine in the water would make her eyes burn, she opened them anyway and reveled in the sight of him swimming with powerful strokes beside her, his hair rippling.

They had been married for three weeks but had been back only a few days from a trip to the Cayman Islands. Cole reached out and pulled her against him as they surfaced, rocking the water against the tiles. The pool was a small one, the villa just two bedrooms, but they had their businesses to build and they were insanely happy. Bree and Manny were running Mermaids, and Cole was transitioning out of rare wood paneling to building sloops and teaching others how to build them, too.

"Easier to float in salt water," he said, "but this is a heck of a lot safer. Nothing to get cut on, no storms, no sharks, no bombs." He was kidding about not taking risks, since he still dived with her on jobs from time to time, even sometimes with the new guy they'd hired.

She pressed herself against him with her arms around his neck, and he clamped her even harder to him. They always melded perfectly, chest to breasts, hips, thighs, though her feet dangled partway up his calves. He slid his hand along her sleek, arched back and pushed her bikini bottom down to cup her with both hands.

"We've got a while before Ben and Amelia and the boys show up," he told her, his voice a delicious whisper.

"Mmm. But we've got to finish dinner and put up the Congrats On Your Reelection sign for Ben."

The election had been three days ago. Marla Sherborne had won back her senate seat by a landslide. Josh had withdrawn from the election. His party had put someone else up to oppose her, but to no avail. Ben had said Josh had turned down an offer to write his story and was starting up a *cachaça* business to produce bottles of caipirinha for a cane company that was in competition with Grand Sugar. Josh had also started divorce proceedings against Nikki, who was awaiting trial in the Collier County jail along with Ric—and Verdugo, for human trafficking. His desire to bring gambling to Southwest Florida had gone down with him.

"Oh, yeah," Cole said, playing her game as he unhooked her bikini bra. "We've got to set up the snorkeling game for the kids. And wash our hair..."

Bree laughed as they came together. Cole swore when the doorbell rang. "Why is Amelia always early?" he muttered. They both knew if they didn't get out of the pool now, James and Jordan would run around to the back of the villa and look in through the netted cage around the pool. "Batten down the hatches, matey, 'cause the kids are here. Just when I thought I'd make a kid of my own."

"At least you're not sleeping on the sofa anymore," she told him, trying to sound normal as she looked for her bikini bottom and bra in the water. Every time Cole DeRoca looked at her that way, touched her, it was as wild as a lightning strike. After being in the water during the distant bomb blast, her hearing and her sight seemed to have returned to normal, but nothing was ever normal with Cole in her life. She would always miss Daria, but her husband completed her, even as her twin sister could not.

Cole threw on a robe and left her scrambling to get back into her suit while he answered the door. He loved the boys and they him. Amelia had even let the two of them take the kids to the Swamp Buggy Races and didn't scold anyone when they came back looking like they'd been playing in the mud. Much of Amelia's efforts were now focused on spreading the word about human trafficking. She'd taken care of the Guatemalan girl the night Cole found her, and she was going to testify against Verdugo at his trial.

Now where was that terry-cloth robe? If Cole had taken it, he'd look like a giant in it. Bree barely made it back into her suit and wrapped a towel around her waist as the kids arrived.

"Aunt Bree, Aunt Bree, can we do that snorkel game now, where we find the coins in the pool?"

Both boys hit into her with hard hugs. "If your mother and dad say so."

"Not only do we say so," Amelia said, putting down a tray of cookies and brownies, despite the fact that Bree had told her she'd fix everything this time, "but—ta-da!"

she cried, and produced a snorkel and a mask, both of which still sported their price tags.

"You're going to join us?" Bree said, walking over to hug her, however wet she was. Amelia didn't seem to mind. Ben was off in the corner already, talking to someone on his cell, but Amelia didn't seem to mind that, either.

"Leftover desserts from the fund-raiser luncheon," Amelia said. "And, yes, I want to join you. It's better than fighting, I hear."

When Cole hustled the boys off to change into their suits, Bree and Amelia stood arm in arm. Amelia had explained everything that had happened the day Daria died. Bree had been furious at first and blamed Amelia for leaving Daria vulnerable to Nikki and Mark. But it was Daria's own mistakes and lies that had made her vulnerable. And perhaps, Bree had told herself, it was the morning sickness from the pregnancy that made Daria slip, not anything Amelia had done. Amelia had believed that Bree would surface soon and, as ever, care for her twin. Bree's conflicting feelings of love and hate toward Amelia had made her understand the torment Amelia had lived with most of her life.

The first month of Amelia's psychiatric appointments, Bree had gone with her. They'd worked through the past. When Bree had hugged her even then, Amelia said she knew that she was loved for sure.

"In the pool," Cole shouted, clapping his hands as the boys jumped in the shallow end. "Lots of fun things can happen in the pool, and we don't even need to be afraid of getting in the deep end," he said, with such a funny look at Bree that Amelia laughed.

"I have a feeling we interrupted something," Amelia said. "Maybe that's really why I want to get in the water. Ben and I have a very nice, big pool, and he's been much, much too busy lately. Maybe the wide-eyed honeymooner can give me a few tips."

The two of them giggled together, as if they were just silly, happy girls again.

A salsa beat shook the walls of the Garcia Party House in Immokalee. Nearly three hundred people crowded the food tables and the dance floor. This *Mexicana quinceañera* celebration with family and friends touched Bree deeply. She was proud to have been one of Lucinda's financial supporters to help pay for this beautiful party marking a girl's "sweet fifteen" transition to womanhood.

And it turned out that Daria had helped to pay for it, too. Manny had admitted that she had given him money to keep quiet about her pregnancy—and that he had spent it on a partial payment for the party house. Bree and her new junior partner had been through a lot of discussions on how they would run things at Mermaids, and they had come to a much better understanding of each other. Bree felt she'd been in the forgiveness business full-time lately, and was a much better, stronger person for it.

The Salazars had selected a Cinderella theme with pink and white bunting, and a Disney Cinderella, no less, on the five-tiered cake. Cindi—she'd asked Bree to call her Lucinda today—looked half bride, half prom queen in her white gown and upswept hair with her gold tiara.

Manny had said that she'd taken five required hours of pre-*quinceañera* counseling classes at her church about everything from family responsibilities to sexuality and religion. Besides that, the Salazars' meeting with Luke and his family had helped a lot. Manny had thanked Bree for her part in that and for visiting him every day in the hospital while he was recovering from being hit over the head with his own wrench.

"And now," Manny announced proudly over the tinny PA system, first in Spanish, then English, as his wife and even his ill, rake-thin mother beamed, "you all invited to dance to this Mexican waltz. Its name, *Mi Linda Hijita,* for our non-Latino friends here, means *my beautiful daughter.*"

After Lucinda's teenage supporters demonstrated the steps and everyone applauded, Bree and Cole left their *padrones* table to join others on the dance floor. Luke was partnering Lucinda this time, and she took his hand and led him over to Cole and Bree, dancing cheek to cheek in a corner.

"Thanks for coming, both of you," Lucinda said. She looked radiant. Luke, bless him, looked proud. "I just wanted to show you this bracelet, Bree. Every *quinceañera* girl gets one, 'cause it stands for the unending circle of life."

For a moment Bree wondered if Manny had told his family she was pregnant. Bree had shared that with him, not only because she'd need more help soon with the business, but because she didn't want to shut him out as Daria had both of them.

Lucinda went on. "Look close. I put names on the charms of people who are gone, but still with us in our hearts. Here are both my grandpas' names, and I put Daria's here, too, see?"

Bree's eyes filled with tears. Cole's arm came around her waist as if to steady her. Wordlessly, but mouthing *thank you,* Bree hugged Lucinda, before she and Luke danced off together again.

"You okay?" Cole asked. "Want to stay?"

"Of course I do. I don't want to miss what she has planned for Manny next. The look on his face will be worth the price of admission."

One of Lucinda's friends carried a chair out into the center of the dance floor, and she pulled her father out and sat him down in it. Another friend brought out a huge pillow, which Lucinda sat on at his feet, amidst the puffy softness of her full skirts. The band quieted and, looking up into her father's nervous face, Lucinda said in Spanish, her voice wavering, "I want to especially thank the main man in my life for sticking with me through tough times—and for this happy day and others to come."

On cue, the band began to play some song Bree didn't know, but it made Manny, macho no more, cry.

Bree turned to Cole and whispered, "I want to especially thank the main man in my life for sticking with me through tough times—and for this happy day and others to come."

Cole looked as teary-eyed as Manny as he put his arms around Bree and patted her belly. Bree put a hand down to link her fingers with his. She liked to think of her baby inside her, swimming already, safe in her own little sea.

* * * * *

If you liked BELOW THE SURFACE,
don't miss CHASING SHADOWS,
the chilling first book in Karen Harper's new
SOUTH SHORES series...
coming soon from MIRA Books!

Author Note

Since I've lived in Southwest Florida for thirty winters, I know and love the area. I have, however, created Turtle Bay. The book's characters are all fictional and not based on or inspired by actual persons.

Dying sea grass has been a local concern for years. The city of Naples and many Southwest Florida scientists have studied and worked on this problem for years.

Since I do not sail or scuba dive, I am indebted to our friend John Hawkins, who does both and who kindly read the sections of the book dealing with these endeavors. Any mistakes are mine, not his.

For anyone interested in the fascinating tradition of *quinceañera,* a good book on the subject is *Once Upon a Quinceañera: Coming of Age in the USA.* This "sweet fifteen" celebration is becoming an American event.

Special thanks to my Florida and Ohio friend Mary Ann Manning for her very own brand of PR for Karen Harper books. Best wishes to our Naples condo friends and, as ever, to Don.

Karen Harper

Join FBI agent Craig Frasier and criminal psychologist Kieran Finnegan as they track down a madman who is obsessed with perfect beauty.

"Horrible! Oh, God, horrible—tragic!" John Shaw said, shaking his head with a dazed look as he sat on his bar stool at Finnegan's Pub.

Kieran nodded sympathetically. Construction crews had found old graves when they were working on the foundations at the hot new downtown venue Le Club Vampyre.

Anthropologists had found the new body among the old graves the next day.

It wasn't just *any* body.

It was the body of supermodel Jeannette Gilbert.

Finding the old graves wasn't much of a shock—not in New York City, and not in a building that was close to two centuries old. The structure that housed Le Club Vampyre was a deconsecrated Episcopal church. The church's congregation had moved to a facility it had purchased from the Catholic church—whose congregation was now in a sparkling new basilica over on Park Avenue. While many had bemoaned the fact that such a venerable old institution had been turned into an establishment for those into sex, drugs and rock and roll, life—and business—went on.

And with life going on…

MEXP1987

Well, work on the building's foundations went on, too.

It was while investigators were still being called in following the discovery of the newly deceased body—moments before it hit the news—that Kieran Finnegan learned about it, and that was because she was helping out at her family's establishment, Finnegan's on Broadway. Like the old church/nightclub behind it, Finnegan's dated back to just before the Civil War, and had been a pub for most of those years. Since it was geographically the closest place to the church with liquor, it had apparently seemed the right spot at that moment for Professor John Shaw.

A serial killer is striking a little too close to home in the second novel in the
NEW YORK CONFIDENTIAL *series,*
A PERFECT OBSESSION
coming soon from New York Times *bestselling author Heather Graham and MIRA Books.*

REQUEST YOUR FREE BOOKS!

2 FREE NOVELS FROM THE PARANORMAL ROMANCE COLLECTION, PLUS 2 FREE GIFTS!

YES! Please send me 2 FREE novels from the Paranormal Romance Collection and my 2 FREE gifts (gifts are worth about $10). After receiving them, if I don't wish to receive any more books, I can return the shipping statement marked "cancel." If I don't cancel, I will receive 4 brand-new novels every month and be billed just $24.76 in the U.S. or $27.96 in Canada. That's a savings of at least 29% off the cover price of all 4 books. It's quite a bargain! Shipping and handling is just 50¢ per book in the U.S. and 75¢ per book in Canada.* I understand that accepting the 2 free books and gifts places me under no obligation to buy anything. I can always return a shipment and cancel at any time. Even if I never buy another book, the two free books and gifts are mine to keep forever.

237/337 HDN GLDY

Name _____ (PLEASE PRINT) _____

Address _____ Apt. # _____

City _____ State/Prov. _____ Zip/Postal Code _____

Signature (if under 18, a parent or guardian must sign)

Mail to the **Reader Service:**
IN U.S.A.: P.O. Box 1867, Buffalo, NY 14240-1867
IN CANADA: P.O. Box 609, Fort Erie, Ontario L2A 5X3

Want to try 2 free books from another line?
Call 1-800-873-8635 or visit www.ReaderService.com.

* Terms and prices subject to change without notice. Prices do not include applicable taxes. Sales tax applicable in NY. Canadian residents will be charged applicable taxes. Offer not valid in Quebec. This offer is limited to one order per household. Not valid for current subscribers to Paranormal Romance Collection or Harlequin® Nocturne™ books. All orders subject to credit approval. Credit or debit balances in a customer's account(s) may be offset by any other outstanding balance owed by or to the customer. Please allow 4 to 6 weeks for delivery. Offer available while quantities last.

Your Privacy—The Reader Service is committed to protecting your privacy. Our Privacy Policy is available online at www.ReaderService.com or upon request from the Reader Service.

We make a portion of our mailing list available to reputable third parties that offer products we believe may interest you. If you prefer that we not exchange your name with third parties, or if you wish to clarify or modify your communication preferences, please visit us at www.ReaderService.com/consumerschoice or write to us at Reader Service Preference Service, P.O. Box 9062, Buffalo, NY 14269. Include your complete name and address.